CW01497440

The

Omnibus

Penelope Shuttle

VP Festschrift Series:

Volume 1: Christine Brooke-Rose
Volume 2: Gilbert Adair
Volume 3: The Syllabus
Volume 4: Rikki Ducornet
(Edited by G.N. Forester and M.J. Nicholls)

Reprint Titles:

The Languages of Love
The Sycamore Tree
The Dear Deceit
The Middlemen
Go When You See the Green Man Walking
Next
Xorandor/Verbivore
by Christine Brooke-Rose

Three Novels — Rosalyn Drexler
Knut — Tom Mallin
Erowina — Tom Mallin
The Greater Infortune/The Connecting Door — Rayner Heppenstall

New Fiction:

Mirrors on which dust has fallen — Jeff Bursey

other Verbivoracious titles @

www.verbivoraciouspress.org

The

Penelope Shuttle

Omnibus

Penelope Shuttle

Verbivoracious Press

Glentrees, 13 Mt Sinai Lane, Singapore

This edition published in Great Britain & Singapore

by Verbivoracious Press

www.verbivoraciouspress.org

ISBN: 978-981-09-5982-1

Printed and bound in Great Britain & Singapore

All the Usual Hours of Sleeping and *Wailing Monkey Embracing a Tree* first published in Great Britain by Calder & Boyars.

Rainsplitter in the Zodiac Garden and *The Mirror of the Giant* first published by Marion Boyars.

Contents

Introduction

FRANCIS BOOTH

Penelope Shuttle was born in West London in 1947. She began to write seriously at the age of fourteen and finished her first novel when she was seventeen. Her early novella *An Excusable Vengeance* was published by the prestigious Calder & Boyars in the collection *New Writers VI, 1967;*[1] they then published the first of her four full-length novels, *All the Usual Hours of Sleeping* in 1969, when she was only twenty-one and had only previously published one volume of poetry with a small press. After this she received a grant from the Arts Council of Great Britain which enabled her to give up her part time secretarial job and move to Cornwall to write full time. In 1972 she won another Arts Council grant and an E.C. Gregory Award for poetry. Calder & Boyars (later Marion Boyars) published her next three solo novels, all included in this volume.

Shuttle published several volumes of poetry with small presses[2] and in 1980 published her first full-length volume of poetry, *The Orchard Upstairs* with the equally prestigious Oxford University Press. In 1975 her play *The Girl Who Lost Her Glove* was broadcast on BBC Radio Three. Robert Nye said of her: 'it becomes difficult to escape the conclusion that no new English novelist since the late Ann Quin has started out with more promise, or already accomplished so much.'

Shuttle also published two novels jointly-authored with her husband, the poet Peter Redgrove, whom she met in 1969: *The Terrors of Dr Treviles: A Romance*, 1974 and *Glass Cottage: A Nautical Romance*, 1976. The two also published a joint volume of poetry: *The Hermaphrodite Album*, 1973 and *The Wise Wound: Myths, Realities, and Meanings of Menstruation*, 1978, an attempt to break the taboo that has surrounded this difficult subject since at least

Leviticus.[3] The epigraph to *The Hermaphrodite Album*, from Goethe, is, fittingly: 'My work is that of a composite being, which happens to be signed.'

Shuttle's solo novels merge poetic language with the novel form unlike virtually anyone else before or since. This was a problem for many reviewers at the time, especially as the writing contains many strange metaphors and obscure words which hardly serve to move the plot of the novel along, and the novels do have plots. One is reminded of TS Eliot's comment on Djuna Barnes's *Nightwood*: that it needs to be read twice, as the second experience will be very different to the first. Eliot said that *Nightwood* would be best appreciated by readers of poetry, though he was not advocating poetic language and was quick to point out: 'I do not mean that Miss Barnes's style is "poetic prose". But I do mean that most contemporary novels are not really "written".'[4] However, in her review of *Rainsplitter in the Zodiac Garden*, Victoria Glendinning argued the opposite to Eliot: that it 'must be read fast, with concentration and sympathy; if one does not cooperate, it disintegrates into a barrage of fragmented images.'

> It is not entertainment; and it is not poetry, although Penelope Shuttle has an established reputation as a poet and takes a poet's licence with language. Rather it is an invitation to trace the mythology of a mind that has left the scheduled tracks and timetables.[5]

A rather less kind (anonymous) review, of *Wailing Monkey Embracing a Tree*, titled 'Strictly for the Bards', said of it:

> Often the reader's imagination is likely to be shocked without being convinced. But images and phrases do not entirely suffocate the story, while the uncommon poetic speech in which the narrator and the conjugal protagonists themselves present their meditative perceptions and reveries has the effect of mythologizing

that familiar theme in contemporary fiction, a stale marriage.[6]

Perhaps surprisingly, the language of Shuttle's novels is more difficult and dense than that of the poems; the novels use more obscure words and are in many ways harder to 'read'. Also surprisingly the novels seem less personal than the poems which, though never confessional in the mode of, say, Anne Sexton nevertheless do obviously refer to herself. She certainly seems in the poems to be the 'dancer stuck between the moon and the earth'[7] and, like Sylvia Plath[8] uses both the moon and blood as recurring symbols: 'Around the moon, / my dreams cluster, not moths'.[9]

Shuttle's first full-length novel *All the Usual Hours of Sleeping*, 1969 is a large and dense work, full of rich, poetic imagery but at its heart is a love story involving four people: the lawyer Tomas who is currently in a relationship with Herma,[10] who was introduced to him by his former partner, Rachel and Rachel's new partner, Daniel. Rachel has left Tomas to travel abroad and has met Daniel but is not committed to him. Herma has had a baby which died shortly after its birth. Rachel returns to Tomas and tries to win him back, despite the presence of the almost irrelevant Daniel. Herma eventually kills herself and Tomas and Rachel are together again. Although the underlying plot is relatively conventional, it is the use of language taken well beyond its normal descriptive function that makes this novel stand out.

> The distance between them, although composed of only a few feet, is, in another sense, made up of intangible areas as impassable as the hyperborean fall of avalanche. A regiment of months holds them rigidly there and has no intention of letting them go free just yet. Sun moves. Sun flees. The faience of sunlight slides gradually down the walls until the lavender disapproval of dusk encloses the man and woman. The weight and drought of this dimness binds them further to the room. (p.3)

The limits of this rich style are revealed in two areas: reported speech and writing about sex.

> He throws some cushions on the floor for them to squat there, semi-nude flimsy ruined inhabitants of a precarious world. They rub their bodies sensuously together, fumigating the flesh, suffusing, stuffy air clapping hands over their outstretched mouths. Her breasts make a figure of eight. His sticky balls are two old crabs. (p.38)

There is an inevitable bathos where the grossly physical facts of sexual encounters meet the language of myth, or where obscure, slightly comical words are used to describe sexual passion. 'Her cascading body awaits the impetus, feeling him shuddering like a spillikin and she arches herself for the happy entry' (p.54). The reported speech hovers between the allusiveness of the prose and the everyday ordinariness of actual speech and sometimes also jars; do people talk like that?

Tomas is only seen, and only seen to exist, through his relationships with the two women; as a lawyer he is surrounded by the mundane, among which Herma tries to maintain her faith. Rachel can never seem to find her real self, and perhaps needs Tomas to complete her identity. She has to travel constantly, both literally and figuratively, to be constantly in motion. 'Rachel, the watcher in the doorway, is the motionless figure who will never find a field a road a sea upon which the sole of her foot might rest.' (p.205) Herma seems at times only to exist as a pawn in the game between Tomas and Rachel with no will or power of her own. She regrets the loss of her childhood and the loss of her own child. 'I didn't want to be left behind with this emptiness I can never satisfy. Why does it seem that I am watching myself vanish into thin air?' (p.104) At the end of the novel Herma kills herself in a vivid and powerful passage.

> she falls on to a shore of salt and ice and her body is carried out to sea. She sustains fatal injuries. She lies there supreme and sacerdotal. She has warded off

perfection. She has entered an ultimate clime. A region where the hunter and the hunted are extinct. (p243-4).

Wailing Monkey Embracing a Tree, 1973 (the cover informs us that this is the Chinese name of a sexual position, though it is not otherwise mentioned in the novel), dedicated 'For Peter', gained a number of reviews in the serious press, some hostile, some more positive. 'Penelope Shuttle writes the kind of prose that gives poetry a bad name. To read *Wailing Monkey Embracing a Tree* is like eating a meal of which every course is smothered in clotted cream.'[11]

> It could be that Miss Shuttle has become the prisoner of her own verbal inspiration, so that the language is telling her what to do. It could be that I have not yet perceived the relation between the rhythm and the story. This is not a book which gives you all it has on one reading. On the contrary, it is *designed to be reread.*[12]

Indeed, on rereading, some of the writing is evocative and very beautiful. 'In their house by the sea they exist with all the bright useless energy of a circus.' (p.254) 'I swallow the preceding year. Now it has gone. I take a sip of blood, a bite of jellied bone.' (p.259) 'Moonlight leans against sea, a membrane of metal and bone.' (p.290) Elinda[13] is the centre of the book; the narrative switches between third person and her first person thoughts. She is married to Luke, whom she does not love and who does not love her. 'Elinda and Luke are both substitutes. Both are seeking supine consolation upon a randomly chosen breast.' (p.252) Elinda wants to leave so that she can return to her former lover Matthew. Most of the novel consists of scenes from Elinda and Luke's aimless and unsatisfying life by the sea in the 'strangeness of a dying world'. Like Rachel in *All the Usual Hours of Sleeping,* Elinda has no unambiguous and well-defined sense of her identity. 'There is the Zouave[14] woman she pretends to be, there is the Salome creature she longs to become, and lastly, the aimless girl she is. She lives her life in instalments.'[15] (p.251) Also like Rachel, she has no faith in religion or anything else. However, unlike Rachel, she wants her freedom, even if it comes with loneliness. But unlike Herma, Elinda cannot contemplate killing herself to be free from disappointment: 'A painless death is what I want, thinks Elinda on this Caucasian morning. But I cannot end my life with a stilted suicide. No, I must go on presiding over myself like a mechanical muse nourished on acid.' (p.260)

Luke cannot express himself as well as Elinda – 'he discovers that he must approach the parapet of language but he does not know how' (p.268-9)—and is reduced to crude insults, as Tomas had insulted Rachel in *All the Usual Hours of Sleeping*: 'bitch, cow, vixen, tigress.' (p.284) Again in this novel the issue arises of 'poetic' writing about sex, the only thing that binds them in any way: 'Now the lovers are grasping flesh and their bizarre bodies melt together, the avatarick heartland slowly infiltrated by genitalia.' (p.259) After she eventually leaves Luke, Elinda does try to kill herself, despite her former denial, but the attempt is half-hearted. 'I wanted a cleverly contrived death! But I was not brave enough. I had too great a fear of that unmuscled decent. I could not die'. (p.312)

Rainsplitter in the Zodiac Garden, 1978, Shuttle's third full-length novel, has a different tone to the previous two: the prose is bleaker, harder and more direct. Again there are two women, one strong and central, the other weaker and more peripheral. And again the narration moves between third and first person, though this time we also occasionally get the first person narrative of the principal male, Micah—an Old Testament character compared to the New Testament names Matthew and Luke we have had previously. The story and the prose have a mythic quality and seem to exist in an ahistorical or trans-historical continuum of time and place, which is sometimes brought into the present by cars and telephones. The sections, each an independent scene, are numbered not named and can again be read as prose poems as the narrative is apparently not linear. The central character is Faustina[16], whose fear of pregnancy and childbirth is the central theme of the novel. Micah, who has been involved in a war, sometimes confines her to the house and dominates her until she finally finds a way to break free. Faustina has a friend, Anna, with whom she has a close, sometimes sexual relationship, though she introduces Anna to her brother Stefan knowing they too may form a bond. Faustina feels physically and emotionally distant from her origins and her unrealised self; she is frightened of Micah and distant from him. He is a grim presence to her rather than a person to whom she can relate. 'For me he has no names. Poverty of me. In our bed he wrecks me, enters me, knows me: but I know nothing.' (p362)

Faustina is not just afraid of pregnancy, she feels fated not to give birth, but Anna tries to show her that pregnancy gives her power over Micah. 'You hold his child a prisoner. Think of it, Faustina: in his house of secondhand furniture, you, for the first time, possess your own wealth.' (p.451) But Faustina thinks of getting rid of the unborn child. 'The removal of the foetus is a simple matter. I reach into my womb with a chisel. I find the blood and bribe the ghost to rise up out of the grave.' (p.472) Faustina is rightly afraid of the violent Micah, who hits her and accuses her of witchcraft as he forces himself on her. 'His penis strained upwards to terrorism. He promises himself that tonight he will couple with her again, even if he must behave like a thief.' (p.376) However, sometimes she seems to welcome sex with him, especially at her brother's funeral. 'When I was naked my voice disappeared. He turned me round and touched my buttocks. He moved his hand between my legs. Then I didn't want to wait.' (p.427)

As in the previous novels, the women are represented by moon symbolism. Faustina tells Micah that men have landed on the moon, walked upon it.[17] 'What am I? Mindmooncandle. I am watertight inside a dozen wombs.'[18] (p.385) There is related symbolism of white/moon versus darkness/blood[19]: 'you will recite to him your prayer of whiteness, the death colour: describing moon, snow, white skin of the youngest canephore[20], white words of an old song, unlit candles, chalk hearts.' (p.384) In line with this ancient moon symbolism relating to the power of the feminine, Faustina sometimes appears like a pagan priestess or shaman. She tries to end Anna's relationship with her brother Stefan but Anna has chosen Stefan over her, male over female, sun over moon: 'please Faustina, understand, I want to know the language and customs of a man.' (p.445) Anna eventually deserts Faustina: 'I am finished with Anna because her ash-white mouth has become servile towards Micah.' (p.395) After Faustina leaves Micah, her brothers try to return her. As men, they cannot share her 'uninhabited world'. It later seems that Faustina is not her real name at all, just what Micah calls her. 'Why do you call me by that name? You know my old name. Call me by my old name.' (p.488) She does not say what her old name was but she identifies with Jesusa, the female christ and the title of her 1971 poetry collection in the penultimate section of the novel.

Shuttle's fourth and last full-length novel, *The Mirror of the Giant*, 1980 is subtitled 'A Ghost Story'; this has two meanings: Theron is haunted by the ghost of his dead wife Vellet—literally, as Vellet is a character in the novel—and his current wife Beth is metaphorically haunted by her former female lover Ash, whom she has not seen for five years. Another major character in the book is the giant at Cerne Abbas, whom Vellet consults and on whose gigantic carved penis she has formerly copulated with two men while still alive. It is less of a poetic novel than its predecessors and more a fantasy in the mould of Angela Carter and Emma Tennant. In his review Andrew Motion says that is is a novel of two very different halves:

> her opening chapters abound in sentences of excessively wrought luxuriance . . . while her closing ones adopt a tone of more tightly disciplined naturalism.
>
> This is partly explained by her decision to cultivate purple patches when emphasizing elements of mystery and surprise—since these necessarily diminish as the action unfolds, what has been called her "Shuttle-music" inevitably becomes simpler. But it is also due to the fact that she seems to begin writing a different kind of novel half-way through.[21]

Vellet—the 'beast-girl'—has drowned while her husband watched and did nothing; unable to find peace she has come back to haunt him. Most of the time it is only Theron who can see Vellet. 'So is there a dead woman?

thinks Beth. Or does Theron wallow in some dream?' (p.561) Vellet comes to Theron mainly at night and he apparently has sex with her, but when Beth witnesses this she can only see Theron masturbating. The giant gives Beth a vision of Vellet's orgy with two men to show her wickedness when she was alive. Later on in the novel we find out that when she was fifteen Vellet had been the mistress and model of a local artist. The giant tells Beth she must 'grip the thorny veils that bind Vellet, grip them and tear them off' in order to free her. 'Remember, Beth, in the giant's mirror, all broken creatures can be healed.' (p.625)

ENDNOTES

1 The same issue also contained a novelette by Carol Burns; Calder & Boyars also published Ann Quin and Alan Burns.

2 Including: *Nostalgia Neurosis*. St. Albert's Press 1968; *Jesusa*. Granite, 1971; *Branch; A Poem*. Sceptre, 1971; *Moon Meal*.Sceptre, 1973; *Midwinter Mandala*. Headland, 1973; *The Dream*, Sceptre. 1974; *The Songbook of the Snow*. Janus, 1974; *Photographs of Persephone*. Quarto, 1974; *Autumn Piano and Other Poems*. Rondo, 1974; *The Songbook of the Snow, and Other Poems*. Janus Press, 1974; *Four American Sketches*. Sceptre, 1976; *Period*. Word Press, 1976; *The Orchard Upstairs*. Oxford University Press, 1980; *Prognostica*. Martin Booth, 1980; *Child-Stealer*. Oxford University Press, 1983; *The Lion from Rio*. Oxford University Press, 1986; *Adventures with my Horse*. Oxford University Press, 1988; *Taxing the Rain*. Oxford University Press, 1992; *Building a City for Jamie*. Oxford University Press, 1996; *Selected Poems, 1980-1986*. Oxford University Press, 1998; *A Leaf out of his Book*. Carcanet, 1999; *Redgrove's Wife*. Bloodaxe, 2006; *Sandgrain and Hourglass*. Bloodaxe, 2010; *Unsent: New & Selected Poems. 1980-2012*, Bloodaxe, 2012.

3 Redgrove and Shuttle subsequently published another book on the same subject: *Alchemy for Women: Personal Transformation Through Dreams and the Female Cycle*, 2005.

4 Introduction to Djuna Barnes, *Nightwood*. New York: Harcourt, Brace & Co., 1937.

5 'Blood Sisters', *Times Literary Supplement,* January 28, 1977

6 *Times Literary Supplement*, February 15, 1974

7 'The Dancer' in *The Orchard Upstairs*, p. 2

8 Plath's 'Thalidomide' for instance has 'Oh half moon' and 'blood-caul of absences' . . .

9 'The Orchard Upstairs', p. 49.

10 It may be relevant that Shuttle and Redgrove's 1973 joint collection was called *The Hermaphrodite Album;* the word hermaphrodite comes from Hermaphroditus, the son of Hermes and Aphrodite who was united with the nymph Salmacis, combining male and female in one body. However, there is nothing in Herma's character or behaviour to further this idea.

11 John Mellors, in *London Magazine*, June/July, 1974.

12 Robert Nye, *Books and Bookmen*, November, 1974.

13 The name, Like Herma, sounds like a character in Greek mythology and is in fact a Greek name as well as the character in an Estonian folk tale.

14 The Zouave were Algerian soldiers in the French army, exotically dressed and renowned for their bravery.

15 A possible reference to Prufrock's 'I have measured out my life with coffee spoons'?

16 The name may relate to the Faust of the Faust Book and its many retellings; it was a common name in the later Roman Empire—Marcus Aurelius' wife and daughter were both called Faustina—and there are two saints named Faustina, the later of whom founded the Divine Mercy mission in Poland. Elizabeth Bishop had a poem 'Faustina, or Rock Roses' in her 1955 collection *A Cold Spring*; here Faustina's 'sinister kind face / presents a cruel black / coincident conundrum.' Emma Tennant later wrote a novel called *Faustine* and Shuttle elsewhere uses what may be a feminine version of a male name in the poetry collection *Jesusa*.

17 This was in 1969.

18 The neologism mindmooncandle, like moonmoodlight in the previous novel is reminiscent of Paul Celan.

19 *The Wise Wound*, about menstruation, was published the year after this novel.

20 Canephores are the women with baskets on their heads in Greek festivals and the stone caryatids supporting beams in Greek temples.

21 'Overblown Apparatus'. *Times Literary Supplement*, February 1, 1980.

ALL THE USUAL HOURS OF SLEEPING

To Amanda

PART ONE: FLAW

One

The man and the woman sit face to face. But avoid looking directly at one another. Their eyes hardly ever meet. That is what is so noticeable about them, that and their stillness. The distance between them, although composed of only a few feet, is, in another sense, made up of intangible areas as impassable as the hyperborean fall of avalanche. A regiment of months holds them rigidly there and has no intention of letting them go free just yet. Sun moves. Sun flees. The faience of sunlight slides gradually down the walls until the lavender disapproval of dusk encloses the man and the woman. The weight and drought of this dimness binds them further to the room. They are ashamed of their restriction. But they keep still, just the same. The room waits for them to commit their fanatical crime but is already reproaching them. Even if science is their excuse. Without moving, they beseech each other to break the silence. This particular silence is shrill, a long drawn out note coming across the fields, without obvious identity but immediately personal and demanding individual sorrow. Only the woman's fingers move, they work and cavort on the arms of her chair, seeking the correct way of holding herself strong, or if this is impossible, then of simply remaining still and sober within herself. She watches her moving fingers abstractedly, without caring for them, her head held slightly on one side: whilst through her mind drift the disconnected fragments of the profound sighing words she had intended to use, which she had so laboriously thought out. They spin away from her and out into the dusk. Only those attitudes and emotions which she has chosen to call her own keep her on course, hold her to her primary decision, the taking, after so long an immobility, of a first step. Only a strength like that of an opiate stops her from resisting the impulse of her arms to reach out to him. Her fingers writhe and twist. But she grips them tightly together, until her knuckles are the shade of obsidian. She remembers how avidly she had made her original decision, had undertaken that servitude to an ideal joyfully, how her eyes had been as eager as her hips and ankles. How she had smelt an orchard in the early morning. But now she does not look at Tomas. Although she is viciously aware of him, the new-born way he is sitting, slumped, so evasive and defeated. Unlike her, he is without any hope of flight inward or outward. He does not comprehend the importance of different objects set in a dimension nor see the way ideals can shimmer. But in spite of these disadvantages he is the first to speak, he asks her why, in the voice of an emergency, why is she leaving . . . ? When he has told her time and again, repeating the words, as in a sensuous nightmare, that he does not want her to go. No truly he does not want this to happen now that the moment has come. The severity of her body makes him speechless again, drying the words up in his universal mouth. The fidelity of the pluperfect shadows thwarts him. When his withered voice returns, it is normal, firm and steady, very clear and precise. But the adjusted calmness makes no difference. Because she can sense how at the central nerve of his vocal chords, at that soft place, there is a wild and tempestuous shriek living a silent life of its own. When she strains she can hear it. That shout of uncleanness.

O I must go because I am incomplete here
she answers
> because I need a kind of landscape that cannot be superimposed on this garden. I'm lacking something vital in myself, of myself, the longer I remain here . . .

To him, her words feel like snow and ice, cold metal, a frosty bronze: the repercussion of them inside the bone cage of his head makes him brace himself, even his fingertips, to withstand their force. This parting will damage him more than Rachel, he thinks. The fire of resentment burns in his veins. She finds it all so simple, doesn't she, there's no anguish in this for her, is there? He glares at the traitor but when their eyes meet his mouth falls opens. Her mosaic eyes confuse him. For her this action, of travelling to a new self, is instinctive: he can see that. She is willing to obey. When the order is her own. But it curses him. The cedar of his backbone shakes. His throat is scraped by omniscient wire. He says hoarsely

Rachel, Rachel, why? What makes you say things that are so vague? Can't you even streamline your excuses? Why don't you tell me if you feel anger or jealousy or boredom? Tell me.

She shakes her head immediately, he is still speaking when she denies what he says. There is a short convulsion of his limbs. Night falls further across the hemisphere. Her face is a pallid disc of skin, her features lost among the shadows. He was almost right. That guess at her motives was a near miss. Her recent humiliation, her contemptuous mourning of one dead, the return of the nightmare of the children, all these led her to her departure. His uncharacteristic acuteness, caused by his shock, makes her merciless. But she doesn't protest, no more than to shake her head and only sighs and says without any compassion

It goes beyond anger or boredom . . . beyond any tendency to abuse you. I just feel so untidy within myself. I've told you I feel incomplete.

Her hands are relaxed now. They lie becalmed as dead fish in her lap. He moves violently and imperfectly and sits forward in his chair, stretching out to grip her wrists. His touch is warm but messy. Outside in the garden trees lurch in the wind, like conning towers about to crash down.

But I've finished with Herma

he says urgently, measuring out the need and love in his tone and attending to the syntax too carefully for her liking. She shakes her head again. Where is the yoke? Her hair gets in her eyes. Its contradiction. She pulls her hands away from him and flattens her hair back into place. Jerking her shoulders, she gets up and walks to the window to stare at the dark blue wintry spring night. He watches her, a darker shape in the gloomy room. Caressing the glass with hard and expressionless fingers, she says.

No. You haven't. And you're free when all's said and done.

Nothing is legal between us.

Does the lack of any real traditional bond still pain her? Is it this that sends her away, alternately praising and damning? If it is she is too numbed by it to notice it or accept it and tells him in a cold voice smooth as stone or moon through glass

I must go, Tomas. It isn't a retreat from you or a penance for either of us. It is, more than anything else, I suppose, discovery. I have to look for something else. Myself perhaps. Or something more than myself.

He should cry out now. This is his cue. She is waiting to hear him cry out loud. She wants him to shout no no Rachel stay with me please stay, to hear him bellow it out. But neither move, neither speak. They both stare at their hands, disregarding the opportunity to seize one another. Estrangement: its distorted power is thoughtless in its exercises. The wind hisses like geese. The inability we have to live out our lives, Rachel thinks. His mind moves in such limited formal patterns, his ideas are so superficial and biased he cannot realize how aware she is of the dense emptiness everywhere, of the almost mystical stretches of nihilism in her world that extend far beyond the haunts where they have always met. But her nature is not blameless. Does she know that her faults are just as clumsy, just as much the cause of the trouble? She will not deny or rationalize anything once she perceives it, not even to survive. She defies it and takes what is potentially dangerous out into the deathly open where it will rage. She cannot forget secrets. She cannot forget another woman's stillborn child. She cannot forget the hypnotism of the past. Both this woman and this man reject the black night's simplicity. In point of fact, she is drawing the curtains now and she switches the light on, ending everything. He stares at her unencumbered back, visualizing her meaty entrails. He knows he has not been a model companion, that he has not fulfilled the hopes he encouraged in her: so why should the recent death of a comparative stranger, with all the carriage and appearance of an outsider, change and influence her more than his neglect? Why had the news of this death roused her? He could understand a birth angering her. But now everything was over. The senseless woman with her back to him is cold from neck to instep, she feels his stare, she swings round in a balletic curve, she returns his stare, returns it, in memory of some things.

But it is these last few months? What's happened lately? She nods her upright answer and looks relieved now they have arrived at this difficult section in the hour, where it runs away from them and down into the future.

I couldn't just pretend to be out of breath,
Although her voice is tattered she goes on

I was crying sometimes. And such shocks always seem to demand a violent reaction from me, I've noticed before how they require an absolute change. Not just of air. Yet it does go far beyond you and Herma, and into myself: it concerns both of you only peripherally, the way rain falling through air involves the air without choice.

She screws her face up as if staring into this strange auspicious ether. But he does not believe her. Not that he had ever expected the truth.

Rachel, why? Look, you're going away as if these last three years meant nothing more to you than a few days visit with a casual friend. Everything is over with Herma. How can you just go. . . .

His mouth is loose and moist. This is his way of crying out. She has overlooked it, she cannot recognize it. When she replies, after crossing the room and sitting down again, it is with an authority she cherishes yet is hardly aware of. Watching her thin titanic body, he wants to shout at her, to tell her all right go, try and find your other immense gardens, go on. But he cannot. His voice is a dark silent negative. He merely listens to her.

How? Perhaps because it is as easy as that, perhaps the difficulties of going away sink out of sight knowing I am not ready to confront them yet.

You might regret it later then?

I might regret it, yes.

But no, she has not even thought about it. Questions of failure and doubt are bare and puny: she scorns them.

How will I know if you change your mind? If you did, say, come back?

O you will either hear or you will not hear

she shrugs. He looks away from her. His eyes are blunted by her inconsequential yet solemn way of speaking.

Aren't you afraid I'll forget I ever knew you?

he asks in a thankless anger. These half-tamed words tend towards permanence in her. The enquiry pierces her. Bewilderment mars her polish. Will he ever forget her? As if she'd never existed? What will he do after she has gone? What kind of a self will he be left with? What of Herma? Rachel's independence is checked by the thoughts she fears most. Her own hand becomes illegible. She bends her head in honest doubt, uncertain just who is the inferior of the two. But then she whispers

Yes . . . but you won't forget completely. I mean, I'll always be on one or another of the horizons you face, won't I? Audible or not, visible or not, I'll be there? Somewhere? You won't forget that.

He stares at her as if she were the ghost of his mother. But she does not attempt to touch him or soothe him. She does not comfort him. Every time she tries to reach out to him, false painted locked doorways present themselves.

Can't you wait a few weeks more?

he says softly. This makes her sad and makes her smile. She even laughs a little.

Wait

she echoes

O no. Everything says no. Everything says now. Although I have been happy with you, on many occasions. Or thought I was. Which amounts to the same thing.

There is little apparent irony in her tone but he cannot take her seriously, she has made fun of him before. He replies gently, his voice quilted with sadness

Rachel, it's all wrong.

But brave now that this stage is over, even if it is only a preliminary, she says loudly

Tomas, you'll be happier without me, you know, without my discontented face.

When he stretches out his obsolete arm she draws back.

No

she says and sounds glad

don't do a thing.

She waits for a moment, perhaps steeling herself. Her figure suggests a sculpture, one that bears down on his eyelids. Then she stands up and puts her hand on his shoulder, the rings on her cold slender fingers refined, quiescent and bright as gilt. He does not look up at her now.

When you look up

Rachel tells him

I will have gone.

Morning follows morning. Each hour has the dampness of primary colours. She does not return. There is no letter, no telegram. He does not know where she has gone. His acclimatization to this bleak and unexpected scrappiness in his life would take the form of a loud and passionate utterance if he did not restrain it. The silence of the empty house sounds staccato. Whenever he recalls the day of their separation, he feels guilty at his lack of real dissent. He is stretched out now to the psychological extremities of himself, a cartographer mistaken in his latitudes. I was so inadequate, I should have made her stay somehow, forced her, even by plucking her hair out at the roots, I should have been tougher, he admits to his long black gesturing shadow. Both at his work and in solitude, he clings on to her salient memory, doing her a dumb dusty honour, which is by no means exhausted yet. At weekends, he remains alone. He wants no visitors and no distractions. Because he dare not abandon the thought of her, not yet. Tree branches fray in the air and flowers march noisily across the earth. The brazen-footed summer is firmly entrenched, heavy with its seed and gossip. But he walks quickly away from it over the standstill wall-eyed lawn, sun-streaked birds scattering under his feet, as if it is imperative he tears himself away from everything, he cannot remain at peace in this season which gives no shelter. Since she left, he has been trying to understand her motive: what had been wrong if it went beyond the business of himself and Herma: whether the reason was, as she had insisted, merely her own dissatisfaction with a life in one place. As she is no longer present to be questioned, he works his way through the lickspittle memories with his hands tied. He has to find out whether he can be excused his guilt before revoking old decisions or making new ones. A concrete absolution is what will satisfy. Otherwise what is the use? What is the good, Herma? We must wait. He cannot accept a counterpart immediately. For the first few weeks, he went through the days mentally frozen and chastened, his body stiff and angular as a mathematical T-square: but he is becoming softer each day: soon he will begin to assess conditions and starting-places even if he cannot alter them. So, troubled yet enrapt by the solstice, Tomas walks towards the sun, carnivorous light raw on his eyelids, turning the landscape to blood. A pattern of leaves and sun and flowers and flashing glass, their mingling which means he cannot tell one manifestation of nature from another, jangles around him, recurrent and harassing. Birdsong is a twittering of parrots. There is a scent in the air of a salubrious bed of roses. To avoid the malaise of this he goes out of the garden and down into the fields. The houses beyond the fields are miniature models, blocks in a game: toy town. They have nothing to do with the real world, especially when exposed by this sun. For Tomas, both the day and the night are hard to get through safely: but shade matches his indignant grief and even in the afternoon he ferrets out a snare of darkness, the murk of shadow where time filters through a silence that is itself like a clock stopped or the photograph of a dead forgotten figure appearing sudden and swift, face up and smiling from a drawer that is opened quickly when searching with decisive fingers for something else. Everything that he keeps in his head accompanies him into the weedy dark wood. Until he has absorbed Rachel into himself and neutralized the ritual of waiting for her reappearance, he cannot resolve this state of tense uncertainty that exists between Herma and himself or give his second girl any protection against unhappiness. He cannot think of any one else whilst Rachel's memory continues to plunge into his side. All idea and faces seem unorthodox and dishonest. He tries to explain this emotional stagnation of his to Herma and comfort her, because she is also bereaved: but whenever he begins to speak the thought of Rachel hinders him. He cannot tell Herma yes it's over and we're free. It is not true. Like a clapping of reversible hands, a round of applause condemning him as vulgar, a liar, shreds of Rachel's voice call out across an old courtyard as they come back from their lectures and classes. Reminding him of all the obligations he has to their time together. So that all he had been able to say to Herma last week as they stood in the car park staring at one another across the bird dung on the bonnet of his car was, Herma when infants die it is only like being covered in bloom. She had looked at him with a weary open mouth around which her narrow face was a white reprimand. On all sides the buildings, banks and offices and shops, the people and the brass band, swayed beneath a watery and serrated sky. Yes but he left me behind . . . she said in an exempt voice and walked off. Her slow doggerel feet groomed the gravel. On this dry sandy path leading through the wood his footsteps are quieter. They leave their outlines behind them so that he will be able to find his way back. O what is the difference between plagiarism and absolute theft? Which of the two has Rachel got fixed in her mind? Tomas lies down beneath the cancerous trees. The moss is fuzzy against his neck. He closes his eyes. His face is in shadow. Rhythmic compulsive thoughts vibrate in his mind. He cannot switch them off nor gain any breathing space from himself: there is no mental intersection at which he can pause, at twilight say, to just watch problems race past him and off into the preferable distance. He is too involved in commandments ever to get entirely free. Whereabouts is Rachel? In some shared and confidential room listening to the jokes of a stranger? Alone and walking along a tow path by a high river? In a corrupt dress shop? He snipes at the images. But they still make contusions appear on his eyes. Her voice rises then dies away, calling him, giaour, giaour. It is impossible for him to relax. When it comes sleep is artificial. And its ripples soon end. He is awake again almost immediately and when his eyes open he sees above him the gimlet branches, allied to the sky, symmetrical as ninepins. Without warning they are slowly taking control of him. He tries to count the branches and so subdue them but there are too many. They insinuate. They make him want to grovel and whine. He is sure they are pinning him down and he cowers away from their cut-throat shapes. He stares up at them again, as if they are a mirage he daren't take his eyes away from, his face cropped of all expression and those eyes huge and drab and purposeless. Hot lewd branches. The linear branches. Burnt by the diameter sun. O branches o branches his hands grip the green earth and soil punches his fingertips. He goes down and down. Down. His skin coated with branches. Until he jumps up from the hoax of his eyes, springing haphazardly up and running. From them. Runs then back to the domesticated garden whose exact orderly smallness reassures him and steadies him, like a jet of cool water. He balances, a human Argus under the sky. He stands by the gate, breath still overwhelming him, gulping the centripetal oxygen, and looks at the empty house, its windows open because of the heat. No matter his agony, the fugue of dejection nailing him down, if she'd just appear it would drive his grey exhaustion from him. Whatever Rachel thinks, for him at least some irradiating weeks and months of their time together had been a time of life becoming luxuriant, that is how he sees it, in spite of the opposition of the trees and his imagination full of tricks. Had she left him because his imaginative vision fell short of her expectations, because in spite of his acknowledgement of what perfection was, he could not point to its location nor forget his own mild but true pessimism? Because he could not let go of ordinary daily life to the same careless extent as she could? Was it that inability to reach the depths of freedom in him which had so often made her sullen and cruelly boastful of her own nonchalance, her voice when she was angry like a rusty tambourine? No, no, he dismisses these ideas as too fanciful and summery, sentimental and transparent. Flippant emotions are always liable to self-destruction in him. For an instant the thought of his son causes him to despise Rachel. But it does not last and she re-occurs just as potent a symbol, even when he goes on thinking dutifully, poor Herma, flesh racked and torn rudely for nothing, or rather for an everlasting pain the other side of nothing, that unirrigated pain. He walks towards the house, crossing the square garden. Rachel had never known the control and discipline of that pain. In spite of everything else, that had not summoned her. Or she had refused to respond. But because it is still Rachel he prefers to love, he will not admit that it was inevitable she should eventually leave, and so abruptly: that she might even have planned it long ago. He will not accept that they are unable to manage a life together, that they need towns and miles and seas between them in order to preserve the truth of themselves. It is a bargain Rachel is trying to keep. He does not understand the consecration of distance. For him, emotions must be clarified and explained and then accepted: he does not see the wrongness of this, or at least is not brave enough to think about it. Indoors. He goes indoors. Closing all windows, drawing all curtains. And moving into and through rooms of an obtuse and to him almost azotic melancholy which closes down over his face like a vizor. Is it four months? He finds it hard to believe. Nothing seems at all different. Only superficial nature has changed. The season is hotter. Hot as Egypt. Hot as monsoon. But the news in the papers remains the same, the riots and the strikes, the wars and the fashions. The crimes being committed are still the same, his legal transcriptions of the wills and divorces of strangers do not change. He is still hemmed in: a parenthetic limbo: or a playtime of statues with no sing-song voice to release him from his own grimalkin shape. At midnight he sits alone. He listens to the winds blowing from the sea. When he sleeps he dreams of orifices. During the day at work he withdraws into testimonies. At lunchtimes, in restaurants or cafés where violins play solid little tunes and where waiters lunge among the customers like gangster-acrobats, he stares at Herma across a number of tables and a succession of tablecloths as she speaks, her voice more resilient than the music each time. She needs repose. She says. She wants all this to be settled. She entreats him. Like a ballad. But his face stays startled and poky and afraid. She hates his indecision and the atmosphere of the dust-bowl city: the waiting and the way the streets direct memories at her. In fact, her whole inhospitable life bores her. The strain of it tires her because she is still weak. She burns as she plays cards through forsaken hours. He knows all this but when she asks why not now? he has to look away from her and stares at the violinist instead. He tries to agree with her but when Herma uses Rachel's name as an argument in her own defence and says she's gone, she doesn't care, it doesn't matter about her, you don't even know where she is, this only inhibits him more than ever. The ardent image of Rachel always gets in the way, her monotonous hands forbidding him whichever way he attempts to go. So that he cannot confirm anything to Herma. Who nearly moans in discreet corners of these restaurants or cafés. He is constantly unnerved. He is unable to say the word 'love': it becomes the heaviest of words. Neither can he play the fool to cheer her up. He has lost the skill. Even in this cool silent room his eyes ache as he thinks of yesterday and yet another constrained scene, their hissing restaurant voices, her quivering mouth that has a red life of its own. His brain demands payment, it works slower and slower. Sitting beyond the range of microscopes, he is conscious that there will be no refund. His bald elbows are restless. He turns the pages of an out of date magazine and, fingering them hungrily, looks at the women and the cars. Then he throws it on the floor. The pages slither. He cracks his knuckles. Then he tries for the second time today to read a book about the Magna

Carta. And the barons again swim away from the king on the island. He hates these difficult weekends. But for the present time he is caught up in his own wizened past, decoyed by it, soured and cheated because of it: and because it is his own must work it out during these motionless weekends, complete in every detail: must decide whether to accept it or forget it, one way or the other, absolutely, once and for all. To examine the hiatus of roots. The heyday of stones. To plant or exhume. Seeds. In the time of the unwilling roses.

Daytime: she accepts the pangs of the light like a second skin. This place is a new and unfamiliar city. She arrived yesterday. It is studded with very beautiful civic objects. For instance, the statues so heroic and the cool clear clean fountains. Its administration is purity itself. Trams occupy it. It is very famous. But it does not interest Rachel in the least. A sediment of brownish light covers the pavement. Her feet plod through it. Around her, the dappled serenade of traffic whines. But to her, the uproar fades to a blue-print of its loudness. Time has fallen lingeringly through her hands ever since she went her own way in the middle of the deceptive spring. She walks sloppily, in a drawling manner, her hands stuck in her pockets. A celluloid figure marking time in a passive syncopation. When she glances sideways at her reflection in the shop windows she tries to see the face of her great grandmother there. But her poise is tainted. Immediately after she left Tomas, she made sure of fastening a tight intellectual crupper around all of her recollections. Power is the ability to bury dead things, she had said bravely, taking refuge in the year. She watched the months run wildly forward, believing she was well prepared for the challenge, of facing the anguish entailed in learning how to pass the night alone: prepared because her life up to date had been a whole series of broken promises and she was used to overstepping loyalties, quite unconscious of impediments. But wavering and more than mortal, she over-estimated her capability to survive on her own unquenchable terms. Now foreign words dance sorrowfully around her and are too quick for her to catch. Corrupt vowels, syntactic arches, ranting diphthongs: their sense only comes to her in snatches, benefices, particles. It's the inward edges of words I must listen to, the disturbance in them. She repeats her own encouragement. O but what when everything can have a dozen different meanings, it makes even commonplaces sound like the ideas of a genius. An absurd imitator of compassion, she gazes at a howling child but does not stop to comfort it. If only days were not so unanimous in their blankness. Nothing can take root in them. Lazy twisted sloth, relentless hours of ease, imperial silence revealing the smell of time, the dregs of the soul, the loss of spirit. In the satirical summer mornings she used to sit beside the powerless vases around which the antics of space dismissed the cobalt sun and search through the daily newspapers like a vengeful deaf mute: slavish to the photographs of others who resembled him, scanning the print for his name. Until one day at the end of summer she changed tactics. She left the country and now like a ner goes from place to place, watching for hours gondoliers and sailors, to see if they will turn into Tomas. Sailing on a dry sea is more clever than courageous. But solitary. O yes. Prison without bars. Some would shrink. Or pity. On the basis of laws perhaps false: or else merely foolish. The ten invisible fingers of her mind wriggle to wrench fears which protract aristocratic images. Some silent words filter through her jawbone. Loss and separation only underline the extent of her own incompletion. This real loneliness stuns her. It is so different from its photograph. Mentally she chides the air around her, in protest against her compulsive role as a creature that wanders and goes alone. But whenever she thinks of returning, to depose Herma and prepare herself to accept again a comparative if impoverished security, her own voice still says loudly no, no: because it is cowardice: only travelling in the cold dry sickly world of this loneliness will prove what she is now reluctantly beginning to doubt: that she was right to go, that she can somehow exist within herself. Only this reassurance will satisfy her and if not this, then nothing. It seems. Fortified during a short clement interval by the thought of her aphoristic ideals, she crosses the road, strutting, her backbone aesthetic. She is a heroine made for highboots, without scruples, a female patrician. She will win. In this irregular autumn light, her yellow hair is strident, apparently possessing all the tactile propensities of gorse. But she cannot maintain this phony cheerfulness nor persuade herself that she is not already at the very dead and calm centre of failure. She sees herself as oval in heart and snake-haired. O the impenetrable strength of the tomb, she thinks wryly, but we are not all fortunate enough to be able to imagine that we have our deaths available to us at a moment's notice. For me, it's true, death is a subject meant only for comedy. It must be. Otherwise it would be a constant reiteration of temptation. Her lungs stifle her like a nocturne. She had been so determined to cut herself free, of Tomas, of her own secretions of unused emotion, of Herma and her quiet concentration of blows. To be free of the history which Herma stands for, every time she forgets she must not think of Herma and her crippled sombrero. History and its spasmodic obscenities. At one time she had wanted to become incapable of shedding tears. But her desired immunity has been engulfed by too much emptied time and too much intensified thought. The actual acknowledgement of failure had come about eight or nine weeks ago. She had been staying in a spa town, up in the mountains. For the views. Because she is healthy enough. In this town, while standing on a bridge, watching the noisy white water gush below, light-hearted for once and confident of approaching happiness, she had realized, in a cursed unction, that the time of disintegration had come: that nothing of yourself can be utterly shut out. It is not allowed. After all it belongs to no one else but you: who else will take charge of its history if you do not? This idea of responsibility had recurred to her in every other town since, so potently and realistically, in so many different streets and climates, it could not be denied nor put down to a mere geographical fantasy. So that now all her attempts at amnesia are useless. This city like all the others is threadbare, its buildings have as much meaning as fishbones. O she had told him, other gardens. Instead it is the garden she has left behind which continues to trail her. When she walks in the mornings and afternoons through streets in one strange city after another, she keeps her eyes fixed on the cunning light that fetters and muzzles the horizon. But she finds nothing. She moves n an isolation, whether it is through the neat gardens of a public palace or cities dangerous with maltreated deities where in spring and summer flowers appear at the windows of even the most mercantile buildings. It is the appalled square garden and the fields beyond which are always spreadeagled before her, preventing her from understanding anything: the nature of air, the privy purses of emperors, the durability of the sky: they are all forbidden to her. (What if there is nothing to understand? Perhaps you must treat the world with more respect and just be content with what can be seen out of the corners of your half-shut eyes? No. She will not share in that pessimism.) Autumn burns with its own fine grained heat but her bare fingers are stiff elegies of ice. She crosses another street and begins to walk back to her hotel. Head so full of unimportant shallow details. But from time to time there is a homicidal flicker stinging her or annoying her in the form of an itch or worse a sinewy headache that pricks at her eyes like the nib of a pen. A festoon of cold dust makes her eyes smart. Going back. Yes. The first of all her memories then. Sand dunes, all moving, softly and slowly, towards the crooked sea, blown towards the revelatory waves, fragment upon fragment. And a recollection of sea pinks. Ephemeral. But thorough. Uncompromising. A particularization of colour which transfixed. And then a long list: of parties, schoolrooms, tragedies and prudent white confirmations, lies and mountains, kyrie eleisons and station yards, rubbish dumps and cinemas. And somewhere, at some time, she had visited a desert: rocky: a terrain out of her past that, skimming her mind, does not pause long enough to have a name attached to its contours. Only a glimpse, a tang, the arrangement of a long lost landscape. To find a way towards which, or back to, is unthinkable. Near to a strange insult. She just holds on to whatever scent of the place remains with her: hot, dry, a temporary sensation of futility when she watched Herma walk away from her and the rocks for the first and last time: helpless as if they spoke different languages. She shakes her head agitatedly, slatternly tears fly duskily, she looks embarrassed. But no one sees. Memories graft themselves on to her. The most recent seem the oldest. All the pictures of Tomas present him as the tidy urban equivalent of a rustic king caught and slain in his own prolonged nativity. But in spite of this she cannot renounce or abolish the memories. She walks on laconically, body swaying to one side, a vessel compelled by the wind. The slow indistinctness of the resigned day she had telephoned Herma: her fingers had slipped off the dial because they were sweating and quivering: she had forgotten the number and had to look it up again, the pages violent in her hands. She had stabbed her cigarette out exhaustedly. Had it been anger or fear or relief, that emotion she had felt? Even now the prevalence of solutions makes her feel sick. At the other end of the line, the phone rang out. You must you must, she told her, there's no room. O I can't, cried Herma, he exists between me and myself. The receiver slid across the burning table. Then Rachel had gone to Tomas and put her hands on his shoulders to stop him from going out of the house and to her rival. This brief persuasion against leaving. She brought her face close to his and inserted her tongue into his amazed mouth, her eyes greedy, her tongue curling, a powerful liquid organ. But he spat it out, as if it had been pitch, and seized on her wrists as evidence. And they both froze in that hot house. They remained standing there, the rearing flowers in the vases making the only colour there was in the room, the clock ticking out the great distance that there was between them. Until Tomas turned away from their squalid union. Now the bombastic evening citizens race past her. They shove her out of her retrospective subjectivity. She looks around her almost crazy in her painful dolphin privacy. She is embedded in solid air. The filigree no-man's-land of sky is smoggy and full of a mist that descends slowly to cover the world with a damp vaporous mist that blurs the scene to frosted glass. The negative stone fields return her body to her own hands, they want no part of her dangerous mock-widow life. Her promenading along the highway comes to an end. She returns to her empty hotel room that is always full of eyes and ears. Its interior is clean, depressing, obdurate. She stands before the mirror for some moments, attaining a false composure. Then she goes into the snow-white bathroom. The grains in the glass bottle promise to cure the pain. So she swallows two of them, staring into this other mirror, groaning quietly once without reason, unless headache is a good enough reason. Whenever she looks directly at her face in its expedient bondage, she is repulsed by the sight and each time thinks how she hates spending the night alone: she curses all the old lullabies. The night spent alone is sweetish and abominable, much too sweet to relish. This conclusion had come to her recently, as suddenly and sharply as something objectionable that the eye discovers but the burdened mind tries to keep hidden, an obscure and remote generatrix. Now she acknowledges that she wants the taste of other mouths. Sitting on the bed, she waits uncertainly. Her hands are restless in her lap. 1st voice: has she just left him? 2nd voice: o no, it's been over six months now. Her despondency becomes imperturbable and masterful: she lies on the bed with her palms upturned. She cannot find the essentials inside anything and is conscious that she only plunders life, with harm both to herself and to it. Reluctantly, she examines the idea of taking another sea trip. Tomas's intrusion into her once strong and rebellious life obsesses her. She thinks of him both lovingly and resentfully, the carnifex of silence upon which she is stretched. It is him she blames for her invalid world. She lifts her hands very slightly, an economic personal apology. For not being able to save herself from this extortion. The rudiments of data drain her, the complex ways she has to conduct her mind, the rushing droning language in her head, a distrait painstaking parlour game where her monologues scandalize her. She often shuts them out, blocks them, channelling them off from her brain: writing letters instead to friends, lawyers, herself: or sketching eyeless faces in the margins of the newspapers she does not read. She believes that maintaining this neutral zone performs the job of appeasement. But this is too critical a view. It is the interrogatory perceptions and the long intervals of meditation which relieve the cramp of her elaborate solitude by forcing her to analyse the diligent pain of it.

Night-time: when the style of loneliness crumples against the flesh, her flesh. Her nights are fractured and the dark pieces knit together badly, By refusing to settle in one place, she forces herself to speak in riddles. The adder that ascends the tree. Hahah she laughs quietly but bitter as hell. Hotels are all vast hives, with their multiple humming cells. They worry her, the thought of the other rooms accosts her. Although on some nights the moon, bare as a shinbone, calms her with its wash of ivory light. At a time when she has broken and abandoned nearly all of her other talismans, thinking them heretical, she keeps this. In an almost sarcastic frame of mind. Yet with a touch of urgency. There is no moon tonight, however, no support from the sky. She cannot sleep, she gets out of bed. Her eyes feel sticky, as if claret has been smeared on their lids. The way the white sheets break into the setting of the black room pleases her but it is a very limited pleasure. Rachel sits by the window in her unlit hotel room. She is pale in an official manner. This night without a moon grinds down hard against the glass. There is no landscape at all to which she might resort. For her, love means decay, whether that love is perfectly stated and alive, or casual and puzzled. The season of reconciliation has ended. There is no hope at all of cornucopia. She looks out at darkness upon darkness, roof balanced on roof, star set at a tangent from star. The night fascinates her like a wimple. She feels homesick for a place she has never seen properly. The night's silence holds her motionless, a mirror into which she involuntarily stares. She wants to be purified and cleansed. With the back of her hand, she rubs her cheek, her forehead, her anatomical mouth.—We all love our faults excessively—she thinks, waiting for the dawn light to appear, to see what it will do to her,—and perhaps one of my worst faults is that I keep hanging on to a fading or faded identity, constantly demanding proof of it, as if I had a right to something concrete: and I can't rest from it. I must know why all music turns out to be a dry epithalamium for me, dry as . . . as what? fire? I don't know, dry as fire yes perhaps, yet fire can also mean ecstasy and so it is wrong because I know ecstasy is not involved. I must understand those ancestors of mine, those betrayers of me, so far off in their future. I could have stayed with him, to look for understanding, I suppose, tried to be content with dissatisfaction. I could have. Perhaps lived in that large supremacy of familiarity. But no. No, there's always this anxiety to move on. Valediction is denied to me, self-denied. I know what I am, always a guest, just a polite stranger travelling, on the way somewhere else in a week or so. That's all.—She closes her eyes. In this absolute darkness, she remembers all about desire and disgust, those bony and stained nights. She stretches out her arms that touch nothing. She still smells on her hands an arbour of relentlessly aching blossom, which is real and not merely a forced justification she needs to believe in. She lets her arms fall and rests her forehead on the glass cold as seawater.—If I am testing myself then perhaps I should remake my life without pity but the thought of it makes my head mew and I feel dizzy every time I consider moving purposefully forward to meet that next life: even though moving backwards in a detour also injures me.—Sleeplessness makes all of her muscles throb boorishly. She feels wooden. Why does the day always lead to the acting and process of night? What is the purpose of the contrivance of dawn? These paradoxes and the strain of the allegiances which she imposes on herself keep her awake night after night: between them she notices the days come and go and the suns rise, each one dispassionate and dishevelled as a maniac. But she obliges them to remain untouched and unfulfilled, without distinction.

Some autumns thrive on extracts from the other three seasons. They appropriate the blue pectoral fins of winter's dawn ice, the impulsiveness of dusty summer afternoons that dart in the sky like birds suddenly startled by aeroplanes, the moody weepiness of fluid spring evenings. In this kind of an autumn, he asks Herma to come down and stay for the weekend. We can talk, he says. And relax a little. Standing in the uncertain position of an observer, in the open doorway, his hand is on the door knob, but his body is still turned and drawn towards her, a warm climate running parallel to the chilly hallway, her balsamic scent both parching and refreshing him: harmonious, in keeping with his ignorance of her. At times, most times, she is an unremarkable girl, ordinary, no more than average in her judgements or her merely pretty appearance: but at other rarer moments (such as now) there is a splendour about her, so easily missed, so often unnoticed until the sensation is almost gone, like a fog horn sounding in the estuary and heard uncertainly and vaguely far off on the land, that she becomes metaphysical in content. Thoughtfully he commits her to memory, part of a list of components that will form the petals of the flower in a different more exotic colour. Yes, we'll relax, she says. Her dark voice overshadows her face. Her world is frigid and hard as bullion: for her, this is a time retrieved from desperation only by huddling herself around the warm fire of her ambition, which is their marriage, of great importance to her. But she makes no comment about this. Her smile has a deceptive quack gaiety. For the limitations of her cosmetics have been troubling her. She has not felt herself distinctive enough. He has been withdrawn and moorish lately. All her tottering grace is failing. And she has been expecting her second decline at every twist of his mouth. But now, tonight, his study of her seems less reproachful and his eyelashes even quiver a little. They lull her. Her iridescent breasts swing under her motley patterned dress. He watches their movement more impersonally. The nocturnal world is empty of birdsong: the silence is too ashen. Her lips are adhesive and shiny. She has lost her aura. He smiles blindly at her. He's not liable for the performance of his eyes, surely? She opens her distant mouth again. Yes, it'll be a good thing, she tells him, leaning towards him, her jute hair swinging forward to touch his face. But something in the atmosphere, a sly recanting of his tenderness, sets her burning. She wants a drink, perhaps. Their goodbye kiss is a tired neutered kiss, a caress belonging to the daylight even though it is private evening that skirts them. She listens to his car driving away through the darkness, the engine beating out an unmusical drumroll. Then she turns back to the reformed apartment, to gather and groom herself into a tawny perfection of the body. To force herself to blossom. She walks around herself slowly and carefully, trying to work out systematically just how their lives ought to go during the visit, how she should behave, talk, smile, act. But building up false situations and then making calculations based on their wayward events is not her speciality. Nothing resolves itself in her mind. On the Saturday Herma wakes at dawn. How cold. For autumn. There is ice on the windows. A threat from afar. Monopolizing her, putting her in jeopardy. A lacuna of cold where she feels her body. There was an old woman once she sympathized with. Years o years ago. Who wept. And pulled her into the shuttered room. Held up the dead body for her to see, saying, look look! At her last gasp. All the stubborn corpses, perishing to the bone, that litter the world, with their gravestones and all. The frosty fields garnished with ice. You will go then? Primavera calls you. Yes I will go. Whatever. Only at the last moment does she decide to impose a restriction on her eagerness for action and advocates the maintenance of a calm face, the exhibition of a trust: because she cannot force him to obey her, she has tried before and it does not work. Now she can only rely on the jessamine acuteness of her presence in his life to influence him, rather than her old repetitive arguments which burden and disappoint him. Which she shuns. And she will not use her dead child as a weapon. Will not flaunt that suffering. Will not even mention the name Rachel. Because her mouth goes lame now whenever she thinks of the mantissa violence and whiplash body of that woman fortified by scorn. No, she'll ignore her, pretend the memory she has of her is just a hoax. She will not remind him of her first downfall. Exile from first paradise. Her rosy broken body then. He opens the door to give her access: and faces the outer world, its coldness, all the elements of autumn baleful as the field of the disengaged sea. They smile. They greet one another with almost sincere voices. She walks into the house out of the icy hazy morning thinking of this place as a haven. If she has her way she will never leave it. She walks through the dark hallway: a square cage of amulets: there are so many pictures on the walls: sketches and photographs and collages: the knife edges of the frames excite her. She ignores the high walls which surround her, a dangerous area bricking her in. Tomas and Herma both have excuses prepared should they be needed. They stand facing one another, awkward at the outset of their meeting, creatures halted in flight. Then she takes off her coat. To begin with, her voice starts, and she tells him about her journey. Idle talk. Solecisms. It had taken her about an hour. By car.

Yes, very good. The roads were very clear.

Yes. Just as if the countryside had been abandoned to a leaden band of invading soldiery. She looks at him directly for the first time in this shadowy room. But his face gives no evidence of his thoughts. Is this visit to be a test for her? Part of an experiment he has carefully devised? Mock encounters do classify skills. She has to succeed whilst Rachel is absent. And she is well aware that the act of rejection is in itself autumnal, that to demand the token of marriage if Tomas is still restrained by guilt could destroy the foundation of their relationship for good, leaving her as the sole object of his detestation. And what does not come safely to maturity blazes out neon in the mind forever, she knows. Sit down. They sit down. They talk. Heavily. In words of pulverised marble. The conversation is an effort for her. To be honest, she is exhausted. She thinks of keys scorched by time making a conflagration of locks—firing squads incorporated into places of annexation. The somewhat sad almost trite expression which flickers across her face at the end of each long sentence disturbs him. All the virginal ghosts in her head frighten her. They twist her tongue, make the words foolish, cause her to blush. And she has slept badly for over six months. Her fermenting dreams boost and demolish reality throughout the night. But she is not going to tell Tomas about them if she can avoid it, she will not describe to him those networks, seascapes, pearls and corpses which continually appear in her sleep. She keeps them to herself, packed in ice within her brain. O he would sympathize. But they would disgust him. He is a rationalist and would consider them as tedious as the conversation of a noisy and verbose speaker in an overcrowded room. So she keeps to a sober absolute spectatorship. Just watching his hands move when he shows her letters and books and souvenirs, looking at his mouth which contracts when he tells dirty jokes. Making the responses. Laughing. Every time she thinks of a permanent separation from him, the roof of her mouth tastes of charcoal. She cannot understand how Rachel could go, leaving her in sole possession: could go calmly away from what Herma seeks with such a high-pitched gravitation, all her muscles and emotions tugging her in his direction. Tomas's fingers can be like the priest's, blessing, but in a rakish way. Her hybrid love for him works silently to establish herself in his life forever, making it their life. This requires a delicate and minute series of negotiations, far more skilful than any other kind of smuggling. Her words lunge in gymnastic arcs of invisibility that shift their weight and uproot their anchors, crafty and explosive. She moves in these choppy waters, grabbing at his body, for a shoulder, a tongue, an eyeball. To cling to. Because of the child. For the entombed child. Perhaps. What she wants is a stable relationship: yes, to join the twain together more firmly, to mould man and wife into her own insignia. She compresses all this desire deep within herself: but it is a ceaseless microbic activity without any relaxation. She allows it to manipulate her from the inside, creating a bias, an automatic reaction to everything that happens. Late late in the afternoon when the melting weather is forgotten for the sake of cross-examinations, silence arrives. Their faces are cloudy. They are serious. Everything else fuses out. It is such a time. A drastic sharp cough. Then silence. A youthful vertical weeping remembered. But then silence. All else ends. It is one of those times. She looks at him. Afraid, cautious, expectant. A woman at an ancient point in time. All women come to it, whichever you stop on the street. Any woman, any street. Her eyes betray it. Will he do conjuring tricks, produce doves, paper flowers, the flags of many nations, reveal the schemes hidden in a pack of cards? No. He stares down at his hands where no tricks bounce. And then at her: who can hardly bear the system of that gaze, the warfare that they are shut up in. For a period. His methodical hands, freckled like sun bleached cotton, shake.

Herma, what is it you believe in? Please give me some hopes, some speculations, tell me what experiences you have of . . . meteors . . . any meaning you've found in life, at the height of your pangs . . . what was it gave strength to you besides yourself . . . ? . . . what else is there besides our bodies . . . ?

The marshy blood in his head twines in the white mockery of afternoon. In his eyes, an expectation of half moons spirals wildly. To be born innocent, how unjust. He opens his mouth again.

Souls Herma souls. Is there anything outside the precise world we inhabit?

He is begging, drowning in a celebrated formal sea where many others flounder. It is because the words are genuine she is pained. She stares back at him. He is a sort of spectre. She remembers the mad night when she crept bitterly to their door, his and Rachel's, snatching at their voices, herself gelded by isolation, her small head soft as a peach. At times such as the present or at a death you are left alone stranded in such flaring dried-out places of difficulty in the world you think is crucial to you: where that flare strangely enough lets in no light at all. Then, then you need someone there at that moment to hold on to, like an apparatus that permits breathing to continue. If so desired. So her diminutiveness, her helplessness create the remote lonely tension that poisons her. Her faltering voice dies down and vanishes like an old keepsake. These are such unlikely trials. Of all questions, these. Such unanswerable questions. Is he out to trap her? It is a transposition of cruelty then to judge by his strained face. She must speak. With her too brilliant too moist mouth. But she cannot. His words still stand out, too loud, too symbolic. They are both embarrassed by the speech left there in the room's centre. The sound echoes and balloons out, it is far more gigantic than when sheltered by his mind. But he will not allow the subject to grow flabby. Not now. He needs to know certain things before he can clarify their domestic relationship. He must know what makes her answer in one particular manner and not another. Test her reflexes. Swiftly and roughly, he reaches out and kisses her with half-disgusted lips. She draws back, then grips him in an ornamental way. The solid dense crags of flesh settle against one another, in the pulpit of this room: their watery lava limbs buckle together. Until he pushes her away. But gently. He waits for her mouth to go black. But only he sweats. As their eyes shudder. He turns his head away. The privation of shrivelled lives, the waves of the sea, dead brothers and sons, all weaken him.

 O is there anything worth believing in, apart from days and and people
  and buildings . . . ?
he asks pathetically. His hands straddle the air. She considers, leaning back in her chair. Her eyes take the retinue of ice cold sunlight now breaking into the circumcised room.

 There's faith.
As she speaks she nods briskly. Her voice is offhand. The answer is pat, a foregone conclusion that takes no notice of her cajoling plans. Strategy is lost. Any harm done? It's too soon to say.

 I believe in faith.
Still nodding, as if the whole matter of his doubt is settled. But he just lets himself go limp and grins at this. She must be fooling. With the grin, his seriousness loses its value: is eaten alive by the ceiling he grimaces at. There's a refreshing change in the atmosphere: but it is not required by her at this time. With a forged laugh, he says

 Hope and Charity?
She looks directly at him, pacing into his laughing face and open mouth.

 No no. I'm serious. You asked me what I believed in . . . so . . . it's faith.

 I've got no time for alienation.
He almost trembles at her display of clear thought, the firm purpose of her words. A court of enquiry heaves itself into the room. He studies her, his face repaired, set for the historic event, re-tuned to gravity as he amends again his opinions and ideas. Her head is a carved fuselage. Has she always been capable of making statements like this, of maintaining stances like her farewell in the hallway last week, her body always as graceful as this? And has he always just failed to notice? Did he always just nod and say o yes yes of course and let it go by, what now seems priceless? Whatever the reason, it catches his attention. It is a clue to an unsuspected mystery. Since Rachel went, he has been thinking about various beliefs: but only to find them narrow and lacking in substance,

because he is not prepared to admit that the obscure can only be defined in terms that are themselves obscure. He does not want to discover that Herma's belief is also susceptible to this literal animosity of his.

Faith in what though?
he asks.

O no exact visible system or institution, not yet
she says, in the same tone of voice which insists there can be no other answer
> my faith is pure and undogmatized and anonymous: but should I come across something worthwhile, then the scaffolding of faith and devotion will be there, prepared for my ascent.

She smiles at him, accomplished and safe on her own ground, her face tranquil for the time being, chequered by the neat autumn sun.

But in the meantime, how can you bear the uncertainty? he says sharply, exasperated by her private constellations. The debate has resulted in a trumpery analysis of their two natures.

O it's easier for me than not bearing it. Tomas . . . ?
her voice rises, her patient hands gesture at her hair . . .
> . . . Tomas why are you asking me about the way a universe works when surely the problem is just between the two of us?

And then her face splinters at the indecorous words. He stares at the carpet, its tall blood-red flowers. Immediately they both realize her question expresses her own desires too plainly. The words show so blatantly the way she wants to go. She has broken her vow to stay dumb about their future. Her guile is still shaky in spite of all the times she has practised cleverness. But she cannot reword the question or alter anything: there is no way of extrication unless she changes herself into a seraph and disappears amid jupiter flames. O Henna make fun of it and make it sound ridiculous, make a joke of it. But she sits there in a silence which keeps her locked up in her own impetuosity. The tension is powerful: two magnets dragging them further apart. Tomas looks away then gets up to sort through some papers. He is searching, he pretends, for a magazine which carries an article bearing out his almost brutal pessimism and underwriting his tantalus belief that only visible objects are real and that even they are heading for violent destruction. Also he turns his back to avoid her question. A marching tune thunders on an old keyboard. Its muddy confusion is irresponsible and ragged. She can't drown the song or remember where she first heard it or think of anything to say to him which would show the kind of fatigue she's feeling all the time.

I know it's our problem

he agrees after a pause, a respite, a silence during which Herma glimpses a school friend's wedding begin, a procession of whiteness opening up a traditional still almost medieval territory: from which Herma at first flinches but then approaches in order to identify the familiar yet unfamiliar pert girl's sugary face amid the satin waterfall that will not rub against Herma's cheeks

> but you see we've had so many scenes about it that it occurred to me we ought to try and talk outside of ourselves. On grounds of security at least.

The incantation of this excuse sounds mean to him. She nods her head, however, and although she knows he cannot see her, still has his back to her, she feels it serves her purpose. He cannot find the magazine, perhaps it was imaginary, and he comes and he sits down again. All his ideas are secular: he must know if the possesses anything within her heart more valid than his own nemesis collection of facts. But he won't grovel for it. Not that performance again.

His voice comes angrily

> I don't see how you can trust your faith, trust to something eventually being there, which might perhaps, if you're lucky, be worth all the effort of preparation.

At this challenge she looks inertly around the room: groping for a covenant. She cannot break down her principles into slick maxims and hand them over to him for inspection. They are too heavily loaded upon her to be surveyed objectively. She is too accustomed to them to see them from that kind of angle and she shrugs, not rudely, but entirely matter-of-fact in her attitude. Her fingers probe the air, her lips hiss out a sigh like shantung. The vitreous timbre of her body again impresses Tomas.

To have 'nothing' at all, that is what is such a dreadful monster to me she explains, hesitant and nervy, not putting too high a value on the words: afraid to place an excessive emphasis on any of them

'nothing' is dangerous, its emptiness devours you before you can slay it. So I decided I had better be my own judge and do something, even if it was only to prepare an ambush for what I can't comprehend.

His head jerks up afraid of a blindfold.

Not a god?

he asks suspiciously.

O perhaps. An indication of one anyway, in order to defeat the nausea of 'nothing'.

Her voice so uninviting. The words are miles off course. She sees him capture them and destroy them. The words have too mechanical a sound and they are unable to support the truth which she senses. They are exhausted by cruder uses, driven out of their minds years ago. Even she is somewhat unconvinced by them. A good part of her is also still awaiting ostentatious proof. Even more so than Tomas at times. A primitive voice cuts across hers.

When did you decide this?

But she has never cited the distance to herself. The complication within her mind amazes her now: she's always been a nomad in abstract worlds. So when she touches this ganglion inside her head, trying to unravel it, she makes new assumptions, finds unexpected policies emerging. Her voice goes slowly through its own defeats and winnings.

It has always been in the background, I think. But lately, more so: it has increased. After the baby. Tomas. You know.

He doesn't like that.

Yes yes yes

he says quickly. Something decomposes within him. They both fall silent. The room is packed with changeling sunlight.

No I'm not convinced

he states when the silence becomes ominous as a bunch of keys and dimensions begin to slip from his grasp.

No?

she repeats amused but unsmiling. He glares at her, he's a retailer making sure he is not being cheated. If he is, he will shame it away with his grinding eyes. He snaps proudly

What if this 'nothing' turns out to be all you're offered in life, what if everything you regard with hope turns out to be false, Herma, a liar's exhortation, what then?

His mouth shuts tight. He is absorbed, crouched forward in his chair, intense, all concentration held and focused on her sitting plausibly there. Because he is jealous of this revelation of knowledges in her. The subject scorches him, a piquant salamander. Again she shrugs and says without looking at him, almost chanting, but her tone without lustre

Then I suppose my life is just a slip of the tongue.

She is unwilling to say more. No more. She would feel the same weariness even at midnight. But she hides her tiredness. A sudden aloofness on her part now would be a disfigurement even if it wore a smile. What they both need is to close their eyes more quickly when they sleep. Herma sits very still, not unharmed by all these obligatory words. A sibling's anger and her own griefs suggest to her that survival, in a personal as well as a collective sense, depends on learning how to balance weaknesses with strengths, on recognizing that it is a mistake to imagine one virtue more important than another, to ban sluices from life. Partisans must accept subtlety. She shifts away from the perpendicular discussion and his see-saw opposition, to leave the burlesque alone for today.

Let's go outside. For the air. Before it gets dark.

With a successful brimming smile.

Some days in late autumn are scabby and harsh. But this afternoon is observant and oceanic as a nymph: gelid, enriching. As they scuffle through the rotting fallen leaves, he notices a partial easing in this tension of this radical year.

I've never seen any of your neighbours you know

she says. Out of the blue.

Neighbours?

Yes. Your neighbours.

Her saffron dress curls up in the wind as she walks away from him, her hands poised carefully as if she is carrying salt in her palms. She peers over the wall into the adjacent garden. It is a miry place, crammed with broken frames of glass once intended to protect tomatoes and cucumbers and strawberries from the weather, the frost in particular; and then two old cars rusted to yesterday; and boxes full of other boxes; and silent tables and chairs. There are also flowerpots left upsidedown, overgrown trailing flowers, weeds, and sprawling rhubarb. Fruit has dropped from the trees and gone to mould so that the earth itself looks foul and degenerate there.

What a mess. Don't they care how it looks?

She moves along by the fence, agile, an eye ready for snares. The garden is aromatic for all its neglect. A maximum scent.

I've no idea, I've never seen anyone, I don't know. Come on, Herma.

He stands impatiently on the lawn, fidgeting and waiting, a victim of her sentimentality.

No. Wait. You must have seen someone at some time. It's occupied. The curtains. See?

Herma looks back over her shoulder at him, frowning as if condemning him. Courageous in the open air. And the blistering energy that results from sheer exhaustion activating her. To outline an image for him to keep.

O yes then, I'm sure I have seen them. But I didn't take much notice. I don't gossip. Come on.

But hands on the fence, she ignores him and takes another look. An explanation, a reason for the state of the crumbling garden, comes to her, hat in hand. With a pretence at nonsense, she creeps towards Tomas and lowers her voice to whisper childishly, out of her throat, deep down, a pearly distiller of the truth

Perhaps they are thieves or escaped convicts hiding out. . . .

Herma!

Clips from dusky old movies exclude the fishy sunlight. He laughs briefly. But the short laugh is more of a reprimand. He walks on, expecting her to follow. But she doesn't. She stays there, watching him. Then she contradicts his dismissal, shouting after him

Don't laugh don't laugh

even though she is laughing sleekly herself, her laughter hanging sideways in the sky

they might be desperate men

(points her fingers like a gun)

. . . bang . . .

He comes back quickly towards her with an ape's grin, laughing by remote control

I doubt it, I expect they are guilty of no more than neglect, letting things drag on, that's all. They can't be bothered and why should they, whoever they are? Leave them alone . . .

She shoves him away.

Stop it . . .

His arms grabbing at her. . .

Stop it . . .

Still laughing. Her head off. But shivering in this exalted wind.

But they should be bothered. Gardens are meant to be pretty . . .

Tomas rushes at her. They're really playing games now and he twists her around and talks into the back of her neck as she shrieks merrily in a monumental sham that for some would be cause to weep . . .

It's the owner's right to see ugliness from his window, if he wants.

All the time he licks her neck between words, his saliva running down between her shoulder blades, in wet strips. She wriggles away from him in a water-proof manner, still chuckling.

It's everyone's right to choose

he says suddenly serious, indignant, controversial, drawing back, making his confession, taking up his own stand, to repel attack. And she just stands there, with breasts of stone, her face a stone likeness, caught out by logic.

O

she begins but cannot go on with the sentence.

Come on

He pulls her by the wrist: then puts his relenting arm around her shoulders, conventional as a guard. Leaving the vague quarrel incumbent on the grass, they go on down the path, soon chattering and giggling again. Before them, the fields and the wood are almost bare, prepared for winter. They bump into this landscape constantly.

Who lives over on that side?

She points away to the left, her hand fearless. Perhaps because of the coral plumbline of sunset above them that is free from poverty, fear or disease.

I don't know much about them either. They're an old couple, I think. They stay indoors mostly. Only come out to fetch the fuel or the milk. Or to go shopping.

He dismisses them abruptly in a burst of vowels. A spell of conversation at a time like this has to be short. Tomas and the finite body of Herma go on walking. They are on a mutual excursion. But take no account of one another's differing speeds. Shadows of mid blue fall in a mezzotint. The thought that an idolatrous unreal Rachel might be a sort of Trojan horse he is feinting with has not escaped Tomas. All Sunday it rains. Cold drops, romantic, passionate, aquatic. The sky is in a state of constant flux, like a great pool of water set in motion when disturbed by a stone. But sea or sky, abstract vision is a fugitive from the land. So she dare not attempt to codify the scenery. As it challenges. By its incoherence. She turns away from the window, but is already infected by the incitement of the morning. Moving in a sprint, she settles down on the floor, her limbs forming a sort of free rectangle. His eyes discern her, momentarily, rims dry as rind.

Are you going to be working all day?
she asks smoothly, almost insinuating, twisting herself around. She is ready to dance, to become supple, all the units of her body prepared for nails or flames, her white face caustic with her own heat. Their eyes meet again, then once more both parties abscond from contact. He is sitting at the table in a clutter of documents, files and papers. His concentration and bent head are tantamount to a ban on laughter.

Perhaps. As it's so wet. And I've a lot of work you see.
He begins to write, the pen in his hand crunches against the lined paper. His fee looms. This is Tomas as notary.

O yes
says Herma. Mumbling. Her head falling forward to rest on her knees. She'd expected this answer and does not feel it is dangerous. Perhaps it is even a safeguard, to participate in this dull routine arrangement of an over-long day. But that remains to be seen. For the present time, she is bored. With the two of them. They are so efficiently turned out, both of them slender and lustrous: but the world, it could do just as well without them. Her arid hands tighten around the day. She has an indeterminate but virulent feeling that if she gets up and looks at any of his papers it will be like sniffing at his breath. Or spying. To end in a brawl. Her voice strops the silence.

Can I do anything then?
He stares across the room at her, distant as a miser torn from his golden cogitations, his self held up high before his eyes for him to examine if he so wishes. Which he does not.

Can I help?
she repeats
is there any telephoning or typing?
He shakes his head and goes straight back to his work.

O no. Thanks though for offering.
The three bars of the electric fire burn and blaze. Red-eyed. Tomas smiles at his papers and scribbles affectionate notes in the margins. Embezzlements, evidence, liability, statements, Limitations, persons in

debt, persons taken and given in adultery. He ticks them off on a list. The wind and rain descend the scale, a ponderous cello. She fidgets. Hang on to it, she thinks, this invisible faith. Others before him have tried to make out it was only a hallucination and she has been told often enough in the past that it is foolish to invest faith in anything: heard that even to think of it is damaging to the precious self. But she wants to. She is always on the lookout for that single moment which will sound like a serenade. She goes on looking even when disillusionment blots out the effort with its oily rags. She has an obsession for clean straight lines, moments of encounter, total and correct, for the proper recognition of any state: is eager for it to be seen to be accomplished and outwardly demonstrated as true. She wants marriage to exhibit their love publicly: and an angel with wings to prove heaven. All this before she can rest. The rain creeps through the air. Herma shuffles a pack of cards, doubtful of their shiny surfaces. Three quarters of an hour pass.

Herma?

he asks in a disjointed voice, preoccupied, still writing, not looking up

have you any idea why hatred at times can become so attached to love, so close to it that the change from one to another can hardly be marked in time? Why do you think it happens? And how?

She lets the cards collapse. And clutches at her own immaterial fingers.

Who hates you then?

Her voice academic and unnatural. He finishes writing the sentence. Then he laughs. Getting up from his desk

No one. Not much. No, it's the people in all these cases, the divorces

he waves a hand at the papers

I told you about the way they attack each other. What do you think of it? Why does it happen?

She looks at him. Her voice now is slow and guarded. You have to take the scum off the question. Must not offend against codes.

Hate is supposed to be love's other half, it's traditional, everything works in pairs . . . and when the protector, man or woman, goes, then the love once borne towards that person is replaced by a hatred for a dispossessor.

She does not look at him when she finishes speaking, but blinks at the ungainly wall. He leans down and touches the polonaise of her hair. As if this is a sign of disapproval she turns on him, kneeling but on the offensive. She shakes her head and says breathlessly as his hand falls or she flicks it away

No there isn't a standard answer. Because you can't judge the extent of bitterness from the outside.

The surprise on his face is transparent. He soon lets it go.

I was afraid of that

he says unsensationally. She watches him. She does not move. Not when he stands over her like capricorn. For a moment, a devout venetian silence. They stare. The rain treads down leaves. Her skull is heavy inside her head. He lifts her up by the wrists. She is lighter than disapproval. Her bare feet grip the carpet. As he lifts her, a perfect hermaphrodite image comes to life. A joke neither of them can recall laughs at them. He sits down. She crouches between his legs, her hands on his shoulders. A sordid farcical confusion is in all their movements. Afternoons indoors can be so sleepy. She yawns in in his face. In the faint distance, a train moves desperately as a runaway slave. Tomas waits for her to stop yawning. And then fiddles with her nipples. He touches their hard vascular carapaces. He kisses her. At first, a gimcrack. Then an experience for both of a mouth of evocation, reaching a promontory of love. When he lifts his head from that residence of heat they both remain quite still in the inspiration of improvised nuptuals, breathing rapidly. The true goddess is known by her walk, even when disguised as a flamen: and lust is only made of clay: but these two gaze at a harvest of the future with fertile swelling hides. Imagination memory desire. You can't wash them away, not even by weeping. He throws some cushions on the floor for them to squat there, semi-nude flimsy ruined inhabitants of a precarious world. They rub their bodies sensuously together, fumigating the flesh, suffusing, stuffy air clapping hands over their outstretched mouths. Her breasts make a figure of eight. His sticky balls are two old crabs. The vegetation of their bodies expands out and beyond usual flagrant dimensions: until the rite is no longer a soliloquy. Fire bugs show their finery. The firmament thins. Their heads rest on the flowery carpet edged with green woollen leaves as their bodies talk in a kind of sleep. Even their skeletons glaze in a cunning joy. They hover before gongs. They come: with a concord of friction. But when noon and the room wheel around towards them again, he feels the extreme heat of the fire on his arse and jumps up with a shout of pain. At which she also draws her knees up to herself in defence.

Apart from this, the weekend is a success, reasonably gentle and pacific. But it achieves nothing. He says nothing of their future. They kiss goodbye late on Sunday evening. She watches their varnished figures in the hall mirror with a tacky melancholy vanity. Her liberty suffocates her with its loneliness. She returns to the cold wet city knowing he is still not adapted to his freedom. It is a world of night and rain. The windscreen wipers flip from side to side, clearing out a segment of vision through which the road appears shining, all black, pvc, an ebony arrow leading straight into the cerulean blue eyes set in her slotted head.

Void above, void below, long unending afternoons. Shadows are the very essence of threat. The empty house is full of closed doors and stale far-fetched books. This is all that remains to him. She had told him once—it won't work, quoting dead men won't help you—and at that particular confident time he had laughed, blundering like a renegade through life, misunderstanding the tempo of existence, seeing the world in the same distorted manner that a normally quiet mind, when invaded by fever, will see what is not there in the bedroom. But now he knows interwoven words and all old worlds are useless to him. As Rachel had done when she quietly warned him, as they sat together out on the lawn, her short hair plastered with sun, strands and wisps and locks falling into her eyes and mouth, making her hawk and choke. He is looking out of a window. Even the dull green rough lawn is safe within its fences. Gales clatter around the house. Low, cloudy, aching, the sky presses down against the top most branches. The trees make the house even darker, so much wood surrounds it, it is almost a pyre. Had she suspected the approach of this unusually dry winter, so frozen, inactive and languid a season? Had she known such listlessness would result? His crestfallen fingers touch the glass. The cold sensation is too intimate, it is too reminiscent a coldness. He turns away from it. To where the flickering muddy bodies of the rugby players lumber across the screen. The crowd screams silently. He attempts to follow the game, staring at its artful patterns, which seethe. But all he finds himself thinking is that the difference between a regiment and a mob is the same as the difference between silver and steel. The pack tears from one end of the ground to the other. And again, and again. The volume is turned down because its noise makes him visualize chaos and disorder, a world leaping joyfully out of control, martial and resounding with war-cries. He cannot keep track of cheering voices nor understand them. So he watches a silent game. The flat grey afternoon is never going to end. He winces in its leviathan atmosphere as he forces himself to sit and concentrate on the game even though his brain is spongy and his balance prodigal, not to be trusted. But he scents self-pity at once. What of Herma then, what of her experience, she must have known a far greater stress, the franchise of childbirth, so harangued in a bell of labour, her stately complicated fingers covered in blood. The agony of the womb-grenade exploding. And the child dying less than a month later. He is ashamed to draw any comparison between their endurances: even to himself he appears petty and worthless. O the mendacious iron act of turning his back on Herma. And the moon under which she'd forgiven him. The crowd throws up its arms and howls possessive and insurgent without a sound. He distends his face. But the sob is abandoned like dung. Ghosts are everywhere. He is captive in their impure web. Yet he admits that sometimes it is he who hangs on to them, allowing them to take over, willing them to: so that he can think about the dead son of whom he knows nothing but who separates so numismatically one woman from another. It is an almost instinctive morbidity. Afternoons alone encourage him, they are so profane: these times of solitude can be tropical: they wait for calamity to emerge, the world to spit at the universe. O no, it's not in the night, he thinks fearfully, not during that theatrical pre-dawn era, no, it's in the afternoon when everything is silent and dulled, that is when tragedy comes, it is an even worse fox-hole than morning (which is also a nefarious time, bringing wretched light and the promised threat of afternoon). Afternoon itself is the time of maniacs and throttled gantries, that is when the strong but weak scream will come, the simple immediate over and done with death of millions, an afternoon with a fiery red perplexed vibrant height and heart to it. And it is always alone in the afternoon when I realize this, the truth, not in the safe darkness of night. Night is too much fun, an escapist's resort, waiting for Santa Claus. He sits restlessly, listening to the dripping of the silence, waiting for the rhythm of it to be interrupted. But for a while, at any rate, it continues whole and complete, neptunian in its grandeur. He switches off the television set, still waiting and watching. Yes, the images shrivel up. Now slowly he wanders about from room to room. Which horizon, which way? The fields are stale. So is the sky. Is there too much waiting? Into the kitchen. He cracks an egg. The red dial on the stove pierces his eye. The salty garden is another quadrangle, a steelyard by a forgotten river. In retrospect, he has the impression that all the time he had been watching Rachel and waiting, not exactly with anxiety, but watching and waiting, prepared for anything: as if at any moment she might have burst into flower, or white flame extend suddenly from her angelic fingertips. This ambiguity, the recollection of it, still worries him. Rachel had often made him feel uncomfortable, tense, even inwardly violent. In Rachel's company, there was no such thing as security. She gave most pleasure: more pain. He has to agree with his own criticism. She had none of Herma's ease, zest, gaiety, nor courage: not even the relief of Herma's quaint ideas. Take that first time he'd danced with Herma, she'd thrown her head back as she laughed at his jokes, carefree, alive, not dry and agitated like Rachel, not prickly and clever and shining out. He can still see her. But Rachel, never.

She would never have thought of making fun of a dead garden. So why does he continue this tribute? He shakes his head to get free, like a dog with a cankered ear. Dizziness makes him fall foul of the table and he knocks his head against it, loses control, almost landing on the floor. He gets up, cursing, the day undated. O no. If he goes on like this, madness will begin to edge up on him and hell it's bad enough to fear corning face to face with your dead son without the additional terror of seeing yourself crouched on the ground, drooling and singing and raging. He must transform his world and accept that he is not suited to this incipient role of being set apart, mourning deserters. Seeing dangers everywhere, he will advance anyway, hoping he can parry them. He needs to resume that other self, to regain the ability to use and corrupt emotions, instead of being ruled by them. He has to end this stagnation of the heart: he and Rachel parted almost a year ago but still days of regret linger in his life taking up valuable space which Herma's occasional visits cannot succeed in salving any more than she can fine Rachel's stinging censure down to an impoverished echo. Only by taking drastic action will he regain a proper background to his life. It must be soon. This framework of trivial and senseless time stunts him. However much he aspires to tragic passion, common sense always reveals itself in him, demonstrating the fussy outlines of reality, that world of which he is a member and Rachel is not: and with which Herma flirts, skipping between fairy tales and sharp unsentimental pain. Well then. He can catch her and take her with him. The whole tone of his personality is that of a lawyer. His mind does legal exercises best. Rachel has been gone too long, she's left it too late. There is a limit. He cannot wait for ever. Tomas sighs. But fruitfully now because he has decided upon a substitute. Even when he and Rachel had watched Herma walk away with only her hair loitering on the wind, her honey nectarine and vinegar body (which Rachel had hidden from him) clamped to the sky-line, moving like a habit along a cloister, a gingerbread girl in dank apparel, he had felt ashamed. He had felt even then like a poacher who puts out the eyes of larks. Yes. He owes her something. He eats the fried egg. It warms him. Trees are black liquid, pouring this way and that.

Disciple to none, he thinks of Herma with a condescending affection: he rediscovers her. Never mind that he knows names and memories are extinguished best of all by deep exhaustive groaning. Never mind that now. Time marches on. And all follow.

Two

Winter turns milky. Oblong snow storms soon melt. Mist is like a gauze expanse of kelp stretched over the muted narcotic days. Light searches out a foothold. But darkness still hangs around enquiring in a rough diction. It has to probe dawn, whose rays taunt it and scatter it away across time. Just what is this dawn trying to prove? Why does it always linger in the corners of someone's eyes? Why, even at noon, can you still find it, skulking at the bottom of the garden? This is a frowsy day. There is little or no excuse for its scruffiness. Fog pares its dirty fingernails. Birds fly through the porous air. Intimations of morning crash gently through the house. Hernia is already out of bed, she is downstairs, she has lit the stove. Hear it roar. She is cooking breakfast. But it is so early and it is so short a time since she awoke that she is not properly adjusted to the daylight yet: everything is too giant shaped to be tackled. There seem to be an unaccountable number of clocks ticking, ordinary plain-faced clocks grandfather clocks small goldeny and glass clocks wooden clocks fanatic clocks metallic clocks: all churning out hours. She wound some of them up last night. O yes, that's why they are so full of energy. She looks sleepily across the garden, over the grey fields, to the houses wrapped in the fog like old women at a seance. Lights shining in odd nondescript rooms in the early morning are just like the yellow eyes of cats. Why do the faces that look out of windows at this time of the morning always belong solely to history? Herma's face does. And her expression says no matter how early you get up you can never quite find the real world. It is only the lateness of salvage and wet velvet that you find when you arrive panting on the scene. She turns back to the stove, calls Tomas Tomas in a painstaking voice, sets the table, starts another day rolling. In the evening Tomas writes to Rachel, drafting the end of laws and customs, as if this will suffice. He has been putting it off for over a month. But Herma told him, you must. The hasty words are cold and comfortless as a passage out of a novel from some other century.—How right you were to leave me—and as he finishes it with—you must come and see us when you're over here—he says to Herma, his witness, who is reading this letter over his shoulder,

I hope this reaches her safely, she is still travelling and it has to go poste-restante.

Yes

says Herma

shall I sign it as well, Tom?

So Rachel only needs to glance at it once. Because it means exactly the same thing no matter how many times she recites it over to herself, dust gobbling the lavish air around her. Spider on the rose, she wonders of exile, realizing that her life is still full of promise but parched and unpalatable. She waits on in the crowded festive town for nearly three weeks longer than she had planned, listening to the instruments tuning up for the different recitals, walking on snow, hearing the harps and comets, waiting, just in case there should be another letter. But he is to write rarely after this. Not even trifling words. As she packs, with aching fiduciary hands, she tells herself, remember, he is newly married, his work always did keep him busy, litigation always occupied him, he's not unfaithful only tired and forgetful, what else did you expect? But his silence, correct and dutiful as it is, seizes at her roughly, hurts like a hard brush going through her hair and rasping her skull. But it is correct. She runs the edge of her finger along the razor blade. Her fingers are like stalks, waiting to be plucked. But she puts it down and packs that too. The absence of midwives permeates her impure limbs. What journey will there be now? Undergrowth of jungle or rock of mountain? Half-empty hotels, towns so out of fashion they are reptilian and eerie, every monolithic station that resembles the last, strangers, losses, emptiness, laughter that is apocryphal. Rachel learns all about them. The silences in each of her successive rooms remain untouched. She does not explore the silence. Its torrid sparseness does not shelter her. There is nothing in it for her. After replying to Tomas's letter, she does not contact him again. But Rachel goes on believing that in spite of his marriage Tomas and she will continue to move together through time, like two trees where the branches are so inextricably entwined together neither growth nor decomposition of the one is possible without the other also succumbing. Aren't you afraid I'll forget I ever knew you? On this servile dreary half-drunk evening, her room is numb as a cupboard. Sleeplessness is a hand shaking her whenever she dozes. So she takes some pills. And pills. Ah Rachel she is calling her own name now o how she is stretched how she is torn and rent asunder how full of stone. Tons of blankets lap against her lips. All objects are magnified. Everything speeds past her slows down wheels and then comes at her from behind. Hearing, vision, thought, feeling: all change places unceasingly. The drugged horizon mutters at her breast. Her eyes are the colour of laudanum, they look round the room constantly, raking the walls. All the tumult of day buried, all that could be purchased, all merchandise: gone. And she's left with only this lack of clarity that cannot be annotated. She had demanded everything: but she has discovered only its manikin shadow, its impossibility, how at the centre of everything there is merely an imitation of some other sapphire, some other meadow, an older fortress. How at every house doors open irrespective of knocking. How there is only emptiness within each house, cataracts of spotless emptiness. And also villas and castles. From a distance, from her mechanical trance, she contemplates the thought of Herma and Tomas married and the impact of it reaches her even there, it grows and grinds and hurts her. Its pressure is like a granite headdress. It is even more of a blemish to her because she knows she is the cause, she is responsible, she made way for what she was sure would never happen. This marriage proves her wrong then: and no one had asked for her opinion. There is nothing for her but silence and the dry mouth that won't sing, solid and dense and searing, the body forced back against a barrier of good wishes. He'd written them down. —We'd love to see you, sometime.—Just that, and a few other phrases, cutting like sickles, to console her, a retainer of solace. No blood spitting or spilt for her, no guilt on their hands, no reason why they should think of her. It had been a voluntary and too conceited a departure, expecting to be followed and dragged back. Why, no .one had even invited her to return. It is her own fault that she is left with the agony of jealous ice at the brain and the hugeness of madonnas waiting to enter her. But that acknowledgement makes it no easier. O his calm fibrous bride. Her old companion. How well she knows the other woman's horoscope. By her own actions, she is debarred from that small area of love: on her own initiative shut out. Rachel lives alone inside the sockets and joints of her rosary bones. She lies absolutely still, thinking how did I ever come to choose this flamboyant exercise? She had been foolish to believe in a dilatory wonder, in the counterfeit of thunderbolts: to which she had stretched out her hissing prominent hands, accepting fire by the fistful, ignorant of the dangers that go beyond burning. But now she stops. This is far enough to come seeking out a non-existent future. Help me for god knows I'm in need of some kind of aid I'm desperate to climb out of this place raving with my own hope of migration o don't say no there must be a time for me to end my polished travels how can I drive Herma away that perverse girl willing death on the child she never deserved even to see die how can I change the shortline? why do I urge myself on from one country to another always digging myself up regarded by old friends as long lost seen by new friends in as transitory a light as I see them: it could have been so different if he had tried did he try why didn't he try he must have longed to rid his body of his weaknesses to overcome the smallness of his mind. How can I express any love for Tomas now, apparently separated from him so willingly? But the love, such as it is, is impossible to shun. Although for Rachel labour has always meant her own still-born identity and never a child, still there is pain. The ungainly voice of the drug prolongs the cruel interlude before sleep. Don't hold on so set me free even if it means dislocating me impairing me breaking me down as I struggle in this artificial world inundated by it. Skinned and deprived of courage what else can I do but narrate a less courageous future for myself? There is no other way but back. This universe is like a village hall. Conspicuous and known to us all. Enraptured knights riding their hands relieved of swords weight are eaten up by their ponderous time of grail wandering swollen and starving in armour. . . . I'll backtrack now . . . So what she is, bursts forth. Sends her beyond purification. No libations. Just that need to somehow conduct or interfere with the lives of those touching her, even if her methods are vicious, even if her morality does depend on the weather: because she can no longer pretend to be interested in art galleries, museums (like temples or water companies), corn exchanges or race courses. She is as out of place drifting through the remnants of Europe as a lioness on the seashore. Rain squirts all night: rattles on dustbins and junk heaps and corrugated iron roofs. It washes away a year. In the morning, she buys a plane ticket and begins to plan the future as coldly as she knows how, to deprive a garrison of its guns.

Another morning comes, all in a rush, the clouds like hafts of knives worn down by dangerous hands. Stripped of leaf, the trees are scandalized by their own bare branches. Frost is in command of the air but weak filbert sunlight spills over it. The yellow December day has an edgy invisible darkness about it that purrs with the advent of jazz in the evening. Ah but it is no use grumbling, you must accept days at their face value, you cannot take them back and change them nor refuse to welcome the cadavers the sun gives you. Daniel knows this. The marble zone of reality frightens him but so far all through his life he has managed to withstand it, by qualifying its power, by saying, I need never encounter the sort of inner and outer life that threatens men, not if I'm very quick off the mark, I'll always manage to head off in some fresh safe direction, I have the potentiality of escape. This is his eccentric blood money. He has a bitter aversion to the truth of daylight which dries him out, soul and dream and all, eroding him, until his skin seems to have a texture about it similar to that which falls from your hands when you have crumbled rose petals between your palms. The sky is lined like an anxious brow. From a third floor balcony, he surveys the hardware world, automatically accustoming himself to his familiar duty of expounding its false scriptures, its fashionable calamities. But he's a clown, petulant, mediocre, wavering like a paper kite. He suspects this: and sometimes, when rain falls in a grey jeremiad, is humble enough to admit it to himself. All the time he makes experimental gestures that are dishonest, that do not want anything to do with the realism their eager motions pretend to seek. He always speaks fastidiously. Always misunderstands answers. Always moves quickly, as if fleeing from a city of the sick, its plague gutters. But new creatures are approaching him. Today starts off like a day of summer but the air is chilled as the wine which pours through the tittering glittery evening. A prayerless woman with beige hair and green eyelids (a set of second eyes, lizard eyes) and red fingertips, that flap like wattles around Rachel's shoulders, beckons to him and when he politely approaches introduces them:

Now this is Daniel he's a journalist that's right isn't it? The woman speaks straight from the shoulder, out of lips bright as a fire-engine. Her introductions are always well esteemed. The crowded room smells of drink and hair lacquer. Her voice runs on without pause, a clattering treadle treble. The rules are immortal for her.

And Daniel this is Rachel she's one of life's inspectors and keepers aren't you Rachel?

The woman smirks at them and then vanishes into the molten party.

A journalist? Is it a vocation do you think?

So Rachel intends to charm him. For no real reason she can think of: except that she has always had this habit of awarding people (seen on the other side of introductions) good or bad marks, awarding ticks or crosses for their conversation, face, smile, cruelty, temper etc, as shown in the space of an hour or thereabouts. And she must begin this round suave as a diplomat. This old game endows something of a motive to her life now that she is back home and has no new horizons or heroes to occupy her.

The non-surrender of this singular ritual means that she has still not shut out all the alternatives to silence. She has to find out his distinguishing features, if any. With a pungent smile. Which Tomas would have called frenzied. Ah but then no heroes. As she speaks, the lost elaboration of fans comes to her sharply. Her face is exposed by its too many bones. O the plumes of birds lax and airy as lawn. It has a sedentary smile, his face.

No no: carelessness in letting myself be trapped. Perhaps destiny is involved somewhere . . . but no, no, just an accident.

He smiles, gloating over the pat words. It is a peculiar smile, as if the muscles of his face have long been fixed in one neutral attitude, making it difficult for him to switch to another expression. His eyes are just about intelligible. She can read them.

Most things are.

Yes, she can read them. Noise in the room is the sound of chaffinches gone mad and their sentences clot. So they speak loudly. But no one can overhear them. All are busy shouting. Rachel and Daniel offer one another small glib tempting details of themselves. They communicate with the animated immediacy of strangers that gushes out at parties like this in too undisciplined and expansive a manner and that is always regretted later. With a head aching. She observes him, as if from afar, cheating. She sees already how he treats the world, as merely a part of his own reserve, a private imagination, a make-believe world. To a degree, this puts her out of his range. So she believes. Rachel talks elliptically. She doesn't see the shortcomings of a mirror. She hopes now for a fitful extravagant summertime. She investigates him with growing delight tucked up her sleeves. The information she is getting relates to a collected and complicated sequence that is going on within her: and that increasingly has a more serious purpose than merely passing the gizzard months. She injects questions into him: the usual subjects, of course: the aggression of various nations, the sanctity of lives, the morality of law when it touches the heart. For his part, he tries to catch a glimpse of her but it is like waltzing over ice. You leave your movements behind and forget them. He thinks he's home and dry but he is misled. The woman he studies is deliberately acting out of character. She conceals her strengths, camouflages her more dominant and victorious self by hiding behind ruffles of lace. She emphasizes a loneliness (which she truly feels if to a lesser extent than she pretends) and her need to overcome it which she admits

. . . . I can't help feeling . . .

is parasitic at times. O she wants a replacement for sadness, she tells him that, more or less. She manipulates the pair of them with legerdemain. And she fools him. He's caught. She sees this with grubby self-satisfaction gripped between her criminal teeth, her tongue dry with excitement. He is moonstruck. When he first saw her coming quickly but cautiously into the room, he had experienced a forceful sensation of nostalgia, the way a man who, after spending nearly his entire life in a rich but alien land, suddenly and rashly recalls his native country, vivid as a gun fired repeatedly through the silences of night.

I'll get you another drink.

Yes. He wants to appropriate this image which she so carefully represents. For years he has been looking for one like it, to make a contract with it. He sees her as the means to an end: not the most suitable characterization for her. Before meeting her, he had always believed that to accomplish this, the completion of an old fantasy never allowed trespass by him, he would need a phallus of solid iron. Now it softens to a deflagration of flesh. Her robust fragrance is an original source, it is what will nourish him. He does not think about the likelihood of miscalculation. It would be too brackish and austere an ordeal. He roves back to her through the hogwash of people.

This isn't a fancy dress party is it?

he asks her tartly, handing her the cold glass. Senseless topics suit both of them. In this revolving evening they are indispensable. But laughter deceives them both, weak and strong, winner and loser, into a trust that forgets the malevolent insight gained from past frauds. This is the dark time before rhetorical light condenses them into blotched copies of what they really are.

No no why?

See, over there, at the bar, there's a soldier serving drinks.

See?

What a contrast to the idea of celebration. Her face wrenches like an incubus. Beyond doubt, it is. Thoughts in her are not to be put into words. She has to slug for a smile.

I suppose he must be a real one then.

Her laughter swirls tenaciously. If there's any consternation in him, he sets it apart. To deal with later.

Anyway, he's in the heart of the battle. It's the right place for him, I suppose.

Her eyes of north search in corners for another warrior. But there are none. So she smiles again at Daniel, a heavy intimacy of the lips. Whose saliva is made of marzipan. He is not often interested in the people he meets. He rarely discovers worthwhile qualities in them. They never seem to differ very much from one another. Being close to black headlines, interviews, disasters, elections and revolutions deprives him of a clear unbridled view of any one actual separate human being, one with a nervous system and a sensitivity of its own, a memory, a past, present and future. But Rachel is an exception to all uniformity: because even he realizes that she inhabits an autonomous state, one she has raised up for herself. His quiet voice grows dramatic.

Are you in a battle then?

She finishes her drink and consumes his minute sarcasm. Both taste like sap. She is grasping all the time her idea of a fierce involvement with this man. After so long and dry and shadowy an incarceration in herself, she is fearless as the count, she wants the sexual reunion Daniel has already hinted at, the achievement of sweating, her body pressed flat against the vice of sheets. She looks at him. Puts down her glass. Holds out a hand to him. Offering? Dancing is a trim and permanent condition. It is short and it quavers but while it lasts it is total in itself, the frivolous docile art.

What did she mean, one of life's inspectors?

The music produces its wasted chords without revelation, without affection: the stony warbling of a caryatid. He holds her like a thousand others tonight. his hand unfolded on her back, careful and sentimental. The room is hot as a canyon at noon. Walls frame this collection of dancers grudgingly. After a long time of watching lovers from a cruel angle which debarred her, Rachel is addicted to the reality, of touch, of smell, and soon of the cry. It saves her from the blasts of the retreat. Her legs swagger in a circular longing. Her eyes are closed. Her blue genius eyelids wink.

Because I go from place to place, town to town: I'm a kind of an explorer, you see. Not of any learning. Just a visual traveller . . . looking at things . . .

When she sums it up like that, so brief, so broken, so interrupted by grammar, it does sound scanty, she knows, a glut of nothing. But she is unable to give him the innermost explanation, cannot croon her secret: cannot confront this minefield of mutual incomprehension: so naturally the sense of her words is lessened.

Why?

Now he organizes judicious questions.

O various searches . . .

Escaping. . . . ?

She sighs in place of repartee.

I hope not.

They dance. Now to a single sad blue horn. Moving around in a very small area, as casually yet perfectly as they know how. The chromatic shouts of others are boundaries of no interest to them. Both amphibious, they move towards one another instinctively. Yet that very similarity is what could antagonize. In meeting, they will find their own twin selves on the revered doorstep: too violent an occasion. But now she just touches corduroy, he watches silk seams. The night is both sweet and carnal. And in either instance it contaminates.

You enjoy travelling?

Perhaps he does not believe her, perhaps he cannot bracket her with desperation. She looks at him. But the byronic expression on her face is muffled by the darkness. She sighs again.

> I think all people who travel, pedlars, tourists, journalists, or just the homeless, all become indifferent to change, don't you? So enjoy? No. In fact I find it hard work always to be navigating. I'm thinking of staying here, this time, for good, in this place, the old home town.

He shakes his head and smiles: if he is admiring her it is without understanding. She laughs quietly. A half-crushed laugh.

> O well.

They dance in abrupt little jets of movement, around and around. Her body gives off internal sparks, a whetstone in a trance.

> Do you like your journalism?

> O not much.

> Why go on with it then? You're freelance aren't you?

He retraces some granaries, their contents.

> Yes. Why go on? I don't know. O I'm always going to change. Yes, I'm constantly on the brink of giving it up and becoming perhaps an archaeologist or a diver but then I think jesus there's no glory in anyone dying or winning if no-one knows who died or who won: so I go on with my job, repeating what's already happened, deaths and all, to let everyone know what happened yesterday, or the day before that. Archaeology is too far away. And diving's too deep.

At the mention of archaeology she thinks of Tomas and his amateur measurement of the past, the bookish allotments of history which fascinate him, dead attendants and crowns.

> It is a vocation

she insists. He laughs. His face gleeful. But only temporarily. Because tragedy hangs from her thumbnail.

> Have you any ambitions Daniel?

He stares at her. As if scrutinizing an injured eye or a damaged machine.

> No

he says quietly

no they all fell away somewhere. I just have a sick mania for rumours. Pure glowing metal this room, no way of defining its contours at all. But as they encircle other bodies Daniel and Rachel are gazing at one another, planning an erasure of it, their faces soft mild smooth rosy cherubic and erotic. Because Dancers perpetually mean desire. There is a sylvan cesura between them: it is a germinal pause.

Shall we go somewhere else?

he asks

yes yes

says Rachel, in retribution.

Innocent moonmoodlight whitewashes the darkness. They walk up flights of steps, kindred stones, clinging to one another. They have exchanged lifestories of sorts, first at the party, then in whispers as they walked along by the river: at least enough information has been transferred to mean that they must go on together tonight, each movement of their bodies making a daguerreotype, an engraving. There is no other way to go. This episode is moderate and already resembles a dubious fable: but the illusions of the darkness and the drink encourage them both to believe (even careful Rachel even careless Daniel) that a transfiguration of gait is possible, that soon they will win a personal independence from their worst depressions. Now they embrace on the bed in a naked federation. She bites the palm of his hand. With his other hand he touches the back of her neck, an action as tender and continuous in time as that instant when the sky breaks into light, a whole terrace of showering blossoms. She looks at him, her expression tired and cold in the cold room but of abnormal lust Her arms are smooth as bamboo. She lifts them up and laces her fingers together. The light filters through them, a lunar light. She says in a swoon:

see how the light comes through my fingers Daniel?

He looks.

Yes like a Chinese lantern.

His words are hurried, stilted as a tabloid. He is sharp as a bayonet against her side, ready to espouse her. Her cascading body awaits the impetus, feeling him shuddering like a spillikin and she arches herself for the happy entry but at that pulsing moment all her ancestral fears drag her away from him, chaining her to them: she stares at his strange assaulting face, her hand under his chin, holding him off.

Were you ever in a war?

Because she notices his skin is rough and granular, as if the science of artillery has at some time or other been his background: sulphur, nitre, naphtha and napalm.

No I just watched.

True, somewhere there is a memory of bullets, blood and dysentery, watching deaths that meant more than the end. But he dodges and goes again towards his oblique saddle. He begins poking their bodies. This is what you wanted, she says to herself, staring at the brown peruke of her pubic hair. The light: now Rachel switches it off. In the darkness the ceiling is inverted. He scrambles breathlessly on top of her. She reaches out for him. Her wavering half-open hands indicate a brief kriegspiel: of the emotions and of the flesh, in a struggle unending. Two bodies meet to make a rigid diphthong. Sinew and muscle stretching, with the wiry nature of shells. O to call by name, aloud. All her stratagems fail. His incendiary posture, crouching to screw her, becomes barbarous. That penis of his should have been a muscular apex, she should have been able to balance on it like a ballerina, it should have released her. But he thrusts too hard, brutal as an old mandarin, touching her gender in a cheap fashion: so that she obtains only bloodletting instead of the nice skedaddle heaven she used to know, is left wanting, swindled, making silent clubbing references to anger, biting her lips, clenching her fists to form two obituaries. The dereliction of his oily fondling oppresses her and the rhythmic sound—crick crick—of Daniel's pleasure is as unwelcome as insomnia. His mouth squeezes hers dry, sneering and superficial. She flinches and sweats too much. At the end, she gives an almost simian cry, a growl, a groan, a sob of dead and deadening fever. What I must do, she thinks then, in scarlet words like weals, her torso torn by briars of fingernails, is to get hold of that ability to work out my life as icily and accurately as an equation, I can't reject it any more, I must do it as harshly as this night's work, Tomas and Herma and myself: equals what? Daniel sleeps and snores, but she lies awake till dawn, in a humiliating draught, sore and damp and partitioned off from everyone, the zigzag night littered all about her, lousy dregs of alcohol swilling around in her mouth, unable to think of any way yet of doing the sum, of freeing herself from the constabulary of unhappiness, no way of using her head full of secrets, no way out of all the identical rooms closed up by brick and glass, no escape into the shameless baby pink sky.

Wind hustles along streets, scraping paths with iron impact, the natal day of a machine gun. The light of the city gives a hard feline glimmer to all surfaces because it is like the light a frosty pond reflects. This afternoon is colourless as piety. Anyway that is how it seems to them, as they walk swiftly, apparently in a hurry, with steps long and lounging: it could be moorland and heather they are tramping over. Which is not the case. Her unnerved laughter rattles, forced, dry, exhausted. He met her outside the zoo where she spent the morning, staring into the cages, at the straw. The hours there puzzle her. She is troubled, she has found a great disease of her species there. What is it that bewilders, stupefies and ultimately governs all? What links one object with another, places one creature supreme? Everything is lost without a name. Where do names come from? She walks with him apprehensively, fingers dove-tailed to her two cold hands. The wind tarnishes her hair.

Out of the country you say you've been?

She nods peakily. The tigers in a duel with their keeper. O.

Where?

Rachel ignores him. The parrots of red, the vultures of black. The children pointing their fingers at the apes. Their nasty nail-bitten fingers, the rude quicks. Beaks, bears, humps of camels, but most of all giraffes humorous coquettish giraffes with their long silky necks.

Remember those games in the museum Rachel?

He squeezes her stiff gauntlet hand, trying to reach her by recalling that happier afternoon when they had raced down the corridors, not looking at the thighs of the statues but at their own, their laughter aslant and all alone (it seemed) in the echoing mausoleum that she said reminded her of a stage castle, only a month ago. The day after which she'd gone, without a word, and no clue left for him in her deserted neat apartment: and then he had only memories, like an emanation, a condensed form of herself she kept sending to him, from wherever she was. Until yesterday, when she had returned: with no explanations: only the sharpened face of hibernation. There are things in her life he is excluded from. Fair enough. He's glad: because he is already involved enough: o he wants her: or rather the honeycomb images he dredges from her personality: but he doesn't want to know about any old alliances she might have hidden away. Keep them hidden. So he doesn't press very hard for answers. Though he'd like to know why she won't go to bed with him now. This is why he speaks like a conspirator who's forgotten the plot.

    They were crazy

she says, with a sudden auburn glance at him, her eyes shouting huzza for a second, then falling inanimate again. He cannot tell whether she is tolerant or regretful. Sincere? Sincerity is only for half-wits. He lets go of her hand. They walk on in silence. A stray dog follows them for about a hundred yards, then loses interest in them. A horse tethered to a cart of junk and rubbish, rag and bones, pulls a lengthy face at them. Above: no sky, only a sagging net full of cloud. They go down the steps and walk along by the river again: but heading in a different direction to their first walk at midnight. Boats sail on their own faint winter shadows, mockingly frail. Like biographers, Rachel and Daniel stop and both stare at the dirty water. Her coat is a macaroon colour. Motionless, the man and the woman are lost in private thoughts as well as the ice colony of winter. Their feet are millstones for a time, impossible to lift. But, the ophidian water surveyed, they turn, Rachel first, and begin to walk again: more slowly now, as if a pattern of movement has been successfully agreed upon. They make for the park for which the city is justly renown. At this season, the ground is hard, it is like a frozen lake, and there is a precocious antiquity about the trees.

Are you going to stay in the home town?

She doesn't seem to mind this question. At least she smiles, shrugs, and takes his arm. Perhaps she is not listening. She is counting cartridges and the firearms. Anteriors are her concern.

What have you been doing?

she asks briskly, a moment later, without warning. Like an indulgent courtesan.

Nothing much. I've no ties except you, my name is interchangeable with a dozen others where work is concerned, we all look alike, any one of them could replace my professional life with his . . . and my private life is not worth the question . . . so nothing has happened.

He swaggers carefully along, listening intently to himself.

Are you sure?

She does not believe him. But it is a plea not an accusation. In spite of his boasts, he is a keeper of personal skills. She hopes. And wishes him to reveal some substance.

Yes,

he insists

one thing is as important or as unimportant to me as the next, you know how I feel.

She knows. How angry it makes her. This is the one thing she can't forgive or understand, the lack of any territorial emotion in him. It is the place where they go their separate ways. She looks on his withdrawal from the fight with distrust, like illicit hemp discovered under the floorboards. For her, there is always a goal ahead to be possessed. Whatever she does (even destructions) she does in a complete manner. Always must finish the game or the attack. Does not have his ability to live in the freedom of apathy, the soft haven of non-alignment. He is content if he makes enough to live on each year. Beyond that, nothing. It calls for her contempt. She doesn't realize he might have been worn down to the bone years ago: that the bone itself might be in danger of snapping like a dry twig.

Daniel, aren't you aware of any responsibility at all . . . haven't you a duty of some kind, to yourself, if nothing else? Life can't be just mechanical and uncommitted.

Her sparring voice recites some doctrine he once recanted: she touches things he too has hidden away in his darkness. He jerks around to face her, like a marionette on a wire, so abrupt that her arm falls from his arm. For a moment she thinks it will fall right to the ground, leaving her body, like some reptile's tail.

Duties?

he asks violently

do they really interest you? No there's no duty in my life, I've always believed in keeping myself free from everything, because if I participated, the process, in time, of setting myself free from a certain prison would be much too painful.

As if he is defying her. In this foreboding climate. Where mercury contracts.

How would you know if you've never had to try?

She tries to trump him but he doesn't look at her, he just grimaces at the air where fiends squat. A concise negro passes them, staring not at them but at an imaginary misshapen sea. Nor do they see him. Rachel and Daniel each hold a part of the silence. Her face is snipped both by the wind and disapproval.

Don't you know that bloodshed of one kind or another can follow some people from the moment they become freethinkers?

He sniggers:

Who told you that?

But she goes on without paying any attention to his remark, her whole being directed solely at this central fault in him, no barriers between them now, no failure of communication allowed.

What if you turn out to be one of those people?

A snarled eloquence. She sounds so certain that he almost blushes, hands almost steaming with sweat. Sometimes she can make him feel so dejected. But in the end he always grows angry. He walks away, fury causing a partial blindness, with out comment. Leaving her there. She left him for a month. And now won't sleep with him. Keeps on criticizing him. What does she expect? But she follows him, trailing him. The cold wind beats at them. The crust of frost is slippery to walk on. But she catches up with him easily. They go through the trees together. When they come to open ground they are talking of recent history, examining the register of deaths.

It was a disgrace, he lost half of his army and was then given medals, why?

Rachel asks bitterly.

Because he also managed to kill three-quarters of the enemy's army, of course,

he replies, with a claymore laugh. It is the truth. Cordial truth. Which does not touch him in his protective clothing. But to seem brave he adds

I was there.

She smiles but not for him. She is thinking of other things: retrocession among them, minerals, inflammations, transitions: she falls away from him, letting the conversation slide on without taking too much notice of it. Her righteous head is working out cruelties. But when she is satisfied with them, she returns to him:

What do you think about betrayal Daniel?

she asks, her voice penetrating in the emptiness of the park, emphasizing the abstraction from its life of any heat whatsoever. Not thrown by the question, because he is beginning to know her, nevertheless he again grasps her modern hand hopelessly and has no immediate answer: after all it is why he shelters, to avoid these speculations.

I don't know

he says quietly as if they were in a mosque

I can't look anywhere without seeing evil, not even your face: so I try not to look closely at anything: and perhaps whenever we do look closely betrayal is inevitable. So Rachel, who are you going to betray?
No one
she says brightly
I'm planning to be the victim.
Fire-water and panthers, he thinks.
Honest enemies are the worst, remember
Daniel tells her.
Isn't that rather like the difference between latitude and longitude?
she asks, gently for her, her eyes nearly full of reactionary tears. A few minutes later, they part. He walks back through the trees towards the park gate. The icy air creaks through her waving hand. To not want a war requires greater love than hers. She longs for mementoes of battle, to regain lost trophies, to make new treaties.

Three

Now it is time. YES. Time to leave. But her own face in the glass is a sultry reproach. And those horrid soft motionless fingers of her gloves ugh she won't wear them won't have it won't let that death of ceremonial leather touch her flesh. But Anubis made use of a sheep's skin. So one adapts to circumstances. And as the time has actually come she might as well accept it. She picks up her gloves and slides her hands into them teeth antagonistic o honey sweet and far too rich are their crude perspiring interiors. The sexuality of the ten tubes, passages, entrances. . . . Admittance. Of several kinds. After all the plans with their decimal accuracy this should be an easy action. But it is not. She finds it hard to retract this last most attractive part of her dwindling exile. She is not doing it very gracefully, she is no mannequin with arms held just right there yes hold it. In a way, she feels that she is admitting an imperishable failure: to return is a concrete symbol of being wrong in the leaving. You will hear. Or not. Yes she knows there is a basic inability in her temperament to retain the submissive pose of an exile: which sends her out of the city. This time she goes and says goodbye to Daniel: the words gash his weak heart. It's only for a few days. She hasn't time to be dexterous: she sees how the corneas of his eyes dry up like peas: but she has work to do. So she dashes away. Now unfavourable currents of wind chill her, sleet hurls down, triangles of ice chime. The mild middle of winter has caved in and hobbled everyone with icicles. Bleakness and a raw temperature do not help Rachel. Even in the car, frost follows, eyeing her greedily. Blood heat only makes her shiver. She takes the journey slowly, along roads both deserted and congested: black ice is belladonna for wheels. This journey then: it is the second of two courses open to Rachel: this alternative which she has chosen is perhaps an inherited decision: it is neither divine nor noble: but at least it does not burn her eyes: even though its gross possibilities do press down on her almost fearful but compulsory eyelids. Its momentum sends her on her way. Her life's no longer a lyrical carefully saddened epoch: it has purpose: the way an epic has purpose. She arrives some time towards evening. Light still reveals the essential outlines of objects although they are now buried somewhat under dusky dark monitors. She switches off the engine and sits in the car for a few minutes, pressing both hands to her head. Which aches like a leonine heart. No: one comes running from the house to see who is arriving. So she gets out. She leaves her empty gloves on the car seat. She listens. Only the wind pocking the silence. The edges of the stone steps leading up to the front door are cracked and broken. Weeds flourish, their roots in the cracks. The steps have the appearance of ruggedness and yet there is also a touch of the makeshift about them, a hint of the circus. As she locks the car door, she glances at them, humming to herself. But she had forgotten the way they looked. That month of preparation. Wasted? Hurriedly she walks up over them. Then stands, looking at the door. Her hair blows smokily in the high hibernal wind. Her excalibur mouth has a deluxe steel hardness. She rings the bell but can hardly hear it, it is embedded in the wind, inseparable from it: and she trembles in the cold because no one comes to answer her, no one opens the door. She rings again, keeps her hand on the bell, keeps on ringing. All she hears is the god-forsaken wind. All is eternal and abandoned to eternity. She goes down the steps again: one two three. But her initial strongly affirmative attitude leaves her now, she becomes uncertain of which foot to use, how even to walk forward: because in this wounding cold it seems so much more than a failure, so regressional, this trip. Their encounter will be difficult and surly. It may not succeed. There is no guarantor at large. She might be left for dead. Her stomach is a smelting core of flame within coldness. O she is only here to try herself out. But today all the other roads seemed to terminate in harbours: only hers rushed inland. The sleet is sinister. The wet discoid sky makes her feel abject. Everything is shabby. Including herself. The wind sneaks along the ground. O come on. She is going straight back to the city of thermometers and miniatures. Not just yet though. She goes along the side of the house. Beneath the stark unapplauded clown trees. Into the back garden. Damp fists of cold pummel her directly she comes out into the open. Now the sky above her is littoral. It is immense. In the cities one sees only segments of it, like strips of blue canvas stuck to the air somewhere high above the very top of the buildings. But here is the whole cornelian expanse, its lithe and lumbering contours. She stares up. But soon feels blinded. And looks down at her hands mauve with cold. Gloves, she mutters, turning her head erratically from side to side. She is going to shout for someone in a minute. Then the hymeneal couple appear before her. They are coming through the gate. Well, are they real or ignis fatuus from the marshes of her mind? No. Real heads down before the wind, they don't see her, her face flushing to a shade nearly henna: but then the blood fades, leaving her skin white as glair. They have been out for a walk, across the fields, through the wood. And now they are coming quickly back to their warm house, cold feet snapping the cryptic frost on the lawn. Conversation has been battered out of them by the wind. All about their heads, foggy zephyrs of ice air hover. The desecration of flowers is at its utmost. Winter. Tomas looks up, he sees her. Systole. He stands still. For the sake of pictorial effect, Rachel also stands very still as she calls and waves. Hi! A mere pretence of surprise. Inside of her, exultation and fear tumble about, then couple together. Equal parts. Shared. She avoids looking directly at Herma, who has now raised her head to see Rachel's flat talkie face, because Herma's eyes always contain that one cruel superiority she has over Rachel, her own particular role flaunting itself, the place which she alone has visited, the cutting power of her knowledge, of her woman's privacy. Which Rachel can't bear to face. Tomas feels his guts twist. The runaway stands before him. Her narcotic body. At once, he lifts his hand, returning her salute, the significance of which is not clear to him, and walks towards Rachel, without saying a word to Herma, not even saying, for instance, o look here's Rachel come unexpectedly. No common exchange before he moves. Away from her. So. The complications already. The deflections from the real. The way he greets Rachel, a kind of unconscious homage. Herma understands it. What is meant. What is desired. What is to come. Sleet falling on her head and neck and shoulders: icy fingertips. No medicines for such cold. The sky is darken-, ing, small rungs of evening make a ladder not for climbing But she is too intent on Tomas and Rachel to concentrate on it and begins to approach them, in her turn. Slowly. She watches them meet. A wretched superintendent. Against the apache air, they stand together, runners familiar with the race-track. Their hands reach out to touch helplessly. The clasped hands try to create a centre that will draw them together again, weld anew the broken elements of their varied relationship of apples and textbooks and quarrels and refugees. But the understanding between them, which they both still believe in, has gone for good: they stare drowsily at one another, unaware of the force of what no longer exists, of the power of the void. Each is magnified by the other's gaze. The mutual gazing goes on. It takes in even the astringent shape of the pores. But nothing can compel the past to shatter. It is boss, it is more authoritative than the counterpoise of an army. It records events. It does not however return to them or renew a once rejected gestation. Tomas welcomes her like frankincense, he can't help himself. Although he knows she is a threat, a possible apostate to himself. He longs to touch her, just the same, all over, to crawl into her, heat in a cold garden. He lusts after her until he almost gasps for her limbs to move like white fronds, for naked capers out there in the colourless garden. This suffocating longing is communicated to her. They stare, Punch and Judy, in serious stillness. They hardly notice Herma as she walks up to join them, with the air of one who has seen what she expected to see. The distance towards them is a short one. But filial dross makes her drag her feet. She anticipates an interlude of bedlam which will have to be endured, to which they must yield, until its silken ocean dries out. She does not look at Tomas, but she is shrilly aware of the tension in him. The way he had reacted to the sudden (and to her) macabre appearance of Rachel. Almost springing forward. Grabbing her hands. Writs dealing with the body's possession do not stand firm. There is no way of implementing them. She knows. Why it happens. Her mind moves slowly but burningly. She already feels trapped by Rachel, cornered in the stoppered up mouth of illegitimate winter: an unacceptable situation, like a pistol pointed at her head. But she smiles at Rachel, says hello, how are you, where have you been, although her bare hands are throbbing as if they are full of tar. She spreads them out on the sea-cold air, her palms extendeds webbed bones straining. Already isolation administers it sallow justice to her. Bereavement is like venom. She looks at Rachel with a sightseer's accuracy. The woman is thinner in the face but the way she moves is just the same. Tomas is letting go of her hand and begins to talk and grin, his breath making lassooes in the air. Herma stands a little way off from them, to one side: imperceptible the distance, almost unnoticeable. But it separates. Paramour or pilgrim? she thinks as she gazes at the shoddy sky, the fierce myrtle green tint of it, listening to the grave harmonics of the wind, stamping her feet to keep warm. She seems rehearsed, aloof, a piebald mirage, censorious of the other two. As for Rachel, she hardly glances at Herma: no more than is necessary. She knows Hernia has recognized the adversary. Who comes at her from such an unscaleable unsuspected diameter. Who consists of such an unrivalled energetic bundle of enzymes. Who she will not ward off no matter what effort she makes but who will gradually sink down into her mind to make excavations for the final collapse. Her eyes are constantly frowning when she lets them touch Herma. Any speech between the two women is strained and brindled. But Hernia behaves as if Rachel's visit had not come as a great surprise, as if she had been waiting for her, expecting her intervention this weekend. Rachel's conceited manner towards her (when she uses a tone not apparent when chattering to Tomas) leaves her unscathed. What hurts her is Tomas's acceptance of this, of Rachel's approach to her: the way he shuts her out with his accustomed mirth at the old private jokes from years back, the names of people and places familiar to them but unfamiliar to her: the strange contents of another life. The knowledge that Rachel might deny her all grace turns Herma's nipples into nuggets: they are unbreakable as hours: she knows they are closed up for an indefinite period.

It's cold

she says sadly and walks towards the house. They follow her, words still pouring out of their pitiless mouths. He with his grin is behaving like one shipwrecked now rescued. And Rachel is encouraging him. To Herma, the wind is a collapsible sea murmuring in the distance, not concerned with this dingy season, but hinting at the dangers flowering from potential growths in the future: beyond the limits of rose-beds: beyond horticulture: beyond arboreal schemes for the garden.

Rachel's dress is of a soft desultory blue silk, a shade similar to that much favoured by the Gallic painter, J. M. Nattier. Tomas studies its folds and frills all through their unhealthy improvised dinner party. So: now he realizes that nothing wholly ceases, that the furtive despondent apparition of the past (slashing at every object in view with its punitive arms) never dies, that the pressure of its violences both old and new stay in the mind forever, draining the province of all its energy. Before her arrival, he had just reached the relaxing emotional stage where he found it difficult to visualize her face: whenever he tried to recall it, the languid image blurred like some old newsreel, merging into reflections of other women, becoming powdery, rouged and unrecognizable. But now this immunity has gone. The reality cancels out any protection. His deferential yet depraved attitude towards Rachel, cleverly practised and continually supplemented by slight but significant movements of the hands, twitches of the face, half accentuated words, is an attitude ready to oust Herma. As she watches him nervous truths thump Herma. She sees and hears exactly what he means, the exclusive palaver that again reduces her to a substitute. She is no longer his nucleus. Her bleak eyelids are nearly closed. They are haunted by this purdah she's enclosed in. She has to move, she must interrupt these two veteran voices. She draws the full-length red velvet curtains across the darkness, then stands before Rachel and Tomas, holding her hands before her, gripped tightly together, like an actress uncertain of her reception, gauging the volume of the bravos. When they look at her, she has to speak. She swallows, sick in the throat: her own pathetic frugal voice makes her head loll in shame.

Tell us where you've been Rachel.

Rachel leans back in her chair graciously: slowly she smiles, with her netsuke teeth showing.

I remember the sea more vividly

she begins

than any of the islands to which I was sailing, I remember standing by the rail and staring down into the grey water thinking of all the bloodless ghosts it contained. The rucked-up waves were so powerful, they surged violently and there was no way of avoiding the salty sacrificial air. . . I was glad when the ferry boat docked. But as I say, I don't remember the islands, only the seas . . . .

You've done a lot of travelling?

asks Herma too solemnly. Sitting down at the table unsteadily. Sacrificial. It has started. Rachel's campaign against her.

Yes

says Rachel wistful and tense

yes for nearly a year I've been a perpetual tourist, I've seen so much that's put on show expressly for people like me to look at . . .

What have you seen?

Herma's voice very light, very mild. Tomas' eyes on her, cold as chain mail.

O monuments tombs relics

her tidal voice trails

monasteries golden altars churches urns temples parliaments museums all manner of habitations: I've examined everything, even the identical statues with their one white face that turns up in all the major cities . . . talking of statues . . .

she turns to Tomas quickly but an ante bellum movement just the same, her voice gayer, making it clear that it is him alone she is speaking to

    guess who I saw in Haifa? I saw Walter, you know, who married that girl, o she was a stupid loud girl, remember her. . . ? She liked to buy shoes by the dozen. But I forget her name . . . what was it? . . . .

She snaps her fingers. Herma draws back.

    I know who you mean

Tomas says excitedly, picking up the conversation at once

    Jo, that was it . . .

Trespass trespass pumps a balloon up in Herma's head. Her eyes grow protuberant.

    Yes that's right, Jo, well she was there, with Walter.

    Still buying shoes?

    O yes she was. And sandals.

They both giggle, a fragile union, indicative of understanding though, particularly of those areas unrevealed to Herma, a late-corner. Who takes the brunt of their mirth.

    So you've been to many foreign places Rachel?. . .

she cuts in with a centurion's precision, antagonistic, ill-tempered.

    O yes

laughs Rachel offhand

    almost every place that's worth visiting.

    And have you seen many churches?

persists Herma.

    Churches? O yes. They always have to be seen. Churches. I like the big cathedrals best. I long to sing Knees Up Mother Brown in them. Just for the sound of it, you know, and the echo.

Tomas roars with loud laughter that is not a denunciation. It disturbs Herma. Her eyes flicker from one to the other, man to woman. Her own laugh is one left out in the rain, shrunken.

    O no you don't have you ever?

Alarmed by the illogical insult

    No no of course not

says Rachel with a sharp coarse look

I always want to though. That's all.

She is thankful for any lead: she is observing every move, both of her own and theirs, the tenants of the house. Externals. Characteristics. The boat floating or sinking. Between islands.

I like churches

says Herma dreamily

my favourites are the country churches they're enchanted addresses there's one in the village here. I always go into the graveyards and read the old fashioned names on the tombs Martha Eliza Hannah and the rest.

Tomas and Rachel nod thinly.

Once in a church I saw a cross of black wood it was very old and on it this almost naked figure of a man lolled and the cracks in the wood looked just like black blood the juice of the body I thought. . .

She stops at their dense silence. They sit, the three of them, a cabal about to whisper.

I expect it was a christ

Tomas says hungrily

Or a thief or john or peter

suggests Herma, her voice still dreamy, and yet acute, as if she knows she knows what she is talking about. The rusty wind whines.

It may even have been a spanish christ

Rachel shudders, but humorously, playing camp:

you're morbid, Herma. You're just like Mathilda used to be, isn't she Tomas?

Yes she is

he replies

let's go out for a drink, girls.

It is an evening of interstices. At which they variously halt, pause, hesitate.

When they come out of the jaunty pub into the hollowness of the dark night, they are silent, having run out of jests. Their heads are heavy as butter and as thick. Tomas is flanked: one woman on his right, the other, his clumsy wife, on his left. They jostle him. It is a cold night. Following a cold day. They go down through the trees. The wind is at the back of them, driving them on with a royalist fervour. Their thin masonic bodies sprawl through the olympiad of the night as if this journey is customary, a once a week affair, an expedition in common usage: instead of a haggard artificial situation completely out of the ordinary. Rachel has precipitated this: and she intends the others to become addicted to strife beyond the point of satiation. Too much to drink slows their passage, all three of them in the drunkard's gazetteer world. It puts a glaucous bloom on Rachel's forehead. Her feet slither on the slippery moist undergrowth. We all face the firing squad, she thinks boastfully. Inside Herma's head there is an unwholesome tyrannous dialogue unwinding itself. Otherwise, silence. The path narrows. So now Rachel walks a little ahead of them. After all she knows the way. After about five minutes, she stops. Turns back and stares archly at Tomas.

What is it?

giggles Tomas, swaying, his hands skull caps.

Yes what?

says Herma savagely. Speak, before the moon goes in and it becomes more difficult to see your liar's face.

Let's play hide and seek!

suggests Rachel, her eyes round and rustic.

OK

Tomas says, her satellite.

You hide your eyes, Herma

commands Rachel. Herma stares at Tomas, her hands sweating. Her forked loins are in a nightmare.

Why me?

she asks tired and scared. The stalactites of her heart are hexagonal.

O we'll all take a turn

says Rachel

don't fuss, go on, close your eyes, count to fifty.

Tomas stares up at the conchite moon. Taciturn needles of fatigue prevent Herma from protesting. No indignation. She turns her back and puts her hands over her eyes. Begins counting aloud. Rachel grabs Tomas by the hand and they run unsteadily off the path, away through the trees, lurching, crashing into branches, then swerving off again. Herma can hear their laughter. But she counts to fifty, then one hundred, then one hundred and fifty. Which is time enough for Rachel to lead Tomas into obese trouble under the pine trees. Tomas is too drunk to notice the end of a world, whose fragments will tell nothing of its past, its old old glory. He pulls Rachel forward: her compressed chalky body glides around him.

Tomas Tomas

she says and bites into his neck diagonally, her face crabbed in the darkness. He takes big handfuls of breast and bum, the flesh feels like barleycorn scattered through fingers. The King can move one step only at a time but he can make his move in any direction: forward, backwards, laterally or diagonally. He has the distinctive privilege of being himself exempt from capture. I'm a printed picture of a carnation, Rachel thinks, my head's as fluffy as a flower. The Queen is by much the most powerful of the forces. She has the advantage of moving in straight lines: forwards, backwards, and sideways, to the extent of the world, in all directions. She laughs a dribbling lingering laugh. Herma hears it. But does not move. She is struggling for supremacy over her unwieldly devotion to faith: is fastened to the damp path: the supine conflict keeps her counting angrily for a long time. To protect her from seeing the other two at their slanting play. But not long enough. She puts her hands down and holds them out in front of her, bloodless as leaves, just as veined. She begins to walk automatically towards Rachel and Tomas, as if guided by her sense of smell rather than her eyes. The Pawn moves only straight forward (except in the act of capturing). However, it is permitted to go two steps when first played. The Pawn is the only one of the forces which goes out of its direction to capture: and which has not the advantage of moving backwards. She creeps up on them, almost lecherous, a little indifferent at heart but, having special knowledge of pain, ready to extort full compensation. At first, looking through the trees, she does not see Tomas astride Rachel: or will not: but sees instead the child's face at a school prize-giving; or a baptism: she searches out the strange child's future and dwells on it. But a moment comes when she has to watch the other two. Lord, she can almost taste their bad breath, the beery chromy stink. No: it is hers also. Her head is not, full of cinders. She watches the kneeling couple, a hundred yards away. Their arms around one another like lovers. Rachel opens her eyes by instinct of the blood and with her horse-shoe eyes stares at Herma who cannot hide in time. Their eyes meet. For an instant. Tomas mistakes her tension. And only clenches her tighter to him. Rachel stares at Herma in a murderous reverie. Who is stone or salt, god knows which. Then Rachel closes her eyes. She falls back on the ground and stretches open her violet thighs. Herma sees it all. She wants to call: Tomas Tomas Tomas. Make him turn and see her and save her. But her mouth is cursed by its saliva of sea water and her lips stick together. She sees. Hidden behind the trees. But cannot run forward. Is broken by that sarcastic glance, the defiance of it, the strength. She can hear them murmuring. She feels lifeless. But when Rachel takes up Tomas's prohibited rod, fingers it, and then manoeuvres it into position for him to fuck her, Herma howls silently in an old chequered torment. And whilst the other two receive each other in their exposed delinquency, she too mimics the womb's act, leaning against the tree trunk. Her hand scourges the sterile place. She is leprous. Beyond cure. So she comes forward, fearfully, treading lightly, as if on parole. These two bodies are still strained and rigid: they do not hear her: she waits until their connexion is finished. Spawn. They stop. Tomas' mouth is ready with a superfluous rebuke. But Rachel's teeth are content. She had been aware of Herma behind the tree but was not going to warn him. She wants sudden panic to grip him now. Now that Herma stands over them. But when Tomas sees her, he is at first almost too tired to care. Who cares about her childish crucible of hate, her silly spasms of pain? Yet from the ground, Herma looks tall as a giant: or some sort of an approximation to one, at any rate.

She stands over them in a frozen paroxysm. Her legs are stiff. She can hardly balance. Their equinoctial lust insults her. Tomas hesitates, not used to the new status of his body and its mind. But he gets up and mechanically covers himself with his hands. His lips swell. He faces Herma. Now he realizes she is military. He sees a whip in her hand. Or rather the significance of its absence. Rachel stays stretched out on the ground for the time being. Her silk dress is ruined. She is glad. She points a phallic finger at Herma.

Without breaking the skin
she shouts. Then slowly she gets up. Her face is the perimeter of her mind. Herma understands. The impossible nile pacing across the desert. She stands between this man and this woman, a fulcrum of bone. Only the trees are alive. She turns her back on him and faces Rachel. He shivers, does his clothing up, does not look at Rachel's amused face. Everything hushes. Silence is palatine: it knows the uneasiness of the situation. The painful night heaves. Darkness and the trees surrounding them: a laborious stockade. Herma lifts her hunting hands. Which force their way up through doctrines. She is sore between the legs: she thinks of it as a wound inflicted on her by them. Her faith may flower or die. She does not care which. Rachel stares at her. Does not speak. Is sworn to secrecy. It is a strict rite they are inventing. He watches them, his body the attorney. The freak wife uses her hands to encircle Rachel's throat. The incestuous stallion and mare, those ancestors, are present. They do not move, no more than Tomas, Herma or Rachel. Rachel's breasts shake as Herma moves her hands. The wanton hands tighten. Again their eyes meet, these two: they go down into the darkness of pupils, Euridice & Euridice. The hands. Tomas takes a step back. No musician. His hands tremble. The hard sober blood pounds in him. But his foreskin is limp. Rachel grips Herma's wrists. She holds on to them. For dear dear life. Herma does not release her hands but she stops squeezing. Just remains. Metal solidified in the mouth. Arms growing tired but not falling. Tomas watches cunningly. Herma begins to shake her head cretinously. Where is a clean place? Not dead any of this group, nevertheless, they are skilled in the death that is a

living death, that is an ignited death on fire. The night pricks Rachel's skin. Her eyes are still round. She pulls Herma's mute hands down. Whose heart contracts as she gives way. Rachel glances at Tomas. But he is staring up at the heavens. The cavities of stars.

Things are reduced

says Rachel but even she sounds subdued and goes hurriedly away through the derangement of the landscape. They both turn to watch Rachel go back to their house. When she is out of sight, they move towards one another simultaneously. There is enough of a union between them for that. Perhaps heathen. But a union. No sound, no token, no sign between them beyond this. Only a recognition of disease. Words at this time would annoy them with their brawny verbal cartilages. They have different views of the same events, are as faulty in

judgement as historians standing in a conquered city. He backs away from her, back through the horizon. To obliterate is what she wants: to return from this night a different way, to be safe from it. Tomas stares at Herma but, in place of her concussed expression, he sees the great culture of altars, little churches and huge cathedrals, the sacrificial alms, the gold: for the first time, he glimpses a way in which life could become a succession of achievements instead of chance blown and scattered by a haphazard wind. The peerless but truculent idea, which is the very belief he has been seeking, for so long that he has almost forgotten it, hovers near him, tantalizing, just out of reach. Understanding is almost within his grasp. A solution. Knowledge. He forgets Herma. A strangership. No affinity with. He is grasping at a new order. Where all the answers are. He lets Rachel congeal within him. He flees from Herma into this byre. But Herma is still aware of the present, she is still colonising that sight of them on the ground. She speaks: to shatter his light:

Think of me.

Darkness again. As his vision withers, the new hope drowns, the joy of his blood turns to a weak weary serum. It is her fault. His contempt for her is as strong as her fury at her usurpation. The thought that she has been a spectator maddens him. Was standing there watching. Looking over his shoulder. O it leaves him at freezing point: shows him the distances he can't hope to travel: in the polar depths of this night. He can see Herma now. The slightly maizy quality of her skin. Her dull eyes. Her numerous stupid faces. Which follow him when he looks away into the black boundaries of night for a lost world: but where he sees only her and feels only the coldness. His teeth are fixed in anger. He moves towards her. He can't speak. But he remembers a giraffe he once saw. With great accuracy and in silence, he unzips his fly and shows himself to her again, holding the flesh up to the fringes of night. Bovine, sickened by the proof of this evening which he holds in his fingers, Herma retches. The lazy undisciplined wind blows ropily. This is a crisis of the flesh. But she can't take her eyes from it. He empties his bladder at her feet. Urine flows in a god-killing whisper. Steam rises in the pulpy dark cold. There are no concessions. Herma turns and runs through the night, with one scream that demands the sun, that warm blossoming.

Early sunday morning. A day, alkaline in substance. Fields blanch in wet mist. Flights of birds tilt blackly across the sky. Scrappy light slopping into her lap, she sits on the bed. Impassively. Her pelvis is sluggish. Ungainly, slouching, humptybacked, she stares at him. He is cold, the room colder. In an attempt to clear his hangover head, he stands straight and soldierly before her, his hand resting on, then gripping the bed rail. The sportiveness of her hair is a thing of the past, now she just lets it fall lank and dry. Tomas wants to use the proper words, the adequate, no, the sonorous words, to tell her how afraid he is of another direct confrontation with Rachel, of the perjury that might mature in him before long. He wants to apologize. He wants her protection. Save me. He wants her to realize how much he needs her assistance: now that their plain but comfortable world has been invaded and is being turned into a transient glebe. Rachel is dangerous, walking so slowly, neither dancing nor singing, manipulating Herma so subtly that in the end, when the end comes, she will appear to be the one to blame for any destruction of a whole kingdom of hours. He understands this as well as he understands he will believe it himself; in time. O he knows Rachel. And how to handle her. Until they stand face to face. He can hardly bear to be deserted again. So he has to explain to Herma that behind his first greeting in the garden yesterday had been the history of the wilting plant, intimations of blood to be spilt, broken glass on the bedroom carpet: to say that Rachel has the power to trick him . . . so please help me . . . in spite of the renewed knowledge of the past which Rachel has brought us . . . The vanadium light hovers around them, unsure and cautious, somewhat lost. In the room there is only this cold dummy silence. He sits down at her side. She looks away from him and into the mirror and down at the floor. He puts out a hand to touch her. But does not. He fears the contact of the raw angry flesh. He just speaks, the words of an itinerant preacher

Herma (my child)

which he does not say but she hears it just the same

Herma some of us have to live out our own brazen age . . . we can't help it . . and we spend the rest of our lives either remembering it in even wilder colours than those of the reality . . . or else trying to forget it, absolutely. I'm one of those . . . I'm hoping to forget it . . and I don't want to have to relive it. Not the way Rachel wants me to.

Her nightdress has no sleeves. The company of heaven call out at the woman's name. Her bare arms are icy and clammy. As if scales are growing on them. He swallows. His tongue is rough and dry.

You must try and understand what I'm trying to do . . . don't you see how difficult it is for me?

She does not speak. Rain makes a fortress out of the house. Her straggly unwashed hair wrecks her face. It makes compassion hard for both of them.

You must

he repeats defensively. Tell her you are still tied to Rachel, unable to reject her, how only Henna can help you to free yourself. Tell her. But it is too fragile a relationship to support words. It becomes buried beneath them. There is a good common land somewhere. From which he is barred.

By his heavy wife. There are barriers. Of many kinds. How can he begin to anneal? A portcullis of silence is down, a drawbridge is lifted. Anything he says to describe his divided loyalties, any way of beginning, sounds like a confession. Which is a breach of his own self-respect. Yes. He has that. O Herma. Her dead silence and her very way of sitting hint at a private devilish spirituality. Perhaps it is just an external form of his own guilt. But it overawes him. And puts him on guard. Anger tastes sweet.

Herma if you want me to kneel or weep then you're wrong he says loudly, standing up again. She ought to understand his unabridged dilemma, without this prompting. He has adorned her with explanations. Now he takes her by the shoulders. Shakes her until the morass of her hair flies in his face.

My god can't you understand!

This brigand's voice frightens him. It is a travesty. It is not him. What has happened to me? He lets her go and backs away. He can feel the blood pulsing and pouring through his body. She lifts her head to look at him, her eyes half closed, puffy: throughout the night the street of dreams has become a metropolis. She nods, her caramel hair swings, then she sinks back into herself; refusing aid. How can he give this situation the warmth of touch, the relief of a mutual forgiving? He leans down over her.

It's not that I . . .

but he stops, checks himself; coughs, touches her arm

Herma you're cold

then feels embarrassed instead of sad, removes his hand and walks to the window

I'm not making any promises . . .

Sharply. Because he feels that something is being wasted, being allowed to slip through their fingers. What this is exactly he cannot say: but he knows that he is part of it and it is part of him. Priceless. Whatever it is, he cannot grasp it. Its nature is unknown to him. Perhaps Rachel knows what it is. Perhaps it belongs to her.

I'm going down

he says. He has to get out of this room. Cannot move quickly enough. The door closes.

o god

she says. A voice like a bee's wing. But without so much expression as a good morning, to the postman, the milkman:

o I'll never die.

In this same tone. Once, in an optimistic mood, Herma had told herself secretly, my life is unfolding like a flower under the falling down raining down of time. Now she disbelieves herself. She knows that there is no possibility of forcing Rachel back: the woman is victorious. Incessantly. Always has been. From the beginning. Has the weapons on her side. Tomas has gone. She stands up and rubs her eyes dry as cypress. She goes and looks in the mirror. She is that young. She stares. Impersonally. She is that old. No matter what happens she will always find herself every morning greeting this too honest and faithful a representation. It is useless to challenge Rachel. No gloves thrown down. Crazy. It is too cold a season for one thing and besides she has her dreams to handicap her: dreams that give her glimpses of insatiable worlds flying quickly away leaving behind a suggestion of the suspect presence of golly-wogs or a rag doll wringing its hands or Generations Of Vipers or faces drowning in the evening or the agency of burnt metal searing her nostrils and the fear of all these things plucking at her like dying hands. No no I haven't the courage to expose my dreams to the daylight and the test of open air. They mutilate her and deceive her, they wake her up just when they are about to speak aloud and explain their purpose in her life. So that all she hears is the silence of her own mouth. This last night she dreamt she stood, wearing a breastplate (which weighed her down, of course) on a beach of grey stones, surrounded by a herd of white neighing rutting horses. And as she was stretching out a hand to touch the mane of one of these horses she awoke. With her hand outstretched. Towards the window. That is all. But for those first few seconds she had been all ready to get up and go and search for the horses. But Tomas's sleeping body was lying in the way. And she soon realized that the horses did not exist, anyway. Which made her body feel empty and disordered in the frugal dawn where it was already raining heavily from clouds of livid grey. She puts her hands over the reflection of her face in the cold glass to cover it up. Her hands shake. These dreams curtail all her modes of communication (even mime) but what can she do? Day knocks them down but it does not cancel. She dresses. Her fingers are lumpy with the cold. Damn this clear light of morning which conceals nothing except dreams, light moving cleverly and slickly over all possessions, bright or dull, the morning which always returns too eagerly, too early, enemy of the individual, dragging its dark afternoon ominously behind it. Sometimes overnight you become stronger, if your dreams have left you alone. When you wake you reach out to strangle the feverish light of dawn. This time you are going to defy it, you've got the courage, you'll beat it this time. You lunge at it. But it turns out all you hold are handfuls of air and space. So best stay asleep. It's too early to live. She undresses again. And crawls back into bed. In surrender. It's early. When you do wake and live, time will sweep you on. It's a train that will not stop, won't give sanctuary, won't pause either for open field or battle ground. Sleep is a safe cage, with all those locks. Without it, you'll be abandoned up to yourself. Even dreams are preferable. Herma tries to sleep. Turns and tosses. Light catches Rachel's tired eye and rouses her. The sight of this room is a grim yet glorious ritual of rediscovery for her. Her breasts feel like gold, heavy and shiny. Yawning, she turns over to verify this impression, but her hand finds only soggy flesh, that is like candy to the touch. She closes her eyes and attempts to grunt herself back to sleep. But how the rainy light gleams. The rain slaps on stone and whirrs between sly blades of grass. Wind and trees are engaged in a noisy dialogue. So she gets out of bed and walks shivering to the window. Coldness. She hears Tomas's voice, raised, expelling all the anger from his heart . . . any promises. . . . She smiles. The coldness encrusts her limbs. She lets it have control of her body. Her teeth chatter, tilting her smile. This is a day when waiting is the hard work. Waiting, for results. Waiting, with ear and eye in trim. Cocked. On their mettle. A vigil for the daytime. Though it could easily be night, a dark day like this. Septic day. If her luck holds. Castellated sky. Sensitive to misery. Herma's. Hah! A seminal day too. Estates are bequeathed on such days. Great events are perpetrated. On a day like this illegal bodies must cling. They must. Before senescence begins. When friends, lovers and enemies are just old bones inside sepulchres. The cold is unbroken. Its ravages go on. But she is a match for it. Such a specimen for its examination is rare. Few of her kind. They make a difference to the general body. She is alien and masked all the time. But she is proud of it. As another is not. And in such a way that another, who is ignorant of such morbific matters, could not comprehend. She is made for lingering on in life: a realm she enjoys. The listless months of exile, Daniel, other cities, old ambitions, all are meaningless. Who cares for lanky wedlock? Down in the garden, the tangles of mist rise as high as the fences. The gardens on either side are ugly, disciplinary in their raided desolation. Over them the mist also curls. Uninterestedly, Rachel studies the monkey-tail patterns it makes. But as she watches, she sees Tomas come running out of the house and through the mist across the lawn. He heads for the fields. She smiles again. But he is not making his escape. Merely taking exercise. Also he is measuring bravery. Or what to him stands for bravery. Clouds fan the sky and move fast as a merry-go-round. The rain baptizes him. He goes on running. He has no use for transport, not even a sea horse. He barges through the chinks and cul-de-sacs of the mist. The rain and wind are loud as corncrakes. Daylight eats into the face of man running woman at window stone sky earth and tree. The impact of the weather makes him stumble, he is struggling with his own peculiar loneliness, there seems to be a rotting herbal scent everywhere, far worse than the usual decaying odour of rain. Perhaps it is this garden. He wants to turn back to the house. But he feels it will be cowardly if he goes back indoors so soon. He does not see Rachel watching him. He slows down and walks across the fields, his fingers numb, his legs aching. She waits until he is out of sight. Then she goes slowly back to bed. He wanders. He has no destination. What does he feel? First: impetuous hostility towards his wife. After all that had been implicit between them, to give in, without a fight . . . Rachel has only sparked off their trouble: there has been a fraud right from the very beginning. He veers off the path, moves wildly between the trees, knee-deep in wet grass. Never want to see either of them again. Deliver me. From mine. Enemies. I'm not fit for correction even. I implore. I do. This incompetent sky. I command. No. No. Rain falls. But I do not fear. What's Herma doing? Her gentleness should have forbidden . . . Herma sobs and whines under blankets. Her penance. For nothing more nothing less than inexorable birth. O Rachel, I'm confused, I'm tired, I can't say goodbye to you, jezebel, virago, boadicea, madonna my own. This little Herma, the young, the stupid, just a girl, what's she to us? With her, picnics. With you, banquets. God. Some laws. I call for them. A pillar of fire. To lead me out of the wilderness. No. I forgot. There is nothing there. Nothing visible. Nothing empirical. Rain smelling of joss. Again running. Running. The two women lie in their lily-white beds. Walls, a corridor, and their lewd libretto separate them. He runs through the wet wet pale green dark green brown. A forgetfulness of colour. Dripping. Leaves of linden smell fresh. His vervain head opens to the freshness. Like mead. Under this tree he falls down glad and thankful to the soaking still and contemplative earth. Ah. Mere. In all my troubles. Lady for me. To improve me. To hide me. From visible objects which must be described, gods, decisions, philosophies, beliefs: all medicinal, ended by your sweet sound of still silence. He rolls in the wet muddy grass. An orgy of self-pity. Which he should fight off. But will not. For once. Medullary tears stream down his cheeks. The nacre mist wraps around him: and soon he begins to shiver. Then he sneezes. What am I doing? There is a long day in the house I must endure. The conflict is there. Not here. A felon returns to his booty. Like a limpet his life sticks to the bones of him, to his knee-caps. He goes back under the unemotional trees.

Sunday is an onion day. With a silent oval shape, having false tears attributed to it and the taste of ammonia. Shrapnel rain falls. They spend most of the day in separate rooms. The two women stay upstairs. The tenderest of them cries real tears. By noon, both are dressed in gay colours. But Rachel in her white sweater and orange skirt and Herma in a bright yellow dress stay hidden behind their doors, as reluctant to emerge as any real sun. No one bothers to light the stove. So the house remains cold. A moist saturating coldness. That does not amalgamate them. Continuous hunting goes on in each head. But they keep as far apart as possible. Half-eaten food lies on dirty dusty plates. Today no one feels like eating. They had too much to drink yesterday. Afternoon inundates them. Herma wants to strip everything down, to tear things open, to take them all down with her into an even more private dwelling. That darkest descent. But she does not know how to start breaking this silence. Let alone hearts. A necklace of pearls, a ruff of shrunken moons, encircles her throat. She fingers them nervously. She's fragile as a minaret, a reduction of hands to helplessness. Who cannot explain herself. White flower of bone, dark roots of eyes. She stares and stares in the mirror. But it's not enough. A collection of compromises and errors makes her a non-runner. Amongst these winter hunters. She should have thrown Rachel out the minute she'd seen her. That would have broken the spell. Tomas would have been proud of me! Why didn't I look up and see her first? Why didn't I throw her out? Because I am frozen, because my will is stiff and unmanageable. Because I still cherish the memory of the friendless unicorn. Back, beyond the dry desert of the past. And closer still, the inflorescence of death. Bile and bitter her mouth which falls into a horse laugh now and then. Demolish the rainy horizon. She is the assassin already laid out in the mausoleum. Until she turns away from her mirror. When she becomes a dancer sleep-walking. The white cargo of her flesh crouches on the floor in a cold sweat. Plant seeds in too shallow a box . . . she murmurs through a breviary of tears. BUT. If nothing changes, I'm the winner! So Rachel: in her room at the end of the corridor. Silently she waits, recalling coastal towns, the spray, various weary revels, odds and ends of geography where unwanted flowers nestled, caves, cafés, cages and grubby floors, an old rennet stripper covered in scars: without regret for the sufferings of others she thinks on and on and on: if nothing changes I'm the winner! Yet, standing by the window, she sighs, rataplan, unawares, and she has about her the quaint air of utter boredom. Downstairs, Tomas listens to records uncritically. The volume is turned down. He doesn't like noise. So the songs can't be heard upstairs. If either of the women hear a phrase, they think it is the wind. French songs, slow, a tempest of sorrow. His head, bent over a book, is the crumpled stone head of a philosopher. There's a way out, if only I knew. He thinks of the wet explosion on yesterday's horizon. For which Herma mourns. If I could, I'd prophesy deaths for us all: she plans worthlessly, stuck inside her coniferous phoenix body. At about three in the afternoon, Rachel leaves her room, banging the door. No one has come near her all day. All normal social behaviour has ended then, she gloats, in merely a matter of hours. O what power, how she sparkles. Tremors pass through this bony earth because of her. She wields her body like a sceptre, guarding her breasts as if they are roses, free from death, and goes along the corridor and down the stairs with noisy steps. Herma is listening at her door. Just like old times, she thinks. But no. I was healthy and strong then. I fought. Her dulled face sucks its cheeks in and contorts its lips but she goes on listening. Rachel goes straight into the kitchen. A bowl full of cups, saucers and plates is waiting. Grease floats on the surface of the water. Rachel makes a face of disgust. Then she goes through the cupboards. She finds a loaf of bread, stale, but it'll do. She cuts a slice and eats it dry. Then takes out a dirty glass, rinses it out, fills it to the brim with water and gulps it down. Aah. She kisses the back of her hand reverently. The wet reserved impressionable world is a place for walking. She shall walk. She gets her coat from the hall and goes to the back door. No. Wait. Again, her quick step taps the stone floor. She hears the music. Sacred songs? No. Symphonies? No. Lovesongs? Yes. She opens the door. Tomas is standing at his desk, his youthful back towards her. She resents it. This is the only warm room. He has the fire on.

Hello Tomas

But he does not turn. The way his shoulders heave is a thrusting away of anything more to do with her.

Where's Herma?

Upstairs.

As if he gags at the word. Still does not turn.

Thank you thank you

mocks Rachel, laughing recklessly. Then he comes across to her at once, face wet, eyes deep yellow. His doodled mouth is slack.

You leave her alone.

Rachel pushes him away from her with as much force as a punch. Why should he interfere with their lives . . . . ? Her nubile bulletin of anger comes out in a strong muscular voice. A short answer: of obscene currency. Her lips form the monstrance. He flies at her, why he's been in a coma ever since she arrived last night, his rage is a colossus, who is he protecting from insults, Herma or himself? The back of his hand slashes across her unnatural lips: whipcord flaying. Her jaw is aflame, a comet of pain. There is a pretext of tears in her eyes. In this instant, he is patriarchal. Then loses his chance. He cannot follow up the first blow. Rachel laughs. She can taste blood. But she laughs. Upstairs Herma hears the raised voices, the blow, the scream. One long pithy shudder goes through her: an oxidation. She rushes to the window, tripping over a pair of old shoes. Leans her burnt forehead on the cold glass to cool it. Then stares at the bedraggled fields. As if they could grant a reprieve. O god o god she whispers what's going to happen to us? Unwelcome sanity remains inherent in her. She pleads for instability, the relief of madness. She'd like to be able to roll and scream on the floor. To bite the carpet. She'd like to foam at the mouth. But there is no revolt of the brain. No black-out. The pain goes on. Just the sternness of reality. She hears Rachel's excited laughter. The blow has made a companion of Rachel. She is involved now. She is no longer just a visitor. Blood tells her, you're one of us again. Her happy face tells him this. He turns away. He feels sick and hollow as a bell. He disbelieves in honey. He hates afternoons, with all their tendrils and tentacles. Banging doors, Rachel dives out into the garden, her coat unfastened. She is in the lead. So the colour of grass is beautiful. The whirlpool of rain is wonderful. She runs towards the fields where no cattle graze. Feeling sorry for himself, his nerves suppurated, his head reeking with howls, cowardly and trapped as a czar, he goes back and forth across the room, looking for a doorway that is not there. He is incapable of making sense of this fierce world. I can't keep a journal of a voyage like this, thinks Tomas, I'm no Marco Polo. The vendetta of winter is directed against him alone. Cold, shivering, his jaws bristle, the dampness penetrates the bones, the bones flinch. Herma bursts in on him, a refugee from herself, she's seen Rachel run off, her eyes are regalia, what does it mean . . . ?

Has she gone has she gone?
Scrivener's animus: he reels round he staggers round he kills off any idea of being a refugee his head is full of soft black mud it oozes out of his eyesockets he wants to slice the skin from his bones to cut his face off where are the scissors: the sclerotic meteors of her eyes enrage him he screams

Go to Hell!
And she goes, to sip the hot desert wind, obediently.

Rachel soon comes back to the house, an expert on falderals, a philanderer soaked to the skin, curtailed by the sharp-witted wind. But she is still satisfied, her determination now as hard and rough as emery. Gloria. She goes and gets out of her wet clothes. What a cold house. She puts on a dress of vermilion wool. Herma does not hear her footsteps this time, she has fallen into a samite sleep with no dreams. Rachel makes a pot of coffee. She leaves the washing up and uses clean cups from the shelves. Her short wet snaky hair is a flat wig of marmalade. Evening is falling. She switches on the light. The music has stopped. She takes a cup into Tomas.

Thank you
he says softly, not looking at her. She sits beside him, drinking her coffee. She smells wet and clean. The room is warm. Quite like old times, he thinks. The music plays again, it is about summer nights on a river. It is

romantic and good-natured. But when the record finishes and the coffee is drunk they find themselves sitting hopelessly in a corrupt explosive modernist silence. He does not put another record on. Small bodily movements embarrass mutually. A difficult stoic hour. During which all she says is

I must go tomorrow morning.

He nods. He does not know yet how he will feel then.

You must come down in the summer

he tells her. Yes. Quite numb. Lips phantom. She nods. Then no more. Soon after six o'clock has struck, Herma comes into their black and white solitude. They are glad of her entrance. It means she is still alive. But her face is blank: and all she says is

I'm going to church now.

She only attends on odd occasions, harvest festival, new moon, Michaelmas. Because Tomas never goes: he always asks, what for? it's only echoes and candles lit when it isn't even dark. Her pearls are jittery.

Coming, Rachel?

Herma looks challengingly at the other woman, who is reclining in front of the fire. Rachel hesitates, schismatic.

No . . . no . . . I believe it tempts me even more . . . besides . . . the weather . . .

She seems half asleep.

Goodbye then

says Herma and kisses Tomas goodbye. The room is full of mouths during that caress. Rachel is smitten by the lusty grey bodies touching. But says nothing. And Herma also without speaking goes, leaving the two of them alone in the house. They hear the front door shut: then the engine start up. Tomas almost yawns. He feels like falling asleep too. But what with the noise of the rain and the knowledge that Rachel is watching him he knows he will not be able to sleep even with his eyes open. Wasted day. At which he feels annoyed. Like the day he had swept all the dead leaves from the lawn and the paths: the garden was cleared, he had piled leaves on the compost heap, prepared for fire. And then it had rained.

Poured. As heavily as today. He could never get over the idea that he had been cheated. He feels the same way now.

After all you said when you left I didn't expect to see you again so soon he says cruelly

what happened Rachel?

She looks at him sorrowfully in the dim room, some of her triumph gone. Inamorata. Her voice is pure, deceptive as pretended sleep.

Soon after I went springtime came again as I had known it would, and I was alone. The lawns were green and empty in front of the strange houses. Days grew longer and skies higher. Or it seemed as if they did. Everything became remote. You know the feeling?

He nods, his heart already a tingling mass of ice that will be tray him. She goes on, eyes closed, in the same restrained manner, with the same sleepy clarity.

Every night I slept badly. I was prepared, I had the know ledge of myself clutched like a passport in my hand, I . . . but . . . I . . .

He touches her arm of cold arum.

Rachel, don't . . .

A voice from the undistinguished crowd. She waves a congenital hand at him, not letting him stop her.

Please: you wanted to know what I did when I was away, now I'm telling you. I could not go it alone. I longed for a substitute for you, I couldn't stop myself, there was the great racking desire of that search, mornings when I ached from the harshness of it . . .

She grips her hands together. The room is hot. But her hands are dank. Outside, evening clouds flap like capes in the sky A choir sings.

. . . . and it was such a dark spring, I could not find any light, it seemed I was in a dungeon and I could not break out of the too soft fleshy prison which held me, my hands full of wet skin . . .

O Rachel

he says almost swooning

I was here all the time.

She opens her eyes. There is an amelioration of herself at this point.

Yes. I know.

She does not look at him. She makes a shape with her fingers that becomes the shadow of a mallard on the wall. Watches it. The shadow. Laughs. He does too. Then mammoth seriousness returns. Her hands collapse. She looks at his hands.

I know. But I'd got a kind of stage-fright about any relationship by then, I could not come straight back here to you, or go on into the future to find a stranger, not at that time. I was squeamish . . .

She pauses again. Fundamental shadows are between them. Psalm number . . .

One evening I cut my finger with a kitchen knife. O it was an accident. Truly. I put a plaster on it and forgot all about it. But during the night the plaster worked itself off and in the morning, because my hand was lying close against my cheek, the first thing I saw when I opened my eyes was the dead dry skin of the cut finger. It was whitish and flaky and it made me think of the grave, all dry and dead. I was so afraid . . . .

Rachel looks at him for a long time, fierce yet with a hint in her eyes of a slavery, that is perhaps only visible when she is disturbed. He tries to sympathise, to give her some security. But the tableau seems bleak and beyond his control. He feels tired and as void of sympathy as an empty cylinder. The shadows consume him.

Fear is normal

he says shakily, looking at the fire,

at some time or other we all discover it, hiding under the bed, out in the crowded city streets, by the traffic lights, down a deserted dusty thoroughfare. It is part of us, Rachel, it can't be burnt away, just as if it were paint.

But his elegiac voice and wincing hands give him away. The words are unsteady, as if he expects her to flaunt a noose at him, as evidence of all the morgues. He does not fool her. She knows he is only minimizing the truth. But she pretends to believe him, nods yes yes, says so in a rasping thorny voice. Darkness approaching more than ever gives her the sensation that all objects move on a prattling sea of air. Blood rustles silkenly in her ears.

But in time

she returns to her story

I began to look for a way out, I went to parties and operas. There was one party. Whose, I forget. But there I met a man. I danced with him. O Tomas. He was so curious, mysterious, detached, and yet ribald. Far off. And yet familiar. As if he belonged to me. I thought. We went walking along by the river that night, we whispered and kissed. Then I went home with him, I let him . . .

Tomas grimaces expectantly at the hated moment of hearing. But worshipping it also.

. . . o you can guess. He undressed. I undressed. He told me . . .

she stops, sour and ill, not from the carbon heat in the room, but because of old climates. Her bitter monomania closes in on her. She puts a hand over her mouth.

What happened Rachel?

he is worried, there is hardly any light left in the room or the sky, darkness is about to cave in, fantasy figure, guy stuffed with rags and old newspapers. She is too involved to appreciate the situation with her usual irony.

I was expecting so much more. A total experience. But it was just belongings scattered by a flood, shock, my tongue feeling like a frog's. After so long a solitude, a privacy, I resented this reconciliation which I had myself instigated. And I felt so bruised and hurt, icy, unmoved and shunned in the act. A good night's sleep lost. . . . because I was awake until dawn, until darkness was running away and everywhere had a silver tinge, air, land and faces. And the world then was different, as unknown as a hell. I felt I'd been through a burial. I was changed, perhaps for the better, perhaps not, pale and doleful because of the night-time. I stayed with him a few weeks, then I left, saying nothing to him, was away for about a month, went to another city . . . although I went back to him . . .

His voice is a blunt metaphor, defacing her sad story.

Did you make some discoveries, the ones you talked about? Yes, it is contempt she can hear. But love-birds are cheap fools.

No. Not any to speak of. But I had to do everything I did. Am doing. Don't be so austere about it, Tomas. Try to open your mind for me. Let me in. Don't you understand? That to achieve the identity I wanted and still want, I had to break away from everything else, I had to do it. I'm not like Herma, I want more than the simple truth, a pat explanation. I want the whole picture. I want what lies behind the whole picture.

She hurls the words at him. He resents the fact that she left as much as he resents the fact that she has returned. Hates the way she shows up all the evils. He recalls infantile curses. In his imagination he grabs her pettishly by the hair.

But you did not succeed.

As if that proved anything.

I had to risk the failure.

Tomas gets up. He switches on the light. False knobbly daylight clamped in steel wires. Standing by the door, behind her, he says disappointedly, handicapped by his lack of correct terminology for this occasion,

Are you proud?

At once she twists round to look at him, not angrily, but shaken, caught off balance, and says breathlessly, gabbling:

Yes in a way. Yes. Whatever it is, no matter what, makes us suffer, well, we are proud of it. It's right to be proud. O I wonder

he says without moving. Neither of them move. Until he comes and kneels down in front of her, hands crossed and resting on his sloping thighs. He stares at her.

I wonder.

She touches his hair with crescent fingers. Herma prays on her pale knees. The cold festival of evening. Heat hard and salty is on her lips. Sing Sing Sing.

Tomas it isn't only pride for its own sake. It helps loss to be bearable. Loss I'm so capable of, because I'm no longer invulnerable. It's like a priest, formal when it gets at you. You cannot be insulted when you're caught. You accept it. You cannot be insulated from it. But you can try to protect yourself. The things I do are protections for myself. I do them because I think self-knowledge means an absolute and total trusteeship of one's self. That's what I wanted. What I still want. As far as I'm concerned, not wanting it is a fault, it's a weakness. Beyond question.

She places a strait hand on his shoulder. He cannot get free of her influence. But he goes through the motions of argument. Sermon, a tasteless odourless stunted discourse on a candlestick text.

Rachel, it is not a weakness. You put too much stress on that inversion of knowledge, you want too much that doesn't exist, you make others suffer for it.

She lifts her hand.

Do I? Still? Do you think that?

Intermediary, her mind, her body, that parallax.

Yes. Yes you do. O we all want knowledge. But you, you've always wanted light that's too strong, darkness that's too absolute, you demand a freedom that's too great. You left me, and you never thought of my loss, you never protected me from that, did you?

Gripping hold of her wrist. Livestock.

Perhaps not.

The thought still does not seem to bother her. He sighs.

And it was you who gave me Herma, Rachel.

Yes

she says loudly in her confession

but I wanted dimensions to be stated. That's all.

Rachel, there aren't any, you can't do it, you should have stayed here: or if you had to go, you should never have come back.

Although his kneeling voice is luminous in reproach. How can she tell him about the high hoarse command of the night that had driven her on?

It was self-guardianship I wanted, Tomas, as I do now. I go after it diligently.

Sad as a cathedral, that statement.

O I'm not judging you.

The hardness of his voice is hot as loss, she is sweltering, what she has always regarded as courage is being assigned to a zoo, a curiosity condemned by him.

Tomas

says Rachel, pulling her wrist away impatiently

I've learnt that there is never any time in the future that is going to reveal answers, you can't plan ahead, it's now that matters: personal reformation is demanding, the necessity for it is always here, it doesn't sit waiting somewhere else, at some junction along the way that we can only see faintly in the distance or in the clouds, we're not allowed to prepare for it, it is here, ready to attack or be attacked. Parting isn't a release either, I've learnt that too, it's just the beginning of the journey, a time for hazards to commence, now or never. And never means death. Tomas that blistering white light that broke us up was me undoing my brain!

I can't see how

he says coldly

it's a mirage that you see and a phony exile like yours doesn't help to convince me

Aah

she says swiftly

you want to use my failure do you to win the argument and hide your own failure?

I've got no failure to hide . . .

No?

she laughs, shrugging and jerking her head back, holding on to his wrists to prevent him from standing up, laughing as if she has dismissed the subject, throwing it in a furnace, then moving to kneel down beside him, no longer versatile, argumentative or reserved, her hands held out to him, gentle, awkward, girlish, yet somehow incongruous: stupid and white as full-blown roses. A vicarious image has relayed itself to her brain and she capitulates to it. Demons will have reality to play with. She beckons towards her crooked thighs, places his hand on an unshaven stereotype and claps her legs shut on it. He leans away, struggling to get free, but she pulls him, she is stronger, her strength is loathsome. There is a struggle to gain possession of orifices. But in fairness to Rachel, she is remembering a day of foreign summer, of his lips then that had no exact language, no messages. It is for a resumption of this that she scrabbles against his body. But his lips are dry and perplexed. The hot dissolute air of the room intimidates him. He cannot move through it, get through it, or pierce. When he flops down on her, it is like some parody, twisting and writhing without accomplishing even the first glassy splinter of an erection and her statuesque voice cracks miserably in the room her hand grasps the vacuum of flesh as he curses loudly christ cleaving them apart.

Decisive, severe, Rachel's shoes lying on the carpet go blacker and blacker as night gets later and later. They have all the tension of a marching song, she thinks, Tipperary, it's a long way, a long way, don't they . . . ? Too long perhaps. But never mind. I don't really care. I'll imagine that valuable bitter diamonds peek out of the toe-caps. Tomorrow morning will be like a blue trapeze swinging and the sky will be slippery as a dance floor: or so I hope. In the afternoon, trolleys of wind will bear berries from a totally imaginary and green country (greens of many different shades which dwell in and depend upon the light for their lives of sedulous lime or eye-burning emerald): and now right now out of this land of primroses and procreation comes a tame cockatrice wearing a hood fashioned out of cobwebs and newspapers. Perhaps it hides a world under the network of that hood, a world it wants me to share? No? No. No it's turned away, it's gone, it's caught sight of an old friend. But just that one glimpse makes me think about junkyards and fireworks and the faces reflected in a square of tin hit by the sun o years ago years: when we were children: o christ: and each of those faces could have passed for humanity's one true expression: though like the trimmings of king queen knave or pope they too relied on masks, on hoods, on the tenuous yet unshakable evidence of newspapers. All do. All of us do. Otherwise individuals fall flat and crazy on the ground or else disappear down the mouths of coke bottles and defiant lovers. Crying irrationally, all the shabby offenders, who looked the other way when the proper world said watch me fools, are judged unfit to have names, they must be stripped of their names, consonant by consonant, over continent and continent, until only their soft soapy hearts remain, the result of disfigurement. Pelted with tombstones, the radio bulletins on all of our wars terrify me, their barking damages my morale. And no calm lawyer, no economist, rephrases the shock, says that yes things are bad really means no all's well. Everything taints, the word whispered in the ear, the hand laid stealthily on the body, the gay blithe song so slaved at: we are lame cassowary birds, destitute of all our attachments: if we so much as challenge our rivals we lose touch with them: they forsake our lips and love for ever more. Door bangs. Here she is. At Herma's question, Rachel looks up from her book, resentfully. She is dazed, torn from her colourful inner world. But her expression changes at once, shutting off any hint of the lilliputian world within. Disdainfully, she gives Herma the facts. No explanations or advice.

He told me he had a headache. He's gone to bed.
Methinks this god is a lie, Herma moans to herself. But a sadder fate for Midas. She fingers she sleeves of her arrowlet dress.

O

she says, just a sigh scratching the room like a quill. Rachel reads her book again, ignoring her. A goodheart, though clipped, compassion and pity flood Herma, changing her passions. She understands the gloomy cramp Tomas is experiencing. Noble as some stranger from camelot, she goes up to him, leaving Rachel to talk to the moon again. It is sadness and shame that have gone to his head like liquor, making him lean against the wall and close his eyes. He hears the car and then her tread on the gravel. The door opening, her voice, Rachel's voice answering, then more footsteps. He himself is footless, unable to go on any further like this, unable to act the part. He keeps his eyes closed and puts his hands on his head. Descriptions drawn from fables occur to her as soon as she sees him, silhouetted there. She comes in and stands by the shut door. In the drab darkness.

Why are you in the dark Tomas?

Bare shrubbery of earth turns on its axis. Through magnificent circles of silence. The night surrounding them on all sides makes them stand crooked, ill at ease, too conspicuous to one another. Herma's mouth is dry as a moon. The craters of her brain ache. She fears the vehement understanding which Tomas and Rachel share, and of which she falls short. The way he had lifted his hand when he caught sight of Rachel, in an almost classical salutation. The dumb leader. Anywhere on the globe, recognition, a hand held out. O it doesn't matter which way you march, so long as you are out of step. Who once told her to believe that? Tomas looks only half life-like. He is hunched up in a personal disparagement, she doesn't want him to move, she knows he would shamble, and can't bear to see him humbled. So now she comes and clings to him, despite the vulgar rainbow, comes and kisses him with her showy lips where prayers have recently been. He does not stop her. He does not participate. He leaves his arms up in the air, his hands folded on his head, thinking only of a cold grey sunless room where there is neither the haunch of love nor the bequest of indifference to hasten time away. The room sways with threats. From now on, wherever he walks, he suspects himself of limping. He is covetous of the way Rachel sails through life, by virtue of her relentless heresy to it. How she can play with worlds so sinfully, so faithlessly, so inventively is beyond him. It hurts him that he alone is left to live with all these tensions of banishment: which are by right hers. Herma touches his face, stroking his hair back from his forehead, pulling his arms down and putting them around her. She kisses him again. But he is longing instead for Rachel's thick spiteful mouth against him. Perhaps it is the apprehension of this that makes Herma detach herself from him and walk across the room. She switches on the light. He almost drowns.

Herma wheels round, her face flushed: and begins to protest through thin lips, spawning bad language, a recantation of all her gentleness, specimens of her invalid-hood.

But what am I supposed to do
he whispers in a rambling sentence
throw her out?
I don't know

she mutters pointlessly. She crosses her wrists in a crucifix. Not even the appearance of dragons would surprise Herma, everything flies out of control so suddenly, the crew of winter mutinying at the last moment. So that spring is never reached, green harbour never seen. She sits down on their bed. Once again, she feels as if she is going through life constantly glancing over her shoulder. Endless threats. Outside, the darkness is stiff and bland and unreal as a sheet of black cardboard. Sunrise has hours and hours of its solitary and brilliant journeying yet to go. He senses that the darkness crows over them. As if it has won a victory. An ashamed corsair, he holds her terse unhappy body. They sit together in an atmosphere of incandescence. Silent tocsins ring all around them. Eventually he says

Tonight I looked beyond the lame edge of the moon to where the majestic night stretched out its legs. The church spire pierced the heavy darkness glassily, seeking angels and revelations. I was looking for you. The stars, tawdry as spent sovereigns, did not burst into flame. The night went on. I was disappointed. In the darkness everything rustled like a swarm of bees. Whether I do worship in some way, or whether the adoration of heresy is my lot, the wooden ends of my fingers are still unable to say. So I continue to move through my own ugly confused paradise. Forgive me, Herma . . .

They kiss. Although they are both deeply disheartened, they find consolation in one another. Fading saints, their icy fragrance sustains them, for the time being. It's strange, how at the very moment of descent, an uprightliness staggers you. It makes even misery acceptable because it sharpens your sphere of existence. Their stale sexes dampen. Regulated anarchy swells. Their ascent is tumultuous. It contains them as they strive. Even though it is probably a false start, it comforts. Downstairs, Rachel puts aside one book and takes up another. Downstairs, Rachel clock-watches. She reads. About the collapse of empires through sedition and siege. Her shoes glisten in the centre of the room. She waits for him to come downstairs. Midnight is reached and charted. He does not appear. But she goes on waiting. To accuse him. To impress him. Something of this nature. Later in the night, Herma wanders through the dream's greater darkness, a member of a cavalcade of shrouded figures who move through an endless garden where slothful flowers bloom eternally. Whose scent is terrible like the glare of a tiger's eye. Whose odour is the quintessence of a threatened soul. Causing her to suffer a morbid over-activity of the heart. And when she awakes it is to a nameless sensation of falling. Herma's defiled scream lifts its voice up into the night out of the dream. Its cessation is just as sudden, it leaves an equivocating silence clattering and hammering on the air, a forerunner of dawn. Rachel drops her book and runs eagerly upstairs. She knocks loudly on their door.

What's happening?

Murders? It would spoil everything.

What's wrong?

When Herma hears Rachel's grating voice, her amorous shallow tone, she pushes Tomas away and lies there flat and angry, stranded half-way between the moonlight and mudflats. What she wants is instantaneous mimosa. She will not admit it is out of reach of the hand, beyond the art of the mind. He turns the light on. She closes her eyes.

It's nothing

calls Tomas depreciatingly, not opening the door

Herma had a bad dream, that's all. Did she wake you?

No. I was still downstairs. Is your head better?

Yes it is. Thanks.

This ironic little conversation slashes Herma. She sweats. Her nightdress sticks imperiously to her circumspect limbs that shift in the bed.

I'll lock up for you

says Rachel.

Thanks. Goodnight.

Herma has not said a word. The sour vibration of their two voices adheres to the ceiling. Rachel, you came upstairs, Herma whispers to herself without consulting her memory, in order to make him even cooler towards me, just to make me look foolish. Couldn't you find an alternative? No, I suppose not, not you. But she keeps her mouth shut as Tomas turns back to her. Darkness, as he puts off the light. Clocks click. Pebbles falling for time-pieces. Her uninsured hands unfurl. Now she understands Rachel's old promise to materialize. Her hands touch her husband. Dreams! thinks Rachel as she descends the stairs, I learnt all about them years ago, learnt by heart the way they come like lightning, making cracks in the fresco of the night. Dreams! Everywhere in the house, she slides the bolts, turns the keys, switches off the lights. Her own room peers at her. The first thing she does is to open the window and breathe in the clean strong cold dark blue air. The moon pussyfoots among heavy cloud. Slates of sleet blow into her prostrate eyes. Air turns rancid in her mouth. She shuts the window then clamps her lips hard together, walking into the centre of the room, hitting out at the air, fists clenched, veteran face churning. But the open eye of night does not blink, it stays open wide, bright as fine weather that satirizes the likelihood of rain. The black horsehair atmosphere of the dark house bristles. She remembers she left her shoes downstairs. But can't be bothered to get them now. Tomorrow will do. A clock strikes against the darkness. Not even the moon helps. Dreams! Yes, I know all about that faltering towards nightmare, my body has experienced enough whirlwind . . . The faint silver of the mirror tinkles in snow-moonlight. The straight-backed chair beside the bed reaffirms Rachel's despair at her own obsessed severity. An absent whiteness begins to fascinate her, like a totem. She goes and touches the back of the chair, running her fingernails along the grain. Then she folds her arms and stares out at the nightfall. Eventually she undresses and lies down. Silent censure rules her domino hands. She sighs when she feels fatal tides approach her. Up and down the night and her body she searches for a motto. But she cannot reach far enough or deep enough. Night is a lonely place. Muscular spasms merely encumber her travels through it. She closes her eyes. But a stern hour and more will pass before she sleeps.

At first, she sees a dawn full of crystalline fish. Because Rachel is still partly caught up in parachuting slumber. She turns agitatedly from side to side. By the time she is fully awake, the incidental fish have disappeared. She sits up. Her ringless hands reach out for a cigarette. She watches a red angry sunrise emblematic of blood poisoning. The rays of light have hardly made it to the distant roofs before rain rattles down in long narrow lines: it sounds as if a relay of sprinters unleashes the morning. She stubs out the cigarette and lies down in bed again. She doesn't want to leave. Panics. She is afraid of it. Perhaps they will forget her again. She can already imagine her farewell, both of them saying, goodbye Rachel, goodbye, see you in the summer, goodbye. As if the trenches had not been dug. That veiled smile of Herma's, smooth as calf skin. she can see it already. But no, she does not see Hernia. Because Herma stays in her room until Rachel has gone. She needs a place of security. A young crone, she is dependent upon it. She lets Tomas say goodbye to Rachel on his own. Paper roses clutter the green walls. She gazes at them. And then she asks the opaque edge of the sage window whether or not the pagoda of silence is free from traitors yet. Rows of books, piles of books, their leaves are sheaves, concealing the dead doll behind the wainscot. Needles ofpine trees rustle down there in the wood. Their mosaic labyrinth keeps hostilities hidden. O one day one day, she prays, let me awake to find my hopes utterly fulfilled and all the dream houses of the night available as pyramids with especial keys made for me to unlock the wavy doors. But now invisible silver chains manacle my wrists and encircle my throat. Within the portrait gallery of my head the wooden animals are full of lice and the puns revolve spiral fashion around waste-paper baskets. I know that if I look out of the window I will see through the sleet a hidden passion play that may only be a rehearsal. Tomas says to Rachel, he croons:

Before you go, let's walk around the garden.

Beneath a winter sky they go, a winter sky of immaculate grey. They walk down to the fence: and back again. In silence. Finally, they arrive in the conservatory. It is a natural abode for her. The floor is stone. Even in summer, its cold air makes a frost out of every movement. His eyes are like doves' eyes. He opens them very wide as the words flow from his mouth. Silence. He whistles. And then he talks again, about his duty, to Herma, he must stay here, the time's gone by for us, it's ruinous to hope. Phrases of his defence are theological. She stares out at the sky, at the sleety snowy drizzle which is falling, knocking against the glass: and wonders if meditation will ever bring her a knowledge of actualities. Her empty ungloved fingers, gnarled and malformed by the cold, sum up her own rashness, the way she had let days and weeks slip by before coming out into the magnetic arena of action.

Who was that man you told me about?

O no one you know . . .

When she looks directly at him, he shifts his glance away, a debtor faced with saving both money and honour.

But perhaps you'll meet him. If he could come down with me, in summer?

Tomas shrugs.

If you want.

I'm thinking also, I might marry him . . .

she says with her most winnowing puissant smile. Then she takes his hand. This is a line of impossible conduct after what she's just said. Her touch deprives him of whatever innocence remains to him. He pulls his hand away and looks at his watch. The minutes have a sense of scale. They know these two are standing at the margins of a compound sea.

You said you'd go

he says. But softly.

Yes. I'll go soon. In a second or so.

Although she takes his hand again and gives no sign of departing. She stares at him from an inner eye of indigo that reaches across the seas. She is trying to compel intuitive wisdom to have a concrete result. But again he withdraws his hand, symbolic of an ending, without unnecessary words, flowers, or formality. This movement of hands is only a technical expression of feeling. Considering their mercenary idyll is officially over. He moves away from her. She follows him out of the conservatory. As they stand on the lawn, the igloo sun shines faintly through cloud. Shadowed by the trees, boxed in by coldness, they feel themselves tautened by the loss they now realize is greater than they imagined, as the magnitudes of a fuchsia are not realized until it is plucked. They are overwhelmed by pain that amounts to a total desiccation. An interstellar wind blows.

I'll go.

They stand amid icy rain. They are steeped in ice. To the heart. To the bone. She looks at the frozen drops which balance on the branches. The wind shakes them and they fall. She smiles. But she does not leave him. She looks up at the drifting cloudy sky, the greaves of pale light on the horizon. Then she seems to gather herself in, relics and wrecks, to move disabled but forcefully away. The mortar pain kneads her breast-bone. Merry-thought. Cold torpedoes of sleet catch in her hair. She goes. With deliberate strides. But turns back to him, a spasmodic acute movement, and stretches out an arm to him, across the precinct that separates them, her short damp hair serving as the invariable crown above the surfeited face. She says nothing. But stares for a long time: a maritime stare, cold, with a willowy flowing texture (copied perhaps from the weather) and a semi-cylindrical shape that, as he goes on meeting it, appears to change to other shapes, expressing a hatred for his weak eyes. Or what he does with them. Opening instead of closing. A bracing mesmerism. When she speaks, her face softens, coaxing him to prevent her from leaving.

I haven't had much chance have I? And I haven't given much attention to . . . no . . . . it doesn't matter . . .

She breaks off, again she has not made the right response, for a second time he has failed her, the flesh is allotted its true self, the trembling mouth is uncertain. She walks quickly away, not looking back, avoiding any closer contact with the truth, leaving a widening space between them like that arrogant emptiness between two opposing armies, an emptiness which invites the foolish to essay dangerous and mawkish rebellions. The icelandic goodbye is over. But in that ornate wintry atmosphere of devoid crystal, her voice echoes and resounds through him, its discontent inflexible, solitary, suspended: almost a prayer. From an upstairs window, Herma watches and sees Tomas waiting and listening long after the car has gone out of earshot. Herma is not a participant in any such idolatry. The palatial fire of that sweetness would kill her. Few could stand it. Or understand it. Whenever she approaches understanding the industry of past generations threatens her. That is why she is the only one weeping. That is why her mouth is now full of the vomit of a doom she cannot perceive as she watches him waiting below, his hands despising their emptiness. Opening wide, her mouth screams in an utter silence, screams the soundless twanging sound of its bondage, tongue a hot coal, not purging. Twain dwell and move in a cold cold season. Where all aid is holy but posthumous.

Part Two: RADIX

One

Dream moves like some prowling animal moves, a leopard maybe, slow and stealthy, with the emphatic threat of larceny. Herma knows darkness is rent. She sits up in the ridged bed, very carefully, so as not to disturb night or Tomas. Who breathes deep and easy.

Yes

she thinks feverishly with a dry mouth

o yes my dreams are growing up, truly. How the darkness growls! It sounds different now I understand the words. And I fear night now. More than ever before.

The moon is calm, all of a white composure in the sky. But she does not glance at it, not once. She stares at her silvan fingers that clutch at darkness.

I wish I could have another chance. I wish I could recreate my old childish fears. I wish I still feared shadows and drunks singing in the street. Instead of myself. Not singing, not drunk, not a shadow. But whole body sweating and inflamed in an uncouth way. Myself, the meeting-house of fears. I wish that all the formal symbols of my childhood had not faded, I wish my own child were not dead. I did not want him to die. I didn't want to be left behind with this emptiness I can never satisfy. Why does it seem that I am watching myself vanish into thin air?

She looks down at Tomas, whose wrists are twisted as bribes. She touches her breast. The glaring strokes of midnight enrapture, charm and horrify her.

O christ, let me be beyond time, without a past. Take away the future, free me from the awareness of prophecy, let me escape from all the encumbrances, the distances, the flashes and the breasts.

The garden of night is barren, its hedgerows lack thaumaturgy. She cups her hands and covers her face. So: there is to be no thanksgiving for her. Night filters through her fingers.

Stop this tenancy of night from hurting me!

The violent silence bruises her. With its thumbscrews and hot irons.

Why? Why must I be the dream's domicile, the dream's host? Why can't I stop rubbing my hands on the purdah of broken glass? Sometimes I'm brave. I'm not afraid of Rachel. Tomas is. But I'm not. I'm not afraid of leaves scattering across a hampered sky nor of the saucer sunflowers. I can relate these to their sources: and the rationalisation helps. I can relate Rachel to her source: and that helps. But darkness and dreams . . . I don't know and I don't want to know the fortress town where they reside. What bravery. How I distrust this heroism of mine. It lacks honesty, it is only a relegation, a coward's trick to avoid uglier beasts, preventing my eyes from turning inwards. But now the time has come when the heart . . . my heart . . is the prey. I hear it howl. Yes. I hear it. My nightmares have grown up, my god, how they have grown up. How big and strong they are. I hear antiphons, all the world's troubled evils, prayers of the fascist, shrieks of the tortured, all their mad antiphons. I can't bear it. No, no, I can't. Not alone. Not in this dark.

Once again, the scream in the dark. After which she has to explain, to answer his questions. And the dream is no longer what it was. It collapses amongst the other births and deaths. But she must speak about its antiquity and await a verdict. She begins to tell him, thinking, this is real now isn't it? this isn't still part of the dream is it? I'm not a ripvanwinkle girl am I? I'm still young aren't I? But she can't ask him that. So she says

. . . I found that I was in some dark place or other that was almost medieval: the tension of the place was aged, I think it might have been an apothecary's shop. Or else a mock-up of one. It was very dark. Pitch black. And more than anything else I had the impression of cold stone: stone floor, stone walls, stone steps leading up to a gallery of stone. It was very dark. I could not see the ceiling, even if there was one. I don't think there was anyone else there besides myself. My breath was so loud. Like a forest fire. I could just make out that this place was full of cabinets manufactured from a thick smoky glass. And in these glass cabinets I saw weird objects, dried and rotting herbs, weapons, snakes, old books that looked like savage treatises . . . but . . .

Her voice, the agate off-spring of sleep, falters and goes dumb. They both sit bolt upright in bed, staring at one another, ignoring the hot summer night, unconscious of its influx of provocative air. His arms are thin sticks of solicitude. He arranges them around her. Assuming responsibility. He thinks His face is intent, sharp and involved as a regent watching a coronation.

These cabinets . . . . ?

he asks, half embarrassed, half eager. She sighs and the tempest of her voice builds up again, melancholy as a sonnet: but it goes on, in spite of a door banging downstairs.

. . . worst of all these cabinets also held dead or dying creatures. Unidentifiable crawling creatures. Embryos. But of what, I can't say. This sight was the worst of all, Tomas, I stared and stared and then I screeched . . . and woke myself up.

She groans. How can she translate the odour of the place?

It was so strange, Tom. Do you think it has a meaning? (This bit isn't a dream is it?)

O no

he says quickly, clinging on to her, curving his body. He must be right. Feel his strong arms.

No, it's just in your imagination. Have you ever read anything about a place like that? Recently?

His hands touch her body, procrastinating.

Perhaps

Herma says faintly

> but not recently. A long time ago. Years. Years ago. Quite often these
> things reappear. Unexpectedly. From the past. Don't worry . . .

he yawns, letting her go, drawing away from her, lying down again and
closing his eyes

> . . . don't worry . . .

Be like me. I've slept too long without remembering my dreams to bother
about understanding or superintending yours.

> I'll try and forget it

she says, the earthenware terror hidden from sight. But how to catch at
the real meaning of the dream? The scheme of it, its ambitious design
confounds her.

> O yes you must put it out of your mind

he mumbles

> try and sleep.

With the exquisite vampire-neighbour trapped in her brain.

Try to sleep.

Watch the ramshackle night go by.

Try to sleep.

Until.

She sleeps.

Comes floral daybreak.

Green light, cool and plaintive, a minor tune played by the left hand on a
piano deep inside the dimness of a house. Green light, an unreal dawn, a
paste gem. Greenwood of summer. Green dawn grainy as wood. Sun rising
amid mists as if bound with a garland of smoke, an old-young yellow.
Clouds moving like flamingoes. Ghost shadows of trees shake in the light,
haunted by the flowers of the evening. In the house, a continued sleeping.
The only movement, oriole sunlight running up and down the stairs,
crossing and criss-crossing the walls and the floors, the tops of tables and
the backs of chairs. Birdsong, sun, green lawn. The world is an obsessed

green. The man and his wife hold coffee cups in their epic hands. They read newspapers. Then the woman stands up and says a few words to her husband. Who nods. There is a self-consciousness, a precision, a nervousness about all their movements. Sun jelly pours over the morning, the pressure increases until the house is like a jungle captured between four walls. The man in the house kisses his wife but she turns decidedly away. And then the man leaves her alone, he goes off silently into his study to await the arrival of the visitors. The woman in the kitchen is also waiting, her eyes still medieval. Sun-silence, frightful as a broken vase, spills its huge flower shadows about everywhere. Geographical trees wave and are reflected in the glass fronds of the windows. Small breezes come and go. Westwards the sky is landless, harbouring a denseness of rain. In the east, a secrecy of islands. Over the bland roofs, sun's river flows uncharted. Clocks pound out minutes. The tattoo shadows of man and woman do not meet. When the man or the woman looks out of a window straight into the centre of the sun, its strength devours. Such power. It is impossible to avoid its vigilance. It holds conventicles all the time. Their neighbours have gone away. The man and the woman must not disobey their shadows. They practice being like them instead. The young woman follows her shadow out of doors. She is wearing a sun hat. She thinks, I'm walking out this febrile morning to look for a jubilee. Beneath the rose-trees stones are sick of fastidious petals which criticise the land. When Herma woke up this morning she had the memory of a foreign language in her mind. Strange words that would sound tantalizing even in a grocer's shop ordering merchandise. Beyond the escarpment of her ears invisible bands of musicians scrape their bows. The chords fold around the trees. She closes the garden gate behind her. As she walks she kicks up the dust. On the days in spring when rain fell from a cloudy sky the leaves had flashed like pearl and silver knives. But now it is summer. The safe guardianship of spring is over. Tomas's impatience to see Rachel again has given the months of June and July a rotten apple taste. That dream of . . . glass . . . No. Forget it. Walk on. Gaudy girl. She walks on. Yes, gaudy girl, almost sane but too fond of a haven, too vulnerable, her body is artificial. Like a model's. Yet it must be real because I feel its breath, my ghost, my soul, abandoning me. Across a street once, a black-eyed boy had grinned at her and waited. The arching of an eyebrow became suddenly tudor then. But she looked away. But I looked away. O world, I move apprehensively around your centre, I whirl like a pageant. Motion encourages motion. What if my return this morning should find the place, the house I needed empty, the lover fled, away to the arms of another? What then? Then? Then there could be no more hurtful nor more fitting an answer than that emptiness. A harsh judgement? Yes, but the truth. I want to divide my life into skeins, strands, slogans: to make a proper pattern, to make time cohere, even unto eternity. On my ear a foreign language. The sun nudges the trees. Herma sits down slowly beneath a willow tree. A fallow stream glitters in the sunlight. O I am so afraid of that figure at the window who drew the curtain forever. Dates and appointments nested in her, never triumphing in termination. Instead a mad capricious movement back and forth across a shrinking world took their place. And a shriek began to pierce her imagination, a train approached. O mother why did you give up? But no, not me. I'll go on. I won't give up. Because such suicidal figures always hang and sway until they rot in too correct and odorous a fashion. And then the coffin lid is pricked and tormented by the nails. At the moment where the opera ends silence replaces . . . My salvation lies in the merciless falcon world which I inherit. Beyond the escarpment of her eyes bands of musicians angrily lift their bodies up from chairs. Whose backs go on clutching the air. To whom Herma will not be slave. I will not be a slave. No one's slave. I'm ready for her this time. My wicked eye winking. She walks through the fields again. Noon and midsummer grip the land. Earth and air entwine close as mating snakes. No sea for miles, no smell of it, no ozone: instead cloudless sky, roses red as butchers' hands, the flesh of soil shrivelling. The lawn is dry and hard as flint under her feet. This season is not temperate, dust blows everywhere, without chivalry. Shadows move like dice. The thought of lustration wanders abroad. Herma drinks some cold water then sits down at the kitchen table. She sweats, she drums her knuckles on the table, she waits for something to happen, she feels the heat grate against her bones. In her mind's eye, deserts and branding irons. She goes over to the dresser and gets the pack of cards: she sorts through the septic cards, pouncing sadly on aces and the faultless knave. This heat is unlike the heat of that foreign summer, the olivine summer when the homeless rift between the two women had been finalized, the other summer day when Rachel, white-lipped as waves in storm, voice sour as a love potion, eyes wide open but blind as a kentucky fish, had told her the secret. They stood side by side in the tourist's desert. Then Herma had thrown herself at Rachel. Shaggy woodpecker, howling dervish. Demanding revenge for the desecration of her life, the bites taken out of her particular garland of flower. Mourning the end of a golden world, intolerant as a rebel army. She blamed Rachel for the end of a civilization. She sees again in this kitchen the brown shadow of her own raised hand. In an empty country. She hears again the sound of her own high-pitched ashamed voice, refuting the suspicions which Rachel had just verified, her squashed voice threatening to rip open her own throat: and let the longed-for blood escape. Her voice, denying the knowledge that wherever she went she'd never forget what Rachel's confessional tongue had told her. Herma looks at her hat on the table. She'd thrown a different hat away then. Telling herself, it was not true. A silver medallion touched her throat as she ran. I wonder where that is now? She tripped over the grim milestones of rock but did not stop. She had no warning, not of this ground. Her eyes were weeping. She examines the aces. Looking back, she realizes what an actress she'd been, all those mad gestures departing from a stage. When all along she'd known the truth. O yes. You can't hide such conduct, not even after a hundred years. You can't avoid it. You're born knowing, suspecting something of that nature. It's in your blood. Or else you guess, from hints, certain silences, a twist of some lips, pierced ears, hidden bracelets and lost names. Amongst a confusion of papers one day when you're fourteen you find a love letter and it tells you everything and you scream but there's no one in the house to hear you and so you hide the letter away in your turn and never look at it again but also you never forget the words, the terrible endearments. She had guessed. From her inability to love Rachel: and Rachel's exorcism of any real affection for her, her slight withdrawal from any caress of hers. No. There was never a chance of any other world for them except their abortive adaptation of it. The thin doric wind of the desert blows through the room. Again Herma, shuffling cards, feels the nausea, the pain, the speed at which she had gone running through the rocks. Then the inevitable return in silence, the drive back to the city. She had fingered the silver medallion around her throat with its two engraved horses' heads, as if it might protect her. Manege. Today, it's so hot today, she longs for something equally cool to touch, an amber globe say, such as ancient ladies used for keeping the hands fresh as dawn flowers. The drive back to the friable city. The untranslatable silence between them. Both mesmerized by those skeletons. Whose bones prise open the lives of the two women sodden with heat, their italicised minds aware of a mutual electric resistance, a repugnance, a desire to get as far away as possible from the only other person who knows the private language they speak, its verbs, its grammar. How Herma had hunched her body together, body not yet filled like a barrel of rainwater with the unborn. The sun's glare, like the souls of the dead. Back at the hotel, they had said goodbye. The ice revolved in the glasses. Goodbye. Forever. And a turning away from hunger. But after an absence of five years, they met again, suddenly and unexpectedly coming face to face in a liberal world. Each possessed a new name, a false surname: but they recognised each other. How they had stared, motionless, like goddesses on naked pedestals. They stared. Words plugged the wounds temporarily. Rachel wore a crape dress the shade of sea water. Herma can still see it. A week after their encounter Rachel had taken her to meet Tomas. Told him, look, an old friend. No more. He knows nothing about the enactment, the partnership. He does not know the truth. Rachel had brought her to Tomas. As if now that they had met again, they must struggle together always. Herma goes over the memories, brooding, preparing herself to meet Rachel again, to hand over love. Memories, coloured fragments, tasting of fire: a mimicry of sense.

Tomas is ignorant of their cloven relationship: he must remain so: they must keep it hidden under leafy shadows and holly bushes. That is the important thing. The two women are not able to leave one another alone: they keep chasing one another, the protagonists constantly changing places. Fighting to douse the wedding torch. Herma chokes on her own anger and runs out of the house on to the lawn breaking that symmetry at least. The sun burns her skin dark and discordant as basalt. But its macabre brilliance almost solaces her: it mocks Rachel because whilst she is shut out, encased in jealousy, only a visitor, Herma belongs here under this sun: conscious of the stark columbining sunlight everywhere, Herma acknowledges her own particular shy courage. Heat squeezes her lungs and ribs to prove it under the mentor sky, encouraging her to prepare against eviction. She turns, is about to re-enter the house, has her foot raised to the step, when a sensation of unnatural stillness catches her and holds her immobile between the house and sky, the inner and the outer, a stillness that is Tomas watching her so that she belongs to neither one nor the other, is split between the two, the man and herself: and although it is only for a second, although almost immediately she goes over towards him smiling tensely, she wonders and thinks why do I continually turn to him, why do I sense him watching me all the time, why do I feel so shapeless under his gaze, even during bulging nights, why do his eyes follow me so closely. Herma and Tomas walk through the garden smoothly as if painted on glass. The heat, the distinct yet simultaneously hardly noticeable pandemonium of the leaves, the elegant cultivated beds of flowers, confident yellows and introspective mauves, the red claustrophobic roses, all turn and rotate around them as they walk with slow royal strides. Regal steps. By this movement they spin the garden on so that the landscape cannot crash in to the horizon or crumple against the fences.

They'll be here late in the afternoon.

His proverbial tone is a blind. She does not even bother to nod. It is not necessary. He has said this so many times during the last week, with so many different emphases, that there is an end now to her reactions.

Will they be staying long?

Her bored voice eventually pricks the quiet voraciously.

Three weeks. I've told you, over and over. Three weeks. At least.

Herma ignores his nervous irritation. But she coughs. The air is a dead weight. He puts his hands behind his back and stares at the rocky lawn, the fields, at her feet.

What time is it?

she asks, screwing up her eyes and staring through the mask of sun at him. Light makes his face fierce before her. She does not want to know the time. She speaks more in order to break the rotund silence: she does not care how long the morning is, how short the day.

I don't know.

As if he is apologizing for not knowing. Although it's nothing. But he can't think straight. Not beneath the diadem of summer. And the memory of Rachel.

It doesn't matter.

In this silence she can hear clocks ticking and booming out all over the world.

We should have a sundial.

Why has he said that? She flies around to face him. Enraged.

Her voice hurts his tongue.

What when there is no sun?

He is drained by her inexplicable anger, by this heat.

O it's hot

he says. They turn. Canvas faces. Before them, the house conceals a part of the sky. Each slate on the roof is a deliberate act of sabotage against the sky. Its boulevard rises unashamed. Only the open windows and the banging of the unlatched side door reassure them that there is a real house there before them into which they might go. They approach the french windows.

Change, never ending change, nothing does not change, nothing stops changing.

But his vague down-at-heel assumptions leave her uncertain.

Yes it's true everything changes, but only back to the beginning:
her voice brightly dark and hard
it all reverts.
Net curtains are stretched tightly and tautly over the glass doors,
fastened by a brass bar at top and bottom, like a child's hair slide. The red
velvet curtains hang limp and rabbity. Herma and Tomas come into the
room, towards the corners of bookcases, the mantelpiece, the chairs,
away from the musket denomination of the sun. They are not hungry.
They sit and wait for Rachel and Daniel. At the height of summer. In
weather unruly as a sea glaze. With a hot wind swishing like sequins.

Daniel sighs again as he watches Rachel's agrarian hands on the wheel.
Daniel: who was once in the past nicknamed Adonis Barefoot: by someone
who had Rachel's hands. Is it safe for me to remember her now, after all
these years? Or isn't it time yet? Can I recall that I once called her the
fairest of all the world, yes, with a conscious affectation, I called her that,
can I remember and be safe? No, perhaps not. But I do remember. That
whenever I saw her I gasped and I sighed. Whenever I saw the imaginary
white boarhounds and the flute players at her heels. Now every heavy-
eyed morning I say to myself; o who remembers Adonis now, even if he is
not completely dead? No one. No one hails him now, hey Adonis. How are
the mighty fallen. Because this is a different world. Where Rachel holds
him in an impotent fascination. Partly because of her hands and partly
because she has the rare ability to capture the spirit of any creatures who
try, who dare to examine her too closely: riveting her with their eyes,
they are the ones who become the captives, trapped like Daniel by her
odious courtesy. Yes, one day he found himself cornered in a saurian
existence, an asexual relationship that left him dangling, that took away
his conditional acceptance of the world and set him adrift. Rachel makes
his sky dark as a concert hall. He comes down to visit these friends of
Rachel's, a reluctant and complaining guest. In burning climes, fallen is
the throne. No. I must not think of her. The days that stretch before him,

even though they are dressed up as holidays, are penances. As he undergoes their hours, their festivities and tragedies, his personal stability is doomed: there is no neutral ground left. My life once had neither sharps nor flats, it was like a dance, the days and the footsteps, all of a slow and easy tempo. Now Rachel introduces an element of allegretto I don't want or need but cannot avoid. He knows that his old way of living had not been admirable, that his escape from cosmopolitan hermitages was long overdue: he should feel grateful to Rachel for having liberated him. But he cannot. Nostalgically he longs for the deceits and falsehoods of that existence into which Rachel is an intruder. Rachel's personality annoys and disturbs him, it causes an emotional reaction in him, a backlash that means they invariably live on bad terms. During the past six months he has come to realize that Rachel is not the sort of woman he can use to extricate himself from his mental lamination. She has a slight physical resemblance to his first love: but that is all. Now he cannot get away from her. And he still awaits the deliverer. Yet somehow it has changed, it seems like a bad joke now, not a goal, not a life's work. Rachel's voice is sometimes crude as street music. But he goes on listening to it. Sometimes he wants to marry her. Even a second-class relationship is better than nothing. Basically he is disunited even with himself. Child of his time, he is not suited to the role of knight errantry: he wants no adventures, glorious or otherwise. But Rachel leads him on, the inventor of no new world: because aimlessly idling about life he is easily used. He cannot decide on any means of defence. So he is helpless. Eggs, angels, footballs: are merely objects to him, he cannot make them cohere. He is not even able to destroy a world: he accepts it as it is, without definition. His investigations go unrewarded. Yesterday he read through a yearbook for sailors, an almanac containing tidal information for navigators. But it did not help. After long waiting, after much close examination of her own choleric naked shadow, after gathering up querulous strength, Rachel is returning. For a resurrection. For a collage of flesh. That will include and crush the ache. Before order and victory are gained she knows complexity must rage, a storm whose fire catches the deepest nerve and shakes it, depriving the body of gravity, sending the blood hungering back to its source She's waited for over six months. She's watched roses cruise the rain. She's fought with Daniel. And others. Dead and alive. She's discovered that time does not sooth the sinews. Her clutching mouth has fingered both words and silence until her tongue is clumsy and swollen. Now she's returning. Asp in the heart. Scorpion in the mind. Her perfume is too lambent. Gusts of it reach Daniel. In more esoteric moments he imagines that it is the odour of an embalmed body. Necromancy. The word rolls over in his mind. Necromancy. It is a long drive. Sun beats down on the nape of his neck. They quarrel. He starts it by repeating that there is no need for him to come is there? after all, he doesn't even know them, does he?

Sometimes you behave like an astronomer of the universe she yells at him finally but softly

you're so aloof and conceited.

When she speaks like this, she hints at depths which automatically threaten him. It does not encourage him to look forward to this visit. He bristles with satire but cannot bring himself to speak. They drive on through trees dark as a forest of horse. Rachel is nervous and exasperated. She is pursuing a necessary part of her life and the time already lost, all the months, disheartens her. She needs Daniel as a prop, to help her regain her balance. Will it be possible for me to resume contact? Traffic lights: they are so red red red. O come on. Hurry. Change. How can it be easy? It will be like meeting foreigners rather than . . . what can I call them? . . . with no knowledge of how soul or language might have altered. Talking might prove to be too difficult an art. Communication breaks down from day to day in this or that world. So what chance do I stand? And now she is completely alone, with no double for reference. Her sister exists in Rachel's mind only in the way the dead do, a formal mental expression of grief, almost a reflex, certainly no longer an emotion. She cannot carry a stiff icon through the world any more than she can mourn one. What's he saying now? She snaps at him. Her hair, recently bleached, yellow as lemon or primrose or gold or sulphur, is short and untidy. She shakes her ebony ear pendants with an apprehensive gesture that betrays the dislocation her kind of temperament can suffer. He sees the movement out of the corner of his eye.

A voluptuary has duties which ordinary creatures cannot know
he says grandiosely
rigid and demanding as any religious office.
Because she is driving too fast for his liking. It is not intentional. But he is sure she is doing it on purpose. The car chisels through air. His teeth feel weighty as onyx. Afterlives of saints depend on the manner of their deaths, he thinks.

In time, you know, everything becomes unimportant.
he points out, half-holding his breath.

That's all right for you, Daniel. With nothing at stake.
Her voice fashionable and leisurely. Daniel gazes at motifs of nereids in the air. Her reprimand drops in his ear, like a prologue to this rubber season. The miles take them south.

Come on, get out.
They stand amongst shadows of castilian gold down-pouring, like deer hunted away on to the necessary air. Rachel does not go up to the house straightaway but stands in the forecourt looking at the landscape to which she is again joining herself, the quarry a haven, much more than temporary. Trees, dusty road, a hidden cart track, sky darkening now but it has been so many delirious and tearful colours in the past, saffian fields, although from here she cannot see them or the paths going through them, bisecting them, leading limestone across the land, the cracked steps, the door. Silence and dawn, silence at midnight, a world in silence. Green perplexed bundles of leaves on the trees. Evening is coming on, weaving around her, coiling around them, she a figure of contemplation traditional and exact, he already emaciated and sore in the throat. There is no one she can call as witness to her time spent here in this place, no values or photos she can show and say yes yes look, so far she has only

ashy remains, invisible leftovers, the ebb-tide of time and thought and hunger.

    I must move

she says aloud, in spite of Daniel by her side,

      for I am becoming the ghost's ghost, am growing into a product of my
      own heat, my own enemy and pursuer.

O why this teeming prey in her, who has no guards to fetter violence? Then she walks on through the shadiness to the house, troubled, but capable of existing in a new climate.

Two

Dawn slithers from behind the moon, half ashamed of betraying the night. The laudatory richness of sun begins to blaze. Daniel is sprawled out in bed: suppose it to be the sea and he tossed into it, overboard, man overboard. When he opens his dry eyes, brittle sunlight jabs them. World, what world is this? Icarus. He is thirsty. Another morning. He feels he'll be here for ever. Days are an over-ripe victimization. He does not believe his salty neutrality can survive in this unnatural landscape of flaking celandines and decrepit August roses, dusty facades, peeling paintwork and old moustached fields. Such proximity to decay disgusts him. The thick voluminous countryside is far worse than the debris of cities. In this mediocre atmosphere he becomes more than ever obsessed with his own weaknesses and his own poverty-stricken character. He wants to leave. But he can't walk out on Rachel. This is one of the penalties of being a fool. It is his inability to change his skin which he hates most of all. He speaks to people in a monotonous singsong voice. Unrealities, reveries, tension, fantasies, his abstract necrophilia: abnormality haunts him. That his mind should be cloudy and mazy, so formless and indecisive, is as grotesque as inhabiting a fictional version of this house where stone falls constantly from stone. Rachel's hamadryad friends leave him alone: what has he to offer? Neither effort of the body nor flagellation of the will can help him out of his stupefaction. He can only dilly-dally through his life. However lofty or aspiring he tries to become, he fails in the daylight. He remains a slave to himself and thus to anyone who passes by. He is too exhausted by life to be anything other than totally innocent. I am perhaps an irrational part of nature pre-condemned to live this way, Daniel thinks wanly every night before he is entitled to sleep. But every morning there is the same reaction: distress, anger, self-disgust. So the contrivance goes on. He begins to wash, still viewing his life fearfully like a soldier whenever he thinks of a battlefield. The despised blue of the sky is burly as a bailiff. He only glances at it. His back is bent under the weight of day. June, July or January, they are all the same to me, he mutters, and I know cowardice's red and stained hillsides are my only way out. There are two other themes to his philosophy. One, he believes that getting drunk is a blessing. Two, he believes that to revere a woman would be superb. Herma's nature, her potential coldness that promises so absolute a frost and her hidden fever too tropical for rainbows, is too close to his ideal for him to be able to ignore: already the fantasy starts up again with her. In all seriousness, he is going to rehearse, to act, to prepare to carry the stage on his back where it hurts his heart. He learns nothing. Sitting down on the unmade bed, he grumbles to himself; brought here, a stranger, a homesick reluctant guest, my pleas are too weary to dance and sing their petitions. The drifting icefloes of my heart, its emotions, are in my way, they hamper me. O why even in this place do I have to tug myself and my memories around with me, like a trolley full of rocks or a sack full of drowned kittens? He closes his eyes. He catches his breath. Then he sighs. He is neither happy nor sad. He sees her, from his unhallowed place: She moves in the manner of old. On all sides, darkness, duplicity, silence of a great war approaching. No way of telling where a hand might halt, on what a coldness fall. Never to rise. Air grows warm and fat as velvet. Then blows cold again. Remembered words, phrases, questions, in her head. As time-no-time goes on, things become hazier. The learned talkative boy sounds foreign to her. This xenophobia frightens her. And she begins to fall through this dead air again, falling, spiralling, falling, trying to land on firm ground. Which no longer exists for her. Yes, there she goes, Cassi with the wind of ages in her hair, falling forevernever until she wakes-sleeps and then what boy with bloodstains on your hands like Lady you remember yes there goes Cassi o what a sin Daniel to fall in love too soon and too late and how sad for Cassi flung headfirst into tomorrow because of your red-faced lust disguised as a tenderness of song. Does shame still make your hands shake? Yes of course it does. And don't your hands tremble when you shuffle the cards? Yes of course they do. In a world where laws themselves are the tools of lawlessness, what hope is there? O none none none. Cassi didn't know about such things, she never heard such riddles. She was no fool. But it was just too easy for her to drift mirrored in all those classic afternoons on the river and not wonder about the confusions of time and place, life and death. So she was unprepared. Where has she gone? Into your head? Yes. That is where she has gone. Where did you hide the ivory body? No, not in the undergrowth. Inside your head. Yes. Forever more. You fade Daniel but this voice in your head never fades never stops. No matter how many modern dawns sweep cinematically in. No matter how many magnificent nights you watch and wait. Her golden hair falls like a wig: and where is it now . . . . ?

Daniel smashes one fist into the palm of his other hand, grunts, swears, moans, thinks . . . everyone has a few ghosts . . . but conscience is not satisfied and he goes on sitting there, hearing her say over and over again Adonis Adonis Adonis . . . . .

Meanwhile on this purgative morning the other three walk down the garden beneath a mirthless gospel sky. They are silent. Truth skulks in the green slime at the bottom of the waterbutt. They do not look in it. They walk on. In a silence that bores deep into the heart, dark and unnatural as the smile at the bier.

Last week, in town, I saw something unusual . . .

Rachel attempts to ignite them. Anything to break this deadlock. Herma walks like a martinet. With her head held up high for inspection. But inside she recoils. Tomas nods though and of course asks her to go on. Were there any immunity against outcry in me, thinks Rachel as her own mouth moves arbitrarily, the sterility of this August would send me packing. But disreputable stoicism is too much a part of me now, any good humour I had's gone, long gone: like this hot hard bloodily executed summer I will not relax my grip.

This fat old woman collapsed, she went down like an eiderdown, it was awful and yet funny: you see, I thought it was a film someone was making, but no: it was all real. Suddenly she was flat out on the pavement. And I just watched, I thought it was a gag. They tried to get her on to a chair, someone brought it out from a shop: but her body wouldn't centre on it, she kept sliding off.

Rachel is learning that courage is needed by the breakers of promises: because they have to live with themselves long after the promise is forgotten by others. Her story goes grimly on. In a carefree and holiday voice. Hernia gives her a fierce duelling glance. But Tomas listens open-mouthed. His rugged walk. Lamentations track Rachel down, without even offering her the compassion of an old classical style: they open up before her a sunny avenue of despair. They do not even give her the satisfaction of saying, ah but it is a fine tragedy, this suffering. They know, she knows, it's petty, it's crude, it's nothing, it's everything I have. And she is burnt to her centre. So the desires of mankind inevitably mislead them. Even tender good souls, even majestic personages, those of character: or the evil and the foolish. Huntsmen, queens and judges, all fall victim to themselves. No matter how sober, wise, extravagant or corrupt. The removal of liberty will only sustain their strength. These three know all about the symbols of madness: they've learnt at second-hand about the staring eyes, the arbutus flowers, the dummies and the zombies. But nevertheless they will not turn back from their too provincial season. Half a century might separate Rachel from her desire, a rigid mile might lie between Herma and her love, a strange language might deafen Tomas: but their graceless passions will still go on trying to somehow break the lock of the distance: not even scourging the flesh by way of correction would persuade them otherwise.

. . . . and I suppose she was dead. Anyway I walked away. Silence again. Rachel's sophisticated logic is as comfortable as the deserts of Arabia, with the same lack of shade or green life: it has the same dryness that eludes the eye and avoids containment in the hands. It weakens the strong, it attracts and blinds all with its perpetual light.

O no

says Hernia, denying that she herself often wants to dismember

it's too horrible.

It happened. I saw it. I was a witness . . . .

Rachel says with a savoury defiance.

Yes but . . .

No, Herma is not so strong. The words leave her with her hands foolishly outstretched and sinking down through the air. Nothing is so stupid as the theoretician caught by the tail running for shelter: nothing except hysterical women who have no explanations except in Greek. Corybantic. Tomas grips her until she stops shouting. Her head hurts. What? She stares at their two shocked faces and at the brilliance of the falling sunlight which burns both heart and brain.

I'm better

Herma mutters. The blood is still resonant on her cheeks. They resume their walk. There is a compulsion about it. As if we go through life in italics. Call this condition irrelevant, say it has no qualifications, cry it has taken no examinations, repeat it is absurd: it makes no difference, we don't listen, all attempts at denial die before they get to their feet. Time may exhaust the strength of the parties involved. But for the present, this imperfect unity exists, matchless in its irony. Herma breathes in the orchid air. Her thoughts seel her eyes, as in falconry. The indistinct fickle conversation ambles on.

Did I tell you?

laughs Rachel

Daniel used to play the piano. Very badly. I made him give it up.

Her hands remain hidden in her pockets: their imaginations must take the responsibility for that image of power she has just set free on the air. They walk on through the poisoned fields. Mooching shadows accompany them. They go through the squirearchy of trees. Hunts are harmful. Strictly speaking, a hunt is a race towards an objective not always in sight.

The hunter must employ methods of both intellect and instinct. The heart of the hunter will fall sick if the quarry escapes: if he does not gain his first fox, he will turn for his prey upon more ambitious game and the outcome of his subsequent hunts will be tragic and irrevocable. Solemn games both inspire and affright the child. They all mark the glances and impulses which flicker through their insularity. All are primed. The threat of retaliation is embodied in Rachel's bent head and quick step. She puts the future under glass, to force it. Tomas awaits his liberation in an academic excitement. But Herma can't stand it any more. She turns on them both with eyes of phosphorus, her face like a meringue:

O stop it stop it

she shouts and runs back through the curry-comb fields. Tomas moves after her but Rachel catches him by the arm

Let her alone, she can't hurt

she says softly, squinting through the sunlight at him. Her obligatory hands pull him on. She smiles at him until he smiles tentatively and dismisses Herma from the landscape.

By the afternoon, Herma realizes this game of partners is antics gone mad/bad. She can't stop thinking of that winter greeting Tomas had given Rachel. The horror of his hand gently but immediately raised had been confirmation, to an absolute degree. Out of the window she sees blank white hot space: keeps on staring at it: the sky. Everything is white and still. Nothing moves. Except the voices. Her body, the furniture, floor and ceiling, the afternoon: all are white: a wedding cake white. Her outstretched hand is white. She has cramp in her left leg. Rays and angles of light slice into her. Hordes of white butterflies. She shuts them out. Long curtains drool down windows. Fat breasts of air nudge her, old women's tits. She walks stiffly to the table. She sits down and after ten minutes she writes

. . . Ah but the days will stay the same and in them we'll continue to behave as always fulfilling the hours transfixed by our gestures our waxen faces never melting our hands never touching any real substance . . .

But she is estranged from even the consolation of writing. She stands up unsteadily and walks restlessly across the room, back and forth, back and forth. She can hear their voices, harsh and coarse. She ignores them: goes on walking. But finally their surmounting influence defeats her and she goes to the window. She watches the three of them laughing below. It is a time to view the disintegration of hearts. Not to spy on okes. She glances at the flowers. Then pulls the curtain across again. O no, not this. The memory of piercing colour is a glass bell cracked for no good reason. Is it inevitable that she should feel so incapable of conveying her feelings to Tomas, is there so great a separateness between them that she can only reach him by violences which he misunderstands, hedged in by his own desires? She kneels down in the middle of the room to pray. But barbarians and jokers drown her out. And the heat pouring from the crotch of the sun does not relieve her spiritual chill, it does not revive her, it is only like first-aid gauze scraping her flesh, she can only whisper to herself

Ships are sailing even on the land, but no one, not even a sailor, walks on a lake.

The volatile stolen world of negation welcomes her. She gets up murmuring, she waits only to fold up the piece of paper and lock it away in a drawer before going downstairs, out into the vegetative full-blown summer which has nothing to do with the early morning sunlight she had watched, it has nothing to do with the genteel azure tint of dawn, nothing at all. This light, this glare blinds her, at first she has great difficulty in seeing. Then it clears to blue sky, pulled tight as a corset, and big roses as red as it is blue. Violent contrast. Shading eyes with her hands, she makes out the figures of Tomas and Rachel and Daniel walking away across the lawn. Left behind, Herma experiences a kind of secondary sunlight that has a blinding byzantine charm. Her coffee shadow is self-evident behind her. Clever lies confuse Herma. But she knows that when the sun sets it will leave her and her alone beneath iron adamantine cloud. She calls to them. Slowly they turn and call to her. O this ridiculous afternoon, thinks Rachel and goes on talking to Tomas. They walk slightly faster than the other two. The distance between the couples increases.

I'm enjoying our visit

says Daniel mildly. But Herma ignores him and maintains an acrimonious silence. She is acute enough to see Daniel for what he is. She walks swiftly, to draw level with the others. Rachel glances at her, sideways, on the pretext of a smile. Has she accepted that insulting discovery yet, has Herma realized how insatiable is the need to cling to the frothing ship that has no use for a horizon?

This concert, is the conductor Hungarian?

Rachel asks sociably

I hear he's excellent . . .

As far as Herma is concerned, the voices click meaningless as castanets. She looks up at the sky and sees the elongated reflection of a great bitter lake, a submerged blue, accepted as clear water. Tomas looks quickly from one woman to the other. Herma, the younger of the two: she walks awkwardly: though upright enough she leans to one side rather delicately: her face is sun-burnt and her long hair has the dark tone of muscadine. Rachel is taller and walks more gracefully: is pale-cheeked, as if she had spent some time recently in total exclusion from the sunlight, her eyes are chokish, her lips closed up tight. Always, the same expression appearing on both faces would denote differing emotions, alternate energies. Nothing can mitigate the disparity between these two. The enterprise Rachel is occupied with commemorates herself alone but it feeds mostly on Tomas: this is why Herma stares at him so seriously: this is why Daniel is in this place. Tomas yawns. He cannot penetrate this atmosphere of exaltation and fear. He yawns again. Just lately he has been sleeping badly, he has become familiar with the dog-watch of the night and recognizes for the first time the ebony characters of night: trees chairs fields garden statues cars houses sky silent wife also lying awake or half awake in the tinny rays of moonlight blinking like a somnambulist. So that come the late afternoon he often feels dozy especially when light moves falteringly like today and there is no shade. But what can he do besides walk lazily on? The fringed sphinx of the sun remains the summer's most muscular element. Beneath it the afternoon is leaden as medieval sin. But they shimmer across this garden resembling a stationary hearse of flowers and huge ripe silence hangs on them, fearsome in its weight. All the morning after she fled back to the house Herma had moved from room to room, her vivacity compressed into short jerky strides, as if expecting an eclipse of this sun. And now Rachel tries to analyse her own brand of jealousy. How, in spite of saying to myself o I can't bear it, how do I manage to get through each day, to complete the structure of a whole year, to go on ploughing through the seasons of drought and monsoon? But I do go on. I do go on assuming animations, moving too elaborately, a little like a pandora, my clever brave mouth shedding parrots and slanders: giving as much light as a roman candle, sparks scattering uselessly and liverishly across my dark mind, leaving again the darkness and my own self clothed in furniture and clocks. But this does not diminish her jealousy nor persuade her to let go of Tomas. Herma senses this regirding of the will. O god, she thinks, don't let it be the wrong mirror into which I'm staring, don't let Bethlehem turn into Bedlam again. O the child. Actual symbols, crosses especially, and blessed water, all plot their movements carefully and skilfully, I know. So I too plan my steps. Please please help me. Perhaps I should just keep my eyes closed: open they see so much that is spoilt and rotting . . . O love's merry-go-round and rumours of a god. . I'm so afraid, so afraid that I'm walking into, no, Rachel's pushing me, forcing me to enter an uncompromising devoid room where all the memories are kept: nasty stinking carrion whose claws I know are more dangerous than death. This fear makes her hands seem not her own hands but a part of the body of the day surrounding her like a sarcophagus and from which she must withdraw, she cannot stop herself. Daniel is cautiously watching his three silent companions. I've unfolded the dog-eared pages of history. And all I find is suspicion. So now I await the flames in a cave of lust. Dispassionately he watches Herma grip Tomas's arm with both hands. Holding him. Until he looks at her and sinks down into the calyx of her stare. Then wordlessly they both turn and go in to the cool dark house. Moving so slowly they seem almost bored instead of burdened and bowed down by the dead gods and heroes which they are carrying within themselves. They leave Rachel and Daniel standing there, not looking at one another, but still much too solemn and surprised a couple. They are bound in the tight angelic wings of heat. They sit down on the lawn. Perhaps glad of a respite. Besides there is little else for them to do. Under the circumstances. Impressions of this first week: she thinks of mornings and afternoons merging together to make one long vista of sunlight. O the ordinary transactions of life go on, meals and newspapers and involuntary smiles when someone sneezes. But noone is fooled. They are uncomfortable and out of place in one another's company, never sure who will come into the room or down the stairs or out into the garden and catch them off guard. She gets up and leaves Daniel. Who seems half asleep anyway. Great red and white projections of roses stain the air and blanch or bleed the grass. There are paths along which she feels compelled to walk. Or glide. This is one of those long boring afternoons which grip her heart until it sweats. And there is a pain somewhere intangible and deep. It can be cured by travelling and acts of bravery. No! That time is over. But flickers of its grandeur beset her. There is nothing here besides the ennui of plants and the numb lawns. Again doubts seize her. But the masterly examination of the sun puts an end to them: it limits her cleverness. Again she returns to the struggle. So far she has not been able to probe Tomas as thoroughly as she had wished: in this light he prances out of her reach, like the strangler at confession. And the way he had followed Herma this time. Is all pleasure to be forbidden then, forbidden or resented? Her long red mouth that is not quite real enough bends and splutters towards Daniel, trying to convince someone that she is a priestess.

I could have told you she was wrong.
Daniel goes on reading or rather gazing at the book whose words convey only a sense of sudden illiteracy.

What?

She was wrong . . . about the weather . . .

Oh.

She said there'd be a storm. Herma. She was wrong.

But it is very close.

He closes the book and lies down. He shuts his eyes. She gets up again. And rages and ranges about the garden. She goes to look over the fence into the next garden: where there are only wild flowers. So she turns back to the cultivated roses. The petals babble incoherently. She listens: but is diverted by other landscapes. O her aura of desolation . . .

Because indoors, upstairs, behind locked doors, a nude eager Tomas and a naked gay Herma cavort like a golden lion and a tawny lioness, smashing against the gold shadows. She knows that they are. And she is on the outside. She will not scrimp on imagination. Marching up and down the garden, she can see it all. But as she prowls, a far less fitting ceremony occurs, there is only mutual indifference between them after the blows have been exchanged, an atmosphere of anti-climax after the hooded conversation is finished. The strained intense silence will not even permit arguments.

> You might as well raffle life month by month to see if it is worth keeping

says Herma bitterly. To her galled hands. He does not answer her. Whatever does Rachel think of their departing, just going, just leaving, just like that?

Tomas?

Still he does not answer. She gets up and stands over him. He ignores her. Deeds accomplished and planned, implications, threats: all impersonate one another. She turns and rushes out of the room. She clatters over the cold stone floor in a tumult. She is burning. She kicks off her shoes and cools her feet on the kitchen floor. She drinks some water. Then stands. Watching the couple in the garden. And listening. The clock ticks. The hands of the clock move. She stands there, watching its loneliness. It moves. And yet it does not. Just like me. Standing here, I lack both compassion and courage. It is late. The pyretic sun shines. Predestined and unhappy, the hands move. I am it. I recognize it. Like knows like. Its own kind. She watches the clock. It might be her own heart. I must go away and live my life free of this control! But she cannot. She's the target: not the arrow. Rachel stands by the roses, the leaves are lean, they tantalise her. Even roses burnt by the crisp summer sun can harbour cold doubt. Then they cease to smell sweet. She turns away. The air hums motets. YES. She can hear the two of them up there in that room, to which she fruitlessly demands a key, grunting and yelping as they come, caught together in the invigorating pressure, tucked flexibly together. Her lips are emollient, she tingles and her own genitals sting. O the summer, you can't escape it, not even by swimming. Her eyelids fall beneath its waves. And the somnolence, her cerise hands . . . . She moves slow as waking to go back into the house out of the flaxen heat but when she turns she finds Herma standing there waiting, her sunny face in the way as if she wants to block the way.

O

says Rachel

O Herma.

A thick heavy voice from cromlech lips. She just stares at her. Opposites meet but do not match. No. Not on this highway. The furnace air gags them both. Maxillary flies buzz around them. Herma seems tongue-tied. Unsure of Rachel's wide open eyes and her assumed amazement. When was she ever genuine? Anger keeps Herma dumb. But then Rachel relaxes and laughs, twirling a full-blown rose between her fingers. The petals scatter.

I thought you were indoors, you made me jump.

Herma smiles pleasantly. Almost humble. An overdose of good manners sickens Rachel. But, as her hands are relatively cool now, Herma jerks her hair back indecently. Despising Rachel's prurient eyes.

I'm having a drink. Do you want one? it's so hot . . .

Rachel nods. She throws the remains of the rose away. Sun is tireless. Nothing can be hidden long in this most true of summers. It burns and burns until even dust is aflame and a trinity of heads are on fire. The two women wake Daniel up and hurry him into the house with them. Soon evening will flutter and dusk mash the sun. It cannot be soon enough.

The dinner table is ornate and sprayed with silver. They spring upon it hungrily like hunters. But above their grasping hands, their faces are unexpectedly ordinary. Tiredness and the lack of fairy-tales show up in their eyes. For the first time there is a certain amount of intimacy between them: perhaps because of the evening rain and its coolness. This conviviality repulses some of the tension. The room contains many voices. O their own voices yes: but beside the volume of these, other voices can be heard, crammed in with them because they belong to them in various ways: they have been laughed at or with, cried over, listened to, ignored, obeyed, two times four is, three times six is . . . all through life.

Perfect weather until now.

O but I'm glad it's broken.

The wine goes through Rachel like an outline being drawn, a firm hand. She watches two trails of wine seep into the white cloth. The wine tastes of surprise chocolates popped into the mouth, it makes her smile and smile down at the bridge of her nose. It is fermentation which perfects wine, she decides, wine protects you from pain or thought or avarice. Herma's glass-sharp voice pricks the air.

Then you two stay

she says decisively

I know you'll only be bored by music by music by music . . . Rachel looks at her unsteadily: but cannot see any hint of violent disturbance, no subtlety in the eyes: only calmness and a kindly face. Tomas avoids her eyes ringed with charcoal paint. Pavilions of grey silk, the sky, a light rainy wind swabs them, the couples part at the front door, go their separate ways, Rachel and Tomas watch Herma and Daniel drive towards the gates of the limp city.

Goodbye goodbye . . .

Brown light. Shadows multiply. Herma sees how the house recedes into the driving mirror. It wobbles, becomes a miniature lodging-place. But loses none of its importance. She knows the eye does not always comprehend the hand's evasion nor does the deepest ear always listen too carefully to the contagious lie. Between Daniel and herself, the present silence is binding, the appointments it must keep. The straitness of these two fools is a moral crime: it leads to a situation changing farmland to marshland, viaduct to silt. But he cannot act after so long an absence from activity. And it seems she cannot stop herself putting Tomas to the test. She drives towards a finale. Every corner demands caution. The street lamps come on, one great lantern. He fingers his tie nonchalantly. The other evening is in a turmoil, disturbed by the nomadic motion of their bodies. Her short hair is spiky and fanatic. His fingers have swept through it. Barer than rocks, her hips. The sound of rain locks into the silence of the room. The friction between the man and the woman is cynical, familiar, laconic. Its brightness is forced, in spite of the final rapid flood of lucidity which results in one of them gasping as if mining a vein of gold. Now they separate. Without looking at one another. He sits on the edge of the bed. Possession fails by such a voracious margin. Her stretched-out body tries to decipher what she has gained.

Rachel, leave me alone, leave us alone,

he says, his voice underground. She lies quite still, her hands at her sides, sated with fretfulness. The uncomprehending room is anonymous as a station.

Rachel?

he says questioningly. Short dead interval of silence. The pearly feldspar of her motionless body gleams in the rainy half-light.

No

she tells him indifferently

it won't leave me alone, will it?

He asks his question again. Less politely. She looks at him once, motherly. Then away again. Her tongue is like the tongue of a bell.

I've told you of my travels, haven't I?

she asks very wearily.

Yes, you've told me.

In a tone of deadened bitterness.

What do you think of Daniel?

Nothing. What am I suppose to think, what did you intend?

Leaning over her. Void of tenderness.

What should I say?

He takes a handful of hair, pulls it tightly until she curses, then then lets go. He dresses and lights a cigarette, his face anxious and gloomy. This evening has a post-dated flavour. Is more remote than the moon. He roams about the room. Then comes down and sits beside her again. She is exacting. He puts his hand on her moist belly. But turns his head away from her and closes his eyes as he says emphatically

Rachel, I used to think, when we were first together, years ago, at the beginning, I used to think that there was nothing out of my reach, or your reach: our grasp. But since then times have changed, new conditions have developed, unexpected factors have led me to doubt whether that first love ever existed, whether either of us ever occupied that warm wet flowery world after all: yes, I doubt whether we really did giggle our way through life the way we think we did. We could never have been that carefree. And even if such a world did exist, its finished now. I've grown out of that simple kind of love, that easy refreshing sort of desperation. No no

says Rachel loudly and angrily, sitting up, gulping, pressing his hand against her flesh

No Tomas

But he does not open his eyes or move his head. He pulls his damp hand away.

No

she says more softly

No Tomas, it is not true. It could be just the same. It is just that you've slid into an indifference since then, an indifference which is too austere, which denies the possibility of that kind of sweet love, yours and mine.

Words slitting the air.

O no, no, its just another excuse

he says coldly

love doesn't just come and go, it doesn't endure unless it is a reality: and ours was no, no, nothing of the kind, remember, Rachel? It was so unreal you had to leave me in order to find realities . . . and it was you who went away, not me.

Rachel, the laughing-stock, sits upright.

It's true, Tomas, I was wrong. That's why I keep on returning.

Her gentle candid eyes. He turns to her and stares urgently. Then questions her rapidly.

Is it Rachel is that why is there no other reason Rachel none at all nothing to do with anyone or anything else just the two of us is it is it?

More depressing than the bedrooms of the chaste (once she was) are those of the adulterous.

Why yes

she says lightly and lubriciously, a sudden change of manner, shrugging, eyes half closed, reverting to her customary attitude

yes of course

the bewildering impatience, the boredom. His face feigns sickness and he stares at the wall:

I think perhaps o perhaps it was so once Rachel yes once: but now . . . no longer. You're in the wrong place, Rachel, what you want won't be found here, you can't grab it and take it away with you again. . . .

If all that you say is true

she replies and coldly now

why do we go on trying to rehabilitate it?

looking at the same wall. But the wall is not a good enough symbol.

No

she goes on

No, it could exist: but I think Herma has tampered with you somehow, she's changed you: now your whole being demands too controlled and yet also too contorted a love: it demands a communion between lovers that is too radical to last, too dangerous a love. Use mine, instead, don't let Herma fool you with her faith, use my love and disbelieve in hers!

He slumps on the bed and sneers:

Of course: Herma. Is it all her fault then? What about your greater gardens?

But she has a defence.

I said I was wrong. I'll admit I was wrong. But will Herma admit what she believes in is wrong? I've learnt to deny and ridicule them, those gardens. Will Herma deny anything! She wants you to desire this additional dimension of love, spiritual love, because she desires it: she knows it's an impossible desire, never to be fulfilled: but she wants you to suffer the way she suffers.

Rachel places her palm on the small of his back, pressing down just for a second. He moves away, he walks to the window, shutting her out. He is shaken. He won't give Rachel an ovation.

She wants you to suffer

Rachel persists

she does, she does: look at the way she went off tonight, just to torment me. And to tempt you. You'll be trapped if you don't save yourself and come with me . . . o why won't you admit it. . . . ?

her naked limbs scalding and dried out, ready to break at the slightest pressure.

Tomas . . . ?

No

he says

No no, I can't, get dressed, they'll be back soon.

Tomas,

goes on the warning sybil voice

    Herma's taking you in a strange direction, towards everything you
    hate: altars, hymns, visions, everything . . .
He turns around, contentious but laughing nervously
    What a fantasy, Rachel: Herma doesn't want to be laid by a god.
The dark flowers juggle in the night. Rain stops. She comes, her
nakedness like a douche, and stands besides him, her body inset with
strong hairs at its angles.
    Tomas, our internal struggle is so great. Out there
she points at the woolly sky
    the loss of a battle
and she underlines the word by placing her hands on his shoulders, one
chinese finger-nail scratching the back of his neck
    is a national catastrophe, journalists like Daniel rush to chart its
    horrors, to count the dead and wounded: but think —here between us
    it is just the same, the impact is no different. Just because we do not
    live in headlines does not soften the blows. You don't realize how
    much like a war everything is.
He does not answer, he has no intention, no words, no saliva: is there any
difference between these two women anyway?
    I suppose legal terms would suit you better than the military
she says, less articulate now that she is growing greedy. Although her
strength is still great. But surely she had not wanted this strength? It has
been forced on her surely? See how it drags me down. Is hers a pure
uninfluenced love? Or is she using it to serve her need to gain the upper
hand over everything? The sockets of her eyes ache. What would it be
like, to be set free of her obsessions? O the pervasive memories. Outside
damp summer air spins full of night. She stands, cold body very pale and
still. She waits for a moment. But he is still staring out of the window. Her
voice prangs out, she lifts pride in both hands:
    We're like fire and air, Tomas, pearl and oyster: we're indisputably
    welded.
Now he turns, he laughs, a witty broncho.
    You know, you sound just like Herma

he tells her, shocking her for a change. Her marine ideals are all at once tertiary. She thinks of them pitifully. She says no more, naked she awaits snow, then she dresses hurriedly, she makes the bed. Does it matter that he can't differentiate between a madrigal and a shopping list? And if it does matter, what then?

Come to the ruins tomorrow?
he asks from the doorway, calm, unconcerned, as if nothing vital had happened in this room.

Yes, I'll come . . .
she says, a descant. Often, she used to refuse. Once she had mistrusted the too silent apparently dead pedantic past. Now it does not matter. For the past there is, was, shall be no apology. It cannot be ignored. Its aggressive relics abound. Often they cannot be seen for tears. Now it doesn't matter. She follows him downstairs, to sit and wait for the return of their deprived partners. To await another greeting, the bad blank stony good-night. Arpeggios descending, stinging singing octaves. Night has taken place when they leave the hot concert hall. Music still pollutes the air. But they walk away from it over wet pavements that shine under the street lamps. The night smells of a stable. Faulty reception disturbs these receivers. But no matter. He shakes his head. According to the season, it should be warmer. My hands are cold. O we'll soon be back. After every concert he always feels he has left something behind. So now he walks along like a mourner. Silently the night narrows down. Her sloping back cuts the darkness in two as she walks across the rainy road. The planets in the saline sky glitter like burning flowers. The plough is covered with black grass. The evening star's gone, silvery and boasting of Venus. Now other stars of mesh hunt in packs. The moon hangs in cosmic gas. There is an endless rurality even in the universe's furthest points.

Look
he says
the moon's on horseback.
They both look up. She smiles a little. Her real laughter is reserved for puns and victories. If he'd been a few years younger he'd have winked. Or

even a few years older. Herma just smiles. The music still churns in her head: she is oblivious to everything but its blue-black rhythm. Daniel whistles a tune from a symphony. Don't don't don't she says to herself. But he goes on whistling as she unlocks the car door. He wants to reach her somehow. The darkness is stamped with lights from cars, houses, street lamps, traffic signs. None of which clarify the withered city. She braces herself for the return. To be able to defend her praying noon: and not to fall. To keep the sanctuary clean.

Rachel upsets you. Doesn't she?
Then he swears as she over-takes another car and only just avoids smashing into an on-coming lorry. Between her shoulder-blades there is an ache. Is it the nights which worry her or their threat of daylight? No, it is both, their divided unity: too reminiscent of Tomas and herself. She does not answer Daniel. He's just a stooge. Why bother with him? Her silence prompts him. There is a sudden cruelty in him which he has not felt for years and which he does not try to rectify. He ignores this reluctance, this obvious pain of hers. Even the speed of the car is unimportant.

She does upset you. It's obvious. Why? What's the angle? Ah all those voices shouting for sacrifice. She slews the car around a dangerous bend. The car skids on the wet tarmac. A screech of brakes. But she rights the car somehow. The music is still loud. He is watching her slyly. She has contracted and curled herself up inside his words. Which have revealed her inefficient camouflage.

Yes then. Yes she does
Herma says, a cold faith in her words
yes.
With her hands holding on tight to the steering wheel. Barbarians lie in wait. To devour. She turns the car into the drive. She knows she would have been afraid to come home alone. She smiles at him. Then looks away. Self-consciously. Down at her awkward ingenuous hands. They sit in the car awhile. In spite of welcoming lights in the house they do not feel inclined to enter. With stark frippery he says

Is there any reason?

As if he were an expert. All at once she turns ultimate eyes on him. They are the lees of an immortality. He is afraid and unsure. Only the happy are safe. She says with pure expatriate sarcasm:

I've known Rachel a very long time.

She gets out of the car hurriedly. Who said, my death will cost you? She can't remember. She is just in flight now. He watches her go through the howling summer night where abusive rain is falling a second time. Why are you scared silly, Daniel, he sniggers to himself. But it is not funny: and he knows it only too well as he also goes reluctantly into the faithless house.

Three

The ripe cavalier sky, surly casual light, the multiple slender shafts of heat falling to the ground with an aromatic tang: all goad them. He at least is becoming anadromous. In an enigmatic sense. An enigma based upon the source of the air. They are crossing the lawn. He walks a short distance before her, as if to protect her from any dangers. The mica earth burns, it feels vigorous, brawny and wavy beneath their feet. The unmoving green garden is stiff and threatening, its atmosphere belongs to the same frightening category that includes wands and rodents. But they do not notice, perhaps the heat has stupefied them, perhaps they just do not care, that this stagnant air is shrilly full of innuendos. They wander into the fields, chalking out their own isthmus. They learn little of any real value from their concave studious pilgrimage. But the bodily movements alone console. Their heads bisect the arc of the afternoon, they are its central focus, sitting in the wood under the shade of a linden tree. Her hair is a flambeau of jet. In spite of her sun-tan, she remains somehow snowy, that is the impression given: she is not at all strong, still so damaged that she is only able to act intuitively, is exhausted by her own history and her memories, the way they sweep her to one side of life. He glances at her. The music of last night is coaxingly wet on his lips. She has hardly spoken all afternoon. This woman beside him is a stranger, gritty as a figure seen in sleep. But he has to touch her. Tomas's neglect burns her, hot as a simoom wind. Is the situation in any way open to negotiation? Her face flushes to sienna when she realizes how Daniel is studying her. His touch is unsought. But he had to touch her. She turns to him. A rebuff. In her eyes are grains and flecks of light that make him think of grace abounding. Saliva bubbles in his mouth. He imagines the gaudy passage of boats through the water. She does not speak, she turns her head swiftly away again to look back across the dry fields, as if she had caught the sudden movement of shiny broken objects there, out of the corner of her eye. He watches her, fascinated by the shroud of shadow falling over her. And touches her wrist again. But even under the sheltering leaves, the cubic sun is far too strict and burnished, the leaves themselves too savage and gory for her to defy. As far as she is concerned, there is too great a distance between the two of them, there are swords of gold and apothecaries' dead rooms, she won't risk not being able to reach out far enough. Her withdrawal quells this other stranger and compresses any thought of going forward to a shrine. He is like dark wood inflamed, the skin pulsing that resembles the colour and texture of skin found at the base of the beak in some fowls. He needs to find a way out of the menagerie. Even though she flashes away from him every time, merely by sitting, massive as a giant stamen yet slight as a girl.

I myself was born

begins Herma unexpectedly, speaking rapidly and very quietly

in a far-off place with which I am sure you are not familiar. In my own room, at the back of the house, I could always hear, every hour of the day and night, the trains as they came in and went out of the station. At that time they were of course steam trains and they blew their whistles in long exhausted cries. You might imagine hearing such sounds in a desert, a wilderness. But for me they acted as a lullaby. I keep awake even now listening for them. Half the night sometimes. The winters of my youth, my childhood, were always long: but mild, clammy and transmarine. I enjoyed them. They fixed limits for me. You see?

He nods and the nautical shadows go nodding also.

Did I ever tell you how much nakedness disgusts me? she asks, in a sudden cry, an intrusion into the precarious but otherwise calm sentences, a red brilliant cry that burns itself out . . . .

. . . and o I did not live then, I did not move freely through the years: I was domiciled, set in place there, just like a tree or a stone or a lake: no . . . less than a lake, for it sparkles in the sunlight. And was I any more wicked, wayward, disobedient, badly behaved or indecent a child than any other? No. No.

Now she speaks half to herself, almost inaudibly, shut in to herself.

Nakedness does not disgust me

Daniel tells her

I could protect you from your fear.

But greater fear hops one-leggedly across her face and she replies swiftly

Protectors are often jailors in disguise . . . . Why didn't you go to the ruins, I thought Rachel said you were interested in such things?

He basks in the sun.

Rachel's wrong. I'm over my craze for the dead.

She flinches.

O I'm not

she says but without conviction. Sun travels in the sky as scruffy as a goldsmith.

What is a marriage supposed to be?

she asks half coyly.

You're married, you tell me.

With elation. Now we're getting somewhere.

O there is no prototype

Herma tells him, in a changed voice, cautious and serious, unfastening her hair from its plait and twisting the freed hair around her fingers. The sky above them is full of orange branches. Silence flows like water from a mill wheel. Except for the persistent song-bird who mimics the song of other braver birds. A mirror image of Rachel beats Daniel with sticks and whips and thorns and prickles: iron bracelets on both wrists, legs strong, muscular and vermilion. O Cassi. He reaches out and touches Herma's cheek, as if about to hint at something. But gradually she is disappearing into herself, hands gripping clods of earth, rocking herself slightly, to and fro, repealing all kindness to herself. He drops his hand.

Tell me about your child, Herma

he says, with no emphasis or expression whatsoever. She does not move. Except her head, which quavers minutely, darting in the air.

Unhappiness is like a mirror: when you confront it you find yourself reflected there

she says in a fatalistic and shy voice

and the authority of midwives is not always benevolent either

but it's a steady voice, as if she is only continuing a conversation which has been building up and increasing in her mind for over a thousand hours, built up with the skill of the quarry man and the integrity of the mason, the dual actions of weathering only toughening the words.

I can hardly remember him, it was so short a time I had him to myself. But I can remember my . . . lamentations . . . o how I cried out to know all about him, his curled-up unravelled life, the potentialities . . .

Then breaking down, trembling, cursing, she stands up, hair hanging like catkins, and runs off into the wood, reeling from side to side under the weight of her trouble and letting her voice go, wailing and squalling away from her. Somewhere far far behind her, the hooves of black iron horses stamp: and great wheeling kites caw and scream. A blind bespangled girl dressed in black dances and sings in an infamous slang tongue. He watches Herma, thinking of Cassi and real mushrooms and lust. He does not move for a moment. Then he runs after her, runs and catches her, pulls her around, shaking her until she is quiet and there is only the hysterical echo and their breath upon the silence. He looks fixedly at her, like the camera seeking its image: the proper stance, the light, refractions, depth, focus, exposure. Soon she lifts her head but slowly. It is heavy and she is almost ready to curse again: yet the words do not come and so she smiles an intoxicated smile. She leans against him and their foreheads touch. She places a cool hand on his cheek. They both smell the airiness of dried orchid roots and hear the triple chord of a hurdy-gurdy, an instrument played without much skill. They kiss with wide open mouths. For want of tornado, they do not end this embrace. His spade fingers kneel between her legs: all the time his face is growing agitated as if going beneath the waves, the brittle exact declension of waves, whilst his body intensifies, solidifies, becomes in sensation almost neo-realistic. Her face is compound. He says her name, temptation is greedy for jewels, for a moment she crouches like a crescent moon to let his jocose wooden hands bray up. But then her body fizzes and for her the tableau under the leaves cracks, desire falls from her and vanishes, ludicrous and theatrical. She drifts awry, away from the nail of seduction, writhing in her own pained dew. Leaving him dethroned on the outskirts of the ritual. As she clenches in on herself, he breathes out, he puffs angrily and then takes his rejected fingers away. Sensitivity ends. After the manner of something valuable shattering.

I'm sorry

she mutters. But her view of all this is restricted to a voyeur's eye, peering through a small hole in the thin wall.

It doesn't matter

he says, his voice uninformative as a nicely written thank you letter.

I am

she tells him forcefully. The fixed eyepiece wants too great a freedom. Under the leaves of the oaks and the lindens. He does not move. Herma hesitates then begins to walk back to the house, she keeps on walking and does not look back over her shoulder at him, no, not once. Passion is only giving, she tells herself, only a pouring from one vessel to another. She does not look around even though normally the thought of escape would seem petty to her and she would deride it. He remains standing there, staring down at the unreadable parchment of the turf. Herma is a chantress in a fiscal chapel. Herma is a stupid conceited cat. Which? His indecision is evidence of a weary unexplored distrustful man. How was he supposed to know she had no love to give to anyone? Yes: but he admires such a lack of interest in her husband's affair with Rachel, such stony isolation. Perhaps he could free her, this static sleeping beauty? But he can find no way of reaching her. Does my own negation have riches? O yes. It does. In a very valiant sense. Of course. These stiff meadows know. This negation is a kind of conquest of emotion. Like Herma's. It does not matter that for him it is easy, merely a clinging on to personality: whilst for Herma it is deformation, an agony. He will not consider this, it would spoil the dignity of his masquerade. He will not accept commissions of guilt. His eyes have looked down too many trivial streets to see anything. O Cassi!

Rachel walks doubtfully, dubiously, through the ruins of the amphitheatre, under an eagle sun. Is this the same place or a facsimile?

    All roads lead to Rome

says Tomas foolishly. He is ashamed of his voice's echo. She turns slowly, hypnotically.

    What?

It might have been the beginning of his life story. Both know this visit this afternoon is a prelude.

    Nothing.

She gazes thoughtfully at him. But the light blinds her. Its cardiac rays. The taut hot wind makes her hair go bushy. It is metallic. He expects to hear it clank loudly, lock against lock. Her mouth looks like a burn. As he watches, the outline of her body seems to merge into the heat-haze. A young couple, arms around one another, lips touching, pass without noticing them. Tomas cannot avoid her condemnation of the boy and girl. He accepts it. The rocks are dormant. Their shadows form scabs on the ground. Rachel blames her failure to survive her own search for something real and perfect with prominent spires, true flowers worthy of this sun, on the whole world: even the strangers walking away from them. It is the habit of the very cold. She knows it. So she holds a hand out to Tomas: so she smiles: in remembrance of her purpose for returning. He does not take her proffered hand immediately. But leaves it to crawl on the air for a blazing moment. A sensitive itchy part of his flesh feels like a syringe ready to spray. As they stand there beneath a stationary blue sky, they feel the dense encumbrance of their limbs. Rachel is prepared to destroy hers, for the sake of victory. But Tomas will not take the chance, she doesn't even try to persuade him. Instead she holds out her other hand, to make a pair. He takes them. He smiles too. Both relax, sigh, and walk on, hand in hand, like lovers. The flavour of love will not be so good this season, it will be too acid. But she does not care. She is determined to plunge them all into a hotbed of dirt and chagrin, if necessary. He does not understand that unglazed callousness is the strongest of her emotions. At their feet, growing wild, celtic worthless white flowers, like broken friendships. These ruins are crowded with the shadows of centuries. They say, nothing is final. They're right. Lifelines do not snap even when hair is rotted half away like rope. Shadows of Rachel's forebears tell her how short a distance they have gone away to hide, how little a journey it is: and yet how far a distance she must still go on no matter how unwillingly. Her dress flaps in the win. The recurrent memories of a dry landscape where sun forced them to their knees, the dabbing hurt, the raised hand, the horizon of surrealism stabbed with blood dazzle her: a lethal conclusion makes her heart pant, her glass limbs shake, she says, gauntlets of sun push her down, she cannot withstand the pressure. He catches her.

O Rachel Rachel . . . . .

But her eyelids have collapsed. The wilful shadows congregate around this couple, she fainting, the man kneeling ineffectively beside her, wishing Herma were here. Brazen girl stranded in a place where the air is red hot and the attitudes of the dance are rare, Rachel cannot find a way of controlling or defeating the spirit of malicious majesty, no matter where she walks, at whose side.

Rachel Rachel . . .

An unceasing endless motion, a rocky ownership of moons, predictable mornings, eternal shadows, alone, and not alone: swirl. Have a haunting dryness. She knows: bountiful straw and the capricious lamp: brought together they burn and destroy. She opens her eyes to a flame green light in the middle of which his face eventually appears, hackneyed and irrelevant.

What's wrong Rachel?

He hides himself in the wood of words. He holds her wrists loosely to keep her there with him.

What?

Careless masses of stone jut out around them, illustrations of history, bones of those left dead by drought. This place, this landscape brings me no comfort. Would dog roses and delphiniums? Her eyes half close again but with a defiant strength she forces them open and makes her famished body deny its current havoc.

What's wrong?

Wrong?

Voice amid blistering shadows. Nothing can enhance the rocks. I am near enough to touch. But dare not. Of this emptiness, a sample alone kills.

You just fell, Rachel . . .

O the heat . . . it focuses here.

Her dehiscent head throbs. She gets up slowly. The feathery dust bumps around her.

Help me . . .

Tomas supports her. Her hands reach out and cling, her memorable skull bobs in the air like a cork, she almost falls again, she leans heavily on him. Deified rock jostles the precious words of explanation in her brain . . . . I found a tomb . . . she moans in a flowerless voice . . . and a place of birth also . . .

What . . . you found a what . . . ?

His loud voice is so calm and indiscriminate.

O nothing. Nothing. You can let me go now. It's over. They stand together, faces shadowed. The quilted sky of quicksilver and gunpowder cools down. So it seems to her. Its cruel needles leave her alone, trespasser, in contempt.

Are you sure?

Yes yes. I'm sure.

The atom in his heart is bulky with fear. But too deep for her to discern. Now her face is smooth and cleansed of frailty.

Yes. It's over.

She laughs, an airy arid sound which deceives him. The earth spins on its axis. She walks on, she goes on through the jasper world. Follow me. And he obeys thankfully. She saunters on. Suppressing the bitter vision even god knows is too hard to bear. Bullets and brickbats and blood. It's a strange life but it's the only one I have. Empty subterfuge. They walk on, eyes open but unseeing.

You know why I fell, what's wrong, the trouble?

No

his voice curdled by the sun

no I don't.

I'll tell you then: it's the shadowy inconclusive portions of memory that owe allegiance to a dark gothic history which influence me every proud day: the heat of the summer has nothing to do with it. It's the darkness. Can you understand, Tomas?

No. What darkness? What history? Do you mean the war? The war? What war? O, I see. No. Not that war. A kind of . . .

But persecutions and motivations keep Rachel's mouth shut. She shakes her head slightly. The domains of her oberon world are impassable. Her patriotism must remain a secret between herself and Herma. The principality is a trap: which either will not let her go free or which Rachel herself is unable to leave. The sun heaves in the sky as if it wants to rid itself of all its burdens. No. Exposure is not possible.

O it doesn't matter.

Rachel's history has the texture of stone and storm, not satin and silk. She can't inflict it on him. He is not able to bear it. Let this false unity be all, let instinct be all: let him ask questions she'll never answer, let him be worried, suspicious, inert: but keep him free of all this dissolution of hers. In silence they watch the summer's dry primordial dance. All achievements are vanity, she thinks unoriginally, kicking at stones. Which are fractured by time.

What do you think?

Her reticent eyes query him. He explains:

Now that you've travelled, I mean, does this place strike you differently, do you like it now?

She is silent, a fizzy mocking sound. She renounces weakness, she forecloses its charm. Her tutelar demon is at work. She turns away from him and speaks over her shoulder, a malediction.

How mysterious all the things I see, all the curiosities I calmly absorb, all the forbidden things that creep over me. All so strange. I've come beyond my own ground to your land yet I did not march. Am I unwelcome in this favourite place of yours or was I long awaited?

She pivots round, a parabola of flesh. Who gets no answer from Tomas. His disappointment could kindle a fire. A moment ago, they almost met. Now he merely takes her hand, trying to put them on an equal footing.

Answers need voices, Tomas.

But still he won't speak. She wrenches her hand away, an association with unsplinterable glass on her mind. For some redemption, she appeals. But takes the unuttered words away with her to the steps. She sits down on cushions of saxifrage. Rachel folds her hands on her knees and stares at them. Inresplendent sterilized sunlight she breathes: the paleness of her face is comic in this cyclamen weather. He comes and sits beside her.

What are we going to do Tom?

she asks without looking at him, her voice fragrant. Almost timid. Waiting for his answer.

We've said goodbye once

he tells her with worn-out words.

So she stands up and begins to walk away. Octagonal heart pounding. But he follows her and takes her hand: again they walk hand in hand. Strangely, there is a considerable ease and understanding between the. He embraces her in a masonic grip.

The body needs a,warmth more emotional than blood can give he tells her gently

and I can't deny that Herma can give me such warmth. At times.

They walk on in silence. Rachel's mouth is fluvial. This is her only reaction. Externally.

And Rachel you know any execution means more than the simple pronunciation of one word, the movement of one uplifted hand.

She nods obediently.

I can't just go to her and say, I don't want you any more. There are bonds, Rachel.

As if she did not know.

You yourself know how strong such ties are.

O what clever tactics. Have I taught him so well?

More than locks. Any treasured possession has to be kept within the imposition of limits. In spite of what's between us, I treasure my marriage. I do. I need her. Rachel, don't laugh. I do. But you know I can't send you away. I can only ask you, please, go. Go quietly. Please. Don't make trouble.

She shakes her head.

It's made

Rachel says softly and restlessly. He stops walking and stares at her with unlucky eyes.

Please . . .

But she walks on with her skull steadfast and orderly.

Think of Herma

he says doubtfully, following the curve of her eyelid. Waiting for the anger and the shock to shake it: which it does: like a corroboree.

Herma!

she hisses, swinging round

Herma! O listen to me. Listen: the head hidden in the urn is too ridiculous a passion: you agree? Yes. But that's Herma for you, that's where she wants you. Dead or alive. Just to gloat over. O Tomas: I've often wondered and now I'm sure that you do resemble that old man who thought whoever commanded the sea commanded the empire. Remember: there are many entrances and exits to every sanctuary. Remember: And look! You look!

Rachel gestures at the ruins. Then she tenses again and her body becomes quite stiff and pointed, nose, breast, elbow, knee:

All Herma has to offer you is a crazy aura of light no one's ever going to be able to cling on to: or see by. You'll find yourself back in the dark. We cannot and must not let ourselves be fooled by her. We must not sit around waiting for an ascension or a reincarnation, the way she does. You can't play at being a faithful lover, just for her sweet sake. I told you once. I wanted a total trusteeship for myself: and I need you to accomplish that . . .

Her voice already loud, now she shouts, with authority

. . . and now you ask me to give up . . . o no!

Hooks and grapnels, he runs away from them. He feels the dry pieces of air, sewn roughly together: they rub against his lips. He groans when he hears Rachel call after him

We must accept the situation for what it is, if we are going to understand anything.

He stops. He doesn't want to, but he stops. He turns and looks back at her. The air seeks captives. She comes down the steps towards him. He waits watching the manner of her translation from attacker above him to girl beside him.

I don't understand . . .

he says. She smiles flatly.

Let me tell you about something I saw in Italy. Two stone bishops lying side by side on their iron tombs. I thought then, there is a fine indication of all our futures, so strong and honest I doubted whether I could bear it. But, I thought, I will bear it. I will live with this knowledge. I held the divine water in my hand and it was green and stagnant. I saw an olive branch but the vines wound around its throat to strangle it. I knew then that I was on my own. That we are all on our own. That we are everything: it's inside of us, our world, our god. Temporal only. And Herma wastes life by looking outside. At nothing. I tell you, she's wrong. Get rid of her!

And what if I tell you I hate you?

he asks abruptly. A hot wind again lifts Rachel's short hair.

O christ

she laughs loudly and coarsely, dancing and cavorting away across the ruined stones, danding and laughing

O then I'd tell you that the marvellous and incredible stories of travellers darling are often false.

He laughs too. And chases her: and they dance in the sunlight like kids. Until the dance slows and the sun dazzles and the dancers they look at one another with pride and love and envy: before they embrace and kiss.

With her eyes closed, Rachel says blissfully

O Europa: I've studied her to absolutely no purpose. The inheritance of centuries is awesome and lyrical and pure and useless. A series of dead objects set apart in museums. Open to many eyes.

They kiss again. Until he breaks away angrily, his face ugly as a golliwog.

You tricked me

he whispers dismally

Yes that's true

Rachel answers wildly

Yes this speech of mine was meant to entice you both spiritually and sexually. Why not? It's more fun than kissing Herma, pious saintly Herma! What images does Herma put before your eyes? O no, don't tell lies, don't turn away, what does she give you?

She grips his arm:

What images do you get from me? Tell me?

That he sees a gorgon covered in blood?

I don't know I don't know . . .

The past or the future: which way for me? I've put the blade of the knife against my throat and I still don't understand anything except that the sunrise is a token of burning: And he breaks away again and runs off and does not turn back this time nor does she shout or run after him but walks slowly in the opposite direction towards the trees where it is cool. For her there is going to be no intermediary or compromise. No hope of relenting. No abatement now.

Close stuffy evening: a room, two women in the room, one of the two women wearing a perfume, the scent of rushed lavender. The face of one of these two women is scratched. Herma has just tried to carve permanent scars on Rachel's face with the sharply filed points of her fingernails. And screamed get out. But on realizing that sudden actions without warning are cheap, she ceases. She thinks of the bodies paralysed in the black coffins. Rachel's face smarts and burns and bleeds, red on white: but she smiles. Fraud and artifice, out of these she constructs a cold way of life that is destined to last about as long as the display seen on the windows any frosty morning. But which the euphemistic summer supports. One day her chilled existence must fail her, all the transparency and caprice must end: and then she will fall victim to the sea-sickness of withdrawal: so Herma hopes. Rachel's martial temperament, a synod of evils, is roused. Now she shouts, striking out with words: her incessant wailing voice grates on Herma's insecurity. None but a true foe could derive a pleasure from the battle.

Farewell is cheap Herma but my mouth won't say so for nothing.

The roses of Herma's lips sulk and droop. Her hands are a sort of death split up into ten pieces. Rachel goes on

Love is a two-headed coin and you're not going to spoil my flaxen dream. Don't ask me for reasons, don't touch me again, I've got a thin invisible knife in my head and I'll use it if you force my arm. But I'll drink a toast to you anyway, shall I?

Extortioner

says Herma dully, with a blank face, a bleak delicacy of tone. (As if anyone could be guiltless, so hallowed as this woman: so Rachel thinks with a precision like the sound of the muezzin at sunrise.) Ill-blood between stock: a malign sanguinary situation. It is a mistake to meddle with lineage: the result is a stone dropped to cause deaths, to put a mode of life out of sight. Rachel is running a hazardous course, in danger of tasting the salt sea, that raw biting damascene taste. She is wrong to aim only for the most extrinsic rapture, absolution that will right all. She may give the essential final victorious thrust, may scream with joy for a second. But then she will fall into an immense metaphysical abyss, out of which there can be no ascension. She pours herself a drink, saying

There was a dragon once who fell in love with a princess who spurned him and

Don't tell me that story!

screams Herma, turning away, flinging her body through space, no, she can't stand it

Don't don't no!

Rachel's unkind voice broadens out into a laugh.

Just a joke

she tells her. But pain is deeply etched into Herma: and like a novice, she has a solemnity about her. She stares at Rachel.

I know scorn is a weapon you like

she says in a tired manner

because you know it makes me nervous, it upsets me. But I tell you I know something you don't. I understand the unseen, the miraculous. I can go beyond the everyday. I know about faith, I know it must lift up its head and make a representation. I know what faith means. You don't. Other things I don't understand much, far less than you. Perhaps in the end there will be nothing there, nothing at all, only darkness. But I'll know how to bear it. You won't. Remember, I tried to find out, one way and another. I tried.

O and is it all a test then, is it any good cheating . . . ?

laughs Rachel sublimely

Let me tell you, Herma, all your ideas are just on loan, when you're finished with them, you'll send them back to wherever you got them, thank you very much. But mine, my ideas that you ridicule and despise, at least they are my own. I chart their progress myself.

Jumps up, poisonous girl. The rhesus factor divides. The jaw snaps to, it is learning how to refuse the bait, it has found a way of saying, enough, goodbye, goodnight, I've had enough of you. And Herma has gone.

Four

The two guests sit gravely on the crural lawn. Rachel is humming a folk tune to herself as she plays idly with a handful of small reddish stones: perhaps the outcrop of a razed volcano: which glitter like the backs of tropical snakes. As she throws them up in the subjective air, she thinks, after all, another definition of chastity is to become sacred. Yes. But what good is the god's name to me, does he have any references, employ any under-writers, have the right credentials? Ah I doubt it. I doubt it very much. Also there are guns and things, for instance. All to be considered. Taken into account. In the final analysis. She smiles unfairly at her absorbed companion. What's life? More than anything else, I suppose, it is a search for something, some tiny thing, which is real: a hedgehog, parsnips, figs, yes even those rotting figs that are left ungathered on the reddening garden wall in autumn. The afternoon curls brownly in the heat. Daniel goes on reading his book, about Indians, their habits, their gods, under their own sun. Complaisant accents can be heard inside the house. They grow louder and sharper. They disturb the peace. Laughing but too wildly, voices raised against one another, in opposition, Herma and Tomas come towards them. Surreptitious as a law breaker, Rachel whispers to Daniel, nudging him

Look at them: aren't they fierce?

Daniel glances up at them, grinning. Herma, the empty-handed, smiles back at him as she sits down on the sordid grass. Rachel's pale skin is like enamel. Cavatinas of light deceive. Replete shadows seem to slumber. Tomas squats beside Herma, possessive and threatening But he also leans towards the other two, ready to seize any chance of escape from a dungeon he is only half aware of occupying.

Hello. . . .

He has a taste of snow and salt in his mouth. The blenched light makes even the superficial resemble a matter of some importance. Rachel watches him quizzically. Your move.

We've been talking about our beliefs, about survival. All afternoon. And we still can't agree . . .

he states, trundling the words out as he looks from one face to another. The heat has made these two sleepy but he's going to wake them up. He has the unnerving cowboy sensation of being the only stranger in town.

Do you think any of us has a future? Is there any evidence in the world at large that justifies hope? I say no. There is nothing. I think we're approaching the end. Herma says the danger will pass, she has faith in a future. But I say, no, I say

and he brings his hand emphatically down

that anticipation of, expectation of, fear of and preparation for disaster cannot be prolonged indefinitely: one day they will all be dispensed with: and the event, the last war, will happen.

His apocalyptic eyes shine. But he still sounds like a lawyer. Daniel thinks he's heard this speech before and seen the same extended noisy face at some rally or other, in some city. Then it had been raining. Or had it? Rachel admires life and death struggling in his dark heaving brain. Tomas looks challengingly at them all, especially Herma: who just smiles tersely at him however and begins to bite her fingernails. She will not reply immediately. Or will she? No. she won't. Herma will not risk a recapitulation yet. She wants to hear another opinion first. So she sits tight and thinks of the terrible prophecies, of time and of chance. She looks slyly at Tomas. Then at Daniel. Is love just an absence of hate then? She glances back at Tomas. Is all that emotion needs simply a proper direction? A sense of futility goes out of control. The eye of god, the sun, says beware. Summer shakes and sizzles and mourns, caked with open-mouthed sculptural shadows. Rachel lifts her head as if she is about to speak, her voice flowering out like a siren. All afternoon she's had something on her mind, something which baffles. Perhaps the horizon unnerves her, its sophism of distance, that thin spendthrift mirage both timid and triumphant. But the movement comes to nothing. She does not speak either. Instead it is Daniel, no pruner of trees, uninterested in soil, life neither a comfort nor an agony to him, who says in a slow, careful, even and level tone:

I agree with Herma: although probably for different reasons. I think, Tomas, you are a person who sees everything in terms of a beginning and an end: so of course you will see, on present evidence, a world ripe for destruction: either by internal or external pressure. Pessimism is the logical view. Because disaster is logical, you expect it. But I am far too afraid to be logical. I cannot face the idea of my own death. Because I cannot, I don't, I turn away. I refuse to await annihilation: I say no. It may be colourless and cowardly. But that's how I feel. I repeat, the danger must pass. It must.

Silence, like a datafalque. Then, contemptuously, Rachel picks up the stones and begins to play with them again, throwing them up in the air, too high, too boisterously: and then catching as many as she can on the back of her hand. Herma watches, counting how many stones fall to the ground. She sees it, the battleground, every bloodied detail, the world drifting like a phantom ship.

But I don't understand how you can turn away?

cries Tomas, his mind frogged to the idea of catastrophe. He's built so much on it, he's excused himself so much because of the coming disaster, a fake Noah, he's been living with it so long he cannot bear to relinquish it now, what will he do without it? Daniel sighs

Mainly because I'm one who hides and because I'm afraid of so many things. I can't change myself: only protect myself.

Eyes wide open, pupils of coloured water, Herma reaches out, across the sunlight and their shadows that are like slaves kneeling around them, to touch, words warm in her persistent mouth

You believe me

she says earnestly
> he won't nor will she. But I know we safeguard the future by not condemning it and what which seems fragile is often what is most indestructible.

Rachel juggles with the stones.
> And the reverse is often true . . . .

she tells Herma in a soft aside. But Herma does not hear and goes on
> There is more to us than we know or see.

Tomas laughs, without music. She lets go of Daniel's wrist. Rachel makes a bored face, a lamia.
> No

says Tomas bullying her
> o no, I can't accept that, you've over-estimated us . . . there's more to us than we know or see . . . !

he mouths.
> Why can't you allow any room for innocence? The soul has its curiosity. . . .

This time both Tomas and Rachel laugh out loud, she drops the stones and cackles, a mouthful of noise: and even Daniel smiles in a creamy melancholy.
> Ah but what else is there except faith?

she implores, hands helpless in the air. Her humiliated flanks are mannishly stiff. No one answers her, they are not able, they might lose their way. Each reply turns into mist, curving like ostrich feathers. Despite the brilliant light, the marjoram vapour fools them.
> I cannot say

begins Rachel's sour voice
> but anyway, like Tomas, I won't be tricked by myths.
> We're tricked as much by ourselves as by professional mystics

Herma snaps, still dabbling her fingers in the air, a sign of nervousness
> and just because judgements are always restricted does not mean we should give them up.
> O words!

Rachel spits out tiredly, railing at her. Daniel and Tomas watch the two women. This world which might destroy them and about which they squabble is at all times a veiled world. For all their talk, both brave and cowardly, the future has no reality for them, there is no likelihood of their confronting it, it will not take precedence over them, it is constantly postponed. Both men know the outside world exists, that it is there. Although their reactions to it differ, they know of its material being. But these two women veil it and distract them. Both men are shut in by the barricades the women raise, day or night.

    Yes, Rachel, words, all words are important,
(Daniel looks down at the illustrations in his book)
        they mark the expression of a personality, they make thoughts obvious
        to all, you can't deny that.
Speaking calmly and firmly, Herma is proud of herself.
    Yet we all make sure we devise words that go the way we want them to
    . . . .
continues Rachel, equally collected and composed. Tomas interrupts eagerly:
    Don't you think . . . .
But unable to follow this inverted conversation with any sort of clarity, with no ambition to do so, no delusion, he had once used the same words himself, in another garden, Daniel closes his book and stretches out full length on the grass, gazing up at the dangerous body of the sky, its astral design, trying to gauge its depth. They go on talking. Tomas is saying
    . . . . it is impossible to believe in reincarnation or ascension . . .
Daniel is distantly conscious of Herma shaking her head time and time again, as if covered in embers, and knows that she is arguing with them, that the standard of her feelings is probably superior to theirs although her ability to instruct them or move them is negligible: but he turns away. Sun, a stupid chronology. No wind, only a series of hot cracks opening and closing in the afternoon. All at once, as their voices lull him, he thinks, but I am illacerable, cannot be torn. On deciding this, he looks at them again, his face set hard, a stunned jawbone, the expression of a playing

card: and sees how their long oar-like shadows thrown on the flat planes of the lawn reduce their bodies to gesturing figures playing at a philosophical discourse in some stranger's imagination. And he wants to call out to them, to warn them that they too might become trapped in their idolatrous images: but his impulse cannot transcend gross birdsong or the impractical celando of the leaves: for him only apathy is real and anyway these three annoy him, they are just pictures for which he is trying to find a caption. He closes his eyes in revulsion against corpses which have just died of a contagious disease: but also he prepares to return to them, that migratory world, with or without end. The starched malarious sunset unfurls. Daylight's flowers of silk are gradually obscured by the growths of darkness. Conversation peters out. They are all afraid to move. When the day is at its earliest flight, the golden body's journey through the clear grecian fields of spring is precise and trained. But later in the day, it becomes slow with wisdom and the unsuspected weakness emerges.

I must post a letter

says Rachel suddenly.

It's almost past collection time

Herma tells her, with a menthol face. As she stands up, Rachel's cotton skirt crackles like corn. Why hadn't I noticed that before?

I'll drive you

offers Tomas. Daniel is mute within his book.

Would you? It should go off today.

Rachel brushes the grass from her skirt. Her limbs feel unlimited, as if she might be capable of floating.

Bye . . . we won't be long . . .

They go towards the house, talking about the time when they had been students, in love with youthful inviolate selves, without any grasp of conflict: they are relieved to get away from Herma and Daniel, leaving them behind in the dusk, with no incentive to move. Evening, an elegy in memory of a dead era, is indefinite, as if plunged beneath tulle. The long white face of a portrait painter, dead as any of his patrons, flutters in

Daniel's mind, he can't think why, perhaps it is the weather. Herma's voice terminates his search for a name.

What's the book?

This? O anthropology.

What?

It's about Indians. A tribe. Their life.

Primitive?

Yes.

He hands the book to her.

Happy people, they look.

She turns over the pages. Meeting their smiles.

I doubt it.

Daniel speaks loudly, almost jeering. But she takes no notice. It was an ambiguous remark, hers. It upset him. Perspective depends upon the stability of lines and objects: this limitation is necessary. Otherwise distortion takes over. He desires the safe clear-cut image above all else: the surface which takes care of itself. He thought she represented such an image. Now even she becomes evasive.

Why do you doubt it?

she asks eventually. She looks at him. He shrugs. Was it a joke? Did I misunderstand? But after all, why doubt it? How does he know how happy savages are? Or are not? They are both silent. There is a moment of appeasement. Subtle clouds are characteristic of the zenith. Birds flying in the sky are in formation. Home from school, thinks Herma childishly. She closes the book and gives it back to him. Picking up Rachel's stones she tosses them from one hand to the other. Her hands are elegant. The air is still warm. He stares at the sky, considering its rich monotony. He does not open the book she has given back to him. He thinks of Rachel and the sponsorship of a life with her. Now he would be lost without her, having known her. When he looks at Herma again, he sees that she has bent her head and that she is crying noiselessly: she has taken her misery into her arms, like an infant, letting it devour her, sallowly and gluttonously. Crocodile dreams, atmospheric repercussions. He doesn't know about them. But he is not surprised at these tears. For days she has been wracked with tension: for which even he takes some of the blame, realizing that her isolation is more complicated than he thought. He does not say a word: but waits until she seems to be finished. In the meantime, he looks at the photographs. Happy. She takes her hand away from her eyes. As he closes the book, he asks her

Is crying really as frail as it appears?

Because in spite of his other weaknesses he has never cried: not even when she left him, that other surly girl, not saying a word to the soldier he wasn't: and so weeping is a strange sight for him. Herma grits her teeth at this question, as if to prevent herself from swallowing a mouthful of raw meat. She wipes her face with the back of her hand. Before replying she looks across the lawn at the angular stanzas of the trees, the calligraphy of their movements, trying to sort out the overworked words and shake herself free of their vocal grime. Chimerically she tells him

Crying is often a freak . . .

but stops. For a moment she thinks she is going to break down again. But its exhibitionism restrains her

. . . it is often no more than an occasional accessory after the fact, it fits the moment, makes a direct but disposable reference and that's all. It's just a temporary aberration . . . . .

Her voice almost whines away. Words move heavily in her, burdening her, as if moonstones and agates flow in her blood, circulating ponderously. And the explanation, the acres of ill-lit arcades which it conceals, does not satisfy him. He feels that she is minimizing something of vital importance, that the knowledge of it, which is denied to him, is too great a secret for her to reveal. The relegation of her emotion looks like usury to him. But perhaps he should not have asked. She is mourning after all and it's true, it is a strain, being loyal, whether to a prince, a lady or a lover.

I'm sorry, Herma, I didn't mean to embarrass you . . .

She shrugs, watching the birds in the sky: her lips move only to fill up a silence

No, I am sorry, you must feel I'm using you . . .

The pomp of her benediction.

> No, I don't. It's just that I've always thought of crying as a predatory habit. But seeing you weep, I'm not so sure.

He's losing touch with his customary self, he is feeling too deeply, how can he retrench himself? He cannot stop probing amongst derelict fever.

> No

she says puzzled

> No, it is not predatory. It's not like that at all. Why does it intrigue you, why do you think of weeping as something so strange and involved? It's just a release of tension, a passing emotion, an impermanent treaty with sadness . . . it passes . . .

Cerements of a breeze bind the two of them together.

> I've never come across it, not in myself.

> O you're a stoic

Herma tells him playfully but ill at ease.

> No: weeping just looks slightly sinister to me, it always has . . .

He cannot qualify the statement, he cannot simplify it, he has to sit and endure her bewildered stare.

> Why involve it with a depravity or a venom which it does not deserve?

she asks, becoming animated, her hand skimming the air

> All it is is an excess of emotion: perhaps that is what you cannot understand.

At the end, her voice cuts a little.

> No contest, no victory you mean?

> Yes, that's it. . . .

He picks up several of the stones and bowls them away through the grass without thinking. But she has already forgotten about them. Although she keeps one in the palm of her hand.

> Do you know what faith really is?

he asks quietly. Offended, as if he has divested her of some part of her identity, she says rapidly, her face flushed

> Yes I do, it is a struggle to hold one's self upright, in the cold open places where we are each on our own.

He shakes his head.

No, you are wrong. It is not a struggle, Herma. It is a slavery to yourself. I have no faith. But I have freedom: it is a freedom I took without guilt or interrogation: absolute freedom, which the individual bestows upon himself. I looked at the world. And then I set myself free from it. Freedom: clear sky, light heart, no weeping.

As he speaks he throws his arms out wide, to show her what freedom is. But her laughter is angry and she argues, opposing this emptiness he threatens to use against her.

There's no freedom, Daniel, no clear sky, no light heart anywhere. When I lived in the city, it always seemed a haughty place, it made me feel like an outcast. I longed to leave it. I thought I would be free then. But even here, away from the city, where superficially it is quieter, there's still no freedom. If you believe in a future, then you're tied to it: if you care for anything, you are tied to it: you live, not in freedom, but in fear: fear of losing the loved possession. Fear of losing a husband to another woman, fear of losing a world to marauding armies. No, there's no freedom. O times come now and then and you think yes everything is going to work now and you say to yourself no more worrying no more caring: but it never works, it all comes back to you, the weight of the fear.

The stone she grips in the palm of her hand is a small pyramid of ice. He is quiet: he does not answer: he feels remote from the surface of everything, has no rendezvous with anything. It is bituminous thoughts like these which once made him commit a crime. So he must joke with only a placatory inflexion towards seriousness says

We all have to fight with wild beasts eh?

Her temper wanes because she wants to laugh and she does laugh, a frolic, facial muscles relaxing, her unstable gentleness and romanticism returning.

Yes, all of us, that's true

she says cheerfully

if we are going to mean anything.

They sit there in the redundant evening. But the next thing she says is hoarse and less therapeutic

Daniel, I'm sorry about yesterday. . . .

It doesn't matter

he says softly taking her hand listening keenly for the sound of Tomas and Rachel returning but soon forgetting them because a momentum of desire burrows in him deeper and deeper o right through him increasing stepping up its intensity until he feels what he feels is point-blank lust so much of his vision no all of his vision is Herma both of them shaken in a heightened horny state both of them they want to touch if only they weren't so exposed out on the lawn who knows what eyes are on them: It doesn't matter he says again wanting to hold her he touches her hair still warm from the sun that's gone down and he twists his hand in it says one or two words that afterwards he cannot recall but now at this particular moment interpret themselves on their own bringing the man and the woman closer together making their surroundings unbearable because they separate them protocol their energies demand more room the flesh demands privacy they gaze they are touching hands meet their bodies strike outwards for land it seems endless the chips of their nerves vibrate and the effulgence drugs them her closed jacaranda body is subordinated but in protests it protests and he feels this what right has the sky to censor them to force a purity of conduct upon them? like blows well-delivered their desires wind them the rigmarole of adjournment frets the surface of their eyes their eyes these difficult circumstances are rude and lusty like scrolls her fingers are decorative she is not afraid of anything is she is she? perennial humility has deluded me he absorbs her he tastes her on his palate lurking deep in his unresearched heart is Cassi her eyes of alpha she knows compassion is an added danger Herma's mouth is in a fracas she gasps: Soon they'll be back we must go indoors soon they'll be back she wants to move but the enclave of grass has her and her sex has opened like a duck's beak and she is squeezing his hand crushing it almost:

He carries the book under his arm. Walking across the lawn, they are playing a sad game, itchy as if smothered in potash. They don't know any more than does the hunter what lies in wait for their guns. Evening, like so many cages, receives them.

Five

Languid and malicious, the way she walks, that idle step of hers, the way she has of gliding as if through a cold forest of glass amid glissandos of arctic light, is especially noticeable in summer. Her hair resembles lemon peel. Rachel confronts them. There is the coldness of self-love in her scrutiny. She sees Herma and Daniel huddled together on the ottoman, sitting close as twins, both looking miserable as sin: and she begins to laugh, confused and tumultuous mirth, forcing him to open his eyes and look at her and suffer the brightness of the withered noon's light that hurts the irises until he longs to bury his head in the softness of Herma's lap. Herma, who stares down obscurely at the carpet. The anarchy of this summer splashes Daniel with the sacrificial: it ends his entombment within himself. Now every single action demands great care, the relics of some forgotten Caesar's defence. He longs for the past conglomeration of banquets he once took for granted. Herma grips his hand. To pillage a ruin. It is the mock drama of Daniel's repudiated identity which amuses Rachel. Her cold spruce attitude is unbearable to Herma, she springs up and walks away, to stare out of the window at the cloudy fiddle-shaped landscape. Light fuses the leaves and lawn into a mass of green. The day buzzes. Heavy cloud and a sycophantic sun.

Enjoying yourselves?
Rachel asks. But gets no reply. Not from the morganatic girl at the window nor the man in the centre of the room who stands and faces Rachel. They both understand Rachel even if they cannot defeat her. They keep quiet.

Are you?

she persists sweetly

Are you, I asked you, are you?

When there is still no answer, she snaps at him, her good humour gone and her eyes a mottled shade, making the air unshriven:

Tell me, are you, fool? Are you enjoying yourself?

Her ravenous voice establishes crimes in the room. Steadfast and narrow at the window, Herma makes a gutteral sound in her throat but it does not turn into words. Daniel remembers that the recollection of the short hot pleasures he extracted from Rachel's body last year disgusts her, how she regrets the rotating connexions, the way that unemotional uncommitted sex deprives her of an absolute charlatan's superiority now. His gaze is silky and attentive.

You tell me, did you ever enjoy me? Once? Did you? No, you always winced, didn't you?

Impatiently she pushes him aside and goes towards Herma, searching for a hassock: a misapprehension. But she feels thwarted, childishly naked, degraded, very pale: a failure, as if after a long search she still has not found any surface that will reflect her own image successfully, without distortion. Both women ignore Daniel's insipid laughter. Rachel touches Herma's shoulder lightly. Herma turns to her. How the woman unnerves her, to Herma she seems wholly nourished by ice. Ardently, he too advances on Herma. Rachel speaks through thin harpy lips.

I've always thought of you as a moralist, Herma, with a blundering inconsistent morality perhaps, but nevertheless . . .

You think you were wrong?

Yes. I'm disappointed. . . .

Why?

Daniel stands by, with comic dignity. They search one another's unpainted eyes, these two women, their burning quadratic bones making them both short-tempered. The advent of rain soaks the meridian.

You know

says Herma in a dentist's voice but herself unconvinced

don't you that envy is an emotion that likes looking behind doors, that
enjoys spying on an empty room?

Rachel glances meaningly at Daniel, carelessly she implies: whatever will
she say next, I don't know! making it clear that Herma's remark is not
worth bothering about, as far as she's concerned any research into the
origin of the sentence would be fruitless.

But the essence of society is built around it

she replies lazily. Herma stares out at the roof of air, the falling rain. The
existence of mermaids somewhere, perhaps. How little Rachel prizes
innocence.

Are you going to make him marry you?

Herma asks, almost shaking.

O I don't know. . . .

In a loud despairing voice. But not harshly. This time she does not mean
to be unkind, it is just that she is experiencing a bluish nostalgia today
(yes, blue is its colour), an indefinable sensation of memory that has a
certain haziness about it, preventing her from saying yes or no,
threatening or reassuring. But she does not take Herma into her
confidence, she lets her think the worst. For Herma, this is too tough. Her
tears are like knobs of wax, the way they form on candles lit on birthday
cakes.

Herma no

Rachel goes on quickly and compassionately

you must learn that always wanting to know the truth is dangerous,
this looking for truth is like looking for a sunken continent, it leads to
frustration, misery, madness. I cannot answer one way or the other.
Beside, we both know that this search for truth is in fact quite the
opposite.

Herma looks at her in defeat. She suffers passively in the ambient air. Her
caricature of a face angers Rachel. It is a danger to her own strength, it
affects the force of gravity. She feels hot and dizzy, her hands are wet
although it only rains outside in the garden, all around her every object is
foggy, tables, chairs, lamps, all lose their distinction. Through the open

windows the sky shimmers, sun on water, the sea itself: it takes on a ghost-like attitude, a tone of none-ness. Her head seems chock-full of ornate flowery decadent spikes. She almost falls in a faint. The matted sound of rain drums in the background. She breaks out into a tirade against Herma.

Herma, throughout the tranquil warfare of your life, darling tame creature of god, there is hardly a fault anywhere. Hardly a fault. How splendid, how praiseworthy, yes, you'll go to heaven, that's for sure. But tell me what's wrong with vivid depressions, arguments and struggles why not curse a heart when it gets in your way? Why not sleep until noon, why not be cruel? No. Not you.

Herma listens, fearsomely intent on hearing every word, quarantined in these words.

Not you. You'll never leave that desert, Herma, you'll go on making footprints in that sand.

Did she just tremble? Yes, at this gala of hate.

You'll never be free of all those old friends of ours, those bitter-sweet secret conspirators working and plotting in a silence so stiff no one heard them twirl their voices at midnight although all ears were sharp as lice. O you turn away, you do, do you? You go pale. Indeed. They're my friends too, but I've got them under control. But not you. It is an evil you must endure, I think.

Daniel pushes in between the two women, Rachel had gripped Herma and was shaking her, he has to stop it, he interrupts,

No, Rachel, it isn't fair . . .

he tries to shelter Herma, whose face though intact is cowed. Rachel turns on him.

O look, entrance of an astronomer

cries Rachel sarcastically

an astronomer called Daniel. Daniel: a round name, a brave name. But he's no hero, are you Daniel? No you're no hero.

Herma startles them both by shouting back, her voice a veto

Heroes! O no, Rachel, you can do better than that! Heroes! We're better off without them. Even the soul is happier without them, without heroes, Jesus, Faust or Prince Charming. But it is difficult to rid ourselves of them. We all conspire to their creation and their greater glory. It's a vicious circle. We make it and then we find we can't break it. There's a point at which we ought to turn back whilst there's still time. But we don't. By fairy tales, swords and spells, books, princesses, dragons, images of knights and the enpurpled bodies of slain lovers, we are bewitched. I've examined these heroes that trap us. I tell you, they are not like us, these heroic monsters. They arrive in our unaware hearts, secretly, by night. They stand on the threshold a minute, hesitating politely, their empty suitcases between their knees. Then they rush forward. Just like you, Rachel. And by morning they have settled in for good. They are always with us, telling us what true bitterness really is, what true love ought to be, what passion really tastes like, how the graves of the dead ought to be cared for, how we'll never feel the way they do, so deeply, so absolutely. Just like you, Rachel, just like you. I've become host and associate to you, you're hollow and meaningless.

Then Herma stands and waits. The unexpected eye of Rachel is destitute. When she answers, her voice is quiet. But dismissive:

That doesn't matter. None of that matters. You don't understand Daniel. He is playing possum. He and Tomas are a fine pair of lovers for us, Herma! One a fraud, the other pretending sickness in order to be able to die in peace, with his histories and globes and telescopes.

Tugging at her kohl hair, Herma laughs and cries and screams hysterically. Daniel says o no and flees from the steep tremors of her mouth, leaving Rachel to deal with it. She slaps Herma.

No no no no: gay laughter is wrong. For us, everything is a malady, a malaise, an awful real sickness. Pity us on our uncalm bloody field. Where any perturbation increases fever to a deathbed. Where no warrior can defend himself. Where all wounds are self-inflicted.

Clinging together, both women weep. Their knees touch. Their breasts brush together.

O christ O christ

whimpers Rachel

haven't we already shown you we are incapable of bearing such gentleness, why don't you shake your fist and shout at us instead, like funny old Knox, bawl like Luther, punish us until we are fainting from victory. . . .

Rachel shoves Herma away from her and shouts frantically

He must become a conscript in our dirty connubial ranks, he must decay like us, with us . . .

Rachel's face, spattered with tears, contorts and makes satan-faces. Herma runs out into the garden, whispering grimly to herself, yes, love lies bleeding, leaving Rachel to stumble upstairs, permanently in a region of snow, her demeanour fleFh's shipwreck. Sprays of rain showering damply on Herma's head give her a terminal grandeur. The lime-green brilliance of the day calms her. She hardly notices the rain. So nothing is simpler than walking through it. She does not think of it as real rain, only as an effect that is being stage-managed. That is why she lets it drench her, why she walks on through the brandishing flower garden. To the spectator, watching at some distance, from a window, her circuit is disturbing. Her feet crunch against the gravel path. She still does not notice the rain. She is too lost to notice, too preoccupied with her thoughts that are declining away to nothing. She does not take shelter. The figure (too far away to be identified even if she saw) opens the window and calls and shouts look you're getting soaked the rain it's pouring but she does not hear. Perhaps she is testing her own ability to endure discomfort. Perhaps she is saying to herself you know my girl don't you that Daniel is just another one of Rachel's experiments. just a temptation, a deflection. Perhaps she is preparing to under-go the cutting away of the heart from the mind. Perhaps she is just sad. Perhaps it is all of these things. Anyway she does not hear and goes on walking away from the waving figure at the window, further and further away, until the window is banged shut and the figure of the spectator goes angrily out of the room. Herma does not realize that her passage might well turn out to be merely an ironic flight from a false alarm. So she goes on, seeing, through the rain's cloudy lorgnette, gardens and other seasons in which she moved more serenely, a boastful arethusa. But the docile calendar has become an enemy. Tomas runs out of the house. Rachel watches Tomas go towards Herma and an abysmal fraternal smile without a heart touches her unsinging face. He treads carefully through the mud towards her.

O you

she says in an ochre voice that shuns him

I thought you had a migraine.

It went. I saw you

Tomas tells her noisily. A pause for memories. Lips and eyes give way to them.

What was all the shouting about?

he asks.

Nothing. No more than usual, that is.

Let's be brave, Herma . . .

he suggests, as if this were again the marriage-walk the wedding-march in the cold bright benevolent morning

Time will sort things out. Be brave.

I'm not interested in courage

she says desperately and turns away from him, crying out suddenly and loudly in a renewed sense of bereavement. She recognizes loss at any rate. Full of wet leaves the garden rattles. Air is accurate as an hour-glass. Time will sort things out. Long thin white stamens wave like the careless arms of young girls. After the one agonized reflex, Herma holds herself upright again even though her hair is spidery with moisture.

You must tell her to go, now

she cries softly, keeping her back to him, cold fingers hacking at petals. But he does not answer. His agile homage to Rachel tires him yet enchains him in an almost child-like dependence so that he cannot even reach out a hand to console Herma. Now that he has to choose, she seems wholly immaterial, she is a superfluity, someone he has to get away from as soon as possible. He says nothing. The frail existence of their love lacks sustenance. Images of harvest disperse.

Tell her

she says, turning to him arrogantly, not begging but commandeering, face screwed up like nickel.

No no you must accept it. . . . I can't do anything about it. His litany of selfishness.

Tomas, it's unacceptable. . . .

I don't care

he says abruptly

you'll have to put up with it . . . its rough justice, I know, but . . .

It isn't justice at all

she shouts back. Their wet bodies flare hotly as they argue. But words are stupid as silence.

Go and talk to Rachel but don't tread on my heels. . . . he says finally. And walks away quickly under an unnatural wrinkled sky. The morning is over. Systematically, Tomas sets about forgetting it. He's a fire-worshipper with an unlimited supply of matchboxes. She stares after him, her face twisted in what would be a saint's ecstasy if it were not so tormented, ravaged and livid. The morning is over.

During the afternoon the rain stops and the sun comes out and turns the sky a fiery bishop red, buckets of blood flowing into a river after a battle ten days long. Or gored toreadors. From where he is standing, the horizon seems to be disintegrating. Wispily it floats after the morning rain, gleaming venomously. But no, in spite of the redness, he will not believe it is the end of the world hurrying towards them, like some fatal tidal wave, some great dry wind. No, he will not. He feels he should make some sort of effort to control his own future. This is a familiar feeling. At times it makes Daniel twirl guiltily around: to find no one there. He should make an effort, even a superhuman effort, if that is what is needed. He wants to be shown a safe route to the nearest civilized horizon. But if not I myself, who else will discover the way? He cannot go on aimlessly waiting for a miraculous dawn. But what holds him back is a worse enemy than fear. It is memory. Herma is an extension of his own revived conscience. And its botanical investigations sicken him. In this unintelligible world. He leans against the side of the house, trying to push it over. His life is worthless, he might as well be a sailor, alone and drunk in a strange town. O he must clarify himself. In the shrewd conservatory Herma plucks the warm-skinned tomatoes. As her fingers move, she also struggles. She tries to free herself from the mythological morning: to convince herself that she is moving towards a holy apotheosis of life, that the biting vigilance she feels denotes spiritual progress and not a loss of faith. But the derisive mimicry of birds, her fingers unpliant as the stems of dead flowers, and Tomas's cruelty all go against her: and the charade of youth tells her that working out these monodies and genuflexions is just a joke. Her jagged face scowls. She moves long-leggedly to the door. Bloody pastorals, she says to herself. She is going to weep or whip them out of her heart, shedding that responsibility. She goes back to Daniel. The couple stand motionless in the light tensile as silver paper.

Where's Rachel?

asks Tomas, approaching diffidently.

Here she comes. . . .

Daniel says too fastidiously. Mirrored by the dud eye of jealousy, whe moves on expanses of bevelled glass. The strained pink flippancy of despair makes her lift her head brave as insurance. I will go slowly this afternoon, for intemperate flight mars the landing. She comes across the lawn. There is Tomas waiting for me. And Herma and Daniel, standing robot-stiff. The light glares, all its jewels on show. It hurts my eyes. I am saying something to Tomas. He laughs. On the whole I dislike jokes. We say goodbye. They both look terrestrial Why can't I set them free? This morning dawn's thin moon scared me and I still do not like the look of the horizon. If I were to scream . . . if I did . . . I should be defeated. But it tempts me, a scream. Loud yes . . . but polite as a minuet. No. I must go on, the way I planned, the way I promised myself, the one promise I can't break. I must go on following dead footsteps, grandma's footsteps, go on, knowing that there are no more maps anywhere, not even on the palms of my hands, but going on . . . And this, is it a willing duty? Wait and see, you'll see. The days are ready to be slit open. Yes, but who's keeping the score? Left behind, the veins of their hands are joined together like stone. Herma cannot stop shivering even in the heat.

Herma

he whispers, as they go through the green wood, walking very fast, his voice without that nervous laughter which has sheltered him for years, that stupefied sound failing him now

Herma, you know, one of the worst things that happens to me as time passes is the way that beautiful objects, people and landscapes in general become no more than a vehemence of trash.

They sit down under the trees where the turf is almost dry. It might be the fenland of the lonely heart.

What shall I do?

he asks

Rachel clings, she battens on to me . . .

I know

says Herma involuntarily. All around her blasphemous air coils. The parables won't go away.

So what are we supposed to do then, without rules, or practice for this game?

the gelatin man cries out. The art of making and judging anything (sundials for example) is, he knows, traditional: but does any learning pass down from generation to generation with complete accuracy? No. And this is why we have no chance of disarming Rachel. We are caught in the nets.

I used to think in definitions once:

he says more quietly

I thought you must either be free or a prisoner: do exactly as you wished, or obey orders. Now god knows. . . .

A mallow silence. Until Herma says thriftily

I want a touchstone to judge the horizon. Can you help me? He meets the repose of her rock crystal gaze. The man and the woman clutch strong but amateur fingers. He shakes his head.

No?

she says gently

Never mind. I want a world, pure and clear as the flower within the moon. But I am clumsy, oh yes, I slash my fingers on time's rough glass, all the care is wasted. I want to be delicate when I touch . . . .

her face becomes disabled and her tone gets stringy

. . . you don't know what it feels like to have a creature crawling around inside your womb. Ugh!

She shudders, all the horror that's accumulated within her comes to the surface, he sees it, he observes it. Then as if parodying Rachel, she says ironically

I could show you the quickest way to ruin a life-time.

But Daniel is the expert. He needs no advice. He has mastered the art.

Love always cringes away from my interrogation

he says

for me life is largely a hit and miss affair. I repeat, discoveries are no longer magical, you know? They merely sadden me. Days fade and die, they make an ice-rink out of the ceiling. And that's all. O occasionally I get thrown a renegade garland: you, for instance. But that's all. Does any of this help you?

She smiles.

O yes. A little.

The savannah afternoon is still. Then Herma moves, she kneels, she stands up, her body clean and sharp as lime. She walks and wanders about. He watches her go abroad and pick wild flowers abstractedly here and there: and when she has a dozen or so, drop them: reds, mauves, yellows, white, purples. He watches her hair float, a dark lacy shawl behind her as she goes through the windless air. He stares at her, as he would at the blinding place on the sea's horizon where the sun actually touches the water and makes it bleed. Then she turns and faces him, holding her arms out carelessly yet with an intricate need in the gesture which he construes as love: and speaks, as if she and Daniel are alone in the world, contained in their own storm.

A brazen age . . . . ?

he repeats. But he is unreceptive to riddles and he dismisses it. He laughs at her and pulls her down on the grass. She laughs too. At her wasted seasons. At discovering her own clandestine depravity. They lie embracing on the grass. It is a sort of waterway. The silvery green grass stains them. She closes her eyes because of the acrid mandarin sun.

I suppose the sun is neutral

she whispers

but somehow I don't believe it. I know it's mineral but it seems to have a personality of its own. Which opposes me.

O imagination

pants Daniel. As they nestle all the land edges towards evening. It does not occur to them that time might relax its grip on them, it does not occur to them at all and so they keep trying to run in front of it.

Yes that's all

says Herma, exposing herself. Her grayling body moves, her buttocks crush the grass, the ends of her fingers go crazy for a second, but there's no equilibrium between these two lovers. Because their love was made for them, prescribed, it is not genuine. She hears the sound of the voices in the procession, and the candles, how long ago. Is he surprised to discover in Herma such intense sexual melancholy, is he intrigued to find that her climax takes the form of a requiem? If so, he says nothing to her as his hands caress her neck. And when they get up to return to the house, he does not refer to her dissonance. She is silent. Herma has begun to think of herself as a monument to the dead. And if this is freedom, it troubles her, it neither elates nor kills, it does not begin to satisfy her, no, no, no.

Torrid magnesian evening: Herma is storming her way through a parthenon of books. She does not notice Rachel's entrance. Her neat fingers probe old theories, worlds balanced on tortoises, vamps and a few queens, politicians and infirm tubercular poets. Her narrow h ands turn the pages. Rachel, being one of those rare creatures having excessive cannibal vices, knows how to disown any kind of weakness: o she witnesses and accepts the agony: but hides it, keeps the pledge of silence. She knows the value of the motionless minutes when all words are bringers of doom. She can strike the messengers dead in her mouth. In silence she watches Herma. Yes, even tenderly. But Herma looks up sourly:

What do you want?

In this house, bowls of fruit crimp each room and vases of heavy roses shed buttercup shadows. O the helpless flowering, nature's thoughtless hourglass. Rachel looks at them distastefully, they irritate her. Then she points at the books and says exactingly:

Spy out all these old faiths, go on, read them. And you'll still be none the wiser.

Her laughter needs renovation. Herma takes notice but goes on reading, using the book as a shield. Rachel examines the books, Plato, Kierkegaard, Hobbes, Carlyle; Sartor Resartus.

Sartor Resartus

she sneers, throwing it down.

No one's asking you to read them. . . .

Herma remarks coolly, sneaking a glance at the future behind history's back.

Don't you worry!

Rachel turns to go, feeling a pulse vibrate in her throat. Then stops.

Outside, the rising moon is a silver coin in a despised dark sky.

Love

she says ominously as she closes the door and comes back to lean on the table

Love: love holy and merciful: what kind of a world would that give us?

Herma puts the book down and looks at her moderately, ready to separate the grain from the chaff.

A different one

she tells her firmly. The zoo and Rachel. Flatulent antelopes. Skinny elephants. Herma's bright voice scrapes her nerves raw. To the roots.

I'm trying to understand the world, life, everything . . . the girl informs her

. . . . and you can't stop me.

Rachel shrugs. Stratosphere turns, she encircles her own path of journey.

Love can't stop death.

The foreigners' days are here again. Herma is wounded. Yes. Her heart is daubed with elegiac poplars, an unsociable wind blows this sultry evening, she lifts a soundless voice for succour or for spring. This diamante attack shames her aspirations, they are in the dust. She says nothing. Companions of silence, the two women meet head-on.

It is bred in the bone

says Rachel softly. Herma looks at her fingernails. Then she turns the radio on. A single violin soars, a hawk or a wind-hover. The moonlight spills on to the lawn. Rachel's voice deepens and becomes repellent again.

What does your belief exist on? Mere legends.

Emphatically and with a slavonic gesture she pushes the books off the table. They lie there on the carpet, a tumble-down library.

Look at all those books. There are a dozen different ultimatums there. A dozen christs dying a dozen nasty little deaths. Which one will you choose?

No answer. Her lunar mouth is closed.

I look at the facsimiles of saints too, Herma, but I don't allow my imagination to live my life. I've got no time to waste!

Herma stands up. Nightingale summer breathes all around them. The season is hidden though, concealed within a confusion of events and hours and weathers.

I want to find the world

she says kinetically

that's what I want.

Two women, internecine ambassadors, different worlds.

O the world, space, time: Herma, they're all in your head, you don't
have to look them up in books.

Herma sits down again, she turns away, she is hoary all of a sudden, has
taken refuge in an internal devastation. She whispers

O yes I do Rachel I do need to look you mustn't blind me please. . . .

(Why have you turned this pleasant room into a charnel house?)

A man on the radio is declaiming the relevance of the book of Genesis, a
cry from the labyrinth. Impatiently Rachel flicks the radio off.

This situation is unacceptable, Rachel . . .

says Herma perilously but her tongue is whetted.

Only for you.

Spicy rain falls to the shingled lawn and the broken circles of moonlight.

Of course for me. . . .

It makes a lagoon of flowers: evening rain has the smoothness of hot wet
angels.

I never asked you to come, why don't you leave us in peace. . . .

Rachel's lucerne heart is cruel.

You're only a second best, and, Herma, if you want to be happy you
must begin by tasting sorrow, even if it does have a queer taste.

The room is full of the damp odour of rain. Herma acts like a lodger in it.
But for Rachel, any place of anchorage will do.

I've tasted it

shouts Herma dramatically, jumping up, her cheeks sonorous

and I say, you must leave: it's unholy, what you're doing to us . . .

Rachel sighs and says in a tone reeking of boredom

Unlike you, Herma, any form of god is abhorrent to me. Which one do
you want, Tomas or Daniel? No, don't answer, you don't know. Would
you like me to tell Tomas the truth, would that help . . . . ?

Threat stands out like a basilisk. Chiaroscuro. Herma hits out at Rachel

O you bitch

she cries softly but Rachel has moved out of the way. The force that
sprang up in Herma dies. Anger still pricks her tongue with as pointed a
touch as that of a needle: but Rachel's calculated unjustifiable smile

makes Herma feel prim and sweaty. Her eyeballs dim to marble. She won't look at Rachel. She turns to the window and watches the summer ebb away: she herself longs to escape into the autumn: in a four-wheeled carriage of fire. But this woman remains, a burden, damning coherent thought. Rachel comes to her and stretches out an arm to touch her cheek. Hopelessly. Herma will not be tricked: she considers this caress in terms of an abstract idea, willing to be fair and let Rachel ascertain essentials. Confronted by such acceptance, Rachel lets her fingers drop sadly, wanting to clap Herma on the chest, as if she were a horse, to see if it is possible to get through that reserve and come out on the other side, to see if she can exhume from this body the real girl who is at present hidden in the summer. But she restrains herself, admitting the need for and the propriety of a more laborious method. Perhaps they are never to be yoked together. Neither speak. Until Herma, careless because of the moonlight, says with an arrow in her voice

We're equal, Rachel, we're opponents well matched.
And then trembles because of the falsehood. But Rachel nods as if satisfied.

Tell me your troubles
she almost sings. But Herma is busy hatching apostolic dreams, seeing apparitions of death, going hot and cold, finding feet of clay in her shoes. She turns and stares at Rachel in amazement, expecting to see her clasped hands turn into swords: to match her temperament. She expects to see the chill flesh turn to warm steel. But there is no metamorphosis. Puzzled, she opens her mouth but only gasps in oxygen. Tension attacks all her pulsepoints. She wants to move unfettered. Somehow. But it's madness. Even to think of it. Herma goes away through the wily sheen of evening, her golden inertia converted to gymnastics by her tension. Rachel narrows her eyes, assessing that straight back. Absence, boredom, travel, loss of feeling and of a name: over the years they have made her astute. During a challenge she feels, as always, that her own security is at risk: but in spite of her fears she is lucid and sees the pitfalls and temptations for all concerned, the company at odds, their faulty lyricism. She closes

her eyes and smiles in a dreamy gentle languor. Herma walks on up the stairs, taking care not to stumble. In their bedroom she sits down beside the sleeping Tomas. Once she would have woken him. But not now. She is a gull catcher trapped by her own skill. Night is the colour of copper. O the charm of that always disguised always anonymous prince who by rights should belong to the carnival and not the soul: how can she avoid the two men who are his earthly representatives? Their faces are inlaid in her mind, imprinting their contours on some defenceless area of herself, like portraits once seen in a provincial art gallery and never forgotten, that seem to hold some unfathomable significance, a scarecrow sense of kinship. Her eyes are wide-open, in a mortified humility she stares at his face that is like a death-mask: but her distant gaze goes far beyond him. She is trying to see herself unfleshed and passionless. Would the role of saviour suit her? No, she doubts it, she possesses only the faint echo of courage,not its substance. Her fitful sentences do not amount to true prayer. The vision is gone by the time she swoops down on it, it leaves her only the taste of sorrowful rain, the scent of damp yellow leaves, rejection, the shape of deceiving. Rachel has remoulded her, she is no longer a country-side of her own making: depth of rock, emotional geology' all the climacteric conditions have been altered, the indigenous creature is ousted from the mediocre Eden and sent into this heterodox place. Even if the god she hunted was genuine she has lost it now. Is flesh a stockade out of which she must go or else remain clogged, without cultivation? Her youth is useless to her. She remains unsmiling, disenchanted with everything. Everything which had once seemed priceless, which she had believed in. Now she and Tomas are drifting so far apart, they have lost contact with one another, he snores, he does not open his eyes: she has revealed her dreams once too often and now the delusion of sleep separates them. Herma hears voices somewhere in the house and stands up, but it is just the radio, a chorus rising and falling tediously, praising the harvest queen. How can she describe truth when she is not close enough to it, how can she accept platitudes of salvation, how can she break into her own silence. She sobs, what is it I am too far out from myself to see? Her intimacy with conflict gives her no rest. And is there no limit to giving? she asks. Tomas does not sit up and tell her. Her prayer resounds limply in the room. No, it is not a prayer, it is just one woman's spiteful comment on another woman. No, there is no such thing as rest, not where the altercation of good and evil is concerned. No.

Six

A scarlet circular sun shoots out rays of morose light. A few leaves fall, just a handful. But Tomas does not notice the first signs of autumn. A hard icy wrist of migraine holds him down, a prisoner in a darkened room. Pain curtails his vision, like shutters bolted down during bad weather, storms of a clerical blackness. Herma carries the proof of his helplessness away, clutched to her solemn mouth like burnt fingers. The day is raw as salt on open sores to her. She lets Rachel be his nurse. Her privilege. Outside, a shriek of birdsong amid shining foliage. But he does not hear. He turns over. The room is still and dark and lacks any true nature of its own. Monotony of time, a hand rises, hearts beat, objects go claustrophobic. Corruption runs like a thread through this summer, tireless, brainless, afflicting the season morbidly, crippling it. A cry, far off, a whisper, unimportant and unrealistic in this airless room. Sunlight sways: it is syncopated, this hot imperfect soiled day. Herma sidles out into it, going into the metallic ormulu light with a sort of bravado because she knows it will give her a pain hands don't cure. Its presumptuous clarity makes prophetic shapes around her. Turning, she looks back at the house. The emolument of glass flashes, light marking window after window. This power of enchantment, it injures all of its demonstrators. She feels so tainted, she is amazed when flowers do not wither at her touch, her hands shrink from their own flesh. The blue limestone sky acts in liaison with her spiritual darkness, reflecting it back like stagnant well water. Her shadow trudges on behind her, slanted, black as vulcanite. She walks across the rough fields, an intimidating expression on her sun-bitten face. She goes through the wood. Under the trees, figures of fallen warriors jerk. She glances at them guiltily. Then passes on. In an hour's time she will be playing tennis with Daniel: a stalwart occupation that insults the serious intent of the season. Tomas is unconscious of the angola weather, the dry malachite heat. His head is sulphuric. In his weakened condition, perceptions intensify. As he looks at Rachel, he is struck by the strange similar greenness that is to be found in both eyes and deep waters. He follows Rachel's vulpine gaze to the floor. He feels like an intruder, out of his depth.

Whom are we betraying, Rachel?

he asks croakily

Herma or ourselves?

If she is afraid that this means the end of her sherrifship she does not reveal it. Her sacrificial red dress hurts his head. Then she smiles.

It's the migraine makes you ask. It confuses. . . .

And she turns to him from her archepelago of conceit, exercising a cold authority. He closes his eyes so that all he sees are the shadows of shadows. Tomas knows this is an obstacle race, the winner of which will not be known for days yet. Herma's ellipsoid face, her heavy body weighed down by its silent quota, he sees it all again: sees his hand laid possessively on Rachel's arm, dismissing the younger woman, long ago, in a stubbled winter. Guilt. Yes, guilt. He groans and opens his mouth, groping for a breast. It is a pleasure to sleep, to go marching down those dark gypsum corridors. But she is still sitting there when he wakes again. How she'd hollered at him once when he remarked lightly on her obvious romany blood, not because of the colour of her skin but the bone structure beneath. How she'd screamed. But it was only a joke. Once more, sleep. When he wakes for the third time, his attendant is still there, circumnavigating his vision. She sits like a figure carved from the moon. So pale. Time is torn up into little paper triangles: past, present, future crazily pave the air. His head aches, it is full of scorpions. Reluctant bones grind. Cockroaches hinder his thoughts. But at length an old problem reaches the peristalsis of words. He heaves himself up and begins complaining about the way the world is being cut to ribbons by all the generals and their brave boys. She takes no notice but looks down at her festering hands, a smile of summer on her repulsed face. For as one susceptible to the cold, summer is wine to her, she loves even the lees. Suppose I had a knife, whose throat would I slit? thinks Tomas, not my own surely? He cannot lift his head although it feels light as a daisy. Yet there is something he must know. Only a fool waits for the river to run dry before he crosses.

You never met my mother, did you? No, she died before I met you. In some ways she was very much like you. . . .

She nods vaguely

O yes

but she is thinking of something else, a smile still on her lips, half transcended by some unseen beauty.

Yes, she moved like you. And she could never leave bunches of flowers alone. She would pull the petals off, one after the other, whilst boasting about her domestic abilities. I've noticed you strip flowers. You and Herma.

None of us are perfect

Rachel says, still abstracted.

Poor father. He was well out of it. One morning when Mother woke up, he was gone.

Rachel's hands become significant.

He was a weary man even then. I was about seven or eight. We never saw him again. I wonder if he's still alive?

Scraggy silence props her up. His voice swoops down though, questioning, demanding

Why, tell me, Rachel, why did you always refuse to have a child?

A sad look composes itself, is embossed on her face. She turns to him. Her eyes are the shade of water hemlock. The heart of even a sentry breaks. The compass of the brain loses its bearings. She knows the very young are sweet to sacrifice. But does not tell him. What she does try to say sounds lame. But it is not a deception, it is honest, a confidence.

It's the thing I fear most

she whispers. His eyes shut. It is a mark of respect to her, a repudiation of his doubts about her body and the way it works.

How pedigrees make us suffer

he says in agreement. Her face changes colour at once, as if she is wearing clinical rouge. She goes to the curtains and stands there, her fingers made of sawdust, her eyes of coloured glass. She repeats to herself, I made this arrangement in the light of an old state of affairs, necessarily preserved from and yet in spite of and because of that subsiding earth of mine. I must have the rigour of a phoenix. But she does not explain this to him. Instead she goes on silently making headway against time, reason, memory, history. . . .

It's why I married Herma, you know,

his poor thin voice floats across to her like another name for Apollo

so that there should be a child. After that business. Yes, that's why I chose Herma. Because she lost the child. And it was my fault.

Our fault

mutters Rachel.

Yes ours then.

But she doesn't mean him. Her mulatto stride brings her back to his bedside. He opens his muggy eyes. The man and the woman meet each other tribally.

She'll never have another child

says Rachel quietly, without any excitement. But with all her strength behind the words.

O yes she will

he says sleepily

o yes

and his eyes close in a sick sleep. A prussic frustration snaps her body in two. She almost shakes him and screams the dirty truth in his face. But her hands stop in mid-air and her face grows wan. It is of little use, his knowing: he is of more good to her kept in ignorance. She's sure Herma never told him her life-story. She shuffles uncharacteristically out of the room. Wounded in action. He dozes, approaching that stage in a minor illness when one begins to enjoy the sickly warmth. But he is not at rest. In this spasmodic half-sleep he can still hear the enforced silence in the house and he imagines invisible objects falling to the floor or lavish papery conversations: until he sits up groggily and finds himself alone listening to an empty house, hearing doors bang and swing open and bang until his head is a bladder and he mutters as he sinks back into bed . . . there is no peace. . . .

No, it is not his question—why did you always refuse?— which torments her but the coming again of autumn, the return of this ironic season which highlights her loveless endless childless pacing of time. With its golds and half-remembered dreams o how it clashes. Today is Rachel's own birthday. The worst of all days. This is why she surveys the sky with a fermenting black ache in her womb and the devil of an angel's spear thrust into the onomatopoeia of her heart. The falling leaves all say to Rachel, get going, Death's girl, get on with the search, finish this sequel. Walk along the perimeter of your alienation. Get going. You are guilty of hurting them, your three companions, with your eyes that won't close. What do you mean? You have no choice? She thinks of all the other women she has known, ranks of them, regiments. Were they ever uncertain of their own birthrights? No. With their odoriferous breeding bodies smelling of saxons, they had no need to fear for their daughters, not the way Rachel would fear. With an oriental bearing, she faces the coming of autumn and the most difficult of all weathers. In spite of the plush yellow sunlight, it is a hard acid world with a sky of stone, o what a high and stony sky it is, a blue infinity invaded by birds whose wings make an ebony circle and imprison all the songs she recalls. Rachel looks back at her life and sees that her path through time is littered with salvage and treasure, broken bridges and dry rivers. The rigid penis of an anonymous man fell limp when she touched it half afraid of her own courage and then her body shuddered and she felt her emerald eyelids heavy enough to fall. She goes on back through landscapes, through the great dry tracks of the mirthless sand, sees Herma running away, her discarded hat falls to the ground again, for the thousandth time, the grains of dust still blow in a cuckoo wind: the wet flowers on the grave, the draught-horses standing in the rain. Yes, she hates all the remains. She hates this life of hers, where all the conditions are prescribed, where every restriction is urgent and immovable, where there is no possible scope for satisfaction. She wants a child. She deserves a child. I deserve a child, Rachel thinks. For one dilapidated instant she believes it could be possible, she would take that chance. But then the fear returns. A message should break out of her slave's body. But it will not. The boss Death lifts his invisible head of frost and commands Rachel to go on with her hallucinatory journey, to spend another day searching for her great-grandmother's green and mildewed coffin. Once she had looked in different exotic lands, palaces, fortresses, fields, factories, churches. Now she goes through the dead hallways of the wood, where there is no scope for love and where shadows fall victoriously upon dank voluminous air. It is through such places that the sinful long-dead couple wandered, the girl in the white dress and her lover, the girl with her white dress falling to the ground like a mist: yes, now they are both dead and they should be no more than an echo on the staircase: but they deafen Rachel, the folds of the white dress are draped around her head and they suffocate her, the whip of flowers held by the dead hands beats her. Because of the dead couple, joy is something she only glimpses through a waterfall, a gay garden seen through a waterfall, a garden she can't enter. For her, there is only struggle and silence as measured as her stride, her steps taking her away from not towards the outstretched hands. Branches infringe the air. The bad lovers went wandering through the same kind of landscape. The horn of the dynasty deprives Rachel. Until all love broils deranged. Her dredged state of land can result nothing but fatal in its effects of grain. She stops and to avoid the inner silence listens to hidden children screaming with laughter as they play hopscotch and farmer in the dell. There are waltzes for some of the living, all the sounds of a world vibrating and warm. But she is cold and waiting to come face to face with her great-grandmother. Who stands poised on a flight of stairs which lead nowhere and come from nowhere and which Rachel cannot climb. The past is beyond even the camera's rage. There is only sunlight dancing, brisk air wholly fine and charming. There is no place for the dead couple's footsteps to fall, no place for their cold lust to outleap spring. Rachel's abstract judgements cannot hope to contradict the facts. The scars cannot be rationalized. Autumn flowers. She bends and picks them. She holds a withered bunch in her hands, they precede her, clearing a way through the marathon of her ultimate exile. She walks on amid all the various trees.

Talking to herself:

> Before the black knowledge touched me, I stood on a good land. Ah it was mine. I knew its boundaries. Since I lost it I have to make constant reductions. The land shrinks so. Once upon a time, days used to be strong. I could rely on them. Life was sweet. I took such pleasure in the lace dresses and the wine and the invitations. Even now I can hardly accept the knowledge. Although I neither blame nor pity the couple who created all my distance. There is no room. Sorrow and self-pity are my only real emotions. Flawless. Sharp as a diamond or an axe. The two lands of the living and of the dead cannot merge. Yet because of the dead, the living live in pain. O the black crape! Once all things, all objects, all hands were warm: the grass was soft beneath the tread of afternoon, stars were whiter in a deeper night, the friendly horizon the haft of a likeable sword. I lost all these. The terrain was swallowed up. The place I live in now is tougher than real stone or the ticking clock's dominion. Each travesty of a day runs riot. Because of that couple, I can never offer the breast, it would not nourish a child, it would poison first. Yes then, yes, I am angry, I do blame you. O you with your gulping cunt that's dust now, how can I get even with you, how can I hurt you, how can I punish you . . . . ?

She throws the flowers away. They fall in an ephemeral heap. Antagonist perpetually struggling, this furious angry deplorable enemy who bears her hatred like a witness, lamenting old lust and the violated body, who sees the flash behind the sky, who awaits relief from all the suffering and yet who creates hurt and barters treason on all her sea-trips: she who is lost goes indoors where the coolness does not cool her brow.

The first day of autumn concludes with a loud penurious storm. Strange discomforting weather. For autumn has a duty: to be mellow, a last fragrance of bounty, the romance of ripe fruits. But in spite of all expectations storm loiters between sun and moon. Evening: and Herma stands out in the garden, piles of damp abridged leaves around her feet. She is thinking, this whole experience, these events should give me the courage to work my way towards some new life, to achieve something along those lines, I should be at a starting point now, not approaching the end. But events don't encourage me to act, no, they stun me. Sunset is a purple square in which she is framed. Wearing someone else's scarf. Lightning disfigures the skyline, shocking as a departure from virtue. The thunder that follows is an extinct reaction, quite dead. It leaves her unmoved. Rain blots out the fossil of sunset. A wild shedding of leaves accompanies the rain. They whirl around Herma, leaves of bronze and tar and iron, all imaginable shapes, mowing and despoiling the air. Branches of trees heave and creak like ships at sea and each spout of lightning is a warning beam from a lighthouse pin-pointing the rocks of her peroration. She runs towards the house. Its atmosphere is of people just departed. The storm gains ground, is centred directly above the house. Where are they? Have they all gone away? Is there no one left? A door bangs. But no one speaks. The storm is absolute and demanding, breaking the air apart: lightning is a white bedsheet held up over the sky. Herma shuts the french windows. There is no one in this house, not even the sound of footsteps running away ticktacktrip down the path: isn't this what you wanted, to be alone, why are you scared? The blank walls are deathly-looking glasses. Outside, the storm. Inside, the vacuum of the thundery house. She stares back over the fields. Everything is too astringent, she wants someone to take the blame, someone to be responsible. Where is everyone, why are there only shadows? She calls out softly. The sound is of little comfort. Thunder absorbs it anyway into its own roots. All at once Rachel is coming towards her. Her face is a curfew. Her dress is of formal silk. It makes Herma feel second-hand, a clump of discontinuous bones. Rachel assesses her coldly like a mercenary.

You'd better change

she says intrepidly

look at you, you're. . . .

But before she can finish, Herma goes away from her suddenly, the patina of rain vehement on her sun-tanned face. Paschal, she goes away, driven out, her eyes smoky. She goes upstairs into the bedroom without switching on the light. The rain is falling slantways, grey, delicate and melancholy. She stands and looks at its falling, a statue with arms uplifted. Ah but I am not in a movie, she says sadly among the dying storm. There is no moon, only grey and dun clouds, bitter quadroons. The mind is a close cousin to the soul, thinks Herma, the length of years, the values, the accumulations, the memories: is it possible for them to add up only to nil? Is life only a hibernation, a headlong race to no goal whatsoever: no peace anywhere? Branch of tree, unhappy sky, both complain to me, we are not free. Yes, I know. Everything that she is turns her away from life, with a haste that does not prove how essential or inessential it had once been to her. Is the creature inside her going to emerge more wonderfully than ever before? Or is she only waiting for Rachel's sake, hiding out in this room just for her? Rachel meanwhile shrugs and goes on her way, ignoring the offhand westernized girl soaked to the skin. Daniel's careless use of wine this afternoon sets boundaries on his head now, he is an infatuated slumbrous heavy figure, he meets the garish night reluctantly, with a hard mouth. At the moment, he is trying to read a book about astronomy. But the light is too strong. He can't concentrate. He is too much a part of this other starry discord, this universe of uncharitable strife. Senseless, he mutters to himself.

What's that?

asks Rachel entering the room softly, on tiptoe almost. He peers round at her.

Nothing. Nothing.

Trouble. Which might involve the loss of honour. But this does not make him forgetful of the outward terrors which soon might explode in their faces. No. He remembers them even when Rachel stares at him. Where can I live? Nowhere. Where can I go? Nowhere. Because the tragedian is misunderstood, accepted only as a clown, with a clown's shallow constant identity. He sees it in her eyes.

Have you ever watched a bull-fight? O I have

she says in breathless spindly words

I have. I am fascinated by the actual spectacle of killing . . . But then she shuts up, all of a sudden. In horror, perhaps. Anyway, she checks herself, returning to a verbal abstinence where blood is concerned and goes on as planned, suffering unexpected fatigue like a bravely earnt forfeit. He watches her shadow. As if without it the inhospitable world could not be borne. The lonely hands he stretches out wordlessly towards her are soon submerged by the air. She pushes them away from her hips. Her indemnified gaze is enough to repel him.

Poor Daniel

she says with a smile

he built a house on the sand. Now he must go.

The last words are wooden. She walks across the room, strewing silk, perfume, anger, fear.

No

he says watching her pour out a drink

No, I won't go.

You might just as well go quietly. You can't enjoy living

with enemies.

Herma is not my enemy.

No?

But half-disinterested. She ignores his defiance as she has always ignored the neurotic drift of his silly jokes. Her frown constricts him. The clef of Rachel's voice is higher, ringing out now, critical and free from confusion.

You must go.

She is wearing a silk gown of pure green. It takes in the light like glass. The silk furls over her adroit breasts. Daniel stands up, jaunty but clumsy.

I'm not going

he replies. She stares at him in a kind of ecstatic coldness. And she sighs.

Then I must tell you

she says in an irrevocable voice

that Herma is my sister.

This ultramontane confidence staggers Daniel. What of the world now, it does not grieve for him, why should he care about its safety? He stares out into the dark garden, looking for Herma, as if the sight of her might explain this knowledge, this arsenic secret. But the microcosm of the garden explains nothing. Lacrymose, he sways and then sits down. All his self-doubt reacts to her words: he is angry at having been drawn into this billet. The realization that everything is over comes to him. But Rachel? Where does she stand? Danger. Nothing is wise. All is dubious. The situation is sand-paper. It puts him on trial. His moist hands trap him. Do I want her or not?

She's my younger sister. . . .

Rachel looks down on him serenely.

I don't understand.

No, you don't. Your voice is retarded and weak. O you could understand an assassination. A war, Outer issues with clear black edges. Rachel turns away, hands clasped together. She says nothing. Everything hushes. It quietens down. The fertile garden sickens her. She comes back to him. She can't go on staring out at that fulfilled darkness. In spite of the silk, she's Spartan.

You're both so hostile

he mutters

so antagonistic. . . .

We're not responsible for that hostility.

But her bright voice is broken somewhere deep. Daniel stands up again. He licks his lips. His mouth is full of glass. His legs ache. He wants to laugh.

Sisters. Then who is responsible?
Her face goes almost scarlet. It is today's sun as much as her blood. She turns half away, hesitant, winged.

I only meant you to watch . . . just watch . . .
she says harshly. But it is a slight defeat.

You haven't the right to question me.
Her voice is tired. But now she turns and grabs his wrist. She digs her nails in good and hard. He winces. As if the accused.

Did I ask to come? Did I?
he asks angrily, pulling himself free of the degradation of her fingernails.

In a way
she sneers. This apostasy is like rime, so cold it burns. Her eyes are oriflamme. He backs away. The wall blocks his way. He is afraid. The stupidity of the fear is hardest to bear.

It's an untypical relationship. Very private. Tomas does not know. I only tell you to persuade you to go. . . .
She comes too close to him. Her breath is too much like a jungle. She stifles him. The priestess holds a pitchfork.

I should have picked up another woman at that party.
he says quietly, crooning his disgust. She shrugs. Almost prudish.

But I need . . .
he begins anxiously. Paraclete, goes through his mind. O Herma, O Cassi. And Rachel laughs at him.

You can't tell one of us from another!

I can, I can . . .
he shouts. From a battlefield. With tears in his eyes. She puts the palm of her hand over his mouth. Mockingly. The dumb show. Excessive fear takes hold of Daniel. He pants. She keeps her hand over his mouth. He edges along the wall. She comes with him. He stops. They stare at one another. Annexed. They've gone beyond jurisdictions. He takes her wrist and pulls it down. He lets go. She draws the hand up again and slowly bites her lip and slaps his mouth. She feels his automatic horror. They stare without

moving. He opens his mouth without speaking. Must force accompany all of her actions? Then he says

Rachel, the madonna without offspring . . .

With a greedy hatred. She looks out of the window, without any visible sign of distress. Although a single stone is deformed within her. He does not see that. She turns eyes of monochrome on him now.

It's not too late.

Bacchantes free from conversation. Sisters. It explains her distaff paranoia where Herma is concerned. If there's no love, then the opposite must take its place. But why does she torment him? Her lecherous prehensile expression tyrannises him. He has to get away from it. Where can I go? He must escape. Anything to avoid her eyes. It may look like disgrace, his departure. But he must go. There must be a homeland. A city of gondolas, of balance. A safe gouache world. To rest the eyes, to slow the brain down. Where locusts do not hunt. Where the purblind are safe. Lacking in venery. The bones are a burden, heavier than scales. But they move. He runs out of the room. Honour is left behind. Its coruscations, its laws. Enabling Daniel to breathe his freedom.

Say goodbye to Herma

Rachel calls out after him and laughs. Her heart is air-tight. But his flight from her sensual propaganda increases her nervousness. A nervousness which is buried deeply within her. But which if tapped would gush in a black uncontrollable spurt. His revulsion prompts exhaustion to work itself loose of control in her. Drowsy in the craven evening she sits down. A sensation of personal unreality immediately overwhelms her. Her odyssey head falls, she sleeps in an improvident state of mind, in an indiscreet attitude. She dreams too, of the cavalry, those rescuers, riding out towards her across the desert. Daniel looks for Herma. Who is living from one day's tension to the next, in the tilting yard where a rash thoughtless act will bring violence crashing down upon the unguarded heart. The manes of her particular dream horses tangle and twist till dawn. Then she walks away from the dream at dawn, telling herself she expects to awaken soon. But she does not: she clings on to both its exterior and its soul, she clambers back on to the dream's lap, as if the battleground and the shiny hooves alone held some hope of release. Manege. He climbs the stairs and finds her in the dark fustian bedroom. He tells her.

I knew she would send you away.

Her veins are autocratic.

Yes

says Daniel

I'm that sort of person. Will I ever see you again?

She turns and touches his russet hair. His avoidable body waits. For the vertex of the farewell. Her hair swarms about them both like a black flag denoting irregular soldiers. He holds her listlessly. Without loving her, she is certain. Possibly without pleasure. O I'm sure. He'll forget me in a week. Cassi where are you? Give me just a memento, I'm sorry for being unkind to you, so sorry. He clings to Herma. But she is vernal and does not concentrate. He lets her go. She says to him

Perhaps one day we'll begin and try to find each other again. And I hope then, next time, we meet under more floral circumstances. Come, let us separate.

She kisses his cheek, soft as childish genitals. He goes away. As I move the cold air moves and the paper flowers on the wall move and the sky moves only the floor is steady and I'm not certain about that. Hours are like the beats of a metronome, their close formation does not fool me any more than this cold air or the dead flowers or the sky's cloudy fiords beneath which Cassi stands alone forever. If I were to shout why the whole cargo would be ruined for the flock of admirals manning the boats are not sailors, all the cruel crew are lost, the icy ocean grinds their limbs, scattered and lost their hard hands grab my fingertips as if I knew the way home. The door bangs, he walks to the gate. Herma watches him go. What colour is the eye of the fountain that shimmers in the town whose baroque structure is like a gate locked and I beyond so angered? All the seers are cut to pieces and compel the god to bring forth his seed alone in the abstract blackness where clambering swans reach a summit and then descend to golden mud: the tidal air overwhelms me. A strike of lightning comes crude and too opportune. Rain shocks Herma by falling in these black storms like tears wept because of eternity. She feels her mouth disappear and knows she'll starve. She flings herself on to the bed and lies there broken and therefore harmless.

Seven

Diaphanous jiujitsu afternoon. Autumn is a week old. Its fires are already burnt out. Tomas is counting his debts. He thinks of autumn: autumn, the third season, the season of decay, the time of declining power. And he thinks of love, hot, burning and fiery: yet double-dealing: it demonstrates at every encounter a divine apathy towards its subjects. It dominates us, an ocean which we have to swim, a newfound continent which we have to conquer. It makes us cruel and immodest. And when the act is over, it leaves us with an icy coldness deep-rooted in the marrows of our bones. He closes his eyes, he lets the papers fall to the floor. He wants some peace of mind, to abandon this physical study that has too many affinities with serpents. Rachel and her hood-winking, her intensities, fade into absurdity as he recovers from his sickness. He turns back to Herma, he wants her covert nimbus of sensuality. So now he is going to defer lust to legal decorum and a darkened room. Now it is simply a question of sending Rachel away. Rachel, once his centre of being, accepted and honoured with almost the same dedication that the art of selenography demands (because so much of its essence is also taken on trust) will now be rejected. He cannot go on avoiding a settlement. He wants this rivalry to be brought to a conclusion. His life is with Herma. The thought of its neatness soothes him. For this he is prepared to overlook the fact that she thins his potentiality as an explorer down to almost zero. Zero is at least a stable factor. The thought of sitting down to work at a desk again, of having a clear head, thrills him. It is enough of an adventure. He gets up and roams around, trying out his regained freedom. In his new estimation, Rachel is a woman who has willingly lived out her entire life in a private cage of unrealities: he believes that even if she were to be liberated into the greater pyramid of the world she would remain unchanged, still hold herself to be the only law and god. He no longer feels tragic or afraid when he sees her. She comes down the stairs in a rage.

Where have you been?
she shouts
where?
But he only looks at her calmly. He's holding an atlas in one hand, as if he has been planning a journey somewhere.

Shhh
he says
Shhh there's no need is there?
Although Herma is out wandering through the inclement leaves, amid the naturally occurring elements. He walks into his study. She stands silently in the hall. Air is heavy and rheumatic. The nape of her neck is muslin. She follows him into the room and props herself up against the table, admonishment a dead weapon in her thin hands.

I'm sorry
she says quietly
I didn't mean to go for you. . . .
Tomas shrugs and begins to look at the atlas, those expanses of blue for the sea. She speaks gently, confidentially, sadly. . . .

You know, when I left? A mile later, an hour later, I longed to return. . .
With her hand gripping his wrist. But he has made up his mind. He passes easily from one woman to another.

No, Rachel. It's over.
Over?
She stands up without the support of the table, black shoulders drooping, homeless and severe, a rose covered in black lead, gothic and dramatic: ancestry is slyly devouring her, the fact of inheritance is avoidable, it is the spectrum of her sun.

We alter the surface of our lives but underneath there is always the same shape. To which we must finally revert . . . .

he continues peremptorily. Rachel looks around the room. The door is open. But there's nowhere to go. There's nowhere to go this great stupid afternoon. Inasmuch as temperament is visible in her air and carriage, he has judged her.

O yes

she says with expertise

Yes I know. Sometimes I have to go and look in the mirror to see if I am still there, to make sure I have not wasted away. I know what you mean, Tomas.

They stand together, executioners devoid of victims. Her cathode hair is in disarray.

But I'm telling you, you must go, all the same. There is no future between us.

His pedantic jargon. But she will fight the snare. Her hands pirouette, her phonetic voice begins its journey. Away from the skull and cross-bones.

Tomas, no, it's not possible. Look at our two lives, what we share . . . all the disjointed images we'll save, that we'll never forget, we'll always hang on to. Out of them we both make a polished nostalgia, some sighs, half a life-time. We cannot tear ourselves apart. Memory holds everything together, it solemnly kisses the dew. You remember, the blue seashore that greets us both daily because the waves were almost but not quite my grave? And do you recall a time not so very long ago when philosophy was the hobbyhorse we both galloped on? You must.

But her appeal does not make him adjourn.

Stately frozen swans still litter my mind, Tomas, after ten years or more. Can you believe it? You see, I can't help being like this. I have to shout, to prove I'm still here. Besides I still taste the salt sea at the back of my throat. I have to stay, Tomas. If I go away, I have nothing left. No, you're wrong

he says thickly as if the stipend of air is insufficient. He stares at the atlas. What I'm doing . . .

Tomas pauses, struck by his own inaccurate voice: but he continues

. . . you must go, you don't belong here, you're queen of the traffic lights, tsarina of the night-cafés, empress of LSD yes: but there's no room here. Not for you.

How he stares at the frontiers. Ice at the poles expands. To be always experiencing the spring is dangerous. In the lexicon, no word to save her.

O the cafés, the cafés . . . .

she says excitedly

. . . Before I came down here, I often used to go into that café, you know, the one by the university: I liked to talk to the students.

Yes. . . .

I escaped to them. Because they know all there is to know about meaningless things. All the things we used to know and have forgotten. And then in that café there were also the ex-soldiers with their enmured eyes. And other awkward miscellaneous men. Exiles. I asked one of them, where do you come from? Because he had an accent. Ah, he said, I am a refugee, I have no home. I thought after that I would not visit that café again. But because I have the heart and temperament of a penny-weight, I did, I visited the café again and again. Especially when it was just past midnight. I used to sit alone and think about our time together,

her voice softened and rounded, longingly, as if the thought had come to her by chance, numbers in a lottery . . .

sit and think about the two of us.

Oh what a cynical pantomime, thinks Tomas.

Nostalgia's no good, Rachel,

he says in a hard-baked voice

it has only unreal images which contrive to make us lonely and pine for them. They have no new existence of their own.

This new mastiff voice of his frightens her, she sees veils again covering the mast. Bitterness jostles her. Now she realizes: he believes in the fatality of their affection. Herma is winning. He thinks that the antedote to nectar is a fetid poisonous liquid. His words deny not only her but an idyll: perhaps giddy and from which (had it been abused) evil might have sprung: but nonetheless an idyll. He will not take the risk of happiness. He values only tepid security. She turns her back on him. I love and hate. She begins to talk unevenly about the merits of stars and planets as lucky charms.

> Although they are just meteorites they have a profoundly depressing effect upon me

she says and then turns and slithers towards him, taking his hand and placing it against her soft underdone breast. She holds his fingers so that they make a starfish shape.

> Tomas, am I only an apparition?

she asks glibly, breathing deeply, beneath a sea. But he compels the hollow of the hand to be empty and blindfold. Cruelty is nothing to him, he fears brisk insensible calamity so much more, crimes of passion, the end of the world. Cloudy emotions turn to tock in him: the granite forms a landscape in which he cannot stretch out, to which he is not equal, dogged by nightmares which have nothing to do with sleep. Under these circumstances her breasts are as tiresome as a false and mistaken idea of colour submitted by a blind man.

> O Rachel

he shuns her like an unwanted comet shooting across the sky

> I once thought that wounds could be healed simply by being filled with new flesh, I thought that was enough: but I was wrong, life was not so. Now I have to live out what reality is here with Herma. I know there is something that weaves you two women together, that holds you both, something more than myself is at stake. But don't speak, don't tell me, don't make me a witness . . . .

his voice borders on a whine. He controls it

> No knowledge you have will help me. I don't want to know any of your secrets. I'm not fascinated any more. I've cut the shadows down. You must realize, it is the facing up to life which is the hardest task, not the rebellion against it.

Rachel jumps on him, she kisses him, sabotaging his mouth. Again, the taste is of pitch. It is all over. She must go in the direction of nothing, anonymous and unwanted. She panics, she sobs. The reckoning alone in the dark waits for her. The aftermath is hers. Dogma and explanations to herself. Obeisance to a failed life, a neuter world. She doubts her own equerry's identity: is too disheartened even to plan an envoi. She sees how his expressionless face resembles a sundial and yes it's autumn and she just wants to go away and investigate the fluffy dwarf world of solitude. So she stops crying and looks at Tomas unemotionally. Lifelessly she says, in a stammer

I can't catch your eye any more, can I?
He shakes his head. The slipshod afternoon shivers. Time plucks at his sleeve.

The struggle has grown monotonous and dull now
she says with dignity, her faultless eyelashes stiff and sloping, the words heavy. They burn. Like sin, guilt, misguided anger at the wrong moment. And yet symbols of righteousness. She feels a dark twisted heat move slowly through her veins. His eyes are methodic ice. They pierce her with a heavenly ceremonial silence: silence she cannot remit. She stands stock still.

I no longer feel I'm attacking a citadel full of secrets. she whispers
All I've been doing these last few days is to stroll past old stumbling blocks.
He watches her tense lips compassionately.

And yes she turns sharply away.
She gasps: (I can't distinguish between bread and stone, velvet days go by and I bury my jewels. . . .)
But he's gone away. He leaves her, he closes the door behind her, he goes out of the room. Leaving her hands modest. The palms dry. She hears the door click shut. Silence twines around her fingers, a silver chain. The room is full of yesterday's stale air. A grey wind blows a flat sky into motion. Scaly rain falls in short spasmodic billows, leaves churn like so many tops. The summerless sun comes out. She clings on to her own

hands. O the dead, the young men slain in battle, antique revered sleepers, grinning philosophers, warriors, ancestors, angels, atheists and lovers: all the dead, what do they care about us? She stares at the atlas he's left on the table. Inexhaustible numbness. This breaking away pushes me too far out to sea to be forgiven. Now the air itself will be unapproachable where I am situated. Troubles knotted into my hair recall me to their intention of throttling. She is so shocked she is crying again. But after all when the enemy is found already dead, cut down by another, then shock is only natural. And o it was the wrong sort of a death. Her sad abandonment is without humour. To think, at one time I was said to have resembled her, my great-grandmother! She laughs a tinkling laugh, an iceberg on an oily ocean. Soon she makes a movement amid the shades of afternoon that now are dark as night. And meets Herma in the hallway.

I'm going, Herma.

Rachel smiles. Is dog-tired.

Going?

No. Why it's absurd. Herma's hands fly to a praying gesture. Don't go. Not yet. Not just yet. All that dwells in the air belongs to the land, the land climbs to meet the air.

Yes, I'm going.

Rachel remembers, once she fell into the arms of the sea. Herma says nothing. Her succulent tongue won't move. She edges past Rachel into the room and stands by the window.

Before I go, you must tell me, do you still believe in love? Because the silent girl seems wrapt in some mystery. She is thinking as she grips the curtain why the inevitable nativity, why? But committed by heart is the branch of the tree: tree of everlasting stone. Rachel always feared that Herma would be the first to discover a way of resting. She must know the answer. This is the dark quick moment when she admits to herself that she fears the reproach of Herma's jewelled fingers, the elegant tripods of her hands.

Herma?

But nothing can axe the ice from her younger sister's heart. Rachel, the watcher in the doorway, is the motionless figure who will never find a field a road a sea upon which the sole of her foot might rest. Her very stillness sums up the difficulty she has in being simply her own self, the plain object: it gives away her inability to represent her nature openly for all observers to deprecate or adore. Each individual has its own rosebeds and high walls: its atlas and its economy. She does not understand this. She waits. The atmosphere seems far too thin for ear or eye to hold: if either woman moves, it will crack, shattering and splintering into a kind of emotional shingle. Herma realizes this is a truce: but simultaneously sees how those who command the slaughter of the innocent (even when they are suspected to be otherwise), how those who give the silent signal that means no reprieve, never forget that actual moment of supremacy. So she looks up. But says nothing.

I want something to be confirmed or denied, one way or the other . . . appeals Rachel wearily, devoid of energy. .

Help me, for god's sake: would emptiness confine its opinions, supposing it had a mouth? Just because the wheeling air has no tongue to curse with, no teeth to whistle through, does that mean it has nothing worth while to communicate about liberty or love? I'm threadbare, Herma, I can't understand the world any more, hemispheres fly away, I am . . .

She wants to say: Herma, I am an enigma and am not to be taken as wholly pure or evil: what I say is neither truth nor lie. Not one hundred per cent. But she cannot, not even now, give that much of herself away. There is a concremation of silence. Until Herma herself with a cetacean effort says

Love: even if poor reward is all, the mention of love will always exalt the heart of man, year after year, century after century, millennium after millennium. O love makes interpreters like you uneasy because it is too earthy. But all things are held in this sediment: praising its body gives us the repose of fire!

But quietly, subdued, the words no longer engaging all of her sympathy. Rachel guesses this. She comes into the room, she has granular hands, she pokes with her fingers. She is struggling with herself. She shakes her head. The words were not enough. Her failure (is it her fault?) to understand condemns her to a savage hostile land.

In an age of simple mowing and reaping maybe, maybe the mind and the body do belong near the ground. Without argument. But our world is not so simple.

Herma keeps very still, this conversation becoming clear to her: guilt and shame and the rough surfaces of words all add up to a kind of motionless hysteria. From which she cannot escape. O the gradations of, the bounty of, the wrongs. Her buried. The grappling mastery of her child. At last it has her. As if Rachel would ever have given in. Herma's face closes up. But the damage is done. The words are all finished. The worlds are all finished. Just the coldness remains. A coldness that holds her more rigidly than a dancing master or a vow.

You are cunning, Herma

goes on Rachel, not seeing the lattice of Herma's face, still preoccupied with her own problems

But let me tell you something. A few years ago I went to Athens. You don't need to be told that I'm a pagan. . . . I went to Athens then. Ready to be spellbound. By the ancient gods and goddesses. But I found nothing special there. Nothing. The city, the atmosphere, the experience I had expected, the gods and goddesses, were present only as a dream. Unreal.

Dreams are unreal then?

asks Herma from the depths. And turning.

O yes

Rachel tells her, eyes narrowed, sharp senses marking the change in this other woman, it could be of importance if only as a postscript . . .

Yes, quite unreal. Athens skidded away from my fingers, dust blinded me. I don't like ruins, I discovered. No more than you do. Neither of us like the past, do we, neither of us care for slavery?

Her pewter voice throws a shadow.
 Herma
Rachel says with the rapid passion of munitions now
  what is it that makes you think you are any different, any better than I
  am?
Herma cries out once, a non-vocal sound ascending a colossal scale
 No no
and culminating in a briar scream. Then she is silent. Her rosy pink face is
reflective and slightly puritanical.
 The heart of man
she whispers. Her briny sister stands over her and finishes her sentence
for her
 is hard to believe in.
The stone and flesh are present only as in a dream. Both faces are
inwardly emaciated. Rachel kisses Herma. Who does not move. Remember
the station, do you? Rachel wants to ask. The groynes will no longer stop
the sand and waves shifting, the faint growl of the tide approaches.
 Do you remember the station, Herma?
Rachel says in a voice like a groan.
Herma makes grooves in the air with head and hands, meaning yes yes
how could foundations be forgotten, how could she eliminate that day?
The stolid prosaic station. The grey epicene platforms. The spiky-fingered
town. The train. The woman with the hysterical hair who jumped. The
mother. The faithless castle beyond the town crumbled. Quarry and
pursuers. She had jumped. Leaving behind her two little daughters. Hectic
geometric tragedy. Fourteen and eleven years watched time harden. The
actual statements of fact only proved it. Strangers gave them candies
tasting of sharp lemon. I wonder if it hurt her, Herma had said. The first
comment. Rachel had slapped her face. The first real blow. As they sat
waiting for their father. In a nice sunny place, a parterre. He never turned
up though. So that it had been a complex kind of weaning. Now they sit
waiting again. For no one, for nothing. But waiting. Sitting in this house.
Living different lives at different paces. Having since that morning of

realism learnt with difficulty that no human heart thrives on decay, that decay always brings forth a further decay. It is an emotional moment, gentle and close. As their eyes meet. Their two impassive faces acknowledge this. And that they are no longer bound together. Apparently.

I'm going

she repeats. The campanology of sound falls between them. They draw apart.

Be good to Tomas . . .

Herma looks up with converted lips, an insurrection in protest at this finishing touch. But it is weak and fails.

I don't suppose we'll meet again.

An affidavit from Rachel.

No

says Herma, aground, shivering, could have been called an ague once, now no longer, why this is a fresh start.

Goodbye.

Rachel drags herself out of the room. Herma does not mourn. Although dead figures of both young and old with raw deceased faces sneak up to her, black and funereal, horrid as yews. This is the ultimate age: when the drawn and quartered image is commonplace. Herma stares at her hands. Which are empty. Rachel has gone. Because her job of destruction is finished. Yes, she has gone, laughing at us both under that pale mask, gone with her achievement hugged tight to her breast. A heavy load but she needs no outrider. Without reservation, she's locked the door, wound up the timebomb, lit the fuse. And gone. She, Herma, does mourn. From a sardonyx heart. Because she knows she has lost everything. Love of man, love of god. Is this barrenness all, is this empty space all, is it god, is it only god, is this all man is? Why must I revive a past I do not understand. Understand? No, nothing. Light should have broken in on me before night fell under a train. Now it is too late. I am destroyed. Yes. Rain and wind. But I can't believe in the curve of the horizon any more. Flickering and pastel, it has died. O Rachel is this all, is this all? The world pushes its bloody way into tomorrow, a dark and difficult birth also. Herma covers her face with hands of rock and weeps for many things, the end of simplicity, the ruinous clarification of her erotic responsibility, that peculiar flight, the shadows becoming more and more the real thing and silence the noisiest tumult. All the waiting I've done for renaissance, that great rebirth, is wasted and useless. I am unable to bear the pretence any more, my heart has rotted clear through to the soul. In winter I sweat, in summer I shiver. Siva. I don't know what it is I serve, I turn down all the images I'm offered. It's all just a bad joke. The chair that supports her might as well be a rough sea because it bears no relationship to her: her lips of gnawed stone bleed: but the stone will not blossom into actual flesh and join with the air's brave emancipation. Tomas comes cheerfully into the room to tell her, Rachel's gone at last, everything is over, we're free: but one look at her glacial body crouched on the oblique chair warns him off and he goes away. She does not look up. Her ancient stillness is constant motion.

He stands at the foot of the stairs. Walls have the astringency of bars. His cruel face does not stir. I had a walrus mentality once, now I've lost it. Lord o Lord. The way she had crept out of the house. The way Herma bows her head and arranges her hands. Everything is changing, his future seems to lead him towards outposts of infinity. He would like to rush back to Herma and say help me, please, everything evades me, everything eludes me, what's my name? But he feels so constricted, he is mute, vague, darkly inchoate, liveliness remorselessly stripped away from him. Doors disturb him even when he has the keys. Stairs confuse him. He feels fatigued and is irritated by the tiredness, just'as if he had forgotten to shave. He glances at his watch. Time rocks the afternoon. Is this pain I've got really mine? My loyalty to a wife stretched beyond its limits? Regretfully he begins to go up the stairs, slowly: he does not notice the familiar smells of the house (wine and dust and floor polish and herrings) but counts the steps five six thinking my feet do not move agilely not like dancers or ten eleven twelve soldiers they cannot leap over the princess no I go like a servant in twenty four agony. When she comes into the bedroom expecting to find it empty she is surprised by Tomas standing there, white, bony, naked, still wet from his bath, smirking like a boy as he dries his privates. She almost cries out. But represses it.

Aren't you cold?

she asks sniffing.

Yes, but its good for the circulation.

She picks up a wet towel from the floor.

Any more dreams?

he asks balancing on one leg. Being alone reduces little of the tension between them.

No

she says, coming towards him, making prickly gestures with her hands

Here let me.

She rubs him with a dry towel. His back, his shoulders.

Rachel's gone too

Tomas tells her briskly. Is he grinning or glaring at her? But Herma is not going to laugh. I am not going to laugh. I am not. She knows that if she laughs her chest will split open and her heart will fall out and hit the floor with a bang and roll away and she'll never find it again. She goes on drying him.

I know

she says impatiently. Silence. Tomas shrugs concisely. She stops drying him. She is beyond minor lacerations now. The sky drools alcoholicly, pretending to be clever. A chorus of silence. Then he reaches out for her roughly. But she gets out of his way. Avoids him nimbly.

Get dressed. It's cold

Herma says, her voice the genesis of winter. He was only experimenting, he doesn't really care. He looks out of the window. Those magnificent trees. They are just like sleepwalkers, they don't care about anything, they just let things happen, why can't we be like that. She follows his gaze.

Yes

she says

they're much too high, they darken the room, we must get them cut down.

Why?

he asks unwillingly.

I've told you, they make the room so dark. Often we can't see in these rooms in the afternoons.

Do you want to?

Don't be stupid. We must have them lopped.

All right, I'll try and get something done.

He dresses but she stands and stares out at the alluring white sky behind the stilled stern poised black branches. Her eyelids feel like lichen.

Tomas

she says quietly

I was lying.

He looks up. Shadows ride between them.

What?

I was lying, I had this dream, about a week ago: but I didn't tell you.

She comes and stands before him in a commemorative pose. Her face looks chipped, like an old cup. He sits down on the bed.

Come and tell me . . .

After hesitating a moment, she does, she sits down, clasping her hands. She looks stable enough, he thinks. She studies him for a moment. I'm a fool. I shouldn't have told him. But she sighs and begins

It was about a week ago. . . .

Why didn't you tell me?

You were ill. Besides, it did not seem so bad at the time. It's only now, I keep on thinking about those plants . . .

He strokes her granary of hair.

What plants?

he asks tenderly.

O all kinds . . . saxifrage, moonwort, brownspar, samphire, strangleweed, hawkweed, bryony, cherianthas:
like a catalogue
they were odourless in this dream of mine: I keep on thinking about them, they were so bristly and uncouth, beneath a tightly stretched coarse sky. And the ground they grew out of was unnatural too, it was made up of the unlikeliest of minerals, shale, hornstone (all shining by the way shining like burning gas). . . .
She stares at him piercingly for a second
. . . crystal, feldspar, zircon, bronze, nickel, iron, quartzite, flint . . .
she begins to recite automatically again. He strokes her hair all the time.
How can you remember their names so well, the plants and the stones? he asks, listening to the grisly autumnal sirocco wheedling around the house, Rachel is gone, she'll never come back, I'll never see her again . . . .
. . . how can you recall their names, Herma?
I don't know. But it all seems so definite now. There's no doubt at all in my mind that I saw all these plants. It was a hoary crustacean world.
She is subdued: but inwardly agitated because the essence of the dream remains sealed within her. Like a doom.
But what happened in your dream?
O I just stood there and looked. I felt so tainted by my proximity to it. It had a physical impact demanding I memorize it, you see: the whole scene urged me to record what I saw, as if hundreds of lives depended upon it. But then it faded and all went black and I fell down between the blackness as it went Tomas what shall I do I'm afraid to sleep to close my eyes. . . .
But her voice is gentle, it is not hysterical.
O no don't say you're afraid, that's giving in . . .
he says almost gabbling
dreams are only . . . . dreams. . . .
He puts his arm around her like an elder brother. But sh does not notice. Because she is still deep inside that dream.
What shall I do

she whispers staring at him touching his face. But he cannot become a substitute for her in the dream's abode.

    Ignore it.

he tells her urgently. Ah the acreage of commonplaces. But h must parry this silence. The insensitive clocks begin to chime. He interrupts them.

    Ignore it, it's just some unusually sly mirage your unconscious mind
    has thrown up. It doesn't mean anything. . . .

She holds on to him, is it night or morning, she cannot tell, but she wants to protect him from such a mutiny of knowledge.

    I suppose it is just the residue of my imagination

she says speaking with a forced smile, a dealer selling a mood not an object.

    Yes, that's it, yes . . .

he says, relieved at her brave exterior

    are you ok now?

    Yes

she smiles

    yes.

But it has profaned her, this confession. There is no exorcism. The mineral desert glowers in her memory with the strength of an absolute reality. As if those plants had been the dying roots of time. Jejune.

Eight

Another snowy timorous evening gathers. High summer is long gone. The leaves of autumn are almost forgotten. The November is obvious. Tomas sits thinking of two women. The difference between them. How to define it? Ah, it's the difference between sunlight and moonlight. That's it. He is pleased with this definition. He lights another cigarette to celebrate. Clever, apt, to the point. Is it? Then it strikes him. Which is which? And o god have I chosen the right one? Herma looks surreptiously at Tomas. She sits thinking of that other evening when she stood in swollen silence before the tribunal, Rachel and Tomas: how they had tilted her pain away from them, how they had drawn together. Without comment. How she had gone and cried floods of superfluons tears: which in the middle of her pregnancy she had fancied were made of myrrh. She looks hard at Tomas. Her old cringing jealousy, which she had thought dried up withered dead and witless, constantly returns with the green life in it bursting into feathery fronds, missiles showering over her, tormenting her. She is still bound to her jealousy, in thought she is bound. But word and deed: no. The seersucker sky darkens. Has she broken the sequence yet? Or will Rachel again turn up one day with her crooked smile and confident jousting gait? With her head like a gourd?

You've done no work . . . Tomas . . . .
she reminds him softly. He does not look up from his magazine.

Lack of hope robs my hands of the urge to labour
he tells her sarcastically. The lassoes of print fascinate him. He does not look out of the window. At the water's edge of sky, time hangs and sags. Tomas looks old and tired, shabby, destroyed by a vehement desire to

hold stars within the palm of his own hand. Although he does not suspect this desire. She watches him. He sees other worlds, mink-lined and indecorous. Which he rejected. Shall I tell him? Will that break Rachel's spell? Or wreck the garden already more rugged than any other rose-bed? The arms of maniacs always go for the throat. Herma stands up leagues from the land and walks quickly out of the room, an operatic retreat. I thought the world was going to stumble: but no: it was merely myself. She has a headache. Time slips slithers disappears hour by hour and years fall flat on pretty faces and line them: sleep hides the progress but is still part of it. What do I do with time? Thread needles, smile, fall over, get hurt, pretend to cry. As she moves through the draughty house, the confusions remain. From his side, once longed for, I flee. I drift. Such a necessity to do so. The world once travelled along-side me: now it has sunk down deep within. Where the darkness is mortally stern and heavy. There is no such thing as victory, no such thing as defeat. Life encircles, enfolds, ravishes and finally carries off both protagonists. No, no, it isn't finished, it isn't over! Winter, silver and black, must still be strewn from a high-held arm. She goes upstairs, nursing her headache as if it represents her pride. Downstairs, lost as a king amid too many courtiers, he awaits forgiveness of sins unnumbered unadmitted unknown perhaps even uncommitted. The boat rides across the lake. The water blazes. There is no sound. Only forceful surgical silence. The picture afternoon floats. The land to which they are going shimmers in the heat. But they are shorn of any place which could be honestly named as their own. Which makes things worse, which preys on their minds, this man and this young woman who does not understand his language, whose eyelids are sore from the heat. The man is staring at her but he does not see her. He rows the boat. The young woman gazes down at the water. She would like to jump in the water, it is so green and cool and restful. But it is more than cool, it is icy: and the pregnant young woman knows this and this also has something to do with her sadness. The way she sits. He cannot relax. He wants to reach land, he is afraid they might be stranded here in the middle of the lake. He slaps angrily at a swarm of gnats. The light is so cumbersome, it makes his head feel triangular. The sky is judicial and prophetic. It is very hot indeed. The young woman manages to tell the ferry man as much and he nods and agrees with her. Yes, the sun is like a glass ball, an orange glass ball suspended on an invisible gossamer thread. If the thread snaps it will fall: and if it falls it will devour them. Will there be a landing stage or will they have to wade ashore? The young woman clenches her fists, her son leaps inside her womb, her knuckles shine o so white, she is praying that their boat does not resemble a warship. Outward show is so important. Their throats are dry. But they have made an agreement during their silence, that they will not reveal their privations. Accordingly they dispatch their emotions, they send them away, in different directions, dismissing them swiftly, without error. They dare not risk error. Apprehensively the boat goes through the waves, leaving two lines of white foam in its wake. Neither the man nor the young woman had planned that their lives would include this trip: they had not wanted it. But this crossing had been made compulsory, there was no alternative course to be taken. The young woman is heartsick. How much further? she wants to ask. She tries to ask but she cannot. Her mouth tastes of salt, as if this were the sea, not a lake. She is dizzy, her head falls to one side: then jerks back upright again. The man looks at her anxiously. She nods and half smiles, to tell him, I'm all right. It is all such a waste, he thinks. There's no shelter at all. But there had been none back at the place she is leaving, the life she is fleeing. He is glad when he brings the boat safely into shore. And he delivers the young woman to her husband who is waiting for her and watches these exiled ones embrace. They have overcome wood water everything intervening. How often had his mother told him that story. How often he had heard the story of her flight from the war, carrying him within her. It is his only dream, the boat crossing the water. Tomas pulls a face, brushes some ash from his sleeve, does not dare close his eyes. What made him recall his only dream, from years back? What drew him and the past together again? An inborn tendency to delve and reconstruct? What?

Winter landscapes, the meridians of the desert, heights of spring, dry harsh autumns. And now this city, angular as a black umbrella. The cold is hellish. Herma Goldstraw, alone and without the chains that had bound her and held her safe in one place, lacking the strength that her faith had once given her, comes slowly out of the station, trying to look both watchful and elegant. This is a dangerous journey, as the loop of the airman is dangerous: a calculated risk of the incalculable. She stands on the pavement and feels the vibration of the traffic, the fierce dread of the people as they move like migrant companies before a plague: she sees the mutton-coloured sky: and all she wants is some means of escape. O let me go home, she thinks. But where is home? She remembers that this disfigured world knows no limits to sacrifice. She feels outcast and looks for some means of flight. All she sees are avenues of wreck, ruin and desolation. Violence is the customary manner and sensation of the city. To avoid it she waves down a taxi, cautiously as if instituting an expedition. She is taken forward, on through streets of grey, past towers, glass monuments, people swathed in velvet, billboards, ultra-severe finance houses, buskers: the city is a barracks run by the indifferent, the mercenary. But this is what she has to face, for a time. With her eyes like umber. The taxi stops. She gets out and again stands staring at her reflection in the shop windows. Cold, cunning, consecrated, the city is a receptacle for emergencies. Why do I walk as though haunted, as if the shadow that tracks me down is not my own? Minute by minute, her own seediness disgusts her and she feels unreal as a wax dummy. The hallway is rubbery and smells of lilacs. Smooth and oiled, the lift moves up. And her colloquial life goes with it, even if it means the extinction of the blood. Leases terminate, save what can be salvaged by the bare hands. She forgets how long this lease has to run. However, rather than relinquish her rights she will set the property ablaze. She bites her lip as she walks along the corridor. It is inevitable that she should make this hissing sound in her mouth, that she should feel weak, that she should confine her eyes to the darkness of their lids. Dumb blood is on her tongue. She recalls the childhood day she beat her sister in a race and they had both been helpless with the force of their bodies hitting the air. My bones are now somewhat less malleable, she thinks, my life shuts in on itself like a conceited camera. I have no likeness to conform to and I will have none. She opens her eyes. Rachel's face is pessimistic and delphic-hard as ever.

Herma

says Rachel in a matinee tone, a foreword.

Rachel

Herma replies unemotionally and walks into the apartment.

I'm sorry to disturb you

she says

were you busy?

No, no, I was just finishing some sketches, they can wait. They do not look directly at one another.

I haven't slept for over a week

says Herma carelessly. She looks around. All the furnishings are either blue or green: they give the impression that the, apartment is situated some feet below sea level. Rachel closes the door.

You must see a doctor

she says slowly.

No . . . . it's a trivial thing. . . .

Herma kneels down by the fire, holding out her cold hands to the warmth. She is conscious of Rachel's eyes levied on her like a tax. The space between the two women is musky. On the table a bowl of white roses, their petals shaped like lozenges. The godless hour strikes. Both women are unsure of themselves but neither has lost their footing. Herma is dressed in black, her arms and legs petrified by the blackness.

Wandering?

Rachel asks her mildly. Herma laughs, almost snorting, blowing down her nose. But keeps on staring into the fire. The flames are graphic. She maintains a profane silence.

It's your own business

says Rachel in a kind of distrustful musing. Then she comes and stands behind her sister, putting out her hand and smoothing down the unbound hair. The weight of her hand is like oil, annointing. But Herma gets up at once and walks through the apartment, moving bewildered through the watery light. Graceless and unsymmetrical she turns in a doorway and looks exhaustedly at Rachel, her eyes aggrieved. Rachel is no candidate to bring anyone forward for acquittal but she asks Herma to come and sit down at least. She hangs her coat on the back of a chair and sits down. Glass, stone, flesh, cloth: all separate them. Time is a rose thorn. Outside, the traffic echoes like sin and repentance and sin again committed. Herma wants Rachel to say, it is not your fault, this world, you are not to blame, you have not sinned, I absolve you. Rachel begins to speak but after a fraction of a sentence she stops, leaving Herma in a garret of silence. Is she surprised to see her? Rachel's full sleeves fall down over her wrists. Herma has introduced a brittle pressure into her long pattering afternoon. Various kinds of silence are dispatched. Both women are foragers: yet not withstanding that, they need to be held in a certain safety for which they are still rivals. Rachel knows her sister too well. Her manner towards her is always influenced by the fact that she believes Herma is too fond of herself, a spiritual whore, who would be insignificant but for her talent of appearing gentle: a talent which, although secondary and tired, always defeats Rachel. So that her white hands clutch together, converting one emotion into another, not allowing Herma to see that she is enduring negation. Herma has forgotten why she came here. This meeting allows her to reason through a variety of problems but does not help her to understand Rachel. Rachel curbs her instinct to be sarcastic, to be deceitful and prevaricate. She waits for her sister to speak first. Failure and flame have taught her how to wait. Herma's sudden arrival puzzles her. Perhaps she too is working out some internal plan which she is not prepared to reveal until it is complete in every detail. But why should she? She has no reason, she is in possession. Herma touches her black skirt tenuously. Its destituteness is painful to her. She tries to separate herself from its sombre pigment. But does not speak.

Are you going to see Daniel?

The silence was getting dowdy. Rachel could not go on excusing it. Herma shakes her head. Still she says nothing. But stares out of the window. All her life doing this, staring through glass. My theories are constructed only to be broken, thinks Rachel, going into the kitchen. Herma drinks the liquor as if it were medicine and then hands back the emptied glass.

I'm seeking a shape for myself, Rachel. . .

What do you mean?

Putting the glass down.

I mean a harmonic relationship to myself.

Herma's face is everlasting pain, confined by some slavery to some thing which had not held her so rigidly last time they confronted one another. The emptiness beneath her heart is cold. Four years ago the blood had been packed tightly inside her to feed the cretin. Rachel touches her sister's forehead with one cold hand. But Herma takes the hand by the wrist and firmly removes it.

Not just love . . . but its meaning . . .

she says. With compressed nostrils. Rachel smiles but Herma does not see. That the smile is gentle. Their hands are still caught loosely together. The slight grip acknowledges mutual dismay.

You think there is one then?

Herma lets go of her hand.

Perhaps I should say I want to be free of artificiality: I want the reality itself, earth, iron, truth. . . . I thought I had it once, but it was only a decoy. . . . I want reality. . . .

Rachel's single heart responds.

But Herma, all that lies at the bottom of artifice, beneath it, nowhere else.

Artless and clumsy, Herma turns to her, consumed by many brooding sleepless nights

Rachel, yes, yes, it's what I feared all along: that I should have to march through the passions to find silence when I can only find common passion in my own silence. . . .

She speaks with great rapidity, almost in awe of herself. Rachel looks squarely at her, bored and disapproving

Herma, how you can talk. . . .

her voice direct and grating, her face sour as a blackmailer. Herma's fingers spurn her, they fiddle with her skirt. Although her eyes feign acceptance of the criticism.

I know

she says, quietly and orderly

But I can't alter it.

Rachel picks up her glass and drinks. It burns her throat.

Why come here, Herma, why to me?

A cessation, a surrender if she answers. But at once she says

Because you see me so clearly.

Do I? See you? Clearly? No, I never have done . . .

Yes you do, you recognize me because I'm your opposite number, you understand me by instinct, on your own terms. Perhaps

says Rachel doubtfully. She pauses, still angry about the strange quality she cannot extract from this girl, angry about what she cannot quite catch hold of: then she adds cruelly

But I understand Tomas better.

Herma's body goes slack at first but then she gets up and crosses the room, freed of land that had been disparagingly mortgaged: she goes to the empty bedroom and flings open the door, with a movement as flamboyant as a ringmaster.

That's your knowledge, that's all.

Her voice trembling as if she used obscene language or made a crude gesture. Rachel stands up, on cue: she is shaking. A viceroy's dignity sends her across the room, her face a rash. She pulls the door shut without banging it. Their faces are rustic. The room resembles a tomb seen sideways.

My knowledge

say Rachel simply

is greater than yours.

But her voice is tough, a warrior with a spear. Herma knows it. She stares at the point in the air where their eyes meet, all the rays converging. Their spirited animosity is resumed again. Herma jeers at her, walking away, pointing a finger at her and saying in a mocking see-saw voice

Ahah so the enemy trembles . . .

but this time Rachel does not reply. All at once she is disinterested in Herma and the afternoon: and she walks to the fire because anger has left her cold. She sits down. When she looks at her sister again, her face is precise and stationary, she has it under control.

We must be sensible, Herma, neither one of us can delude the other with tricks: it isn't worth trying. . . .

Restraining the clanging inside her head, relaxing her defensive attitude, Herma approaches: as if the fight had not been disciplinatory for both of them, as if there is no cause for alarm. But then she is afflicted with a fit of weeping that will not stop. And she kneels down beside Rachel. Rachel grips her by the shoulders. When silence is resumed it is like a delta.

O Rachel, Rachel, how diversified and full and yet how barren everything seems. At one minute we are engaged in the development of something valuable, a great achievement: and then, another time, another day, this ability we had to hold emotions together, to make everything cohere, it just goes. Do you understand?

Herma clings on pathetically to Rachel's wrists. But she pushes her firmly away and stands up. Black, thin, divested of both courage and dignity, Herma looks up at her. One hand on her hip, her body slanted, eyes narrowed, interested, penetrating, Rachel nods and says

Life is harsh and difficult and stern but you must find the right place for yourself in it, a way of getting yourself correctly positioned.

From the fastness of the floor Herma asks

How?

And without enthusiasm Rachel says flatly

O Herma I don't know. In time perhaps it comes . . . as though overnight. . . .

Since her departure in the autumn Rachel has suffered for all the times she thought Herma only worth looking at with one eye, lacking any intelligence. Her own tendency to dramatize led her to overlook the resources of her rival. Seeing Herma is a rebate of chagrin. Her voice hardens.

I don't know.

Icy rain begins to fall, like sweetmeats. Rachel draws the blue curtains.

Its like being in a grotto, all this blueness . . .

says Herma affably. Rachel nods. The pale indigo light does not flatter her, no matter what angle it falls on her head. Her dyed hair is shaggily cut. It is the colour of nicotine at the roots. She runs her fingers through her hair, leaving it confused. Her face is memorable for its new lack of exultation. From the floor Herma watches her doubtfully. She wonders how many times Tomas deceived Rachel before her own advent. Rachel's sulky moping figure is like a song without words. Why Herma? thinks Rachel, remembering that when she heard of the marriage her tongue seemed to swell and she almost retched. To be superseded by the lumpish cheerless Herma; a joke in poor taste. Dregs of anger moved loosely and astonishedly around inside her, culminating in the seditious game played with Daniel, that recalled the inferior kind of adoration paid to some saints, some deprived angels. Herma has no comprehension of the good relationship that once existed between myself and Tomas, as balanced as weights swing in the hands: a relationship which Herma has eaten into with her distilled body and preposterous unfair mouth. Why did I take the risk? Herma gets up and comes towards her quickly, as if Rachel might break a fall which threatens her. Her halting awkward yet charming way of moving, her stupid face and perceptive hands are all so different from Rachel and yet nonetheless there is a reminiscence about her, like a mirror unexpectedly there in the room, that jerks Rachel back into the coldness where all her judgements are frozen. Herma sees her face go pale and knows that the time of approach is over, that she is strange as a lascar again. Herma sinks back to the floor.

Perfection,

she starts, her voice percussive

does it keep any of us safe, does it satisfy us, what is it? I've tried to find it, do the trick, kill the ghosts that reduce life to a feudal tenure, take the field against them, no matter how feverish it left me . . . and so have you. But there's a deadly quarrel that repels us whenever we try to solve it, together, alone, or with a man. Rachel, do you know what I mean, what I'm saying, does it make sense, all this nonsense about lights moving in the darkness?

Herma sounds overwhelmed, beyond tears, her body lax, clustered on the floor.

If you mean excessive thirst, accelerated pulses, excitements that don't need a swoon or an orgasm to complete them, yes, I do, but only glimpsed in the distance, like mirages.

And her sister turns her head away.

Ah no

she says

you don't understand, Rachel, and you're freer than I am. Rachel laughs shrilly and frigidly

Free! There's no constitution that can give me freedom, Herma, I'm not conscious of any freedom.

Herma lifts a black arm towards her.

But you are free enough to move alone, to leave hiding-places, to shackle others with your desires instead of giving in to them: you can use any method to find out what you want to know, or to get what you want . . . a garland of flowers that never die, people who are afraid of your name forever, unhappiness left behind you. . . . You can do anything, Rachel. But I cannot walk away from myself, the way you can. I'm always trapped by what I desire, I do not master it. . . .

No no

Rachel pushes the words away and comes to kneel beside Herma. She shakes her slightly as if she had fainted

No, what I do is only a way of snapping the fingers at a fetish, as if to say, there, so much for you . . . but this stratagem of getting up and going does not work, it is only a rehearsal for enduring the return and the failure to succeed.

She lets her go. Herma's elfin hair smells of spring.

But, Rachel, at least you do move, you are independent of everyone and everything. O how I envy you. I only perform duties laid down by certain conditions. I'm a slave. I don't create the conditions. You do.

Rachel disagrees. She says no. Softly. Evening outside is nothing to do with them. They must go on trying to construe a disease from its symptoms.

No, neither of us understands the other, Herma.

She looks at her younger sister, her own face beginning to wither. Herma's fingers are piano keys. But there is nothing else musical about her. She is tired. She regrets telling Rachel anything. She should have not announced her troubled state of mind. Rachel's calmness, her lack of reaction, annoys her. Where's the old spirit?

Was Tomas faithful to you?

she asks suddenly, in a loud tac'less voice, pretending to gossip. . . .

Before me, I mean?

Rachel breathes in sacramentally. Herma waits for a sneer or a blow. But it does not come.

God, that's a romantic question

says Rachel artfully. She is playing a game which will perhaps leave the victor free from the past. Rachel enters into the darkness of explanation, that is odourless and without energy of its own.

Sometimes he was

she continues disdainfully.

Is that all?

You want to know it all, don't you, o you always did. . . She sounds amused. Perhaps reproachful. Certainly not bitter. Although she is.

You've wanted me to tell you for months. Years. When I say sometimes I mean, yes, remorse always caught up with him. Love tends to behead you. But not me. I counted them up, one girl after another. I was impartial. He came back. It was the others, including you, he cheated. Not me.

No

cries Herma sharply. A pause. A clock ticking. Both of them noticing it for the first time. Rachel's hands are morocco. Then she attacks

Do you suppose that I waited innocently? You probably would, like a standard bearer awaiting the flag pole. No. I had my pleasures too.

But she stops almost before she has begun, voice failing, with no more to say.

Tell me about him.

Herma will not let her stop. It is a command, the way children asking for a story at night command. For her to leap into a tottering past, ramshackle with heat, broken glass confusing her, scattered about her feet. But she goes on, lacking sparkle, not even mournful: but forthright and gutteral. From outside, the sound of train wheels.

Very well. But you won't understand him, no matter how much I tell you.

Herma says nothing. Rachel tugs her sleeves down over her wrists, coldness is radiating out from her mouth.

I first realized what was happening one night about six years ago. It was a summer night so hot I could not sleep. Tomas was sleeping but badly. Suddenly he woke up and recoiled, you know, the way you do, when you wake in the night. He roused himself and looked into my open eyes. He closed his eyes at once and pretended to go back to sleep. I thought he was kidding. So I kissed him and crawled on top of him. But he tried to push me off. I hung on and then he shoved me roughly away and got out of bed. I asked him, what's wrong? He grunted. As if I had molested him. At once, he was sequestered in himself. And it was as if a gun had been fired inside my head. I knew what was happening, it was clear, he'd been ignoring me for weeks. He went to the bathroom and left me there. I felt as if I was being hauled over a flame. I waited for him to come back. When he did, it was the most greasy thing I've known. Almost. He inserted himself bad-temperedly, it was hasty, strained, there was difficulty in fusing. Whenever that distance erupted between us, I knew he was gone. I got used to it. What else could I have done about it? After all, until you came along, it never lasted.

Silence salts the hurt. Rachel stands up, her mind happy no that it is freshly delivered of its half-truths and fantasies.

Are you shocked?

she asks Herma, with a touch of her old tartness. What were their names? thinks Herma, what did he call them, those women?

Maybe

she says

Maybe. Although Tomas has never behaved like that to me.

(Are you sure? Are you certain, Rachel?)

O it's true

says Rachel angrily as she looks down on her, insinuating, humourless, uncompromising. Blood is not enough to secure loyalty.

You know who Tomas really is, don't you?

she asks, her voice scarred as a stone. Herma shakes her head with a clambering movement of the hands as accompaniment. No. She has never believed it, not even when he said things only she and Rachel could understand. No no. She wants to scream. A grace-note. But her mouth is dry as latin. Nascent understanding fills her belly. Yes then, yes, she had always believed it. It is real and true as placenta. And that truth was the attraction, the fire in the breasts. Yes, even the middle ear understands it. I am no better than Rachel. No use my saying, Rachel, it's your fault, you should have told me who he was before I loved him. It would have made no difference. O sin, his father, our mother, pairs of lovers, children. Desecrated, no longer the sweet infanta, she swears insolently at her sister. This ember day is taken over by devils. The syncopated rhythm of the hunt throughout history makes her sick. Finally, very quietly, as if communicating something celestial, Rachel says

Did you know that on ships the block used for stretching shrouds was called a dead-eye? Or that some orchids are called dead-man's finger, thumb or hand?
Herma looks down at her own exaggerated hands and then up at Rachel. Her face is vestal.

No

she says deeply enamoured of the thought for it is a quasi absolution
no, why did you have to tell me . . . . . ?

Herma stands on the causeway. The molecule city is unencompassable. It is beyond even a rural deity. She whispers again, o home, home. Pigeons collide in the air, anxious and weary. It is a cold creamy day. The sun is far from her. Showers of meteoric sleet dash in her eyes, small hard stones. She walks along slowly, involved in and yet denying the impulse to grieve. Children shout at her, encircling her with their game, a gruesome game copied from warrior adults: these kids play in an unthinking desperation. But she does not notice. How can Rachel bear such freedom? Or is her freedom a sleight of hands? The edelweiss air is keen and cutting. Herma is not surprised to hear that Rachel used to act as a kind of procuress. But the idea of Tomas blazing like kerosene in girl after girl shocks and frightens her. For all its penalties and rites, their marriage seemed strong enough to withstand anything except Rachel. But now she learns that other women have taken his hand and let him release them from their hives. They have let him work upon their missal-like groins. If Rachel was telling the truth. . . . Conversations with Rachel are always incomplete: the fag-ends of truth. The rudimentary eldritch accompanies Herma, she feels it move in her empty womb. Her puffy eyes blink: sleet is the pretext. The two sisters, travelling through Europe on the train, years ago. The affection between them, pure love, which sends you into a gentle sleep, is gone forever. She climbs the steps, goes in past the students, the tourists and the old men. Perhaps it is another race, she moves so rapidly. Her footsteps echo: separate her from all the others. Cripples, she leaves them behind. If she shouts, there will be another echo. Her hair is dark as pluto in the nightworld. So much of life is waiting and it seems like antiquity. She walks to the centre of the gallery: she is aware of stone which gives no indication of the shape or size of the carving hand. The wet light is ecclesiastical. Herma drifts from block of stone to bronze sculpture to iron maiden in pursuit of something which might affirm her belief in the adoption of death. But she finds only the scraggy underbitten smile of Daniel who states cleverly

I thought you'd come here.

She nods expressively. But says nothing. She is too chilled to be argumentative. Is she fond of novelty? Her head is tautological.

Hello, Daniel.

Hello. . . .

His voice is bright as a comedian. The cursive mouth of silence sneers with wisdom.

Did she send you?

asks Herma. An aztec voice. And moves towards a symbolic buffalo built up from an immense mass of bronze. He does not answer. He scuttles after her.

Just look at that painting . . .

he says. A portrait of asperity: and yet of violence shattered by violence. In it she finds no revelation: there is no vision: it is just oil and canvas sanctified by a frame.

I have one of his works. . . .

The artists. . . . ?

Yes. It's of the madonna.

She turns. Pariah. Two bodies at rest. No, not at rest.

Madonna? What Madonna?

Daniel moves neatly, on the balls of his feet, testing the question.

Tomas's madonna. Don't you know it? Haven't you seen it?

He has no extravagant notions of diplomacy.

No

An excerpt from his smile strips her of hope.

You must come and see it
he says, bending over her.
No
she says but he ignores her, his lips almost touching her hairless cheek.
He is ready to make a bargain with her.
 You must. Now. Tomas originally commissioned it and then gave it to
 Rachel. She gave it to me.
His voice is shrill, handing out information. A new wilder voice.
 You must still have been at school.
He jigs around her, a horehound dance: is this homage, is this what you
call it, is this how you do it? He does not regulate the pitch of his voice.
 I thought you knew all about it.
 No, But it doesn't matter.
The volcanic rocks are graven idols.
 No? Anyway, you must come with me. Come on.
He drags her by the wrist. A momentous act. He dives towards the door,
moving like a lynx. His eyes are wide open: they beckon. And Herma,
drawn not by Daniel but by her desires and her own faulty circuit of
personality, follows him saying yes yes yes: her thoughts are colourful as
a dorado: perhaps she is even prepared to kill. Has she ever thought of
this? Of her hands being completely used in such a way? Yes, she has. But
she is not telling. She goes out with Daniel into the glucose city. In a
sense, this is her first entrance into the world. Debut. Herma and Daniel
go up the stairs. His flat is on the third floor. Noises are everywhere.
Something clatters and bangs. A machine for making flowers in winter
perhaps. The long thrusting interval of sheared dumbness in the taxi has
tired them. So they go up the streaky stairs with slow steps. He opens the
door.
 This is where I live.
The first thing she sees are white plastic flowers in a black vase. They
make her think of a chessboard. Daniel touches the asiatic medallion she
wears around her throat. Chemical silence. Taste of quassia in her mouth.
This obeah couple are sworn to tell the truth.

Where did you get it? It's pretty, with the horses . . .

This? O it was a present from someone. From Rachel.

Under oath. He turns away, he touches the roseate plastic flowers.

A long time ago.

The dolour in her voice pretends to be gay as a goshawk. Chatty even.

There's the madonna.

He points. She lifts her eyes. The semester of black outlines, the face, leers at her.

She gave it to me. Obviously she likes giving things.

he says, curiously waiting for the reaction. Herma stares at the portrait of her sister. The tarsus fingers.

It's inappropriate. Such a subject. . . .

Herma says quietly. And her complicated face is not to be probed. Her lips are purplish-blue.

You should have stayed

she tells him sadly. But with a cannibal bitterness.

I don't know

he says. His eyes are half closed. Through their slits the pupils shine cautiously.

I don't know. When she told me that you were sisters. . . . It shook me.

You should have guessed. It was clear as daylight.

Greasiness in his eyes, desiccation on his lips, a sub-kingdom is his only possession.

Perhaps

he whispers. They stand on earnest furious legs. Angry with one another for not understanding the barrenness of each other's soul, the descent which they have both suffered.

You didn't know we were sisters? All summer. I thought you knew. Or had guessed. Or would guess.

No.

He smiles a normal smile. She tries to respond, a smile wavers and purses itself eccentrically on her lips. Then it is severed from her mouth. She trembles and shivers. His crinkled hands are very still. A large glaring eye, a wall-eyed dead stare, he thinks of this. But his hands are very still. He forces them to be still. Her torpid voice again:

Our parents weren't married, you know that?

He shrugs.

No. But what about it? It's not unusual nowadays.

No?

she repeats, suspicious and uncertain. Then her face draws itself in to the heart.

You see, my father was already married. But he had left her.

So he just lived with our mother.

A torrent of words, incoherently pronounced.

It's a common situation.

Is it?

she laughs, unruly and noisy

I suppose you're right, it is. . . .

A pantomime horse frightened me once. But o it makes me laugh now. Molten eyelids, a disorderly countenance, she holds his shoulders parasitically

Tell me, will you marry her?

He thinks of spiders.

I don't know. I can't understand any of this . . . I'm . . . I don't know what kind of conduct would satisfy either of you.

A pit yawns pinkly. For me to fall into. So I will keep still. A pinchbeck philosophy. But safe. Keeping the pinions free, unclipped. Thin, hungry-looking, ancient pindaric eyes. Yes, Herma is haunted. Her youth is past renewal now. Now he sees one sister looking out of another's eyes. That same love of phalanxes and warriors, that same hatred of flowers. She says in a breathless pasternoster

You know what I want. You said you'd always dreamt of some one like me. Here I am.

He bites his knuckles. His meagre wrists jerk.

But I thought that of your sister too.

Her hands fidget and tremble. Kama in the abstract sense: inside her head it spits its imprecations. Her hands: she strikes them together and all her past gentleness explodes in that gesture.

You know what I want.

She emphasizes the i. He looks away from her in a dream blindness.

No, I don't. I don't understand your world.

It's the same world. Whatever.

She uses up the wasteful obstinacy of contempt on him.

No. There's more than one world at stake.

He walks away from her to the bookshelves and runs his finger along the spines of the books. An atmosphere of pessimism, the sensation of imminent disaster circulates around them, like an outspoken rumour. Under the influence of this obscure tension, their conversation grows vagabond. He is numb before her land, her territory. His anger at his own inadequacy returns. The fences between himself and Herma are laughable. But deadly, electrified. Her face, the avatar, is worn down to the bone: the cortege gapes at her. Toil and feuding leave her cold. She walks to the door with too mathematical a step. Leaving the surplus lover behind. But he runs, he catches at her hand, he bites it helplessly. She cries out. A shrike. They struggle. Gauntly. Then he lets her go. She stares at the broken skin, patched with blood. Sodden with violence, he groans. The man and the woman raise their eyes and look at one another indifferently. Then he walks to an inner door.

Please. Herma. Come in here.

His eyelids twitch. A morbid lust wriggles in him. She follows him in and closes the door with an hysterical bang. He forces her back against the door. He kisses her with a cruel admonitory rawness. She submits to a crucified pleasure. His hands are smeared with the blood of her oxide hands. She looks for somewhere to kneel. But nothing offers itself. To have nowhere

for the smarting dusty body to rest is what hurts. Her distracted hips sway in his red and white hands. The shortness of her unnecessary struggle amuses him. Now they pump up their bodies. It is a variety of discipline. Their incarnate fingers rub and press and pull and squeeze their diabolic privates. Their white bodies coast along on the white bed, turning mechanically with devout motions. Prey runs in a straight line. It is revered and then they consume it. The angular relationship between their two bodies recedes then clenches close together then widens again. Herma watches their wrenched extreme bodies as the heat unbends from them. Later, they dress in an almost purified silence. Until consciousness of the state of danger and tumult in which they exist mounts in Herma, distending her. She must compel him to help.

Won't you fight?
she asks Daniel. But he sweats. His face is wet. Even his eyebrows. He has many faces. Now they all fear her.

Tomas and I? Why should we fight?
he replies with intense control. Not this girl as well.

O not Tomas.
Herma spreads her hands out in the air and lets them appeal to him. Her comely mouth smiles. But to these suggestions, he is immune. He turns away. How can I recover what is long-lost?

I've unmasked you
Herma tells him furiously. No votaress, whe leaves this flat, thinking of plane trees. He has a nice convenient life. With no totems. No lepers. He has everything to live for. She halves her heart. Her shoes rattle on the stone steps, like unanswerable riddles. She still feels the vehemence of her body. It makes her think of the act as a shedding, the body a shell, a husk, a tunnel: she can never forget the bashful womb from which the ticking bloodied creatures emerge, time and again. So she stops. She holds her body in check. Then she turns and goes back up the stairs. He stood there listening to her footsteps, feeling the dampness of his face. He recoiled from it. Now he hears her coming back. She walks towards him, a malpresentation.

Did Rachel tell you anything else?
she demands. He shakes his head, dull and careless.

Not about our great-grandparents?

Again, the movement of his head that is heavy as a wheel.

Then I'll tell you. Our great-grandmother never married. O there were many proposals. All the local young men were suitors. All were rejected. She died young. In childbirth. Perhaps it was the climate or the boredom, god or the devil, who knows who was to blame. . . But the child was her brother's. Which brother, it is not known. Probably the eldest. So: what do you think now? Rachel's a fine Madonna. And what about me?

She speaks quite merrily. Then she is gone. Again, her feet echo on the stone steps. His wide open fixed incredulous eyes are asterisks. His staring gaze sees all manner of forgotten things. Quite naked things. To disgust him. Originations. A luminous stallion in a metallic race. He stands very still. The false waxy flowers in the vase begin to sing a blackish song. His kidneys ache. In the dungeon the dead sleep. The inhuman walk the earth. The inimical, the insane. Touching his flesh. Kissing the lips. This flesh of his was always grubby. But now it rots. Grubs drill their way through the muscles and the nerves. Making cavities in the bones. His skin crawls. He is on the verge of a world. How did I get here? He falls forward on his knees, ready to vomit gallons. But his throat stays gummed up. He kneels there, waiting to be canonized. Only to live for a day, he whispers, carefully inserting the words into the room. He writhes, tries to stand, falls on his face. Everything makes sense, the cohesion of that queer triad. The black and white space he occupies is faithful. It holds him close whilst he cries. The flowers stink in their sweaty vase and the murmured conversations of his neighbours, who shriek with laughter or yell in anger, go on even when his undistinguished teutonic tears have condensed and he sleeps because there is nothing else to do.

Herma comes to an open field strewn with crosses, a terrace of ice beneath a gravestone of snow. She walks with a chillingly regulated stride. Her eyes deepen and darken, are the shade of a sky the half second before it breaks into night. She drags her body to her son's grave, the snow falls on her shoulders, white, she is a swan, the swan. Pursued by tempests. She stares at the grave, masquerading as a bereaved mother. She stands like some statue erected to no particular kind of posterity. The dyke is at a dangerous level. Hurry. No. All my ambitions are here. I can't leave yet. No. Not yet. She spreads out her ungloved blue fingers. Everything she endures is in those hands. She holds them against her heart. The heart is ungladdened. Because its themes are shattered, never to be mended or consoled. She puts her hands in her pockets. She shivers. Not from sunstroke. That treeless desert, where no torrential rain or epidemic of snow ever falls: how she is locked to it, a composition of skin and bones, immobile, polemic, already half dead. There is a great grey stone weighing her down. Which curbs her desire to strike out afresh. She jerks as if in sleep when the dream hits home. But she is still standing there, awake, ulcerated, no longer aware of the meaning of fortitude. Coldness. And the utmost area of time finally reached. Snow rails at her. Then ceases. All things in their own season. She looks at her hands again and wrenches her fingers back as far as they will go. Somehow from this vast and minute desert she must make her escape. A voyage. Risk the boat of the brain sailing too far out of the harbour's reach. No. Sail like a schooner! Change occurs in many ways, says Herma slowly, it is not always marked by the directions printed on a calendar or the closely written pages of a diary. The words freeze. The silence is hardy. Loud strokes resound from the church tower. After it, silence again. She smells under the snow the extraordinary flowers which grow from the seeds of dream. Heavy seas appear. Beyond the ends of her fingertips, that is where she must go. The waves are so tall. The seas wail. Seas of an unborn world. What kind of a death is allowable, Herma? Can you fight for it? Her eyes travel from the gravestone to the tallow sky. But its idiot mouth has no answers. She has a gentle talent for evil. Goodness came to Herma once but she combed her hair free of its burrs. Asinine utterances staple her to the snowy ground. She kneels down on the snow. It soaks her legs, the hem of her coat. She runs her fingers through the snow, she puts some in her mouth, to taste death's coldness, o no, yes, that frozen reflection in no one's mirror. She recalls the shape of her happiest head, the swing of her carriage then: now like a pirate, she must run events down to the very last deck, plunder or be plundered. The afternoon's white chandelier sky stays stupid above her bent trapped hereditary body: the graves, silent as pomegranates, hold assembly around her, stony, crumbling, mildewed, not praising her. The cold cruel wind, how it blows, hear how it blows. Her eyelids are closed fast. She grips her hands like oaths. Her knees ache and sting. She chatters to herself in the rhythmic strife of the quite mad and the very jealous. Metallurgy in her soul, full of acid, warped by thieves and villains. Her long oppressively mournful hair, damp and classical, hangs down loose and incumbent on the elongated air. The unnamed children, the generations lost to her. She is cut off from them. Her uneven hedonism shackles her to lost pride. She calls to hounds. She laughs. She groans. Her capriole hair catches the wind, rises with it, limping, a pendulum of silk and ash. She stands up, reeling. Her feet crunch on the snow, it sounds like sand. She makes a sudden sound of loss deep in her throat, a metal spoon twanged to make a dull note. She trembles goosily, her wet legs burn. Her contagious heart hurts. She lives now stripped down to nothing, nailed to the earth, stake driven through her heart. Homicide stays with her forever. She almost falls to her knees again, wilting. Her eyelids close on a slaughtered carcass. Nothing will pass through her body towards a new athletic life of its own. Only the spinal remembrance stays and betrays. She bites her lips, she feels the invisible muzzle. Question: why had she slain him? Answer: because he was a travesty. Comment: that is no excuse. Her own voice flays her. Drunken roses on her lips taste of a tired life. Scarlet with frost. A simpleton emerges from the past. With repellent strangling fingers. She chokes on a wax tongue and turns again to her prodigal journey: she runs lamely out of the burial ground. She hears a fugue of frogs. And outlandish hallelujahs. The train snarls through the stone foliage of the city and past the flower-gardens of the suburbs into the iced dark of tunnels, buffeted by the vituperative endless night. But all the time her eyes are closed, like the eyes of the dead. Pieces of a dead map, her sister's fetishes, the pressure of her eyeballs solid as rubies, bismarck history, a snake tightening around her throat, archaic dirges: all of these preoccupy her within her jacket of skin. Although when the train stops she at once is standing upright as a maypole, eyes open wide. There is darkness rent with lights. She can see serpentine branches moving across an almost full polyglot moon, branches darker than the sky they accentuate, she can see all the dead bandages of a great putrid war, she can see another church tower, she can see the wind, she can see Tomas approaching, anxious for recognition. She smiles narrowly, walks towards him, a pair of cold hands held out, bequeathing herself to him. He kisses her cheek only faintly suspecting that he is kissing the face of a clock: and this feeling he suppresses as unclean.

Back home. Yes, back home. The aperture of escape closes up muscularly. Herma sits at the table, trying to compose a letter, an epistle to Daniel. Her bare white arms make an abrupt contrast to the long red curtains and the shiny brown surface of the table. This room is cold as nails. Outside, genuine snow falls. She folds her arms. Her cusp elbows are dainty. Phrases are cropped by the sharp sickles of emotion. Her mind is impoverished, she has no words, as if the alphabet had never been invented. To begin by saying, dearest, my own, would be wrong and would mock the extent of her tenderness. There is this empty space within her between what she feels and the shaping of it to move externally and seize him. She is uncomfortable in the bastille of sentences. But she sighs, pushes her hair out of her eyes, prepares to make a start anyway. Two gold bangles slide up and down her arm as she writes, a cold simplicity. Her busy fingers make ornate capitals: which are no cause to grieve over, which offer no balm. She has them in her vexatious grip, she overpowers them: but she knows that she too is held, that her body is trapped, that she is permitted no room to move, that in this winter world there are no leafy branches under which to take cover. Yet she goes on writing. She thinks, o brethren. The words take on a totalitarianship of their own, runing everywhere, across the table, around the room, knocking the vases over, making for the door. They have an exhausting effect on her. She wants, wants. . . . To explain herself to him absolutely, down to the last pound of flesh. Daniel. After the deluge, goodbye. I was afraid to say it. This goodbye. And yet I must. I realize the longer I maintain this sullen companionship of eyes and organs the more painful it will be: to begin: to end. How cruel though. When the past is recalled. Remember the day I walked away from you, back across the fields? And you watched, almost senseless, but knowing you had come too close to all of us ever to be safe again? Safe or free? You became attached to an intoxicant. Like all of us. Once I made notes describing events, when and where and how. Inscribing them on random sheets of paper. I can't understand them. Not any more. The relentless rhetorical commentary is null and void. Time has jettisoned meaning, the events are just history to me now and emotions glittery and stupid as sequins. Perhaps you'll accept this necessity of mine for saying so, on its own terms. Perhaps by writing this letter I'll make an enduring summary. But will you, half-way through it, stop reading and turn away with so much more than pain, turn away to your mirror crying out for the sake of these profane words and your own silence? O doubtless. Daniel, I'm sorry I told you the only true terrible thing I know. I'm sorry this letter is so evil and tense, I feel that it threatens to break away from me, to let fly, leaving the anticipation of flight behind it, tasting like celery. Now in the one heart we nearly shared a more casual thinner blood flows. Yet how can I staunch the heart's slobbering flood? I can still see how we might have lived, happy fools running side by side, laughing and never speaking the truth. Love sounded us out but our skulls were like stone. Our empty eyesockets scoured every horizon but all we saw were shrouds flapping in the wind. We turned summer into a crocodile and let it devour us alive. I shout something obscene in this empty house. And that is all. My head seems to be going off bang. I confess, I confess to whatever it is my mouth trumpets. How callous it all is. I'm barren and sad and devastated by time. Don't come near me. You promise? Don't come near me. It would set me on fire and I don't know how to quench or damp down despair or desire. Poor soul, me. Too weak to fight. Not able to slash out a path through this corny secular sabbath. Dogmas, boundaries, bodies, their sudden coldness: instead of these distortions you must stay away from us all and you must try to live a life: be brave, be obedient, be silent, be a good soldier. I have no rank. All I can do is to define us as two who clashed. I have no love to give you. Did you think when I came to see you that I did? No. I just had the desire to touch all enemies know. Blame doesn't exist. Not for us. We all have our problems. We all carry our burdens, our backs bent and crippled by them. We all cry or fawn or command. According to circumstances. And at the end there is just the arrogance of a message no one took and no one received. Herma reads the letter twice. She folds it. She goes and stands by the casement. The snow has stopped. The aerial stillness is primal. She holds the letter in her hand. She tears it to pieces. It was misleading and honest. Not for Daniel. She will not write. Perhaps by retreating into the pyriform world of the self she can be saved. She has a kind of cold dedication to herself which enables her to accept this pain. She will not write. She will send him a christmas card, a religious card, Madonna and babe. When infants die . . . Yes. A christmas card. After all, hadn't he once said, Herma, yours is such a yearning mouth. The truth. He'd think of her silence as a yearning, he would realize what she is striving for, that moment of illumination which Rachel had stolen from her. That moment which is also a life. But would he also suspect that her suffering creates an oasis in her head? She fingers her medallion thoughtfully. How strong is the innocent lamb: can she mulct him of a heart? O yes. She blisters with clever frustration. She'd like to be complimented on this even though praise would be the act of a huckster, one seeking gain. Momentum builds up. She sets fire to the letter. The ashes are grey. Herma knows the fears and fate of all whose idea of perfection is too effusive. But almost gaily she goes out into the silent garden of snow. Her eye discovers winter: she respects the clean break its air makes with the horizon, colour all cut sharply away: unlike the crooked indentations of her heart. She admires the discipline: so the clearness of sky is regarded by sailors. She walks across the lawn, snow clicking under her feet. She has no coat. She shivers. The wind begins to blow, a dark veil. Summer means more to her than the loss of a landscape once strewn over with gold and now stained and blotched with the grey wind. She shivers again and thinks, me, an ice maiden! And laughs out loud. And the cold crazy sound appals her. Her face goes hard and imaginary. She tugs at the winter jasmine and takes the branches back into the house to arrange in vases. Winter flowers. So bright a yellow. She sits down to admire them. The table is shiny as a mirror. She is unhappy. Once I was an authentic if lackadaisical girl. Now I acknowledge a cold desperate temperament where the shadows of the dead achieve too substantial a ghost life. Suppose the child had an ambition to become an infantryman? Or suppose he had turned out to be just an absurd imitator of his father. Then he would have been no loss. But what if he had been a herald, a giver of knowledge. No no. Dreams dreams and makebelieve. I know what he would have been. And monsters deserve extinction. She stands up with her hand over her mouth, she staggers and runs to the door: opening it, she faces the darkening evening sky: she almost cries out as she watches the ambergris light being struck to the ground where it lies as precisely as the fluting on a classical pillar. Somewhat angrily, somewhat foolishly, she turns and goes back into the house, the dias of silence. These are the worst times, when she thinks of her dead son and time just hangs around her uselessly in a pestilent vapour. Death. Its oaken ship needs no anchor to keep it steady. Its benefits otherwise are few though: it gives no rewards. I do not ask for much. Only forgiveness. She removes her shoes. She takes the flowers out of the vases and carries them upstairs. Her bare feet nuzzle the carpet. There is no tyranny greater than that of the self. It is immense as a massacred sun. Last night Herma dreamt she saw a spoonbill use its beak to castrate a man whose face, although strange because of its contortions, she recognized as Tomas in disguise. In this dream she had been perplexed but cool and contemplative as she listened to the forlorn high voice call out, the mortified body enduring a kind of colic. But on waking, an hour before dawn, to a world black as coal, she felt hot as a maiden stitched to a tapestry. She stands still. She looks down in surprise. Her arms are full of flowers. Remember, you and he picked them this afternoon. Their languorous stems wave in her arms. As she goes on upstairs she drops them, one after the other, their wet stems and the leaves smudging her, she just dumps them on the stairs anyway, she just wants to get rid of them: when she looks back down the stairs the carpet resembles a broken and invaded flowerbed. She just drops them. Then she goes into the bedroom. With empty arms. She moves in a dry indian summer of the brain. She walks to the window. And through the window she sees this year and all the preceding years where coffins wriggle like worms, where darkness is, the litter of darkness. Her hands touch her breasts as if they were still full of fresh milk. She sees a family tree dead at its roots and all confirmations broken. She touches her medallion. The horses neigh and rut. Solid glass her hands, two blocks of solid glass. Trials are a rarity. She cannot demand release or bail. Time supersedes her. There is a need for penitence that she has always recoiled from. She sees a replica of transgression, the crimes of killing and living. Her glass hands rest on the glass window. She waits for her hands to break into fragments which will never be trained to the reins, that will refuse briefly but irrevocably. There is a lack of succession, no new year: only stylish obituaries await her, only the impartial cemeteries. The loaded evening has a musty occult crack-pot scent. She closes her eyes. Angels fold their wings and turn away. Anything done blindly will be fatal in execution. A surfeit of bloom, a fatal surfeit. The decline of empires. Plunder of soil. And soul. Animal bodies, consumptive through the ages. Our broken divinity. Servile creature, you must be totally and brutally banished, to a formal and pious exile. A pilgrim's impeccable journey! That's what you always wanted. Did I? Was it this I wanted? The dove wanders and dies on the wing. Anarchic language stunts the hymn. O I can't carry my bereaved infamy any longer. O no. And forgive? No. The begetter, the begotten: never consoled, never healed, never forgiven. The whirlwind of ice equivocates but the temperature cannot escape. Siren song. Her violent stretch of ascendancy.

She leans forward. She stands at the edge of a long hidden long restrained desire. Her hands bless. And no more. O outlaw. She falls and feels the real and sharp and broken glass rip and gash her: a yoke of glass tears her mouth with no lips to remonstrate. She falls forward, her ignorant torn face brushed with red tears. She falls forward into the hedges of snow. The air meets her, the stony ground rushes up at her, cold waters of death flow from a broken dam: she falls on to a shore of salt and ice and her body is carried far out to sea. She sustains fatal injuries. She lies there supreme and sacerdotal. She has warded off perfection. She has entered an ultimate clime, a region where the hunter and hunted are extinct.

Eventually he slept. But the world revolved and brought yet another morning. Like a machine. Tomas was awake before dawn. A bare room appeared, a finished charade, whose emptiness was as mocking as the echo of too capacious a humour, a cold laugh ringing bitterly out in this stillness. So he went out to look for her in all the usual hiding places, the garden of dew, the rose bushes, the windy courtyard, the calm formal shoreline of the objective fields, the illiterate lawn. But he could not find Herma. People had come and taken her body away. Strangers. They have buried her body in a tomb. Whither hast vanished Beloved and hast left me full of woe? Like the saint he cried out. The complicated ovality of the landscape frightened him. He stood on the lawn and sobbed, angered both by his sleeping and his waking, incensed at his failure to inhabit the short fleeting image of her dream. Now, too late, much too late, he acknowledged his responsibility and recognized himself as the too willing partner watching the eager fighters. He admitted it: years of roaming with the eyes shut, selfishness and sloth had caused him to be the soul-mate of destruction. Yes, he heard her voice, Herma's voice sighing, a brazen age, the true voice, the warning wailing voice hidden between the wind and its veering: and he ran across the lawn, past the lifeless rosebushes, across the fields and through the blind branches of the trees, not stopping until the immaculate sky overtook him. But no. The flight, the sacrifice was not real. He had neither the courage nor the strength. In the real world he still stood on the lawn: then turned on his own shadow. But no one was standing there, behind him. Not wife, nor son. Inside the house, at three in the afternoon, he stares in a mirror. He sees the ceremony. He and Rachel following. Private passion hits out at public display. O the carrying forth of the body, the hearse, the conveyance of nothing but flesh in the hollow box, the hollow mourners' hands frozen to wedges: the procession moving across a tabinet sea of air, knowing full well that dead love could not sail it, not such transporting air. All emotion routed and overthrown by that day. And now his inanimate heart like an empty house, stripped of decoration, without ornamentation. His bones endure their burden as a realm. Will stagnate all winter. Forever. Permanent tenancy. Daniel had not come to the funeral. He sent a wreath of exotic african violets. But he could not bring himself to attend any more than he could have read expired letters from another dead girl propped at a window. He did not want to see the act of interment. The action of the knight is peculiar and not easy to comprehend. But when the decade ends he will shoot himself. Peace will come from the muzzle of a gun. Rachel's womb knows no fertility, her blood serves to irrigate nothing, her face is pale, expressing the harm and misfortune which touches all faces at some time or other. She looks out of the window at a row of trees, bare, black, representing nature without hope of spring.

> Ever since Herma's death there is nothing for me to measure up
> against

Rachel tells him in a strenuous voice, folding the last of her sister's clothes, which are to be sent away. Tomas nods all the time muttering

> yes yes yes yes yes yes yes yes yes yes yes yes yes yes yes . . . and look Tom although it might seem selfish and cruel of me to speak as if it were more my loss than yours surely you must see how hard it is for me. . . .

Her voice breaks, jarrs, wails.

> . . . so hard. Look, like you, I divide my life in two: before, when Herma was alive: and now, the aftermath.

Yes but Rachel

he says queasily (the way she had been sprawled out, he'd almost driven over her, the brakes had been one long sound of polecats)

you were always so far away from one another, you were never close, you two, you were unlike old friends, your lives took different routes. There was no love. You were both constrained and embarrassed in one another's company. When we were all together in this house the authority you both tried to exercise over one another made you both overcast and angry. I avoided you both, you were so involved in antipathy. There is a difference in the relationships, Rachel.

Her fore-runner, her predecessor, her successor, her uterine accuser and judge, says

Yes . . . but I needed that rasping in my life, I could only move when it was she I moved away from or towards. Now . . . now I have no direction, every day it is the same blankness I face.

His fingers are hot, need snuffing like candles.

Yes I know. Life becomes a series of divertissements.

Yes.

The conversation is like a star-chamber. She speaks very quietly, he can only just hear her. But the words fill the room bloodily. There is even the smell of blood. Her lips are clumsy.

I've been wondering who must take the blame for her death, you, me, Daniel? Or whether we should take the responsibility collectively. I think we are all to blame. We all drew her asunder from herself. Part of her, I think, was very ordinary: it ate, drank, talked, argued, copulated, signed cheques, spoke to grocers and doctors, prayed, cried. . . But she lived on the inside as well: far more than most people, Herma had an internal existence she was trying to hold on to: yet which she simultaneously questioned and repressed. I think we all strained her beyond the point where she could control this inner world. Especially after the death of the child, she was vulnerable and open to invasion. We divested her of her ability to protect herself. In order to discover the truth about herself she had to engage in death. Her stock-in-trade as a person was exhausted. There was nothing else for her to do.

Rachel sits on the bed, distantly menaced by sleeping sickness. No Herma the place you've gone to you'll never return from I'll never see you again.

Her head is bent, she is watching the floor, she travels an icy vocabulary:

So Herma eliminated her outer limits.

She picks up the medallion and twists it around her fingers.

She had a kind of divinatory power. That is what took her. I believe we should have left Herma alone. All of us. Left her alone as we do the mad who keep reciting a little verse over and over again. We should have left her alone with her natural world, instead of pretending there was something else, something special, she had to search out and prove.

O Rachel how could I have left her alone?

he asks guilty. The flame burns but will not illuminate.

How could I? I was her lover, her husband, we had a child for a few days. How can you suggest I should have left her alone? Didn't she need love, a touch?

Without noticing it, Tomas pleads. He is under continuous fire. I don't want to be foiled at a time like this. But Rachel shakes her head and says, her voice a soft liar, telling a fable to comfort or frighten (it depends upon the century) temperamental children before the long speechlessness of the night

No no. Herma could have survived without us. It was we who needed to rise with her for a second, rise into the sunlight: and then we dragged her back down with us into our poisonous calcined atmosphere where we could breathe and she couldn't.

Noises and movements in the crepuscular house. The whole place is wrinkled, ghostly and fragile. As if the house were made of paper: walls ceiling roof floors furniture: all paper.

But what else could we do? What other way of living was there?

Rachel stares at their enterprising stilled shadows on the floor. The six weeks dead lie quiet now but when the photograph by the bed smiles there is no sun. It is annulled. It has no offspring for incubation.

Leave it

she says, skilfully cutting short their communion, feeling patient, cynical, victorious: but already dogged by a macabre imaginative culpable heartbeat. Time shifting its weight will bring her no forgetfulness.

Are you hungry?

she asks him, lighting a cigarette, looking at herself in the mirror, appraising that reflection, proud of her regimental eyelids and sherry lips, fascinated by her houri face, its georgette majesty.

WAILING MONKEY EMBRACING A TREE

For Peter

My thanks are due to The Arts Council of Great Britain for financial assistance which enabled me to complete this novel. I also wish to thank the novelist Sylvia Bruce for reading the manuscript of this book, and for making many valuable suggestions.

ANCESTRESS

Almost every cold noon she finds herself standing before this enraged ocean, her lips wind-chapped and sore, her hands lacking authority: as if brought here not of her own volition but drawn by the ischiatic tide. All my life, she thinks, I have been waiting like this, standing at the brink of some shore. What solemn vista am I demanding? Am I waiting for a withdrawn spectre wearing offal gauntlets? A ghost at whom I will stare curiously and then suddenly embrace, without flinching? She shivers, realizing she cannot claim infallibility. I wonder what the horizon foreshadows . . . Will I see the faces of uninvited vermin one night? Ever since Matthew left her, after an artificially prolonged summer, she has undergone the drudgery of pain. She knows the pillory of alienation by heart. This new year promises her nothing, she who is aching for a revolutionary moment so long expected that anticipation has wrung all reality from the prospect. Yet she waits, spellbound by herself, awaiting the rescuer.

The rescuer who, the antiseptic rescuer . . .

And where is Matthew? Who holds him now?

Waves crash against the repentant breakwater. So, turning her back on the grey stereophonic sea, this girl looks across open country, sensing the invalidity of all skies. The war-memorial emphasizes her own inability to give to this landscape any more significance than that of a skull left behind by mummers, the result of a fake death warrant. There is a threefold tension in her: there is the Zouave woman she pretends to be, there is the Salome creature she longs to become, and lastly, the aimless girl she is. She lives her life in instalments. Time and again she turns imploringly to the sea, to the meridians of ice. I washed in fresh water at New Year's Eve. But there is no help for me. And like that doomed wandering woman who laughed at a christ she walks away, apprehensive, wistful. She thinks angrily of Luke: and all at once her body takes on a regardant pose. For his sake, his sake. Yes, but her eyelids are heavy with equivocations and Elinda is drowsy, tired of these ursine depths, requiring a long dreamless sleep to erase the recollection of the interloper.

COMPLINE

What is your secret then? he asks almost humorously, is it that you are a natural child or a thief or are the fingers of your hands webbed like the girl in that strange book I told you to read? She does not look at him. No, Elinda says, clinging to the boughs of the tree, no, it is none of those things. She touches the little gold crucifix strung around her neck but is not apprenticed to any master. He asks her no more questions but studies her chamfered body, no longer laughing.

INCURABLE MORNING

Thinking of sharp-set tragedies, Elinda stands by the window and looks out at the strangeness of a dying world. Four months ago, this girl, whose face has the uncertain pensive expression of an outcast, married Luke Beckx. Elinda and Luke are both substitutes. Both are seeking supine consolation upon a randomly chosen breast. One brutal day in the arch of winter, Elinda combed out her long modest hair and married Luke. They made their responses in quiet severe voices, voices which were the envy of the strong and the weak. Now, gauche and nervy, she fidgets with her unkempt hair. Already there are some evenings when he turns away from her, swearing. And then her body becomes unnaturally sensitive and she touches his arm questioningly. Too often their limbs clash and then she listens for the undercurrent of another voice. Elinda feels that instead of marrying she has merely assumed an alias. Their nights are a fruition of sweat. Luke considers their two opposing natures and begins to fear the future. Frequently, long silences divide them, like terrible rumours they are unable to deny. An atmosphere of constraint hangs around them. Elinda, obsessed by her stellar memories, is conscious of an unevadable peril. Because of this there is often a redemptive light in her eyes. But she does not suspect the seasons of columbic weather when their antagonisms will leap into actuality. When, night and day, she will long for a hallowed life. When she will squeal, Jesu, Jesu . . .

VERTEBRATES

The husband and his wife stroll hand in hand. Are they invalids? They have no appointments to break. Both sun and moon are visible in the early sky. The sun is violent. But the moon is pale and legendary, a weakling, the result of genetic experiments. Luke glances at sea and sky and body-snatcher wife. He longs for a respite from hallucinatory emotions. He thinks of the scrofulous Gideon bible lying unopened on the table. He thinks of a young man dying from an addiction to heroin. He remembers cremations performed on the edge of town. When he speaks, his lips are stiff, the words elephantine. Elinda's elfin gestures disgust him now, reminding him of sleepless reflections in a mirror. If he realizes that the framework of the soul is unmoved by the petitions of broken bones he does not reveal this knowledge. He stares into distances, hearing volleys. He wishes he could fling himself out of this thyroid marriage. And yet, her cloistral hands, her surly breasts . . . Elinda glances at him and thinks, Luke and I are like those hunters who awaken under the observation of a kaffir and know our blood is taken. There are shadows of sombre leopards at her side and the seashore is a sub-lunar desolation. Remote wars, mirage deaths, annulment of betrothals: these grieve Elinda. And again she remembers Matthew's renouncing words: *The drift of darkness hides the truth, Elinda. We are finished. Our brave brash day has ended.* The sea still echoes these words of farewell, mocking all their ebony associations. She thinks of a girl who never really laughed. Aberrant shadow birds swoop from branch to branch. Elinda lives in submission to an army of clocks. Luke's silence fatigues her. We have our first summer before us, with its jigsaws and juntas of flowers. But I will not forget Matthew's raptorial face, nor the military arrangements of his mind. Luke's voice is lost amid the sound of the banal sea. This serious girl raises her voice of organdie, unforgiving as a mastoid madonna.

THE SEACOCK

Luke and Elinda, this thorny near-frenzied couple, continue to conduct their lives at a great distance from the splintery stars. In their house by the sea they exist with all the bright useless energy of a circus. Their snowstorm faces are anonymous as those abandoned ones who stare for hours out of barred windows. Now their language of siege solidifies. They communicate with increasing difficulty from their galactic positions. Alba roses wilt in untidy vases. For Elinda, euthanasias are out of the question. Tonight I will be gentle and there will be about me an atmosphere of dream and mistiness. I will become stamped ineradicably upon Luke's memory. Whatever the future does to us, he'll never forget me or be free of me. I will become as desired as a fortune-teller. We must prove to each other that we are not misfits, freaks or strangers. Luke's mouth is smiling coldly. Elinda sees flyspecks on the windowsill. The legacy of locked doors will eventually be theirs. Clamped in an explosive situation, they are trapped in lives of imposture. Why, they hardly dare move. He suspects her of conspiracies and of secret meetings with a mortician. Then he checks himself, subdued by his own wildness. When they confront each other in the bedroom their eyes are sad and their mouths gape, sensual and unsentimental. Luke! cries Elinda, weeping, advocating obituaries, you're wrong, you're wrong . . . We cannot live like this. It is turning us both to stone. He rebukes her venomously. Elinda, have I denied you anything? Her face is swollen, she accuses him of bigotry. When he tries to touch her, she wrests herself away, eking out her passion. But I am not free, she declares. Now the silence is infected. He breaks into it by laughing dispraisingly. Free, he sneers, thinking of knucklebones, who is free, Elinda? No one is free. Free! Now she looks at him differently, with an arduous expression. Her voice is husky. It is useless to hope for freedom from the ice, then? He smiles coarsely, preparing to enslave her. Yes, Elinda, useless. No one will permit it. We will all say no. Take care, Elinda. Not even your dreams, in which you become an Irish princess or a hermaphrodite hero, will tolerate your demands very much longer. And that silence returns. Before their marriage, these quarrels were followed by swift reconciliations, body touching body, arabesques of flesh. But now they turn away, not attempting to caress, moving into darkness with an elated obstinacy. He stands over her whilst she lies buried in mundane midnight sleep. And he thinks guilefully, if only I dared tear you limb from limb. But I am not destined to become a poet with bloody hands. Even in her sleep, Elinda turns away from him, sighing, mumbling stop-press words. He prays to a timeless succession of ghosts. And clutches the darkness in his gelignite fingers.

BRINE BATH

There is something deceitful about this July afternoon. Something that slouches beside them, smelling of brimstone. They know this as they trudge through the shadowy woodland, climbing upwards, astronomical miles from Sparta. What is it from which they seek to escape? Is it only each other? She moves amid pyrrhic flowers and possesses a corrosive melancholy, reminiscent of the moon and of the hunt. Sunlight flickers between the branches, branding the forehead of this tense man, the throat of this woman. Now, under the leaves, it is time for the lewd outstretching of his arm. But she resents his surgical probing of her body. She shrinks away, not caring if he does interpret this as yet another proof of her infidelity. He sees in her action all the emotional confusion of a revolutionary. Elinda examines a servile wild flower and will not answer his questions. The sea, ancient and uncouth, enters their future. She mocks him with her diffident sexuality. Nothing is wrong, Luke, she murmurs. And is silent again, thinking, why, the shifting headstrong light that falls through these entangled branches comprehends my troubles more accurately than I. I look at myself and say, who is that strange listless creature, who is she? Wearing such a prejudicial frown, wringing such cowardly hands? Her mouth is crammed with complaints. But sometimes I think I'd like to have a child, she tells him, betraying no one. Her humid words surprise her. So it is this request I have been memorizing for weeks, she realizes. It is this desire which is the reason for my bondage. Otherwise I fear damnation. Now Luke doubts her suitability, the forgetfulness of her hand. He holds her wrist roughly. He considers the deterioration of her breasts. I always saw Elinda as a woman apart from apparitions of pregnancy, not even capable of bearing a child, immersed in herself, cabined amid recessional thoughts. He looks at her, frowning at fecundity. Not yet, he says shortly and walks across the beach, into the sea, mastering the waves. Elinda remains in the shadow of the cliff. My life is the game of some seraph chieftain. Why can't I conclude it? She looks up at the loser's sky and shivers. She is submissive to sun and serpent. Horizons mumble Douay prophecies. A baronial fatality flows through her veins. Her head aches from injustice. She shudders, thinking of a future drowning, an act to which her consent will be demanded. She sits very still, contemplating the possibility of his abdication. If only my memories were unsullied by the altercations of national flags . . . I cannot see who is holding the spray of flowers. Who? Dripping wet, Luke takes her by the shoulders and tells her harshly to keep her mind off the natal emptiness of her life. He tells Elinda he will keep her from the night. She opens her eyes. His head is a skull lighted from within. His anger draws all resistence from her. The touch, of his farrier hands burns her skin. She nods, allowing him to frighten her, and accepts his embrace. Even though he is not the one I wish to have, to see and hold, even though a longing for some other suitor preserves me when he spurts into me, I'll stay with him. Because then even if all other fulfilment is denied me, I will not be completely alone or jewel-less, secluded in my own recumbency. Assenting, body plastered against body in the sand, they become gentle with each other, temporarily escaping from belligerence: so that finally they can leave the sea, forsaking its notions of fornication. But their reprieve is to be short-lived. For it possesses that insouciant beauty full of a crazy larceny which endures little more than a few hours.

HECATOMB

Light wastes away, swooning. Evening. Unstilled cravings return. In a corner of the formal forbidding lounge stands a life-size statue of a naked slave girl. Elinda looks into the cruel face, fascinated by this other girl. Matthew never writes, not even dying letters. My skintissue memories peel and rot. Elinda, the archivist of ivory fish, stares at Matthew's photograph, trying to evade their separation. Always, every anschluss hour, before all else, it is the memory of Matthew which she cannot dismiss, the image of Matthew in the marina morning, walking slowly towards her. Elinda bites her nails. Yes, Matthew, you still exercise a surveillance over me. Why am I denied your slanting eyes, your braying sex, your trucial hair? When I committed hostilities against you, I did not realize it was my own self I ravaged. That the blood in my veins would seem to cool, the very denial of love present here within me, indisputable proof of an apostasy. She hears Luke calling to her. When he enters the room, she faces him without lenience, concealing her alarm behind a depilatory stateliness. Luke has been planning voyages and the examination of new landscapes. Perhaps, he says excitedly, we might even visit Africa, you said you longed to go there. Elinda glances down at the ring on the first finger on her right hand, the unfortunate opal in its romany setting. She is silent, her mind slashing messiahs to fragments of ice. She fears journeys. The gaps they make. I have to stay here, in case he returns. Must stay here all the time. Including twilights. She shakes her head carelessly, refusing his offer to take her travelling. She sounds bored. No, no. I want to spend the summer here, Luke. Why should we rush halfway across the world? We are not to be satisfied in such a way, you and I. You have no need to make up for this afternoon. I survived, didn't I? Luke reproaches her. We are too isolated here, Elinda, we must involve ourselves in other relationships. Even his voice falters before her new gaze. I prefer this life we have, she answers fearlessly. And he looks at his wife, the female hero, perceiving a sea-change in her which troubles him so much that he reaches out his arms, pityingly. But only images of razors meet him. The lethal sharpness of her anger is his only reward. She tells him that she senses a menace in their animal bodies. Hoarsely she tells him that their lives are the only lives they deserve. A mute Eve burns between these halt movements of hers, but Elinda does not relent, does not smile at Luke, nor touch his cheek. He goes out of the room slowly, discovering that his wife's anger is real as the ritualistic spindrift. Once I saw a torrid retinue of gypsies, he thinks, the eyes of their children expressing all the disconnected pain of their line. And so with Elinda. He leaves her to the silviculture of her loss. He walks along the shoreline in the rain, afraid of understanding Elinda. He sacrifies his shadow. And for Elinda the evening becomes a medieval allegory, complete with punishments and pilgrims. I'm not strong enough to bear the burden of these tocsins, thinks Elinda, hearing the church bells. How long will Matthew play truant? Or is he forever lost, the dying member of our consortium? Elinda stares in the mirror, furiously dreaming. When she hears Luke return, she runs to him. Listen! she cries desperately, I cannot stop making grievous deductions. I am always cold and I flinch from everything. There, I have told you. Told you all . . . All? Look out at the wild sky. Look. Look at the sea. What am I always watching the waves for? Why do I stare for hours at the pock-marked sky? Because you deny me. Is everyone like me, listening always to the zoom of atomic clocks? No. Does everyone search for the meaning of that golden aura surrounding the head of christ? No. Are we all hoping for some silence to utter a final suzerainty? No. It is only me. Only me, Luke. Because of your cruelty. Moaning, she clings to him. He tries to calm her, to stave off her sudden humility. The summer night darts between them. Tell me then,

Luke, tell me what is it that causes me to fail us both time and again? she implores, exhausted, lost. He mouths words of denial. But she tears at her concubine's hair, she utters postponed threats. Her husband catches hold of her. Now the lovers are grasping flesh and their bizarre bodies melt together, the avatarick heartland slowly infiltrated by genitalia.

SHEWBREAD DREAM

I swallow the preceding year. Now it has gone. I take a sip of blood, a bite of jellied bone. The great hall is shadowy. My incantation speaks of summer but my ankles are frozen. I was running once but I fell. All that is made of gold — coins, hearts, crowns — I threw into the sea. My mask is too tight, it hurts. My cloak germinates a harsh nature. I remain motionless, a scarabaeoid silence upon my shoulders. I sit on an oaken chair. He will come to me. I am waiting now but soon he will come. He gave me his hypotenuse promise. He will come and dislodge me from my pain. He is the truthful one. My necklace is heavy, an iron fish pendant on the chain. I am hungry. He comes to me. He speaks of the accelerations of time, his jeopardy entangling him in old words, chafing me. For he does not smile. I distrust images of the retina and try to touch him. He does not allow it. He damns me but without vigour. His aspect in the mirror is angular, his body juts into the shadows. I do not believe his stories of a remote and cold planet. I refuse, I will remain terrestrial. I reconquer myself. I hear myself telling him that another year must pass before we go before the Blind One. I tell him to return to the Maritimes. There is plunging fire around me but I do not give in. He is silent, savouring his wound. Yes, he is very silent, he stares at his destiny. But no, now he is calling me by my second name. I tremble. I am cold. He approaches me, repeating that name. What can I do? Great numbers of birds cross the sky. He is at my side, his breath on my face, the master of speech and song. In this huge room decorated with papist flowers, crowded with candles, he is sacrificing me and, taken into night, my eyes closed, I become night. The grasp of his hand forces me to accept the mucous journey. I lie on the couch, touching myself, finding my way back. He is standing by the mullioned window, inventing history. Another year? he says. Yes, I say, holding my left breast which burns. The branching of the rib, he begins but breaks off, staring at me intently. Come with me, he says. No, I say, no. You must leave me, just for this one last year. He looks at me still, as if I'm a lunatic. Jesus, he says softly. Then he runs up the flight of steps and leaves me, amongst the brilliant candles. But I know this to be a dream and go on sleeping. I do not flinch.

HERMETICA

Elinda casts an eyeless shadow. The waves move without sponsors. She wears a gold bracelet on her right wrist, a gift from Matthew. The sea, hiding deformities, creeps up to her thighs. Beneath Elinda's feet, pebbles sprout. Yesterday's all-blazing afternoon: and she shrieked, protesting at Luke's sexual coercion. If she laughs nowadays it is with the convulsive mannerisms of a spastic. She listens intently to songs broadcast over the radio, expecting to discover her own sundered life mirrored there. But both the facile chorus and the oratorio fail her. A painless death is what I want, thinks Elinda on this caucasian morning. But I cannot end my life with a stilted suicide. No, I must go on presiding over myself, like a mechanical muse nourished on acid. I used to think: one day I'll awaken, smoothed out by rhythmical sunlight and say, look, I'm complete now, I can close a door on everything ugly and move freely with an elemental grandeur. But now I know such a day will not arrive. I will never be exempt from bewilderment. No. I'll never transform myself into the equivalent of an ancient civilization. Yet that is what I desire. To become Mycenian . . . my hair a conversion of petals.

ANGELS

And so the long fiasco days crackle around Luke and his wife. Inconclusive waves break upon the shore. Dolphins patrol the horizon. The hours are minor rosaries. Twilight lingers, encircling Elinda's ankles. Lawful night falls. And Elinda is afraid of going blind. Of suffering from contagious magic. The arms of a blind germinal god are full of rivers of dark flowers cropped in the rise and fall of night. His abominable decrees haunt me. If he touches me, I will walk coweringly afterwards, all faces and futures hidden from me. I will cease to view rebellions, space voyages and murders. Every night I descend into this androgynous underworld. And now even in the mornings, when I stretch out my bravest hand, I feel forsaken. When I walk in the old-fashioned garden, with Luke at my side, I still feel illegitimate. I am unreal, trying at all times to achieve reality. I ask myself whose image I should worship in the exhaling light of dawn. But I find no answer. She looks at Luke. He is a stranger to me. I know nothing about him. He has spoken only once of the desolate yet comely land where he was born. No more. His silence is a clenched hand. Without mention of mother, father, sister or brother. Bearing this in mind, Elinda approaches him with clean hands and ensnaring questions. Luke, please, be fair. I have told you so much about myself. I have told you about the orphanage. I have related my triumphs and my misfortunes with truthful tears. But I know nothing about you. Tell me, who are you? Sometimes you glow with fire, sometimes ice shapes the flames. But who are you? Everything is hidden in consort shadows. But Luke only laughs. Compassionately? Elinda stands up, her skirt of herbivorous green inheriting motion. Who writes you these letters? She tries to take the letter from him but he forestalls her. Why do you hide them from me? Are they chain letters? Now he frowns and folds the letter up. Elinda, there is nothing to tell. Nothing. He is no longer a casual spectator. He grafts his hands to her shoulders. His eructation words should have warned her. But she persists with her questioning. He shies away from her entreaties, warding her off. The fingers of her clasped hands are cold. She peers at him suspiciously, determined to go on challenging him. Until finally he forbids her to continue, shouting profanations at her like one who was begotten howling. She sweats with nervous laughter. I could die laughing, she gasps. He turns his face away. I already see you seated astride the moon, Elinda. An inarticulate anger economizes her lips. Flushed, she stares out at the jilted evening. Caustic images nag her. Once I could avert pain by prayer. Now not even fasting can help me. So, we enter upon a new phase in our decline. Elinda frets and worries. She is like a wavering goddess of fate bearing a shield of skin but overshadowed by vineyards, already sensing her own oblivion. She knows that any intimacy between herself and Luke is false. They are both luckless. Both are locked within their own private calamities. Whenever she cries out for help, the farness of her own geography displaces her. Her voice is a death-house whisper. No one told me my marriage was morganatic but this is what I suspect. I am prepared for lamentations even though they are insubstantial things, devoid of courage and lacking any hope of telecommunication. Only an adult tenderness transferred from body to body can help us but this becomes more unlikely, more goblinized every night. So Elinda broods on the instability of wedlock and the falsifications of memory: the flowers that will not die. Before her is the centaur's sea. Ships mock her. She watches them sail out of sight and then looks again at Luke. A charred memory recurs to me and I was going to tell you about it. But no, I have reconsidered. For we are beyond the beginnings of night. Our braggart lives leave little time for the rites of confession and absolution. He notes her reformative glance and asks, what is it now? Intending to crush her with his words. Nothing . . . she says. Elinda, tell me. She closes her eyes. Shall I deceive him with trailing words? With ghost-words? I'm just wondering why we're living under false pretences, she says loudly. And looks upon the sea, already regretting these words. Her hands wish to strangle the moon. But she has disowned her fingers. He too is looking at the skin of the moon. And he laughs angrily, a sterile sound. Elinda won't stay in this room with a man she considers to be her pall-bearer. She runs upstairs, leaving the wine drinker to sit alone with his fears of oligarchies and one-armed bandits, hearing the twang of a mandolin. But he thinks gleefully of a dove pent in a barbed wire cage and wanders out into the garden. Meanwhile, Elinda, leaning against the mirror, remembers submerged flesh, her once holy belly. She is degraded by clairvoyant memories. Yet she still longs for the accurate lover smelling of cloves. Whose body she grasped, one hushed summer. Now only Luke lies beside her through the nights. She thinks of shard bones, of moaning and of mistrust, of the lodestar which attracts her to a sensuous death. She studies her own facial bone structure with a thoroughness more normally associated with the study of a specific language or race. I must bring a rigidity into my life and rule over Luke. Yes, I must veil my own thoughts, keeping them subordinate to my own will. For I remember how once before my life split open because I did not keep my point-blank thoughts to myself. I must find the axe to hew this summer in pieces. And I recall Swedenborg's words: *There are also angels who do not live consociated, but separate, house and house: these dwell in the midst of heaven, because they are the best of angels.* O how these words frighten me. Yes, they reverberate through me. Until in a slow motion of mist I watch my hands wrestling death from libidinous snow crystals and libellous clocks.

RITES OF PASSAGE

Moonlight like a hurricane lamp. She is seated by the window, crying over the impact of night, holding a rag doll cradled in her arms. He comes towards her, silently, powerfully. He takes the doll from her amber hands, throwing it on the floor. Then he touches her flesh, without tenderness, embarking upon a first crusade. I won't be your victim, he vows thoughtlessly, not seeing the shadows around them. You must remember that our lives and our souls are joined by the church, Elinda. She is not listening, she is on the brink of darkling seas. Yet she does not move, still sits there musing upon the night, bands empty, her throat an incarnation of pearl. Watching tier, rediscovering her loneliness, his anger dwindles, expires like smoke-runes into the air. Awakening at length from her absorption, Elinda rejects false gods. She speaks to Luke, fawning over him, touching his shadow. Luke, there is something I have not told you about myself, which now I'd like you to know. I feel the time is here and must not be delayed. She stares at the interceptor of sperm, the etiologist of night. Then she looks down at her hands and goes on. A year or so before I met you, I was living with a boy called Matthew. I know, you thought I was alone amid my fluttering mirrors. But it was not so. Yes, Luke, I know. Do not shout. Her admission involves consequences. He curses her. He pushes her aside, afraid of her strength. His tongue is wedged in his mouth. Reactions agitate his bristly body. She steadies herself, one hand on the wall. She still has sagittal words to say. You are shocked, Luke. You wish to denounce me. Or to translate me back into your dreams. But why? Matthew has gone away, he is travelling overseas, he has forgotten me. How did it end? All at once there was a great starless distance between us. Echoing around us. Parching our lips. Dividing us, like a circumcision. We felt the arrows of fear. Luke will not answer her. He once had ideas about life, as something classical: emblems, images, a youth half-naked in a myrtle grove, a myriad meek flowers, leafy diadems, all that nonsense. Now she has broken the spell and he has lost all veneration. Her besmirching voice goes on. It was the end of a legendary journey for Matthew and myself. When he left, after he had gone, I (who had grown fat upon stearic sexual beauty) felt he had taken a piece of the distance with him, leaving me utterly bereft. You know, for ages afterwards I was not conscious of anything around me. I existed merely as a flea-bitten symbol, a dejected memorial to the woman I once might have become. One ante-nuptial evening I thought I heard him calling my name.

Calling . . . I was to triumph after all. But no, it was only the north wind. On another evening I saw myself in my mind's eye, sitting alone at a mediator's table set in the centre of a huge empty room, the head-quarters of courageous fascists. All around me silence shone like the end of all dimensions. Yet simultaneously time stretched out into mendicant infinities. After this, the days wailed past me. Matthew did not return. He did not even write to me. Look, this is a photograph of him. Coldly and gravely, Luke examines the photograph of an alert equestrian boy. Elinda smiles, like one eager to flatter. But she will lock the relic away and hide the key. I slowly realized, Elinda, deprived of lustre now, continues, that my welfare was a matter of indifference to Matthew. No, wait, I haven't told you everything yet. Let me tell you how the affair ended. As autumn approached, I went into town to attend an auction, leaving Matthew here alone. I returned late at night, exhausted, in a curious frame of mind, dissatisfied and envious, of what I could not say . . . desiring that which I could not decipher. I came thriftily into the room. And I found him in bed with a strange girl. When I told them to get out, he defied me. And the girl with the bleached hair only laughed. How she laughed, bergamot laughter. I still hear her. So I ran out, not weeping, unprotesting. You see how weak and passionless my true nature is? I still hear her. I spent the night sleeping rough on the beach. It was cold and the sea guessed everything. Early in the morning, I dragged myself home again, my aching limbs moving stiffly through the mist, like a mountaineer. I found Matthew alone. He was drinking a glass of milk in the kitchen. The radio was blaring. I turned it down. We argued. I tasted saccharine on my tongue. He laughed at me. I could not forgive him. He boasted of the other girl's angel sinews. It was then that I hit him, shouting in a disarrayed voice. And what he said to me then, his last words, I will not repeat to you. That same morning he left, driving my car. And since that leave-taking, I have not set eyes on him. Luke is watching Elinda closely in the ominous room. Sometimes I think I belong in the tomb, she tells him in a bloodsucking voice, yes, I should be lying there . . . The following winter, Luke, I met you, and decided to bury myself in you. But it has not worked, has it? She springs upon him, her fingers claiming him. But he is ice: births and marriages and lies have numbed him. His scapular muteness frightens her. Slowly she lets him go. Adversity reveals their true selves. I spoke to Matthew but he would not answer, not even when I called his name, not even when I crawled, Elinda whispers. His exacting gaze gives her no assurance. All Matthew said was, leave me in peace. He wouldn't say another word . . . Elinda adds brokenly. So Luke reaches out and takes her hand in his own immolating fists, touching her fingers. Her next words pour forth, without cessation. I wake up struggling but there are no real arms holding me from which I must be free. I cry out, let me go. But no one is there. No one of any importance. No one hears. There is only you and the ailing sea breezes and the adherence of midnight to suffering. I think of him constantly now that he is gone. But would I welcome him again? Or is it only the distance separating us which is of significance and Matthew and I just impeding objects that mar its backbone landscape? Do I really want him back, laughing at me? Would it not be better for me if he were dead, breathless, his throat slit open and free? Luke, you must kill him. Kill him. Run my errands of blood. Now she is talking hysterically. Nasal words torn from a sanctuary of pure silence. Emigrant secrets set adrift, launched without a horizon, no sun at which to stare. She recites declarations of shrouds and moans about the miscarrying wombs of her friends. But beneath all her words, time . . . Time convened in lawsuits. Trespassing into lazar harbours. Judgement hours. Precarious days of waiting for the webfooted one. And for Luke time is running out. Angels of marble, mechanical priestesses, cities destroyed overnight: Elinda's gravity equals all these. She tries to tell Luke, do not mistake my absence from fever for a sign of health. But it is too late. When I wash my hair, it is a banzai baptism, she howls. Perhaps he is not listening. I am the juggernaut who destroys, he might have answered. But he does not. He, who is a proud man, looks at her as if she were an odalisque in a public urinal. He strokes her face but rejects her antiphonal distress. Having put aside all explanations for the darkness of the night, afraid of the world's exfoliation, she dashes her bloodless body against him, violently, a haunter of wells. Sensual images motivate them both. Yet by exhaling each other's worn out breath, they are simply passing through another stage in their deterioration: their combatant thighs move towards trial. You must forget this man, Luke advises calmly, just put him out of the reach of your mind. He's just an object of senseless veneration. She lifts her eyes, freeing herself from him with a shaky gesture of repudiation, the slightest movement of her hand sufficing. Now she rejects him. Jesus, no, she cries, this is not what I want. No! Why did I tell you about him? Why did I let you know me? Get away from me. We are at a point opposite zenith. And she backs away from him, her whole being a dilatancy of horror. She runs out of the trembling room. This house is a martyrium. Anchor bells cry: only a killer can save you: now only the strontium sun can heal you.

FIRMAMENTAL FISHERMAN

They breakfast late this Sunday morning. For Elinda the day is a wilderness of swans and shadows. She speaks with her mouth full of greedy molasses. I was thinking of the census in the desert . . . Language of ultra-violet rain. Her husband nods, breaking bread into small fragments. O yes, he replies, dismissing her, looking out at the sterile beach. Elinda notes this primogenial hour for future reference. She frowns immaturely, glancing at the newspaper. Elinda, the ovarian, the bereaved, confiscates the emotions of casual strangers to feed her micro-fantasies. Yet she is capable of mouthing obscenities. She gulps down cold lemon juice, the sharpness of little curses. The night, how it danced with a wishbone. I suppose even coffin-makers take a pride in their work . . . she murmurs. And you can neither live nor die for thinking of it. Her leafless face is white with day. He studies her closely as she copes with her ibis thoughts. He still hopes to understand her turmoil, the meteorology of her blood. But she regards him as a trespasser and falls silent, compressing her lips on the raw words. They finish their meal sullenly. At eleven o'clock, Luke goes to the gymnasium, leaving Elinda alone with the vases of flowers, their quietude and colour. Slipping from their reach, Elinda sun-bathes on the beach, brooding over her humiliations. Sand is echoing obstetric dust. She dreams of plaintive landscapes. At noon, her hand, the hand of a britannia strokes her buttocks. But I must not abscond into riddles, she tells herself, entering the plastic kitchen to prepare her mouth with redness. Elinda sits with her undecided head in her hands, the amino taste of wine lingering in her mouth. The clock strikes, suggesting hands, and she moves to the piano, playing a slow asteroid waltz, unaware of Luke's return, a surveyor. A hawk's head. He lounges in the doorway, watching her, preparing to utilize his strength:

and he thinks, our state has become that of a Berlin, bizonal, tense. We blunder through cypherless days and cobalt nights. When he speaks to her, her hands falter, the octave aborts, his voice penetrating even beyond the inner ear, reaching into that empty area where once her soul dwelt. If only you could sleep calmly beside me, Elinda! I imagine I hear you weeping in the night and am about to comfort you: but then I realize it is only the silence quavering so acutely and, roused from perhaps a sacrificial dream, you look at me with indifference, as if you hoped your sojourn with me were to be brief and soon forgotten. And my hands ache but dare not touch you. It is that depleted silence which out-distances us, is it not, Elinda? But she only shrugs, and resumes her playing of an occidental tune. So Luke licks the breasts of the spying statue. He bullies the stone limbs. Why does Elinda's music accuse me of hypocrisy? Why does she dislike the shadow of my body? I long for a harmony to exist between us. Elinda is the dominant theme of my life, she is the pattern I follow, my only real movements are made in accordance with her wishes. This is why in the afternoon free from angelic hosts, he speaks in nocturnal words. But she is only sighing, studying the japonica flowers out in the garden. Always she is conscious of both their heartbeats. This is why she does not answer him. She is listening to other sounds. The complex arrangement of their lives frightens her, draining her of power: and this is why she does not touch him nor allow him to touch her, but turns her face aside, the scandals of the deaf consuming her. Blood and dirt everywhere. Plateaux of mud. It is only when she catches sight of her segregated face in the centre of the mirror that she forces herself to answer him, sifting the fathoms of her hair through idle fingers. Desire for a new life (cruel as the life of a pterodactyl? Or a hellenistic life composed of three primary colours?) troubles her, like the old absence of a dowry. Yes, Elinda longs for a miraculous future as desperately as a dying person who stares into the darkness beyond the young priest's hand trethbling as he offers the final sacrament. In the past, Luke, she begins, seeing herself as a novice speaking tentatively of a cult that promises to enrich life and vanquish fear, I have been deeply wounded, my strength taken, and so you cannot expect good conduct of me. Yet I will try, I am trying to act according to accepted standards. But even while talking of constancy she rebels against her spiritual emaciation. Her next words are cold as an emanation of ice. Luke is whispering advice to Elinda. He discovers that he must approach the parapet of language but he does not know how. So he lifts her hand to his contemplative lips. Elinda, you've become unreal to me since the winter. You seem to think of your life as some laboratory experiment. Why? Is there a future you alone can visualize? Is there? No. You are deceived by your naked eye, Elinda. Luke makes a beginning but cannot internalize their two slaveries. He knows that Elinda and himself are both susceptible to the myths of fire and all such sudden and resistless calamities. They remain motionless in a three-dimensional silence, their own namesakes, her hand still pressed to his lips. She has the pomp of a prioress. Their inaccessible faces deny nostalgia. There is nothing to worship. There are no dispensations of mercy. Only gestapo disillusionments. And these vandal lovers suffer and there is no compensation. Her inability to endure a marathon is challenged. Elinda sees how her isolation stunts the growth of her affection. Now she must abandon her curdled memories. Can I? She touches Luke's shoulder, unwilling to trace her life back to its earliest origins. His body is pituitary. Rain taps against the windows, asking for succour. But Elinda only laughs, then yawns and turns on the radio. Tunes of a harpsichord censor her lips. Her head aches with half-civilized elaborations of blood. The markings on a water-colour flower no longer satisfy Elinda. Do I possess only portraits of ghosts, their perpendicular hearts plugged with stakes? Luke, she whines, why is there no real answer to my voice? Luke refuses to hear a distress call. He approaches her with the sole aim of satisfying desire. But she drifts away, borne on a tide of gloom, leaving him to pilfer eroticism from anger, the envisioning of moonknives.

THE LIFE OF A CANDLE

He touches her by mistake and is flooded by the odour of flowers enfolding her. He senses her hymeneal thoughts of animal limbs having a perfection of their own, an albumen glow. Smoke hangs over distant hills. A sky without bone-clouds. He assumes the erectile victor's role. She cries out again. Help me, Isabelline! But he only mimics her fear of a locked room with impulsive accuracy. She has a vision of the ballistic angel. He laughs, his penis touching ebony silence. The deceiver eats a peach, licks daylight lips and fades into the dogstar future. Elinda is jealous of a kestrel heiress. Her poverty-stricken landscape is of snow in summer. She stands with her back to the wall like a wraith, clutching at some unattainable zombie ideal. The barbs of a nun's head-dress prick her. O the cobra tension of wanting you, Matthew, it demolishes my courage. Yet she faces Luke bravely enough, the wallflower of a fiesta. Emerald rain drips from the leaves. In our family the youngest son inherits, he says. I am trying to get within the womb itself, she answers. The eye is bleeding. He grabs her, opening up a new route to misunderstanding. Anticipations of sexuality have long since been quenched by repeated epithalamiums. But their two bodies will sprawl on the floor. Her eyes retain his image, like sensitized glass: and she sees that there is a tough heartlessness about him now that promises them both moonless nights naked and alone. She fears that it is this fontal evening she will recall at the instant of her death. I want to find someone who saves, she thinks. Their lancinating bodies sweat. She smells burning strawberries. How many mirrors do I want? And what kind of saviour? What beguilements are awaiting me? Complicated fever pours from the throats of birds . . . And soon she opens her mouth and gives in to the mediumistic flesh, adhering to its commandments. A snake bites her left breast. Remembering the hanging gardens, she receives him amid a diversity of rain colours, her hair flung out into the homeless evening. A promiscuous anchorite is crying: someone who saves . . . A murdered pope, maybe? But she slumps her bones beneath Luke and stops questioning. For the shadow there is no end but venom, guile and coldness. She knows they are both phantoms condemned to haunt middens from now until the end of all adieux.

RESPONSE

Luke looks out of an upper window. In the moonlight he sees a naked woman crouched on the beach. Her short hair is fluffed up like a cockade. She is writing words in the sand, an elegy for the death of conspirators. Ah no, she fades into the bright moon and then into the dark moon, a hallux mirage of the shore: leaving him arrested in the midst of chained thoughts, angry with himself, recalling he must not betray himself. He reconsiders his sperm. Time sucks at his puny cock. Night enters his body, black seeds of plague. He flinches from his own imagination, his blinded arch-enemy. Double stars strike the sky. Navigations are all around him. And he stumbles downstairs, his body's freedom uncertain. He stands enviously in the doorway, marooned on the atoll of exorcisms. He has a slouching shadow. He wonders if the platonic year is a time of suicides, whether the amnesias of the slain are comforting. The prickly stem of the cactus fascinates him. He fingers it with a sensation akin to the subsiding of a madness. Futuristic summer out-foxes him, with its tulipomania. Want a drink? he asks her. No. She taps her empty glass with a long heedless fingernail, still intent on her book but thinking also of the broken necks of simian swans. No, I've just finished this one. He belches thoughtfully. Closing her book she begins to sing a sadly-cadenced song, an elucidatory compline: to which he listens transfixed, losing his grossness. But it is a false amnesty. She soon withdraws into silence again. How to endure her own carbide breasts, how to free her mind from myths and tombs and flocks of turbaned whores? And on this evening of stale heat the sea comments farcically on her difficulties. It's so hot . . . she murmurs, dust and ashes clogging her skull. I am vitrified by this summer. Gazing at her, Luke sees two images: one is of a chaste expeditionary woman, the second is of a magdalen swaddled in black veils. Wary of retaliations, he does not speak. Knowledge of tribulation exists in her ectoplasmic heart. She lolls discontentedly in a chair. Her body awaits bruising. Suddenly she rushes about the room, like a slum dancer. Now she is singing unpredictable adagios. Glass-blown, she parades before him, twirling her skirt with its pattern of goitrous moons and declaiming, my sexy skin is silken but I crave more than this! For ours is not a safe world! Then she gives out a carcinogenic moan and hurls her glass against the wall, where it shatters, lustral splinters falling into another universe. This offends him more than the condemnation of a false witness. He looks with heartfelt abhorrence upon this woman who is drunk with despair. And as his gaze casts a massacred shadow upon her, he thinks *and lured me towards sweet Death* . . . Like scripture, Elinda sinks to the floor, bowing before her own sharp and bloody work. But he raises her to her feet, momentarily achieving an unrivalled glory. And for an instant it is her secluded mirror image he views. Yet only for an instant. Then she touches him, thriftlessly. A passage to sin. The contaminated waters. And once again he sees her potential insanity, the venusian flash of colour on her cheeks. So even now he does not recognize the biblical woman quivering before him. You used not to be so unhappy, he says gently, helping her to her chair, regardless of his irritable heart. She looks up at him, vehemently. No, she answers in a crabbed manner, but perhaps it is only recently that the time has come for me to exhibit my sadness publicly, to adopt the stance of one duped and defrauded. Her eyes glow with the promiscuity of an inner captivity. He guesses the future will not rehabilitate her. Such sesame bones are in her body. I have no secrets, he says falteringly. But she only gazes savagely at him, dreaming of an army's fealty. The night distracts him. Outdoor requiems deafen him. He draws the curtains against the liminal darkness. The tips of her breasts are illegally sore. No? she queries, proud of her unruliness and of the way her rings gleam on her nicotine fingers. Silence resumes, drenching Luke and Elinda. Tomorrow, he thinks, I will give my lecture on the vanquishment of a Kaiser, and, as I speak, Elinda will fade, lose all importance and her strength will be outgrown by my circumsolar speech, only a dark patch left in my mind. And she thinks, O Luke, even if, for my sake, you endured all the torments, it could not make me love you, not now. How is it that all through one long night we can hold each other, hold and adore . . . and yet next morning not care if our lover lives or dies? She listens to the sound of the real sea as it escapes towards the horizon. Its alliance with the moon annoys her. She desires no affinities, she fears that field of combat. He looks outside again, disturbed by night yet needing to be within it. Why won't you come out swimming, Elinda? It's hot tonight. The water will be cool and produce echoes. His voice is determined to go on speaking. She fumbles for a cigarette and lights it with unchaperoned hands. Can't you see your questions are crushing me? Yes, her eyes are wide open and she is angry at the fetters she sees, whose implacability she is now discovering. Yes, I'm shackled. I'm sullied. A fatigue like that which follows striation dries her and her mouth. But she only shrugs. Is silent in the twofold room. He accuses her of wilfulness, telling her of his own cowled ghosts and gestations. But she still refuses. No. I won't venture out, Luke. The night is full of assaults. It is a caricaturist's land. I might burst into whelping cries. Find myself back in that first garden. She is offhand, smoking a french cigarette, admiring the gold bracelet Matthew gave her, his birthday gift. Luke does not see the psychic murkiness surrounding her. This is a moment etched with the pain of salic centuries. Elinda is longing for widowhood. She sees that, for Luke, her identity has fallen into arrears, even though his fire-opal blazes on her finger. Why do you say these crazy things? he asks his alkalescent wife. She bites her thumbnail. Let's say my reasons are my own, Luke. Now, will you have us go on talking till cock-crow? I'm tired. Yes, she is weary. Her imprisoned skin burns. She thinks of the shore where the other dead wait. No, I am through with ancient undead lives. With trees and their crimson flowers. I will toy with them no longer. I am finished with the corrupt juries, a thousand lovers fruitful with gonorrhoeas, the sound of steel keys turning in mormon locks. I am through with frozen theologies and impassioned demagogues. I want nothing more to do with them. For Christ's sake, how many lives am I living? I will invade no more birdcatcher eyelids. Her laughter is shrill and unscheduled. There is a stampede of proverbs in his head. He yanks her up by the shoulders and shakes her until she cries out fearfully, no, stop, fool, for I might die. He releases her, saying a farewell with obscene words. Panting, her hand pressed to her side, she gasps, the texture of this life, why can we not capture it, Luke, why does it evade us? He is thinking of a bridal day. I don't know, he says simply. Cowed by her palmistry words, he yields to her silence. They are sweating, these two, saving no one, compliant to no duty. But mortally wounded. There is somehow an absence of light in this room even though the lamp blazes garishly. I am trapped in self-strife, she mutters, I am empty, empty, void of meaning, having a keel-less breastbone. She is reciting her encyclical to the soldier (a distortionist of lands) who does not believe she exists. Escorial doves half-heard one bloodless dawn . . . Again their bodies are stilted, two enemies holding a parley whilst active hostilities are suspended to celebrate the lunar new year. I looked at the open sea through my closed lids and that damn pig ocean has marked me for life, thinks Elinda. Luke moves around the room slowly, touching the walls, a peregrination without meaning. She asks him to pick up the newspapers he scattered on the floor. Now she is houseproud. But he does not seem to hear her. Under stress, feet hoofed, he is compelled to encircle this room, looking for more penalties. Words recoil into her throat. An informer's silence flows from her to Luke. Neither of them is lulled. Never again will he see her as part of a dynamic dream. She observes her incurable husband unemotionally even though he is hemmed in and menaced by all the dangers of gun cotton. The night becomes more crazy. You do not seem now to be that same linear girl I first knew . . . he tells her sadly, his accusation searing into her repose. She gains no remission from him. For I loved your calmness, once you had the dormant grace of sacraments: but now, Elinda, when you behave wildly I have no excuse for you, not in heaven nor on the earth. And he shrugs, his life backsliding. I'm sorry, she says humbly, approaching him with all her damaged slenderness. But he turns away from her, staring into that endless mirror, hardly recognizing his own face. Neither am I the same person, he murmurs. I know, Elinda whispers. Mosquitoes are present at this undoing of a bond. White sericeous flames touch her. Her eyes meet his in the mirror, feigning nothing now, neither honesty nor purity nor courage. If, she goes on cautiously, touching his hand, using no protective figures of speech, we were to have a child, perhaps we would recover our lost godhead? But now he is a descendant of chastity. He hates foetal atmospherics. No, Elinda, no! You can't fool me. You? You aren't fit to have any man's child, let alone mine. Solstitial guns and stellar bullets . . . When she shrieks out her flashflood pain, he raises his hand to strike her. But he is not brave enough yet. She waits in vain for the beautiful blow to fall. His disguise, that of a husband, is quickly resumed. He leaves her to her quicksands. Alone and resourceless. For a while she touches her appetitive sex. Then she weeps. She has undergone a cabbalistic ordeal. Is there ever to be an end to it, this watchfulness between us? Will my head always say, he too is the possessor of a secret? Will I always suffer depressions, backache and nausea? *Ever an end, ever an end, whispers the ensanguined sea.* Will night always gobble up my days? It is the toxin time between our copulations that denies us the union beyond flesh which would make us equal to an acceptance of deaths. Crippled yet hand in hand, Luke and I are approaching an unapproachable glebe. Elinda thinks enviously of the mad reapers rejoicing in the field, those who believe . . . But I hear only a series of laments, elegies, threnodies. Even Matthew's name is lost amid recurving wings of smoke. Air fire water bread wine: all conspire to my downfall. Is my name really Ultima? I'm tired out, dead beat. Who will guard me from guillotines and rescue me from racks? What paraplegic guitarist can I depend upon? Who waits amid the flowers that grow in moist places?

OBSERVATION SLIT

Exodus hours pass, turning Elinda into a lonely freemartin. Sheltered by black trees, strangers of celestial substance come to a savage crisis. Darkness conceals Elinda's face, releasing her from the custody of burning-bush lamps. Elinda stands in primitive nakedness, nubile yet prey to excerebrations. She hears another ammunition train trundle inland. A cigarette between her fingers, she remembers the gateway, her own dissevered nudity. Perhaps she is remorseful. Regretting the dehydration of tears. But her words are brave, a geometrician's defence. I must remember my obligations to myself, Luke, and bear the burden of the flesh. Plucking adobe words from the night, she lives by memory alone. Her womb inhales echoes. Miles away, a thorn lizard is dry as a bone. Elinda worships a manchu god. Is the course of life to be determined by the haphazard fall of a tossed coin? asks Luke, goose-stepping out of the bathroom. He places his proprietary hands upon her body. A bright angel. And how will you deal with those pitch-dark areas of which you often speak, Elinda? What of those intemperate elements in you? How can you control them? What of you, wife? He whispers his dangerous words into her dumb ear, frozen prayers. Dazed, dreading the bloody mutilation of the opal, she pushes his hands away from her purplish loins. She talks esperanto, foiling him. She leans against the glass and closes her eyes. Immortality is nothing to do with me. I have only this foliage of flesh. That cavity called my heart is cluttered with the fallen masonry of old emotions. And I do not even want to lip-read. I reject idle lay-figures and senseless mandalas, Luke, she says, quelling her own doubts, for it is wounds of blood and imprisoned revolutionaries alone who are real. Now I must survive without stimulants. I will analyse the poisons in my bloodstream. I will defeat those interrogative ghosts flaunting their vigilance in my face . . . She accompanies her words with pharisaic gestures, frightening him. Why, you weigh less than a german wolfhound, he says in the voice of weeping. But Elinda's flesh is not to be soothed. She longs for an accomplice (a demi-god) to help her pick specimens of Aaron's Rod. She loathes the spermary sea. A xenolith girl without breasts, she quakes. Residual radioactivity may be detected after the explosion, she thinks, and o what mournfulness will gather in those clouds, monsters, half bird, half mauve lion. No, no, she cries out aloud, throwing back her premonitory head, I will be brave enough, I will face everything with a complete lack of censorship . . . Now as the clocks strike the half-hour before midnight she touches him with both her hands, searching, seeking, like one newly blinded. But I'm tired, she croaks. And he laughs, emboldened by this sudden surrender, despising all rascally human faces this timeless night. Aah, he sneers, and I suppose you want me to invent you a new world, a libertarian world. But no, I'm going to risk your hostility and tell you it cannot be done. Especially not by me. This is crystal clear to Elinda. She glances at her fingernails, long slivers of horn, stained red. A rock-haunting weeper with a basin of blood in her hands. Luke, I have attempted to re-invent the world myself, she sighs, I know it cannot be done. I know also how difficult it is to renounce . . . And I would sooner suffer any quick agony than this continual dull ache, always summoning me. She expects no improvements. She is tearful, she drags her hair unthinkingly back from her scalp, she lets Luke guide her to bed. Without felicitations, they lie down side by side but not to sleep. The head and trunk of a woman and the rough tail of a fish, thinks Elinda. His breakable arms attempt to shield her. I feel as if I, and only I, am groping clumsily through the world. And all that is most desirable and beautiful is being kept from me. Speaking bitterly, she continues to amaze him. It is not so, Luke insists. Her rodent mouth wearies him. Elinda, your longings are of an impossible nature. They cannot be granted, not even on a leasehold basis. Wiser ones than you and I have questioned darkness and they too crept back at dawn, defeated, abused, derangement glinting in their eyes. Her lips press against his cheek. He fingers her body grudgingly. But darkness taunts me, Luke, it has a compulsion in it, curiosity forces me to go in search of fragmentary answers. And other passions burrow their way into my flesh like hookworms. Uncovenanted impulses. He holds her with no intention of adoring. He can remember how she picked up aguish stones from the beach. Elinda, you must say to yourself, there will be an end to this exploitation of myself. You must reject the imaginary ocean which is drowning you. He gives his orders and ceases to fondle her. She thinks of the foetus of a war-goddess, growing, a long summer adjournment. If only I could, she answers, knowing that a metallic mirror freezes her image forever. You can, Luke promises. Stillness enters their cranium heads settled on the shared pillow. He thinks she is asleep but when he edges away from her she says, no, don't move, you must not move. Thinking, do I need him, do I care for him, have we nothing to fear except fear itself, and who am I anyway, who has charge of my disposal? She touches him with unwarranted fingers, accepting nothing. Who mentioned an adulterer's name? Then silence again with its semblance of moonlight clinging to the roots of life. So that he thinks of all the relevant associations. Imaginary dancers parade through a sub-kingdom. Suddenly she cries out, take pity on me, Luke. I must bear a child and it will be my salvation . . . She tastes camphor on her lips. She shudders and shakes: Luke is too tired to blame her for anything. No, I cannot permit it, he tells her, the liquid in his mouth tasting of lava, the forces that lie within that domain frighten me now. Elinda. He thinks of the death penalty unexpectedly announced by the smiling warder an hour before dawn. Elinda's demands also are more than sexual. But, Luke, you must help me. I'm forsaken, even by myself. Say some prevailing words! Ransom me! She clings to Luke, quailing before the prospects of melancholia. This is like meeting the corpse. He repeats her name over and over again, squandering his consolation, but he is too overwhelmed by Elinda's debased likeness to another woman to help his wife. I am not equal to this indecent night, he thinks. I can speak only as a skirmisher. Elinda, calm down. It is only this handicapped summer night which upsets you so, setting you afire. Hear my advice. Proceed more cautiously through life. Become hesitant. I tell you, all of those who rush forward through life shouting: more, more, give me more, love me more, tell me all the secrets, be perfect, reveal truths to me . . . believe me, Elinda, all of you are foetally broken. One day you'll kneel before the mirror to witness your own subordination. He strokes her with his hands now. Life is a series of failures. Accept it, Elinda. Ultimate moments? Ecstasies? They are always in the future, always unattainable. We are not strong enough to capture them. The truth about ourselves would destroy us. We are never as brave as we think. Elinda covers her face with pleiad hands. A recoining of death. The long weeping of Oceanus. Then she plunges into a prophetic sleep. He is exhausted by the exhaustless body lying at his side. He hears Elinda call out in her sleep, from some unpiloted dream: No, no, no . . . Amoral words of power: warning and weaning the man who listens, an onanistic eavesdropper.

BIRD PRINCESS

Bird silence in gardens of childhood. She brushes her albino hair. Rainy weather with pimpernels. If I have done wrong, she thinks, if I have sinned, then I confess to whoever bothers to listen to my braided silence. Bad blood runs through her veins, scalpel pains rouse her. Kneeling on the bathroom floor, she inserts a tampax with expert fingers. Luke opens the door and laughs at her, mocking her leechcraft. He begins the crossing of crevasses. He calls no man master. Elinda turns her cat-clown face towards him, stares at him reproachfully, conveying the fallibility of her life-line. Time is end-around. Yes, I know you are my guardian, she says sadly. For her, images of glass grails appear. But he thinks he can see through her talismanic fantasies. He does not notice that she is participating in spinal warfare. He thinks her clayey vulva needs a nickname. Don't sulk, Elinda, he says, again laughing his clerical laugh, just because I won't let you turn our lives into safaris. I'm going now. I'll see you tonight. He does not touch her. Just watches. She washes the blood from her fingers. It smells like anthracite. Perhaps you'll see me, Luke, and perhaps you won't. She trembles, she who is searching into the presence of a god. With veins of sulphur. Wings like enemies. Burning books in his hand. But Luke is equal to all her challenges. He too uses an inflexible vocabulary, not stammering, pointing at her. Elinda, what I can't understand or forgive is your indiscriminate mingling of truth and deceit. In the same sentence, you utter promises and lies. Do you know the difference? This is not the life we intended to live, is it? This is not what we planned to be. You think it is my fault? Perhaps it is . . . But you also have evaded all trust. And he looks at her with a tri-partite longing. But she remembers the failed quakeress eating an apple. So she turns away from Luke, not celebrating the silence. He shrugs, a lord of creation. She examines her outstretched right hand, measuring the maximum distance between the tip of her thumb and her little finger. He grips her hand, his heart of bessemer steel, and spits a mouthful of summer at her. She follows him to the garden gate. He drives away through a landscape of modern scaffolds. Rain falls upon Elinda, walking on the lawn. Alone, she listens to an inner voice. Now that cloud no bigger than a murderer's hand casts its shadow upon us. She smears lipstick over her mouth. She sits cross-legged on the floor amid all the fiends. Some weeks ago, disquieted by the interior miles separating her from Luke and Matthew, Elinda began to keep a diary, to write down clues and lists of suspects. The entries are brief and aimless. *The hidden transcendental hand touches me . . . silence . . . I saw a dwarf on the beach . . . electricity in me how it snaps . . . there is no godhead . . . look at me . . . find Matthew . . . tell Matthew . . . thin untrustworthy ice . . . Luke and I quarrelled again . . . the dragon's mouth opens.* She closes the journal, detesting futures, wanting to weep cold embezzled tears. Who is Luke? Where did he come from? What unscrutinized sun shaped him? O I could burn this house to the ground. An intercostal singer wastes a song. This was Matthew's favourite tune. But it is replaced by news bulletins. What did Luke say to me yesterday? Now I remember. I once came through this town ten years ago, after I escaped from borstal. That is what he said. And I jumped up in amazement, but glad, already prepared to betray him. He only laughed! And said, hey I was joking. Joking! What use are jokes to me? Doesn't he guess that if I am denied a child of the womb, then I will take possession of him, all his hours? Elinda suspects Luke of travelling through subterranean lands to attend dawn conferences at abandoned aerodromes. I am sure that he keeps secret matters from me. The september rain still streams down the windows, a mesmerism of weather. Why does Luke refuse to exorcise me? Elinda stares out at the greasy ocean, her breasts swelling. And her thoughts are little vivisections. In the afternoon, she reads the letter she stole from his desk. It pins her to the professional cross. All defences desert her. *It is difficult for me to get away and meet you, Hagar, more difficult than ever. She is getting worse. Often she's violent now. Yes, Elinda is like one of those wild mares the king fed on human flesh. I'm afraid I must soon start looking for a suitable clinic, one especially equipped to deal with sick people like Elinda. After all, I can only stand so much . . .* Her curiosity quenched by powerful poison, Elinda slowly crumples the airmail letter in her hands. The nails and the spear, the dancer maimed . . . So, she thinks, we do live under the laws of our own making. Luke is an enemy. Luke is the enemy. Unhearingly, she listens to the shrieks of the seagulls and the ringing of the waves. For over an hour she does not move. Her aortal fear is great. She leans against the wall, groaning. All the ills that flesh is heir to . . . As if I care! But I do. A fatalistic orphan drags her body across the room, striving to make sense of herself. She is not frittering away this interval: she is trying to survive. Shall I begin to prepare atlantosaurus deaths? For myself? Or for Luke? Or for the whole world? She feels hysterical yet apathetic, too weary even to open her mouth and howl. She suffers a self-warping, rejecting sleep, neglecting prayer, either of which would help her, if only she could reach out the little distance to take hold of consolation. Perhaps he wrote that letter, knowing I would find it. He wanted to frighten me, perhaps. Perhaps he never meant to send it? She stares in the illusionist mirror. O Luke, let our frailties embrace us. She touches the basilic bloodvein in her arm, cursing all flesh. On her tongue, a foretaste of sacraments including contritions. Her tarot brain shouts. At length she moves, galvanized by self-pity. Elinda wishes she were a giantess. The radio gabbles: anti-personnel bombs, earthquakes, casualties, neanderthal deaths. But Elinda turns the volume down and caresses the statue shamelessly, touching the old cunt, pretending to be a pioneer. Then she picks up a glass jar containing slanderous artificial flowers. Holding this in claw hands, she squats on the floor, listening to the rain, in jeopardy, deep amid caisson thoughts, motionless, watching over a still-warm corpse.

THE CAPTURE OF THE SAVIOUR

The loamy evening and at nine o'clock she puts aside her book, a biography of Charlotte Corday d'Armont, and looks into Luke's smooth selfish face. She sees that he is already moving away from her towards another world, to a loutish life. She senses that he will leave her to her own captivity. To her bathyspheric sexhood. Playing music of a refrigerated accuracy, she can no longer do as she is bidden, and lifts her hands from the cold keyboard. Insolent silence winds from her cigarette. He watches her and then he frowns, armed only with braille emotions. What are you going to do, Elinda? She turns to him with a diphtheritic smile. Do? she queries, for she has a magnifying-glass mind. Yes, Elinda. How do you intend to pass the time? You have been idle for months. Who gave you your do-nothing instructions? It is bad for you, it rots your hopes. Why not get a job? To occupy yourself. Think. What do you want to do with the future? He studies her sunburnt hands, examining her rings, leaning towards her, connubial yet jaded, eyeing her graceful degradation. The future? she asks, firedamp. His sarcasm is blunt. Yes, Elinda, the future. The day after tomorrow. We must ensure you make a valuable contribution to the community. So consider your life now, Elinda, and not after you have prepared our delicious soup. How do you see your life? Has it any sort of clarity, perspective, shape for you? Can you give yourself a direction yet? Or are you still a post-mortem dump? I must know. I must. He speaks excitedly now, a man whose sole ambition is to photograph the sun at midnight. Elinda has a longing she cannot share because she is unable to verify its authenticity. She wears an interrupt-mask. Her pains are beyond incubation. You must? Luke, no, let me be free. There is nothing to tell. Except that I love soil and sand, the disintegrated rock. I merely drag myself through the days. Surely you've seen me? I admit that I am weak, I have no spirit. All I want is to be left alone, with no outside interference. Don't hate or hurt me. He laughs slyly. Lines of fracture. Her words titillate him. Hurt you? Have I ever ill-treated you? She moans like a sempstress wearily beginning another seam. No, never. Perhaps it would be better if you had, Luke. I could have understood your fists, I could have fought back. I would have defended the hermitage of my brain. But no, you haven't got the strength to really fight. It's just terrorism and surprise attacks. Yet to tenderize her words, Elinda touches him with a gesture still nuptial even in the midst of this atoxic crisis. Luke takes no notice of this action of hers, that is the pre-cognition of a second and fallen christ. You don't mean that, Elinda. I will forget you ever said such things. Please believe me, if I interfere it is because of love. Mine is not a repressive legislation. So he makes his claim, with panoramic simplicity. But Elinda looks bewildered, she does not understand. The stereo-chemistry of night confuses her. She tries to ask why their lives are truculent, why they dirty every day they touch, why their embraces are flabby. But all she can say is, Luke, I don't understand you . . . Perhaps I should go away? Shall I? Tonight? He shakes his head, acknowledging yet again how their relationship is calibrated, moving from detente to detente, yet never achieving peace. Now they will both submit to their interplanetary fate. And oh to lose all brightness, freshness and serenity, what demonology appears, prevailing in my heart? Why do I always return to a fucked prison? He drifts into a cisalpine mood and says to her, once I saw a painting of a young woman weeping. Her eyelids were matriarchal as she stood beneath the dust-coloured sky, surrounded by jealous rocks beyond which the lagoons of defeat shimmered. Herself blameless, she was holding a probate on love, following its cremation. But she had about her an aviational lewdness. Elinda spins away from his words, haunted and maidenly. For her, commitment is a sin. She wants to speak in two voices. To pacify him. And to dominate him. But it is all deadlock, an emotional lockout. There is a culmination of unsaid prayers in her. She desires phosphorescent feats of horsemanship, she breathes the cataracts of autumn and recites: I remember once, soon after Matthew left me with only shells and stones for company, I watched a man riding a huge horse slowly and formally and influentially across the horizon. Indelible gravity adorned him as he approached the citadel. His unfaithful silver-grey shadow followed him.

When the rider was out of sight I knelt down and I touched the waters, the ownerless sea-wrack swirling around my ankles. And then a long period of waiting exhausted me. Its storms and calms sufficed to occupy my days. Until at length a dozen geometric figures, uninvited lovers, threatened me with their embraces. I ran and I ran into the night, clapping my hands. Then I met you. And tried to stop stumbling. I pushed thoughts of an uncommon death out of my head. I revised my doctrines. All for you. And now I find you have cheated me. Yes, yes, you have. You have deceived me, Luke. Sighing first, then sobbing, Elinda hauls herself about the room, a deteriorationist. Me? I have done no such thing, he shouts at her, a saboteur husband. She runs upstairs and she scribbles spidery lies on the mirror with her crimson lipstick. Can we communicate only by word of mouth? I remember our first ashram embracement and how I thought it would last for ever, Matthew and I like the tangled branches of one sad tree. Luke thinks of the douched conversations of the past. I hate this hostage house. I am afraid of the mycology of love. Does Elinda really want to be a nun, clavicular and cold? I want to smooth life out, to file away the unevenness before death's memorial gardens blossom again. Luke does not understand famine. He climbs the stairs slowly, his body herpetic. Elinda, hearing his footsteps, recalls the rubble of countless emigrations. Luke touches her yet fears her reactance. He questions the validity of her arsenic voyage to a wilderness. Why do you reject me, Elinda? Why do you always turn to me fretfully, in some fever? Gravely, not smiling, she answers him. Because you want me to, Luke. And she is proud of her pudenda. He releases her. This utterance causes great consternation within him, like a newsflash warning of some terrible eunuch's revolution, not optional. No, he denies aloud, word for word, no, no. She points at him because it is zero hour. Yes, it is true. Also you long to fall to your knees and beg me to beat you. That is what you desire. I know. Yes, I know. I know many breath-taking things, Luke. Your eyes are the colour of excrement . . . You . . . O christ, sometimes I wish I had a speech defect to excuse this inability to state my thoughts clearly. I want to hide somewhere, far away from everything and everyone. Lead me to a charitable madhouse! That is what you want, isn't it? And I want that supersonic freedom to become my true self. Let me rest somehow, somewhere. She breathes deeply, her priapism. Against his will he stares at her, his own influence on the wane. You bitch, cow, vixen, tigress. He grits his teeth. Her intimidating composure betrays a true brutality. Her innocence is only indemnification against sexual attack. Yet she is the woman. The blood her heart expels gives him life. Sharp, sour, bitter: but life. She symbolizes his intercepted mythology. And now they are both without safeguards. Technologists of the dark. Luke, she continues more quietly, lapsing into her childhood dialect, I admit that all through the reactionary months of our marriage, I have been compensating for a lost desire. I admit that I used you. But my wickedness has turned upon me. You and I were on a collision course all the time, I suppose, but I refused to recognize it until the very last moment. At first, at the beginning of this year, we lived a slow-motion life: but now, as we approach the windmill autumn, events move too fast for us. We are being hustled away from each other by our own stupidities. How strange . . . For in our short time together there have been quiet times. We did not always exist in these cyclonic areas. But, nevertheless, a reckoning now claims me. And you? That is your affair. All I know is that now there will be lonely tempest times for me when I will turn to the night in peripatetic horror, hands held over my mouth, suffocating in my sewer. And my despair will whirl me around tied to a prayer wheel. We will separate, Luke, tonight or some other night. Yes. Don't deny it. We will. And it is only now, yes, now, at this very moment of breathing and bleeding, as I say these words, that I realize the hurt of such relinquishment. As we move by slow clumsy strides towards defeat, I realize too much. And I am sorry I have sometimes insulted you. I ask your forgiveness. Yes, and you give it. I knew you would. For whatever I have said or might say in the future, you are a good man, Luke, and you stretch out your arms whenever you see me suffering. You would not willingly dissociate yourself from me, would you? But I will release you. And I'll also tell you, you were right. Those of us who demand too much of life, we do creep back defeated into the night, our brains threatening to explode. Now my impulse is to weep again as I see the destinations to which we are moving. I dread the time (not yet, it is not yet) when I will say, please go. Go, go away from me. I dread it because it will be both truth and lie, life and death. And it will signify the initiation of our disaster. Will I ever be able to write in my diary the commentary such acts demand? What passages shall we take to reach our futures? Mine? Mine will be a perpetuity of escapes into one astral world after another. And they will all prove to be pitiless metrologies. I know before I start how it will be. But your future is another world to me, equally sinister, equally sad, which I cannot venture to explore. Quiet now. I've finished. I won't use any more of these cordite words. Why should I? How can I? She crouches by the window, spent, having eliminated herself. Her gold bracelet finds fault with time. Luke kneels faithfully beside her. No, Elinda, no. There'll be no parting. We have not been married a twelvemonth yet. Things will improve. The insecurity between us is merely a symptom of the times. All must face the gravity of this decade, with its trapdoors and its un-festivals. Let us try to live together without forebodings. We shall have a more natural relationship soon . . . But already she is speaking again, interrupting him, twining her utopian hair around naked fingers. Ah Luke, darling, we are too familiar with each other's mouths even to eat together, let alone love. We are too well acquainted with these bodies, too adept, too well practised. We have nowhere else to go together. There is only the parting left. We hang by a thread. We are courting disaster all the time. Menaces loom and we cannot buy them off. There is no haven to which we may abscond, no extrication for us except by saying goodbye. We must part: or we shall be destroyed by what has become too real for us to bear. Luke stands up cautiously, as if he might destroy all fire, he is so cold. Elinda spurs herself on, catching at his hand. Her eyes are ash-coloured. Don't you see, Luke, we will never adore each other's smudged profane bodies the way we do now! We will never cry again as we are crying now! Let us separate, before we overtake ourselves. Her eyes are closed now and she shivers in the subordinate autumnal air. Unisexual shadows repent. No, he declares, this is all too strange. We will put it out of our minds and not talk of it again. We will live together for ever. I'll give you anything. Because . because I . . . But he breaks off and his stone lips withhold the words. Elinda looks at him compassionately. Ah no, she breathes into the isotropic silence, no, you cannot even remember the words that could persuade me to change my mind. How can we presume to call ourselves lovers now? That time has passed. We will even cry differently from now on. In this prodigy night Luke hears himself give vent to a discordant grunt of grief. He touches her breasts and knows that although they are white-fleshed they are also offal, bursting with argent malignities . . No, I will stay, he promises, we will make a new start. And regain our confidence in each other. Despite your doubts. She shakes her head, knowing the temptations of exile. As you wish. But I'll take no responsibility for what happens now, Luke. She looks at him passively, breaking curfew, scared of owls, adders and toads. Her submergence in shadows is complete. Her wounds gape. But he has no anti-coagulants. Leaving her to her double-edged gospels, he wanders downstairs and out into the garden of falling leaves. He is trussed in silence. Now he senses, beyond all silences, the interrogations of failure and the remotest subtleties of introspection contained therein. He scents the laws of necrosis. And he bows his head and weeps, differently, as she predicted. Because of the descent from the haemostatic cross.

BREASTS OF AUTUMN

The sabbatized sea watches. The roqual garden is afraid with colour. Her hand touches his breasts. She is refusing. No more discipleship. He speaks words made from another language. But she refuses. Zenithal light weaves into her hair. So that her hair blazes, the public burning of a heretic. He is hardening under anger. He makes noises like a goliath frog. The anti-coincidence of flesh frightens her. She hates his target language. She half turns from him. Opalina escaping. But he won't let her go. He scrapes his body against her face. He wants her; coeternal. What used to be the sun, an easily burning dome, goes over the edge, falling, beginning something else. Something dendritic. He uses devotional weapons of war. A threshold element arises. His lips summon. His hands keep jerking at her. She is destitute of flowers and fossil footprints. And so from her, such a cry, surrendering, complying, submitting. And her body is gone into the mattoid game.

KEEPER OF THE WOMB

Thermometers, amalgams, mirrors. There must be a candle lighted, the colour green must be worn. And she smiles. Because she is strong again, the planetoid one. Emerald and olive. Declarative statements from her. Dagger prayers from him. Time-sharing is hard, digging always into the memory core. She listens to his message of errors. But this time she outwits his scrota. Frees herself from his watchdog embrace. Now she has major control. Must you be so selfish? he bellows, fierce in his frustration. Elinda watches him silently. In this dim light, her undernourished face is classical, a deltoid beauty. He slams the front door, hurrying to the cinema where he will gloat over Barbarella. Leaving Elinda to meditate on her obstinacy, a proto-martyr wandering in the breakaway regions of the heart. Now it is the time of Libra and she knows they stand on a final threshold, looking towards a landscape where the focal attributes of mirrors will reflect the endless infertility of celebrants. She drifts through the cluttered rooms of her house this illegitimate evening, licking her wounds, watching her own shadow. I am losing my psychic hold over my life. Soon I will be possessed by hypodermic couriers. Appolyon's slimy tongue is in my mouth. She bites into an apple and flicks through the pages of a railway timetable Luke had been consulting. An envelope falls to the floor. A letter sent under private seal. Elinda stares at it for a long time. But it is her own unsmiling face she sees, reflected in a thousand breaking mirrors. A woman's head for a monolith. She puts the half-eaten apple carefully on the table. Ghoulish fingers run wild through her hair. The mesmerized clock strikes the hour. Slowly she reaches down through the air to pick up the envelope in a damp hand. She reads this second letter. Why are there witnesses and replicas of witnesses everywhere I look? Why do they flash identity bracelets at me? Mocking my strength. I remember Luke and I stood beside the sunbright war memorial on the eleventh day of November and he touched my forehead with his Buddhist lips as he obediently answered my questions. No one, he said, there is no one else. And then he spoke flirtatious words. Again, one bleak day in January, only a week prior to our marriage, I asked him once more, as we walked along the deserted beach, do I have any rival? And from that wilderness of discarded coca-cola bottles, he looked out to sea and murmured pastel words, like someone returning a kindness. But he lied to me. When I was half awake, he lied to me. When I wept on the iliac marriage bed, it was lies he comforted me with, just lies. Elinda re-reads this undated letter cautiously, dwelling on every word, a vigilante. She polishes her griefs. Whether I go to the future or to the past, it is all the same, pain always welcomes me in its nubian embrace. I am caught at the orthocentre. This letter is from Hagar. It is an obscene document, scribbled without restraint, in large bladdery handwriting. Hagar begs Luke to return to her. She implores and threatens, a violence of words. Her nostalgia is coarse, reminding Luke of too many uncharitable acts. She describes their love, a kind of gargoylism. A smelting of lust. Words of sickening precision. Such details require special knowledge, thinks Elinda, inaugurations of the flesh not to be condoned. Beneath Hagar's signature, Luke has printed one mature word: *reconsider.* And it is this word which shakes Elinda, subjecting her to a microsurgery of fear. The photograph attached to the letter is a holiday snapshot. It shows the two of them, their arms entwined, laughing, carefree, the world at their feet. In the background, a black sea basks. On the reverse of the photo, the same untidy hand has written possessively, Hagar and Luke, summer 1963. Hager is aged about thirty. She has a journeying expression, cold licentious eyes and dark close-cropped hair. To Elinda's mind, she is a woman bred in a land of continuously dry weather. Elinda senses that, beneath the lifetime of her skin, there is something strained and unnatural about Hagar, many troubles that her smiling pose cannot completely hide. I may be a sub-standard woman myself, Elinda thinks proudly, but I am better than Hagar will ever be. And I need him more. To stand between me and anchoritism. He is my shield against butchery. Without him, there is only the sea and the sky and the crane-fly haunting an empty room. In the darkness, the ferocity of her fears grows. She curls up in her favourite chair, silent as a slave. She listens to her heartbeat and thinks of valvular disease. Cold-storage dreams. I will put Luke to the test. Innocent or guilty. Or guilty! A formidable test. How these uncanny words steer me towards the lawless rapids . . . Once I thought my life was capable of all kind of beauty. Now I know better. Now I am afraid. Suppose all my plans go wrong? And I become the promiscuous quarry, lost in the night? Will I shiver and sweat? Will my triumph be short-lived? She strokes the letter. I wonder if the gutter language of Hagar's letter impressed Luke? Did this perfumed paper (which stinks in my nostrils like insecticide) bring him any pleasure? Is the woman called Hagar the one who is beyond any hope of cure? Or am I the irredeemable one, retreating before these contaminating words? Birthright, inheritance, the conferral wedding ring, the bared body, the hangman's rope, funeral flowers: many claimants to the throne of god spit blood at me. Ah, there is the moon like a fat squabbling woman. I see the half-eaten apple turn brown and rotten. Four burnt corpses, champions of the light. I hear a carillon chime inside my head, a pizzle dangles between my legs, memories of racial carnage appal me! All the angels are on fire! What atomic apprenticeship am I serving?

HAND OF GLORY

Moonlight leans against sea, a membrane of metal and bone. The bars close for the night. The runaway strolls along the promenade, singing with discrimination. His mind lingering on the bird region of the groin, Luke returns home. But to an animalized situation, a dimly lit room in which Elinda waits, devout yet steely, her body rife with anger, her tongue slaked of praise. She believes in eternal punishments. If he is surrounded by fire he will kill himself. She sits bolt upright, her robe swirling around her dramatic as a soutane. A celtic cross hangs between Luke and Elinda. Fury holds her like a gem in a ring. Her averted profile is capable of black deaths. What is it? he asks unhappily, sensing the paraplegia of his hopes. The parentage of his love is put at risk. What now? Will she make me violate graves? She looks coldly at him. She is cursing the maize girl. He is drunk. No enthronement for Luke. What if I tell him I have just foaled? Her pharyngeal rage rules her. Who is Hagar? she demands in a photuric voice. The finding of votive arrows . . . Now he must be a celibate solomon soothsaying far into the night. Yes, he thinks rapidly, bartering his blood, I have always dreaded this moment but now that it has arrived I will not succumb without a fight. I will defend myself even if it means we must both ape our true selves until we have no truth left in us and have become hardened to all vulturine ways. He takes up his desperado's stance in the doorway, almost smiling, like a wearer of jackboots. Five years after death she still whimpers. Who? he asks perilously, not looking at Elinda in her witchdom. O for god's sake, she shouts, revelling in his guilt, eating up his hungry soul, don't make me harangue you, Luke. You are powerless, because I have found this letter and this photograph. She holds them up triumphantly. I have had all my suspicions confirmed, Luke. I am not a complete fool. Now she understand all apartheids. She stands by the window, trembling. Luke will be a military monk, she tells herself, for I am not in the madhouse yet. But this knowledge does not make her happy. She knows that he is not afraid of her surly mouth nor of her haemoglobin words. He thinks of the mailed fist and hardens his heart. Here, she says spitefully, thrusting the evidence into his hands, ignoring his glance that transforms her into an arid governess. Read her letter. Read the words of a prostitute. There is no grandeur in your Hagar, whoever she is. Luke stares at the envelope for a moment, then tears it in halves, quarters, scattering the pieces on the floor. Elinda gazes at him with maggoty fear. But I've still got the photograph, shouts Elinda. And she laughs gleefully. He does nothing.

Except light a cigarette, striking the match with an infamous hand. He looks at their decapitated shadows on the wall and thinks of all that is at stake. Tell me who she is! Elinda struggles with her task. He considers. No, he will not speak in a romance tongue. Why should I retrace my steps? He twists his face into a gnarled warning. This is where the benediction ends. Where the deicide begins. Why should I answer you, he says with quiet venom, yes, why? Just to satisfy your dirty desire for forbidden fruit? No, you must stop this interfering. Don't you speak about Hagar as if she were any more evil than yourself! He paces up and down the room in a tired frenzy, telling Elinda she is infected with a spiritual myxomatosis. She shrinks from him, groping for words of defence. Shadows reproach their loud erupting voices. Night blinks. But treat me with justice, Elinda asks, distraught. She has a forlorn dignity and he gazes enviously at her. How he stares at the veins of her thin hands clasped in prayer. The climatology of her being . . . I only ask to know who she is . . . she murmurs, drifting in her own loneliness. For now the unquenched summer makes a low moaning sound in Elinda's heart and her thoughts are burning in the crimson candle. Icelandic knives damage her skin. The bitterness of a sore place spreads over all her body. Her aryan roots hold her. The sun's absence makes her ashamed. She cannot look her husband in the face. The throng of the future . . . How do I dance? They that carried us away captive required of us a song. The trinket around her throat casts its own nipping shadow. He is asking: what authority have you for these questions? She thinks of very early times. But finds no answer. She is whey-faced. Did his pedobaptism give him this zeal? She frays her head in her hands. The accuracy of the calendar taunts Elinda. Did Luke once examine his brother's ashes, himself disguised in a turquoise mask? The heart of heaven is at the northern edge of hell and a host of moons snatch the sky away. Now she narrows her eyes and makes prurient, suggestions. He sighs. I need a response book. Or a familiar. But he keeps these thoughts to himself. Look, let us forget about Hagar, he says more gently, controlling his temper, using all his straw strength. Don't get fanatical, Elinda. You're too quick at seizing. I won't tell you of my secret migrations. I won't talk about Hagar. It is all in the past. Like your affair with that stowaway boy. Or is that different? Now, come along, sit down. He kisses her cold tyrannical face. Elinda, listen. Despite all our harsh words, I still think of you as worthy of worship, a creature whose amorous implications are immemorial. Please, don't spoil things. Why must we destroy ourselves? What is sown in your heart? Slowly she shakes her head. She is determined to give splenic pain to herself and to him. She must taste the bilbo fruits of the season. Swallow the anti-orbital autumn whole. All extravagance is on bended knees now. Don't try to distract me, she whines, edging away from him. We can't make ourselves voiceless. If we are going to remain together, Luke, I must understand you. And to do so I need to possess all the major and minor details of your life, intimacies and sins, goals and crutches. Otherwise there is no hope for us. We will be only figureheads, not lovers. Please tell me the truth about yourself. It is only fair. For I've told you everything about myself. I have spoken openly of follies and transgressions, haven't I? But he merely looks at her with regret as she flits joylessly about the room. A cloaked aurora. So, we are not to have our Indian summer, he remarks throatily, wondering where he hid his passport. O you fool, she shrieks, making libidinous gestures, tell me! Silence won't help you when I'm dead and gone. The movement of her heart is a witness. Still he stands wryly unmoved. He will not protect her. Nothing will protect Elinda. Looking at her as if she were merely a goitred third person, he says, let me be blunt then. I've had a bellyful of you, Elinda. I've had enough of your bloody-minded love, your obsessive praying and prying, this constant tension. Hagar was my first wife. Whom I once loved. What a passerine silence. Her pallor is extreme. Luke takes one step towards her but the curtness of one upheld warning forefinger holds him off. O believe me, love, now there is only the sad echo, he says, only the faintest ghost of an old vendetta between Hagar and me, but you will not believe it. You will always see the darkness. Elinda trembles again for a starveling moment. We may be ill-mated, you and I, Luke, but I will not let you go. It is my vow. Even if I am robbed of desire, I will not set you free. I will be loyal to winter. Elinda examines the photograph again, foisting pain upon herself. She hears the prohibitive cries of an attacking army. Now I am saddled with this image of Hagar, tormented by her impetuous brows, the uneven carriage of her shoulders. She is my penance. I know she can foreclose upon me. I know she watches my enslaved life with an air of privileged insolence, safe in her scalding freedom. Now when I think someone is walking behind me, carrying condemned flowers, I know it will be her. When I lie on the threshing-floor of the earth, she will be watching. I can't bear it! No! Because I am weak, capable only of falsehoods and collaborations. She flies at Luke, blood-letting her ambition. It is time for the fugitives to grapple. Her intonations go on challenging him. She hurls the photograph into the fire, laughing at Luke. She shouts at him, lashing out at his octaroon silence. My name is Elinda! I dreamed up entirely new solar systems, o yes, I invented a celestial sovereignty to be shared with you. Just you. You! My rosewater body touching a fool! You touch the fire then! Lunging forward, she grabs his right hand, trying to thrust his fist into the flames. Her pharaonic crucifix glitters and she memorizes the war. Enraged by the sublimated smile on her face, Luke clouts her roughly on the side of her head. He is hardly aware of the birth of violence, thinking only, I will not be subservient to any newt of a woman. She cries out incoherently, looking up at him with crazily staring eyes. In her concussion, she is beautiful as a heraldic heiress. Luke looks down at her, respectfully. Then he laughs at the wingless female. His hand wounds. He pounces upon her shaveling body. When he rapes her, he is metamorphosed into a spouting barbarian. He is intent on a thievery that will commemorate this stark evening. After the rape, he feels deodorized. He carries her upstairs, staggering under his burden. He dumps her on the bed, brushing his hand against her hair. She is still unconscious. He runs downstairs, lighthearted, whistling a snatch of an old song. But almost an hour later, sitting in his study, he is overcome by a neolithic mood of depression. We do not walk in the light, he thinks. In the night seasons we exercise our shame. He considers gassing himself. But instead he writes to Hagar, telling her there can be no more wagers between them. It is a long and cruel letter, contravening many laws. He signs his name and falls into a kind of deliberate coma, marshalling his thoughts, searching out interlocking moonlit detours. Elinda recovers consciousness alone in the bedroom. She wonders where the day has gone. She touches her crucifix. My body aches. Was I thrown from my horse? Initial vagueness gives way to recollection and a tightening of the lips as she recalls Hagar. She rebukes the man. Scared of the merciless mirror, she examines her missionary bruises. Slowly she gropes her way to the washstand, splashing cold water on her face. She is drained of all doubletalk. She retches. I fear that tomorrow I shall die under the great weight of my armaments. She waits for a voice. She becometh a tree.

TOMB PAINTING

A feastless night. She maintains the pose of a tree. It was you, Elinda, who said you would take no responsibility for future events, says her godling husband, asking for absolution. She does not answer. She sees a man and an ebonized woman dancing in front of an animal. She is the climax of night and fears her own sexlessness. He forces her to look at him, at the face of Jack Ketch. He speaks with care, a brother of the albino princess, and squeezes her breasts apprehensively. Your ring, the opal, which I gave you as a token . . . You'll still wear it? She agrees, half-smiling and half-sneering. She examines the bodily results of correction. A great storm rises out of the south, coming on scaffold feet. So, I am punished, she whispers, a clean bone wife, but I pardon you, Luke. In the fields of the Middle Kingdom grow flowers of uncertain identification. He nods bashfully, escorting her across the room to the bed. She asks him for easement now, frowing in her passivity. Luke, don't go. I want to talk. Perhaps I have been foolish . . . She makes her brief apology without opening her eyes, the petition of a dancer. Yes, Luke, I was foolish. You have a right to your own life. What was I thinking of? You settled my debts. You have cared for me. I owe you a great deal. It is I who am unkind, demanding unlimited freedom for myself yet permitting you no liberty. Luke smiles, he has forgotten the name of the priest who told him of god's crystal backbone. Shall I tell you something about Hagar? She is of Indian descent. Yes, I thought it would amuse you. Her forebears were Crow Indians, members of the Sioux, from Montana. Yes, really. Crow Indians, or in their own tongue, bird people. He laughs and the megaton wind rattles the windows and the doors. Elinda smiles bitterly, fingering the cross strung around her throat like a beacon. She knows about the unswathed ones. And about the sorceress of the Red Crown. All the requirements of the deceased. Why did you leave Hagar? Her pacifying voice goes on the prowl. Please tell me, Luke. It is natural that I should wish to know. I have no sinister motive. He winds his watch meticulously before answering, recalling that he is a money-lender and lord of two lands. I left Hagar because she was perverse and unfaithful. No, I won't go into details. But I couldn't live in the manner she intended. It would have led to an overgrowth of the bones and a gigantism of my genitals. Elinda laughs, a heathen noise. She makes obscene suggestions. Lovers coupling on an ivory bier. He shuts his eyes and prays aloud. To isolationist gods. And Elinda reaches forward and touches his groin insinuatingly. In the protracted silence that follows they perceive the sacrifice of their two antinomian selves. In his hand he holds the list of the priestesses. Elinda, my marriage to you was and is loveless, he tells her brokenly, I admit that and you cannot deny it. We both know it and suffer from our knowledge of a nuptial flight into the darkness of nowhere, of our rush towards plebiscites and emergency exits. Yet my marriage to Hagar was far worse. It was not only loveless but friendless. You and I are free to go through life together in a solemn and proper manner. We have our few comforts, our callipers. Even if we are not abundantly happy, we can face the future together. We must find new ways of approaching our problems and not follow decoy-lights. Who am I? Do you still wish to know whom I am? Elinda, I will tell you nothing. Nothing. Except that I have forgotten Hagar, memories of her are just pennies in an offertory box. But why does he hear Hagar's granular laughter ring out in this room with all the old arraignment? No, Elinda says thoughtfully, raising her head and looking at him, a black mirror showing the dark figure of a man breaking his connexion with truth. No, Luke, now you are lying. She is still important to you. Like the eucharist. You still think of her in the thin moments before dawn. And you still go to see her, don't you? Even if she were secluded in the menstrual hut, you would crouch in the doorway, wouldn't you? Her psittacine anger condemns his voyages. Yes, he admits to this ichneumon night, yes, I still see her, about three or four times each year . . . Elinda stands up experimentally, still aching from marriageable suffering. Without guidance, she can think of Hagar's undraped body and rehearse her jealousy. She touches her own breasts with her fingertips. Luke, I feel like the victim of a practical joke. How can you be finished with Hagar? Nothing is over between you. Yes, you have both made a real fool of me. She hoards anger instead of bracelets. Her heart is achromatic. Outside, the storm breaks amid the lamentation of animals. He mooches across the room. Grow up, Elinda! You must know by now that life is not an aquatic afternoon. Even you must realize that one side of my body is subject to phobias. But now her stentorian silence compels him to move huntedly around this room. He throws open a window, desperately snuffing up the damp night air. And she holds on hopelessly to the bible, thinking of Matthew in this same room a thousand aggregate years ago. Matthew, who in one topiary summer engendered a new mode of desire in Elinda. Who told her oceanic stories. Who exacted from Elinda an adulation that had about it all the lover's archetypal anxieties. Luke glances at her and distrusts her, all her accessory nerves. He thinks of the anagram tree of Jesse. And he makes a returning movement. No, she says, refusing his baptismal embrace, let me speak. Very well, he agrees. He will not veto this. Perhaps she will speak of the miraculous. She pins back her hair and smooths out the folds of her long swanky gown. Between birth and death, she sighs, what bargains we make. We try to reprieve ourselves for just one more day and we expect it to last for six months: and all because we cannot bear to let go of our lives. If only we dared to let go . . . We find emancipation in a flower garden but our lawless eye is tempted by other landscapes. And we soon lose our courage, our youth. We find ourselves weak and insufficient at the critical moment. Our plots are unsuccessful, our pledges crumble and all the rest of our life is an excuse. My body hates fleshly earthquakes. You are afraid of the reality of the womb. And what are we to do, with this other wife of yours straddled between us? How shall we pass those insensible hours when we are both thinking of her? No, don't go. Please, stay and listen to me. I know you're divorced from her. But it is not enough. You will not stop seeing her, will you? No, I didn't think so. She remains our ghost-girl. Luke, when I think of her, I long for her death. We'll not preserve her body in a pyramid, either. Oh when I think of you crowing above her, the pair of you spread-eagled beneath the sky, I desire your death. And then I long for my own last sleep. But I cannot reach out and clasp the knife in my hand. Our raiment is in shreds, Luke. Our old life was a poor one, but, compared with our future, it will seem like one long unclouded summer's day. Why are there so many sins? Yes, and there's cold, pain and grief . . . You must forgive me, I did not mean to say all these things. Elinda looks atoningly around the mute room but cannot stop her own words. I am confused, Luke, I am still shaking and my eyes see only disguises. Is it the truth I spew out? I don't know. I need a listener and you are the only one. Yes, yes, you must not tell me; I realize I am without a gift to give. She stands before him, headstrong, contrite, an amuletic figure. Her passion is justifiable. He does not question the powerful ambiguities implicit in her speech nor try to evade the fears she reawakens in him. She stares at him, the tenanting goddess who is always greedy. But Luke recalls the virtueless white blood cells and knows he can no longer mask his anger in irony. Because he fears a living death, he flares up, a snake farmer. Don't look at me like that, girl, he shouts, I'm not stupid, not one who tends parsimonious gardens. And I'm not your confessor, either. You want the one with fiery feet. Yet even as Luke thumbs his resentments, he fears he will be faithful until death. Ignorant of this, Elinda listens to him, snared among the osiris landfalls of her mind, the place where costs are never counted and where all the barbitone decisions are taken. Oh it never ends, it never ends, jabbers Elinda, and when I most need you, when I come to a lake of blood, you are cruel as a pharmacist. You refuse to tell me the location of the knife or the colours of maori visions. No, you don't want me to see another day break. I am dull-witted then and so you despise me. Yes. And all because my name is not Hagar. I am like a female jackal, you think. She struggles across the minefield, coveting any shifty sanctuary. You point a horrified finger at me, Luke, and begin to plan escapes, diversions, a new life in which I mean nothing, I become a stone, a telepathic nightmare. I am in pain, I often cry out: but you do nothing except look at calendars, timetables and newspapers, you do nothing but write letters. You already have a wife. Why do you stay here? Go back to her. Go on. Go away. Don't let her call me a hijacker. Go back to her. I dare you. Elinda shouts at him, a provincial girl almost lifeless from bellowing. Now he is speaking to her in a comprehending undertone. But she puts her fingers in her ears. You go back to her, if you dare. Yes, I know why you won't leave me. Hagar is the kind of woman who'd really eat up your soul and then want more and not ask prettily. Elinda pushes him away, betraying the drudgery of her words. All women do that, he tells her, his tenderness dying a natural death. Elinda would like to accuse him of pederasty. But I fear the manner of my death, she yells, I who once became drunk on holy water . . . No, he will not exempt her from her night. Nor from images of that darkness. So her conversation begins to tell a story. One woman born in one place is a universe, Elinda says and she shivers. There is no help for such a woman, Luke. My depression is like the stench of a latrine. I am buried under centuries of rock. And yet sometimes when I am alone in the afternoon I feel so exultant I have only to lift my hand to touch the sky and stroke that encyclopaedic blue. How should he reply? The nakedness of passwords is not revealed to him. I take nothing at its face value now . . . she spits, leaping at him, wanting to hold him fast in a jugular embrace. Oh why didn't you tell me about her in the beginning, Luke? He shrugs and then makes her sit down while he takes her pulse. Calm yourself, he says, compelling her to keep still, do you really want to destroy us both? What is it that drives you to seek out these humiliations? I think you want a superman . . . She considers this seriously and then shakes her head. No, Luke, I do not agree. I desire ordinary things. Just tell me where Hagar lives. If I could just talk to her . . . He watches Elinda's stunted terrorism. He sees it clear as daylight. I don't think I will tell you. Nile repercussions flood Elinda. But she pretends to venerate him. Why not, darling? Luke is dog-tired, he closes his eyes, he has had to face too many crises of this nature. He speaks wearily, doubting his own sanity. Because, Elinda, you would not survive any meeting. Hagar would maul you. She would tell you the truth about stalags and other more terrible things. You don't know her. Many are the animals she's paired with. Now Elinda weeps encephalic tears. Luke ignores her, he thinks of the electrocuted men. He is out of earshot. He believes that Elinda seeks out pain with the invigilating ardour of any sexual deviant. Now the stronghold of his heart resembles her own. He returns to the firmament. Nothing can save them from their own voices. Especially for you, Elinda, fashionable despair is a game. But you will salvage nothing from the ruins you are planning. Even your crying is a charade. He is too accurate in his observations. Examine a hero and you'll find a bully, she shouts, judging him harshly, putting power in his hands. Again he watches her weep. He experiences no compassion. He is no longer her body's guardian. His loins are dying. He knows their two bodies form a fatal coalition. Now he knows that he is almost ready to leave her. And suddenly he feels like that young warrior king, mournful because there were no more worlds left to conquer, no fresh territory over which to gain the mastery. He is defeated in the arms of victory. Elinda wants to raid him, she wants to fight until the candles are charred. But she is too dizzy to shout now, she closes her eyes, she lets her body lie inert, the cross hoaxing against her submarine breast. Again the loss of Matthew's soul-tired adoration mocks her. Elinda tells herself: tomorrow I will be free and tomorrow there will be silver lances of a great pure beauty raised at dawn. The morphine sky will soothe me. Flowers will stammer their greetings. If I can only reach tomorrow I will be safe. But this is only Elinda's dream. For tomorrow only the deformities of a chessboard will meet Elinda's hard exhausted gaze: only sterile telephones, only the relentless clock ticking too loudly, too quickly. Luke? she whispers, seductively. Luke? But there is no answer. She opens her eyes. He has gone. There is only the amen of an empty room. Down on the beach, Luke stares through rain at the samsonite sea. He fears that he too is dying a new kind of death and will soon be dead. Dead as Stalin's fingers. Dead as Hitler's heart.

NIGHTFALL AND ITS YOKE-BONE

The scene takes place between two palm trees overshadowed by the image of the winged foetus. Her galilean autism writes out assents. Nightfall, cries the auctioneer: and Elinda puts aside certain legal papers in order to watch the moon slither across the sky. Its mythological silence calls to her. She answers: oh I have gnawed at his bones too long. I am an amputee clinging to the nice pain. The swan's pyre blazes turquoise smoke. Muting naked candles burn. All her funerary equipment is ready. But she does not sleep. She lies awake, waiting for the arrival of one as yet unknown to her, still a stranger, with all the serenity and divination belonging to strangers hidden in the night. What if I miss him? So she waits all through the winter night, listening for his shirked whisper. But all that she hears is the frost, indistinct as a widow who will not marry again. Near dawn, Elinda's limbs move heavily to meet the clearance of dawn. Then she dreams of a flightless bird with the head of a faecal youth. Oh Azrael, she whispers, walking across sleep's thrasonical sea. Luke overhears and smiles. He rinses his mouth out with clear water from the well. This hour's stillness is the opening of love's letters. The pupils of his eyes are green like branches and leaves and lighthouse lenses.

SKELETON WIELDING HAMMER

Winter: vandal snow, icefield sky, dead-locust leaves. Elinda coughs drably and desires the happenings of summer. She recalls the words on the hoarding: *Blessed are they who fear the Lord and walk in his ways.* But such sentiments do not thaw her body. She wants to become just a girl picking flowers by the seashore, free of all melancholia. But her dreams are the colour of pigeon blood and she still lingers at that great entrance. Pangs of an approaching orchid disease teach Luke the tricks of ancestry. He dawdles in the draughty corridor, dreading the heyday of the madmen. The last day of the moon is unlucky. Elinda looks up casually and pauses in her self-imposed task of sorting through the soiled linen. She speaks to him frankly. You must go away, Luke. Leave me. The time has come now that it is cold and fires are building. You have my free and unconditional consent to a separation. You can go back to Hagar. Elinda speaks with the faint resonance of a patois. But, smiling dwarfishly, he shakes his head. She wraps the shawl around her shoulders, huddling into the warmth, watching him carefully from the watchtower of a widow's chastity. Luke nudges the cupboard door with his elbow, closing it. He looks at her with exultation. No, I will stay with you, he promises, there may come a time when you will need me, Elinda. She shrugs and grins feverishly. And at that time, she tells him darkly, you will be safer stranded in the Mare Orientalis . . . So Luke touches her sandarac hair, thinking, all that may be forgiven, is. Despite what you have torn from me, Elinda, the heart quarried from the breast, the soul from the loins, I will remit all that you have lost, I will bear with everything you have done or have caused to happen. My forktail body is forever in need of you. What is it? he asks gently, what are you thinking? Just about the rain marriage of a girl I used to know and the clever songs she used to sing, Elinda says shortly. She despises his concern for her on this greyish afternoon. She wants to erase him from her life. But when she tries to side-step him, he won't let her pass. Luke wants to tell Elinda that one night shortly before their wedding he went walking through a wild porcine forest and in the darkness all he thought about was her, her skeletal heart and her sensorium of blood and whether he dared in all honesty marry her. Your strange and curious body, he wants to say. All his past life besieged him that night and in those brainstorm depths death auditioned him: Pools of blood oozed in the moonlight. Crooked crimson hours . . . Only the persuasive dawn saved him, with its sane view of the whole affair. Only the sunrise enabled him to decide what was right. Now he doubts the wisdom of those decisions. He thinks of the cautery of a death in sunlight whilst a zither plays. Once, Elinda, your glance was not a cretinism. Once it comforted me. Now I dream only of the Luftwaffe. But he knows he will tell her none of this. For I am not a legendmonger. Elinda regards him with sleazy suspicion. Why did you come to me disguised as a traveller? she demands remorselessly. For her pledges must be honoured. In a corner of this room there is a chair with a piece of red cloth hung over the back. He stares at it. Disguised, you say. Can you be sure of that? Can you be sure of anything, Elinda? She hesitates. Where are her friends? Then he whispers her name twice, in a coprophobic manner that threatens her clutch on the day. Yes? she answers, yes, what it is, my love? Assassinations in a dark room. Come with me, he repeats, and he descends the stairs in silence, lumbering towards the abortive future, clad in protective clothing. She calls after him, palatal questions. Deep shadows reschedule banquets. Her pawnshop bracelet drags at her thin wrist. But she follows him. Gothic outlines of trees move discontentedly over the lawn and Luke thinks, ah but this has all happened before, I have pursued this moment before, I recognize this waiting and the same chill has fallen fecklessly upon me. He looks at Elinda, seeing her for the first and last time. Judging her thirst. How long have we been married? he asks suddenly. Again she shrugs, a young woman with a face not yet scarred. Accumulating days escape her notice. The molestation of hyacinths abducts her, their fragrance flushing into the room, remote parishioners. It has been ten months. He is speaking to a mythical bride who wears a chaplet of toad-eggs. Inoculations of the past drug him. But, for Elinda, where are Matthew's soothing avian fingers? I want to give you this gift, Elinda. The words are a tiny mouthful of acid for Luke. She sits unmoved, a lioness with a mirror held between her forepaws. I want nothing, she says, just leave me alone to be very quiet and lonesome and cold as ice. Let me enjoy the stone puppets of winter. But he represses all doubt, he still sees her veiled in the betrothals of burning: and he gives her the gift, entreating reverence for his electro lies. There is a blessedness about this kind of mesmerism, thinks Elinda, and normally it satisfies all the crazy girls. So why am I ravened with fear? What is it I fear? Wounds hacked in my breasts? The advent of a spayed gunman? Again I acknowledge my coastal longing for Matthew. Elinda shrinks from Luke's offering, an amber necklace, beads of fossil resin. She fears the dancing of the Melanchroi. She weeps amateurishly. But he fears no totem animals. He praises her womb until light moves through her accepting fingers. Perhaps this gift will compensate for the loss of her numb nurseling dream. Examining the beads more closely, she notices that each bead is carved in the likeness of a bird skull. She looks at him questioningly. Half of what we say is true, he tells her. She thinks of the alive-dead woman, Hagar, unknown and yet hated, the reality Elinda tries to copy. Is this how Hagar smiles? Is this how Hagar moves, guarding herself against God's epilepsy? Between the thought of Hagar and the memory of Matthew, Elinda is stretched out from one darkness to another. She moves slowly, still imitating Hagar, and kisses Luke, celebrating dysmenorrhoea. He has doubts of colour. A sharp sudden pain in his side panics him and he almost cries out for help. But somehow he remains silent and sombre, watching Elinda. She finds a mirage in the bare mirror. I'll tell her now of my long night of incarnation, thinks Luke. But Elinda is already speaking. So Hagar did not want this necklace? she asks, with a vixenish curiosity about the laws that govern their relationship. Now Luke is afraid of his own huge hirondelle heart. No, she did not, he answers, simplicity itself. Luke and Elinda make crash-landings in an epsilon neighbourhood, no hand on the helm. Elinda's amazonian agitation frightens him, like all the childbeds of Europe and Asia. I'm illegitimate, she shouts, yes, Luke, I am! It doesn't matter, he protests, suddenly downcast, the world freezing harder around him, chilling him to the bone. Elinda strops words. What do we reap from our tracheal days? she asks angrily. He looks out at the big white sky. He cannot shelter Elinda now. So he criticizes her clothes, finding fault. He hates his wife. She shouts again, a vox humana. Tell me, what would you like me to wear? A swan shift? A brown shirt? But now he stays silent, not betraying the dynasties of guilt, the dying embrace of the conjurer, not speaking of that fluviomarine music, no, he remains mute. There are ionic miles between them. Elinda kisses his cheek. He performs perversions. She watches Luke make love to a statue and she is not even contemptuous of him. Why do we seek out re-enactments of bruises, ultimatums and alibis? Why, when we know there will be no reward? Oh I sense that something youthful in me is dying, the apparition of a girl succumbs to necrosis and leaves me here alone. Elinda listens for any sound. She will listen to anything but Luke's last breath. Was that a train whistle? Gunfire? No, there is only the sea. Reminding her that she is wearing one of her oldest dresses. He never lies. Now he laughs, a glacial mirth, and stares at her interminably. All hours expire in the belly of the moon. The ageless necklace surrounds Elinda's throat and distinguishes this day, making it a thorax day, setting it apart from all other time. Elinda reads aloud newspaper reports of the indo-chinese movement of troops, their suffocation of ambush. And Luke wonders how it would feel, to fasten his strong hands around her throat. No, he thinks, we must not turn our lives into modern myths. Slow as one who, retreating, walks with the sick and wounded, he crosses the plenipotentiary room to sit beside her. He takes her hand and strokes her flinching palm. He caresses her ring-finger. He looks into her vapoury eyes so that nothing is private. He fears her. Let me tell you something, Elinda. Yes, a confession, if you like. Hagar and I are drawn together by one love . . . His voice is low and yet very real, akin to hosannas. It drains her of all christianity. We do not dare to laugh now, she thinks. We begin our lives with one kind of passion and conclude with another, less melodious, more heartless. What is that love? she asks, her lips goaded. He tells her, without hesitation. A child. Our first and only child. She's called Pardissa. She is seven years old. She is deaf and dumb. Elinda closes her eyes. I see a crucifixion place. Now Luke cannot touch his shock-haired wife. She hears her own ultrasonic cries. It's over! It's over! Locksmith magnitudes stun Elinda. She remembers those who always die at the end of each summer. She runs her cold hands through her hair, becoming aware of her own calvinism. As she rises, slowly but not tranquilly, he is precipitated into an apostle's interlude. Discernment of living flesh becomes a mystery to him: from which he vainly seeks to escape, extinguishing all protestations and trysts and breathings. He sits watching her quest through interrogations, unable to help her. Unable to give her even the strength of one austerity. And he opens his clenched fists to stare at his own unmarked palms, becoming wholly absorbed in their contours. Elinda weeps for her disablement. For her punishment. She is denied even puerperal dreams. So, she groans, bearing witness to the scorched earth, this is why there is to be no child for me? He nods, then flees into words. Yes, Elinda. I will not permit another experiment. I will permit no more falling wombs to accuse me . . . But you know the worst now. I have no more secrets. He smiles faintly. You are safe now, Elinda. Things will improve now. After all, you have survived this far, haven't you? She faces him formally, her flesh the land, her blood the sun, her bones the mountains and her skull the sky. Survived? What makes you think I have survived? Just because I stand here, speaking to you? Listen, Luke, there are for me hell-days when I have to go out wildly walking along this coast-line, miles and miles, until I am footsore, trying to silence a voice which remonstrates within me. Oh the eloquence of it! Its beauty! But I hate it. I just want it to leave me alone. How it exhausts me! I truly believe I cannot stand this voice very much longer. It is a voice which causes landslides, false timescales, cervical cancers. Creatures that have great daedal tusks jutting out from their foreheads. It is this voice which turns lambs into lions. It discovers fire in a forest. It tells me that Hagar is a woman who has no time for death. It says that I am a sacrifice you are making to her. It says that she is permitted a child whilst I suckle only my fingers. Yes, that is what it says. Listen! Even when I run across the fields, it follows me, shouting, *I know where you are going but not even the sea will carry you off to safety.* Then it laughs a bloody laugh and says: *your life is like the circumference of a circle: you go round and round on a quisling journey: yet any supposed reconciliation between you and your desires, Elinda, is a phony rumour.* Oh yes, that is how it talks, this voice which is neither still nor small. It never gives me any peace. It denies me everything I want: gives me rejection instead of absolution. It says that my attempts to love are items not valid . . . In her darkness, she hits the keyboard of the piano with global fists and again she wails, my life is one of violence and slavery. Never use the word survival in association with me! No. The intended prey of myself is my own self. I know that if I succeed in silencing this lockjaw voice I will render myself null and void. If I live with it, I am dying. If I finally die from it, then I am dead. And nothing more. So I live, lodged in a gunnery, where no priest or rabbi or lover can enter in . . . Anger magnetizes Luke and he grabs Elinda's hair. Now listen to me, he shouts, I think you're just a noisemaker! You could go on day and night, couldn't you? What makes you think you're the only one in pain, in the throes of rectal reconnoitres? No, Elinda, no. How much more do you think I can take? And he pushes her away from him. When Matthew's sister spoke it was with an inflectional magic. But Elinda yells at Luke, using ptomaine words. He defends himself, saying, perhaps there have been actions in my life of which I am ashamed. But I have confessed to the proper authorities. What more can I do? She turns away from their toxicosis. If only my death meant more to Luke that a fleabite . . . Elinda's mind is a padlocked mirror. She believes that her marriage is a jail from which she must abscond in order to rule over a new decathlon landscape: she wants to see that pure pilgrimage place where the recoil of a gun is unknown and all reconciliations are possible: where there are no reports of battle on the outskirts of the city and no guerillas renounce the world for rebirth in the certain haven of flame throwers. Some cruel words regarding Hagar come out of her mouth and in their outflow is hidden all her hungering for that pale ghost of a summer where she once sheltered. But Luke hears only her abuse, not her sadness. He does not know that eternities are held within her voice: nor how hard the journey is for her, the metachronal passage towards a self-pronounced humiliation. So when Elinda hisses, how do you know it is your child? he strikes her down, believing that they struggle in a reincarnated hour. She falls, hitting the piano with her elbow. Notes clang out of tune. Sounds for the ears of migrating birds. Yet

Elinda wants Luke, she wants the complicated simony and sodomy of one man, this man to whom her flapping hands yearn, now that it is too late. She wants his homicidal youth and is convinced of the sanctuary to be gained within his arms. She will never kick out at his lies now, no matter how often his faithlessness assails her, making her heart a bloody sanhedrin of bereavement. How postponement of dying has deceived her! Look, their mouths are twisted, criminology flashes in their eyes, this woman crouched against the wall, the man ranting above her. Now there will be only a few more incapacitated mornings frozen into a hypochondriac prelude and then: the crisis, separation, ectoplasm of ending.

THE GODDESS SEKMET

Deities catch sphinx moths and eat ghosts. A javanese puppet takes refuge behind a mirror. Someone hidden in her own darkness signals to the army. A worshipping world hunts for ivory shells and weeps over its last child. A watcher in the hall is declaring names silently. The controller of the houses of the Red Crown remembers a running girl with a long cloak. The time between January and March is an avoided zone. The day the snow melts, Elinda is sitting in a fireless room, a woman of rank, on her lap a closed book inscribed Elegiae. After sleeping, we swam, she thinks.

VISION CLOTH

She writes cautiously in an italic hand, bringing her correspondence up to date. Words vanish into the unpainted day. For her diary, she uses a language of abdications and cloudrifts, establishing her own history as a burnisher. A narrow street on a dark night and we spoke out the names of god. Elinda sighs menacingly. She thinks of Satan's bruises, the broken helioscope and other fragments. She looks down at her new clogs. None of her wounds is healing. She cannot dance. Amber beads lie fever cold and heavy around her throat. And she discovers she has lived a reflex life. So she seats herself at the piano and becomes steeped in dissonances. She never aids the innocent but instead maintains a randomized existence: where only her own image in the mirror and the back-flowing of her blood are important, where all movement is obsessively erotic, ploughing her into an extinct room. She raises the lamp like an instrument of death and looks at him, guiltless. Last night I dreamt a dead man entered my body, she says conversationally, moistening her lips. All her words are saying the same thing, acknowledgments that their shadows are disintegrating. He knows. You've wrecked our lives, Elinda, in a manner not punishable by law . . . he says sadly, recognizing the isoceraunic nature of their cohabitation, how they both will break. Elinda, I believe that now we must separate, even though the ocean will harass our parting by reviving sad and deliberate memories. She does not look at him but murmurs, when you read my helical diary, pray for me, Luke. He knows no remedial language. She is breaking down his heart's patronage. Look, Elinda, there's no one to release us but ourselves. And we must move towards releasing. Are you unable to open your eyes? Have you forgotten your own words? She places her hand on his parricide throat. I will agree to no parting. We are walking, you and I, through a misty land where beaconages hurt us: and we must guide each other out. We are one, Luke. Yet she cannot compel him to stay now. No, Elinda, no. Not even the jointed branches of your hand can hold me here. Her face is dominated by her largo eyes. Luke, what are you? she asks quietly, without cursing. Are you a daredevil or a fool? Are you really sinless, unstained by reminiscent blood? Her puranic learning will not solve her this riddle. Is he an uncrowned king, adrift in the wilderness of my commonwealth? The chronologer of burning wine? Or a repairer of temples? Elinda is capable of cyclopean perceptions but she flees from them, running with an uneven sloping stride that bestows upon her all the dignity of an isolated violence. She goes accompanied by poltergeists. Galloping across the beach, travelling through disinclinations of rain, her flight is a foregone conclusion. Targeteer, she is ranged on the ramparts of the Atlantic. Tasting the cold salt water, she almost vomits. The sea tallies its libations.

She tugs at the amber necklace and the thread breaks, spilling the jesuitry of beads into the ocean waters. She slurs a blessing upon them and they become pebbles. Looking for excuses, dangling her fingers in the icy air, she moves aimlessly along through the faint puritan shades of afternoon, double-locked within herself. She thinks of the first books of the ancients. She senses the movements of old deserts. Please listen to me, Sky. Keep me from the officials of the Board of Punishment. She sits on a rock and calculates methods of suicide, a nun reciting an inferior service. I want a purification of the forest laws! If Matthew is alive, he'll be spending the night with prostitutes. But I must not fear him! When Luke leaves me, will I miss the sound of our bodies' deaconry? Maybe I'll dream of a recklessness stained with blood, the uncalm of a begetting. And wish I was a deaf-mute. Elinda is infibulated by her marriage. Hours later, in a darkness that burns slowly, she enters her bedroom and turns the key in the lock, seeking solitudes, an escape from photospheres. But the first object that touches her eyes is her own tangled wig hanging askew on the blind wigstand, shadowings showered all around. Elinda turns her back on this abomination, she weeps horizons. And again the nilotic sea hails her.

SECOND CREMATION

Helium night: and Luke is suddenly awake, his mouth menthol-ash. Elinda has gone. He is alone in the bedroom: alone in the dusty house. Flowers are turning to ice in a locked chamber. His thoughts are dark and drab, dynamite colours. Midnight is pointing to the north. The wind taints the hard land. She has deceived him. Now he becomes a futurist. He buttons his military coat. Risking the iridization of winter, he ventures out into the garden. Almost immediately he catches sight of her, rushing along the frozen shore, her nightgown billowing around her, her bare arms uplifted, a figurant possessing the mad moonscape. Her breasts are revenant in the moon's accidental light. He watches, motionless, perceiving in his macrobiotic wife the twentieth century embodied in human flesh. He hears the echo of her faint foetus song. Now the distance between them could not be traversed even by astronauts. Jesus, the man says. Soon Elinda comes wandering up through the garden, silent and carnassial, wrapped in an old multi-coloured cloak that belonged to her mother. Her legs and feet are bare. She shivers exultantly. Now there will be a genesis of stone. A bivouac of raw and bloody bones. For he has beaten back the paranoic night-riders. What is all this drama in aid of? he shouts at her. She smoothes back her seaworthy hair. It is merely a last offering, a species of homage . . . she answers, not looking at him, her unanticipated beauty resembling smoke. And she enters the unilluminated house, with no more words, spoken or sung.

A CATATONIC FLOWER

Elinda knows that her deportation is in her own hands now. She stares in the dildo mirror and sees nothing but globs of night. Roots of her hair destroy the harvest. In her mouth, the mental image of a fish. But the sea cannot be touched. The words in her own mouth are sharp against the blade of her tongue and praise the knife she holds in her curveting hand. We met in a desolate place of lapwings, she remembers. The application of her death is only a growling moment away. And she is brave, she is chalcedonic, she strikes out at the flesh. Now I'll see the forbidden faces. Again she hears the singing of that androgen voice. Taiga angels with red tarpaulin wings blood of the dear night nuns veiled in telegrams holding flowers to throw upon the grave of the shepherdess who dies to save six dynasties . . .

FALSE DOOR TO SUMMER

The stranger hammers at the door, hoarse from shouting and recanting, an acupuncture man wary of forfeits. He recalls the haunted caves full of eclipsing birds. He remembers the coldness of the base-camp. He did not hear her hereditary cry. It was the silence whispering in watercolours that called to him so fearfully. We sucked the flowers dry a long time ago. The secrets of his inner-skull seize power and he forces the door open. At first the room looks empty because he enters like one emerging from a dream, not yet able to distinguish between the real and the imagined. He is thinking of those alkaline emotions of hers, the recent exodus of faiths from her myoneural heart. Now he sees her. The dead of the tribe are normally buried but the bodies of those whom it is wished to honour are exhibited on platforms or in trees. The priests pray to a great serpent to show them yams and honey. Bride-elect, her dress of ice-wool is torn and stained by her unleavened sadness. Eaten up by her humiliation, she lies on the floor, one wrist bleeding endurance from a self-inflicted wound. He kneels by her side. Slowly, committed to misery, Luke makes the sign of the cross. Oh Elinda, ashen light is exposing you to a terrible scanning. But you have not escaped, you breathe, you are still a wanderer and have not learnt the age of the universe. Her magellanic life is saved. But this journey between the acts of the moon is not finished. Luke will need more than a radar map to direct them to a warless future.

THE THIRD EYELID

She hears unidentifiable voices vibrating slowly away into the plantations of a dark dawn. The voices speak the language of jaws that can bite nothing. And Elinda recalls her razor dream. Chilling air revolves around the relic of her body. I wanted a cleverly contrived death! But I was not brave enough. I had too great a fear of that unmuscled descent. I could not die. I could not bear to see the true face in the dark. All I have obliterated is colour. I remain alive, with my repertoire of parables and rumours. Now I must face my fever's therapy. God's penalty. Elinda is sedated, held in a white custody. Her subsonic hands are quiet now. But she still hears the clarion call of the sea which arches her body and makes her sick as if she had been insect-eating all night. She tries to get out of bed but falls back, her head alive with pagandom. Oh, she thinks, I must lie still, I must be still. I must become very calm, very still. So still that he will wail and wonder if I am still breathing, so motionless he will forget the colour of my eyes. Elinda is prey to the hypnotic influence of circles, a pre-luminosity of terror she consents to without question. She dedicates herself to a confessional hour. Memories trickle out, filling the amphora of the silent room. I met him by chance, this second man, the one who bandaged my wrist and called the doctor. A crowd of people were at our heels that first day, lawyers, hippies and divorcees. But by afternoon we were free. We were alone. And we walked slowly through the frosty fields. I remember the winter-white boles of the silver birches. And the belated sky. I spoke of elemental beauty and he smiled at me. We stood beside the riverbank and watched the swans. What are you looking for? he asked me quietly. Was it this capillary darkness? Elinda, the unbeliever, opens her mouth. But she has no knowledge of war-cries. Her tongue is fogged. Behind her third eyelid she sees a shrine, significance unknown. She has only just embarked upon her retreat. Her body is one ulceration. I used to be happy. Ah but that was long ago, before Jesus Christ blew into town. Habitual humiliations linger in my mind! I think especially of black feathers falling slowly through the air. And of his other wife. Whose name I cannot recall. Yet whom I hate. With my sinistral hatred. That is like an exploding star. Afterpains of silence rend Elinda. I think of the life-history of the serpent. An aboriginal heart pounds inside my ribcage. Useless animal! Why won't it stop beating! Why doesn't everything stop! Why don't they behead me! I have become machinery, locked in one rhythm. I am of no use. The mirror reptile overpowers Elinda. She raises her voice and raves about tomorrow's apocalypse. Luke opens the door softly and assesses her strength. Apparently frowning, he decides to make a phone call. Elinda sucks the teats of her pillow. Then she lolls in the bed, her body stuffed with cotton-wool. She sees nothing. She thinks of Luke as a one-eyed messenger. She visualizes him preparing his departure, sorting hurriedly through desk drawers, the very image of a nostradamus, glorying in her downfall. I remember once saying to him . . . what did I say? Oh yes, I remember. I made a brief but dignified comment on the confusion of the room, comparing it to the confusion of our lives. But all he said was, christ, Elinda, go away. So I obeyed. I went away. Further than either of us intended. Sawing through the flesh, falling amid blood. Now I am impaled upon my own vomit. Novocaine thoughts deaden my brain. She closes her eyes. She is still surrounded by nudes. I am sinking in the reservoirs of silence. Yet it was I who recommended this dissection of the voice. And again I think of the old sea breaking over the strand in unrehearsed waves. Reality constantly blackmails me. Life's continuous motion carries me towards the desperate ones. Apprehensions of ice are always with me. Rage, pain and grief: is that all? he asks. Why does he refuse to believe in me? Am I paying a debt then? *Yes, of course I am. Am I?* Being lost, she shivers. False faces watch her, selected hands minister to her. And then this hydrophobic girl sleeps. As sad as the gradual extinguishing of all the candles but one, her greyish face flickers upon the zone of evening.

ABSENCE FLAG

All night, mirrors conserve her body, testifying to her inexorable innocence. She dreams of her ukase blood and of making ready for the ice age of grief. When she wakes, she whispers, ah yes, there is still the malnutrition of my heart. I hate morning. Light penetrates my petalled skull. Darkness I've always understood, crept into its arms, been happy to lie in its curative cave. But this untwists the flesh from my bones: and I, alone, trapped in my rockfall head, cannot stub such light out between my thighs. The holy war between myself and the day goes on forever, the corneas of my eyes the bloodless battlefield. Luke brings her food and asks questions but she will not answer, she will not utter a word to him, she stares at the wall and her silence is the extent of their world. He touches her but there is no response. She is too deep in the assyriology of her sickness. She reminds him of the precipitation of his own dreams. There is no peace for him, not even in sleep-movement. Automatically his white passionless hand strokes her forehead. These weeks of broken glass establish his determination to leave her as soon as possible. He needs to return to the land of the apple coven. But always he looks at Elinda pityingly. And extends the duration of his vigil. He knows only the heart of Isis will cure Elinda. He does not trust the doctor who says, let her drag herself down, let her try to measure herself. She needs these vibratory shocks in order to remake her life. She is strong enough to break down. She will arise. Luke does not believe official words. Her gulping face frightens him. Suddenly she screams out . . . I can see a bullet-proof warrior! Once again Luke must guide her away from violence. Behind her eyelids, she watches the drowning of seven seas. She falls from the cramping sky. And the watcher goes on waiting amid brush-fires and wind-whirled pyres. Elinda rejects the rosary he offers her. The shadow in her heart does not need it. Is there no place between life and death where I can hide? Is there no shelter from affliction? Why do I feel multi-sexual? Who is this man, touching me? Is there no directional effigy to guide me, a pointing finger? Elinda is a breakwater, waves of blood crash against her. She sees for the first time the unveiled faces of her jury: all women . . . And she subsides into a trembling. The echoic desire for escape reduces Luke's sensitivity to her troubles but nevertheless he stays with her, day after day, week after week. As Elinda lies exhausted by an incantation, he writes to Hagar, breaking his long silence to tell her how much he admires her courage in returning to her family. But do not let their distortions touch you or the child, he warns, for they can turn you to wood if you are not strong enough. It is hard for Luke to write, living as he does in a world of absenteeism, but he contrives to say that there are new feelings within him which neutralize the counterfeits once separating them. He cannot help but tell her of the strain he is experiencing and how he will not capitulate. He frowns as he signs his name, consciously that of a marginal man. The rain's drumming has produced insensibility in Elinda, she is sleeping, light capsized over her face. She is at peace now, he thinks, gently touching her throat, and perhaps she has given me power over her. All Luke's genito-urinary tension demands a release into his own violence. He hears another exhausted marriage expiring in this room in this house (a house of bricks and bone) and the hand he is resting upon her throat shudders. Her body is the deciphering of maps. But Luke rejects the dementia of a darkening house. He is afraid of the nystagmic god within him. Who makes a dog and an ape go dancing together through the trees . . .

THE BONESETTER BREVIARY

I could destroy you slowly by charring the edges of your photograph, Elinda. His thoughts are dust of the cross-roads. All the dribble of time runs out of mouths and two people almost weep when another clock strikes another hour. Elinda severs dyed strands of her hair from her head and offers them up to the god of gold who fortifies and fertilizes the angel before annunciation. She looks out of the window and sees a strange woman of pure conduct. And she realizes that a portion of herself has been returned to its rightful owner. Now her cantonment of shadow has two doors: one leads to a sanctuary, the other to a precipice. She opens the window and watches the unhated weather. Soon she must relinquish her vice, saying, no more of this delirium, for I am no longer the veronal woman I was. I can no longer renew my indifference to life. Now I'll forget the worship of the ibis. My sustenance is of a different nature now. I have exhausted the old dish, licked it clean. My mouth no longer wishes to cause mirrors to weep. My anchylosed time is ending. I am alive and my travelling will take me on to the time of the winter barley. I'll unmask my phylactery phantoms. I want to see the lion sun presiding over the annual floods. I am not afraid of the throat of the lunar bull. She smiles and touches her breasts discoveringly. She is unable to curb the decay of the talionic flesh but now she is eager to heal. She will forget her fears of mastectomy. The colours of the wind's hoof can still wound me. But I see strength, freedom and swags of flowers — my future when I climb out of the witch's cradle. I shall leave this ravaged area of maximum moonlight. She zips her jeans and pulls on a sweat shirt. Preacher of the gospel, she whispers, walking down the stairs carefully, planting her feet with a calm prudence, the divorce and remarriage of movement. Luke hardly recognizes her, she walks in so chastely. Goatsong, he thinks, and there is a rift among his widows. He cannot delete anything from their imperfect experiences. She touches him taperingly and begins to explain the shy scope of herself. My life began with reproaches, Luke, it has been renegade. I always went from day to day in a monochromic mood. When I was seventeen I met a young boy in a café and I loved him modestly. We hid in dark rooms and pretended to make love. It was a time of hope and the whiteness of shapely mornings. Until I had an attack of conjunctivitis. Then he lost interest in me. A year later I met someone else. We basked in summer. I saw how Matthew was stunned by his own knobbly lust. I remember myself, clutching dandelions. We lived together contemplatively for over a year. An ethereal alliance. We were pyramidists. Then he went away. I travelled from a place of flowering trees into a city of cinders. I consoled myself in latrines. I had a dream at this time. I was in a hospital ward of pygmean women. I was waiting. I touched my throat to find my crucifix but it had been taken away from me and in its place they'd hung a black necklace. Then she came towards me: a uniformed nurse in an advanced state of pregnancy, transfixed through the belly by a great festering nail. She asked me, have you remembered to bring the church keys? The day after this dread I met you. I thought that with you my numbness would vanish somehow, perhaps during one hour of partial twilight beside this sea. Luke watches her, his body remorsing flesh, all his words athwart. He listens, testing the bark of willows and poplars. But it did not work out, Luke. I couldn't rest with you. Every day I felt a murmur within me, of the north and of the quarry forests where I used to wander. Nothing seemed capable of cleansing me. I descended into a glass-cut underworld and I dwindled to nothing. Luke, I prayed to the priest of the ocean. I stumbled towards hailstones, my armpits on fire with a dirty evanescence. And then my hand discovered the moon-knife. I put it to one side and pretended that I had removed the weapon a great distance away, to a place where telegraph poles no longer scouted the horizon. I closed my eyes and thought of perfect colours, purifying tokens. I wanted to be burdened no longer. I remembered all that I had forsworn. But my fingers demanded another liberation. And that cold blade intoxicated me with promises of a safe region. I thought of our criminal conversations, Luke, and I sliced through the flesh like an army surgeon. There was a noise of an animal howling which frightened me. It was my own cry. Afterwards, for a long confused time, there was only a confiscatory darkness interspersed with glaring whitenesses. So I fell into a crypt. I have been hiding in my room all these weeks, thinking about heaven, hell, love, wisdom, the moon, corn, war and the sea. Of this world and why I shiver unaccountably. One evening I remembered how I once stood, without a name, in a church. Our pauperizing marriage. It was a hard catastrophic day and I said to Christ, but why should I waste my despair on you, you dead thing. He stared at me with his spermless self-exaltation but he made no reply. He never does. That night the singer sang his adjustable love-songs. But by then, Luke, I was well on my way to becoming a puppet with cathartic eyes and a weeping womb. I was so afraid of that girl statue. My ghosts terminated in dolmen distances. It is because of old perching despair that I sometimes see truncated moons. They are symbols of myself. Luke, am I at the turning-point? This time last week I was a crazy girl with a coin in her mouth, not even able to dish out kisses sparingly. What kind of girl am I this week? I only know I am different for the first time in a long while. I am being transformed, anointed, saved by my mutations. Am I justified in believing this? Is it true? Dare I leave my despair behind? Matthew once looked at me and whispered of the millennium. Once he told me I possessed the numismatic splendour of a priestess. Yes, I believed him. But since then I have discovered more of the world's nature, investigating its vanity, its cockroaches and the penalties it reserves for pickpockets and the homeless. Matthew! Listen. Do you hear how ironically his name echoes in this room. Yet I told him my most blasphemous thoughts. I begged him to stay with me. I brought him my favourite flowers and glasses of whisky. I cried aloud in an edgeless eternal voice. But no, his eyes were fastened upon an idolatrous horizon of smoke and steel, where shadows of soldiers dominate the sun. He had found hatred within his groundless heart. On that last day, he called me a jingling witch. He left us alone. But I could not live with just my own shadow concentrated in the mirror, could I, Luke? So I fled to a stranger. I danced and laughed and often got drunk and never confessed but oh how I shouted. Luke interrupts her, asking abruptly, who are you, Elinda? For he is lost in her mythoplasm. She is unable to answer this question and she refuses to focus her civilization upon it. Let me finish, she begs him, please, let me speak of my musculature in my own way, Luke, or I shall become debris again. He nods his shriving agreement. I have bruised myself with spites, she continues. After we had been married about six months, I slept a great deal of the time, even my ankles and knuckles were tired. Often I dreamt of the blond soul singer clinging to a microphone, pretending to weep whilst his concubines shrieked at his feet and stretched out their supple murderous arms. One night I found myself at the motherless hour. It was as if the fingers of a parrot had pulled my eyelids off and I saw the paper house burning at the graveside. Yes, I thought, skewered upon my sweat, darkness and light, now I shall be trapped between them, always disfigured. Elinda pauses, unsmiling. Perhaps you were born to be peaceless, says Luke enviously. She shakes her head. Luke, what deceivable words . . . Even before marriage our tongues were rotting as we gibed at each other; and behind all the bloody mirrors, obscene eternity waited, fleshlessly. And on that suicide night of mine, it lashed out at me, teaching me how soon the spirit can break and defeatism seduce that brittle web, the heart. So I fell, grimly bleeding. And ever since then I have been trying to walk again towards the trekking light. Did I walk downstairs? Is this real? Am I becoming alive again? When I married you, Luke, I participated in a sterile elopement. I could not forget Matthew. I thought of him constantly, as I still do, until the walls writhe with lizards. I think of him, with his visions of asbestine gospels. And as I stare hopelessly or hopefully (it has not been decided yet) at the sky, I consider the mercenary's power he still wields over me, cancelling the strength of atoms. Sometimes I wish that the ungovernable bones of myself and of Matthew were buried in the desert. No, do not look sullen. You must understand what I mean by this. It is because I want Matthew and myself to be safe. It is because I know he is not free from the agonies and frenzies we all go through. Because I know even he is not spared the diminishment and the exhaustion. Only death will free Matthew, as it will myself. Yes, Luke, I am recovering. I am calm. I am mantled in the filaments of day. Perhaps in the future there will be other hours of terror but they will be occasional and we'll soon forget their narrowing policy. I will not pick up the knife again. The deaths I pray for are natural deaths. When there will be no impatience, no pretence. How I envy the dead, the eyelashes of the embalmed and beautified bodies lying so still, so breathless . . . It is that peace I wish to know, that ocean of tranquillity. She comes towards Luke. He touches her breasts silently, to learn her lore. But he cannot believe she has escaped her old world's domination. So he is afraid, he cannot speak and knows that he too must devise a new life. Elinda touches his hand and slips away to walk sedately beside the oxalic sea. She believes that her freedom will last. Luke can still hear her alphanumerical words. The murmur of her speaking comforts him. But when she returns an hour later and holds him in her infanticidal arms, he shudders, thinking, this is bone of my bone, flesh of my flesh.

A WHITE NOWHERE

Because of the latency of a lazy vision Luke watches her movements with chancroid suspicion. And his weakness increases, he knows a continued pain that has the texture of a severing. Through the sunlit March mornings she goes frailly and without weeping. She is counting her zeroes. She visits the amusement arcade without fear for the first time in her life. She is learning the distribution of myths. Some afternoons, when rain gauzes the fallen lands, she studies a book with illustrated plates showing curiously-shaped roots and flowers. On Sunday she sits in the lady chapel of the great oratory, gazing casually at a blue portrait of the Virgin. Elinda is beginning a new kind of cryptanalysis and this time she is determined to become an accomplisher and not an accusant.

Meanwhile, the letters Luke writes are of a spectral pleading. He tells Hagar that Elinda is terminating their union. For the girl's unhasped gait troubles him, he believes she goes like one food-gathering in a museum. He sees how she stares at the ripple marks in the sand. He does not know that she is thinking of those tameless rites of passage which led to her revulsive dances, her clasping of flight. Luke tells himself: she is the bisectrix woman with ammonite bones seated judgingly at a halfmoon table. At night Elinda's nudity shocks him. Each evening he fears that her flesh will have acquired a hardness like the skin of a china doll. He does not touch her. He avoids her, believing she has a pestilence of the vagina. Elinda accepts his sexual restraint, interpreting it as a mark of respect. She is not revengeful yet, she is grace-diffusing, she sleeps successfully. Luke doubts all her lambency and remembers that reverberatory furnace their bodies used to fan. Yet still he cannot make a choice between evils or find meanings for their bone-scraping games.

THE AMBER ISLANDS

Elinda, the mosaicist. Her probation ends. Her interparoxysmal calm ends. The spirit cult calls her as she watches slow birds flying like sanctionative women. Luke finds her late in the monsoonish afternoon. She is crouched naked on the floor, talking to the statue in a thin hypercritical tone. Ah I have relinquished all promises, I have disobediently turned from all the epiphany prospects. Why did I do it? Tell me again, sister, I've forgotten. Yes, I'll tell you. I have forsaken everything because I know that everything, oceans and cities and forests and the sunlight and his penis: all these things are unreal, a genocidal trick. Yes. I know. I was once told by a poet that I resembled a genitive queen and that even at dawn I possessed icy involuntary courage. But in spite of that I am trapped again, deprived of a clear hour. Suddenly Elinda catches sight of Luke and smiles up at him craftily, her lips phosphoric. As he reaches down to take her arm, she dodges out of his way and runs into the kitchen, shouting: Luke, Luke, don't you know that my life consists only of spectres? Don't you understand? Don't you care? How I hate this phenol landscape! What happened to yesterday? I liked yesterday. Where's my strength, my peace? Yesterday I sat quietly in this room peeling apples. But now I'm lost, wandering again in the precincts of a great desulphurized desert, falling headlong into fire no ice can soothe . . . Words without meanings resound in my head. In the beginning . . . A crutched man hobbled rapidly towards me but I couldn't run away. I saw his long fingernails. I'm only a sub-tenant of this scrawny body. Today everything frightens me, Luke. Listen, I'll tell you this, my instability is caused by seasons, fears, hands, storms, all the ordinary terrible things. Why shouldn't I be telling the truth, Luke? Don't look at me like that. Lies no longer suit me. They don't help me. My face is not the face of a liar. Look in the mirror. See? Yes, I know. I do look in mirrors too often. God knows why. Luke's surging heart-chamber advocates Hagar's supremacy. Elinda can hardly bear the leaden-feathered ghosts of this day. She talks compulsively. Once, in midsummer, standing in the garden, looking with suddenly keener vision at the expatriate yellow flowers, I asked Matthew to come help me into the house. There were lurking pains in my breasts and loins, fever whimpered like a simpleton through my bones and I ached in a classical fashion. It was a miscarriage. Ever since then I have been in half-mourning. Elinda is quiet for a moment, fiddling with the crucifix fastened around her throat. Luke touches her hand but she shakes him off, almost absentmindedly. She speaks again, defiantly. So I fall into these hours of loss. Am I weeping again? I did not notice. I fear the blind end of a long dark corridor. There are six toes on my left foot. Last night I imagined that a long lost friend of mine smiled meticulously at me and led me into a shadowy summerhouse where she strangled me with her stocking. And then Matthew's sister laughed in my face. She told me I was a fool. Yes, I know I'm getting confused, Luke. I always do. The pieces of my life will not fit together. My inner ear is deafened by martyring. How I've always longed for appeasement. But I recall her face, the face of his sister, strange, uncivil, segregating me. That selenocentric girl always hated me. She survived everything whilst I was eliminated by the first terror. And yet my nostalgia for her (her penitent's hair) still arouses in me an impetigo. Elinda smiles at Luke because of the unspoken serpentry. I know you will soon escape, Luke. I know you are arterializing all your powers. But first I will tell you truths. Which I will make you hear. Before you leave me, I will injure you with these words of decay. Are you afraid? Does it frighten you when I pull faces? No, you are not afraid. You are at a safe distance. You do not need to engage in the researches of forgetting or have to entreat your saviour for crumbs. Why are you winding your watch? During these supernatural weeks, horology has become hidden from me. So I don't know how long I've been talking. I just swoon and murmur of the Passover, of Olympian acrobats. Yes, Luke, I am sworn to honesty. I am one of life's non-combatants, me with my germplasm limbs and dark purple nipples. The sea peers into my womb and finds it packed with the beaks of obsolete birds. There is a fucking interpreter here beside me who thinks he guides my life but I have other silent secrets hidden within me yes in spite of the damascus light everywhere I still have my dark thoughts and I will not even try to bleach them and as for the TRUTH when have I ever uttered truths through my convulsionary mouth? No, never . . . I sip pain, I am the torn dress. Seeing blood on my hands, I think of Lazarus. Yes, I see how your naked eye closes, slowly but obdurately. I am in thrall to myself, my fetiches. Seeing blood on my hands . . . Luke comforts her like a verminologist. Don't be anxious, Elinda, don't be afraid. I'm here. She looks at him with bloodstained eyes. I am shedding flames, she answers. Then the words of the broken oracle cease. Elinda looks at Luke. Her body is the temperature of bleeding marble prior to the formation of the placenta. We will eat together, he says quietly, we will not disgrace bread. Elinda thinks of the war-dance she performed, dressed in white. She looks at him in a tired dharma fashion. I am not free, Luke, she pants, I am only half-free. An odour surrounds me, like the smell of embalming fluid. He pities her, her tears and her blood. Winter days are short, he murmurs. Their bodies touch stubbornly and shake in a miasma of love that expires before its due term. Recurring events taunt Elinda. With a sound of droning in her throat, she flings herself away from him, rent by a fit of weeping, bronchial and harsh. Her sepulchral sun gives forth no heat. And Luke yields her up to herself, longing to be free of her, to live in a less ashen world and stand before the mandira altar where the tree itself is on fire. And yet how can he ever deny his feelings for Elinda or forget he could not love her more even if she were deaf, dumb and blind?

THE OTHER LITANY

All the rivers are frozen, he says. Elinda is reading a newspaper account of the unnamed woman who concealed the bodies of six strangled male infants in her attic. Frozen, she repeats idly. Thinking, titanic fingers perhaps. Of a marooned priestess. Elinda and Luke move through a strafed hour, threatened by puritanical lunatics. Elinda points at the dummy flowers on the table in the café. Luke smiles hastily. At her approaching mouth. He realizes that despite all her recoveries fascisms are still taking place within her. He knows they both occupy a stratum of extradition all the more rigorous for being situated at the edge of the sea. As they walk through the town he knows that time is on the run. We are ousted by the passion of the mother and the invisible sword of the father. Elinda's infinitesimal blood knows the girl's death date. He can remain here no longer, listening to her rocketry slang. He thinks of all water, tears, sweat, saliva, urine, serum: and how the sinful must drown in their own preliminary prayers to become bloody birds of haunting reduplications of pain. He sees the remediless future lying before Elinda. But he knows she will survive all the roots of blood. And he knows he must bequeath her this trial. Elinda thinks about the absence of the kiss. She asks him a question about the pain of urination. And she covers his heart with a second membrane. I cannot abandon Hagar, he tells her maimingly. I cannot totally neglect that ex-lover of mine. She is the first woman. Elinda's answer causes the hand to rush from the bride's breast and deserves hanging. He threatens her with the breaking of her outermost bones. But her averting sigh is remote and silvan. So you can't abandon her, she says mournfully, I thought you could, Luke, I thought you were a man for shouldering pain. As they compose their dispute, a strange young girl with glazed eyes and a raped tongue runs past them, followed by night. But they are intent upon other matters. Then I am less brave than you thought, Elinda. He speaks solemnly yet with insolence. Now Elinda hears the bones of her body grate. In this unwatched street she talks to him pleadingly. In harpoonless words. Luke, I have recovered from my breakdown. Weeks have passed since my last medusal time. I have locked all the dangerous images away in a gaol of gristle. I am almost free. I do not read my horoscope now and I've burnt my tarot pack. I think only of the wintered lovers. Can't you reward me? Please destroy my fear of Hagar. Please. As she speaks, she strokes his mouth with her cold bare hands. Say you will reward me, Luke. Patiently, he takes hold of her. But it is an act signifying departure. He thinks of a moon on the wane, an expiring lamp, the goddess of silkworms, all Elinda's melancholy penitent images. Elinda, it is because you are now whole and strong as the interior of a star that I have no fear in leaving you. You need no safeguards. You need nothing. You have arisen into your self, diminishing all dangers. I am weak. I can't betray Hagar. My hands aren't the hands of a hero. And I can't stay here with you. Together we are tarpeian. Apart, we'll be really free. She shudders with cryogenic fear as an idiot girl and her companion walk by. Luke and Elinda huddle in a doorway. Their cutaneous shrine is scarred. Dusk is dust of an important ancient city. They can hear the trains. One afternoon last week, says Elinda, subdued, I stood in the garden watching a pilgrim sun set over the sea, and I called out to you, come quickly and watch this, the beauty of it. But you just yelled back, don't disturb me, I'm too busy. I forgive you that. I know how hard it is to venture voluntarily into the dangerous places. But that same night, Luke, I was seized by a ternary fear composed of blindness, sex and death. I thought of all grovelling miracles and I was pain. No, Luke, I'm not strong. I'm afraid of interpreting my own dreams. I fear Ice and His spiky fields. I fear the darkness also, that nitroglycerine sky. I still want us to be as one, Luke. I'll be your wife. I'll become a donor of evenings. She shivers in this doorway, watching him remember the nonperformance of all her other promises. He releases her from his arms. It is growing colder, Elinda, let's go home. They walk slowly through the deserted streets, altering the perspectives. She speaks with exaggerated lip and jaw movements. I am past puberty, Luke. If you leave me, I'll become a promiscuous anchorite, my curving fingers prodigalizing the silence I am and I will only allegedly live, even the crucifix around my throat will be a lie. The gale blowing from the sea twists her ankle-length coat around her legs and she stumbles. Luke takes her arm again and she leans on him. You must not go, she says fiercely, we're only at the terrestrial stage. The wind whips through her hair. Elinda, I must. His quiet voice is ultrasonic. She runs to the porch of their house and clings to the railings. No no no! she wails, razing the world, no, Luke, you cannot go, you have no name, you do not exist except here! She turns to the out-of-focus horizon to find only Luke's exuvial gravity. It is impossible for me to stay with you, Elinda, he repeats. I won't have this bannerless captivity. Hagar waits for me. Doves and doxologies force Luke and Elinda apart. Luke resents Elinda's body shape in the mouthy night, like a lepidopterous mother. He blames her for everything that has gone wrong with his world, for the alienation of his friends and for the bankruptcy hours. He sees in her the veining of the arrow that wounds him back to Hagar. Elinda pleads for a healing that will abridge her rituals. I was walking in the snow looking for plums when you arrived, Luke. Don't you remember? He does not look at her. Her mariolatry tires him. He thinks of the unexpected grace of some murders. She is dry-eyed. She is postponing her weeping. It is not whether you are sane or mad, Elinda, she hears him say, I would still leave you. To me you are the urtication of a blunt knife. A faint unstressed smile touches her face. Am I? She pushes the door open, her heart scorched. Listen: she says suddenly, did you hear someone scream? He listens impatiently. No, I heard nothing. Only the seabirds. Ah yes, she says, accepting her habitual relapse into lamentation. And she murmurs, I want to give myself to you. He stands angrily in the dim hallway, an upholder of feudalism. Her lemuroid fingers strive to placate him. But he shoves her aside, remembering, the iron cross, and then hits her across the mouth. The confusing colours of tigers and saturnid butterflies shadow her eyes. She licks her blooded lips, listening to his allegations, the price of his servitude. He rejects her saltlick need. I'm leaving you, Elinda, because you are an isolationist. You should have stayed a virgin. And he is holding some other words in his hands. She recalls the orange sword-lilies Matthew loved. I am an agnostic nun after all. And my grievance is great, a sharp separation from a tropical heaven. Now her breasts are Luke's leavings. She sees her future hard as ruthenium and cold as dry ice during days of prayer, archery practice, the cultivation of her hands. A big empty mirror is displaying Elinda's empire. I don't care, she cries hungrily, you can go! I don't care. There will be no epitaphs. You're just the nullifier. But she still fears the revenge of an icelandic nativity. Listen, Luke, I'll shave my head! He laughs and turns away, wallowing in the ordure of his mirth, causing abrasions in Elinda's non-fleshy shadow. All evening she watches him prepare for his departure to an inadequate destination. She watches without screaming. She obeys his coarsest order. In their bed Luke and Elinda are a fable test and during their last chiropractic embrace Elinda cries out, but there are three lovers here . . .

JAWS OF THE LUCANIDS

Early in the morning when a darkness is still cascading, Luke leaves her keepsake bed. She switches on the lamp. For she had been waiting all night for the morning of past-pointing. Her diluvial eyes know his mouth's durance. He looks at her calmly, unafraid of her knotted hair. Don't go, she says simply. Don't go, Luke. You know I want your laser-beam self. Don't leave me cooped up here. Stay at least until summer. Then you'll see me decked out in my impregnable silks. He shakes his head and goes on shaving, knowing the policy of his campaign. He cannot leave her any solacements. He is not a lame man. She grabs his wrist, a country-less one. Let me see the inside of your hand, she implores. Let me go, Elinda, get back into bed. It is cold for you. He speaks casually. No, she says, no, I won't be left at this ankh crisis. Will you really walk down the highway, forgetting my lacerations? Listen, Luke, I read that in some lands parents make dolls and upon these wooden dolls they lay the sins of their children, to be borne away and burnt. Can't we do the same for our sins? Elinda stares at Luke and beyond him at her own reflection in the amen-glass. When she sees his unborn smile, she is condemned to long tail-less nights. Tell me how I am to accomplish that real burning that still awaits the dead long after the wind has propelled the ashes away on its deathless air. How can I be rid of the dead, Luke? For already you are as one dead to me. And I'm left in a distressed area. Not bothering to answer, he pushes her back on to the bed. She crawls under the blankets, shivering. There are no faith cures for her. I know no death, Elinda. This parting is alive, freeing us both. Together we are transgressors, we would welcome any anti-christs. So we must separate our hippuric lives. He uses a puritan voice. Deaf, dumb and blind, he thinks. But he must escape. Holy thrustings tell him. My hands, your hands, she thinks. I am not going to ask you to pray for me, Luke. Then she mentions the squirrel cage. But he only laughs. And she is so cold. Only burning at a stake can warm Elinda. He opens the door. The left side of his heart is bleeding. She watches him and knows the stagnation of her veins. She wants to recite a catechism. There is a clock on the wall and the hour is announced by the loud appearance of an imitation bird through a little door. It scares her. The wind howls, a formidable hydrogen voice ordering Elinda to bow down, a prisoner struggling to lift the immense weight of an insect's wing. She watches him check his passport and his tickets. A frightened stupid smile is slipping from her face. He bends down, he kisses her forehead. You'll not be dead to me, Elinda. Your image will remain with me, the image of a woman both rowdy and spiritual, a girl whose lonely self is divided and unverified. I'll see you as you have been, legendary in the mornings, often sunk into, plunged into your own particular meditative solitude. I'll always think of you, Elinda, as the girl who accepted a flower from the hand of a stranger and gave in exchange a small cold coin from her mouth. But the afternoon will not see us as lovers again. And our mutual instruction by question and answer must come to an end. He condemns her to the slave trade. Her whole body is incapable of any murdering. Even her lips are of bone now, splintering. Beneath the continent there is a pre-medieval diagram describing pain and Elinda knows it by heart. I'll always fear for you, Elinda, he murmurs. Who made the war? she asks. In the late fields of winter, the wind moves like many old voices through the grass, leaving after-images of emptiness. All my life now, thinks Elinda, will be a cardiac terror. And she teems with febrifuge. At the last moment, he touches her shanghaied breast. And then she spits at him with a genuine zealotry. For he has the face of a pig gelder. The woman closes her amulet eyes. It is all over. He leaves her. Without another word, without sheltering in prelapsarian promises, without forgiveness. Tremblingly he re-enters the world. He realizes that he will commit the same offence time and again, like a criminal, regardless of punishments or the detentions of the missionary. He can never be a real escapologist. So he walks unprotestingly down the street. He does not know whether the next woman will be clockwork or agrarian. But his life is without championing. And he knows that his enfiladed daughter will also reject him. Elinda stands by the window but he is already out of sight. Stars in the sky remind her of the excrement of larvae. Oh something is glittering in my head, a gangrenous angel. I cannot believe that the exchange of our dolorific messages has ended. What good is it to me that I stand museful? For he does not watch me or touch my harelip heart. My emptying is the anguish of the water carrier. What am I to do now that I have lost sight of so many significances . . . ? What am I to do? Elinda is alone and defenceless before the challenge of her own liberty . . . Now she remembers Matthew once saying: *Explanations do not exist. The eye, the hand and the sex take the place of the priest. There are only ever the broken edges of riddles. One day you will be very unhappy. Only years of arachnology will rescue you. Then only labyrinths will lead you to shelter.*

THE ICE FURNACE

Sky of fibre glass. A feast of tombs. No aphrodisiacs. Nothing creates a skin response in Elinda. She is a chaliced creature. Her mother's christian name echoes in her mind, a shrubbiness she cannot evade. For Elinda there is no more happiness, riot even in mirrors. Her papyrus heart rustles. Her eyelids are streaked with colour like maps. All night she heard the sound of phantom weeping. But she can't re-enact the crowning of the king on his two thrones. She purchases a bunch of snowdrops without smiling at the flower-woman. Her thoughts are sewn roughly together. I bestow gifts upon myself. The archives of her blood simmer. My enemies have scattered. There was no amnesty. I have been left with lacteal wounds. And metritis hours, reminiscent of carcasses. I wish to be transformed into an elm tree. Sometimes I think that herbal moment has rescued me but only until I hear the shouts of the children playing in the street and feel the sun ricochet from the glass of my unlocked door. Then I know pythonism and begin to sing in a thin questing voice. Elinda walks to the harbour. Some of the fishing boats bear the names of women. She leans against the harbour wall and looks out to where the grey sea guzzles the sailors. She suppresses her urine. I am scared, I am an emotional whore. I want any flight to a sunflower city. But I am unwilling to ask god for the privilege of quarantine: and so I cannot cure the parasitology of my bones. There is an everlasting breeding of christs among women: why do I fret to join them? Is it my pornographic penance? Am I pledged to that unslakeable crucifix? Why am I trembling? Is it because I miss the violent dance for two people? Or is it the century or the decade or this one fearful moment which paralyses me? Am I the merciless assassin embedded in every horizon? What is it, this recumbency I long for? The sky clamps down on Elinda's adulterine memories. The dark foliage of her head is beyond the time of flowering. She walks on slowly through the rain, her movements lacertian. I remember flooding. The red bridal chair was like a bloody weir.

KISTVAEN

The snouted afternoon has lasted too long. I shall not leave the house today. *All the places of her joy she filled with her torn hair.* Elinda sketches a map of half-mourning. She is a specialist in the arctic art of spearing each hour through the heart, tallying the length of her solitude until her fingers are soluble glass. Having no name, I envy the snail's mantle. My younger sisters write to tell me they envy me my freedom. They don't know that I have lost my bigeminal self to find this liberty. That I have experienced the revealment of guilt and grief. That I fear weather ships. That I pray for their early happiness. They don't know how I despise my christianised body. I write out verses from memory but I forget the secret meanings. Today is such a dark muciparous day: it is a day on which to erect temples to one still living and praise him/her in a triangulation of serpents. How long since I began this rebellion? I burnt my baby in the flames of obsession. I tore up my paper clothes. Bamboo voices of night say I'm double-faced, double-tongued. My first crime was to grow my hair long, my second crime not telling lies. Don't worry about Christ, he can take care of himself. I delve into my remembrances of cardiac nakedness. I myself have almost died because of those related to me both by blood and casual sperm. Elinda has an astrophysicist's talent for reading only the beginning and ending of letters. I remember how he came slowly into my line of fire, his limbs darkening into his shadow. A reliance on relics? No! Forget the hero stomping on lunar terrain. Forget the croaking of neutered neurotics. Her rewardless mouth twitches as she turns away from the window. She wants to discover the second polar moment. She stares at the diurnal clock. Always the shadows of the future, stretching out towards her . . . She tastes the salinity of ghostdom. But, nevertheless, she sits down to write her nervous airmail letters of condolence.

HUMPS OF FLOWERS

A dark room. A flagellata woman. Her voice. An official language irrigates her ear. Christ ablaze in the upper limb of the sun frightens me. I am a branded slave, a barren tree, a flailing somnambulist. I wear brazen bracelets and my hair is braided with adders. Isolationist, isolationist. Because my uterine lifetime was too long, mother. I would like to copulate with Christ. I would rejoice at that catastrophe. And so it came to pass . . . A heron flies white against the black thundercloud. My fingerprints are deltoid. Gradually the climate will cool, they say, and the summers will be a dominance of fishes. I'm tired of this silent treatment. There is no jesus, no god the womb. Only the chafing of my accused sex and the totem hardness of my buttocks.

BIRTH CHANT

Will this be the flood year? I think the weight of the moon in my heart is what bows me down. Somewhere in my heartbeat I have lost more than an astral body. I have lost the fields of tidal flowers, the brigandine stars: they are spinning out of my orbit, leaving me only gaps of flesh. And for this crime not even she will forgive me. Once I could live out one year of autumn in a single day. Now my hours are haunted swings in a rainy park. How long will it take for me to renovate my solitude where the fugues of a thousand universes etherize me? When will the oceans of the moon wash my body clean? The mirror's hand bleeds. First I must kill one bird with two stones.

SHADOWY WOMAN WITH HOOKED HAND

I have such a hunger I could devour myself! For whose conditional consent am I waiting? An old song mewls in Elinda's mind. Her fictional hair is the colour of crying. The embrace in the bath is her terror. How the windows rattle. Celebrating a double funeral. She runs gracelessly to the station, looking back over her shoulder at the long aggrieving miles. I travel fireless circuits without sentimentality or satisfaction. I am running in order to forget his unhewn sex and the breath of Matthew's manual body that took me by surprise so that I never stopped asking him where he came from . . . What I want is to eliminate all my knowledge of his skeleton. But my shame knows I will never forget. Also there are times, especially when it is prematurely dark or when it rains, that I remember the custodial presence and influx of another man's body, entering me without skill or science. And this memory intensifies all my dispossession. I repent my nickname marriage to Luke. What can I do? Can I bury it in the hearse of my house? Can I hide it in the gloryhole attic together with the shell of my head-dress? No. I may have turned to a new direction but I take all my ceremonies with me. I'm seeking out a fresh affliction, equally venereal yet of a more evangelical moisture. I want to make Matthew return to me. I want him to devote his whole life to me. But where is he? In prison? In the priesthood? In Laos? Elinda slams the train door, stricken with a split-face rage. Even when Matthew turned away, without benediction, I did not realize the extent of my loss. It is only now that I sense the vastness of my infatuation. Lost, Matthew haunts me with an extraterrestrial vigour I only half-glimpsed, half-treasured. Oh the gemmation of our north european summer. Elinda is cherishing her memories. They are tender. Yet they are also sharp as new knives plunged into her side, uprooting the blood. In the ice-bound city, she trudges from store to store, buying an atlas, a camera and a box of dominoes. Crowds of people barge into her, bewildering her. Where are they going? Towards what interlunar calamities? Why are their faces bevelled like glass? Elinda sits alone at a corner table, drinking coffee without enthusiasm. Her coseismic heart vows her to chastity. Students, housewives, tourists and lovers chatter in loud confident tones. She looks at them all sadly. She is set apart. A putrescent sobbing in her throat. She contemplates her nail-bitten fingers. She thinks of the initiations of the past. As he touched my body, his face became petrified with lust . . . And once Matthew said to me, hey, do you want to hear a joke? There was this prostitute who smoked two hundred fags a day and she never had periods, just a fall of soot once a month. Then Matthew laughed, mocking his own purity. And I thought of my own thick tenemental blood. Elinda stares abruptly around the restaurant. She is afraid that soon she will cry out and vomit keys. But remember the strangers! I dare not scream for mercy here with these guardians ready for my cancellation. Their festivity protects me from my fatigue. A tense adolescent boy gazes at her with an intensity that begs for an exchange of flesh. Ah, she thinks as she turns her head dismissingly aside, you also, wanting, needing? I know your body hurts. But you are mistaken, I have no pity to spare. The boy comes across to her table and pauses, waiting for her to speak and save him. One word. Even fleetingly. Their eyes meet again: and her coldness sends him away in flayed silence. Soldier boy, your violence, your burnable nights: how the city is stirring you. Elinda lights another cigarette to use up the monstrous afternoon. Vespertine: she witnesses the resurrection of images on the cinema screen, the black and white memories of some other stranger. She thinks of technological crucifixions. And she tells herself: each day of my life is a farewell bidden to someone who will be dead and buried long before I return. She shrinks within her rumoured skin. This daughter of albion is the last to leave the cinema but she must walk out into the cold rain, traipsing through a city of mongols. The train is slow and dirty. She arrives home, watched by hyaline eyes. Her house is empty. She cannot sleep. The weights of scripture are heavy and her prayers are atrophied. A whitlow wraith, she runs along the beach, surveying the rivalry of rocks. Coming to a standstill, she weeps: and her weeping originates within herself. I have looked at Hagar's photograph for days, trying to discover the nature of the woman who lives and breathes behind that icon. I have sucked from her paper boobs until I puked. And the thought of Hagar and Luke, the respiration and reverberation of flesh, their mesentery desire that once shrank from any disengagement. Is he lying with her now? Adding authenticity to my fear? I wonder if, for Hagar, there was ever a time when her own death became a temptation? When the thought of provoking her own universal death was the substance of her every thought, waking or sleeping? No. Hagar would cling to her flyblown life. She is strong. She will never tear her anserine dress. And the men. I see you both, I fear you both, I am raw since our demurrage of loving. What infra-red hardships you both inflicted upon me. Elinda's sarcoma shadow falls upon sand. Sea is tilting and throbbing. Moon is sheerwater. She picks up a spar of driftwood and looks around apprehensively, afraid of a cauled observer. But she is alone here beneath the floppy clouds. The doors of the night sky are closed. She spaces her words carefully. I am alone on this earth with only a jealous javelin in my hand.

THE WEPT BELL

Dawn plunderage in the season of shinto spring. Valonia silence. At the earliest and greyest of hours Elinda wakes from an angrily unfinished dream, her fingers aching to deny all hands heaven. Plasmodium air breathes her. She moves, listening to her little finger. She encircles the blood-stained clock. She prowls her house, her charnel cunt rank. The street dogs bark. She licks the sky with her tongue. The superstitious women drown their daughters. Elinda flings sensual books on the floor, tears her blouse to shreds and rejoices in the disastrous newsflash. I enter into the iron time. Morning subsides into alchemic groans. Roentgen muscles discharge hot urine. She cries out. But what is crying out except another vanity? The firstborn is always enemy, sacrifice, grief. Espoused to a goblin, she loathes food. She stares through windows of retinal glass and guesses the outlines of another alphabet. At the meridional hour the climax of the area is reached and her head bangs and her breasts are anthills. She wants a real live fuck and tears up the envelope smeared with blood. Flute silence encroaches. She stands in the centre of the room, a girl composed of severity and weariness, looking for the ark of her covenant. The slave huddles over her stone wound. Spiders spin Elinda's androidal life. It is spittle trickling into the mouth of the Blind One who is free from cephalic greed. Dismal cries of seabirds limit my understanding.

The positions of my fingers change too slowly. Little waves of lust lick at me. Silences happen in quick succession. Do I concoct false charges against myself? Am I a woman without bone or womb, just the clangour of ancient ice? I am, I am. A swallowing hand, ash queen of Carchemish. Sourness oozes from the sharp draconic stones I used to call my breasts. And inside the rain a hollow voice echoes from the linden tree, rearranging my leprosy, weaving my separation veil. Elinda reads of mythical monsters, half crocodile, half snake, with merciless wings and claws, often breathing fire: these are the guardians of treasure and chastity. She closes the book. A praying in the afternoon. A radiant spectatress as sun touches the rain. But as Elinda prays she hears a little lizard speaking: You will always go along your way too slowly now, Elinda, trailing miserably through life, burdened with tedious possessions, grapnels, nets and harrows: the festivals of my rainy roots are not for you. Elinda rises from her knees, a resonator, having heard the voice of god. She looks at the glittering branches. Her cloacal prayer leaves her void of redemption. Why does she suddenly think of another unhappy girl, sitting alone and listless in a summer-house, restless in her husband's arms yet unable to cast defiance against the cruelty of his card games? Who is this girl? Elinda has forgotten. She does not want to remember. It is too much trouble penetrating the contradictions of her thought. And so answers, pledges, truths and cures are smothered by Elinda's tiredness. She hides in her house amid the intermittency of wreckage. What is it that drags all light from me? she gasps. Beeswax smears her tongue. Late in the afternoon she tries to sleep and her lunar wrist bones entice her to dream of enemies who authorise official inspections of sanity. And so she wakes, remembering that today is the anniversary of her adoption. Closed doors of dusk. And she is the coldness of toads. She is the transformation of libation into witch. Whispering, yawning, muttering, she moves disobediently in a mandala dance. Her body is blanched and bruised. Evening is a broken fountain, dry. Next autumn the harvest will be of white silk. Last night I ground the moon into a fine grit that now goads my scalp. Today letters arrived for me. I won't read them. I'll make other arrangements. I must be capable of a future. Spasms of tallness must shove me forward. I must find another language to describe my special abilities. I'm not a creature of the lowest order, having only one vent for urinary, genital and digestive purposes. I am a woman's body. I'll find an exit from this membranous labyrinth and god the encumbrancer will die! Elinda, the unvisited . . . Who hears the death cry of the male ash tree. Who sucks her ring finger. Who stares at the thousand fragments of night. Until the aeromancy of loneliness thrusts from her mouth a great moan and she cowers before the vampire who is splashing through her veins. There is no accomplice for Elinda to blame, no one to hear her cry: you told me lies! She is calling out loudly: Luke, Luke . . . But her mouth dries like shingle and anyway there is no answer. So she enters her anus with a prying finger. She hopes to discover evidence of love in this evacuant region. But she does not. I cannot stop thinking about the wings of a bird of nettles. I am all second thoughts. I hate the guardian of doors and gates, the flesh of the peacock, the swarthiness of the lion. I fear the desert where sin stones are shattered by the chemical mother. Sweaty hours drain Elinda and the ancestors of her eyelashes cannot help her. They cannot free her from the cage punishment. The mirror bites its lips. I can't exist in the shitting night-time, she cries. And she pokes the spire of the same finger deep inside her sex. I inflict pain upon myself to find purity. But it is as useless as bathing in mud to become clean. I remember a deplumed woman whose saliva burnt me. I can't forget her. I am a dried skin on a gatepost weighed down with pebbles. He has gone. They have both gone. I am the polluting girl. I sick up consecrated wafers. I yield no milk. April's birds of wrath blister me. I remember the sinews of his stones. I dash out into the garden. I touch the outer edge of the sea and I forget my surname. The rosicrucian embryo floats in on the tide. I delight in its bones especially. But I know I am living beyond the sepulchre. Beyond. Now all that sea shimmers. Sand-dunes shift, endlessly anticipating the sea. Blood bawling on the sheet . . . I want a resurrection of sigmoid men now and let them kill me. But the planet with ten moons still forbids me repose. It offers me only a picture of a palm tree beneath which a bound man and a veiled woman wait.

LAMENTING HIGHWAYMEN

Sea of iron. Autistic seaweed. Ancient language of rocks, leading me by the heart. Evil act of listening to my secrets. My father was a watchmaker. Luke was only the clattering mouth of the ventriloquist's dummy. Yet it was my authoritarian concept of love which ruined us. Waves are ruled by the inheriting moon and so Elinda walks by the shore. She keeps on crying. Her crucifix echoes around her throat. She sees the face of the sleeping snake-charmer. All the evidence of her ancestry weighs her down. I must become strong. I must start with a reconstruction of the whole skeleton. Yes . . . But the wings of a malachite sunbird beat blackly inside her head. He went into the desert, the region of the summer stars, intent on the act of burying me, of creating my square grave, shading his sharp-sighted eyes with his left hand. He knew the tricks of making gardens. I can only stand on the harsh ground rising from the sea. And think of distorted explanations. *The body of a man was found at the foot of the spiral staircase at the railway station early this morning.* How do I know it wasn't him? And after I fling up my arms and cry out in thalidomide despair, what then? Elinda occupies a dolorous day. And behold the waters were turned to blood. And she committed adultery with stones and with stocks. Remember what the gypsies say. Satan is born of God's spittle, God's shadow. Spit on your shadow, Elinda, quickly. And she is full of sorrow, as a cage is of birds. Because in the dead of night, she hears the cries of a landlocked suicide squad. Those lamenting highwaymen . . .

ENTRY OF THE OVERSEER OF THE FIELD AND THE TWO GRANARIES

Spiders measure their spittle, whispering her name. Her skin waits for thuggery. Elinda, your black tongue is a closed circuit. Rain burns around you. She shakes her head denyingly. Everything she watches changes shape too often. Her face is closed as she opens the big redbound box full of punishments. She doesn't understand the hissing women who have unfinished memories of stone and snow and silence. Elinda kneels, believing that marital collaborators falter before the metrication of their own thighs and so become alone in the world, remanded in their own custody, relapsing into membranous memories, bodies a solitude of flesh. I am both the alive and the dying. My nights are handgrenades and I move according to a gyrocompass. Who told me of himalayan lovers who dance abstractedly? Was I the aggressor? Is that how Luke saw me? One rainy curlew morning I walked along with flowers in my hand, no monsters in my head. I remember the bridge, I remember the ploughland sea. I turned perilously and went towards him, not smiling, but like a hostage: and it was a rainy morning, a curlew morning. How could he say I was the aggressor? Padlocks on the night and he ran towards a violent moon. But he had no keys to open the cruel locks of darkness. I did not wish him to erase the sky. I was only joking. Elinda is hungry but the fruit trees are old and retarded. The curtain is moving lightly in the breeze, the scantily wooded sky is touching noon. I am contaminated because I have said one prayer seven times since dawn. Now I am listening to the crocodile's heartbeat. All day long I must admire a jubilee of doves pruning the orchards. Forgetting is all I want. But renegade angels sing me a militia chorus. And rebellious gardeners set fire to all the flowers. So that there is an arson odour in the atmosphere causing spasms and foaming even in stone mouths. Sanscrit fingers curve around my body. A warlike voice shouts, I alone can save. It goes on for hours with its trashy promises. But I reject its peace formulas. I plunge down into innocence, beyond night's terminology. But I hear the gate open. Hesperus, I call out cautiously. I hear footsteps on the path. Between two oceans I wait, watching all the migrations. God fell to pieces when I touched him. Flowing with fire he soon was ash. Circumcized women are deceivers. Arrivals and departures accomplish nomadic miracles. I sing my lunar elegy in an hour without a mirror. I remember Giovanna, her graceful ferocity. It is so long since I lost her. And I live feignedly now, a fellness all around me. The three bleeding breasts in my dream are the babies who will not be born. Rain is atoning the grass: but the messenger sent in haste does not notice. Background sky jackets him in airlight. His long journey has been from an alephzero season: now he hardly trusts summer, not here amid the prophetic powers of her landscape. Last night the extinct birdmoon denied his earliest known life with Elinda and in his hotel room he had doubted all his new devotion. The garden is an evicting place. But he sees the shadows of Elberfeld horses. And his mortal body moves to a dystrophic confrontation. He hears the radio voice inside the house: the weather forecast warns him to maintain his watchfulness at all times, to refuse all requests for loans. Now his bones feel hard and dense as zirconia. He fears that she may have a scabby mouth, that her hands may already have grown deckled with age. He is remembering the maze of tidal mud flats he photographed last week. But he forces his pantropic heart to greet his lifelong woman. And quietly he opens the kitchen door, entering the house. He is Elinda's cloven admirer. He examines the scratched-out dates on the calendar that hangs in an empty room. Then he pushes another door open.

Clarions!

Blood of Concealments!

And it is not known whether my blood is flesh or fish Elinda wraps herself in the dead tissues of a wound. You frightened me, she says simply. Yes, the long axis of your pulse (that capacitor) swings and bangs into you. You wonder if you are carrying a whale foetus inside your womb. The margin of the bell echoes in your sphere. You gaze at the talking telamon. You are standing where? Amid the reconstruction of a Silurian landscape, looking at him with the eye of a trilobite. You taste dry leaves in your mouth. You remember your mother standing against a background of flames, her prayers drawn tight across her face, reproaching you. Elinda looks at four fingers and a thumb. She thinks of the purification of the body. I came over on the ferry, he says. He reaches out and touches her tressure hair. Why did you come back? she asks. She does not move. I came back because I heard a voice announce a death in a night shout and I feared it to be your death, Elinda, for there were always dark hours in you. She turns her face away from him. His arrival at her callisthenic frontier panics Elinda. He senses this and smiles. I remember when you were a hitch-hiking heiress, Elinda. Nothing frightened you, then. She looks at him, coldness corroding her. Is your memory that good, Matthew? His eyes are the colour of ashpoles stripped bare. Test me, he dares her. The tempter. She closes the door. He watches her slow movements. She leans against the door and shivers. Do you remember how we parted, Matthew? He glances around the room, searching for letters. He sees the model of a megalosaurus propped up on the bookcase. Do you remember? she repeats. She must question him. Or else there will be major penalties. He goes on smiling noiselessly. Yes, Elinda, I remember. She looks grieved. Images of the black shining stems of maidenhair are wet in her. You tell me then, Matthew. Instead he opens his hand and offers her an oval stone polished by the sea. She stares at the unscarred palm of his hand. Will you take this? You need amulets, Elinda. He holds out darkness towards her. She bites her lips. She hates jokes. She fears laughter. It is a massacre. It damages the rifting purity she is saving for the birth of vows and amazons. Tell me, she says harshly. Matthew does not believe breeding women can attain salvation. He points at her accusingly. Why do you still wear that crucifix around your throat? You should replace it with a small mirror, Elinda. Then you would be protected, your truths would be sealed safe even against abortions and deaths. She comes towards him too quickly, her mouth clenched. She tells him that she has lived through a time of sorrel transformation. He smiles because he is a corruptionist holding precipices in his left hand. I wonder what your name is? His voice is a slammed door. She stares at him stupidly. You know my name, Matthew! I am Elinda. He shakes his head. No, I mean your other name, the sacred name you will be given after death. He watches her discover the speck of fire that is his sex. Neither my son nor my son's wife are born yet you talk of names, she says, covering her face with her hands. You have a face of fingers, he observes. Please go away, Matthew, she begs. He kneels by her side. Matthew separates the parent from the child. He admits the legend of her nipples. I bring no news of death, he whispers, I have come to you out of a great longing for your pity, Elinda. She does not move. He unfastens her sandals and kisses her feet. Since I have been away from you, Elinda, I have been climbing, in my mind, great sweeps of winding stairs. I have caught fish and birds and men but I always dedicated their bodies to you. Elinda lifts her head and stares at him. You are reeking of more pain for me, Matthew. He places his hand upon her orphrey sex. No! My soldered heart hurts me, she cries. You are not allowed my breasts, Matthew. She moves away from him, away from the articulating edge of falsehood. He shouts angrily at her for only she can free him from his nazification. Do I belong to you? she demands. Yes, he says, yes: either you are mine or you are ownerless. The house of dry wood creaks. No, she shouts, no. And she escapes from the devotional room, leaving him in recoil-less shadows. His spermaceti life aches. He follows her into the bedroom. He has no friends. Please, Elinda. I'm in a kind of post-embryonic isolation and only you can change me. Remember, I once lived in this place for a time with you. She shakes her head. It will always be the same with us, Matthew, no love, only a pretended feast with empty dishes. Oh god, he says, you're burning me to three kinds of ash. Just touch me, Elinda. She stares at the colour of this battle. In the room their metabolite bodies shine. Listen, Matthew, the day after you left me I awoke, for the first time, to a consciousness that my body was full of blood. The fortune-teller knew my frailty and warned me against a foster-child, fountains of feathers and clocks of bone. She did not tell me anything about you. At times I have been half dead with the silence you left me. I have realized all journeys are lessons. I am myself on a journey now. I've often thought of your body, especially your hands and the recapitulations of your sperm. My longing for you turned my life into a ruined temple. It was so hard for me, being alone, but I've survived it, yes, and taught myself how to be healed. I will not risk everything again. Please, wait, let me move in my own way. She presses the palms of her hands together. Matthew has many satellitic arguments. But he says nothing. His eye muscles fear bunched stakes of light. I am different now, Elinda continues, perhaps I already have a new name, one you never suspected. I have gone far away from that churchyard where we fucked. My nightly geography has altered. I don't oversleep any more. No, I wake at dawn and nibble apples. Don't you see? For me, living alone is being neutral in a world of dangerous allegiance: I've grown still. Matthew nods, accepting her need for the observation of a landslide. How often did you really think of me? she asks curiously. He does not answer. So she laughs. I thought of you, Matthew. I wanted to make crucibles but your memory always mocked me. Yes, he says, we hollowed each other out. Then he touches the piano, like a corpse burner. Do you still play? Yes, she answers, I still play. On Saturday mornings I practise and in the afternoons I walk to the recreation ground and sit on the childrens' swings. On Sunday mornings that fire siren still jeers its irritable jest. And it scares me until I remember it is only a rehearsal. Matthew, exhausting exiling grief was my only luxury for so long I cannot undertake new experiences of the flesh immediately. How do I know you are not just a summer visitor? I must retreat at first. Matthew agrees, saying with his cartel mouth, besides, I may be your son's father. We must think of it as a rite now. Elinda smiles hurriedly the one whose heart is tied to a rock crystal. He kisses her mouth with an apprehended calmness. Separate the dead lips and their lies with an amulet, she thinks. And have you been alone all this time? he asks. This is his Venus probe. Yes, she murmurs in an unmarried girl's voice. Yes, I was alone. And she thinks, I looked at the church window and saw oak leaves and acorns. In his hand the Child held a small bird of druidic love. And great skies fall back into Ethiopia. The maimed ones walk in the rain, their blouses wet with agonies. Wise men dissect the words of spelt songs. Elinda looks at Matthew, believing, we are web members of a genesis. Bands of colour ridge our foreheads as we face the storm. And the beloved like an ignited candle smells of god.

SABBATH OF SALT

It is hard for Elinda to go into the birthplace room. She puts the box containing her thoughts on the armchair. Matthew is still sleeping, breathing his dismemberment. Elinda stands at the bedside, staring at him with a hard silvery-white stare, thinking, so this is the other side of my life. And Luke was not a bestiarist. Even in summer there is a morning chill and she regrets her early awakening because now she is aware of all anti-scriptural dangers. She looks out of the window and sees an old man walking across the philippic loneliness of the beach. He goes towards the rocks. I made five mistakes, Elinda whispers. First I wore a wedding dress made of eyelids. She hesitates: then she pins a large map of the world to the wall and traces the outline of China with her forefinger. All the time she is inhabiting the stillness that precedes hemorrhage. Spending daytime in a bluish room is a liberticide. I cannot understand the roots of my hand. She studies Matthew even more intently. Is he the mirage enemy tugging his centipede's heart behind him? Perhaps he is the one with extraordinary gifts. But he is also out for blood, he will consume my best fruit and shit on my bible. He opens his eyes and she is before him, admitting no hope of gifts. The roof of his mouth is free of ceremonial defilement. He supports himself on one elbow and says quietly, *Elinda, though a stranger now and at a distance and unknowing you, let me . . .* She is watching the young speaker's lips. He beckons her and she advances towards him, her hair the colour of partly burnt wood, her sex sphincterial. He takes her from behind, he uses her, he knows how. Pervaded by sun, her rewardless mouth fires. Hearses are moving abdicatingly towards her. She is the woman of Jericho. I am afraid. The kinsman brings me shackles for my feet. She lies exhausted on the bed, watching him move around her room. Two candles, one burning, one extinguished. You cling to your old rites, Matthew. He smiles at the adulteress. Yes, he says, your long heavy hair reminded me of a swamp wife. Is everything in Elinda unwept? I don't understand your language of unknown affinities, Matthew. Why didn't you keep your word? Why did you take me and increase our vice? He thinks of a woman holding a dove. Your house is full of grave-goods, he says. Oh no, she answers mournfully, please, Matthew, spare my sabbath. You are still walking along a narrow path, he tells her. Then he touches her tangled hair, making her shudder, and goes downstairs, whistling. After several moments, Elinda strokes her body. And her hand unhinges a new judaisation. Then she buttons her black dress. Gal pierces my foot with a wire. But I cannot shun him. Matthew does not look at her when she comes into the kitchen. He gives her no kiss. She loses flesh and the light goes violently away from her. Why should I drown, the moment he gives me no kiss? He laughs at her in a yelping manner. He eats a grapefruit. He is peaceless. She speaks in a seminal voice. Mine was a puppet performance this morning, Matthew. I've been alone so long I've forgotten how to use my body or explain how I'm burning in a slow and flickering heat. I am like a bride who goes to the house of her husband carrying a bow and arrow. If I make the world look dead, I'm sorry. I have discovered jailers for myself in this house. There is always a ghost in the kitchen. Cold ceremonial betrothals trap me. Matthew lights her cigarette. The kiss of peace is hard to obtain, he says. Elinda has forgotten the planographic children playing blindfold games. Suppose I was free, suppose I was not allied to this secret undertaking I regret but to which saffron has bound me? I often reflect upon such a freedom, its substantial roses, its copious blood. But there is only desolation for the inhabitants of the time between plagues. We can only search our way gropingly through a diagramless land. I see only darkness, Matthew, darkness between lives and lies, coral and pearl, hand pressed to unsuspected hand, hip against hip. When littoral rain shapes the leaves, my radioactive skull remains dry. Can't you understand? I want to welcome you. But I am held in place by this slipstream of fear. Matthew laughs. And am I never to be in your mouth, Elinda, not even at a designated hour? She stares at him, simultaneously promising and threatening. After you'd gone that time, Matthew, yes, just afterwards, I ran out of the house without thinking about anything, I spent the night in the wood, I stayed out all night crouching amid leaves and rocks, a place called nowhere. I cringed under the bitterness of my eyelids and slept, my blood and bones cursing Pharaoh. An hour ago I unpeeled the day and found you again, all your idolatry. Oh I remember you. You turned informer, you went away. Blood swamps my immaculate heart, telling me it is too late to ask you for a truce, a kiss, too late to suggest we work out some quieter graver relationship. Elinda weeps like the white wife in the orchard. But what are you really crying for? he asks, the watcher in the bedchamber. She looks up at him angrily. Because I'm thinking of one I saw lying dead by the roadside. Because there's a ledge in my mind and I call it despair. And because of the sad taste of secrecy on my lips, Matthew. He holds her, tethering her body firmly. Think of the strength you have found in exploring the victimizations of chastity, he says. Elinda laughs too loudly. And he experiences a downward bowing of the penis. I clap my hands when I pray, Matthew! Matthew thinks of seven women with burning tits who killed one man. Let's get out of this house, he says, looking at the urning sky. She has not finished combing her hair but she follows him out to the car. The ploughed fields strengthen the landscape. My skin and bones rejoice in some of this earth, he tells her. Yes, she says distantly. The sun identifies criminals and Elinda is a scarecrow in a garden of cucumbers. The sky moves aimlessly about. Where have you been? she asks him. In a desert killing venomous snakes, he answers, but less violently than you hope. She lights another cigarette. What does it matter, the violence? she asks. It matters, he answers, for we are betrayed. His words are a blind-bombing. The eldest son speaks, she cries, mocking him. You're always identified with pain in my mind, he answers. He is implicating her. She touches her crucifix. When things went wrong between us, she says calmly, I made excuses for myself. I pretended you were a beggar, dancing and beating a wooden bell. When I played chess with you, I lost on purpose. You said, let's go and we went to that harbour bar and it was dawn when we fell into our chiding bed. I never understood the rhythm that fretted between us. There were bonds between us, both of beauty and of oppression, he says. Beauty's oppression, she repeats. But I had a dream, Matthew, months ago: you came to my house and asked me for flowers. I searched the garden and I asked strangers. But I could find you no flowers. When I go to church, I say my prayers thinking of you. Do you? he says, but irritably, as if she had somehow impaired the hour. All his exposure to storms has not satisfied him. Stop here, she says. She is afraid of the poison sac. They sit in the car, looking at the gates. Matthew cannot help recognizing the disturbance of an oriental tree. He is too close to the executrix summer. He asks her for mercy. She touches her opal ring obediently. Silence is liturgical. I don't know how, she answers. The day begins to burn. Perhaps forgetting would be best, she adds. And the shape of her voice shocks them both. Children on horseback go by. He looks at her incomplete hands. He thinks of the thorn's daughter. Childhood brushes against his tomb. I don't believe you've been alone all this time, he says. He is not shouting. He speaks sadly. I was alone, she says, giving him information. Membraned hands serve as wings, thinks Elinda: she is chilled, she cannot adjust to the handwriting inside her head. We've both listened to the secrets of others, he says, isn't that enough to make another bond between us, however unchaste or harsh? Vanished cries cannot separate us now. But Elinda is following the contours of the earth, she says nothing, she reads the name on the convent gates: Les Filles de La Croix. Tension draws certain parts of her body together defendingly. She remembers an argument Luke once used, words involving neither loss nor acquisition of heat in her. Listen, Matthew says, you are no unblemished one. I know you have known others. She stares at him, unafraid of the vibrations of weather. How do you know, Matthew? He taps her wrist like a stranger or an envoy. It shows as clearly as if he had branded you upon the ear, Elinda. His voice is a symbolization wound. Matthew knows the mirrors she uses for her rituals. So we must fight, she comments. She is calm, a bibliolater. No, he says. There is time for us to find peace. Peace! she exclaims, when you are already calling me *Judas girl!* I tell you, there has been no one else. I waited for you. But you and your brothers, truth and falsehood, don't want me. You want to escape into the senseless shadows again. You don't want to hear my truth. You won't listen, Matthew. I say that this besieged language is all we have to offer each other, sweet or sour. But you prefer kiln-dried silence. You always did. And you are losing me again. Elinda and Matthew stare at each other as lies become smaller. My power as activist in front of the altar is lost, thinks Matthew, because she wears a black dress and wants to walk through the fields. I don't need to be under your protection, Matthew. He is silent. The summer is saturated colours. My hands were swollen and no one came to save me from the corpses. Her long dress touches his ankles as they walk. He knows now that she is still devoted to death and that she plays with a day's allowance under the grallic sun. Sweat derides his body. He is forgetting how to be cruel. She makes a pause in their silence to pick wild flowers. He watches her concubinacy. She holds the flowers out to him in her dry hands, smiling, but before he can accept them she throws them angrily into the stream. He expects wild cries. But she is silent, reserved. Last night I was thinking of our old family bible, she says. You're a liar, Elinda, he says coldly. She does not weep. I will bear four sons, she thinks. She points to a hill scattered with rocks. We'll go up there, she says. The great veins of her throat defy him. She shoves the farm-gate open, renewing their journey, but with the look of one who breathes upon a flame to extinguish it. Suddenly she stands still. A vedic woman. Then she runs away from him, towards the ruins of the abbey. Her black skirt blurting through the flowers . . . He does not follow her. She comes back to him, laughing and shouting. Oh you and I, Matthew, embryonic explorers, that's us, climbing impetuous mountains. She throws her arms around him. Their tongues do not touch. Remember how we made covenants at nightfall? Roses bristled. The moon went limp. With you I thought I was safe from everything. I thought our geology of flesh was everything. But you left me living in an ice house. I was afraid of the skeins of dusk. I walked with seas of ash in my hands. She holds his wrists, digging foetal fingernails into his flesh. He observes her with a tiercel instinct. Matthew, I'm asking you questions, I want to know why you went. I don't want this blanched divinity of mine. I want to be free. Tell me why my nipples are haggard. Tell me why invisible accoucheurs shout at me. Tell me! And she is shouting. Matthew thinks of a vomiting child and hits Elinda with all the force of his marriage song heavy in his hand. I crawled all this way back to you, Elinda, through the blood and the ice, but do you think I wanted to rescue you? No. Already I've forgotten the reason for my return. Already I pray for another life, non-tidal, white, a first garden. Christ, she curses, I wish you were sterile. He leaves her to her feminization and begins to climb the hill. Matthew is disturbed by the rocks, like shrines and relics of fatherless saints. At the summit, he looks out across the sea he has traversed and neglected. He celebrates the cult of the bronze axe. Elinda approaches him, her head bowed. My hair is dark because of these fields, she says. I am a diminished vision. And so are you, Matthew. So we'll go without exploring, no longer at the mercy of wind and tide. She smiles for the nine-day devotions. He holds her hand, depicting them as lovers. Always we rest our hopes upon strangers, he thinks. Lamaic barriers remain between them. Her hand is cold. She moves with dignity. In the Apostolic churches, there are prophesiers, she says. And she pulls her hand free. I'll tell you how it has been with me, he says. Without you, Elinda, I was everywhere spilt out like communion wine or amnion waters. My skull was an elaborate hourglass. My hands became an unsubtle fear of loss slurring the syllables of day or of your death, tri-dimensional, gelid, unbelievable. He kisses her, patiently. No, she says, how can you tell me that? Now I must pray for us. The stone-age sky is a shadow on the present. And she kneels, clasping her hands. Her lips move silently. Whether she is beginning or ending, he cannot say. Her breasts are straw cabals. When her body relaxes, she sits carelessly on the grass and her hands become amphibian, touching him. Hour of epidemics. She is constellating his blood unfairly. He sees the dark suspensorium strangers of his war. I entered the house of god, says Elinda, but the madonna had gone away. He does not answer. I long to bleach my memories, she says, looking at him passionately but I have destroyed the moon's gift and I must be punished. We must be punished. Look, don't try to change my mind. Don't argue. He tells her not to be afraid of her own cowardice. His words are too near the dangerous edge of hearing. She censors them. Don't, Matthew. I still remember the long yellow mantle of her hair and I won't go back to that jealous life behind the barbed wire of amphetamines. No. We promised to forget each other, Matthew. Our short time of entanglement and extremity became a routed army of months bleeding in retreat. We died that night in the motel when I said so many crazy things. Yes, and even now in a new act of grasping we turn into others. We have new keys for our prisons. Why am I stammering? You ask why I'm so troubled? It is seeing you like this, of course, so unexpectedly . . . You can look in mirrors, Matthew, or at gods, but I can't. And I don't want you to look at me. No, Matthew. Don't mention my starvation, don't tell me how different I am now, with my hair like an ashpit and my eyes hating all amnesties. We're breaking curfew. No, don't ask me. I can't go back to that dishevelled life. I have forgotten it all, even the alliteration of our migraines. I don't want to be vandalized. Matthew takes her hand and presses it against his body. She feels the size of his penis under the cloth. She removes her hand, shaking her head. It is because we are islanders, he says. And he walks away, leaving her on the hillside, in a thicket of briars, rain falling, a huge sky mapping out her future, calling her Caesarina, not without irony.

BLOOD

Light and shade of a portfire day. Strophic arrangements of sun and cloud create labyrinthine games. There are white flowers in a room equipped for rape. He is shouting at her through the harvest. Elinda, tomorrow I'm going to . . . You're going to do what? she jeers, her mouth stretching, deserving blame. Her leather belt is fastened with a buckle in the shape of a crescent moon. Something untriumphal, I think he says quietly. Like water dropped into my ears when I'm sleeping, I suppose. And she smiles, thinking of the national cemetery. Be afraid of me, Elinda, he tells her. She shrugs, remembering her black paternoster. I am a son of the mother, he adds. Her native language was hoodlike. So he tells her: I gave some of my blood this morning. What did you say? She stands motionless in the doorway, a drowned summer person. This unrehearsed regicide horrifies her. I gave some of my blood to the blood bank today, he repeats. Now he is the lover of a dying woman. Her womb catches small birds. I wanted to protect all the nuclear families, he explains. Red figures are swimming in a red tide. Fear oozes between her fingers. For these are occult doctrines in Matthew's mouth. And her pain develops remote from the site of its origin. She is beyond befriending. Oh god, she cries, are you going to tread me underfoot? And she trembles. Before his salient power. He has caused her to withdraw to her true time. I can live without the breast, he says. Then he leaves her embrittled in this flower-filled room.

Magdalenian as water.

Alight with juvenescence.

At the shrines of warfare.

Covered with the dust of goldfinches.

HEXENMEISTER

Matthew waits for her through the retinoscopic hours, knowing that the sinews of a great phantom war are flexed against her. As he waits the night goes by and he thinks of corresponding bones. He is learning to be a secular priest. He picks up the book Elinda had been reading and opens it at the place she marked. *But if in order to reach it he had to sacrifice, even to the smallest degree, what seems to him the legitimate fruits of his victory, he would then a thousand times prefer battle.* Matthew reads the words twice. Beside them, in the margin Elinda has written: *I am exalted when I hear of a brave man who shoots his nation's oppressor clean through the heart. But such things bore Luke.* Matthew closes the book. A winterization takes place in him. Elinda returns shortly before daybreak. Reciting catchphrases of innocence. She is limping. He smiles angrily. She drawls explanations, old-fashioned as a clog-almanac. He laughs, loud and escapeless. Swathed in lies still, Elinda? Their spiritual incest is planing her skin. Her throat ribbon chafes her. She leans against the door and looks at him tiredly. I am satiated by this summer, Matthew. Her body is terraqueous. He is silence. She drags her words out. Dearest, I am a quarter-evil, quarter-ill. The rest I only guess at. He ignores this. Have you slept? he asks. No, she says, have you? He shakes his head. I'll make some coffee. She follows him into the kitchen. She is afraid. For in the night she saw the face of the maximalist. She fears Hagar's brothers. She found the ghost in the open city. Matthew drinks two cups of coffee but she leaves hers untasted and stares out of the window. Outside, the sky is turning white, recently dead. She looks at Matthew, intent on reparation. Matthew, do you remember how you tore up that picture I had of Christ on the Cross? It was just a cheap brightly-coloured representation of the Passion. But I valued it. And you just tore it up. She laughs bleakly. I saved you from idolatry, he says shortly. Perhaps, she agrees. She closes her eyes against the reinforcements of day. Matthew, one night I dreamt of lions prowling loose inside a huge house, half brothel, half convent. I opened an unexpected door and found inside the red room three lionesses standing guard over the body of a man. I could not tell if he was alive or dead. His right arm had been torn from his body and half-devoured by the beasts. Fresh blood had spread over the mosaic floor. His blood-stained shako lay some few feet away from him. And as I watched, the man opened his eyes and smiled up at me. And I felt so peaceful. I knew that the smiling man was my other self, the one I had to find and save from a real death. I have almost found that other self, Matthew, almost, so please be patient a little longer! She touches his body, begging. I will try, Elinda, he says and rests his hand upon her shaggy hair. But I have no knowledge of this manual language, he adds in a hardening voice. She looks away from him. After the second flowering, the roots decay, she tells him, her voice continuing to sound away into the silence of her eyelids, prolonging her grief. Her life wants to be breathed. But she still waits for fathoming. For his millennialist approval. Were you really alone all the time I was away, Elinda? She smiles. If I gave him a detailed description, she thinks, he'd see me as a creature moving on my belly towards the queenpost moon. Yes, Matthew, she answers modestly, I was alone, without even a cosecant friend to fasten me to the reality of violence and epitaphs. Her words are alive with resistivity. Matthew needs to probe with his fingers. Elinda, I don't believe you. You couldn't live a life of calenture. Someone, a man or a woman, came to you and gave you soul kisses and then left you superintendent of this prison. No, Matthew, she answers calmly, no, no, no. Spectral war arises from every hand but mine. The flowers swagger in her garden. He accepts her halo-blight. Matthew and Elinda embrace in silence. Two calliopean bodies stuck together, floating out to sea.

DEATH OF THE CRUCIFIX

The drawing of a man with protruding ribs represents famine: an eye with tears dropping from it, sorrow. And their bodies are gored by the new moon, representing their transformation from shrouders to Jehovists. On Friday evening Elinda and Matthew walk out of the church into the late sunlight. She has cut her hair short. She looks like her mother. She is remembering: I was separated from the world and you came in spite of the rain: we drank wine. and I was troubled because you wouldn't listen to what I had to say. You are still apt to be silent, Elinda, he says. You still splinter my solitude, Matthew, she answers, closing the lych-gate carefully. This is their second month together. In the lost territory of their house, they proceed without pronouncing sentence. So far, today has been without maledictions. Elinda listens to the assonance of summer outside in the long-distance evening. The skeletography of her sex helves him. Birds in the sky make him think of ancient books buried with the dead. He touches the silk of her angina robe. Decide, Elinda, he says fiercely. Her photograph watches him. Asteroids forsake her. A celestial marriage, he urges. To put us out of our misery. To reveal the nature of the strength we seek in the night. Our savage saviour. A male child. We must make a bargain of horns, claws, nails; then our keratin weapons will protect us. She stands by the window, her body anointed with whitish leaf shadows. Matthew is a man, Mark is a lion, Luke is an ox, John is an eagle, says Elinda. But her mockery does not deceive him. He sees how her nerve centre is reflectorizing his archaic smile. Elinda, he says, touch your true self. I cannot! she cries, I'm still in a darkroom! No, he tells her, you are leaving your impacted wilderness. She looks unhappily at the man who speaks. And now he sees around her a great host of birds, insects, horsemen and arrows, clouds of them, moving slowly. Elinda is pale as a late-corner and she says, an ancestor of mine invented a gun. Did you know? Wasn't that clever of him? His famous machine was capable of firing 1,200 shots per minute. Don't stare at me with such senilism, Matthew. I take no responsibility. All money is blood-money, one way or another. We're all bribed, either to talk or to remain silent, we all live on some kind of carrion. Poets, soldiers. You give your vices pet names, Elinda, he says contemptuously, so that they come like dogs when you call. It will break you. She looks down at her ringless hands, tending his words. Then she turns away. And Matthew remembers the first meeting: before him he had seen a lawn, a flower-garden, a herb-garden, trained trees and, beyond, an orchard. And by the orchard gate the girl was waiting. Blue-light leaves shadowed her body even then. She knew she would never be a true wife. And so she tore green branches from the tree. And the steepness of her heart often abased her. Matthew recalls how he walked towards her, how he was alive to all the sky. And how he would soon give her a miscarriage. You know, says Elinda, eve may be flooded this year. The newspapers are already warning us. He says nothing, he is remembering how she ignited holy candles in a room at dusk. She kneels at his side. Matthew, I am walking alone through a landscape of circles and I have no philosophy to subdue them. Moving about this intricate land I sense pains that will last a thousand years. I am carrying heavy world objects in my hands and these I call my memories. They tell me things in strange words, not suited to personal belongings but to conventions and fastings. And I touch their syllables that have no moisture, carefully, as if they were eleventh beads. She looks up and meets his surveying. I am not for resurrection. I hide at the back of the altar, not even weeping. And I'm scared of you, Matthew, of what you will do to me. It is like the fear of Sparta, scaring and scarring. But I can't be rid of it. There's a caste-mark on my forehead and my thoughts are of one who stands before the night and tells me I'm not safe when you touch me. So I must go on alone towards casualties and fatalities. He swallows rain. No, Elinda. These needn't be last words. I know you are afraid. But there is no need for this expulsion. The burning of the grass is our time. She shakes her head. No, Matthew, no. Once I tried to abridge my horoscope. It couldn't be done. And why should I sacrifice myself for you? You, with your voyages, your arrogance and your runes. You'll soon leave me. Your contra-orbital endearments are addressed to a shadow. He sighs. Shadow? What shadow? Elinda, you have never sent me away before. I won't accept it now. I've never seen you like this. She stands up. But you've seen me at all other times, Matthew, oh yes, you've witnessed me in my travail, all of me annulled in the bloody aftermath of love. That is what separates us. Look, see me sway, giving one great unreformed howl before dropping down into a silence thin as a leaf. His mouth is dry. I cannot go away yet, he says. Then I cannot force you, she answers. And have you anything to tell me? About the life I have not shared with you? No, he says. He prefers not to think about the times when he awoke in the depth of the night, fearful of the ice-blink of the horizon. He will forget the way he went into other wombs, times when he forgot Elinda's passion, times when the remembrance hung like gory flowers around him. He will not tell her about the days and nights of hard drinking, how he spent his time with companions who resembled laughing pallbearers at some crazy funeral in April. He has forgotten the names of the countries, the ports where the ship docked, the refugees at the frontier. Oh Elinda, he says, I want to lie in sunshine with you and be warm. Will I die of grief? No, she answers gently, you will die like a tree, felled or diseased. If she has become a repenter, she has not told Matthew. He wants to sigh into her and smear her with himself. Their minds quake together. She is thinking, last night in the sky, seven bright stars. Odours of tobacco and blood repel him. Without looking at him, she says, this is my house prison. Here I think of the trunk of the tree and the tesseract web of the spider. But you may share my prison. Perhaps you can teach me conciliatory answers. When I run across the fields, you may watch me and see how the birds are startled into primaeval flight. I fear the tegument of silk and the telemechanics of desire. Knowing this, accepting me, you may remain here. And perhaps cage my wingless questioners. He agrees calmly, his future pigmentary. He does not touch her at the moment because he is an evolutionist. We will survive, Elinda, we won't experience another katabasis. She smiles doubtfully as the late sunlight whorls on the ceiling. Her attention wanders to the clock hand and she tells him, Matthew, I was fifteen before I experienced my first flow of menstrual blood. And I was frightened because I knew that now I would have to fight and to lament. He licks her transfinite lips. I think, Elinda, that you want a different life from the one you are now only half-living but that you are afraid to begin such a life. Ah, she answers with unhappy sarcasm, and what kind of a life will this new life be? That is for you to answer, Elinda. I can only go so far with you. The life is already within you. For Matthew the hour has become subastral. The idea of her blood sickens him. Perhaps I can only give you love's offal, he adds reluctantly. His glance flickers high across the ashlar sky and he ceases to concentrate on her. I said that you would be no use to me, she whispers bitterly. And she moves out of the room with the coarse movements of a lacerator. I hope you die in a thunderstorm, thinks Matthew, or in childbed. Elinda enters her bedroom. A bunch of wild flowers lies on the wooden table, not yet arranged in the earthenware vase. A spray of flowers. Symbolic of all that can exist, be done or happen. Elinda recalls that she has, at times, a shimmering resemblance to a girl who died for nothing. She carries the vase across the room to the windowsill. Once I believed myself to be a pioneer. She puts her hands to her throat. Or do I mean prioress? Exultation is constantly promised to me. But I never achieve it. Waiting seems ugly. And for what? A vision, a vow, a victory? But the flowers go beyond my sleeplessness. I am a woman carrying a burden. A withered prelacy of love causes me to need Matthew. Each day now has a prohibited profile the colour of Arizona because of him. He stands in the doorway, not tormenting her. Why are you looking for swastikas? he enquires. She bows her head. She is ashamed of herself. The greek girl and the latin man accept difficulties, their ideological hands ready for labour. Our real enemy is recollection, he says. I can never forget the sea or the dusk descending upon you: when I'm alone I always remember you standing beside me at the water's edge, night's temperature corresponding to our dark sadness. I can't forget how you once turned to me, praising the sun in your eyes. Why were our lives wrenched apart? Perhaps because answers for mirrors is all we ever had. And they dehumanise, those answers. Yes, the trash-ice seasons we spent apart in a world called thanatos still frighten me. We'll travel steppes of broken furrows and captured cities again but can we go together? An hour ago I believed we could survive all dangers but now I am naked in the labyrinth and I know nothing, Elinda. She is a lump of flesh in the yellowing room. I don't know the truth either, she says, and her laryngology chokes her. He breathes rocks. I knew a woman once, he says, his voice falling through laudanum distance, a woman beloved by all who knew her. She was an apostle of night whose beauty rivalled her satire. She had our modern inability to endure solitude, therefore she was always blossoming in public, fearful of any transit to a remoter shore. Yet her spirit, her wit and her trembling melancholy — all that beauty — at last faded and her blood recognized the equivalent of the hangman's rope. I often wonder now, was she seeking a true mirror in which to confront herself? Why else should I feel this guilt? Should I have waited by her side and prayed for her, night and day? No. For a son cannot remain with his mother. I fought to free myself of her for years. Once, Elinda, she offered me a glove filled with wax in which she had entombed a score of maggots. Elinda laughs. Matthew trembles, marks of the dance branding him. Reincarnated birds condemn the inventor of snares. Elinda watches him peel an old moulting womb. Now she understands him. Now she has wedged him between her bones. He is gnawing the lady's taper fingers inside him. Let's play a Japanese game, she suggests cunningly. No, he answers, the music hurts me. It reminds me of the hardships. Please leave me alone for an hour. Please. He is perplexed by the scarlet embroidery on her vagabond's smock. She smiles at him strangely. He presses his hand down hard upon the child but says nothing. He knows her strength will fail. He knows that his strength will always return, pure and flammable. He will wait until his babelismends. And then he will possess all the summerwood dynasties. She walks through the garden, perceiving the kingdoms of skin. The placentation of her life is happening. She kneels on the grass beneath the linden tree and touches her hair, her breasts and her lips. No one can punish me, she crows, no one. I am the ring leader. I am the lady in the chair. She lifts her arms and unfastens her crucifix. It weighs nothing in her hand. She touches leaves. Their night texture is the ruin of a lion's tongue. She hurls the crucifix into lacrimal darkness. Other sisters crouch at the weeping hole. But Elinda's body is spared arteriotomy and shelters her from the barrage of zodiacs.

DEATH OF THE BRIDE

Ice-claw midnight. A lamp is burning. The rain door is open. Elinda abandons the theories of the alchemist. Jesus is dying, she whispers, terrified of him. Matthew stands in front of her. He is the criminologist. The lives of the dead blur and are erased by rain. She sits passively on a low stool, one hand supporting her head. She is without wealth. She is very still. Only her confession lips move in the shadowy room. We once read a poem together, Matthew. It was something about the entrails of a deer and a burning hand. It was written by a prisoner. That is all I remember. And that the events took place on a semi-divine afternoon. Do you remember? She looks up at him anxiously. He shakes his head. No, I have forgotten it. Her cocainism saddens him. Elinda is not weeping. Yes, someone came to me, she says. I lied to you. But I've come to the end of my lying. I married him. I call the time of my marriage the charcoal year. But it was not dark, it was dangerously bright, luminescence drifting over a virus sea. Charcoal was its odour. There are bruises of moonlight on Elinda's shoulders. He listens, recognizing her words. This is my lifestory, Matthew. You must hear me. You can be lover, priest or doctor, I don't care. You are addicted to war yet you have become gentler. You have become the equilibrist. But Luke had a stone receptacle for a heart: Living with him was an insulin shock. Suddenly she looks up at him expressionlessly. Or am I telling you something you already know, Matthew?

RAINSPLITTER IN THE ZODIAC GARDEN

For Peter

I wish to thank the novelist Sylvia Bruce for reading the manuscript of this book and for making many valuable suggestions.

I(i)

In the distance, I see a bridge of white granite. Whistling its tune, night ends, letting in the wasps and sawflies and ants of the day. Micah, the man, woke early, left the house while I still slept, caught up in my blood. All day he examines the desecration of the war memorial. I have noticed his recent curiosity about vandalism. I believe he is planning a cold assault. I sit on the edge of the bed. My instinct is to hide during this season. I have no wish to lose my memory. He has forbidden my conversations with the priests. I find this hard to accept. But he says their usefulness is confined to baptism and burial and that I must not listen to their hoarse abstractions. I sense that even the distant chapelries are at risk now. I must protect my secrets. Ghost mutilations dance in the scapegoat forest. His chattels are the cast-off skins of serpents. Petitionary lyrics deafen him. I close the curtain. The room is cold and shadowy. I lock my mother's letters away. I try to sew. I think of the snow line. I unlock the drawer. I read her last letter. Her words are like the pressure of an embargo hand. I draw back the curtain and cold light's casual investigation tests my silence. Her letter wants to change me. No.

Starquakes in my head. In the market street, the children are shrieking for pennies. My dress is the colour of slag. I fear the taste of poison. Am I in a spiritual cage? Yesterday I had to keep walking around the village. I was afraid of the faces. Stragglers passed me, laughing. On the beach I picked up shells shaped like haunted ocarinas. I received the last kiss of the secret queen. I wrote farewell letters. I saw the shadow behind the lamp, the treaty-breaker's shadow shape. I wept wheat for the pentecostalists.

Micah has the true fear of the son. The stench of the burnings hung over the town for weeks. And I had these bloodless hours. An analysis of the relationship? Is this my task? I must understand. Is he orphic? Or bestial? He is too far away from me now. All his words are made of silence. Crucial silence. His behaviour is timeless. Like a stretcher-bearer. He understands the brightness of disguise. He returns from the deathbed of a young girl. In his face I see so many dumbnesses. So I do not speak and he does not answer. Our long ellipsis goes on. If calamity happens, what barriers will there be left in us for breaking? Tonight he says her death darkens the earth. But also that her shadow is obsolete. Daughter of retrieval, he calls her. For me he has no names. Poverty of me. In our bed he wrecks me, enters me, knows me: but I know nothing. Night. Forlorn departure of beneficiaries. Gates of my blood are locked. Gyratory thoughts again. Dress me in a mask and spangled clothes, my hangman, and I'll shit for you, jerboa excrement. He is displeased by my restlessness, the twitching of my recalcitrant limbs. I say, this is a false pretension to marriage. Please, do not . . .

And in the morning, after that night, she heard the slow ringing of the bell and saw a great number of trees torn down by the wind since last evening when she'd looked out at a wary and silent land, yes, when she'd stood in the doorway, caryatidal. Watching. Seeing a shrine open to the sky. A handmade landscape belonging to the coldest farm.

Micah looks at Faustina. He is trying to understand her jarring remoteness. I know she is a girl of troubled sleep: but I must go through her mists and shock her by telling her to remove her crucifix before we copulate. For my optical memories of her in the firemaking room and on her night sea journeys are enough to encourage a double suicide unless we understand these dismal cries heard through mists, my body growing knobbled as if in her body there is a gathering of salt water. Micah speaks to Faustina. He tells her why these legacy days of autumn are depressing him. Faustina does not look at him but she tells him that she is finding images of her mother in every retardative window. Micah, she is searching for me in the parish of my life, she's like an echo of a war . . . She's a sin eater. She began the tarot battle. Her breast researches told me this: upon the saying of a certain word, upon the performance of a certain action, when a woman enters the room holding in her hands those objects which are not to be mentioned, then the forfeit must be paid, the eyes opened, the narrowness of the vagina violated, the philosopher king slain, the day burnt to shreds . . . Look, Micah, see the astral footprints leading to a golem threshold. Where are we to find our names? And the hours of dowsing, the costumes for the drama of the hobbyhorse, the pain of the swan, what are they for? What's this landscape of fountains and cathedrals with threshing floors and women wearing headdresses and prehistoric kisses on their lips, arranging atavisms of insomnia? I don't know, Micah. He looked at the shadow of his wife and began to say, your mother . . . but then stopped.

I(ii)

Winter is beyond the walls of the house, the wind furnishing leaves everywhere in this northern province, dark branches heave-offering only a deepening chaos for the silhouettes who sit in the room watching the early clock. In their silence she thinks of ten generations. Testamentary shock is beginning. He explains his innocence. She shakes her head. She fears the bloodroot growing within her, about which she can secure little or no information. You are more than the repetition of an echo, he says. She lifts her head, watches the muscles of his eyelids. Her lips won't accept prophethood. The little seeps of their pain fertilize the earth. I'll

avenge you, he says, and transform you into a nightingale. The arms of
the victim are tied behind her back, she replies. He calls her barren. I
brought you across the long umiak distances, he says, but there is no
reward. You are hard and boastful. Her fingernails are like bird beaks in
the opalescing light. You want nativity's murder, he says accusingly. She
touches the sea shell on the glass table. You require avowals I cannot give,
she says. He stands by the window, he looks out at the fields, he sees
besieging out there. Faustina, he says, I keep expecting you to bring your
real self to me. If you were to come to me with that healing self it would
be such mercy, it would be like watching the ice break up on the river, a
debacle of frost, arborescent thawing. But you will not. Perhaps cannot.
His voice is a sane reproof. She looks at her hands. Is the arbitration of the
world held there? No, she says, I cannot accept belonging to or stroking
your body. Not even my prayers enable me. Monsoons fall upon me. I see
the shadow in the mask, death in the country of my enemies: I've lost the
silk culture of the vulnerary bible. These losses separate us.

Micah is touching the silence but cannot beget any omen. He leaves
her alone in the house. Rain: veils of water. And cries of the peacocks, that
he mistook at first for the cries of children.

Dead children are trying to reach you, Faustina. The Sainte Ampule
shatters. Blood. Mother rings a handbell and mortuary figures come
running. They will clear it up. Pewter deer graze on an Italian spyglass.
Two pegasi hover, watching Christ's hand unhinging me from my fire. The
motorcade went silently by, then the film broke, went wild. I waited until
the women stopped praying. Sun held the old men upright. I thought of
black songs, the dry-cleaning of a heart. The lute-player girl lies face
down in the sand, her hands have crumbled, only her hair lives, a solemn
gold. The listening souls of priests and soldiers have killed her. One
thousand men once heard her music. They gave her gifts, a tortoise of
immense proportions, a chinese madonna, a madhouse dress. Now
Faustina's unredeemed eyelids are closed. But she sees the young girl
leading the youth across early morning, both walking slowly because they
are experiencing the same grief, isolated on a chaste peninsula. She

remembers. Faustina is one who hoards frost. She loves the rocky rubble of the valleys. She knows when the heartwood of a tree will begin to decay. She watches the female flowers open, miasmas of colours.

She examined the habits of the adults with the aid of her microscope. She saw bloodsucking in winter, she took photographs of the old dance, went hunting for spiders, leafshapes, the horizon of fresh water, a windswept place, summers of lichen and moss, conversations with the hodcarrier, horizon of lightning from a brief thunderstorm, her words lost in the prevailing wind: she saw trees burning with the quietness of birdsong, the subsong, mist surrounding old damp houses and gardens close to the water: lentic pools. She watched ceremonial courtships followed by reward or penalty, the bloody-nosed fleas crawling.

Oh summer lady, your tresses are confined by his observations, are you extinct? And you unharboured autumn lady, come to the waterside. In a burnt clearing in the wood a creeping lady waits. I recognized the bare ground, winters, and the burnt bird. I saw harvest men moving through neglected apple orchards. I saw false scorpions, fruit bodies exploding, distributors of the seed, salt marshes and grassy places near the sea.

Winter visitors came to our house: leafcutters and medieval midwives, victims of fugues, enemies lacking limbs, no ribs, no jaws, no scales. Sometimes I sat at bedsides of dying people in old wooden houses where flowerheads were turning to dust. I knelt by the altar on the shore. I walked across the white hempfields. I suffered the clawings and scrapings of a desolate girl in a rain shelter amid waters of wilderness. Walk down the churchway where the coarse grass is bent by prayer. The cornground and the thornbrake wait for a festal blessing written at the source of the stream. I watch Micah and the woman, I am at the edge of time, I am at the centre of the playing place, I am in the pupal chamber growing, I watch them. They stand at gateways, they shelter in tithebarns and stables and ruined tin mines. They take passage by water, they wait in the field's stubble corner. Now I've lost sight of them. I go followingly over rockstrewn land, my boundary is that ash tree. Time is arranged like the fingers of a hand, its skeleton is lost at the bottom of a lake, is strong as a bird standing on a rock out to sea, natal as death, a louse on a human head, lives on a borderline between two habitats on the edge of a wood. Felling of trees happens. I see the trees bleed. I go to the zone of the shore, remembering the day I found a hare's resting place in the grass, where it had crouched in the noon.

And time is becoming strong in the white rooms. Faustina speaks to her caged bird. I draw circles: and within the circles I paint images of wild flowers, dog's mercury with its tiny March flowers, early orchids, milkwort, meadow saffron, the sleep positions of the leaves of woodsorrel . . .

Yes, he'll prophesy when he's drunk, surrounded by a chain of fire. But his immortality will become a burden to him, he'll be changed into a grasshopper. Salt woman in a stone house watching the drumlin flow of the ice. Is it penitence that hurts you or the role of the purchased slave? At the louvred window you must stand all day, lycanthropic girl. I cannot see the storm. But the weatherworn eye of the storm sees me. It watches me murder my father. It knows I am neither ghost nor dove. It says holy women do not breed. It reminds me that I am alone and nameless in a strange land waiting for a great storm. I am standing between an elm tree and an ash tree. Labyrinths of leaves do not move. Periptery of storm: solitary blue time slang words: I offer you these. No, I cannot move. I sing a metamorphic song. I watch the sky that watches me. Watch the birth of the storm. Wait for the ripening walls of the storm ovary to break open. My body cell is a quadrillion doubt. I don't believe in the storm nor its wharfage of crying. Sky keeps me tied here among the trees to await the shout that is yet only faint in the blood fizz. Now the leaves on the trees are in motion like feathery leaves growing under water yet the air is dry as bone without utterance . . . I cannot see you, storm. Once I was in a place where roses grew. I don't remember it very well. I only stumble towards rootstock. My grievance is a matter of kinship, renewed by the vigour of a nuclear tension. Rejectamenta of my life . . .

*

370

II

We were talking, mother and I, about magnolia trees when the other storm broke. That was years ago. I arrange my memories in alphabetical order and another storm covers the cold marshes and the slate roofs and the public gardens, dissolving world salt in its waters, falling upon my head, water heavy and sensual as living blood. My wet garments spiral around my body and heresies drip from my hair. And I am drinking the world. And eating the sky. I am lying face down against the ecological earth. Grass and mud against my lips. I swallow bitter roots, I pray. Banks of cold water sluice me. What are they washing away? My oversharp shadow? The place where the venial and the arterial blood flows together is an area of apprehension. Because of this storm I am gemmed with all my clanging heart and the gateways that are flying at me, these are relics of a ceremony, and I relapse into idolatry: seeding of ritual. My anointing is complete. And the thunder's salvoing turns upon the terraces and gusts away — my twin — into the plains of pentecost. At the orifice time I open my mouth and say: it is my impure puppetry which brings storm. My existence means rain, my cybernetic words call down thunder. I am not afraid of my explorations. I'm not scared of the astronaut's ghost. His white incantations stand in the field amid the debris of pity. My mission is of floods . . .

Micah says women deceive their way out of the anxiety zone. I don't know. I don't care about Micah. I forget you, liar. The sky is dark. Ice islands everywhere. Tergum songs in my sister mouth. Dark sky. Acaroid blood forsakes me and I'm cold. Fornicatrix, he called me. Liar. Now the sky is like cracked and shaven frost. My thoughts are black octahedral crystals. Prophesy? No, I cannot. I am separated from each leaf, I am afraid he will pardon my sins. Storm hour absorbs none of my shock. I walk beneath the trees, the hills burn motionless, I heard the air smoke and move, a sound of silk and dry sticks rubbing together, I demand compassion from the stones, I am a plunderer of the retina, the trees yield bark and wood and music of excessive bitterness, pavonine cries fulfil my mouth. Night stopped the storm. Its hour is over. I am glad. For I was afraid. There are many things I have forgotten. Faces whose mouths smile too calmly at me. Who shame me. But how the currents of storm tugged and sucked at me, like great butterfly tongues.

I am walking through wrecked spiritualized fields. Now there is silence all around. The silkworms are sleeping. The scythes drip rain. My body keeps commandments. Moon and moorland are in me forever. All my mirages are safe. I love the old lake dwelling. The salinity of my scriptures . . . Stalagmite flowers were reflected in a cold pool on the floor of the cave. I bent down and touched them with my fingers and they vanished. I go wrapped in my wet clothes. No one sees me. They are burning fires to drive away the pestilence of the night.

I lock myself into my room. I draw little diagrams of my heart. He watches her, he hears her black and white laughter. He sees her sometimes appearing under a high degree of magnification. With all her weanling strength at risk, her face whitened. He sees her as a menstruous woman drinking new wine. He knows she wishes to be the victimizer. In her pocket she carries a handkerchief imprinted with the face of Jesus. He will tie woodpeckers between her legs to purify her. Then her virginity will stop beating its pain against him.

She looks at him. He is wearing his ivory uniform. Deuteragonist, she shouts: you're in my way. Get out! Why should I be sold? My responses are without colour. There is no burning, no shining. Only a bleached feeling, a decompensation heart in me. When I think of you, Micah, I think of scum forming upon a specimen of urine. I can't epiphanize my days. All interpretations throw me off balance. Amputee strangers follow me everywhere. I wedge myself safe against a child. I fear the sight of it, dripping with ice blood, I fear its circular mouth, its one eye at the front of its head, the fusion of the orbits . . . A thermic fever harms me.

He touches her shoulder. But she keeps on crying. Assailed by rumours, he is unsure of her truth. Let's try therapy, he suggests. Is it a game or is it real, your therapeutic event? she asks. I don't know yet, he says. We must tell stories first. I've been told that stories are antidotes.

We need to find where the nerve enters the eye, don't we? We need at least one moment filled with life. Let's hunt down our deficiencies, Faustina.

She watches him. Invent yourself then, she says, shrugging, you can tell lies, it's long past midnight. He stubs out his cigarette.

Listen, Faustina. There is a forest, leaves that frizzle and shadows of psychoanalysts everywhere. Through the trees comes a wandering musician. He is thinking, this musician, of underwater demolitions and of the last rebellion. He sits down under a dead tree and humiliates himself by admitting his loneliness to the twilight. And to the darkening forest also he says, I am lonely. I will play a tune on my violin and a companion must come to me. Smiling somewhat primitively, the musician plays his needy music. Soon a magpie comes down out of the sky, black and white and alone, flying bravely around the musician. But the magpie reminds the musician of a child who scares people by suddenly jumping out of unexpected hiding places and pulling faces. So he stops playing. He says, I don't want you. He takes his gun. He shoots the magpie dead. It lies at his feet. Its feathers still move in the wind. Is he frightened? No. It is not his first death. He begins to play again, a dance tune. Soon a peacock came grandly through the trees, willing to hear the music. Not you either, said the lonely man. And he strangled the secret peacock. And he played again. Louder and louder. A girl came running through the woods. He ran towards her, he held her in his arms, he sucked her blood till she was dead. Then he kicked her body aside and stood for a long time looking at the outlandish sky. When he had finished with the sky, he went walking through middens of lineage. Then he took up his position and began to play again. He longed for his true companion. He played for hours and hours. Nights and nights. Days and days. He didn't like the days. He played and played. He was sick of his music but he was too afraid of silence to stop. No one came to him, not even his mother. He played so long his sense of time became pilgrimatical. At last someone approached him wearing shoes of swiftness. The musician still played. The frost-biter came towards him, listening. The musician played, defending his territory. But the frost-biter listened vigilantly until he saw the three dead bodies. And interrupted the tune with palatized words. Then stretched out his cold-working hand and took the violin out of the musician's grasp. And the musician allowed the frost-biter man to take him away captive into his cold unquiet country.

The story-teller's voice breaks. The listener; she smiles. The sabbath is gone. Is the mystery finished? she asks scornfully. Yes, he says, for those upon the tree, out of the dark places. Predictions from a weeping soldier . . . she whispers mockingly. You are bewildered even on the road you have travelled before, he tells her. But she forbids serenity. And she dips her finger in the cold ashes. Then she goes out of the room into another month.

III(i)

Her hair is of a reddish brown tint, her skin pale, dark vestment eyes and asian cheekbones. She cradles her thoughts amid attitudinal effigies. She stands beneath a wayfaring tree. And to him she appears like a faint star, seen with the naked eye, or that five-winged creature hovering in the face of the wind, on the edge of the axe. She does not speak in a subtle way but nevertheless he is torn by some morning speeches of hers as by wirecutters.

The winter wheat grows, stalks bend, swaying the peninsula. Faustina is half afraid to sleep. What if I wake with another's face staring at me from the mirror: zero frequency of self. He sleeps, he dreams, the stone gargoyle pulls at his lip with a mad hand. Show me the bride and I shall be silent. Let me see her, those breasts of consolation ruling a holy house. I see epithelial pearls around her throat, she will turn her body aside from the pains but strangers will make incisions in her vulva and then there will be sufficient allowance for the birth and she will not be able to prevent it. Look at the eyes of the birds of the night! Sleep, Faustina. Arrange and categorize the veins of leaves all night, go to the world where god is fertilizing wife, sister and daughter. And in Micah's demon glass, you will see your own beauty corrupt and crippled and a hint in the shadows of mourners going down the streets to burning burials.

They both wake to a divestiture of hope. Her answers will always be telegraphese. He touches her hair. You don't belong to the category of the exploited, he tells her patiently. I had one of my deaths, last night, she answers. She pins her dress with a woman brooch. Her finger bleeds. He said that the owls were set flying in a reverberation chamber (an empty concrete-walled room) and their wing noises and movements recorded. Faustina remembered her mother's story about a bodyguard who collected horseshoes.

She said to Micah, even your birds are forgeries of birds. You have opened the next hour of anger between us. She rings her buffalo bell. He laughs. She quivers. He touches her ear lobe, the dolomitic blood moves, you fear the beginning of ossification in your heart, he laughs and locks the door and pushes me back on to the disaster bed, the edge of the ice sheet. You extinguish her, her breath explodes, she speaks musty words, she regards the freighting of flesh without pleasure but he dedicates her estuarine body to the act, fucking her, the friend of the animal-watcher, her face like a medieval woman, claustral, the sun shone directly in her eyes, it hurt, there was no easing of colour. Released, she turns her head away from him and looks out of another window. Seas of saffron move out there. Storm creatures are making disturbances in the water. He leaves her, his mouth paralyzed, the clubbing of his fingers his constant fear, leaves the bed waiting for the next event, birth or death.

Torrid burning flower: I see you from my transparent room. I walk through an old garden of nettles, the stinging leaf-hairs prick me. I may abolish harvests. My weeping is loathsome and ignorant. It holds me back from the future. I know exodus, double feasts and finger alphabets wait for me. Without trembling, I oppose my thirst. Is it god whose shadow towers high above the forest? Fingers are stitching their snares, painting the sky black. Only a dwarf sun shines with a little bitterness. The wild fennel odours the afternoon brownly. The bird cherry tree and the russet marigold flourish in the trenches of hurricane. Second leaves, adopt me.

Someone is shivering: what invisible ice stretches around her that is so terrible? What cape of coldness chills her flesh?

III(ii)

The telephone rang. She answered it. She heard the voice of a corpse-eater. Cut off his toes and thumbs, it said. Scatter hawthorn flowers on the road and he will waste time picking them up, it said. Scatter bird seed on his tomb and he will lose time counting the seeds. You must wear very white brand new clothes, Faustina. You must smear pitch on your hair. You must eat ashes. Who are you? cried Faustina. And the phone went dead.

Old windows rasp in the old house this day of ambushing gales. We have lived here for over a year now. Near the house are trees of an alive wood and a road of broken cobbles that leads to afterbirths and ammunition dumps. I did not choose to live here. I look towards the direction of Iceland, calling out, tell me, tell me . . . I am a drifter in the blue houses. He calls me Faustina. That is not my name. He says he has rechristened me and I do not think he is lying. He says that his left-handed mother was also called Eve. That she was a forsaker. And so my name must be changed. Do you understand? he said to me that first night, looking at the waterjug. I did not answer and he went out into the courtyard. I heard his footsteps. I remember that time, the barley month. I pressed myself against the fireflies and sprawled into a dry season. Yesterday, some time ago, I kissed you with cloud lips. I am afraid of your jackal eyelids. The sun at its zenith always looks to me like a tiny shell fish smashed to pieces against the sky. He waited in the courtyard that night, searching with his hand for the badly torn shadow. He waited for me. In the mirror I saw myself .

How motionless I sat at the white table in the white room. No, I did not move. Not until he came to take me upstairs.

Next morning I remembered the river, watery branches beneath a speckled sky. Then I covered the mirror with my hands and felt my calcining lips parch. A forgetful song ends. I am narrowly dreamed by her, he thinks. Silent, quiet, a live candle bears its suffering. There are no rebels in this passive room. I went out into the courtyard when the rain stopped, I looked at him, I spoke to him, I forget what I said. He cursed his own father. He saw a zombie waiting by the sea. He watched the dew dry on plants. He tolled bells at night. And at noon he rode a black foal through the graveyard. In his pocket he kept a little pouch full of earth from the threshold of his home. He pronounced the names of his friends without pity. He made me sit in the back kitchen disentangling an old fishing-net. All the crooked roads led to his house.

IV

The sepulchress moved the knob rapidly, carelessly along the radio waveband. She heard music and murder, massacres and protestations of innocence cut across the ice cold kindergarten room. She does not require this information but listens to words contradicting the night, broken isolatable music. Her hand razes summer. Ten years ago, she broke off her doll's arm. For her, day and night are both sad roads: they expel cries out of her mouth, unripe fruit. She touches the fleshy coverings of her eyes. Token of surrender: she switches off the radio. She looks at the dark moon through the glass. She is a horoscopist. She kneels down. Distance of moon. Spikes of flowers. Unnoticed, I licked the blood of my lupinosis heart. Help me. Stop the kaolinisation of my body . . . I will pray only when surrendering. His sacraments burnt me and the mirrors suspended above me will betray me. Combust hands lift the fire into the air: they cannot rest quietly in their darkness.

Micah walks towards her. He says: I wish all men on earth had but a single head, then I would cut it off . . . one stroke . . .

The metal bird moved with the wind and the weeds grew in the undecided fields. Long shadows of the morning. I am still kneeling, I am looking at flowers. I see an island far from the mainland. I know the names of the prisoners. I note the position of a bird about to fly. I speak to the woman with the tattooed hands. Prayers on the day of the horse. Secrets like eyelashes. There are still bruises visible on her face, faint traces of his last attack. She tapped the lid of her cosmetic box. Suddenly he hit her. The mandragora hand of an executioner. No, I am not laughing at you. Why would I be interested in noiseless laughter? Skin of my face is eaten away by ancient music. In a cage I saw a tiny antelope about the size of a hare. I am in a private room of fear. Too many colours within my mouth. Species of beseecher. Spawn of rock. I perform a kind of ugly dancing in the street, wearing the lion head mask, reciting the evil customs of a buddhist nun. I dip my fingers in the dew pond. I see your face. You are tired of machines. You lead me to the summit of the hill and show me the land that eats up its inhabitants. You point down into the dead valley where our new house is to be built. I imitate your gesture. Your words are drowned by the roar of aircraft. You pause, wait for silence, continue. He says he desires the pacification of all lands. He says there is no need for war. Maxima and minima are my friends. I answer him in simple words, I smile at him, I am afraid of not satisfying him, the drafter of documents. Smoke rises above the horizon. You are not lying to me? he asks suddenly, his eyes upon me. Woman, these great fields expose us. Our inherited land watches us always. And so I make new promises to him. My words hang trailing and dirty in the mud. The danger of espousal does not leave me. Deceivers; you are all deceivers, I thought. But I answered meekly. I endure time.

Light in Faustina was like the light of beacons and of flares. Shadow in her was the sundial's shadow. When she dreamed that she was delivered of a lion, she awoke bleeding. The bed smelt of the munitions of time. She fetched him rain-weakened days. She fetched him nights like extinct volcanoes. All through the season of commands and pleadings. Beyond the growth of feasts. But she will not turn her body to fruit. Time burns in them like candle coal. They learn the meeting of the eyelids. Visits from thieves, gipsies and beggars do not corrupt them. Her fingers write out every answer but the one he needs. Will another twelve months free them from the bondage of their deceit? Branches of old trees shadow their retreat house. The death of each hour stigmatizes memory.

The new land is cleared, the foundations of the house strengthen Micah's will. Faustina watches from the edge of the clock. The birds on fire encircle her head. Besom summer ends without breaking skin or bone. Refrain of sea burrs. Two winters of candlelight will whiten the tide before the dying starts. Zodiacal lights yearn to scrape the bones. Woods obeyed the seasons, transforming by slow and secret defiances, green and gold, red and black, odours of sky and rain captured there. A wolverene girl studies the creed. Wounds do not heal. Swagging hearts propose riddles to travellers, who are overwhelmed and do not answer. Marram grass grows by the roadside.

v(i)

There are treasonable meetings in empty houses scheduled for demolition. These meetings of the two women are essential to them if they are to survive. Contact is forbidden between them. But they have found each other. They must have an absinthian hour alone whenever possible, without the velvet fiddler. No, their bodies have not touched yet. Their accusers were mistaken. They do not offer each other clumsy hands yet. The two women sit talking in darkness at night or hidden in shadow during the day: they are intent on the deepening of their spiritual life. They talk sadly of the indiscriminate killing of beasts for market. Their skirts are caked with mud. Perhaps they are praying now. Or it may be auguries of harvest which move their lonesome lips. Virtuous ladies relating their woes. Both women are barren. Faustina has slept apart from her husband for over a month. Their mothers wept for the geniture of god. And so these daughters, born after knowledge of guilt, must seek a key to sleeplessness. Shivering in the hallway of the condemned house, they whisper. Or is it a rainy continuous weeping? There is a vanishing argot. We know the dark day's blindness, says Faustina. And her companion answers in a voice of sloes. She says she has hidden a little image of the virgin goddess in the folds of her body. Faustina promises her that their friendship will soon be publicly accepted. But the other girl disagrees. At home her father has criticized her savagely and the old threats have returned. We are slaves fettered to our own breasts, she says, and I hate them for this indecency. Birds kept in sound-proof light-proof rooms still try to migrate in autumn. I understand why. And she swears. But Faustina says, we must wait. Our enemies are visions and superstitions. We must fear the slave ship yet hope for . . . I daren't stay away from the house any longer, Micah will question me. Here. Faustina gives her friend a glass bracelet of crescent moons. Remember, she tells Anna, be afraid but unbelieving. They part reluctantly, agreeing to meet next week in the douche room at the hospital. They go their cold separate ways through the rain.

The rain fell all that night and lasted until three o'clock the next afternoon. Faustina was met by Micah at the door. She was drenched. When she refused to say where she had been, he hit her. And from his loins, she felt foreboding. He smelt her shoshonean odour and this, to Micah, set her somewhere between man and woman: the anger and reproach he turned upon her, when he accused her of obscene witchery, meant no more to her than the replacement of one stamina for another: but to him it was a winter killing. He had received word of Stefan's arrival in the country earlier today and he will consult him about his sister. Micah confined Faustina to her room all the next morning but in the afternoon he allowed her to take a walk. She thanked him angrily. He watched her walk across the fields. He watched her slouching along. His penis strained upwards to terrorism. He promises himself that tonight he will couple with her again, even if he must behave like a thief. He told her she was viperish but he must be the murmurer between her legs, the reacher of her unguarded womb. He watched her walk across the fields.

> *Flood plaints*
> *of the weather shore*
> *and the reversed colours of the mist*

clouds and rocks and stinted trees

Cold wind fathoming me as I walk: through my anger I still see the old year's fossil water, how the sea is denuding the land and eroding the geode hills. Glacier rivers evoke no response from me. I starve. My life includes snow. A colder season will come with the helm winds. If I turn and look inland I will see the thorn forest. But I am held by the territorial waters, sunlessly dining towards me. I fear Micah, his sex will choke me. He demands a son. I ask for another year's evolutionary freedom. He does not answer. Anna . . .

V(ii)

I walk towards the rocks. Her family will judge her harshly. Like minute rift-valleys, the sand moves under my feet. I bend down. Rain shadows cover the seashell I hold on the palm of my hand. The peaty sky decays. And I cry out with the whole of my heart for the wine in the cup which scalds my tongue. And for the genealogies to which I am being yielded up. In the midst of the wind and rain, only one seashell delivers me out of that shieldless place.

Dream: I was singing about the underworld. Hades. About the Lord of the Underworld. Who touched me with cold midnights. Like the fingers of a spiritualist lightly resting upon my new bones. I have given my messages to the sea. The mistakes are made. This time is harder than the grim summer during which I tried to learn the extinct language that used to be spoken by tribes on both banks of the river. Night, night, night; you are beginning to splash me, you are changing the colour of my garden. I look down at the squares of the checker board. He is looking at me. I know. I know his inseverable need and his strength to achieve it. Inkiness of his justice. Bad pain of my hesitating body. He comes close. Inlaying me with his heritage, hawsing my limbs, that ice-ghost, who? you know the one, she lives in the forest, the hazing trees shelter her, her head covered with the shawl and her feet bare. But he'll find her. He'll offer her blood and sweetmeats. Since I have not heard your answer, he says, I do not know what to think. The daylight is almost gone. Why don't you speak? My protectors laugh. I remember I was warned of these dangers by other women. Must I send you out of my house naked? he asks abruptly. I shake my head. My gifts are death damp and pearl ash. No, I say, I'll follow your instructions. He smiles when he hears my faithful words. He sighs. He goes to the bathroom and makes water. He returns and unfastens my sash, my silk trousers.

A little while, a moment, and he'll discover her complex stars, waste of her body, thoughts sloughing from her like skins.

He devours my kimono heart. He grunts. My half-learning pleases him. Did I cry out? No, I am afraid of giving any trouble. What else did I feel? No, I have lost my memory.

In the morning the room was smoky. Turning to the body, he said, Tabitha . . . and with the fragility of a manumitted slave, she arose.

The blind girl is shouting across to the ghosts of the sea. I am afraid of the shadows in the garden, the samurai whispers of the grass. Who is that girl walking away from the man's house? He stole her eyes to ornament his shrine. And in the shrine room dazed butterflies are pinned to the walls. On the sand, the dead man was stretched out: his murderer was running away. When the face of the Woman opened before him, he clapped his hands in prayer: but she fastened him to darkness.

V(iii)

Iris-out day
her pale whipped body structuring no independence yet
still scared of the implements of war
of her iron sickness
of the testament talking to itself
through interlacing arcades of leaf
she wanders without resting
the golden chestnut day

clashes with her tomb marriage

All her insurrectionary fire is doused. Her clocks wait for holiness. Her impulses are for an achingly cold winter, freezing her to a geometric shape, unchanging, living only to savage him with the ice-discipleship of her pulse. *As surely as I shall not forget the lapis lazuli on my neck, I will remember those days and not forget them.** He comes searching for her. He looks sad. Her body bangs against the tree. Her hair crashes against leaves. The nice wet fields hold power. Their dance is sombre. He wears a giant's mask: a mask so terrible that if a child looked at it that child's eyes would crack. There must be no more gatherings in the houses of the dead, he tells her. I understand, she says, closing her eyes. She hides in the cave. She remembers walking along the mountain road. She stopped and bent down to pick up a leaf from the road, a useless object. He shook it out of her beautiful grasp, telling her she was a fool to touch the earth. Faustina fool . . . She had stood there empty-handed and then spat a word spoken only by women. Now as he reaches out for her with his hands stained by the tree sap, she runs. Dewlapped man follows her. Bringing thraldom upon her.

The room is cold because no one thought of lighting a fire. Faustina breaks her silence. Astronauts have landed on the moon, she tells him, I read it in the paper. What of it? he asks. But he spoke calmly. She tells him, it is a reality, Micah, those men have made an unexpected journey. The newspapers report that they explored a fraction of the strange hazardous terrain, set up cameras, planted a flag and left footprints, several bags of urine and other litter. Now, I believe, they are returning to earth. She looks at him moodily. And are they men like you? she asks. He does not answer, she is speaking in an unknown language. I know how a shiver is caused, she says. And he stumbles out of the room. She cannot laugh. I try guessing weather changes, what altitudes will show on the barometer tomorrow. I fail, I am not correct. My baptistry body is unadorned. There was no proclamation. No word out advertising my

---

*   From GILGAMESH EPIC

arrest. They captured me and took me across the country at night. I heard the sea, its pounding sarcasm: and I heard the sharp explosive cries of the guard dogs: but I did not know where I was. Slothful night went through me with the long vibrating beat of a drum. Dark and dark. He met us at the barbican. Did I recognize him? The ceremony was performed quickly. Why did I move as if I had been drugged? Why didn't I use my harsh-sounding voice? My aileron knowledge died. I looked around and all my friends had gone. I was shudderingly changed. We crossed the border, I riding beside him. I was numb, I hardly noticed we were heading down stream into demi-distance, then dawn came, putrid and careless with its corpses, but I saw nothing of it, my eyelids were cast-steel, my hands frost nails, and my body was cramped, sold. Now I only come alive when I am with Anna, only then am I released from the craniology of my prison.

My glass falls suddenly to the stone floor, smashing beyond love's repair. He has returned without a warning or even a pretext of desire. He speaks disregarding words. The spy words. You're alone? he asks. I do not answer, I laugh now. Malice in my throat: but why shouldn't I laugh? As one to whom a debt is long due. An eater of the moon's flesh. Micah is the assessor. He says my words have the shape and cruelty of needles. It isn't true, I think. Night is stiff, narrow, prickly. We can't . . . He bites me with an envenomed tooth. I look at the sign of the summer solstice. He makes candle-bombs. When I lie down, there is a bitterish taste in my mouth, of the canine thistle, or malt dust, I think, or perhaps I am crazy from care. He . . . The power of a promise is becoming obsolete. Elliptical leaves shadow my voyaging. Yet my twilight eye will not close. What is he saying to me? You only imagine you see the world, Faustina. Then interrogate me, I challenge him. He smiles and fixes his eyes on me. What is the colour of your daughter's hair? Why are your troll lips dry? Who is dancing the weal dance? Where is the birthplace of your blood? I said: the heart beats even before it is a heart. I saw last year the skull of a female gorilla, endangering my own transcriptions. Only this morning I saw clouds, suns, mountains and birds of passage: but I was lost and my footsteps demagnetized the earth. I feared that he would make a war cloak from the skins of slain enemies. I'll know you by your fingerprints, he says to me, you'll never burn them away. Then he tells me of my accomplishments and my failures. The mother hurls her mucus into the night. I feared her skeleton and her gooseflesh, I knew she was still standing at the door, I felt the draught. There is the blanching and the blushing of the face, my face. Spastic attacks (more of his words) feed my crises. No. Keep the head erect, be proud, lift the jaw up, the eyes open. Stand in front of the mirror and observe your face, he says, you will see it is a mimic creature. She says nothing, she does not move. Can't you see the hooliganism of your love, you and Anna? he says. Criticizing. She says nothing. Micah stares at her. Is there no vineyard in her? Darkness covered his eyes, he let go the reins and he fell from his horse by the tomb of the king: no . . . ! Why does she move with the menace of the victim? Micah can remember Faustina, running across the fossilized pattern of the fields to meet him beside the pond of the ash tree. Now her joy is gone and he thinks, watching her now, of the element that tints human blood, causing its redness. Why is she so pale? Her face, arms and hands are the whitest of chalk. Does she know how to fly? Does she suck blood from the thumbs of a sleeping person? How can I subjugate her? Offer her bread and meteorites.

VI(i)

Look. Man is pulling old moon down on his head, woman in her clear chamber knows, she watches him wear the silver helmet of amnesiac moon. Some species without eyes evidently spent their lives burrowing in soft mud. In Faustina's wormlike dream, a deformed baby mouse nibbled her hair. Around her waist she wore a flowered sash. She looked at the mountains. Then she awoke. It was still night, wet straw darkness. The firecrackers flashed outside in the courtyard. I opened the window and looked out, I was shivering. The flames collided with the night, the distance between fires extending as far as a call could be heard. Micah grinned up at me, I saw in the light of his fire how he would drive me on. I hated this festival, he knew it, yet he celebrates it shouting.

I lit the lamp and read my frightened book. It said: the king and his son were hunting. It said: the field was covered with snow. It said: he limped from the bullet embedded in his thigh. I close the book. I sit with my back to the window. Eventually Micah and his friends stopped setting off the fireworks. The girl picked the rose and said: I am tired.

House of incantation house of whooping cough house of pride house of translation house of cockatoos house of mildew house of regicide house of satin house of acupuncture house with a leaky roof: a stranger is at your door, boasting of his surgeoncy, lesions on his lips, water flows out from his heart, not blood, sea hard to climb. Besieger of riddles, he wears a priest's coat but his skin is a shire of heats. All night he has been burning the bodies of the dead. He makes her look in the birdlip mirror and watch her mulish nativity. He afflicts Faustina with justice. He shakes with my fear, his journey blisters my mothering hands. I show him a repulsive doll that consumes small meals and I beg him to spare me an arctic pregnancy. He smiles and disappears, nothing is left of him, not even his gonadial shadow. The reaping hook is in my hand. I remember our walk in the garden that morning, no, it was not yet daylight, and how all the frost was shattering our charity with its white deaths. Now I stand by the sea and the sky is grey as the slab of a tomb. I am watching the scarecrow in that field over there. I have in my hands corn-stalks. But I drop them, they fall on the sand, it is the fetish day, the coronach hour, I step upon the water. I walk upon the waves very elegantly. Prayer for the icehouse people. He frowns. She says I am cruel. But I opened my eyes and saw her standing at the foot of my bed, medusal in the pale dawn light, her eyes closed, her lips moving with the unwifely words. She was asking for a reward. She was wearing the blue dress. Feldspathic light curved around us. I was profane, in my speech, in my actions. But for me desire burning with progenitorship vasts the cornered body with blood and has the nature of an omen. Miracle, portent. Even for us. So when she came to me at dawn, I felt that all of her tristfulness was drawing her to me, to that centre of pain and not-victory where we would meet: and when she stood clad in her blue garments, begging me, body supinate as her words, for the prayer I never learnt, for me there was no other choice but the known observances of flesh, nothing but my hand taking her mantellata coat from her shoulders to begin our harvest journey. And for her only silence denying the blind beauty of copulation . . . Why is she always wresting away . . . ?

She cannot tell him she knows the bone behind the uterus is called the holy bone, the os crucis. Curse of myrrh. My wooden wedding dress contains me, like water. I see the priapic hand pointing the way to an everlasting flight of stairs, spiral upon spiral. The ticking of his heart guides me towards the threshold of the splayed house. I looked into the eye of the man and saw blue stellar objects. The down-land moon and the winter pastures remind me of last year's garden, the inscrutable epithalamia of cobwebs. I fear for our safety. Earthshine darkens me. This room is a triangle of terror. Our bodies outcry wearily. I am the clock paradox. I am younger than my twin sister for she remains whole, did not attempt the escape. I am older than my mother, for I have sewn my fingers to rocks. Some hours are longer than others: slow axial rotations. He separates my bright and dark hemispheres. I am impearled. His weapon is the morningstar.

VI(ii)

Kiss the Son, lest he be angry . . .
Inflictor of flame
Singer of reaping contests
Saint of doors and lighthouses
fasten my lives together mend my flesh.
At whose feet shall I fall?

The one who arrives unexpectedly will be the adulterer inheriting your troubled mind. He will already have fever, his eyes will be sunken and his skin will be shrivelling. He has grown a mirror in his breast to guard him against the snowcraft of the other eyelids. You are the snakeholder. He knows. Next day you must meet him before daybreak in a narrow street high above the harbour. It will be winter, I think it will be raining, I am almost sure it will be raining. At first he will not speak. You will both listen to the foghorn. Then he will show you a picture of his brother, the god-begotten, halfman, halfhorse. You will want to hiss contemptuously. But if you desire the prize of endurance, you must accept the soiled picture, bow, loosen your hair into the rain and lead the man to the north field. He will say to you: the trigger of the sinner got raw because there was no joy in his burns. Then you will recite to him your prayer of whiteness, the death colour: describing moon, snow, white skin of the youngest canephore, white words of an old song, unlit candles, chalk hearts. Then he will take your left foot in his hands and bite it gently. You will realize you are enemies. He will name for you the four last secrets. He will recite the pharmacopoeia of ravens. He will describe the twisted grains of death in the sulphonamide night. He'll warn you of the dreamer's persistence. He will say: I celebrate my murder. You say: the victims of my sensuality never lie. Dawn's augur mouth opens. You rub your wet bodies together. When that is finished, you leave him in the field. You will not meet again.

Faustina is afraid of street corners: because of the automobiles, the strangers, the cold women, the faultfinders. I am afraid. If I close my eyes, I cannot walk in a straight line: so I must face them all. Every barefoot wandering ends in a circle. Do I remember my first hour? Drowning in my hormonal lake? They blindfolded me and then told me I was standing in front of a clock. They made me feel the hands of the clock with my own hands and tell them the time. They said it was an experiment. There is no sunlight in my skin. I know foramina pains. Orbiting the penicillin moon. The excretories of my skin are breathing. I have three different colours in my head. I am not to be compensated. Only I can crack open the secret that is so closely shut. Unpitied, he calls me. Exit via the head. The sun has no voice. And I sleep, the sleep of a thief in the daytime. The black and white songbirds unfolded their wings, flew from her window.

She turns over the sheet of music. Hands, thoughts: morbidezza. The room is cool and clean, pine walls, pine floor. She opens the lid of the piano. But she thinks of the gun threatening the world's frosted shades: silver sea, bare honey sky, leaf of haggadist autumn. Skeins of the future clutched in beseeching hands. I taste the hartshorn tongue of the intruder. Because I see strangers approaching me. They are Micah's comrades. Today they are snatching and gnawing all my hours. They said they would rid me of grief and fear: divest me of cold and untwist me of oppression. I made no pledges. I listened to them. They spoke of a guiltless birth. But I knew milk curdles in the wrong breast. So I smiled and said no answer. They spoke of the beauty of his concubine. But I knew that was a lie. I told them they lied. I killed the wasp as it buzzed against the glass. And they watched me, those gluttonous vegetarians. They came closer to me, yes, three siderographists, men without brides. I showed them my bitter blunted hope. I heard their hearts gurgling loud. I was penned in by the witness of their hand. They said, the pleasant wolf pads through the birch grove. Then they spoke to me of the fosterage of the high road. All wildernesses are like that, I said. They kept on repeating their own words. Redeclaring the disguises they offered me. And so I screamed. Screamed and screamed and screamed until they left me alone and uprooted. Sickness and sadness gave birth to me. A flashlight woke me. Ice harps taught me my name. What am I? Mindmooncandle. I am watertight inside a dozen wombs. The salt shore, I remember, and the thin woman bone, white maple branches, god's bloody fingers . . .

I was alone in an empty room, the birthplace of interstellar dust. I did not know the names of his friends. But I knew it was necessary for me to reconceal myself. I am the one who made a vow. It was no rumour. I dare not turn from entreaty and prayer. I am haunted by the glittering gentleness of christ, all riftings, all cleavings are his, all the covenants of unripeness. I will open the door a little wider and look out at the snow. Halfmelted snow clung to the hem of the mourner's dress. From the shrubbery, macrocephalic children watched the procession. Anniversary of a death: a mournful act, to repeat the memory so often, and not sleeping: only deceit's shell and ice and charcoal meeting in me always. She kept the threat at the back of the throat. Leaves fall from the tallow tree. She heard Micah talk to the parasites within the body of the host. There was an open door and seen beyond on the lawn a birdeater woman not belonging to the garden. I saw her in the mirrors of my skin. She knew the ritual of the hand. I looked out through the holes in my skull and I saw her. He stood beside her. He knew her name. The door closed. There was a great cry of seabirds. I thought of the long midrashic hair of the mother and the depilation of the witch.

VII(i)

> *Here is the body stalk*
> *Here is the future spine*
> *Here are the veils of flesh*
> *Here is the place of the heart*
> *the blood island*
> *The heart has been beating for a month*

I ate the wheat of the dead. I had one fear, small, shaped like a fir-cone, hard as a stone. I folded my hands around my fear once a day, usually in the half light of the winter afternoons, its coldness flowing into my imitational flesh: and I heard the fear speaking, calling to me, hagseed, hag-seed . . . But I never answered. I am afraid of becoming his executioner.

Poor sacrifice son. There were other rooms I went into, searching. I remember little of them. Only my footsteps on the uncarpeted floors. Searching. Did I see a portrait of a holy girl, with parrot and lapdog? Or did I imagine the room she dominated? Revolution spoke to me but I was listening to another sound: it wailed inside the stone: little ugly voice. Silence? I did not rely on silence for it often turned into a voice in rage or pain or loud laughter. Beyond that there were only hills churning up the sky and the sea's incriminating waves depriving me of skin and again that bright unsteady light beyond the darkness, compelling my sinews to an edge, testing the framework of my mouth, forming my speech patterns. I am a karst region. There is ice during all my summers. He lures my horizon to long distances of silt. I am trapped on this island arc. I am held in the elbow of capture. What do I see? A second growth of grass covering the fields after the mowing: and the fossil horse grazing at the orbital edge of my eye. And the ephemeral second seizes me. During the last season of the year all the strands running through the centre of the heart go tight, imperative. I touch the candle frame. Haltingness: I can't move quickly across this rust-coloured room, my thoughts are microwaves, body stretched and hurts, I cannot sing for you, no, don't shout . . . Trickery gave you a name, weapons and a wife. Voyages you take are fruitless, you bring back only news of whitlows and altars like iron cages and fires lit on strange coasts. You bring back no new flowers, no cures for profanity, no knowledge to strengthen the year's spine. The yellow archangel hates you for your despoilment. Yes, Micah, tell me the name of the hospital where you got your heart. The branches of the ash tree are very poor specimens this year, he said, as he gave them to me. He looked like the memory of another person. I said nothing. I looked at the photograph of his dead son on the dresser, a remote smile.

That night I heard Micah climb the uncarpeted stairs, I listened to him as he walked along the landing. He paused outside my door. He said my name slowly. But I feared him and all his dead. So I did not answer. I think I wanted to answer. Yes, I wanted to answer. But my mouth was in despair. I stared at the slats of moonlight on the bare floor. Why was I afraid? What did I fear in him even more than his priapism or his bloodcraft? What element in his body, what substance or fluid or electricity so imbued me with this great fear? I could not overpower my drought. I couldn't guess the answer. Minutes later I heard him shuffle along the passageway and close his door. Then I went down through more dark distance than ever before in my room. I heard the noise of many voices. And that night, bridges, rain and blood all burnt with bequeathing rage. I open my mouth and I see the mouths of the Mekong. Transplanetary flux of the respond leaf. Blood. Mildew of queendom. Madwoman madonna pointing north: I look, I see years torn tremblingly bare, the twilights unleavened, the dawns wanting flesh. Queen of the prairie. Arachnoid brain in my head, protoplasmic collar encircling bone. I step on grief glass. Animal mother. Knower of embryology and riddles. The bird is perched on the branch. I watch. Don't make any noise, I want to sleep. His story makes no sense. I look sad, he tells me, like on the first night. I begin to think he has a great dread of being buried alive. Sensitivity may be obtained, I believe, by placing the couple in isolation. Direct carbon light upon them. Soon they will be speaking in the voices. Their shadows will be snarling. She will out-live him. But only by a matter of hours. Then they will be extinct. I do not sleep.

VII(ii)

I turn the page of a book. Blood eats me up. I will throw the afternoon away. He walks up and down the room. He ignores my words. I do not resent this. He is a stratum of fog seen from a distance. He has entombed us. Why has he buried us deep beneath the surface of his heresy? I close my book, I lift my body up, I return the book to the shelf, unread, unlearnt. I see the weather-house on a shelf in my grandfather's house, the wooden figures of a man and a woman moving in response to changes of humidity yes . . . A man who died two thousand years ago watches me: his body smells of peat. His right hand does not move. He listens. I turn over on to my back. The dark room has to be excavated. I heard him move. But I did not move. I thought of the decapitated girl. She left her prehistoric fingerprints on solstices and equinoxes. But what can I do? Tomorrow I will walk silently across the field, with hard thoughts like splinters in my brain. Bringing winter. I move my hand and an endless chain staircase appears.

My dear, he said, have you decided? I turned to look at him and I wasn't afraid of him. I did not drag my feet when I walked away from him. The boatwoman waits. The meeting takes place in a garden at night beyond the voices of rock. Anna brings her an offering of salt water in a heavy quartz dish. She places it in Faustina's hands. With the utterance of a word that sounds like the caw of a bird, Faustina pours the water upon the earth. She wears a robe of bison hide painted with figures of the spider and images of the whirlwind. She takes Anna's hand and leads her into the cave of the children's games. Soon: the interception of a churching. Soon: the inswathement of a moon. And you will forget the leper mothers in their glass castles. This is their district, Faustina and Anna. They have swerved from the path of the night and formed their own allegiance. Their hesitation belongs to this hour, within the zone of the cave. Faustina spreads the rug on the ground. Both women listen for a voice calling their secret callous. But no stranger's word enters the hallucinated world of the brides. Only mist and the odour of the mist and the sarcophagi mist and memories of the death letter and the moon number and the circumciser from the north. Faustina is no longer the guardian of the frost. She sees the faces of the bog people. She touches Anna, her bird pelvis. Ignorance causes Faustina to act slowly. Her whiteness warns. Anna fears the instruments of her body. I am in a place in my mind like before the world was made, says Anna nervously. I have hidden leaves in the forest where he cannot find them, says Faustina, laughing. Anna hears her own cry, the cramp opulent in her body. She feels the drainings of her own darkness flood out from her. She dare not look at Faustina's pallid face bent over her. She listens to Faustina's words but she cannot understand their heaviness. She listens to her own body:

It says: *First, there is the ghost in the womb*
Second, the establishing of the fear
Third, the lighting of the fir candle
Fourth, the coldness of weasel worship
Fifth, the harelip kiss on the finger

Sixth, the burning of the kern baby
Seventh, the dark searching for your lost skin
at the boundary of the unfelled forest

There is a light flickering between their bodies and they are panting. They are in the saturated room of the furnace. Faustina demonstrates the use of her tongue and attacks Anna's cunt. Anna yields but her skull is full of razors. Faustina feels the weight of the clock, she fears the ice cobra. Your hands must learn how to shelter your face, she gasps, and scratches Anna's cheek. The vagrancy of those two girls is an echo of assault. But they are clinging together in their coldness. These meetings at the ravine are the investment of their bone. Ravine bodies are the only bodies they are allowed: bodies not of women now, nor horses, nor tapirs: but furling shapes of reversal, bearded fish, no names for their pale thumbs and abducted urine. When Faustina leaves her, Anna sleeps in the region of darkness until the rawboned men come for her.

VII(iii)

What else do I remember? Days that broke down under the strain and got lost, times when I was like a peg of wood driven into a wall and dragged captive in a net along the bottom of the water. I remember questions. I remember working all one freezing day out in the kale-yard. It was my twentieth birthday. She talks she smiles she cries, they said. Meaning me. And I remember it was a neglected candle in the linen room that started the fire. Buildings, outhouses, barns, fences and trees: all aflame. Birch and rowan and ash tree: on fire. Bird in a well singing but trapped. Cruel marriage after dark, I, the bride, led to a strange house, met by torchbearers. Yes, there were the lanterns, the ones used for walking at night, held close to my bare feet. I know I ought to sleep: but I cannot rest. A duststorm is approaching. I fasten the doors and the shutters.

It was about this time last year that I received the first of the letters. Anonymous letters, truculent, subversive. As I spelt out the unhappy obscenities, my brain went black with the ergot of anger. I wanted to see my enemy destroyed in front of me, to watch the limbs of my enemy stripped of flesh, the bones broken. But then I realized that the hate in the letter was not its fire-centre. No: behind the hate, I saw fear. And a fear greater than any of my fears. A fear of every finger, tooth, hand. The writer of the letter was using allegations against me as a flesh-brush: to excite the body of the writer, not the victim. So I knew I would not be harmed. I would wait calmly for the next letter. Then I would decide who my correspondent was most like to be. I drank my soup that tasted of amel-wheat. I watched the sinewy untiring trees.

> *Woman-eye sees the water child*
> *sees the darkness of the bird*
> *sees the daughter only*
> *eye sees ocean, dog and garden*
> *eye sees*
> *I saw the burnt bones*
> *from the cut wings of two jackdaws*

I'm an apostle of the inner throat. Around me, vapours of deaf bone. The bridge fording the shallow stream waits for me. There is silence and in the gas chamber he is making love to his twin sister. Within my mouth, all colours taste of scurf. The abduction of a woman is forbidden by law, he says. In the margin of my eyelid, a reproach of sun, essenism of light. As I lie in this field, I think of what I saw at the back of the mirror and I am afraid. I don't want to return to that stone house of his. Greenstick shadows catch me there. He does not like me to walk alone, not in the bleaching fields nor the windy forests. He just wants me to grope blindly around inside the house: or at most to sit in that courtyard, reading the books he gives me, with their oaken words that darken every path. No, I want to be able to grab the sky, I want to watch the replumation of the birds. He can't keep me locked up. The satsuma sky refreshes me and the forest teaches me about the sun's shadow. That is what I will tell him.

As I walked home, I passed two women grinding corn with two stones. And I thought of Anna. Anna walks stoopingly through the streets and the fields, brushing against stalks and children. She is a tall girl. Every third week she crosses the valley to visit me secretly. Her young hands are dry and hard, like mine. Tertian hands. She brings books with her sometimes and we try to read the ancient deity language. We would like to visit the chained library in the big church: but it is difficult to arrange. Micah is a poor and hasty comforter. I mend my torn clothing. He will not speak to me. He will not explain my internment. I do not understand his actions. Why am I stripped of all rights? Why can't I go walking in these dawns with their grains of autumn? Is he afraid I will fade away into the millefleur mists of the forest? Why won't he let me have even a small piece of the Host? Does he think the feet of my christ will crush him like an ant? His masters take large mouthfuls of me and hurt me. The door of my room is locked, I am a prisoner, I cannot cope with my fingers, my increscent body is at the beginning of a death, I look at the walls, I misinterpret his gestures. Let's go into the house, he said. He touched my steeple headdress. He brought me to this room. And his bread was mould. I pray for the hepatization of his whole body. He said my contrition was imperfect. A landscape of carbon dioxide snow is what I see. I want to go out and gather my carrion flowers. But even though I am held captive, I still have, hidden in this room, a cloth containing the sweat of his body.

VIII(i)

The table at which I write my weekly letter to my mother is painted yellow. It is an old table. I do not know the history of this table for I was not born in this house but brought to it, a stranger, an exile, a wife. From my window, I see a man-made hill. I know that if I climb to the summit of that hill I can look out to sea. Sometimes the ocean is blue, sometimes grey. At evensong it is green. It makes me blind. There is a book on my yellow table. I will read it tonight, if I cannot sleep. A lamp hangs by the bed. I have my own room. My own bed. Sometimes at night he visits me.

He is cruel. I begin my letter. The floods are abating, I tell my mother. I had a fever but have recovered now, I lost a little weight but will soon be strong again. I tell her these unimportant things. A plane flew over the house, the noise frightened me, but, mother, I am not melancholy. I am not anxious, no, I am saving the daylight up in my brain and one day I'll use it to transform my rickettsia-self into a bridge over the bloody river. All my love. I write my name at the foot of the page. This body of leaves, the transmittable life, moving from parent to offspring . . . I do not say, here, mother, it is perpetually dark, cold, for sun cannot penetrate to these depths and our bodies are strange to us, as though covered with an earthy ooze, a red clay. No, I do not tell her these things. Nor that the effigy of a womb terrifies me and that my bones terrify me and that I dread the time of telling the amberina secret, the nights he visits me, the month when the blood will not come, the day when my body will kill me by a glance of its eye. I cannot get free, the handwritten clocks never freeze. Lost in the fog forest, I add the mystic numbers together. There are flaws in the wind. I see winding-sheets of candles. The afternoon sucks me dry. In the garden a lunar animal is grazing: it should redeem me but there are still the planet depths, the damp haze of body, that caged zone. There is still too much fear. Surgery of the mouth happens. And the petrification of lakes. Acropolis burning. I curve inwards to the point of a leaf. I dread high places. My fears grow, I even fear the sunlight now. I am ancient. A cup of brine to drink. Luminescence without names. In the forest the bicyclist gets lost.

VIII(ii)

When my brother Stefan came to visit us, I thought this would mean a new beginning, another shape at least to the conflict. But I was wrong. Since his arrival my witchhazel burden has grown heavier. But I must not think like this or my head will gape full of holes and I'll go down the snake path, past the dreams of the women, into the split-second world. The tenth part of a second is, for me, very long and contains faces doubting me.

I sat in the plum garden. I wore a long robe sewn by a silent woman who stitched her thoughts into every seam. I was reading a letter from my sister, the plague nun, when he came to me. I was surprised to see him back at the house because it was almost noon and he should have been supervising the work in the fields. He did not look at me when he spoke. He saw trees of blood with their bloody roots floating, he saw the branches shift about the cadaver woman. As he spoke to me, angry, the bone showing, I thought fourteen days make one long freezing lunar night. A village boy with long hair down to his shoulders looked over the wall at us as he passed. The wife of my youngest labourer is pregnant, Micah told me. He accused me of evil. No, I said, no, but he went on cursing me through a century of stone steps. I tried to explain. I am afraid, I said, I am afraid of the throatiness of birth. But he brought the sky down on me, anathematizing, till I was colder than a stampeding skull. He twisted my arm harshly and said, do you use ice as a mirror? I stared at him. How can I unseal myself? I asked. See priests or doctors, he said, repeat incantations, wear crimson coats, eat leaves . . . I don't care. But don't cheat me. Or I'll send you back along the hard daylight road. Here, use this. He handed me some money twisted up in a scrap of coloured paper. I watched him walk away through the little cowering fruit trees. I had sadness for him, because man and woman had concussed him. He was also violated, each day. That was why he could never hear what I said to him. I watched him move among the leaves. Then I put the money aside and tried to plan my first needlework of the autumn.

I was born in a village in another country. That village was situated midway between Cape Disappointment and Cape Flattery, allegorical names, given to the headlands because of the sea and its wrecks. But I was brought here, to keep on crying like an impersonatrix. The people are strange here. They deny the divinity of christ. Every church is in a state of dilapidation. Priests are figures of fun. The marriage ceremonies are secular. The trades of the people are forestry and farming, in the main part, although there are some silversmiths and blanketweavers. These are the people I have come among. I do not understand them. I do not understand their anti-moon marches nor their veneration for the menstruum of a whore. I do not understand.

Faustina stood by the wall and looked across at the ridges of raked hay and then at the rows of sheaves in the next field, ready for drying in the wind. Was she planning her first mutiny then? How much did she know about the place of initiation? Oh, she knew all about the sprawling world of white flowers and agrimony skies. But did she realize how many hundreds of drops of falling stalactite water she'd have to count before she was allowed her freedom? Did she know how real the degradation of her heart would be? No, she didn't know. She kept on looking for a way out. In the darkening garden, she saw the peacock of beaten steel. And she recited the other prayers. He said many things to me late that night. I was caught in a tetrahedral cage and I said nothing. Nothing. Only the vows came out of my mouth. I made vows. He would not relent. He insisted. He gave me a shawl stained with blood, which burnt my skin. But I put it across my shoulders and let the fire disguise me. All the time Micah was shouting my name. This was long before I learnt how to hide in the fissures of my brain.

We stopped our car at the petrol station built at the top of a huge cliff. I said, I will walk to the sea. You said nothing. As I walked, the proprietor of the station came running up behind me. I asked him where he was going. He told me he had to light a beacon for the ships out at sea, to guide them past the rocks. I went on walking until I came to a stone arcade full of calm birds, perched very still. They said that it was sunset but that they did not mind. Early next morning, at dawn, the sterility hour, you gave me some locally woven fabric and a dress pattern. I thanked you and said I would send them to my mother, who would make up the dress.

White light seen on the horizon. White light of violence. Vomiting fire, I am looking for the herb called honesty. I have received letters from a person unable to write his or her name. I am called seasonless. I have not seen Anna for six weeks. So I think she has made her decision. She will not come with me into exile. My feet sink into the muddy sea-ooze. I can picture her, the seared expression on her face, her hands sowing spiritual seed. But I fear another meeting with her. I cannot reach my translatress. I walk quickly, frightening the birds away from the crops. I am finished with Anna because her ash-white mouth has become servile towards Micah. I see that all the toil of the year is lost. The abacist man is harder to live with and I can already touch the crisis. Mother, your world was an array of dates and crazy memories and afternoons in the snapshot dump: but I am not devout enough. I see you, governess of the breast. What do I do, how do I steady my flickering body? How do I protect the bones of my zero-shear hand? Our life is harder since Micah and I ceased to be strangers. Our words are doggerel. What terror fixed in his memory is making me decay? Our inheritance is of dark wharves and I fear our cast-off skins. I make many drawings of gravid females. For my last birthday, Anna gave me a jeremiad doll with three swivelling faces — one sleeping, one crying porcelain tears and one laughing. Sometimes this doll summons me with the force of her arrogant vulnerability and I am forced to lock myself in my room and stare at the doll and at the stolen photographs I have of Anna and murmur the name of the inventor over and over again. And when such an afternoon is finished, I am burned away, as if I have been seated beneath arc-lamps. I don't want to think of her backbone nor of her voice nor of her coldness. I don't want to think of her wedding dress, the rinderpest shade of the silk.

I saw him, I thought he was praying. But when he turned to me, I saw he was very near to the dead-death and I, incarnate in the woman's name and sleep, was left in my automatism. And the maimed door closed on good and evil. We coupled until there was nothing left. Except I saw his hemicrania face . . .

The keys to the rose chapel are buried. Sword and book are lost but birds go flying through stone, the knife pricks the spiritualist raiding the church and I cut witchcrafts out of my body. Beyond the distorting glass, a line of felled trees. I blunder out into the night, my senses hardened by alum. Light falling on the goalgarden hews me down and I bare my neck to the continence of the moon. I go running down a dark street, I am naked to the waist. A man catches hold of me. He says that because I have not protected my breasts I am the property of all men. He caresses me. I break away from him, not understanding my strength, and start looking for you. Now I am travelling upwards on a dark escalator that has no end. The people who are descending on the other staircase pluck at my hair and pinch my nipples and laugh at me, showing their rodent teeth, and I can't breathe. Their sermons hurt me. I kneel by the river and say to all the people, yes, sever me from my synagogues, tie me with ropes to the dead man. They leave me alone, beneath the averting sky. Phototropic words and pilgrim signs protect you, Micah. But the beak of a great preying bird haunts my dream. And you refuse to kill my enemy. Even my memories are like small untamed threshing birds. I think rarely of calmer days. Razors and warhorses: these are your gifts to me. It is three days since you spoke to me. Famine is all I hope to gain from the sunlight. I am afraid of the machinery of trees. Why is this room full of bottles of ash? Why is there blood smeared on the windows? I fault like a broken dancer. My flames are borrowed. Will I manage the demolition of this arctic sea? Tidal butterflies fail my love, their weight heavy and hard on me like the laws of a latin language. Climbing the mountains of the masturbator's afternoon, we deteriorate all the time. Let your blind singing woman lead you by the hand. The high lamps are silent. We await the first male month of summer. We see the growing leaves of the year. We experience silk and a dry room. Micah, you must taste my farewell blood. Because you are travelling, Micah, guided by your umbilical cord which she has fastened to a dead tree. And you must break this cord even if it means flaying yourself alive. Faustina looks at him bravely without attempting to ward off rejections. But he is afraid of the light. He says to her: on this bed that beauty which ought never to have been harmed was rent by your coldness and now your mouth bruises my throat. Flowers seize on my symptoms. Shadows are estuary webs lost to my naked eye. The pain caused by your words is too great . . . You're like a pedlar doll displaying exterminated wares, Faustina. He shoves her abruptly out of the room, the quinsy bridegroom. She leaves the room without weather kisses. She knows nothing is more beautiful than the metacarpal bone of the vulture. She creates the crossroad days. She plunges into the digitalism of the dark star. The eye of the great slave watches. The geographer in the long room watches. Women of fungicide, their hair blowing in the wind, watch. The spell is strengthened if the wearer of the robe is carrying a dead spider in his mouth.

IX

Faustina sits by the wayside watching the first month of summer. She has left the cool house because the baiting mirrors frighten her. Preaxial dust clogs the leaves and her fingernails and the dogroses and the foetuses. She has been watching the road for over an hour. No one has passed. She stares at her wooden shoes. Sun anaesthetizes her. A little door opens in her mind. A little door closes. She holds herself in suspense. Her claims to the landscape are dormant. She is a hobbled witch, has no power. Drought. Not even precipitable water to spare. She travels the length of her optical path. No one moving. Nothing happening. Faustina should return home to finish the laundry but it is too hot, she is too tired, she gropes her hands down into the aridity earth. Esparto fields urge me to acknowledge my duties to the moon. But the quantity of my darkness is too great for me to manage. I cannot move yet. If I tried, I could only go creeping about like an aged woman.

Her elfinwood body receives the shock of dry blows. Dust, whiteness of pleurisy roots, scalp of the land showing through the dead grass like ivory or plexiglass. And because of the partisanism of her eyes, colours are feigning death wherever she looks.

A mongrel dog lurches along the road. She observes the animal. She does not call to it. She watches it pad out of sight. She said: I will see that dog again one day. And the words she spoke out of the hot head of the day were burnt by the sun, kernel, heart, nucleus of hunger and thirst.

Around her she sees the ghost children of the leap year. She remembers his toxiphobia. She smiles. Whispering, whispering through the broken windows. Her isolating language. Grail girl. And she recalls the indifferent faces of the people on the stairs. Like an anchoress she saw circles of fire and of water and the hand of flesh that shrouded the iron labarum from her sight.

She stood up and the sky never moved even though the silence was robbing her of some pressure in the blood so that she couldn't protect herself or fasten herself down to the rock and the terrible gold day went on winding and winding itself around her, tighter and tighter until her head almost split. So she began to walk. She walks like someone bringing jesus to a city. She thinks: I am dark in all places and much out of zone here on the second staircase. Isogon shapes of smoky flowers are pinned to her skirt. So she stops walking. She leans against a tree. The prehistory of her breasts makes her weep. Her tears confirm her suspicions. Yes. Burn the damaged life. They read me letters full of all kinds of terrors imputed to me. She opens her eyes. Micah stands watching her, fifty metres away. Now she is trying to ask him, what do you want? But her mouth hurts and will not speak. Micah does not move. He stands watching her. The longer he stares at me, the more often his shape changes. But it is always Micah. She thinks, am I innocent? Micah slowly lifted his arm. He threw a white stone at her.

It did not hit me. It fell at my feet. Micah says nothing. Now I ask questions. He smiles. He waits. I do not move. I dare not approach him. So he turns away, he walks down the hill, he goes out of sight and towards the sun, and I am alone and exhausted. My lies capture me. I hear the sound of wars and slavery and babies crying but I see only a sky and a white stone. I bend down, I take up the stone eagerly. It is smooth and white. I love it, it is everlasting. But the stone turned into a grass snake with a landscape on its back. The snake entwined about my wrist and I knew it would ban my lips from speaking. But I kissed the snake anyway and it vanished and the stone was gone also my hand cold and I looked at

Micah and touched him then he turned and walked away again and why
the spine remembers I thought . . .

> *and I fear hooks, ropes and nets . . .*
> *I fear the maps of uncompleted faces*
> *I fear the eye in the stone*
> *I am afraid to eat the remorseless fruit*
> *I am afraid of misunderstanding the hoofed word*
> *A kind of silk daughter spoke to me*
> *because of the trilateration of my body*
> *House with its visionary walls always falling down*
> *pictures on the inside of our skins*
> *our other faces*
> *Who eats your magic? Who follows your footprints?*
> *Who comes to the door of your brain?*
> *The others*

X(i)

The two men are wrapped in red cloaks. The woman who is standing
between them is dressed in blue. The time is winter.

The year is not known. She is bearing the unsheltered candle. They
walk slowly towards the gate. Hammering of twilight and the words they
have in their memory and the answers they know they must achieve.
Their faces are intensely strained, as if to hear the word that will save
them. Once a year, the woman tells her brothers, on a set day, I enter an
empty unlit room where I remain for exactly an hour, not moving, not
speaking. This is in memory of my sister. But her brothers do not answer.
So the hooded woman remains silent. The badger voice of the river keeps
saying to her, fear the ghosts of your tongue, their zero phrases, white
mirages: then that sound fades away and they walk through the gateway
and enter into the melancholia of the pampas. There is the plover
darkness awaiting them and they are hiding in their skins because the

descendant of the sea will come towards them soon. The woman stumbles. The tarantism of her body hurls her between north and south and she isn't brave enough. The woman wearing a blue cloak and carrying a black candle stumbles. She drops the candle. She tries to regain her balance as the earth tilts, a rope bridge beneath her feet. No, she says, no, the triangles are all broken, they cannot be joined, don't you understand, I will not touch his dervishhood, no, please, Stefan, break my bones but don't send me to this place . . .

The two men watch her. Tonight she is not their sister: she is a bracken stranger to be delivered to a destination. They cannot share her uninhabited world. They watch her. She kneels, she lies on the ground, this is her termination, dark pours in through the holes in her head, her hair is going to be sold, her mouth swaddles the night with great mechanical cries, she shrieks matrix-hurt. Her brothers listen. But they belong to the future. Star-roots of the sky burn. Moon zigzags. Her storm brothers drag her to her feet, the elder of the two holds the candle. She shouts: I am nippleless. And I am afraid of him. Stefan says, whether you have blood smeared on your forehead or agonies in your uterus when we hand you over to him is of no importance. We know about pain and it is of no importance. We cannot be free of ice. We cannot save you from a cold climate. We know the distance. We have read runic names inscribed on stone and metal.

Weather throbs in her. The cinder festivals burn back to her mother's testimony. She is trapped. She prepares herself for the falsification. Black names grow inside her fingers. But she does not protest. She is a closed sphere. Her eyes are end of day glass. Now she will live stealthily. She will hide within a rock. She will practise machining her face to dullness. She will think of a room in which an axial arrangement of mirrors on opposite walls gives the effect of an infinitely long vista. She will hate the man and when he calls her by name she will not touch any part of her opponent's body.

The two men approach the meeting place, followed by the girl. Yes, she will torture the sea. The travellers wait. Sky-animals revolve above them.

Cold winds blow from the ice. When the other man appears, small as sleeping sickness on the horizon, they take up their positions, she standing between the two men, her brothers, and holding the candle, representative of generations born of embezzled bone.

Next morning, I awoke to the sound of pigs grunting in the farmyard. I climbed down the stairs. In a room of red stone I met an angry angel, the unelectrified, uneddying creature of the mirror. I looked at the objects on the table and they had no names. On the walls were fastened thin flat leaves of clay bearing inscriptions and carvings. I said, I am in the wolframic times. There is retina dream, grass, rain, winter harlots, soldiers, village, farmhouse, musicians. And I am flooded by the leaf blotch of the roses. I am fastened to Micah like a draught horse to a wagon. The astronomer has betrayed me. A flake of snow falls on the army. Because of the fever lasting one lifetime reflected in the eye of the approaching witch, I am silent. On the first morning I climbed down the stairs, my movements timed by a molecular clock. He said to me: you must carve the star designs on the faces of our first two children, the son and the daughter. But my body was still mine then and he could not disturb my dark friesian calm. You are tired, he said. I must allow you to accustom yourself to the new pattern before warning you that this pattern will not change for the rest of your life. I said nothing. I was watching for any change in the clock's rhythm. I dropped a birdbone pin on the floor. He picked it up and handed it to me. I did not smile. He turned away, a sudden and violent dismissal. At the door he said, remember, you must not leave the house. I know, I said. When I was alone in the strange house, I felt ugly and ungraceful. I did not care for my new name. I was nineteen years old then. And lifeless.

The old woman sat in a wheeled and hooded chair. She muttered something as I passed her, and her attendant-nurse smiled at me with a gluey face. I walked for a long time that afternoon, to get free of the faces. Too many people keep telling me they are holy. And you, Lady Hanging Hair . . . Dry leaves blow across the courtyard, like speech in a low fanatic voice. In her clapboard throat, words she can't use. She hears the clattering of brass quoits and Micah's friends laughing. A solitary bird flies into her room and blunders against the walls. Faustina catches the bird. She wrings its neck and takes it down to the basement. There she dissects it and finds that it lacks a heart.

So what remained of the features of her soul? Burns, blindness and death. She watched the ghost-markings of the seasons: and the tides crammed against her breastbone choked her. The girl moves like a catarrhine monkey, without shock knowledge of fire. There are dead flowers in the vases because I cannot be bothered to change them. Ice and the wood of the ash tree will not defeat me. I promised myself I would tell lies. I will not abandon my litanies. I will not identify myself to this man by any visible sign.

Micah spent the whole of the day supervising the tree-felling. He did not think of Faustina's indirect interrogations nor of pain in general nor of the terrible exciting fear that kept sweating through him. He thought about feasts of excrement. He thought of frequent and violent kissing at a funeral. The day is cold, squally. He cursed the slowness of the workmen. He pointed at the sky. Twice he struck the foreman with his fist. Trees crashed to the ground. Axes completed their own echoes. In the evening, he told Faustina how the great trees fell to earth, their leaves clogging in the mud. But she laughed across their distance and then accused him of hurting her trees. He called her by a bestial name. She glares at him, with her range of seven different faces. You only see half of the world, she tells him, you only feel with one side of your body. Your flesh is archival, he says. Then Micah strokes her and begs her to strip naked. She jerks away from him. No, she says, not when you have destroyed the trees of the forest. He grabs her and rubs himself up against her. She is so afraid of becoming horizonless. She refuses to understand the contortions of their bodies. She struggles to get away from him, shouting, you tell me I have no pride, Micah, less pride than a redemptioner. I don't know. I love the hours and interspaces of the glasscutter sky. You hold me and say that there is sanctity in our sexual act. But I do not accept this. I will not know you. And when I tell you this, you say I have a sanbenito heart. But I can't do otherwise. He puts both his hands around her throat. Eye sees. He releases her. Get out . . . Faustina runs out of the room and upstairs, to the toyroom. Micah can still feel the texture of her patagium skin. Each one of her rejections hurts him, a quasi-rheumatic pain. He stared down at the stone floor. After the horse sacrifice, he thinks, the chief wife of the king lay down beside the dead horse and took its generative organ into her body. He shudders. Night tempts him, multiplying its pretty promises. Micah closes his eyes, he tries to think of the flashing lights of a vanquishment of his horror. But even as he turns and flees he is moving towards the other silent bride with her icy skin and artificial eyes. Smell of heavy dark earth excites him as he hurries along and he forgets the living woman. He runs down the unlit road. He sees bushes and firebricks, he hears penny-whistles and silence, but he goes on without stopping until he reaches the place. Then he stops. He is at the gate. The gate is not locked. He looks around him. Yes, he is alone. He hews his way through the fear and is within the boundaries. The sky has never been so dark. There is a feeling in the air of phosphate rock and fossil bone. He is fetterless. He knelt by the grave. For the dead woman in her coffin he has an unquestioning reverence. He lies face down on the earth mound of the grave. He imagines the excavation. He feels his hands tearing the earth up. He loves the gravel and the stones, a new life. His body will enter a lawful wedlock. Now it is as if he has joined her in the grave. He can visualize how still and gentle and welcoming she is: they are so close. He is embracing her now and he trembles. He asks her to make her confession. She is silent. He knows she is innocent, lying there beneath him wrapped in her seedcoat. There is no way Micah knows of praying so he whispers, Eva, Eva. It is as if he is touching her cold untroubled body and tearing her free of the cloths that bind her, pressing himself upon her. And he opens his mouth for silent shrill lamentation. He bites her unseen breast, he knows her transarctic flesh tastes of leaves, he accepts the tautomerism of this love, he masturbates hard against death, he comes, he dies, he reawakens, he reburies his adulteress, he returns to his house and his inherited wife. Stunned, he sees nothing. He does not see his hand on the door. He does not see the food set on the table. He does not see Faustina sitting on the stairs. He feels only claws prohibiting him any sleep or peace. And the fear of his incurability. I have heard unconfirmed reports about your terror, says Faustina casually. But he walks past her up the stairs. Faustina shrugs. She utters a laugh for the dryshod night.

X(iii)

But later next day she screamed when she saw the body of a woman hanged fifteen days after being delivered of a dead son: Faustina saw her rot in the sunny room. She looked at Micah. He noticed nothing. Or he made no sign. So Faustina, afraid of her husband's ill-natured hands, returns to the toy-room. She leaves the rootman to shelter from the cold wind. She does not know that his finger is cloaked in the blood of unclean animals. She leaves him to the narrowness of his skull. She climbs the sleepless stairs. Rain drops from the eaves of the house. It gathers in the rain vessels down in the courtyard. It collects in the hands of the statues who ask nothing. Faustina watches the rain. Woman's monster, man's monster, she whispers. She remembers the candle with its ornitholite shadow. I will not wear nipple shields. I heard the orchard oriole in the rareripe season. I have seen metal moons, leaf jewels, velvet curtains, a candlenut tree with branches of granular ice, I hear the fog bell, I want to share my delusional ideas. I am cold in my cloud chamber. She acknowledges the doorway's sanctity and enters the room where her toys are kept.

What is her strength? thinks Micah, is she the one woman who will find a healer amongst a crowd of ordinary men? But he has no time for answers for he hears again a cold voice husky from grief and passion: and he tastes blood. Faustina, unaware of the duplication of the sabbat bride, sits on the floor in the centre of her toyroom. Her playthings are scattered on shelves, tables, chairs and the wooden boards of the floor, without any attempt at order or tidiness. A second swarm of thoughts vibrates around her. She closes her eyes. O, she cries, I see the fruit of the world gutted of joy and tasting bitter as lavender, I hear the tired prayers of the priests at the time of the first frost and I am a starlessness, darker than my veiling, it is always night at the border of my eyelid. But she must not break. She looks at her grey woollen skirt. She thinks of the command ship orbiting the moon. She leaps above the surface of the black water. I must not fear the limbmakers and the landscape advisers. In order to calm herself, she names each one of the toys that she has collected in this room. Her voice is stronger than bride-theft.

She says: I have two floating boats, a tea set and a dinner set, a double-decker bus, a doll in a cradle, lots of party masks, tricks and puzzles, a water pistol and a trick camera, pretty toy bracelets, brooches, necklaces and Winky watches, I have a magic upside-down toy, a boy with arrows, a cartoon doll with mouse, a large flute, a trick handgrenade, a miniature Bible spy-glass showing the Lord's Prayer, trick biscuits and many other safe non-toxic toys too numerous to mention and one hundred carnival balloons.

She looks around the cluttered room. Now it is easier in her head. Her withered hand is restored, according to the daughter's prophecy. At the far edge of silence, I hear half-shrieks, cries of the unthankful and of the slaves of impure athletes, yes, all the doubts are echoing there, at the boundary of my hearing. And yet, no cry from my tongue because I see futures somehow and nothing can stop them happening just at the ridges of my bone. I am scrubbing out the footprints of the bride on the staircase.

I kiss Anna. She turns her face away. She is afraid of the children's stories. Of the Jester. I told her to look in the sinciputal mirrors of the dead but she would not. And the avalanche wind seemed to blow her away from me. I stand at the wheat shore, the waves of corn are the same colour as her crescent dress. I cross a bridge of ice, my breasts have beaks instead of nipples. From the door of the beach-house I watched the rainsoaked world. I held Anna's hand. That was the terrible day. He called us as he came towards us and he knocked me over the fence with the hand that wasn't holding the gun. I wasn't scared. Not of Stefan. I heard a lot of shooting . . . Anna fell down, not wounded but maimed by fear. That was a bad day. Now I comb my hair. Some hairs come out at the roots as I pull the comb across my skull. I look at these with suspicion before burning them in the fire. In some languages, there is no word for pity. His language falls into this category. It is a small word whose lack will, perhaps, decide my attitude towards survival. What are these things I am saying to you? How many years is it? I am waiting day after day. No messenger ever comes. Is it a short while ago or a long time since I left that house, dragging my body like stolen goods? Micah threw my wedding dress on the fire. This was the first unkindness. There are no shapes of judgement in him and I dread the perilousness of his body. The protagonist at the altar points his finger at me. He speaks: but I cannot hear him. I see how his mouth moves. My desire for cobwebby food is my own business. The expression on his face startles the eternal eunuchs. The wrecked child carries a forest in his hand. I have no answer. I am thirsty, I run away, out into tomorrow and the branches of blood guarding the foster land. Soon I'll wear orphrey garments, be strong, a bonebreaker. It was a fogless day when I saw Anna in the street, she looked sad, she said hello, but she did not stop. I watched her go into the library. She obeys prohibitions, I thought. She must not ride nor even touch a horse nor see any army nor wear a ring on any of her fingers nor tie a knot in any of her garments. She must not light a fire nor speak to a blind man. She must not walk by the sea. Her hair can only be cut by a deafmute and then only with a brand new instrument. She must not touch any dead body. Her feet must be daubed with mud the day the new year quickens. She must not engage in midwifery. Sometimes she must bring back to Stefan the hearts of strangers and she must make a list of these hearts describing them in detail and he will read the list, uncertain of his ownership. In the recesses of these hearts he sees migrations. She must enter the curvature of mirrors. She must kneel to the foetus and pray. She must find all the ghosts. She must take food to the rachitic dwarf-girl. Yes, Anna, when I saw you, I knew.

XI

Micah dreamt of a headless motorcyclist who rode into his bedroom and stole the head from his favourite statue. He blamed Faustina for this. Seven nights of thin medusa silk clothe Faustina. He jerks something shiny out of her hand. It is evidently precious to her for she darts across the room to retrieve the mermaid brooch and weeps bitterly when he confiscates it.

As we argue, I feel the furniture moving with great violence about this conspicuous room. He says I have spoken to childless strangers. What if I have? There was only darkness today: the empty summerhouse, hard pavements, this cold house. I waited with my alone body. He hit me. He left me in the locked room.

Father and mother: stop controlling my destiny. Free me from the white shale garden. Between my outcrop bones, your voices speak too loudly. Ophthalmia memory is copying all my landscapes. Sheaths of my nerves hate him. This is the field of the sword-edge, he said to me. I nodded. I looked at the burnt field. The birds circled above us like daughters of thorn and thistle. This sad and double betrayal of the map was more than I could bear and I went through the door of the vomitorium. I was lost in a city I barely recognized. There was agony at the joints of each of my fingers. I was afraid. I moved like a trisector through the region of the abandoned docks. I looked at the weather-gnawed buildings. I showed him my hand, bent like a claw. Wave traveller, he said, and showed me the remainder of an atom. I saw its double light. Are you the one who can lick my vulva? I asked him. Yes, he said, reaching out to me. I saw the pig girls of the iceberg cupelling the rock roses. Old Vorticella sang her song long after she was dead. I loved it, heard it coming to me through the frost smoke. Even. I heard it, the insomniac child, as I stood there beside her grave, cold and silent until the patterns instarred on my fingertips severed me from the ghosts and I began to lie for the sake of midsummer.

XII(i)

There are trip-wires stretched across every day. I walked through a series of identical and aged rooms in a footfall house, a permanent retirement from the sea, my true skin's temperature just above zero.

The girl shook her head. In the garden the leaves were still. Early morning of the snails. She shook her head. He walked back into the house. She stood quiet in the aquarium garden.

Today being sunday, Faustina receives her blessing. The priest tells her of her salvation. In her mouth, belief scalds, she is a trembler. She walks home across the quietest field. Heart of pyromancy. Poor Anna. Faustina watches the caterpillar cross her path. As she crouches down to watch, absorbed, a holocaustal young man approaches her. When she looks up, startled by his shadow, she sees he has a face like homesickness. He comes up close to her. He smells of seaweed and treetrunks. She is afraid. He looks like a man who supplies false hair to enhance the female pudenda, he sells his wares to ex-nuns and lesbians. He says to her in an expressionless voice, they gather together in gangs, they have no time for me, they will not show me their pricks. You must partake of me. Faustina stands rigid, then understands, then backs away, then screams, her noise resounding as if in a crematorium or the skull of a sperm whale. His words tell her of his mother's body burning. He tells her of suicides, heretics and freemasons. She shakes her head. The sky, forgotten. Whoredom, the man says. In your dark empty houses. In the whitethroat forests I have seen you and the other woman. And on the banks of the river. He takes hold of her by the forearms. I have seen you before, shouts Faustina. Silently he forces her to the cold and hurting ground. She watches him with hewed-out eyes. Oh god, she said. And no one came to save her. No one came running along the footpath to protect her. Only the eye and the beak of a bird are witnessing the act. The stranger rapes her, slow and musicless. He shuts out any imputation of love. He is the disfiguring traveller. He forces Faustina beyond the edge of exhaustion where trees turn into soldiers and the birds become lopsided and dreary. As the duellers fight, Micah lowers his binoculars. When the rapist left her, Faustina remembered everything in her life she had ever forgotten. She opened her eyes. The cowdung looked appetizing. She closed her eyes. There was darkness. When she awoke, she was still alone, it was twilight, mist rising, and she was shivering. We left the city at dawn. As we walked through the empty streets, I felt the silence we had made harden and fossilize, I saw our marriage was a cathedral built entirely of glass, I knew we were two people pulling the bone until it breaks and the winner wishes for jewellery or sieves or sleep . . . Paths are closed between us, I thought. And in Argos the priestess of Apollo Lyceus ran about the streets, crying out that she saw the city full of dead carcasses and blood and an eagle joining in the fight and then immediately vanishing.

XII(ii)

He walked through the city like a forester reclaiming each of his darkened and fearless leaves. Your cervicitis has betrayed me, he said. And up the winding stair she went, not stopping, not hoping, not even thinking about the colour of her journey, she went on up the winding stairs, high up, climbing past each of the nights that had caused grief, climbing beyond the earliest hands that had gripped her, past the vivisected dresses, ascending beyond the shadow of the daughter on the rack, she went on up the winding stairs until she reached the tower room. Yes, she's tired, she's worn out, but she climbs the stairs. If she could, she'd throw a lighted torch into the piled windlestraw and burn all this all all away into the bodyslam night. And up the stairs she went, her hair hoisting into the chill air, and through the window slits she saw the linear motion of a star, and she heard the rifles repeating only a mile away across the snow fields. And the cries . . . that crying, it lived forever the one death so that the memory of the dead belonged to them all. He touched her forehead, her throat, her lips, contacting the diffidence of an island woman. No, he said after she had spoken, no, the fires will not touch us, nor will the rituals of the railroad torment us. All this, the heroic and the unheroic, is outside. We are already free. We're alighting, set free, already beyond lighthouse and hanging garden, beyond the reach of the separatist myth. And Faustina said, I believe you . . .

Stairways
stairways of burnt bones
watergate stairways
male and female staircases
ice stair in which a bird's wing is frozen
staircase of menstrual kisses
and we leap apart straddling escalators of flesh
stairways laden with trinity lilies
staircase of hesitation
the never staircase
the forceps that carved the first staircase
she stands at the foot of the staircase
upstairs she is being born
she hears the sound of a person laughing
she hears the whispering of birds and of grasshoppers

XII(iii)

I am the first home of nobody. I keep trying to be things, places, people. I have looked into the cold where there are people walking wearily, who could be performers of music except that the clock keeps voting against them and I keep losing sight of the supernovae children . . .

He works hard. He spreads the grass out to dry. He sells timber. He says words of what should be. We start our game. The late summer comes ghosting up infield. My red flowers burn. Places: labyrinth of the plateaux. Dangerous prohibited places. And I came away. The walls of the room are angry: their pictures are angry: the photographs are frowning. I send you away. Hawthorns and a series of cold winter-windows, distant mothers and paths by the banks of the river come into my head and make me a different house and there was a girl with childish features who protected me against the ocean and years reached down to my ankles like hebrew words but the pain flew through my body like the first bird of the Jurassic Age and I had to stretch all my bones out to catch myself. I became a branch reeking of the sea. I became a japanese coin. I became an ex-alphabet. But I kept going back to the place where the pain was, where I was the complaining one. I couldn't be a sky or a forest leaf or an abortionist. Couldn't be a bone or even a piece of wood. So I must be the pain. I was the pain. The simplest thing. The pain. On a stairway dark as yesterday morning there was the great pain, the ancient pain, the wife pain. Roots and closed hands in the room beyond the staircase. The pain is not in Orion. It is not in the grass-dedicated garden. First it is in the zodiac. Then it becomes I. You. World. And pieces get torn off. And the staircase is part of the cry. And the room beyond. And the house. And before. I am sending you away into the darkness, you must stay there for a long time. Until I can catch up with you. I am not even allowed to touch you. Because I did not wait and I did not die. She died. You and I are crippled women who have become the mother and the kleptomanic daughter. Slowest grievers.

What is wrong with you? he said angrily. Why are you crying? Why have you shut yourself away from everyone up here in this cold room? His voice suggests other syllables. I answer him like an eavesdropper. I speak from memory. This also angers him. He watches me with the eyes of the professional bodyguard. He pulls vomit out of my mouth with his bare hands. You're jealous, he said and laughed, wiping my mouth with the sponge. I smelt of disembowelling rooms. I am very confused, I said. I am troubled. He laughed again. Yes, you are jealous, he said. He looked at me with curiosity, the pregnant female. I heard the keening of my old laughter. I drank a glass of water. It is almost certain she will not come, he said, not with the wedding so near. I walked across the room, sat down on a hard chair, looked at him. Blood donors question me all day. Church punishments of the north throb in me. I was going to be washed away. The real mother waved goodbye. Then he said to me, you talk in your sleep. I did not look at him any more. I know, I answered. And one after one the rabbits came out of the hole, he jeered. My throat ached from where I had been retching. Don't keep on saying it, I begged him, it's clear now, isn't it. You're jealous, he said.

The body appeared to be that of a young girl. She was found naked in a shallow grave, her head shaved, a bronze collar around her neck. She lay on her back, her arms thrown up defensively. Her throat had been cut. Her fingerprints were carefully taken and the line patterns found to be as sharp as those of a newborn infant.

*

XIII(i)

Why didn't you come to see me last night? I asked Anna, my voice just on the edge of the stone landscape we were meticulously watching. She pushes her hair out of her eyes. She looks at me, aslant. She is the horizon receding as I approach. I am angry and my interrupted heartbeat penalizes her, the tease amid her veils of obscurity. I was ready to come out, she said casually, but then twilight happened, I didn't realize it was so late. Her quelled body makes me forget distances. I give her a catkiss with my mouth. She is still so frightened of our kinship. No, says Anna, no, we are receiving warnings, a million trees in the salt water forest have inexplicably died, the females in the city have been battering their young to death: we must keep our bodies sharp and sleepless. She turns from me and runs out of the quarry. I shout after her, my words make staircases in the air, but she is the first rain that ever fell, a paper kite landing in a moon crater, a grail snatcher: I am unable to touch her, to find her: she spits butterflies at me, she turns into an adobe song.

I walked home. In the courtyard the dogs gnawed bones. The sun is my itchy mouth. Development of summer, my camera head holding its focus on us, our sad duty making us sadder, pinching us harder than hunger. Nothing hurts me more than your inviolability, Anna, no burning could be worse than the bonfire in my head when I speak to you.

Throughout Faustina's life, there were nights of broken sleep and days of uninterpretable strangeness. She held the pieces of an animal's skeleton in her hands and said: silences don't hurt, you see, anyway not like people think they do.

But there were also the days when Stefan interpreted my dreams. When he told me about the earliest wounds of the mermaid. Beleaguerment of the I in a cold room injured by off-balance seas and times that come too soon times I cannot hold in my aloneness that smear me with their hurts because I am not ready and must say No and send them unredeemed out of my cold room and can't breathe. My breastbone is worn out by the greediness of pain-pressures of continents and the words of the bible behold and crush my bone. Look closely: you will see years in me made of lace years made of caution and keepsakes and ice words and astrological charts planned for the lifetime of no one . . . Journeys in every flower, the bride's decrepit airplane, cages approached unhappily, the dumb woman I am and involved in my difficulties, dancer of the ark, one who cheats, fearer and feared and all the times I have sent you away each month, out into the darkness, the dark of petrography, and you wait in the darkness for me . . .

The bed is balanced on the edge of a cold spasm. Our bed is balanced on the edge of a maze. A woman-bird lifts her veils and holds up a finger. Darkmeat of the breasts. Midwinter joins us together but he masturbates into his own hand. He is the thief. The air-map of this night rustles in my hands. He is sleeping in his room. I am walking in the courtyard. The toe-dance of the stars doesn't interest me. I sit on a wooden bench. I listen to the beginning of the war. I think of the time of my birth and I am afraid. I closed my eyes. I saw breasts. I remembered breasts of women. Slow-worm breasts and harnessed breasts, old breasts and a little girl with no breasts. I smelt breasts, odour of rip-tides, odour of horses and of phreatic water. Then I heard Micah's sleep-voice and I ran back into the house. The foreheads of the people are sprinkled with ashes. I suffered from sudden infectious frights that turned me to broken glass in the palm of a strange hand.

XIII(ii)

Wake up. Wake up . . . Now he was touching my shoulder, talking to me in a low voice, telling me, get up, quickly. It was very dark. Mouths and doors were all cruelty. She married my brother. I was pregnant, I knew now. I was half asleep. Micah was taking me to another house in another village, miles away, over one hundred miles away. We had to travel quickly. We had to start early, before dawn, now. Wake up. But I can't look at that day yet. I won't relive the frozen violence of our few words. I won't wake to watch myself forcing one moment past another as we journey endlessly through the cold fields along the broken road. I won't remember the ice explosions. No. A door opens in my night window. I step through into a noisy silence, the black tokens of birth, laughters, and cowdung on my hair. Foetus team named, said the first witch through her water-lips. I stood in my bedroom. You were in the next room. I held my dress in my hands. But instead of hanging the dress in the wardrobe I stood still and panic made me sweat. I thought you had come silently into my room and were standing behind me, a sinister joke. Slowly I turned round. The dress slipped through my hands, it fell to the floor, my sleeveless dress. I was alone in the room. But it was a quicksand room. Night's troy game had beaten me. I called out to you. I wanted to hurl my voice at you but I managed to speak casually. You did not answer. I called again, louder, but still patient. Micah . . . Shadows I saw shadows of burning burning trees and I couldn't get out of my room. You stood in the doorway. You would not enter my loom. You smiled. You were naked. You were indifferent to me even though your penis swelled, ritualistic. I would not look at tonight's threat.

Micah, I did not want to enter your life, I protested. You sent for me. This room is chilly, he said. He stood in the doorway, looking at me, not smiling now, no expression I could name on his face. He touched the door handle. Is he on a pilgrimage, I thought. I wanted to hold out hands to him. I did not. I could not. But for this moment I was not afraid of him. I experienced a short sour freedom. I did not understand Micah . . . or what I thought I understood I misinterpreted. This house is too small, he said suddenly. At the time I paid no attention to his remark. I did not suspect he would drag me even further into the interior of his country. I moved one step towards him. Then I saw his contempt. Then I was afraid. My mother told me I had no courage. She said I was without valour. Do I have to . . . I began to say to him. But he interrupted me. Why are these books all over the floor? He pointed to the books I had just shoved off the table, after Anna's phone call. Did you lose your temper, Faustina? No, I said, no, I was only looking for an old poem I remembered. He laughed, the way he laughed at my refusal to eat. He picked up my dress and placed it neatly on my bed. And then he went on looking at me and I recalled the uneasiness of the day's colours: who has crept into an intimacy with me? He wants something from me, I thought, and I can't react or help or touch. I looked at my hands with suspicion. Are you tired? I asked him. No, he said, not tired. He shakes his head but I know he has failed to love his counterfeits and so can't hear me. He comes into my room, he moves clumsily, knocks the angle-poise lamp over to one side, its light hits my mirror, yet I don't think he's been drinking, he shades his eyes with his hand and then looks at me again and for the first time I saw doubt and even fear in him, like a man unwillingly arrived among people whose language he does not understand. He did not speak to me, his words must have got hurt inside, smashed to pieces against his memory. I said swiftly, let me see Anna, let me see my friend. His face was scrap-metal. Silence, an old sullen ballad. You are my enemy, he said at last, in amazement. Always my enemy. I tried to explain, I begged him to lift his prohibition, she is my friend, I said. But he silences me with a legendary threat. He says I am to abandon my hazardous movements towards Anna. I do not answer. Tomorrow I will tell him lies. Micah stood beside me and time kept exploding and I looked out of the window until I heard him go out of the room and down the stairs and emerge into the courtyard. I watched him illuminated by the moonlight as he went riding towards the bridge, horse and rider alone in the night, authentic, a chaos that will not leave my memory. I sat on the bed, waiting for him to return. But I must have fallen asleep. I awoke at the first light of the almost summer that turned each object in my room, chair, table, dresser, vase, book, into the excavated remains of an ancient civilization. And I thought perhaps my life would be saved. People talk about me, they discuss my heroism. Early in the morning, I closed the eyes of the dead. I touched the socket of her hipbone. I felt my own hand's death, withering to the dry defenceless bone, all my history was distorted, turned to one side, and my hair I used to love was off-scourings of a darkened mind. I turned to my sister, I was stammering with an oblong voice, and she said, no, no, no . . .

XIII(iii)

Early in the morning, Micah woke me. I saw the sun filtering through the curtains. Shadow blink of birds went against the wall. You pulled back the sheet and looked at my body. You touched my body. I felt rickety and half-starved, my life came to an end. You kissed me like a man crossing out a sentence, I have kept the memory to this day. I tried to conceal myself with my east-midland dialect but you had already become naked and your voice was too loud in the room and your prick stretched out stiffly, a serious root, I watched as your body, trained and equipped, confronted mine. You are begetting my death, I said. I could not move. I let you pull me towards you, you called my breasts missionaries and you searched the folds of my body between my legs, pressing your fingers inside me, I smelt the odours of flood and circus now, your tongue reached the back wall of my mouth, you were approaching my flanks, you were too near the rawness, the woman-opening, but the place was no longer mine, it was occupied and controlled by the owner, exclusively kept for his use. Wedlock enters me. I thought, a billion people speak this language and yet I cannot pronounce the first syllable. He mounts me and pushes himself inside me. I feel pain. He moves fast, dead on target, he has abandoned words, I also do not speak but my doubts regarding my isolated position grow, I hurt each time he moves, I feel sick, cramped by hands, legs, shameful voices from the past and the shifting of his weight. Then his rump bone thrust finally, he exerted all his strength and it was finished. I felt him slide out of my airtight body and roll off me. He said something, I don't know what because I was having trouble understanding the distance he'd left in me and I still felt sick. I closed my eyes, I did not answer him, I think I slept and when I woke again he had gone, the room felt greasy and so I got up and opened the windows to let in the outside air. I looked at the leaf notches. Bones and shells and seeds and stems, I thought, wings and armpits and shoulders, roof rats and averters of evil, and why should my body not be part of their beauty? Should I cease my five daily recitals of prayer? Shall I go on stitching my fingers together with my ice needle? Does my sister envy me my adventurous exploits? I wind up the chess clock. Then I go to the wardrobe, take out my handbag, open the purse and stare at the spectral wedding photograph of my parents, seated alone at the head of the table, their faces blurred and fading, reproof in their upright bodies.

XIV(i)

I turned to Micah and said, did you see him throw the dead girl's tongue to that stray dog? Micah stared at me. I saw his unworkable anger. No, he said, I saw nothing. He went on down the path, mending his thoughts. I looked up at the sky. I did not trust the men or the women. Then I ran after Micah. You saw nothing? He crumbled the earth between his fingers. Doorways hurt him. I saw nothing, Faustina. But when he looked at me, what did he see then? A jargon girl? The shadow of a horse-shoe, the crystal thorn-devil? Did he see danger in my eyelids at freezing point? A crime that would have to be committed? By him? I could not tell. I told him about the fall of the leaf. He said, don't get cold, remember the child you will bear, you're shivering, come back indoors. I was so afraid. The months kept going by. I saw trees festooned with unwanted fortunes, but the evil would not blow away and the sky stank.

Faustina sings. She sings of sleep. Of the whiteness of sleep. Enclosed in the shell night, she sings. She wears a blood crown. She breaks the saltpetre silence. She sings. She does not move. Around her, scattered at her feet, are chicken feathers, skins of snakes, old shoes. She sings of knots, the song nails her to the wild and morbid rose tree. The ice hours dangle. She has a memory of the maze. They kept her there, a prisoner. She sings a perpetual song. But stars deteriorate in the sky. As she sings, she passes a thread through the eye of a needle. She hears the rain. She is remote from her body. She is afraid of the martyrdom of the birds. She is afraid of her locked anus. He stands on the threshold. She turns to dust. In the fog forest the little poltergeist girls chase one another through the conifers and your name is like the cry of a bird. Who are you? she shrieks. He slept. A satiation of leaf and sky. He slept. World thorax can't sing. Woman-trembler eucharistically eats the mud of the white lake. Esha watches him. Yes, she remembers her old name. The dinosaur spoke to her. The man stores honey in hives. The man considers the sun is healthy and we must sit in a solar room to quieten our skins. He, Micah, never grows tired of the rough roads of his homeland, the bays and rocky capes where the sea leaves its troubles. But he doesn't care much about the fields strewn with trash that you see on the outskirts of the city. He doesn't know that some spiders construct a tubular nest with a hinged ledge. He catches animals in traps. He doesn't understand my residual stress. He doesn't know what or why I resist.

After the payment of debts, I looked at the shiny flowers with their large round satiny pods. But I saw only darkness soaked with taunting blood. I will restrict myself to the love of lizards, I thought. Although I didn't believe in my crimes, my feet went over the redhot stones. Painhour by painhour, I feared house arrest. I groped with my hands until I touched the blindness of my stilts and I picked the sterile flowers. Grief is the stronger word, I said to my husband as we walked by the river bank but he accused me of trying to mislead him about my feelings. So then there was silence and our body structures were not recognizable any more in that bitter struggling.

XIV(ii)

Open your girl bible. At the edge of a snow-drift I hear birth cries and other looniness. I am too late, I said, for the door seemed to be locked. I thought the dark-complexioned woman belonged to winter but the margins of the tropics transform even the mother. And the fossil foetus whimpered. Twilight like charcoal. You ask me if I have been visiting Anna. I say, no. Lying again, I get inside my musty heart to hide from you. If you're cold put on a coat, you said.

Everyone was happy when my brother Stefan came. Except me. I couldn't approve of his behaviour. I did not know how to speak to him. He struck me with his fist, he threw the silver coins at me. The mountain road is winding up into the sky and I have made a mistake. In the darkness of my room I bumped into the walls, my skin felt like the skin of a tangerine, but I had a secret. Anna left the dead snake hanging on the fence. They treat me like a step-child, all of them. I look at you, Micah, native of this red clay land, womb-filler. I say: yes, I have written the letter but I have not sent it yet. Oh have you? he sneers. Stefan said to me: when you give money to the poor you supply munitions to the enemy. He went on eating raw cucumber. I watch him, squint-eyed. The mourning women are veiled, I told him. I could hear Anna whining and I was part of her sadness. Why is my sister crying? he asks Micah. Micah shrugs.

Stefan, who was driving the car, died outright, but his bride and his bodyguard received only cuts and bruises. What were the words he uttered as he died? I asked Micah. But he would not tell me. He denied any knowledge. He died outright, Micah kept saying. I suspected that Stefan would have whispered some bad words, reaching out through the last of the blood and the darkness. Did he speak of me, reveal my dread of foreign games, my vaginismus, my gluttony . . . Now that his spinal tree, rotten to the roots, has fallen, am I safe? Can I measure my security in water-inches? No. Last year's poverty derides me. The thinness and translucency of Anna's body keeps me here in this room for ever with Stefan laughing at me.

Who brought those two people together? Who called them mother and father? Why did they make me out of the bone and blood and fear of their nights? I was born in a town called Triangle. Years later, I am thinking of triangles. Am I a triangle? An old shrunken woman says: yes. Shrieks are triangles. Layers of skin were the longest street in that town. I was afraid to cross the roads. The trucks and the automobiles thudded into the sky. The words of my family were hemophiliac. Be careful you don't fall. Their triangles held me down. As soon as I fought my way free of one, I entered another, just as cruel. The words of those people echoed from triangle to triangle: and as I ran along the passageway, the loudness was in my mouth, rages of many days. My name was dark as night, or the first word of the morning prayer. When they said their words at me, I stepped on hidden explosives, I dropped the best cup, it smashed to bits on the stone floor, I knocked the flower-vase over, the water dripped on the carpet, the petals turned brown and died. There was a small area of starlight, triangular.

The street shouted. Apparitional mandoggod. Micah grabbed the beggar by the hair and threw him into the road. I watched. I was in the libration area. A black-haired woman appears. She watches us. I am ashamed. Because of her stillness which is made of harvests and streets I've never seen and elegies beginning. I think she is about to speak to me. But she is already walking away, she is holding her body down with her hands like a piece of paper held down by rocks. I hold my soul-stone in my hand and I drink bitter water. I stand in the house of lionesses: my task is not to warn you of your dangers. Mouths open all over your body, he tells me. Cat and pig and wolf follow you, he accuses me. Micah weeps for his lost brides. Where? In the darkness of autumn wheat they vanished. And we touch in a house of metal. I remember the healing of a dumb demoniac. With his hands of bright daylight, my father healed the mad man. But I was afraid of his calf's head. I go walking in all these village streets, I spy on the people bargaining: I follow you and the woman through all the streets all the evil day. Are you blind to my following or do you hope to cure me of my jealousy by walking with long steps, hand in hand with the monkey dance woman? But in his mouth I found no shadow, none of the madness of the waltzer.

I went to the place where men burn the refuse of the city, dead animals and the bodies of criminals. But I forget who directed me to this place. I walked into a refrigerator because of the silent motionless people I keep seeing everywhere. I join the sisterhood of waterlogged girls. I am waiting for the death of my first skin. This will solve many problems. You scrape disease from my uterus and from my brain and you listen for the quail clock's hour. I listened.

I climbed into the womb and listened. As she is very old, I heard them say, it cannot be long. That wasn't me, no. I wasn't born. They were talking about the other woman. The one downstairs. Where the pain had its home.

Arctic seas full of walking fish for the witches to taste. I crossed the bridge. I tried to talk to Micah, I tried to tell him about her, the old woman downstairs, but the room was too hot and the words melted, I tried to tell him where I'd been but the room was too cold and the words froze. How could he hear ice? When I close my eyes after staring at a very strong light, what do I see? I see myself kneeling in the rain, I see the restless scourged day close, I see him burning my begging letters, I see . . . I walk towards him because I am the sifter of morning and I tell him about my lunatic children. Then I wait for him to speak. He says, the ghost screens you, Faustina, you are hidden by your scars. I can't separate you from your unknown companion, not yet. He stands opposite me in the tiny room. I drink from his glass, it is not wine. I tell him, I sympathize with your difficulties. He looked at me like someone looking at the darkest part of night. But I did not break. I stared right back at him. There was a draught blowing in through the broken window, I felt the chill all down my back. Remember the time, he said, we must leave in less than an hour. So I looked at the clock. Remember the softening of the bones, I thought. And jet-propelled sadness was everywhere, you see. This cold world is turning, with people waving their hands, it gets younger every year. Two words come from the same root but have different meanings and I get trapped between them. Stefan's mother is my mother. I am always in these empty rooms smelling of railway stations. When my body is full of such deceits, what am I to do? I look at my trial photograph, I look at my clean fingers, I learn how many times in the year my heart beats but beyond these bargains why is the breathing so loud and why am I all wet is it blood no only our bodies as they meet on the stairs.

All births must be recorded. I string the pearls into a necklace. I did not answer his friends when they congratulated me on my condition. Be careful, the train's coming, don't get too near the track. I looked into my mother's face, it was like looking into the sun. I sat in front of the door facing the sky. The doorway of Micah's new house resembles a medieval doorway. This interests me. He has no explanation for the architecture, however, any more than he can explain the failure of a broken bone to heal. I am happy that the wearing of black clothes is unknown in this northland. When we travelled here, I wanted to set fire to the hands of the clock. Now I sit still. I am quite pretty, I think, only slightly scarred about the mouth, my dress only a little stained with the heat. I can answer Micah's questions, I can face his friends, the men who mistrust me. I can touch the day with my finger. The third month is smoky, the hot weather is beginning. I bite my tongue, the citronella grass burns.

XV(i)

Tomorrow's people do not exist
I have two shadows
myself and my dwarf sister
two shadows
creeping through the ice fog
the interrupted land
is opening its eyes

> *like a fish:*
> *the tributary girl waits for the clock-driven man*
> *he makes charts of the sea-bed*
> *he studies ice*
> *he does not hear its cry*

Here comes the moondust girl. Anna is a melancholy girl whose fiancé suffered castration in an accident. Now he has left her to her weariness. She dreams of wearing torn dresses. In the winter of the trials, Anna, the grain watcher, looked in dead mirrors. She saw men swimming across the river. She saw mothers cut off from the dying embrace of their children. She saw the dust of the rectum. She moans when I ask my intricate questions. She says to me: One day I was writing poetry. A long poem about an untidy dancer. When he came into the room, I hid the poem. It was a rainy afternoon. In the garden, thin branches whittled the air, a repeated slicing of cold knives. My parents were out at the cinema. He wanted to have intercourse with me. But I refused. Not now, I said. When? he said, how soon, in or near what place? His earsplitting voice did not help me. I shook my head. I don't know, I said, not looking at him. He gave me a present, a silver chain with a charm in the shape of a fish. He fastened it around my throat. He caressed the nape of my neck and my hair with his thumb as he did so. Then he said he was tired and would go back home. I wanted to ask him to stay with me but I did not dare. I was drowning in my dress as if it were a lake. He closed the door. I counted the seven small bones of my ankle. I wanted to show him the stages of my nakedness. But I could not. I think I talk in my sleep now. I sense the remembering of words some mornings.

As Anna walks out of the courtyard, I look anxiously after her through the green glass of the window. But I did not think of Stefan then, nor of the dirt that clung to my body. Bird leaf moves against the sky and the son of the bride is waking. The blood I pour in the twelve bowls will feed him, my son. The dry bodies of the females will admire him. I will wheel him in his basketwork pram to the fountain at the very centre of the park and then I will ask myself, who was midwife at the birth? I cannot remember.

I sit in the field of the other grass. I do not see the clausthalite moon. I see no shroudings. Now my claws, my shoes, teeth, gloves and jokes are made of iron. I went through the night searching with my torch and I stole the keys to my mother's gloomy weather. He said to me: why, you are just clothes held together with string, that's all. He went out of the room. In the evening the vampire gives off a pleasant scent. I swear it is true. But then I cried out for my friend. Where are you? My mouth tasted of blood and I saw the flames fingering the glass chimney. I threw a veil over the head of the sea horse. The three women looked at me. I tried to frighten them off by shining a mirror in their eyes but they did not flinch. I ran away, I jumped over the dog.

When we arrived, I felt cold. Don't be scared, he said. He held me by the hand and helped me as we climbed over the rocks. Where are we going? I asked. I could hear the waves but I could not tell how close we were to the sea. Where are we going? I repeated. Where there is no shadow, he said. But then I saw that the flesh of his back was decaying, I felt his hand loosen from mine, I clutched, but his fingers were water or snow and he was gone. It got much darker, I stumbled, sat down on a rock amid a disfigurement of hawks. I still heard the sea, I knew fear, the repudiation of seaweed, and hunger following me everywhere. I wondered where I had left my little son and hoped he was safe anyway.

On the staircase, Micah accosts his bride of two weeks, takes me by the hand, asks me if I am happy, tells me to come with him, encloses me in our legal room, embraces me, breaks pieces off from my body, skin and bone, praises me, fucks me, is tired of me, leaves me here thrown across this common bed, the half-naked apparition who holds out her arms to welcome insomnia. I wrap myself in the mantle of the earth. I run races with myself, six miles along the ocean floor. I take photographs of my mother as a young woman. I work very hard. I get wet and muddy, I am very tired but must keep picking up pieces of broken glass shaped like girls' given names. And I distrust the people who have found answers for all their questions. Perhaps it is because I was born in a chaste month that I see an x-rayed world, its terrors exposed.

The dark shadows of the wet rice fields.

A car crashing against a wall.

The murdered woman of the week.

The kiss of the unmarried, their unrest.

He showed his child how to kill a fly.

I could not open the door. So I quit. The ghost-houses are on fire. He guessed the name of the woman. Mother is a black dress daughter is a white face. The bomb didn't go off. I went around the room, sky-scraping it. I found bleak fish swimming in the cupboards and the woman, the shadower, was still falling violently through her blood's undergrowth. I watched with placental eyes. I was held in the arms of the ghost. She never climbed the stairs, not even slowly, because of the tumour. Who else moved in the first room? I saw strangers with primitive hands. I was afraid. Her eyes found me guilty and I tried to hide on the floor but they took me out of the room and carried me down the stairs and outside into the mist near the pond. The blood within my skull shifted towards distant galaxies. But then they lifted me up and chained me to her. I ran down a street of whirlwinds. I entered a courtyard where a small fire was still smouldering: my clothes were being burnt here. In the kitchen, my mother is washing earth from our plates. She will not let me help her. Beyond the curvature of winter I saw myself hiding behind the door.

Faustina and Micah are expert performers: we tell stories of miracles. I describe weapons of war until I tire him out and his loneliness begins to show. Stop, he says. You look at me. An evening in the home. Place of contests. Where nothing trembles, overjoys or awakens. No time opens for the woman who is afraid to answer the telephone. A woman who tells you nothing. And you rebuild your calendar. My doorkeeper sister dreams. She bakes bread. I move carelessly. Morning language is not here. Flesh madonna is walking in the snow, silly girl, teasing the armadillo in the starlight. Repeat the girl's name so you won't forget. Write her a begging letter. Write an anonymous letter. You must make the pelvic mistakes. Aftersong is dark as night. A long time is what clocks register. A book for old daughters to read. Who left it open on the kitchen table? What's the first word you say to a hero? Look, no hands? You watch me. You come closer. I can't break my word. You pluck my small wounds. Yes. It is a time between wars. Your skin tastes of footprints. I follow. Because I need to follow.

XVI(i)

Micah looks at Faustina. He sees that she has a narrow shadow body, long fingers and cold hair. He hears her harsh cry. He knows that she lives on the thumb side of the world. She holds a radio knife in her hands. She loves grasslands, forests and the marshes. She sits at her table, receiving the moment of inertia. When she first spoke to me, her words were those of a child throwing rocks at the window. She shits as she sleeps. Her skin weaves restlessly over her bones. She wants to take shortcuts everywhere. She cries, shrapnel tears. I do not take any notice. She kills time in the afternoon by smashing her memories against the wall. She is the remnant of a beautiful woman. She has been in a galactic collision. She does not deserve the new clothes I have given her. I will not permit her language of uncertain affinities to be spoken in my house. I will set her tasks. I will beat her on the heart with my hands.

He tells Faustina the list of questions must be answered in full. I will not reward lies, he says. I will punish lies. Listen to me. He points to the centre of the map. She bites the ball of her thumb. He tells her he is leaving tomorrow to supervise the building of the new house.

Micah says I am to remain here at the farmhouse. He will be gone for several weeks. I am glad. Even when he told me the names of my guardians, I did not care. I did not care about the twelve men rescued from a life raft in the North Sea. Do you understand? he said sharply. Do I look like a deceiver? I answered. He did not reply. He laughed and locked the door and rubbed his groin hard. I saw the hand of glory and its candle, the fingers were alight, a candle in a dead man's hand. Beneath the tangles of my pubic hair I felt a warm martyrdom.

The wind tore at my veils the day of Stefan's funeral. They would not let me speak to Anna. After the funeral was over she burst out laughing like someone awakening from a nightmare. I was afraid to look at her. Micah led me away from the grave. He said he hated the smell of the cemetery flowers.

I unfastened my dress, slowly, the bird pecked at my fingers, I mumbled answers as I took off my pants. My lips were dry. When I was naked my voice disappeared. He turned me round and touched my buttocks. He moved his hand between my legs. Then I didn't want to wait. I lay face down on the bed. He crouched over me. His two hands touched my cunt. I was wading through water, I spread my legs wide apart, I humped my body, he probed with his hand, I drew back but he pushed forward, my body shook, I reached for something to hold on to but there was nothing, he worked on me, that man is insane, I couldn't breathe, my whole body was thumping, a spasm went through me, it tastes of watermelons, I yelled wordlessly, he said, yes, yes, and the wetness ran down my legs.

XVI(ii)

The fire is burning. The bride is very young. The people are laughing. I stare at the darkness behind the fire. This fire is to be kept burning so that we may hide our faces. Disease has caused Micah's lower eyelid to turn inside out. He got drunk at Anna's wedding and fell sprawling. Next morning I went out into the tree branches of dawn. The air was unripe, I heard the rustling of water like the song of a skinny child. I picked certain flowers which wounded my hands. I touched my obeying breasts. Shrouded women watched me. I walked along beside the river, past houses and granaries, until I could look out across the estuary. I saw the church on the headland and the lighthouse. I felt the sea moving in my spine, the air-serpent uncoiled itself. The clues returned, carriers of thorn, and I knew I was pregnant because now the taste of sea was in my mouth. The unborn howls and I bend my body to avoid the evil of the coming day but I only take mouthfuls of the old roman year and the women were still watching and I had no room in my mind for myself, I was charring under their gaze. Then my mother stepped forward. I am the disguise lady, she said, I have been following you, on the sabbaths and the nights of the new moon. Now you must learn the whispering. I grabbed for her hair but she had gone. The fish floundered in the net. The pig wallowed in the mud. The bird fluttered on the ground. I saw toads devour the organs of a naked woman and cling sucking to her breasts. Do not touch my hand, I said to Micah. I was in a rage, I sat in a darkness. I must be completely alone, not even an insect may share my room.

She looks out of the window. She sees weapons, camp-sheds and warlike engines. What do you see, Esha? he said. I turn to Stefan. I am wearing my aspen dress. I smile. See? I see houses, I said. I see wagons, ink, candles, many tools. I see ships. I count pencils, bottles, sheets of paper, fur-quilts. I see ropes, roads, rivers. I taste flesh of animals, fish and birds. I carry bundles of wood, old pairs of shoes, clogs, books. I am sick, there is nothing I can eat because I am swallowing my polyspermic fear. The snow is a white tree the birds are afraid of and the cattle are dying. I am always measuring the distance from fingertip to fingertip when I stretch my arms sideways, like this. My voice goes wrong when Micah enters the room. He says we must wait for the weather to clear before our journey can begin. Stefan talks of the battlefields. One live coal still burns amid the ashes. I leave the two men. I'm sick of listening to you, I said. Stefan laughed. But Micah was angry.

I went upstairs to a cold room. I held the stone lily in my hand. I cannot answer the riddles. I eat using my fingers to pull the meat into fragments. I've been with Micah now for two summers and two winters, perhaps a little more. Time of wounds, sickness, desertion and reconciliation. I saw dreadful daffodils on the graves and I thought of my servitude as I walked through the deer park of the holy city.

The night begins. I see a hand riddled with holes from the gnawing of worms. A hand sacrificed at the wrist. I know that if I can grasp this hand I will understand the reality of the hair on the eyelids of the horse and speak like a wife who looks beyond her dowry. I close my eyes. I hear Micah coming upstairs. He is angry because when I was downstairs I spoke coarsely and am not to be trusted. He hits me. He drags me to the bed. I open my mouth, I utter a torso shout. The solitary vireo sang in the night and I said begin begin begin you fucking physician begin you fucker I see you at the end of the road you're keeping my friend from me you are hiding her amid the shoals of the whispering gallery begin you third person with your three dimensional laughter you slalom stranger begin announce all my bankruptcies bite off the head of a living chicken go on begin I'm not scared I am looking with great curiosity as you begin subliming my ice o begin wedge me between explosives make me live in a dilapidated house only begin or I'll outweep you . . .

XVI(iii)

I don't want to be hurt. This trouble of mine is caused by nothing other than lack of sleep and an absence of truth.

I was chilled, I asked him to close the window. I am made even colder by his glance, he hates the lady with hair between her legs. Scarring of my heart takes away the taste of summer and I think, is Anna's marriage to Stefan the reward for my heroism? The outwash of our touchings erodes my strength now, enemies approach me down both sides of the road, I touch the wooden floor with the tips of my fingers. I shove my big body on towards the end of the war. I hate Stefan. Right-handed people kill with their left hand. I will kill with both my hands. I will fracture his skull. I will poison him. I will burn him alive. I will . . . No, I will watch Anna and Stefan join hands. I'll witness the half-shadow they cast. I will remember Anna and Faustina on the sands in winter, standing at the edge of the water, playing flutes, sunless tunes. I'll present the couple with my words of congratulation. I will give Anna a whalebone box and a star catalogue.

Micah will smile thriftily as he glances at my sevenmonth body. I will watch the end of Anna, I will observe the mongolian fold of her eye, the unlearned eyelid and the impure canthus. As I escort her down the stairs, Anna will say to me, in an unhappy little voice that leaves sentences unfinished, but I must escape, Faustina, even to the tasks of a lifetime and . . . Anna looks at the amputated white flowers she is carrying. I think this is a way to protect myself because . . . We will stand at the top of the stairs and she will wait for me to say something comforting. But I will say nothing. I will not make accusations. I will perhaps smile, to show my fierceness. Her fingers will feel cold as ice-bound waters. I am afraid to enter that room, she says. Her dress is the skin of a blue ox. She is dedicating herself to me. It is too late, I say. Her dress is made of nun's veiling. It is too late, I say, and secure her white hood in place. Now she is ready for her journey. My hands felt to me like instruments removing the head of a foetus. The fishy perfume of the flowers slid between us. I sensed the shortness of this summer, I tasted its disappearance. I will let Anna look fearfully at my belly and I'll hear her heart's repeated blows, the tension in her of a dying tree. What I say to Anna now will be an almost voiceless flapping oath. Then I'll walk downstairs. She will not push me down the stairs. She will not dare to be angry. She'll follow me, in silence we'll go down into the september and I'll feel the pittance in my womb shift as I reach the end of another month. I hate Stefan. He is leading Anna out of the doorway and into the courtyard's dry weather, he will take her to the moment of the hindbrain's hurt and he is kissing me goodbye. I am not weeping. I do not look at Anna. I am an unstratified glacial drift and I let my brother Stefan touch me. He is the disturber, he touches the skin of my forehead with his fingertips and I see dark pictures of discalced women among the small birds and felons of Lent.

XVII

I read the adulterer's letter. I did not know where I was standing, nor whose shadow hand reached out to me, bride of desolate places. In the dead of winter you must visit your mother, the words said. No, I said, and ran through empty streets. When the trees slowly escape from the forest, when the malformation of your bladder pains you, you must set fire to your son. No, I cried and all the doors banged. The earth has been declared uninhabitable. Tree shadows were in the wrong place. I was on a strange road, my back to the sun now, and a diabetic fear of love driving me on. You are not ready yet, I said to myself, but I could not turn back yet, I had to find out where that dark whisper was coming from . . .

I walked. I saw nothing before me. I was walking into a landscape without features. There were no trees now, the sun was a long way behind me, I'd forgotten it: there was no weather, no heat, no cold, no rain, no wind. But my body moved, my little finger travelled. And as my limbs edged along the road I thought no thoughts, only the moon shape and the mown grass. When I left the road it was because I was afraid of my infantile heart and I thought somewhere else would be easier. I stood at a gateway. No one barred my way. I entered. Before me, seated, I saw a woman with hair like twisted strands of rope. A woman looking at how time was going. Departing from custom, I crossed the instability line. But she would not answer me. She smiles her housebroken smile. I was afraid of the desert-garden in which she sat. It threatened to swallow me alive. I was afraid because I knew I had to be swallowed up alive and know that experience. But not now. Not yet. I was cold. My disease came from outside my body. I heard singing. Singing of water and invented words. I wanted to know about that song. But I did not dare leave the woman to go find the singer. I mimed questions to the woman in case she was deaf. But she ignored me. The singing, which had been coming from a friendly distance, stopped. I thought of pond water. I spoke to the woman: all those years of growing, I was afraid to go near the pond . . . Because I did not know the names of the unprompted lovers. I want to lick my body all over, everywhere, just like the animals do, I want to drown in rock, I want to taste slaves, I want to bear my unblemished skin to him, you know all this, you waited too, longer than I did, but no, that isn't right, I'm still waiting, don't you see? Can't you answer me? She looked at me and smiled, goldenseed glance, but secret and guilty and all her own strength showing. Wait, I said, no, I once heard you speak. You do belong to me. You must answer, you, the bereaver. She rubbed her neck with her hand, at the place where she ached. Tell me how long you will stay here, I asked. She said: from midnight until noon. Her manner was so vague I could not tell whether she was talking to me or to another daughter standing behind me. When I complained, she stood up and began to walk towards me, holding out amberoid hands. I turned away from her in fear, her eyes were dark as banshees, she returned to her seat. I walked around her domain, looking for something . . . I did not know whether it was a stone or a knife or a friend. I looked almost everywhere. But I found nothing and had to return to the woman. There is nothing for you here, not yet, she said, looking at me until I was a book with only two pages. I was relieved and went out through the gateway, passing under the alveolar arch, into the streets where I began to count the cars.

XVIII(i)

The alpestrine man arranges his collection of insect specimens. For him there are no serpents or flowers, only insects like small shucked-off birth skins. We started our other argument at the end of the meal. It was so hot that day, the house like a furnace of sunlight and concave mirrors, the solar wind unconcerned about our loneliness. I shouted at him. What about the grief arising from my injuries? When he hit me I felt the blood moving rapidly from one region of my body to another. With a few words, he made me a criminal, made arrangements for my life imprisonment. I heard him shouting to the boy in the stables. I stretched out on the floor, re-setting my bones. There are emergencies in every drop of my sweat, there are bells ringing in distances, I see microfossil cities in the cracks in the ceiling, my hands are the unhappy times of the year, their seasons change constantly and I admire my expectation of freedom. I, with my infallible memory for the opening words of my life, am not happy until all the lamps are extinguished for the night. I saw my own skeleton hand, my wedding ring a darker shadow against the slim bone. One day those fingers will scrub the floor until the floor runs with blood. I was a tiny bat crushed against the wall.

He said to me: why do you keep making the same mistake? Outside it was raining hard. I picked up the words that were foreign. The words that clasped and pinched and drew blood. I remembered when I was a child hearing my mother's thoughts: the sound was the crunching and cracking sound of wood or bones being broken. When I heard her thoughts, it used to give me an itch around my anus. I have too much time, I answered, that is why I make the same mistake. He leaned over me with his blind cruel stare. He enjoys my malnutrition. What were you doing walking in the village street this morning, when I asked you to stay home? I refused to answer. I picked up my book from the table. I looked at the separated petals of the flowers. I kept guard over myself. I was afraid of getting soaked to the skin. But his words went on and on. I was a retiary woman, a denizen of winter. His anger detaches me from the safety of my body. I crop the dead fruiting heads of the burdock, I don't answer, I am easily broken tonight, like the wrist of a bird's wing. He says I spin orb webs, he says I am killing his son. He says I must not prevent the conception of his child. I say, no, I am afraid. I am afraid of the fires of the child's skin. Micah says, your resistance against bearing my son harms all my fidelity. It is not just my loyalty to you that suffers but my duty to the land, that part of myself lost to the huskiness of blood: I do not even have a ventriloquist answer from you. And if you do not agree to my demands, I will prepare a day's phlebotomy for you, I'll cure you . . .

I scream. Outside, it rains. Indoors, we each seize our prey. The dissected dancers limp. When you break, secondhand sky, and fall, then we will stay silent and watch the trees, the willow, the hazel and the birch. But until then, it is only our voices that resound in this room, only our anger scratching totem animals on the wall.

They wrapped my body in hot cloths. This was to cure me. Now I am cured. Nocturnal birds tell me the secrets of the parish, they say the weather is still cold and wet, they say your stitches must be neater, they laugh at my over-cropped ear. I heard loud laughter untroubled by my old exclamations and at the last moment I looked back and her skull which I held between my hands and which felt like a birthday gift turned into a penis of frost and the penis melted and now there is only the westward migration which Micah has planned. We will drive our wagons through lanes and on either side of us all I will see is stunted misshapen foliage and rust on the undersides of the leaves and when we get to our new house, I will leave the trunks unpacked and sit down on a new chair and turn on the big colour television set and watch the andy williams show and be afraid as I sit in the orthopaedic chair of the cavities in my skull which contain my eyes. And when Micah enters the room he will see a female figure with outstretched arms and hands held upwards in a gesture of prayer, not equal to zero. We are holding together our bodies in the dark: we grip hands. Micah asks me why I hate the unborn. If I must enter your house like a prisoner, I said, I must make false statements, I must experience treason. The person who questions me asks me for help. Faustina, he says. And I refused. He was angry but he said nothing, not even the first shape of a word. I wanted to release us from the leafless and spiky distress we were caught in but the way was undiscoverable for me, again I could not name any colours.

On a date before true time, when I lived in the flat country where I was born, a man who dealt in candles touched my neck and described to me emotions resembling the pain of tortured humming birds. He said: you are like a lizard whose colour changes at night. Then I ran between the banks of the reservoir and my thinness was shadowing me. And the foetus turned with its long axis across the mouth of the womb at right angles to the birth canal. And the muscles of my body demanded silence I couldn't find, cries and sweat kept escaping from me, the tonality of my body was far away from me, yet diaphanous, waves of burning water and blood and nothing seen distinctly, only shapes of people violating old customs. I am unwinding circles that resemble sleep to tell of what happened during those years.

XVIII(ii)

The rock children became silent when Anna approached them. She comes closer. She walks as if her body is full of dredged mud, with uncanny elegance. And with one unified impulse the children fan out from her, retreating in a birdy fashion to the safety of the cliff path. They watch her, whispering to herself. When she turns around, puzzled, and cries out aloud to them, black words on the white reach of the day, they scatter. She begins running after them, then falters, wonders how to confess, her hands stinking with the stones she almost threw after the children. She stands still as the afternoon scuds around her. Then she begins to walk along the beach, with her head bent down low, she doesn't want to know about the sounds of speech, she doesn't want to look at any of those horizons you've got up your sleeve, she doesn't want to see you wearing your bright tournament dress. She drops the stones. The girl who has no hobbies walks towards hurt. She sees the rocks, she clambers over them, she doesn't care, her feet get wet in the rock pools, the false birds fly above her, harassing her, but when she laughs and lifts her face she sends them wheeling away, black summers blown away into the sky. She approaches the edge of a steep cliff. She looks at the sky again. The sky stirs uneasily. Anna wears antlers on her brow. She looks at the sky and utters braxy words. There are catacombs for her. There is always the dark violent shadow of a breaking-down following her. Anna sees how clumsily the scriptural world is mended. Her tongue approaches the edge. She looks down. Down down down into chrysalis mother and father down down beyond hearing down beyond tired ships down into the cry that swallows seals the howl that tries to be holy. The sea approaches the cold doorless rocks. Anna looks down at the dark carapace of the waves. She stands rigid, her voice is her punishment. She is the high voltage girl. I am underhand, she thinks, o yes, I am stealthy, I deserve nothing. Less than a year ago I was capable of courage. But now the people I see walking in the windy streets and in the cruel gardens know I am cut down, thrust down to the cell floor by my devotions and they look through into my bones and see my filth.

Faustina put food into my mouth, the geological taste of shrimps. She came across the road on a calm and clear day and spoke sadly and cleverly and I followed her because of the sun and I was so cold and we coincided like head-hunters and our love cut grass and outwitted mirrors and I am accused by my own spoken words and unspoken gestures. I have had reminders and warnings, I have seen the way beggars live, I have become afraid of all concealments, I hate my name, I renounce this jungle warfare, I want to be free of the untidiness I have to endure because of the birth secret. Let me see something other than the bare brain, talk about something other than our segregation, let me understand the meaning of my gestures and take my sickness back to the time of the crusades. Down below me, the mixed blood of the sea reflects me, like an incorrect copy . . . I will get free of the invasion of this trinity woman who is standing guard over my body. I will make her lick the tang of the blade.

Sea pours in through the blindness of Anna's body and fearful of her accidental death she steps back from the edge. The wind flaps her coat and she saw that the dark-coloured sky was moving rapidly away from her to the west, she felt she had been standing on this cliff-edge for days and nights and wars and the trapdoors in her shoulders ached with her dammed-up heirs. Then she thought she heard someone shouting in the distance, a long way off, she thought someone was shouting, Anna, Anna, but she couldn't lift her head to answer because of the turbulence in her and so she simply walked slowly away in the opposite direction, no beginning, no end.

XIX

Watermark of spring
swan and shadow
gnaw the tentorium grass
the spirit bone drowns

and down into the night
your shapeless heart
wafts bloodily

This is the thin mist hour when many of the people die and many of the children fall into terror and life. He let me bind his hands behind his back. I knew he would tell me the truth then. Also there was the knife but that was irrelevant in the room, meaningless as the birds and the insects and the poem I had been writing. The shadows made whizzing sounds. Micah spoke quietly. I think he spoke without fear. I listened, the survivor of the night. They captured me outside the city, he began, a dozen men wearing smoke-grimed masks. They disarmed me and took me, together with a younger prisoner who did not speak, across the border. Fires were burning everywhere and I heard women yelling. I spent several months in a comfortless prison. Guards with machine guns patrolled the perimeter. I was held in solitary confinement. My guards were not cruel. They were indifferent to my existence, I could have been a dog or a chair. They spoke coarsely of women. When I complained they laughed at me and threw my meal on the floor and pushed me down into the mess. One day I was visited by an old man who told me I had been pardoned from death but must serve my captors for three years.

He watched me, his hand on his pistol. I asked no questions. The old man was a spy. I gave no sign. I said nothing. I was taken to a grim stinking barracks building surrounded by barbed wire about ten miles away from my first prison and here I joined a company of ragged men. Silent and undernourished, like me. After the ritual bath, we began our training in the lore and love of death. One night I saw the ice collar of the moon. We were each given nine weapons with which to repent. The first enemy I killed vomited turgid blood. After three years service I was again taken to the border at night and released. I understood none of this, captivity or release. I miss the nights of the heavy guns now it is peacetime.

Micah paused. I stared stupidly at him. I had not expected this story. Am I hearing his sins? He has a trespasser's shadow. I think he is lying. I am afraid. I have tied his hands. But he is lying. I am lost. Why don't you say something, he asks. His voice is harsh. I look out of the window, I see many small birds flying in the sky, I am nothing. I look down at my hands. My hands are turning black. My hair falls over my face, hiding me. Don't you believe my story? he says tauntingly. I feel humiliated. I keep very silent. I do not move. Listen, he says, I'll tell you one true thing. I was in a war once. I was wounded in the thigh. I'll show you the scar. His voice is my autumn enemy. Please, I say . . . I am crying. I fear hand patterns.

He asks me the dangerous question. No, I say, I don't want to become pregnant. I don't want you to touch my dress. I don't want to wait months just for pain. I don't want to adopt the stance of that great womb. He spat in my face. I know you, he said, no matter how you try to hide under your careful words and acts. I've seen you walk casually to the fields and watch the farm girls like a shamaness. Yes, Faustina, and you're alert at night, you show me your body, patient and unangered. I know you.

She turned away from him and began to wind up the music box. In the hushed room, the music makes a truant sound. Hurt is leaves blown along the pavement. Three hours before dawn I heard their halfmoon wailing. I say to him, please don't harm me. The spittle is still wet on my face. He says: you've locked the sun up in a steel box. You'll never be forgiven. Then I unfastened his hands, untying the knots. And I let him caress me at random. I took his weight. The penumbral man begins to deform me.

XX(i)

Anna opens the door. She throws the door open. It bangs against the wall. She looks tired and ruinous. Her coat is splashed with mud. She is out of breath. She pulls open her blouse and shows me the teeth marks on her nipple. She says loudly, I will recover my long-forfeited privileges as the bride of Stefan and sing when I burn to ashes on the anniversary of my birth. Before I can answer, she is running away, scared of everything. My fears are skintight. I cannot help Anna. She must teach herself how to become the wildfowl woman.

My condemned sister is quite happy? asks Stefan, laughing, placing his heavy hand upon the nape of my neck. Did you see Anna? I said. He ignored my question. I was afraid of belonging to his evening. I edged away from him almost imperceptibly but he let his hand fall slowly, deliberately, to mock me. Are you happy? he repeated, standing in the doorway so that I couldn't pass. I looked at him but I could not recognize my brother. Why shouldn't I be happy, I replied, because I didn't want to make any trouble for myself. Stefan looked at me without any kindness and I shivered with exhaustion. My voice was thin, unprotected. How did you arrive here so soon? We did not expect you until the weekend. My question made me invisible. I came over on the ferry, he said, and began to walk up and down the room, not patient, not impatient, encumbering me. How is everyone at home? He wheels around, rubbing his hands together the way the victorious have. O gnawing and biting, he answers, cheating and hurting, all of them, you know the family. I asked if I could go out of the room and get on with my preparations for the evening meal but he wouldn't let me so we sat in a severing room for over an hour, waiting for Micah. I stared at Stefan when he wasn't looking at me. Fat hog, I thought, assassin, I thought. No longer my brother. I felt him look at me. Stefan has stolen many things from me. What does he think when he looks at me so monotonously? Or doesn't he have thoughts, does his knowing fall to pieces before he ever grasps it? Is this driving him to madness or is he sane, the narrator of events, a teacher, a master, killing only his enemies? And am I an enemy? Feminine cares and angers agitate this eager woman, said Stefan, not laughing. But then Micah came in and sent me out of the room and I was free to do my work, sweeping the stone floors and scrubbing wooden tables, silently, secretively. Whetting myself against the days. I must tell Micah that this unborn child will be the child of a white father and a mulatto mother.

XX(ii)

An interlunar room: the dwarf woman is throwing back the curtain, exhibiting suicidal tendencies. Through the small barred window the brunt of light falls on to the naked girl sprawled in the chair. Her lips shun comfort. A man enters the room: he has the head of a cat. He bends over the girl. Her eyelids are closed. He turns on the dwarf woman who is standing in his shadow. She runs out of the room, quick as the old moon. The cat-man sits watching the sleep of the violated girl. There is the odour of apples in the room and the whispered report of many voices, the murders of ancient actors. The apex of the sun's way is silent: but the man listens to it: he hears its rattlesnake quiet. In a dark corner of the room he has arranged the playthings of the dead child. He does not look at them. He saw herds of wild silk girls driven towards the precipice. In the sky he saw the colour of white mixed with black. He spoke to the sleeping girl, hornwrack words. In a voice of ill-luck, he told her about the parasites who enter the human body by the feet and suck the blood. He laughed at the extremities of the moon. The girl opens her eyes. She sees her guardian. She hears the sound of people tramping along black corridors. She thought of the fire lady. She stood up. Her head is full of lepidopterous insects and the dates of dark events. She looked for the summer. But did not find it. He told her the name of her cunt. He told her about her vandalism. He told her she was being held under suspicion. She knelt down, she swept the bottom of the river clean, she stood in front of the painted theatre curtain, she covered her nakedness with her hands. He told her about her autopsy. She wept and said, even the heart and the lungs have been removed then? And I am dead? Then she remembered the false accusation and the cancer of the summer solstice and she screamed because the web-footed wife has abandoned her. The man comes towards her, the hawker of slugs. She watches him, the girl puppet with the bisque skin. Will you live to be very old? She asks him. He does not answer. He opens his animal mouth. He bites deep into her flesh, he is eating her shoulder. She shudders with the pain but cannot run away. He is swallowing lumps of her flesh whole. She is already growing weak, is falling to the floor, one side of her body paralysed, but she shrieks once, loud, calling for her mother. And her mother appeared laughing and she also began to eat the girl who is making a harsh grating sound with her contorted mouth until only the bones are left and the bones of the girl are given to the dwarf woman who takes them to the landscape of the arctic circle and buries them under an ice stone. And wails . . .

XX(iii)

I am ready to collide with the river. I am diving. I hit the surface of the water. I go down beneath the cold waters. My skirt is caught around my legs, heavy, but I kicked myself free, I had to swim out of the ovary of the flower, out of the woodwork of the house, away from the woman in her long debtor's robes. I swam fast, my body all one bone, the skeleton of my song rattling against the waters. I had no fear now, I was free in the wellwater, it soothed my burns, it released me from his reprimands. The river bore me up, holy and strong, it was connecting me to some myth, I slid through the water and I was very clean. When I reached the opposite bank, I clutched the yellowish brown clumps of grass and pulled myself upright. I stood waist high in the water. My hair was plastered down against my head. I was happy. I looked up at the sky and I forgot the fingerless winter. I looked at my hands, flesh gloves. I climbed up the bank and pulled off my wet dress. I let the sun dry my skin and draped my dress over a bush. I had taken the day unawares, it was still very early, I'd used my body like a sickle, I'd escaped the black midwife, obliterated my future. I knelt down, I touched the obtainable flowers. I was alive and exhausted. I slept. When I awoke, my mind was haunted again, troubled by the fear of some approaching penance like a meaningless refrain, a church song. I did not believe I had prevented disease. Again, I had to climb the wooden staircase. Dregs, impurities: I live on them. The sky opens: wounded and blue. You don't understand. I have to get the sky right. You don't have to obey these rules. You only glance at the world, at the foliage of shade and fruit trees: and you are safe. But I am not. I am sick, I am rotting away like the fruit stored too long.

Thundery rain of a summer afternoon. I stand on the edge of a plantation of young trees. I am thinking of the tremulous forest I used to walk in, touching each leaf. Rain soaks me to the skin but I do not take shelter. There is no knowledge in sheltering. I endure this saline environment. I see leaf scars. Trespassing, I shiver in the wind, suddenly chilled. A woman with the head and horns of an animal watches me. Cankers appear on the fruit and the twigs.

All night Anna and I shared the same bed. But we were fully clothed. We did not touch. Flesh did not search out its nature by trial. We were frugal.

The land is in its third month of mourning. I say we honour the dead too much. I say we forget the waxing and waning of the moon. But he does not listen. He is planning his journeys. I was drunk, I was naked. There were nights when we saw ourselves crashing, flung against cutaneous walls. Our sweat like grease from a viper candle. Our bodies pitching in the bed, contracting into rowdy unconsciousness. We are like two plagues. We fold up the dead. We stop their backbones from shadowing the living. We close their eyes. We lay their bodies in calm boxes smelling of night. We burn them to ash. Then we open the wardrobe door. We take out their clothes. We fold their clothes and lock them in trunks. We distribute their linen, sheets and pillowcases, among the relatives still living. We sleep on the sheets of the dead. Drunk and naked some nights . . . We felt our way back along the narrow passageway to the dawn. Got frightened of the night eye. The depths of tides and beds frightened us. We stay sober now. And have taken out a lease on the sea. We plan to exterminate the birds. Halfway round midnight we come to the ice shelf. Now I face the meaning of the raven. And my hands deny. Go away, cold child of the abyss: go away, back into your darkness. Be dark, stay dark, stay away from me, no, you must not dismember me and I must not devour you.

XXI(i)

The girl looked in the mirror. She was wearing dark glasses. She saw her shadow self. She saw the birdcage moon. I am young, she said. I am young as my mother was when her shoes creaked and her silence lashed me to her fears. I am young as the upheaval of her heartbeat: yet I do not cry. I am too old. The ground beneath my feet is too muddy. I sleep next to my own skeleton, touching my own perineum. I remember the wingless female emits a shining green light at night.

On the outskirts of the village, hidden by old dark yew trees, there is an abandoned house, with broken windows and a door that won't close. Faustina stood outside. Cold twilight was everywhere, but unconfessable. She said to herself: dancer on the cross. I hate the roman pun. The messengers of my world are creating new flowers out of splinters of glass. She entered the old house. It was hard to see her way so she switched on her torch. The thin hostile beam of light went before her. The floor was littered with rubbish of tramps and sperm of lovers. Faustina sits on a pile of old newspapers. Time sank its little fangs into her but she waits. Once she thought she heard voices and quickly doused the light. Then she heard silence. But did not dare shine another light into the darkness. An hour without any victim went by. She is reading her own mind. I am far from the saint's creek at the turn of the river, I have gone away from the miracle church, I can't get back. It was so good there. The air never had to stand trial, the stones demanded nothing. There was peace and purity, the place you saw when you couldn't sleep or when they hurt you . . . But they sent me away, as if I were broken-witted. Why? In the dark house Faustina watches the dance of the one-legged people. The short leaps of women with one leg sicken her and she closes her eyes against the horning of their tabernacle hair.

I hear a shadow moving. A white owl watches me, here in my bethel room. Is that you, Anna? Yes, I am saying your name. You are the ghost of the cut grass, Anna. I embrace you. Yes, but it is guesswork. Because you are silent. You are smoking a cigarette. The patterns we hold in place with our fingers are not to be trusted. Darkness. Anna? Are you still there? Yes, she says. A tree of the rose family speaks. She laughs slowly and I am uneasy. Are you still there? I repeat. Yes, she says, tossing her cigarette away. Then come out of the shadow, I say. I shine my torch in her face. She does not flinch. I see. You are wearing your new smile, you are changing suddenly as fever, he has touched your forked clumsiness, you have cried out in pleasure, you have kissed the other person. Answer me, Anna. Anna, please. Anna touches Faustina's plaited hair with a stoat hand. I was your overshadow once, Faustina, she whispers. Anna makes the other woman afraid with these words. She fears the deportation of her torturer. Anna says: I am your sister now. It has changed, my purpose. Faustina breaks into grief. But Anna interrupts. Don't pretend to have been blind from birth, Faustina, don't set up such a cry. Let me change. I want to end things between us. They are hurting me. I want to be with him now. Let me go. Faustina stands with her back to the door. The night is murmuring its own terror. She watches Anna's expression change from that of sad concerned friend to writhing girl. She smiles. Let me out, says Anna, her voice a dark bay colour. No, shouts Faustina, no, you're a weakling, Anna, Stefan will tear your skin off with his hardships. She suddenly put out her hand and grabbed Anna's arm. Listen, has he known you sexually? Have you known him? Anna went away through the spider's webs, crept further into the night, with no answer. She has not slept with Stefan. Faustina knows. She laughs unhappily. My brother's name is cobra-de-capello. He sleeps with whores. Anna shakes her head. Many words of yours are lies, she answers. Faustina gives her a blow across the mouth with her open hand. Anna makes no sound. You'll do as I say and refuse to go with Stefan. Anna turns away, the room smells of dung, she is not afraid, she kisses Faustina, she says, the days and nights of our bodies have finished, I must find another year or lose my memory, please Faustina, understand, I want to know the language and customs of a man . . . The two Women are parturient strangers. Anna throws herself forward, struggling with the body of Faustina, the lies and memories. Their ungentle embrace is a pledge to the future for them both, the difficulties, cruelties . . . the geotropism . . . Faustina forces Anna back against the damp wall and kisses her with a compulsion mouth, taste of snake words on her tongue. Not Stefan, she pleads. Anna chokes, then kisses Faustina again, murderously. Then the women release each other. They tread down their hive history, Faustina angry, Anna inaccessible. Silence is squirting them, they are wet with it. There is no more violence, they have separated, they have chosen different colours of vomit. Fuck you, says Anna. She goes out of the house, goes back to her father's house, towards the slow fires of night and the man. Faustina's shock is vernal. She stands in the moon's shadow and cannot understand how her strength has become so narrow, only a sliver of lust. No, she says, I won't try to reach her again. She has left me alone at the frontier, abandoned me to my annular eclipse, the pain. I will not rescue her from Stefan. Let her learn her own lessons.

XXI(ii)

A third woman entered the room. She called me by my name. Micah, she said, Micah. She holds an etching needle in her hand and her eyes gnaw away my deliverance. She wears a masquerade garment with an ecclesiastical hood. She told me about the baptism of the dead. She showed me the prepuce of Christ. She gave me a sea stone with a hole bored through it. She told me to go on a pilgrimage to her angina equator. She wounded me with cold wet hungry tiredness. She harvested her hair and left me. I went out into the fields to look for Faustina. I wanted to hear her breathing. I wanted to be close to her skull-womb. I saw her in the distance, bending over the stream. In the garden with her grand-daughters. Her shadows thin as cat-gut. She waited for me to speak, to dash her brains out. I am afraid, I said. She laughed. Was her body like an old ship? she asked. Tell me what to do, Faustina. She threw the storm-cone into the stream. She was jumpy, nervous, kept looking away from me. No, I am not lustful, I said, denying her accusation. Tell me what to do, how do I get out of this world's darkened room? Is there a key? A key?

she repeated scornfully and moved abruptly away from me, like a horse trying to throw its rider, then she added, my face is the face of a harlot, Micah, my eyes are the eyes of the onlooking mother, my hair is the hair of the weather. I am not yet born. I am afraid also: and my sleep is studded with nails. She held my wrist and took the pulse of my prayer. I touched her forehead. Help me, Faustina. There is an eye in the palm of each of my hands. These eyes see hungry ghosts. I want to eat my own body. My voice became a snarl, I couldn't help it, I smelt her heartbeat. No, she screams, no, let me go, I'm at the bottom of the sea, so let me drown. She jumped across the stream, she ran away from me, she couldn't help me . . . I watch her run, holding up her riding dress. She lives inside the skin of a dead animal. She is not ashamed of the darkness.

XXI(iii)

A long time ago the bridegroom came out of the waters. On the night following his departure, I waited for Anna. I saw the bodies of red ants. I read a book of prayers. When did Anna and I first start trying to work out the rhythm of the stars in the night sky? After Stefan frightened us? Or was it when she gave up her job in the doll factory? She hated painting the eyes and the lips without any theological doctrine to help her. I sit in a room with six small sphinxes of foolsgold and a japanese mirror and a shadow clock. I remember my first few years of unwearying pencil marks. The mirror at the back of the shelf reflects the footprints of the piano. I sit in the censor's room. I wait for the girl of the last crusade.

In a closed hour without windows, we look at the embryos of pigs and rats and men. I knew she was telling me lies. I saw her eyelashes chilled with ice. I knew she was lying. I smelt my brother, his three odours were in her armpits. The strands and chains of her hair were infested with shame. But my body is tremorless. I embraced her. I ate the eucharistic mud. Her eyes were closed.

XXII

It was a cold day of birthright when we travelled to our new house. We drove out of the village with the children yelling after us. We crossed the bridge. I looked at the waterbirds. My hands could not decipher the cold. Micah was whistling a carnival tune. I heard the cries of the horses. Damp oak-ash forest for miles around us. The track was rough, overgrown, it was little used now. We'd been journeying since first light and I was tired. Earlier in the day I had looked across at the abandoned chapels out on the salt marsh. Cold mist wrapped its silence around the moorland and the estuary saltings with a lonely exaltation. But the forest was doubt and darkness and riddles. The wagons jolted on. The cold snatched at me. It came on to snow when we got to the streamless head of the valley. I sat on the unsheltered wagon seat, a confession chair. You are on fire, he said. Look how the hills deceive, I said. I looked at him. He was not the deliverer. But I am not bound to him. Eradicative vows made at a poor temple in a barren night land do not bind us together. I wait impatiently. The blood in the ends of my fingers is stammering. You did not flinch when I showed you my book of obscene pictures, he said. I shrugged. If the child is an imbecile you will not be absolved, I told him. He threatens me with the mad whiteness of snow, cold wreckage of deaths. But I feared the toad midwife more than any of his words. Today is colder than yesterday, I said carelessly. He said, I see nothing between the warp and weft of your two colours. And turned his horse and rode back to the other wagon.

I stood before the mirror with the woman standing close behind me, he said to Stefan. It was the third day after our marriage. Will your prayer be answered? she asked me mockingly. I should not have told her about the musician in the forest. I shut the century behind me. Other, the other sees, I thought. My bones burnt. I locked her in her room. But she went out boasting amongst the ant-hills What should I do? Stefan has explanations for winter. He says, there is a complex and wild difference between men's and women's speech. Faustina's tongue is one hundred years too old. She should be kept in a furnitureless room. She is the spider's silk gland. She made the blackthorn season. You must tie her hands together at night.

Micah rode on in silence and looked at the broken body of the church. He saw her hands reaching everywhere into the cowardice of their life. She has the face of a woman but I do not trust her. Her speech is ice excrement suspended in the air. I believe she is concealing trouble and gloom and disgrace. She rides her cold castrated horse and mine is a wisdom that comes too late. I am an alarmist dressed in dirty linen, I suffer loss of sight even though my eye appears sound. In my stables, barns, fields and factories, wherever I go with orders and examinations, I long for the bodily pain of this anguineal woman who hates our son and who I must follow through the earth, room after room, hammering my great artery into arctic shapes, my brain wasting away as I watch her listening attentively to the cries of birds. We sit beneath an awning sheltered from the sun and she does not move. When we are apart even a letter in her handwriting savages me. Look at her, half-asleep. Why won't she stop hoaxing me? Why doesn't she cut my throat? I have given her gifts, sandals and rings and silk and a white horse to ride. I have punished her, humiliating her with menial jobs, showing her the life of a drudge. But she will not yield. She continues to go into drugstores and look boldly into the eyes of strangers. I hate her freedom.

She lifted her head, gazed at him apprehensively. He got up, walked away, stared at unsubmissive fields. I'm sorry, he heard her say but he didn't answer. He would not look at her.

XXIII(i)

The translator sighs
Trapdoors open
Rain falls without pleasure
The suicides sit on the floor
I read the second book

of the old testament
I am afraid to cut my hair

Trichology of Anna and Faustina and the sky and the trees. Anna sleeps among flames and birds. I look at her. She is made of dried blood, remnants of a sister. I did not dare steal any more of her shroud. Moon whitlows hurt me. Why are you inflicting these penalties? My falsehood dress is thin. My own whiteness stank and the school children shouted. They yelled and shouted. O I am very sleepy, said Anna. We moved across the fields, following the footprints we had left behind. The folds of my skin froze.

He sits and stares at me every evening. But I say nothing. I hide in the region of my ribs. When I washed my hands, my wedding ring slipped off my soapy finger. Smoke rose from the fire in the shape of a lion. I told him about my ring, the strange way it came off my finger at the same moment as my anger really hurt. He said: you find me too many confessions. Spare me this priesthood. I won't wear iron shoes, I mutter.

Anna touches her throat with cold hands. I want to tie promises around my neck, she says. I offer her a beach stone pierced by the sea and threaded on a safety chain. She shakes her head. I offer her a jewel in the shape of a leaf dangling on a gold chain. She says no, she cannot accept. Because of the silver fish necklace which she hates and has locked in the painted wooden box by her bed, the box she never opens, she is prevented from accepting less sorrowful gifts. She is musicless and bangs against window and lamps. She crouched at his feet, she wept unskilfully.

XXIII(ii)

Three sisters guard the region of the autowrecks. Blood came out of his mouth a gushing nebula and he died he died. Blood came out of her mouth. But she did not die. He died. And the cars were beaten into metal enigmas, edges sharp in the above-sea-level air and blood came out of his mouth and the sirens howled and the lights flashed and the bride saw the open heart of her husband and stared at his head smashed in, the youth spilling out, lost day after day, and I felt pain drag me down into moony darkness awaiting the axe and the sky went unbalanced and I knew Stefan was dead and I went down into the darkness and there were wet girls and springtime murderers there and a cold piercing wind and snow, all apprehensions and my blood hurt and blood came out of my mouth and wherever I looked I saw his coagulated body, in the prayer, in the mirror, in the bed, in the orchard, behind the television screen, everywhere. I put on my coat of long life and walked across to the archery ground. I was hanging loosely in the aftermath of the womb. Micah saw me but ignored me. I stood on the path and watched the bowmen shoot at the target of white cloth.

The seafox is thirsty. I am afraid of being imprisoned in the annealing-tower. I dare not approach Micah. I cannot bear being exposed to public scorn. Between the moons, my hands move, gestures of blue shadow: but he will not understand. Each night he grips me with closed fingers. Perhaps we are waiting for the hands of a third person, a chirographer. Uniting our lips and eyelids.

I ran through the damp field where the graves were and came out on to the beach beneath the sky painted in grey tints. I have dressed myself coquettishly: so that when I groan I will sound more frightening. Anna sits on the rocks, her ivorytype gaze fixed on the waters that lap around her. I keep repeating words, teasing her. She said without looking at me, the daytime held in her hands, what is wrong, Faustina? My body was so tense I could have flung it to the ground and burst open the gates of the zodiac. I touched Anna's hand. He wants a child, I said harshly, I saw my own words indistinctly written on the rocks, he says I must become a well from which artesian blood can flow. He has prepared my body for the anatomy of the future. Even now the supposed ghost child may have taken hold of my body. I hate hate hate . . . Anna looked at me curiously. You have missed the real point of attack, she said. I looked at the unhewn stones. I don't understand, Anna. She pointed out to sea at a ship of two hours. She was wearing a bright coloured muslin flower dress which did not suit her. But what about the beginning of my night, I continued, what have I misunderstood? She laughed. If you hate Micah, if you still regard yourself as a prisoner of war, then now your pregnancy gives you power. Don't you see? You hold his child a prisoner. Think of it, Faustina: in his house of secondhand furniture, you, for the first time, possess your own wealth. You can make Micah your follower, if you let him see that swelling protuberance often enough. You'll hear his loud bellowing. You'll control his low jests and his penitence. Anna smiles, heavy uncoined smile that I feel enter my grief and release me. Anna stands up, wanders away along the beach with the finches and the sparrows. I watch her. I am turning from bone to blood. It is difficult but I think fruitfully down past the bone, into the radioactivity of prayer. I hear loud-speakers saying, yes, yes. And can accept the seed entombed in me. Fire wouldn't burn me. Look, said Anna, coming up close to me, look, I have found a stone shaped like the face of an old woman. She placed it in my hand and stared at me. It was like the first time we ever came face to face. The want of knowledge. The fear of white lies, black truths. With child, said Anna, showing her teeth. Then she kissed me, almost accidentally. Let's walk along the cliff path, I said, when she let me go. I looked at the stone I held in my hand and thought of the six open spaces in the skull of an infant. Gradually, one colour blended into another and I felt happy.

XXIII(iii)

Tell me, who are you? Where do you come from? Anna's questions were difficult but I put the stone in my pocket and said to her, I was born in the last year of the fascist regime, just before the civil war began. My afterbrain throbs as birds skim through my memory. But I'll confess, I'll confess. Write it all down in the growan book. I walked between the empty pews in the church, saying, I'm blind, I'm deaf. This angered my mother. As for my father, his authority prevailed even after he was dead, for a long time. His sons persecuted all his enemies, because of the blueness of his poisoned skin. His daughters wore rags. His daughters looked at the loose skin on the ox's throat. They identified diseases. His daughters obeyed the bloodless laws. Our homefarm was built on a neck of land between two seas. I, the youngest, the remotest child, watched the flaying of seals and the flenching of whales. I loved fireworks and candlesticks and ice in the valleys. But I obeyed. I went out into the darkness in my recaptured white dress. My mother was the threshold.

There she sat, sewing. She was brave, with wry silences. Interlocking birds flew into her orbit. But she did not speak to me. Not even out-of-doors. I have collected volumes concerning the sea, I have drawn diagrams of the scrotum, I have woken in the middle of the night and heard the droning sound of the long bone in the arm of man. I have discovered analogies between thoughts apparently unlike and have frightened myself awake to sit waiting on the ridge of an ice field, unable to move until the light of the clock hour approached. Sitting in this darkness, I think of the wife who returned her wedding gifts.

Anna stared at my brink body. We were standing outside the church. The blizzard meditated upon us. Tell me about your brother, said Anna throatily. Stefan? He annoyed a girl who was out walking alone. He replaced the broken mirror. He said, we have to change trains. He said, I am working, do not disturb me, and he hung the lamp on a nail. Once I saw him march down a dark alleyway in the city and drive away a drunken man. He made a scarecrow out of empty tin cans and set it in motion by pulling a string. He is my brother. When he looks at me, I straighten my dress, I knot my hair with mistakes. His body is tall, his eye a cuttlefish, he is the prognathous one you run into unexpectedly in the afternoon when you wanted to walk alone to mend your damage. Anna shakes her head, her hair like tusks. No, she said, no. Are you inventing your own reasons? I ask. No, she said again, long distances have cured him. She turned and hurried away, upset and beyond the protection of the law.

XXIV(i)

I opened the door and Micah looked up from the newspaper. Listen, he said sourly, you must not behave foolishly when your brother is here. I said nothing. He looked fatigued. He ordered me to begin the cleaning and scrubbing of the rooms allotted to Stefan and to supervise the provision of clean linen, extra bread, meat, wine and firewood. When I had finished this work, I was very tired and went down into the basement, into the windowless room. There, by herbs, by smoke, by mirrors, by cards and by the movements of pitiless water, I searched for knowledge of the journeys and the labours and the excuses of the future. I stretched my limbs to extort a confession from the silence. I devoted myself to this science until I heard Micah calling me. Then I went back upstairs slowly, my experiments complex and incomplete, the trajectory of my body not under my control. My skirt of heavy blood weighed me down.

He insists that I obey him. He stands at the point furthest from my eye. I say that my body has already been burned. That he cannot hurt me. Elliptograph grief separates us. The edge of my body meets the edge of a man-shadow. Before I speak again, I think of waves of sound and light bending around all obstacles in their path. I remember a child's name, the splint-bone sound. The sun has fingers, the moon-crucifixion cannot be just a mirage. I am conscious of a redistribution of energy within me. Then I speak to him, explaining the pigpen nature of my world and the fears I feel, the scavenger ibis I saw during that very cold weather. I tell him the legend of my sea brother. I want him to understand the stormsurge of my life. Two nights of insignificant sleep have submerged my strength but I must tell him that the paths of the land echo our murders and that we will drown in our blood streams. I demand the release of the prisoner who bears my name.

He says: I am the husband of a dark-plumed adulteress, I will not be threatened. He refuses to eat or drink with me. I could hear the street. The clock exploded. I stopped talking. I stopped trying to explain. Why are you silent? he asks, do my words terrify you? I shook my head. I could not explain the real fear. The blood hemmed me in. He laughs. He eats black fruit. He reads his comic paper. Where is the eager woman? he adds. I told him about the mortuary. He slapped my face. I heard you, I said. I saw you. All this time I was needing great strength to understand us with any clarity. We were both shamed. I saw the white surface of fear beneath everything. I saw the eyes of the man. I was skinned, all raw. I was in an unmarried cave. The icy birds would peck my baby to death. I had pains in my head. I heard what he said to me. He shouted the same words over and over again. Yes, I cried, hiding behind my human hands, yes, I will come to the wedding, yes, I'll come. My thumbkin surrender. His hands worked hard on my body and he made jokes. He began to swindle me again. Faustina, he said. He said my name three times. He pulled his body back then drove it deep into me, into the pulp chamber. I wondered how to understand this act, the sex act that intercepts my rumours. I start from scratch.

XXIV(ii)

My brother Stefan was a sailor. He went on long voyages across the ocean. It helped his sensuality. One spring when I was a child his ship was wrecked. He was the crew's sole survivor. The muscular tissue of his heart saved him. He was hauled out of the cold waters, a parody of death. He returned home overland. After convalescing from the sickness he took from shock, he went on longer voyages. Two years later he was again shipwrecked. Again he was the only survivor. Since then he has worked on the land. Men are suspicious of him. He keeps declaring his innocence. I do not like Stefan's manner of entering a room, the hydraulic priest. I distrust him when he looks at Anna, his boldness. And I fear the glacial drift of her eyelids. I know Stefan. He gave a book to a blind woman. He smites the firstborn. I have suffered his thuggism. He gave a beggar a handful of worms. But Anna listens to him, laughs when he laughs. She will accept his writing on her skin. I warned Anna, I told her Stefan lived within the arctic circle. She laughed and licked her long fingers. There is an enormous woman who lives in an enormous house high up in the sky, she mocked me. I looked up at the sky. I saw blue and black and silver striped clouds and I had to go away from Anna's harsh chattering. She had the apparent brightness of a fixed star and I was afraid Stefan would turn her into a silk picture of a girl, not even to be displayed on the wall but just unrolled when desired and mostly neglected. I hesitated and then I felt my breasts with my hands: they were white seacows, milk slaves. I heard my voice move through the bent grass.

> *It was the sound*
> *of shaken keys*
> *I live in a flimsy house*
> *the wind blows through it*
> *like a Black Mass*
> *I am not allowed*
> *access to my memory*
> *the bare feet of tomorrow*
> *chase me into a pawnshop*

XXV(i)

Why am I afraid? Why do I live in fear? Why do I skid from room to room, unable to settle? Why do I doubt the existence of free space when I stand timid in doorways and fields? Why do I worry about the upkeep of the streets? Are you listening to the sound of the patient's voice? Why do I fear the opening-up of my bloodcold body? When did I hear my last scream? Why am I exposed like this? What's my poor radiocarbon life for? I am a peat-hag. I watch the hysterotomy of a meditative girl. I run along the crazy pavements of the city. I sleep in a rainy bed. I can be seen in the corner of the mouth or the region of the anus. The children who are blindfolded come towards me. They break me to skull fragments. Why must I crouch down and watch the rate of my deformation? I am looking down the throat of a bird. And there is the question of slavery that lasts through spring summer autumn and winter. No, you cannot avoid danger. Why can't I run away, run past the light and beyond the darkness and down into the plutonic rock, down beyond the bone? No, I am stuck in feeble rooms, afraid, my head blown up like a black carnival balloon: my hair which takes seventeen years to grow and five weeks to die is the colour of a mouse carcass: and I ache with spinal fear . . .

I see ranks of dead women marching towards me under the water, black rifles held in their hands. They march over the harvest fields. I am trapped by the telegraph wires. He would not come with me when I abandoned the ocean. I saw the eye of the peripheral ape persuading me to scream. I looked at the veins in the wings of the insect. My mechanical twin read out my answer. Does this mean a further delay? he said sternly.

Carrying our scarecrows on our backs, Anna and I visited the zoo. It was a melancholy day. The sky like a marshalling yard. We heard six voices. We were afraid of each other. The animals were all dead. I liked the mammoths preserved in ice for thirty thousand years but Anna preferred the delicate creatures caught in amber, butterflies, spiders, ants, bees and flies. We did not argue. We did not stay long at the zoo. The shacklejoints of the fish frightened me. The sad sore animals kept showing Anna birth memories. So we left. Afterwards we went to the movie. He sinned, I told her. He isn't guilty, she insisted. She wouldn't look at me. She had many moods of futurity. I was hungry. Everything was tarnished. I was the old worn-out one. Behind my veil of whalebone. My split-skin. I cannot bear the meeting of the eyes. Always I hear the other heart beating. And something terrible forms in my mouth.

XXV(ii)

The importance of the dance and of christ's menstrual blood belong to us both, Micah and Faustina, husband and wife, accuser and accused who live together. When the fasting was over he presented me with a silk dress. He told me not to wear it on sunny days. My skin was embarrassed and I twisted my hair up into two horns.

Head
Skull
Moment
Thumb
Arrow
And the shabbiness

of his footsteps behind me in the darkness. The rope swings in the wind. Without his consent. Don't make fun of deformed people, he told me angrily. I stopped laughing. Rice insect corpse, I thought. Cries of encouragement from my vagina. All the tribes live there. But the sarcomas kept spreading through her body. Hurting. Bad. I saw the grail's face. Milk flowed from me but I could not believe in the gifts of the holy ghost. Milk drains from me and I weep, lost between two depressions. I look through web-eyes. He said the weather had changed his mind. I am chained to the tip of his tongue.

Stefan called to me from the white room. I will come immediately, I answered, although I did not know the tune or the name of the dance. Stefan took me by the hands and we danced. We danced out into the courtyard and got wet in the rain. We danced to the phonograph's cry across shifting sands and glass Pekings and suspenses of cold. I saw the oval faces watching us. They were the inhabitants of the moon. I did not care about them. I forgot about facing pain and difficulty. We flung ourselves through the throstle night. My horse hair flew shaggily out around my shoulders. I would have danced into water and drowned. I wasn't blind any more and I didn't have to listen to the ticking of a watch. I thought I would never stop rushing through the music. I held Stefan's hands tightly. I thought the old thoughts. I saw Anna standing in the doorway, in conjunction with the moon, but I didn't care about her, she was hair-combings and dust, old darknesses, a speaking clock. I forgot the bride money. Stefan did not laugh as we danced. He watched me intently. Perhaps he was losing sight of me then. My body got strange and distended, I curved myself backwards, I was washed by the waves of night, I felt drunk, I stamped my feet, I was thirsty, my mouth dry, and I wanted to be kissed between my legs, to be touched under the thigh, I wanted to be circumcised by Stefan. I started to shout myself hoarse with the song but then Micah stepped forward and stopped us, he stopped the dance, laughing, pretending to, a monstrous man doll, telling stale jokes and hating me. You're exhausted now, he told me. I leant against Stefan for a moment. Defying them. I closed my eyes so that I could not see any jealousy. My sweat was cold as the moon's age. I was back in the world of punishments. Go to bed, Micah said to me quietly, go to bed now, you must be careful, you must rest. People were listening. Watching for me to fall into the trap. I would not accept their challenge. Micah smiled but I did not trust his voice. I was afraid that the night was watching me now the dance was over and Stefan had left me and was talking to an uncertain woman wearing a dress of green pasture and I clenched my hands together because my sex felt imperfect and I could not recollect why I hurt there in that cunt place . . . Go to bed and keep the door open until I come, said Micah. I hesitated. He observed the anger of my slow movements until I got scared and began to lose my ability to distinguish certain colours. I was afraid of the disease of the children. So I went out of the night with my forgotten face. And I was learning how to be guilty, how to bear a guilt across an earth-night of curves and surfaces and many other kinds of bitterness. A small bird sang with a sweet morbid note in that raincloud night. I heard it as I kept saying, no, no, Micah, no. I said no. His voice came in thin sharp uglinesses. It was a corroding night. But I held on to my one word, no, no, all through the night that lasted through June and July. No.

XXV(iii)

During the days when Anna and I met in secret I was afraid of the first leaf to appear on the tree. The vault beneath the church sheltered us for an hour, myself and the girl who cried, yelping in her first knowledge of injustice. I watched her, drowsily, my body dragged along by shadows. Then I told her that the fear was only just beginning, that our lives will be spent wading through ice and that our stern custodians may never be defeated. It is hard for people to relinquish the map of the world, I said. Anna could not listen then. She did not believe she would be insulted so often. She kept saying, they must let us be free. She did not listen to me, not for months. Yet finally she had to listen to me and hear my excommunications. She rolled her body in the ashes of valerian. I laid my hands on her shoulders, on her hips. I looked at her through the walls of the allantois, I looked at her with my slimy eye until she lurched away from me. Today she looked slovenly. Outside, the day had tasted blood. She sat down and looked out of the window. She looked at the roofs and chimneys. I moved around the room in a closed curve. I kept picking up rocks and looking at the blowtorches of the flowers. I saw her formal profile. Are you afraid? I said. No, Anna said without looking at me. Then she added, but I intervene at these times between the culprit in me and the daughter. I looked at the stone buried in my hand. Are you my friend, Anna? She turned to me, uncertain of herself, engulfed by her easy sin, and in an earlier version of our familiar language, she, the inheritrix, said, perhaps not . . . And she leant back against the wall and closed her equinoctial eyes. You see, I am relating events that took place in disastrous and melancholy rooms. Anna and myself were lying side by side one winter afternoon, our corresponding legs locked together, and we were struggling to sensitize our hazy and venomous cunts. I rubbed her unfreed genitals with my index finger but she was dry and said it hurt, what I did. She touched me once with hands a little too clean. But we only unbalanced ourselves. She cursed me with a warning cry. Her body was curiously cold to the touch, as if her blood were the oldest and rarest in the world and not that of a young and urgent girl. She dug her fingers into her sjambok body and moaned. Then she snatched up her clothes and left the house without saying a single word. Dogsbane laughter. I heard myself laugh.

I hope, fear and expect the mother of the betrayers to come towards me muttering promiscuously. I am learning how bloodred my memory has become. I am losing my foothold. I move objects secretly from one place to another. I fall accidentally and hurt my back. I am sleepless. I see the deity of the pylon. I watch myself. Woman, lady, wife, mistress, servant, widow, antarctic virgin. The wounds I nourish don't raise the dead. He knows all about them. Micah is unhurt and unfriendly. He calls me a white weapon. He laughs because he knows how Anna will treat me. He says she is obedient only to her real protectors. I risk anger when I say I hear the sound of a dying person's voice. But he does not strike me, he only laughs. I refuse the wine, I go out of the room, I feel mad, crazy, can't hold any thought by its real name, have forgotten words that can never be recollected, my bare feet touch the unpolished wooden floor, the woman who suspects herself of forgotten crimes, I climb the stairs and from the attic window I stare out at the new night with its uninhabitable stars. A million years later he will pick up my skull from the floor of an ice cave.

XXVI(i)

Next morning Micah left for the city. He was afraid of war. I did not share these fears. But I live mostly in the early hours after midnight and have narrow views. He went to the city to talk of peace and memory-training. Afterwards, he planned to go on to the north of the country where he would inspect our new house. He says our present house is dangerously close to the border. He left early in the waterlogged summer. I was alone then. Was able to pass my counterfeit coins. Cliff dancer, my ankle perceives the bird's taciturn claw. Here is my stark victory. June's waters blemish my footprints. Hardfaced spectators watch me, my silk strength wrinkles. Darkness withholds sleep from me. I have stopped dancing and I have come to the season of the long days. Before he left he told me about the battle at the gates of Phnom Penh. I was frightened. He criticised my cold womb. He wants to plant death in my body. I said, no . . . I hoped he would never return. I opened my eyes and what I found in the future zones of my years, as far as I could see, were nomads and fatherless children. I closed my eyes again. May I not speak, may I not smile?

She looked at the dresses I had laid out on my bed. I prefer the blue one, she said. The boat faded away into the mist. There are some years when there is a temporary slackening of time and the last part of autumn reverts to summer, as calm as a scientific study of the moon. During one of these meteorological seasons, I was born. Ten years later there was a winter when I rode on a toboggan, face down to the cold. I had a watch with a luminous dial but I lost it. I was held between two inescapable and overwhelming forces, day and night, mother and father. First I learnt gesture-language, then I learn the emergencies of speech. For a time, I was an invalid. But I didn't practise those rites for more than a year. The lips of dwarf orchids suck at me. I shouldn't have broken into the church, it was wrong of us to violate the sacred place, even with the sorrow of our night words.

Spermaceti years harden and I'm standing in a junk room. Watch the appearance of flowering plants. See the extinction of dinosaurs. In my parents' house, I found glass snakes in the cupboards and I voiced my grievance on the stairs. My mother, faultless as a fallow deer, would not answer me. Why did I make her afraid? Maybe she saw herself taking dangerous steps when she looked at me: she saw what she dare not see.

Anticipating disasters exhausted my strength. Then I was alone, I was sent away to begin my wandering tent-life, out in the wilderness. The empty talk heard at the gasoline station. The requiems of cheap cigarettes. Madness of the supermarket. I have seven days in each week to get through. Alone. I have seven nights to fold over and sew in place.

Alone. He writes me brief letters connecting us by drawing imaginary lines on imaginary maps. He rebukes me for my childlessness on postcards. Pictures of the blue sea. He says the city is cold and exhausting. The people are apathetic. I threw his letters away. I quarrelled with Anna. My days were spent in vigilance, exploring, touching and stretching the world. I learnt very little. I saw Jesus walking through the wet fields one morning. He stumbled hesitatingly. I went to a wedding and threw ice confetti at the puzzled couple. During the days I dressed the wounds of the trees. At other times I slept during the days and worked at night. The werewolf left my house when I discovered his infidelity, he got into his closed carriage, and as a sign of grief for someone's death, I wore black or dark-coloured clothes at least for several days but I did not like those old dark dresses, they smelt of mice, and eventually I burnt them.

XXVI(ii)

Photographs: I smile, I lift my hands forever, I am always a child in a fireproof room, my plaits, my dumbness. And I have photographs of my mother taken before she sailed to her safety island. When I come face to face with these witnesses of my earliest life, I am shaken by contradictions, a meetingplace of rivers in me, the waters of Moon Drove. And I have insufficient proof of my own guilt. I ate the flesh of fossils, I drank contaminated water. Outward ceremonies and rites, I obeyed all the rules the world's war made. I lived silently until my skin turned black. I had been working a long time, my wages unpaid. And so I broke the contract of my apprenticeship, and allowed myself to defy him, to run loose out-of-doors, to revive my memory, to understand the feel of mouth and anus. Doors revolved, the blood in me was less sad, while he was away I did not need to hide in clouds of dust and sand, my climate changed, I controlled the constant trembling of my eyelids. I explore the planisphere land, following the contours of water courses, old roads and paths, examining the ancient earthworks.

In her hand, she holds the map of the two fish. She walks along Cinnamon Lane, towards the ruins of the abbey where death and dark crawl towards the virgin. At night the lapidary girl without fingernails sits in the light of the astral lamp. In the empty house I heard someone playing the piano, the executioner's twin sister. In Micah's absence, I found it hard to throw newspapers away. I resented losing them. I liked their company. For hours I stared in fascination at the words, Doctor has no cure for cancer. Or, funerals become a craze. Or, dry day with sunny spells evidence sought.

Anna telephoned me but I hung up on her. The night before Micah returned, I saw a woman shadow on the stair where no one was standing. I sat in the orchard. He was due to arrive at noon. I was not afraid. I looked at the tree stumps. Where's that imaginary enemy? Riding through a forest of eavesdroppers. The puppeteer plays, acting out the sky's story. I have eaten nothing since yesterday morning. Perhaps he will not return. Perhaps he does not exist. My skin has no sense of responsibility. I picked up a child's toy, a small figure that springs out of a box when the lid is lifted. And frightens me. There are no windows or mirrors outside, only sky. Perhaps he will not return. He may be delayed on some important business in the city. Swallows are swarming over the fields. Who was the girl who drowned herself in the river? No, he'll return. My skin laps me coldly. Because of a ghost giantess with red hair, the army flees, scattering like the birds. When he returns, he will say, why are you not wearing your velvet dress? Or, why do you look so scared? Or, have you yet conceived? He has been away for six weeks. I fear the return of sexual desire. I'd forgotten that I am a begging bowl. I forgot that he will blind me. I'd forgotten his cockpit body's force. I'd forgotten the foetal monster with two faces.

I stood by the calico bush and welcomed him elaborately, just as if I had waited from one midnight to the next, praying for his return. We touched our bodies, kissed faces like leaves. I could not understand his words. But I smiled and nodded. He praised my hair, its fragility. The horizons kept rising up and hitting me. He led me across the courtyard, into the dark house. I smelt his fern seed. Last night the moon was very small. I was the body of the victim-witch whose myth child is the personification of pain. I was being dragged outside the sky. I couldn't speak to him, I could only make throat noises and I don't think he heard me. The hard room was full of the oldest flowers. Before he made love to me, he asked me what I had done with my false face. I said, I burnt it after the festival. It kept smiling at me in the dark like an overlander. I could not see his face because of my thoughts. He touched my tarpaulin skin. He said words gathered from the fields. I told him about my abnormal sleep. He hadn't shaved for several days. When the rock hurler touched me I burnt with wrongdoing. When I touched his penis I knew what my sister had known from birth. I cried. We judged space, I heard table-rapping, our bodies jerked fast, we dislodged our boundaries. Spirituous blood vibrated in us and orgasm reaped me. Then he came, stutterer, fornicator. I undid my stitches. We slept, our phossy jaws wide open.

XXVII(i)

Body colour of the ghost
womb of the arsonist
Dislocated bones
of the tame horses

Phasic, the moon barbs my whiteness. He speaks the language of conquest. He deprives me of both my names. I'd rather live in a convent than in his stockade house. Yet my body catches fire from him, even when he refuses to answer my questions. I heard him coughing in the summerhouse. I am hiding, I conceal myself in the osiery: but even when the host is displayed to me I think of his body which separates earth and sky. I scrub the wooden table and listen to him in the courtyard, talking to the dogs. I resent my need for the name he gave me. I tear up lyme-grass which wounds my hands but I return to him. I think of a star in Ursa Minor.

He came into the room. He picked up the devotional book I'd left open on the table. He adds logs to the fire. He watches me silently. There has been an accident, he says. My dress is white and I am calm. Stefan is dead, he says. I look at him. I am outside the methylated heart. I think hard and cannot work out the puzzle. The root of the embryo aches in me. My brother? I said, half-asleep. Yes, he said contemptuously. Sit down, you're pale, Faustina. News of death, I answer. I sat huddled over my voice. I opened the bible at a different page. I read words that would not stop. I closed the bible. I did not know how to give expression to my grief. I drifted through the laminarian zone, not understanding anything. I looked at the smoke rising from the fire and time moved very slowly. Micah began to eat. My hands could not uncover the mystery or hold off suffocation. The garden was flowerless, lichenic. I remembered the receding of the sea. And Anna? I said. I did not look at him. I touched my hair nervously. Only slight injuries, he said carelessly, she's at her father's house. I was lazy, I couldn't laugh. I only had one womb. I saw no reason to continue with the careful nutrition of my body. Are you going to the funeral? I asked. He looks at me appraisingly. He would throw rocks at a woman's head to win a prize. We will both attend, he said slowly. Now I know he is going to hurt me. He means to change me, to force my bones to break differently. I knew this months ago when I watched him at the killing of a cat. My body was being reborn all the time. My hands searched the death-penalty room but found no blood. I will attend, I said. Knowing I could not pass this trial with long strides, that I will stumble on the ortolan rocks, with no protection against the war gas. The duration of the darkness exceeds that of the light.

XXVII(ii)

Husks of promises on the floor, I shouted at him. I said I was leaving him. He laughs. Yes, I see your fingers are touching the handle of the door, Faustina. I threatened to open the door and let all the carnivorous animals in. The mechanism of our marriage never lets us recover what we have lost. I'll go, I repeated. Go, then, he said. Beyond that door you'll find one hundred towns, shore after shore, roads and bridges, sundials and words that will stop up your mouth like so many death leaves. But you will not open that door, Faustina, for you fear it, that world, even when you boast of its love for you. I gripped the handle of the door tighter. Tighter. Yet I knew I would only open death's door. The nightmare of the stairs changed its colours yet I was never free of it. I was afraid of the dope fiend's charity. Why are you waiting? he said, why do you stare at me?

The motionless girl deserved an evil name. The moonless pear-trees stir through our spurning. Stefan is dead. I wait. I am much-prayed-for, Micah said. Yet am eternally full of anger. Night weeps unexpectedly between us. Red and yellow shadows scratch me and the wooden statue of a god in the alcove watches us. He said to me, yes, I am tired out. Yet he did not touch me. There is nothing secret about Stefan's death, Faustina. The car crashed. He died. We must not put our lives into these harsh words. I am proud of you and I am fastening my future around you. You are made of one solid stone. You hold the door handle but you will not leave our inner room. I'll give you the second prize, the fishing net that is cast over two seas and catches the whole day in its cleansing. One woman lives in flames: sometimes she dances, sometimes she cries: sometimes she tells stories about a child changed into a mountain. The other woman simply gazes at herself in a mirror and is not aware of the thickness of her heart. Both women are you, Faustina.

Micah touches her with his left hand. I saw a dog with a torch in its mouth. I saw a girl vomiting my lost blood. Leviathan hides his face. Sky, foliage, gleanings. I walk towards a closed door, Micah. I am not freed from bone. My hair stretches across the sky, can you see, there, beyond reproach.

XXVIII(i)

I still thought of Anna as a young girl who had been born in the city and played the flute and sang. But when she came into the room with a smooth silent movement and began to tell me about her wedding gifts with such pride, I was worried, I caught a glimpse of Anna smeared with the blood of a hare. Anna, stop, I shouted. She would not. She went on to tell me about the hyperborean flowers Stefan had given her. I mistrusted the colour constituent of delphiniums. Love thrown forward from the hand finally takes a backward direction to the thrower, I said. She bit her nails. No, she said, that is just one of your formulas. I shrugged. We ate our secret supper. Wives of the dead. We watched the exhibition games of baseball on television. The great dog of the Parrett river barked. The giant child moved in me.

I am wearing a dress of thermoluminescence covering my entire body except my face and hands, like the dresses the women wear on their pilgrimage. My hair is braided. I will give gifts to everyone, I said angrily. A cloth for a dead body, warmed with wax. A knife for taking the child out of the body of its mother. A girdle of rope for my neck. Water-legends for my eyelids. Shadowsticks for the fire. Clocks for the priest. Killers for the streets of the city at night. Blisters for the skin of a tide water princess. Thready music for the lonely. Millions of thorns for the tempted. A season of snow-prayer for me. A home in the rock and an unhappy marriage for you. And a wolf for mother. A tunic for my nakedness. A secret listener made of hard heavy wood for the god Micah. Nothing for Stefan. An armistice for the Old Year Ghost. I give gifts, I am the jungle ghost.

Anna is yawning. I must go home now, said Anna, her abstinence a private intoxication. She left me biting the coldness. No, I said, when he questioned me closely, no, I have told no lies, I have no secrets. But I kept brownish summers in an old box. Skin is not speaking the same language between us.

Anchorage of sea birds in the town but there is still our untruthfulness to be reckoned with. Its waters around us. And the dusky garden I was afraid to enter because of the deceits. By the evening I was chilled by the greenness of the trees. His wife never neglected the garden. I rushed on past the people, through the streets, I didn't know how to manage. I am imploring him. No, he says. I must remain here. A hand lies unnoticed on the sheet. Who am I singing to? Be quiet. Don't laugh at such things. Look, there is the bridge. And the umbretted bird wades through dusk towards the true cross. Why are you crying? Please don't. Why do you walk clumsily? Why do you obscure the sun? Why are you devouring all the crops and vegetation for miles around?

Cry, shout, scream
of the unaccompanied girl
sharp reproach

XXVIII(ii)

The year Anna was married, the summer only lasted a few weeks. The beaches were deserted, hands without thumbs, and there were several madnesses on the edge of the cliffs. I did not dare look into the distance for fear of what I would see, the woman crushed under the heavy waves, father lying on the sand, the old man walking past him with his white stick and his black dog. Anna was married, had joined the unreal people, the broken people who blemish the clean sheets. One evening in autumn, I walked back from the beach, up the cliff path, thinking of absurdities, scratching my initials on the sky. I came to Anna's gate and without hesitating went into her garden. The curtains were drawn back from the window and the lights were full on in the room. Anna stood by the window staring out into the night and the bamboo grove. She did not move. Her face was sad and shetlandic. I turned away. I felt the strangeness of my skin hurt me, I ran home, a young woman with her face not yet shaved. I rushed into our courtyard: cats and dogs were everywhere and the dogs barked at me. Years and years itched all over my body. What's wrong, he demanded, coming out of the house, his eyes blurred. Nothing, I murmured, but the street is full of evil reports. I close my door, I lock the door, I shut his country out. Certain voices recur, mine among them. Yes, I hear my own voice, distant, sometimes thin and childish, not often wise. He says I take as long as one day to answer the simplest question. Why did he show me those erotic photographs? My attempt to steal them from him and destroy them was punished severely. I howled inside my gourdy head.

I splash down on to an open map. A haunted castle. Landscaping of summer. The foot of a falcon, the hands of a clock. The marriage of blood and broken glass. I said quietly: wife, child, nurse, cat, rat . . . I construct a pentacle of feathers and leaves. It does not protect me. Faceless, without taint of sin, he touched me. I broke my nails with scratching at the locked door, trying to escape. I resemble a trick photograph. But I sent him away. Yes, I did. Another stopwatch exploded, at midnight. Century child, I named myself. But I will not foretell the future. No, not yet. The ghost climbs out of the moon crater. In a forest like a spider's web, I sang a spider song. My crucifix burned him.

He said, the enemy will bomb the city first. That is a cruel deed, I replied. He went on making punctual calculations in a notebook and paid no more attention to me. I had a photograph of the moon and I studied it carefully. Bright streaks radiated from the largest craters.

The woman watched the rushing waters. She didn't like being alone but there was no one she wanted to have for a friend. Sunshine and rain and the shape of my hands are real, she said. But the time was going and she was becoming more distant and even thinner than before. The testaments are worn out and the strangers will never love you now, not even if you start again. There will be no hedge-marriage, there will be no birth dress. You are crushed beneath the left foot of the figure of Orion. You are being chased by the enemy. You have lost the first bible.

When you get there, don't say anything to her about celibacy or death, he warned me. There was a smell of burnt wood in the air, the sky was the first, the beginning, and I was afraid of the lamps that lit the street. I had to run all the way to the river and even then I might miss her and have failed. The moon was a whorled fossil shell. I ran. I could not de-ice my thoughts. I was afraid I would be too late. I heard the shittim songs from the empty houses. I heard gunfire. I heard my own loud piercing cry. The bride could withstand heat and cold, drought and wetness. I did not stop. The direction of the stair changed, I climbed the windswept stairs like a drunkard, I stared in the shop-windows at the secret preparations of the dummies, the wind blew coldly from the eyelids of the policemen, I ran, I was trying to save time, but the prairie dogs left me behind and I was thin and shrivelled and the wooden walls of the houses brought ruin upon me, handcuffs fastened me to the twenty-fourth letter of the alphabet and what could I do? My mouth twisted to one side and I became a refugee when I realized that I was too late, that Anna had gone home or had not even bothered to come to the meeting place and so I could not give her the winding-sheet as Micah had instructed me. Did you hear my drawling plaintive cry narrower than the newly baptized when they appear in their white garments and hide under their fingernails? I was so unhappy and where had the nuns gone? Off on another of their wild goosechases? They converted me by beating me with willow rods and when I showed signs of distress they laughed and said they held no political office. White silk summer, dispose of me after my death according to my own wishes. Semaphore strong messages with my bones. I wandered wildly and my head was a watchmaker's machine. You must speak in whispers or I can't hear you. I saw a man with a nose and two eyes but no mouth and he wore knuckledusters and he thought he knew everything until he got inside my vagina. Melancholy mistakes. I reproved the animals of the water. I saw you, I saw the tracheal rings on your hand, Anna, I watched you stand in the shadows as if the darkness had been set apart for this purpose. As I watched you the sun entered January and the ground trembled beneath my feet. You did not see me at first. You did not see anyone. The married woman is already in debt. You would not confess your crime nor reveal the identity of your accomplice. My moonlit fingers smelt of your flesh still. I was afraid to test your new purity. Your dress is much too near catastrophe. Last night I was brave enough to say cruel words to you. But now I cannot. His wife is also a dwarf, Micah said. He sounded cocksure, as usual. The rumours soon spread of course, he added. I ignored him. I knew his deceptions. I saw a phrenological map of my head. But Anna is staring at the flowers and for her they resemble illiteracy. I heard the synchronized shifting of your heart, I sensed its remote location. Then you looked up, aware of the outcome of your thoughts, re-entering the day. You spoke to me with half the power of your voice. But I heard you with incredulity. I'd forgotten you could sound like cold hands. I went away at once, without answering, it was terrible, I went away slipping between the crowds of slaughtered people. I crossed each visual threshold quickly. I was walking along a cinder track.

XXVIII(iii)

Why did you speak to me in that Frankish language, oh Anna, the months surrounded me with fires when I saw you overgrown with flesh and I could not even find or touch your left hand. Am I the narcotic wife? Why am I smudging myself with questions? Everyone tells lies.

She brushed her hair and looked out of the window. A little girlchild with hushed eyes stared back at her, a burnt moon in her hands. I am looking for the nest of the oriole in old pastures, the little girl whispers. Faustina turns away from the window and clouts the mirrors. Her skyblue birthmarks take no notice. In the clear air of megalithic times, a pause in the singing. I relax out of my trance. I stop collecting electricity from the croonings of the sky. I open my eyes and look at the stillborn man. I visualize my movements were I to turn and run, passing away from him like smoke, furlongs up into the sky. But I did not move until he took my hand and led me up the stone steps. In spite of your beggar lice, he is saying, I am fond of you. I will accept your dishonoured state. I said, am I taller than my sister? He says, why are you neglecting the old year? I whispered my tribe-name to myself and waited for the metamorphosis. I saw the toothed birds flying towards the volcano. Come with me, he said and pulled me after him. He said I was thankless. I saw that man we were talking about yesterday, I said, trying to be friendly. He was silent. I was worn out, my breasts heavy as the thunder. Don't be angry at what I did, I pleaded. He would not answer. I began to cry. I sent a radar signal to the moon and heard its echo but no one believed me. The war criminals ate chocolate. Why am I afraid of a handful of unthreshed corn?

Lithodendron voice: I spoke to the doors and the windows of my embroidress body. The answer frightened me even more than the question. The disease is transmitted by copulation.

XXIX(i)

She is feeding the birds with her chronicles of days, hours, minutes and seconds. I am not making mistakes, Faustina tells herself, I am being very careful. I can explain everything. Whatever I am accused of, I can explain. See, my body is hidden behind the windbreak trees. I am timing myself by the clockwork mirror. The removal of the foetus is a simple matter. I reach into my womb with a chisel, I find the blood and bribe the ghost to rise up out of my grave. Is this habit-forming? No, it cannot be, I don't believe it.

Now here is the death of the first spouse. She screams, the womb earthquake is killing her. She cannot stop shouting. This is worse than my early childhood. I vomit a bird's wattle and the ear lobes of an infant. Blood comes out of my body to curse me, blood smelling of islands. He stood by her bed. I am not Faustina, she moans. I am not that woman, no. It is just that I bear a close likeness to her. But I am an impostor. I am not Faustina. I did not try to kill her unborn child. I did not try to get rid of it. I live in the expectation of more cold weather. The dead prevent me from eating. I had sunstroke, that is all. A shadow was cast on me by the sun and by the moon. A central fire is burning far out of sky sight and causes eclipses in me. She talked very loud and said god forgive me when she had the fever. Not clockwork, moans Faustina. No firearms in the garden. No blood. No osteopath kiss. No. I climb the sea stair. I have no plans. I am falling . . .

Stefan and Micah exchange opinions. Her child has been saved, says Micah, we will not punish Faustina. There need be no punishment. It was her thoughtlessness. She did not know the peril. Stefan looks at Faustina doubtfully. She counts the revolutions of the fever wheel, she marches back and forth over the same ground, executing countermarches, falling, falling. Stefan looks at her. He made accusations. Medieval threats. He says that a lameness should be performed on Faustina. He wants to reduce his sister's night illumination. She is evil, he said. Why should we cleanse her? No, said Micah, she is not evil, she is subject to depressions, she hates weddings and afternoons in the garden, she finds herself in strange places pouring libations for the dead. Punish her! Stefan repeated, prevent her from hating us, prevent her from hatching her memories. Stefan moved towards the sick woman, emitting a fetid odour, but Micah stood in his way, barring the advance. Leave this room, he said calmly, leave me with my wife. Micah is ready to put Stefan in bondage. The men clash in the room, illegitimate sons, the one subarctic, the other an electric dreamer.

No moons, sighs Faustina. Who else has closed their eyes? she asks from the brink of her delirium, her old and little-used fever. With wards of anger, Stefan moves sullenly away. His defeat leaves him with only stilted movements. Free your slave, Micah, he sneers. Then he closes the door. He has already arranged a meeting with Anna's father. The motor muscles of his fingers go haunting the boulevards. He is providing himself with alibis.

Micah leans over his wife. There are no signposts for her saprophytic body. I cannot enforce makeshift judgements, he thinks, preparing to remain awake all night even if his thoughts do get twisted up together and the distance between objects becomes uncertain. Why should I ask you to explain your failures to me, Faustina? Why should you accept me and bear my child? Just because we have built a landscape around you, must you admire it? He strokes her damp hair. She is sleeping now. This is a night supposedly for tears. She will recover . . . Micah tries to pierce the obscurity of her body. He remembers how she has moved slowly these last few weeks, heavy under her burden. He kneels by the bed, he prays she will return to him from the region of unintelligible games of sorrow. There are never many people in the darkness, he murmurs. She is still the one walking along the path of no-time. She is looking at a shoe, a lock of hair, her own soiled underclothes. She is listening to declarations of war. She is watching the elm trees die. She is riding a forgetful horse. She is dancing the marsupial dance. Night takes care of all her forests. Micah watches her. Holding on to his bare and splintered information.

In the morning she lifted her head, she felt sick but not hopeless. The child is safe, he told her. She nodded, she could identify him and the room, she forgives her enemies, soon she will try to crawl on all fours, she stretches out her arm now, moves her stiff fingers fumblingly, he takes her hand, they go back to the beginning and start again.

XXIX(ii)

Photographs of prisoners standing in the snow. In the early winter of my twentieth year, I edge towards the girl I have seen in the distance. She is called Anna. She still remembers her first prayers. She practises her laments by mourning over dead birds she found on the hillside. Her laments are of a treasured reticence. Her hair is a misinterpreted shade of brown. She has never been flogged. She wears dark glasses. Sometimes she walks past our house. The cold moves in her unspoken throat. She lifts her legs uncertainly, conscious of her negligence regarding her own body. Once I saw she must have been hurt in the hand, because of the bandage. She is hovering between hope and fear. I will not speak to her yet. But the hands of two people will rest upon a hurricane. I will not speak to her now because she doesn't even want to wake up yet, let alone listen to my words that exceed the height of a man. But when the weather has broken, I will loiter around her house, half looking in the windows. When she comes out to go shopping, I will follow her, making a clacking sound on the pavement with my leather heels and we'll begin to talk. We will soon reach the absorption area and the sacrament will let us bathe in the waters of its vulnerable ocean.

I have three white bibles and three white prayer books. Bibles are carried by many brides and bridesmaids at church weddings nowadays. I also have a strange black bible from which I hear the sound of downcast thunder. But I do not read any of my bibles for I discovered that the words went too fast for me and the colours changed every time I drew a breath and I shivered and raised my shoulders momentarily in a gesture of indifference and closed the book forever. But I keep my bibles in a safe place, to avoid confusion. I could not understand the windstorm of the parables. I forgot the commandments when I walked into the swarthiness of my own thoughts.

Kisses in honour of the bride and I move towards her, stealthily to avoid observation. I mail a letter to the scraggy moon. I said to Anna, you wore the elephantiasis dress the day we quarrelled about the presence of the holy ghost, do you remember? No, I do not! she said emphatically, flouncing away through the prehistoric flowers. The three days of my vomiting smelt of gipsy slang, on those days the clocks' hands went backwards, hailstones shaped like skulls fell and he said, I can't set those words to music, Faustina . . .

I opened my mouth and vomited my firstborn, the lake-dweller. I saw a white sparrow voyaging within the thin sheets of its bone. I walked slowly. Then there was a heavy dragging pain. I had painted my eyelids to make myself look stronger but my mirror showed me a child beggar. I concealed Sirius in my closed hand. I saw the skeletons of apple leaves. Winter shears me of my fetishes. Whisper your marriages in my ear. Are you crazy? I know the place where thrushes breed. This morning is the size of half a finger, my eyelids will keep the rain off, the girls of the white islands have sent me medicines, today I am deformed by my shameless adulation of the reigning tyrant and my obscene and licentious expressions. Do you think I'm blind? I shouted. It rained all day, the day after my confinement and I smelt of shotten milk and I had nothing to worry about.

XXIX(iii)

He calls me Faustina, a name to kill weeds growing among grain, a name legendary as war-butchery on the sea coast. I open my mouth in laziness, the quail-mother is migrating, the aviary is empty, kiss my little mouth of bone, quickly, I sing the eggshell song but I cannot forget my name, the bird-wing name. Faustina, he calls me. Why? I wear shoes of rainwater. I whisper instructions in the ear of the dying. I add salt to the soup. I tie my horse to a tree. I note the date of his departure. Do not let yourself get cold, he said to me. I saw the ghost moon of the late winter and the early spring, the colour of vetch. I say my onion-scented name. Faustina, Faustina. My name casts a shadow. He is running in a lifetime race. I do not know why he takes part in this contest. He tells me I am not capable of understanding his body's awareness, his scrupulous regard for death. But I move when touched. I am voicing my shrill call near the ponds and the swamps.

Who telephoned you? I asked him. Everything he touched became taboo. He looked at me, doubting his inhabitancy of his house. It was Anna, he said casually. He laughed. The childbearing night echoes. What did she want? I ask suspiciously. Through distances white as the bride's outfit, I followed him about the downstair rooms. She said nothing important, he said, no message for you, no. Leave off asking me. Okay, I said. He left me with the poverty of some potential danger. I am Faustina, I whisper, I am Faustina. I walked up the slow-flying stairs. I hated his house. More than half the rooms were unfurnished and dusty. Some doors were locked and never unlocked. When I opened the other doors I expected to find observers in their emptiness. They resounded with the static of silence. I was afraid of treading on the excreta of animals.

And now there is no colour sensation in me even though I am lying down next to Anna. I am bored. I have written the wrong address on the envelope. She does not move. Her eyes are closed. I can see her wooden slippers on the floor. I see an empty glass jar on the shelf, its lid missing. I see the daylight room in which the aviators are training. I am easygoing, I am indifferent to her moods. My body is pressed between two sheets of glass. I speak to her. But she is unwilling to answer. As I speak to her again, I touch her clitoris. She turns her face to me, shiny and clean and shrewd. She sees no difficulties. There's no one around, she said. Do this in remembrance of me. She stretched her body out, opening her legs to show the sagebrush. The stones skip along the surface of the water. I touch her unventilated sex, manipulating her without a false step, using my stumpy fingers. She crumples her new dress in her hands, she lifts her knees, raises herself, seduces herself, comes so hard that she forgot the meaning of it and was exhausted. She slept. I washed my hands. I cannot see her today. Cannot see her as anyone but a stranger. Last month I would have stretched out beside her and begun the whispers of my own orgasm. But now I feel no desire, am in a hazy room, look at her tailless body, her shabby youth . . . I see nothing of interest in her this afternoon. I am experiencing the isolation of a virus. I look at Anna's weekend mouth and I say no, no crime has been committed. I move quickly, dressing myself rapidly. If you aren't careful . . . I thought. I knocked my bare foot against a chair and swore. Then I held my breath in case she woke up. But she only sighed into her antiwar hair. I wrote her a message on the tornout cover of a book, short unkind sentences, and left it under the ashtray. I opened the door quietly and went out into the street and I could smell the odour of burnt rice. I am always cruel in the afternoon.

XXX(i)

I sent a questionnaire to a haunted house once, to bring me good luck. I looked up at the sky, I felt the calm dead wind move down the street. To put it briefly, I was defeated. And I did not know why. I walked across the road to the church. I did not expect to see you here, he said, speaking through partly closed lips. Hesitatingly I answered, I was looking for you, Micah. We stood in the porch, sheltering from the rain. He looked at me with the forensic suspicion of a herbalist.

There was a call from Stefan, he phoned, he thought you had not received his letter. Micah opened the church door. This is how men try to frighten women, I thought. Your hands are clammy, he said. Side by side we faced the rose window. It was easier to tell him lies here in the dimness. I walked away from him while he was praying and went to look at the great bible on the lectern. I read words I couldn't understand. Nothing changed. I received two messages I couldn't comprehend. I lifted my eyes to the church. I saw rows of empty pews. He stood in front of me. I was afraid, wanted to crouch down ready to leap at his throat. I heard the sighing of blood donors. Did Stefan send any word? he asked. I looked at the bible. Stars in the sky shone, dead ends, blind alleys. I stared hard at Micah. Yes, he did. My voice echoed in the church, I had a war strength. He motioned me down from the lectern. He took me by the shoulders. His fingers gripped me very hard, bit into my flesh.

Who brought these two people together? On what night? May I introduce you to my mother? She is very thick-skinned, you may speak freely.

He stares at his wife. Don't take that road, Faustina, he said. Let me go, she said, wriggling free. He pinned her body against the door, he crushed the snake's head with a rock. I've done nothing wrong, she claims, it is all the truth . . . She speaks calmly. If you are lying, he says, I will sell all your shoes. I am telling the truth, Micah. He watches me steadily. I almost break. But then he opens the door. We walk out into the rain. At the end of January, he says, we are moving to the new house. But I don't know the name of the year. The child touches the earth for the first time and rebels against the kidnapping mother. I am walking with Micah into our first house where the treaties are signed, where the red flag always flies its warning, where I read my unsigned letters crouching on my hands and knees and look out at the tonsure world. The house I see blurred by twilight . . .

We eat our supper in silence. Is that a face at the window? Or is it a miscalculating shadow? The mountain's joke? I spoke to him in Anna's voice and he flinched. Bastard. Snarly photographs of ghosts will punish you. He prizes a hawk of the first year more highly than his wife.

The lady wiped the grass stain on her white skirt with her hand but she could not erase the mark. She walks on. She is very thin. I watch her walk under the sluggish red trees of autumn. She feels her way towards the sky. I watch her. I am thirsty. I mutter obscene expressions dating from my childhood.

What did you say? His voice, sharp, illusionless. The lady is dumb, her shadow is fatal to mice. But I must attempt to answer my husband, I must face him and explain what causes the dilation of my pupils when I look at him. I hear the humming of bees, the roar of a lion in a zoo, the bellow of trumpets, the song of ice. No, I am afraid to say anything to Micah. I run across the road, I run along the river bank, I am running in memory of a woman who has disappeared without trace, not even stopping to gaze over her shoulder.

XXX(ii)

Anna closed the window shutter. The light from the lamp is poor, it deludes us. She turns, she looks at me. She is wearing dark funeral clothes, grey shawl. I note the outward signs of grief, dress and gesture. He is dead, I say, not mentioning the separation between us. The wife nods, unaware of her murder. Thorns in the private places. Yes, there has been a breaching of the loins. The car skidded, she said, the road was dangerous, I kept asking him to slow down. I offer her a glass of water. She drank, gulping. I told her about the shells I found on the beach. I tell her she can have them. But she said, look at my bruises, see, where I was thrown right out of the car, my face could have been cut to pieces. She pulled up her sleeves and then unfastened her dress with fingers of extreme frugality. She showed me the great ferreous bruises on her back and shoulders. Look, she said, come here. She was watchful, edging towards my crowbar silence. I was tired, I could hear only what was spoken to me, I could not refuse her. She took my hand and pressed it against her cloudburst mouth, I felt myself falling downstairs, I wanted to speak hard words but I was afraid of the highways overshadowing me and I just let myself float within my own undesired blood. Like a dancer making pantomimic gestures she bent her body against mine, grasped my wrists and ankles, made our harlequin bones strong enough to survive the winter, driving file on before her. The widow rubbed her cunt with fine sand. It was easy for me to lay a finger lightly on the correct place, despite the clots of blood. Then she pretended to fall asleep. Outside on the verandah, I spoke to my own body. Why are you eating dry stalks? The sky's fertility scorches you. You are standing at another midnight. Your hands won't turn to leaves. You will become weighed down with years and will continue to stare at the bird-wings but still have no knowledge, your hand always held out empty, afraid of hoodlums.

XXX(iii)

What happened in that room? I can't remember. Yes, you can remember. You won't get out of it that easily. Tell me. I do remember then. I remember slattern fingers. Now the blackmarketeer is unwrapping his new corpse. When Micah shouts at me, I am ice, understanding nothing. He is planning to occupy the summer by composing an epic poem on the subject of the first world war.

She walks all day between thin and hungry-looking trees. The whispering of the leaves is like the handwriting of a very ancient woman. Faustina is crying without tears. If hundreds of dead birds were to fall from the sky, she would not notice. Micah's strength is increasing. All his salutations depress me. He asks questions that wound my hands and feet. I cannot hold out much longer. My arms ache with the weight of my own blindness. Two men lie dead in a field. Faustina does not notice them. She chews earth. She is the recidivist, burning her flesh not with words or songs but with silences that he drags out into the open. She cannot escape his attention. He measures distances across the sky and she is trapped. She walks across the saltwater meadows. He is watching her, hidden by the stumps of trees. He is not touched by fire. She walks towards the sea and men drown. She turns inland and exhausts the flowers. He observes her as she rushes from beach to cliffpath to tree to river but he does not approach her, he lets her choose her own hiding places and the nature of her own fears.

Some mornings when I wake I know what weather the day will bring because although it is dark I hear the foghorns. Then I know that when light breaks I will see misty fields and dripping trees and clouded animals, the rain blowing in from the sea. On these days I do not leave the house. I do not answer the telephone. I do not leave my own room. I sit by the window and the mirrors huddle around me. My hands are heavier than falcons, and my hair, tightly bound in awkward plaits, makes my head ache. The damp house smells like his words to me when he is trying to hurt me. Yet sometimes he looks at me uneasily, afraid, a pale robber. And I cry, fitfully.

In the garden she let the man cut off her left breast. She gave it to him for safekeeping. He saw beyond the sacrifice.

She smiles, she swishes her horse tail. Her new breast sprouted, the nipple like a brilliant blue night. Their bodies are living at the bottom of the sea, their skins are standing in the rain. Who's going to stop me? he said and they both laughed. The spider crawled over her child's shaved head. But the photograph did not turn out well. She refastens her hood. The window is opened. She will deny all the accusations. She whispers to him. He smells theological smoke. He pretends to be unaware of his danger.

XXXI(i)

The rusty door squeaked. Anna came out into the garden. What are you doing? she asks, smiling, then, looking from one to the other, feels awkward, sensing the threat of starvation, afraid of their secrecy. Stefan and Faustina stare at the haphazard girl. She is afraid of their bluish-white rain shadows. Their dented faces tell her she is walking on the wrong side of the road. But she repeats tensely, what were you talking about, Stefan? He does not answer. He and Faustina go on staring at Anna until they reduce her to the skeleton of a burned girl. She can't stand it. She cries out. Why are you both against me? She goes away, ashamed. She begins to weep, to take risks. Faustina turns to Stefan, frightened and angry. Anna has made a mistake, she says bitterly. Leave her, said Stefan. He took Anna away that evening.

I looked out of the window and tried to gauge the acoustical source of the rain. I listened, but I couldn't quite hear the answer, the noise of the hovercraft kept breaking in on my concentration. I touched the pine tree with my forefinger. Rain dripped from the fringe of my hair on to my face. My body is designed to deceive, do not worry. Sometimes I take up a slightly different position, to observe the chasm more closely, but my obedience cannot be queried. Do not cut out my tongue, please. I am afraid of the travellers who stop at the house. I am afraid to hear what they have seen along that road, the glare and dust. Later, he was murdered . . . I am afraid. That is Micah's power. This morning he said to me, the guilty heart outtells its innermost thoughts. But I was afraid to laugh at him. I submerge my hair in waters. I wash my body free of gangrene. I write my name on the front cover of books. The white dog licks my hand. Your legs were bleeding. I did not know why. I have not swum in deep marine waters. He says, Faustina, you resist suggestions and commands. I do not know. I laugh during the recitation of the rosary, I admit it, I cannot help it. Because the silent movement of the cold lips frightens me.

At the celebrations for Anna's wedding, we wore masks. Mine was black, a private expression of discontent. I saw multiple stars in the sky. During one single year I was born, lived and died. The salamanders crawled over the stairs. I complained about this but no one listened. On the faces of the poisoners, I see crazy ideas, like colours bereft of blood. Songs for the dead, a crying-out, the tongue like a red rat snake. I see the insect behind his brain. I tripped on the bottom step, the humming birds measure the activities of my body when I am asleep.

That afternoon out on the edge of the marshes, among the tree stumps and the underbrush, after Anna had run off, I saw only children and ramblers. I did not look at their sightless eyes. They possessed the world. They moved noisily, glinting against my darkness, telling one another jokes and laughing, always laughing laughing laughing . . . As I walk between them, I feel old and ugly. I move swiftly through the fog until I cannot hear them any more. I know my way, I will not stray into the peatbog. Haggard birds fly overhead. Gone away, they shrieked, gone away. I said, I loved my mnemonic doll. I remembered the whiteness of the negro. I hope the women are looking after my son properly. I don't want him fed on carcasses. I don't want him killed by the cold. At his baptism, the sponsors blamed me for his hunger. I knew they were jealous. You got the worst of the bargain, I shouted. You, with your hollow horns. But the gulfweed dragged me down, drowning me in icy water. It was Anna who told me that flowers were hermaphroditic. I wanted to turn our house into a forest. But he swept the leaves out of the doorway. I studied the veins of my breasts and they warned me of the conception and birth of my second son. My mirror flies away, a shiny bird.

Faustina, he said. We were standing outside in the yard, beside a low pile of unburnt bricks. Out along the seacoast the fogbranches still hung massive. Trails of mist crept inland to us, darkening his triumph. I shivered but he would not let me return to the house. We were wearing winter clothes suitable to our way of life but I was still cold. I have to feed the baby, I said, let me go . . . He held my wrists. Dark cracks appeared in the sky. You have made a mistake in the date, I said, I have an alibi. He said words backwards. You must tell me, he protested. Why won't you look any further than the leaves of diseased plants? Any further than the hour of the bird's beak? Why won't you look at me? Is it true that you believe I am insensible, a sort of mechanical doll? He was asking me windswept questions. I hated the violence and suddenness of his move towards my horizon. I wouldn't answer unless he desalinated his words. I had no protection against illegal imprisonment but I had my silence. I hide from him in my mud room. Down the wet stairs I go, memorizing the fauna of the region, down past the barns and clays of the lowlands, down past the chalk beneath the hills. I go down into the mud room and he cannot find me. He does not even know how to become a winter visitor. I hear his voice calling me, in the distance, sometimes quite close but never close enough, Faustina, he shouts, his voice shearing the waves of the sky. But none of his mimicry will bring me out of hiding. I know the working of his traps. Did he ever shelter me from the cold? I stay warm in my earth room until it is safe to emerge and watch the birds and count them as they pass across the face of the moon. He never mentions these victories of mine. He regards me as capable of transmitting malaria by a single word. No, I would just wash away his sin. I carry ice-worn pieces of rock in my pockets. I stood on the railway bank and held a winding staircase in my hand.

Anna brings me dead leaves and maggots. I push her away and stare at the remains of the square arable fields ploughed by the primitive early settlers. I watch Anna climb an almost lifeless tree with a very thick trunk. She sits on a low-hanging branch and looks at me. I remembered that today the men would be burning the moorland. Anna and I walked across the mudflats, wading through the intertidal plains. The silence of Anna and Faustina is famous for its humidity. Our bare feet sink into the mud at each step and we have to pull our feet up with some effort to take the next step. Therefore we advance slowly. We are disgracing our shadows. Our clothes are old and worn out. There was frost last night, I say. She turns away from me in dislike, shaking her long sleeves to get free of me. I was tired of the sable skin of my heart. I had not wanted to leave the clinker-built house in which I had been born and had lived for so many years. I had not wanted to marry Micah. I had lost too much. I refused to let Anna escape. I held her by the shoulders, I shouted at her, I told her all her faults, difficult yellow words. She stared at the sky, just to irritate me. I pulled her towards me by the hair and kissed her, her body felt like a summer insect flying into the fire. I pinched her nipple and felt her sweating with pleasure. She pushed me away a moment too late, she was shaking, there is nothing god cannot see, she told me. I looked at the sticky hands of the messenger. Don't let him know, I said, or he'll tell everyone as soon as he learns the language of the region. Anna did not laugh. Your shadow is so thin, Faustina. The words of the younger girl are unanswerable. She lives sideways. I smelt the prejudice of the mud and I tried to express my grief. Between us we shall succeed, I promised. Anna rides a horse the colour of a deer. She takes Faustina in her embrace, to counteract the poison.

XXXI(ii)

Wilderness of rain
Secrecy of drowned sailors
Fifty words for daylight
The daughter burns the night letter
Grass-quit birds unsettle the sky

Horses stand motionless in the field. The rain falls. She lives hand to mouth. The doors all close behind her. Faustina is the river's eyewitness. She is casting off her skin. I will kill his child and feed it to him, she says. Her own face reflected in the other women hurts her eyes. Stefan writes me letters, tells me of bad weather, birds of prey, his inheritance. Words like brain fleas. In the toyroom Faustina can hardly stand upright. She decapitates her dolls. Her abscess has come to its bursting point. She looks doubtfully at her bandaged elbow. The throbbing of her arm makes her face ashen. Played from memory, learned by ear.

Downstairs, far down floors below her, in a hazy room, Anna is playing the piano. Faustina is waiting for the music to become untrue. Her reddish brown hair is subject to ridicule. She glues her thoughts together. This is a complicated hour. Risks are to be taken. She stamps on the trick handgrenade and flinches because there is no explosion. Downstairs the piano is silent. A door opens, closes. Flashes of light are seen near the horizon, reflections of more distant summer lightning. When the reverberation time has finished, Faustina leaves her toyroom, locks the door, smiling to herself, depriving herself of her prison, and carries the key downstairs. She meets no one on the stairs, not even women of the seventeenth or eighteenth century. No one reveals a face to her as she goes from room to room. Her abstinence from timepieces gives her strength. She opens another door and steps out into the garden. Her hoop skirt distends around her. The prevailing fashion. She smells in the odour of the flowers her own stay of execution. The sex moon is creeping across the sky as usual. Faustina plants her key in the earth, among the rosetrees. Dirt and grit get under her fingernails. He will like to see such dirty hardworking hands. She giggles. She returns to the house, singing a requiem for the imaginary tiger.

You can see from this photograph how much I have changed, I said. Yes, he replied, now you have lost the taciturnity I see here in your body. I smiled, from habit. I scratched the sole of my left foot. The room got darker, we kept on tossing the coins. Mother, father, was it easy to send me away with Stefan that night, send away your pinioned and white-hooded daughter? My bones numbered, my hair dammed up into that hood, my hands cold and uninstructed. When the door opened, the night was there, flames roared, waters rushed, I cried aloud, sister . . . Nine years ago, my sister left me. Now I go. My skull changes colour. I wear clothes stripped from dead bodies. I was not aware of my body, my hands or my hair, the way I moved, until he demonstrated to me the existence of extreme grief. Kissing the sea and riding the funeral horse, setting a trap for Anna: these escapes have not worked. My walls are hung all around with mirrors to avoid bad luck.

He said nothing when he was told of the violent death of his mother. He looked up at the sky where he saw a bird like a heron and heard its booming cry. He spent the night in the open, without even a tent, not even a coat, lying on the soft damp ill-fated earth. But why should I tell tales about him? Who knows what a man's life feels like, the white-flowered trees conflicting with the misinterpreted pain when he cannot escape from his body? I hated it when he spoke in the language of lawyers and augury and I disliked our visits to that half-built city, where brick-dust flew in my eyes and on every street I witnessed the unreality of sons expelled from their fathers' house and deceived daughters wandering, losing their way, shivering in their threadbare green cloaks and staring at me with undecipherable eyes. When he noticed me watching them as they loitered outside the stations or the public lavatories, he said, you are lucky, aren't you? Then he took me by the arm and we went down the occultation of those streets.

XXXI(iii)

Where do you live? she asks. Anna's first words to me. She spoke slowly, always aware of the revival of memory. I answered her with lies that afternoon. I explained my difficulties. She smiles consolingly. I am not really cheating her . . . She understands my words. She has her legends. It is unkind of him not to let you have any friends, she says. Now I speak rapidly of the embryo and of the storms of overactive blood. We walked along the afternoon road, dodging the reprimands and the potholes. The soldiers hailed us, waved to us. We laughed. Anna did not suspect then that my mode of living was to steal from others, either openly or furtively. She walked on and did not think of perpetual silence as a means of tricking people.

From January to March the fertilized female cursed. Lock the bride's father in the grey room, lock the door, leave him there. Summer touches the lobe of my brain and hurts. I am bareheaded. I have located the seeds that make me smell like a decaying tree. My troubled expression does not make him unhappy. Look at the pallor of my skin, I said. He said, place a piece of agate or jet upon a heated axe-head and it will move in the direction of the guilty person. Humiliated by the tides of his braying sea, I touched my bones silently. I am holding the candle of the battlefield. I see the ghost of the pretarsus.

Down the steps I go, it is too dark to see the outlines of the steps, but I am not afraid. Anna moves against the profile of the night, within the apprehensive hour. Her heart is thin as a hair and the anticipation of her throat frightens me. She is becoming an edgy heretic. My footsteps echo angrily as I approach our meeting place. She is waiting for me in the doorway. Her arms hold me and she stops my mouth with her tongue, my reservoir of blood splashes against her blouse, rain or snow falls on us, I hear the rapping of the icy spirit atmosphere, her darkish mouth is still hard on mine, she stops the bleeding . . . Our shadowgraph hands clutch at sexual answers but the innumerable small stars of the night deceive us, I tried to sleep, she sat by the window smoking, I was fettered by her restlessness and I feared the figure of the horseman. The poor children of the village follow me through the streets. Already their cries of disappointment are adult, already they play unfriendly games. I turn, I shout abuse at them, they hover, dirty and hard-faced, then they run, laughing, jeering and swearing at a woman infamous for her crimes.

XXXII(i)

I cannot forget the beehive womb. I have not chosen this place. Mechanical words in dark rooms, that is my marriage. Stefan's hand was very cold. I stared at him awkwardly. We stood on the corner of the street. His hand on mine and his warnings upset me. He said, hesitancy won't protect you much longer, Faustina. I bump into his words. I pull my hand free. I turned away from him, I looked at a tree with yellow hanging flowers like waste silk. Do you understand what I said? he repeats angrily. I do not yield. I am laughing. Why call me Faustina? I ask. Why do you call me by that name? You know my old name. Call me by my old name. Don't be ashamed. But now he looks embarrassed, is afraid someone will notice us. As he walked away, I called out after him, go play marbles with Micah. My lips were dry. I saw the lace lizard on top of the wall. The sun shone but I was still cold where Stefan had touched me, and I couldn't get warm. I ate sea-fennel, the smell of wine sickened me, I could not stay forever in the place where the tide comes crying, I had to return to the house, going back along the same raw path. I saw the spittle-like secretion on the plants. I saw the crystalline minerals of the earth. I counted my buttons and ribbons and needles. It was hard to have to watch him cut down the trees, harder to watch him with the young hawks in the hackhouse. Taunting me. Which fist holds the white chessman? I make charcoal marks on the floor. The child is with his nurse. Fat globules of rain run down the window. Despite the rain, the dirty children are still playing in the courtyard. I know that down in the village a noisy mongrel crowd is swarming around the market stalls. No, I cannot be bothered to go out again. I rest on my bramble bed. I heard the child crying along the passageway. I closed my eyes. I'd eaten nothing since early morning, I felt sick, ignored even by the grazing animals. He will come to me tonight, searching for a sexual partner, I already hear his late cry of pleasure. What about my stridulating song? I am silent. I hear the necessary rain. I feed on thistles. We have lived in this new house for two seasons. I have seen ghost larvae and, on autumnal mornings, webs of spiders alive with their extinctions. This house resembles the old house in many ways, the same slate stone roof, the same cruel windows. It is a little larger, colder, barer. Some of the falconer's escaped birds have bred up in the highlands, he said, we must go after them. But when I go walking here, I follow the footprints of the deer and touch snow in summer. He smiled at her with his dog mouth but his eyes were in a coma, shadowed . . .

Seaweed girl suckles a nun's child. She sings a fanatic lullaby. Candle shadows caper against incarcerating walls. The door opens. The astronaut's widow reclaims the child, the sea, the song. Man resting in sun watched by shut-hearted woman. Departure in her eyes. A handful of earth in his left hand. Small bones plaited into her hair. I half close my eyes. I go on journeys through the pre-alphabetic earth. Trials of the children. I throw a stone through the window. Your white skull and the rush-leaved daffodils make a note of my war-mongering. He talks to me, a repetition of metal words. He says I panic too easily. Sea islands the colour of dry grapes . . . The failure of the blackbird cries in the cold weirwater sky. I hear the skin of her face tighten. No, I did not try to kill the unborn child, it was the bad air I breathed when I was near the marshes, it made me sick, I did not reach into my body with the cat's cry, I did not . . . The child sleeps, a thousand years old. I watch him, my unwanted son. I am expressionless, Micah says, charging me with my crime. But I hold photographic replicas of my emotions. My knifeless hands touch your unyielding smile. I stay within doors. That humpbacked sun does not trust me.

> *Time moist as blood*
> *moves years from place to place*

until some penance is accomplished
I am still festering.
returning to the moments and their sequels

XXXII(ii)

Anna dashed into the courtyard with her dress torn, her hair the colour of crotchwood. She came straight towards me, her arms stretched out like a crucified person, half-choking, a false membrane in her throat. I watched her. I couldn't say anything. I knew too many fullgrown secrets. Micah had already told me and the right and left sides of my heart were completely divided. All the necklaces Anna wore around her neck jangled, the glass beads like insects undergoing a bright decomposition. She moved swaying and moaning. I shouted at her, go away, don't come near me . . . She shrieked, merciless, grim, and grabbed the necklaces, pulling them as she shouted her instantaneous snares. The baubles flew everywhere, colours of bereavement and frustration. The flowers I had just picked looked decrepit. I wanted her to speak gently, quietly, so I could understand her, but she would not. I told her I was ill but she took no notice. Oh, she cries, there is no place on my body not bruised or broken or inflamed. I stepped away from her, the glass beads crackling under my feet. Pleadingly Anna said, I can't marry Stefan, I cannot, Faustina, help me. She grabbed my arm. She was deadly. I felt sick, I was unacquainted with this woman. Her voice oppressed, quenched, extinguished me, the child trapped inside me shifted fretfully and I felt my body go damp. Anna, no, I said, I can't help you any more, I am lost to myself now, I've forgotten everything, I have been broken down into simple substances, I sleep in a deception bed, you are frightening me, I feel harmful radiation exuding from you, please, oh please, please, go away . . . I began to cry. She stared at me. Then she screamed, you cheat, you bitch . . .

The sky kept swaying back and forth, the sun, I heard Anna scream the sun down, it fell on me, it set me on fire, I couldn't bear her interrogations and insistings and I feared for my own safety. The dark came and I lost the morning. Stepping-stones led me away across the hours. Micah was supporting me, I was sitting up in bed. He said, you have an archaic sense of danger, and smiled. My head had stopped plotting against me and I breathed the reluctant air of the room. Stefan has taken Anna home, said Micah, it is all settled. I lifted my rubber head, I looked at him, he kissed me on my throat, below my jaw. Do not repeat your words, I begged, this is the third day of my sickness. You are only tired, he said. So I slept. I was no longer a girl who jabbered.

Sun rising above another horizon. I warned her. Stefan? I repeated. She had asked me a question. He will give no quarter to the aged, nor to woman nor to child, I answered. My brother is a liar. Brutality's deformed echo follows him. But Anna said nothing. She smiled. I left her, went to collect the eggs from the hencoop. When I returned, she had gone. I warned her. Nearly all winter I was very unhappy. What is it? asked Micah. I looked at the barren countryside on the other side of the glass. I kept silent, I said to him, all through the earliest days of our marriage, I remained silent all through my flesh's tertianship. I will not begin to speak now, I will not criticise your timekeeping nor your rangefinding. He sighed and said, you are on a sabotage mission. No, I said, I am mapping out a refugee area in myself. His eyes saw nothing. Give me the photograph, he said. I obeyed. He looked at it. What old-fashioned dresses you wore then, he said. I was surprised that he noticed this. He handed the snapshot back to me. I looked at Anna's sealed smile. I saw the sadness of our clasped hands. Anna is a flood victim, he said suddenly, stop memorizing her. I said nothing. I put the photograph back in the envelope. You'd have eaten anything when you were hungry, he continued, but you don't need her now. I looked up at him and remembered that when I met him in the first darkness I hoped perhaps he was a brave man. I remembered his shadow in the mirror. Once we made international promises outside the church with the weather vane that never moved. Once he tore my dress, accidentally. Promises. I'm bound by the promise of a slut. I'll never be friends with you, I warned him. When he left me, I tore open the other envelope, and looked at the letter. The sheet of white paper was covered with ink blots and smears: no words, no signature. I surrendered to the blackness at the back of my eyes. Blood disappeared. He ordered the men of the captured army to be blinded, I thought. The rites of the bed tire me. My hair is nine nights long, it reaches the celtic floor. I touched the child with my unhealing fingers. I am afraid of my nameless son. Only one person speaks and I am tired of her.

Burial brother, why have I achieved this strangeness? Why do the wild trees dragging out the throat of my fever bring rain? The crier calls out the approach of the white morning. I wear my ultra-violet dress today. Micah is working on his tower telescope. He studies solar images today. He is trying to slow down the clock rate. I have my day to arrange, the slicing of the red meat, digging in the garden for potatoes, washing linen, fearing the subgiants of the summer sky, polishing furniture and shoes. But I must break the day's ice. I must find my skin and slip back into it. He lends money on reasonable terms, especially to the poor. He employs bullies to collect his debts, dark-skinned unconsecrated men. I avoid looking into their faces when they come to the house. They look such priestly men, I almost believe they are weary with their work. Until they chill me with their parting words.

XXXII(iii)

People without fear: look at a man and a woman who are failing to give adequate warning of distress: watch them sending letters to the wrong address, cheating the nipple of its pleasure, waking in the first dark stupidity of morning, and moving, mirthless and cold to the roots of my flintlock hair, through infinitesimal rooms until dawn comes performing its routine tasks just as it were alive. I keep coals of fire alive by covering them with ashes. I keep flowers alive by putting them in water. We will postpone talking about it until the day after tomorrow or some other time, he said. This was his answer when I asked him why he wanted to move to another house. Dust and dirt beneath my feet wherever I walk. My own words make me cry. Micah is amused. He helps a wasp to commit suicide. I am sleeping alone tonight, with only the stray arrows of my water dreams to fear. I imitate my mother's voice. No, he says. Where are you going, he says, as I open the door. I resume my seat. I have something to say against you, I inform him. A sneaky look on my face. What is that? I looked at him without fear, no contact between us. You are afraid of war. I spoke coldly. I watched him closely as the words clung to him. He taps the table with his hand. I cannot perceive his thoughts. He murmurs the name of a clown. You are right, he says, I have these fears. He stroked my hair. He said, a journey of a thousand miles is begun by taking one step, Faustina. Then he told me he was going to see Stefan out in the courtyard.

I knelt down in front of the fire. I murmured the rain incantations. I was afraid of thieves and cakes made in the shape of mirrors and of being stripped naked by the enemy and having my breasts burnt with cigarette butts. Then I opened my eyes. I stood up. I turned down the bed quilt. I selected a book to read. I pour water for my bath. I arrange legends. White moonstone words. Purifier, atoner. The water cannot wash me clean enough. My hands befriend me but it is not enough. Now even my hands cry, wrong girl, mute mazer, all wrong. Thin candles of concentration burn down. Darkness. I told him I knew the name of the first widow who remarried. Autumn of you women, he sneers. He pokes me between the buttocks with his finger and laughs. Going to Jerusalem? he says.

A dull rainy day, a fire of parrot coal burning. He looked into my face. I am afraid of the speech and of the speaker. Somebody told me your mother was your first enemy, I said. I opened the night door, I thought I could escape him. But he caught me by the hair, he made me look at the family prison, he read me a story of a harlot with the tail of a bird. Yelping, I crouch on the floor. I am immobile between the larva and the imago. He locks the door. My hands are hot glass. I am afraid of someone who is in the room with me, an old woman who is totally blind but who will approach me, her heart hanging out of her body like the innards of a broken clock. But whenever I turn around, she hides and I can't catch her.

I banged on the door. He wouldn't let me out. I was left alone on a high cold arid plateau. Brittle snails crawled towards me. I spat in the mirror. She is the fallen eyelid. She is the chewing fungus mouth. Anna. She is the silent pianist. I hate her. She will not unlock the door for me. I want to place my fingers against her eyeballs and press parasitic visions into her retina. But Anna has disappeared, is no longer luminous in the dark. At intervals I stare out of the window. Night's smoke screen has hidden all my friends. The dream of the vagina is deceitful. I walk rapidly around my room, my light footsteps have too many echoes, I am chasing the old woman again, there, she vanishes into the wall, like a flying squirrel. Patchwork girl, Faustina, who listens to you? Who passes his hand across your sex? Who strikes you? Only Micah. Paper dolls carrying nuclear weapons will live longer than Faustina. I kneel. I want to sleep very much but the noise the black words make won't let me rest. I bite my lips. I am sweating in a dry room. I remember the seaside café in winter when I spoke to Stefan in my first voice and he said I must never tell anyone else what I told him. A mismarriage. We have written our names on a piece of parchment. We have embraced, hands and limbs, slept together and feared the death of our sons. I mend the creels, I sew the hems of my unexplained dresses. I want to open the door. I must stop counting the cracks in the wall. I must turn that tap off. I will open the door. One of the birds will be white. Early in the morning, protected against injury or pain by my own sacrifices, I will leave his house, I will not have to face Micah again, I will only have to confront easy strangers. I lie on my bed and past events surround me like ice crystals around the moon. Who sprang full grown from her mother's womb? My threshold strength . . .

Part of the church was occupied by singers. I looked but I could not see her. My hair was cold with songs and games. My mother came in and the choir began singing. The key only opens one lock once. The changeling-girl sits in a chair by the window for long periods, weaving smoke through her shell-membrane hands. In her head, she hears a confusion of voices, like cross-talk on a television circuit. The thin oval of the looking glass shows me a photograph of three dead women. So many men with burdens on their backs, bent beneath sacks of coal or promises, so many women who walk for pleasure among the extolling birds, so many other women lost to virtue. No open declarations . . . no shadows to remind me of the speaker, no more hands touching me like a cold wind against my eyelids. The child with four hands does not know that money is paid for the hire of a woman's cunt. Black eyelids that will not stop bleeding. Hands of the sex, blue colour of arctic grass on which she cut her finger. Sleep with a long knife, silent song of lamentation. Anna's dead daughter glares at me.

XXXIII(i)

That summer I was first married was strange everywhere in the world. Innocent bystanders were gunned down. Rats got into the waterjugs. I buried myself in the iceberg, noiselessly. Volcanoes sparkled, such light. I am perched on the carnal tree. I hate the drab clothes of the pilgrims who are saying prayers while fire is burning in the brazier. A leopard and a butterfly expose me to the evil influence of the ruling star. I bite through the birth string. I am not at rest in this crowded dance hall. Men and women dressed in burdenless colours laugh and dance. Unlike me, they do not notice the driving snow nor the intense cold. My clothes are torn but theirs are festive, the midgets dancing around me. I could not satisfy that tribunal of shrill witches, I could not convince them that I was telling the truth. Trying to tell the truth. You're crazy, they said. Send her to the crazy place, they said. So I watch the dancers here without even an antelope for my partner. I cross the unpaid bridge. I shout at my mother. I tell her, your face is the scene of christ's childhood, your face is the hour of prayer among violators. Your words are the radio when the batteries are running down. You lie in wait for me, clutching a small girl's nickname between your fingers. I am not coming your way. My early irish garments protect me. And there are the nights and the blackbirds. Mother. Stop saying my name. There has been a delay, my sentence will not be carried out yet.

The woman has finished submitting to penance. She wears again her dulcimer earrings and all the general outfit of a tryster. She is tall, her body slim, she has got rid of the child, it has been born, she can have her rangy hopes back again. She is keeping her bruises hidden and is intercepting messages. Tannery trees stretch in the sun. But the dryness of the enamellist's earth, the colour of dust, the repetition of it spites her, is an ensilage of doubt for her. She'd accepted her new name and his body's emphasis, and settled upon him her inalienable adventures. But like a collaborationist, or darnel weed, he soon chokes her. She cannot stop pain forming in her womb. She notices how closely he watches the widow, Anna. She sees the shadow of a new infirmity. I told him to put his seed in the belly of hell and he spoke strangely to me, not in the bridegroom's voice. So I ran away. Yes, I am safe here in the snow hut. He said, who is the woman in the locked room? I was frightened then. But the trouble began early this morning. When I awoke, I heard Micah coming upstairs. Will you be at home all day? he asked. How should I know? I answered. I brushed my hair. He watched me, then inspected his hands. I told him he was the only praiser of his mother. Faustina, he began almost calmly, then he changed his mind, broke off in the middle of his sentence and cleared off again. White cat watching a train, I said to the empty room. With my mouth of camphor.

The day went on. The men burnt fires in the fields, fires of magnolia leaves and dung. When the telephone rang in the silent room, I closed my eyes, the hand nailed to my womb writhed. I lifted the receiver. I heard a wolf howling. No, I heard nothing. Silence. Hello? Anna spoke. I heard her peyote voice. Where are you calling from? She did not answer. Can I speak to Micah? she said. She sounded cold. She spoke from the world of the forger. She lives the ballet of the disturbed. Can I speak to Micah? she repeated urgently. She sounded tired. She was hiding herself. She did not say my name. My name is a shadow on the water. He is not here, I answer. Truthfully. We converse, semi-subterranean words. Anna sighs. Her exhaustions resemble my dresses, drab and shy. I do not pity her. He is not here, I repeat. When will he be back? she asks, in a high-pitched voice, venus of flint and bone. She has made her mind up. I don't know, I said. I was in a panic. I banged the receiver down. I don't live here any more, I thought.

A lost night's sleep as the weather coarsened. When I looked out of the window next day I acknowledged my losses. The daylight enforced my darkness. I knew it was dangerous to wait much longer. I heard the offshore songs. I must leave my work here unfinished. My face is black and blue, I must get away, hitch-hiking or crawling. I will turn the radio up very loud so he will not hear my thoughts. I must fight off my illiteracy. Yes, I must escape from Micah. I'm always in some kind of danger. I hate him. He can't defecate or urinate. I held my son in my arms. I remembered what Anna said on the shore when I was pregnant. I smiled. So, after Stefan's death, Anna came to stay with us, a convalescent's visit. She was very suspicious of me and would hardly speak to me at all. She led her own predatory life in her own room. I knew she had a habit of suspending her slaughtered prey upon thorns. At our evening meal, taken in silence, I see how she watches Micah, the twelfth man. Sometimes her silence was broken by weeping and laughing. A different Anna. I did not let her stay alone with the child. Her opal-glass eyes saw bridewell burnings. I was afraid of being supplanted by her already.

XXXIII(ii)

I stood in the garden on the dark winter day. The bonfire burnt sadly, anticipations of evil. I watched him throw my letters into the flames. Anna laughed, nervously. Sometimes she was afraid of me. No, I said to Anna, I do not trust you. I suspect your gifts. She is thinking of the wedding of the delayer. I can't forget, I said, the imperishable angel who aches with charity and who waits in the green and unplagued fields, not knowing how not to hope, despite my resurrection of ice. Anna shudders. I am frightened in your arms, she says. My mouth is stopped full of dirt. We stare at each other, two women, two filching hearts. I am a threatened girl looking at a lifesize picture of her mother.

Why did I turn to the window? Why didn't I remain in the background of this white room, reading my book? But I did look out of the window. And I saw Anna, the druid dancer, the girl who used to walk on her hands. She came into the courtyard, looking worried. She does not see me spying. She does not want to see me watching her. She walks slowly towards Micah. Yet she is not wasting a second of her time. She smiles. They do not touch. It is worse that they do not touch. I cannot hear what words they are using. They laugh. I watch Anna's face. She is a different woman, no longer rocky or rainy. Can she remember the future? Her hands are almost touching Micah's shoulder but never quite reaching him. They have come to an agreement. They have no beginning and no end. Anna walks with Micah into the orchard. I still watch them. Now they have gone. I brush my landlocked hair. I remember the birth of my son. Woman of wineskin I drag dead moons down. I don't know anyone who can save me from the long driftless days of my repentance. Rain is falling in closed rooms: dislocation of the star chamber. As I walked along, looking for safety, I was detained by my mother, her skin browner than usual, her eyes zigzag windows opening back into the past: then my brother stopped me. And then I was accosted by a hermaphrodite. But I threw them all off. I said to them, do not doubt that I will do everything you are forbidding me . . .

XXXIII(iii)

A scarecrow covered with feathers
An estranged husband and wife
and the girl lover to both of them
Anna smokes her cigarette
Faustina holds her son in her arms
It is cruel to photograph people unawares,
she said. The sleeping woman of last year has seen hope murdered by Micah's hand without the aid of weapons. Now she must be alone, must wash the feet of the poor every day. Faustina watches the betrayal. She

stands in the courtyard and hears her own elegiac laughter. Anna comes in through the gate. She does not look at Faustina, the anal-veins of the ex-queen disgust her. Anna walks straight past Faustina. Faustina is the fuguist. Anna, she calls out. Anna turns at the doorway. She is wearing a long rough cloak made from the dressed skins of small trapped animals, a present from Micah. I hold out a malformed flower. But Anna tells me I move in the opposite direction to the sun. She explains why my legends are outworn. She can no longer grasp their meanings. What about Stefan? I asked abruptly, not daring to approach her except with my voice. How long has he been dead? She laughs, then blushes, then speaks angrily. Don't stare at me so stupidly, Faustina. We are both afraid of strangers, I answer, moving slowly towards her because I see her wavering, unsure, thrusting her fingers awkwardly against her face. Vespiary girls. Anna, I whisper. The evening is crowded with summer phantoms. Anna does not move. I kiss Anna. She does not move. She has been standing here for seven years. She tastes of pantomimes. I will scrub her skin with bibles. We kiss in the doorway. I do not feel homeless now. I scoop my tongue around her mouth.

But the forecast of the unhappy came true. Micah appeared, he took hold of Anna from behind, he was silent, he placed his hands over her breasts and lifted her away from me. This was in the fourth month after Stefan's death. Micah held Anna in silence. He looked at me and I backed away, out into the courtyard of the leaves. He led Anna into the house. Silently. Girl with empty hands and gaudy hair. She did not say a word. She moved, hypnotized, she could not protest. I saw his nakedness. Anna closed her eyes. She made silent signals to no one when he entered her. I cannot forget how proudly he lifted her skirt. How dreamily he entered her. Anna held her breath. Anna stretched her body. I turned away, I was being overtaken by nights without authenticity. I walked very slowly, the burning particles of my heart quenched. I remembered Stefan's funeral, the godsticks in the fire. I saw two lions regarding a laurel tree. I climbed the citadel staircase. I knew I had to leave, to go to the scar city where people keep coming into empty rooms, promontories of ice. Thistles sprang from my bones. No, I do not remember his name. I will not see Anna moving in my landscape, shameless, gravid. I will not bear a second child. I will not re-enter the house of the double woman. I'll drown twins in winter water. I wear lunulae of sea ice because I want a truthful body. I want to understand the uranography of blood. I looked at the witchflowers of twilight along the river bank. One word kept repeating inside my head: abort, abort.

I remembered a strange premonition. Three years ago, soon after we were married, Micah took me for a drive in the car one saturday afternoon. We went along the coast, taking country roads. A pleasure trip. On our way back, we passed a girl trudging along the road. She was about my age. She had a haversack on her back, a baby in a sling across her shoulder, and on her face, an expression of determined desperation . . . I thought, one day I'll follow you. Now I am walking her road. I must be as strong as that girl. I must use my documents correctly.

I walk along the road, thinking, if the waxwork figures return to me, if Lammas overtakes me, if the grail castle imprisons me, I am lost to fear. If a man speaks to me, if I guess the moon's true age, if I wear a dress of six different colours, if I gnaw at my veil, I am lost. If I tell you what I saw hovering over the seaway, then I am lost and the hair taboo of Jesusa will find me. If I tell you I carry blood, if I tell you my son's name, if I let you know I stumble and tell you how the girls in the shop are going to watch me with hostiles of eternity . . .

No . . .

I must be strong . . .

Laughs she does

the one behind me the one I can't see, singing your song mother. If I tell you I hear the shouts of the dove and remember the room in the jail, if I tell you about the quarrels I don't forget, if I tell you about these helpless days, the hair taboo of Jesusa will come upon me with its ever summer and its counterfeit blackbirds and its loud asinine utterances and I will know that the weddings and the picnics on the beach and the prayer endings and the mansions of the moon and myself are all going, receding from me. If I tell you of my unsheltered nights tell you of the rough breathing of the eyelid tell you of the heaps of ice and the slow dogs, then the hair taboo of Jesusa will live me or die me and I may not understand even then so I must walk with my thoughts jibbing and sleepless and the child a carried jealousy.

Jesusa . . .

XXXIV

I don't even know what town it is I'm approaching. I don't know what hotel I'll stay at. I think my stolen car is shatter-proof. That woman said to me, we're all frightened now. The baby kept crying. It was like carrying another woman's child in my arms, yet not . . . I went along, copying landscapes and didn't want the world to be quiet or painless. Had no need. Heart liver lungs: I trespass within my own body. It is a worn afternoon. The shops are shut. I park the car, stand on the tarmac, luggage and carrycot at my feet, my mind washed and separated from the two strangers in a garden miles away. I looked up at the sky and I saw thin broken vapoury clouds and as I was looking more rain began to fall, cold, worthless. I shivered inside my rabbit-warren body. Then I carried the haversack and the sleeping child across the road and into the brief mournful town.

Falmouth, April 1971

THE MIRROR OF THE GIANT

A Ghost Story

ONE

SHE moves from room to room in the semi-dark of the house. Torn maps direct her journey.

Some nights she kept herself hidden, very secret, unavailable, lost in a sisterhood he could not understand. Some nights she spent annulled in the orchard, beneath the awkward appletrees. Some nights she waited in a blind alley of flowers.

On other nights she watched him as he slept. She says to Theron, 'A wife is walking towards the sea and a wife perceives the night unsteadily.'

Tonight she is silent. She looks through mist and rain. What she eats tastes like pieces she has ripped from god's body, and the flesh is sour as toads. Her long heavy hair drags her down like a sea. She is icebound but she hears summer calling her. The penis of summer is tempting her but she is silent. She stands by the window, the night moves restively about her.

Her name is Vellet.

In the morning, he studies his books in silence. He is tired. Last night he slept badly, alone, in a dusty room. On his desk, in a silver frame, is a photograph of his late wife, Vellet. He glances at her stilled smile and he wishes for peace. He wishes to be free of her. He wants her zodiac to close its mouth. But I'm being swallowed up, he thinks suddenly, in a panic, and looks around the room, harshly.

Beth woke up, afraid. Fear like an aromatic taste in her mouth, a taste like apples of earth. It was early in the morning but he was already up, maybe practising the art of beautiful handwriting or perhaps mending the garden fence. She sat up in her barbed-wire bed and realized that her life in this place, with Theron, was undesirable to her, alien in every way now. But every solution, every escape that she conjured up in the first light of morning cancelled itself out: the noise in the background of milk churns being loaded on to the delivery lorry derided her with an every-day practical competence that she could not find in herself. She saw again all the difficulties of change, renewal, and her own weakness drove her back into familiar impairment. Rain tapped on the window. Sadly and unwisely she slept again. Her dream went on hurting.

In the middle of the field, a scarecrow covered in fatal feathers is waiting for her. But she runs away, and not for the first time. Her luminous shadow pleased him as he watched her running. He stands at the crossroads. When she saw him, she slowed down and walked towards him reluctantly. Bleak as scripture, the sky darkens. The man and the woman converse about honesty and cannot agree. Your womb is a nutshell, Beth. She sees the ghosts of her retina, pale seaport creatures. Love slips away through the eye of a needle.

TWO

BETH is alone in the pensive room, recovering from a minor attack of influenza she caught wearing her new summer dress for a cold May Day, a shivery celebration. This morning she sits at her white table, painting flowers on a square sheet of glass.

Her husband Theron enters the room. He knows that this is the day of her ovulation. It seems to him that his wife is gradually being lost to his view, that she is a careful mirage he might erase by using the wrong password. He stands in the doorway, deliberating. But she misinterprets his watchfulness and shouts angrily, 'leave me in peace! Let me have a calm day alone! I don't want you hovering on the outskirts of my thoughts.' She sends him away with all her strength. And in the room huge rippling circles of solitude remain to intimidate her. 'Don't play your bloody tricks on me,' she shouts after him down the passageway. He does not answer. She leans against the door, full of grief and anger.

That evening Beth and Theron go for a walk. The moon is murmuring like a pleased domestic animal. Beth stares at Theron, chilled to a little smile that tells him nothing. He grabs her arm and pulls her towards him. The moon reminds Beth of all wives and children. White faces. 'What about the time when you pretended to be dead?' he asks her. She trembles. 'You and I must go our own ways, it isn't working out, there's a wall between us a mile high, two miles wide.' He smiles. She looks more closely and sees the mudstains on his shirt. 'Separate?' he says calmly. 'No. You are the one I have chosen, Beth.'

She looks around her, at field, stream, stone and tree of twilight. She hears the night beginning within herself. He led her home, like a nun approaching the cold cage of holy week.

Brain-tissue of the night. All that night the idea of Vellet's body dragged up on to the river bank, ornamented with bracelets of weed and necklaces of jetsam, all night the thought shuddered through Beth, the night was made unbearable by her own feeble cries for help, her own drowning.

All night she was drenched in elvish sweat. Alone in the dark she thought of Vellet.

Vellet's ghost is tall and wet by the side of her bed and is swathed in the damp colours of Vellet's enmity: night reflected in the bedroom mirror, drowning there.

Vellet, beast-girl, first wife, five years dead. White skull of the girl who has charge of Theron's insomnias bends over Beth, functionless breath of Vellet chokes Beth. Beth carries the remains, the scars of the day with her into a restless shallow sleep.

Without a coat, Theron walks out of the house, into the fields. He is determined upon retaliatory action. He heads for the river.

'It is easy for you to reproach me,' said Beth, 'it is easy to confuse me.' That morning he had given her a long list of her faults. She shook her head. Theron, there are splinters of worlds under my fingernails. They hurt me.

They walk in silence through the forest. Beneath their feet raw pale loppings from the branches are the proof of last night's storm. A midwife is singing somewhere. The song tells Beth that she can be freed from her self-made sadness. But Beth is not listening. Theron is speaking to her. On their way home from their afternoon walk they loiter by the town cenotaph. She's picked a bunch of marsh andromeda from the river bank and at home she puts the flowers in a vase, governs them badly. Theron compliments her on them. She smiles at him. For a time it seems the dangers were exaggerated.

THREE

BETH is waiting for a letter from Ash. Darkness strikes the land forcibly, the moons damage Beth, the unmanageable afternoons come back. In the morning she expects a letter. Every morning. But no letters come. It is no fun, this waiting. It is like an unalterable distance which must be travelled every single day. A silent toxic journey.

Beth, housewife of calamities. For Beth the walls of the house are a prison. She appoints Theron her warder. He has no choice in the matter. She blames him for her own submissions. He is the man who carries fire and laws in his hand simply because Beth says so. Beth says so because Ash will not write to her.

My antagonist changes sex, says Beth. Reptilian mirrors coast me back to the dark. My antagonist changes sex. Theron/Ash. Ash/Theron. He/She/Elohim walks in the woodland of the scissors. And who will ambush me there?

White rainbows will be my downfall.

But the reflection of a spider in a raindrop saves me from the depressions that are threatening. The alternating colours return, the world returns, with its suns and salts, I return to myself, even though I remember how the ghost rotates in her wetness. She gleams with her lifeless smile, with her wintry lace of drowning. She is his companion, she is the wife. I must listen to her legends. When once again there is no letter I sense the beauty of the electric-chair, I know the splendour of the gas-chamber. The dream-road shines then and Vellet offers me the day before yesterday. She whispers: 'God will dissolve your marriage, despite his crown of petals, his broken mirror.' But I return to myself, despite my unhappiness. I return to myself, not to Vellet. If Ash has forgotten me, then I'll occupy that devastation of myself with a purity, not with Vellet's stench creeping in upon me.

Vellet leaned forward and whispered in Theron's ear: 'The wife of Harlequin just kept lying there in the mud, laughing and slaking her sensitive flesh in the mud: Harlequin said, be careful, remember your clothes, they'll get so dirty. The mother of Harlequin's wife stood on the river bank, watching, her face made impassable by the rains. Her gestures were without speech, required none.

'Harlequin's wife got up from the mud and her long hair was stiff, like the black snakes of Egypt. Her shadow was composed of a flock of black cuckoos.

'Harlequin offers her the bunch of red flowers. She smiles, she is shivering. She is naked now, having abandoned her muddy skirt and blouse at the river's edge. Her husband wraps her in a tartan blanket and the trio enter their winter conveyance to drive off along the highway . . .'

FOUR

THE kiss that Beth and Ash exchange explodes into morning and beyond the dream Beth's exterritorial life begins. Shivering in the cold bedroom, she dresses hurriedly and goes downstairs to prepare breakfast, thinking of her dream. Around the neck of the goddess hung painted skulls. The goddess was set in a niche in the wall and her draperies were stone. The stone goddess had Ash's face. The skulls are the skulls of her lovers. I fish for them, and draw them up in a white net. Or was it that the skulls dangled from my long silvery tapering fishing rod? One skull grows flesh and features, smiles at me, it is Ash also.

Where is the giantess in her iron dress? Where is the giantess holding up a mirror, her hands encased in gloves of bronze? I have not seen her yet. He said to me: 'Beth, let the darkness enter your heart.' I cannot forget Jake's words. Jake stands between us, Ash. I can never forget that.

I know I am not the inventor of the firmament. My fears spread out beyond me like branches. I am a tree of sadness and constant winter.

Theron came in and sat down. They ate breakfast in silence until over a second cup of coffee, Beth said,

'When I was a young girl, first experiencing my monthly issue of blood, then I was fully alive, truly responding to all things. Every day was the day of the moon. Every night was an arena of sunshiny dreams. But now I am flung from day to day like a beggar, owning nothing. The whirlwind is too strong for me. My agile ancestry cannot go that fast. Now I want to live on the sheltered side of the east wind.'

'I want to help you,' said Theron gently, stroking her hair, 'but you frighten me, Beth, when you stare at the household furniture like a wife murdered a century ago.'

'I sense a power in me,' she said, after a moment, 'a source of strength and freedom deep within me, but I cannot reach it, gain access to it. I cannot mine the treasure. I do not know the password to enter that region. And ever since I sensed this power, soon after our marriage, I have become awkward in all my actions, clumsy emotionally. The part of me that knows that power is there, presses against the remainder of my life, demanding entrance. But I do not know how to let it in. That power leads to an equilibrium of abilities. With it, I can come into focus and find peaceful solutions to my problems, a detente. But I am afraid. And I stare at the furniture like a wife murdered a century ago.'

Theron shrugged and sighed, and left her in the kitchen. She thought, Ash is my reflection. Her light to my dark, her dream on my day, her answer to my question.

Ash walks in a landscape hundreds of miles away, beside wild Lent lilies flowering by another river bank.

Yet we both shrink back from the looking-glass, flinch from that reflection. Lady Unique: that is how I think of you, Ash. I see you on stairways, in rainy fields, in your herbarium: echo of me, my reflection, receding always, no longer turning to me, to see your reflection in me, always retreating. Yet my need for you will not die down or lessen. It is like an inheritance. I was marked for this from the day I was born. Only you are free, Lady Unique, dancing without hesitation among your children. Heroine, who has led me to a precipice. Jesus dumb, Jesus deaf, Jesus blind, heal me. How long is it since Ash and I watched the dawn horses gallop here, from field to field? Almost five years since our parting, since Ash became an impediment in my dreams just as surely as if in my speech. We came to a frontier, Ash and I, we paused; hesitated, parted, moving unsteadily at first until she began to run across those fields, obediently running. I did not attend her wedding, though I was invited. I long for her yet wish to cleanse my life of her influence. When we were both growing weaker, when Jake became determined to part us, it was she who first said, 'It's no good, Beth.' I had no answer. I remember there were small streaks of colour in the sky. Sunset. 'It's no good, Beth,' she said again and began to run. I watched her. She ran. Is she still running? I think it is a marathon, our race. It is not over yet. There are no winners.

FIVE

CARVED out of the turf that grows on the chalk uplands of this region, a giant 180 feet by 160 feet. The trenches of the giant's outline are cut a foot deep and a foot wide and the rain runs downhill and washes them clean and white. In his right arm he carries a club like that weapon Hercules carried, in his left what might be the hide of a slain lion. He stares bolt-eyed, his penis is huge, a white erection three thousand years old. Beth looks across the valley to observe the giant carved in the chalk of Giant Hill. A spring sunlight illuminates the giant's unanswerable fertility. Beth suspects that the giant knows she has been drifting aimlessly ever since Ash went away. Drifting, going wrong, yet expecting always to remain unhurt. Demanding to see her reflection preserved alive unchanging amid the landscape she and Ash once celebrated. Beth knows that she is drifting, that her thoughts stream indiscriminately beyond her grasp. She knows it and the giant confirms it. She stands on the summit of the hill and watches him.

He brandishes his club like the body of a newborn child. Beth stares at the white giant but will not let him suture her wounds. She remains trapped in the fever of her fidelity to Ash. She still moves via her backward zodiac, and dismisses the giant as a fetish-navigator, long out of fashion; and she turns downhill angrily, keeping her balance with difficulty on the slippery grass of the steep slope.

Restlessly she comes down into the ruins of the abbey and wanders among them. If she is searching, she finds nothing. Ash is not here. Ash has her own house, bright, noisy, modern, far away from these ruins. Does she still concern herself with thoughts of Beth? Or has she forgotten the summer they shared?

On this afternoon in the ruins, Beth swears like a blind woman approaching the source of her own decay. She walks in circles through the ruins until she is sickened by her repetitive journey and goes through the lych-gate into the churchyard. She threads her way between the old tombs, keeping her back to the giant. She is a female prisoner parading among the graves of lust and the rain falls on her, rank as Pharaoh's dream. She will not ask the giant to show her a way out of her trouble. 'Dear Ash,' she had written, 'I wonder if you ever remember our times together, fondly, or even mockingly . . . probably not, especially as you live so far away now. I am more likely to remember them, for I still live in the village . . Ash did not reply to the letter.

Beth shivers, the egg of the woman is like a lump of ice in her. She closes her eyes and sees Ash sewing, hemming black curtains. Like an ancestress, whispers Beth, just like that. Beth feels the rain going through and through her until she is no longer a woman but a rocky island. She shelters beneath a yew tree until the rain eases.

Ash paused on the stairs. She was five years older than Beth's memory of her.

I was never a holy woman! she thought resentfully.

Since the letter came, she had been thinking about Beth. She was worried because she knew Beth was not one to be strong against trouble. Her letter was full of hints of unhappiness. But I don't want to write to her or return to that . . . She heard the voices of her children upstairs. No, she decided angrily, no, I am not going to return, not even for a short visit, not to the village. It would spoil everything. I can still remember the way the twilight falls fingerless on the land there, misting me with fears, blurring me like an outrage. And how cold that Orion is, on the hill, in his white armour.

Ash shook her head and dismissed the thoughts that troubled her, thoughts of Beth, memories of their life together. She resumed her own life and climbed the stairs to her children, a bedtime storybook in her hand.

SIX

THERON was haunted. He was a sympathetic man by nature but he was haunted and the presence of the ghost stood between Theron and Beth.

The ghost was of his first wife. Vellet whispers to him, 'my dear Theron, I know our enemies are beginning their assault . . .'

And then that laugh of hers! Snaking along the corridors, her angry hiccup in his study. He flinches. Her shadow is always there. He is a sympathetic man but necessarily distant in his manner, because haunted, and less aware of Beth's unhappiness than he might otherwise have been.

And sometimes, mistaking Beth for her predecessor, he turns on Beth and speaks to her harshly. Beth is often immersed in her own thoughts and cannot defend herself. She has not seen the ghost yet.

Mostly Theron lets her alone, though. Weeks pass when husband and wife are strangers. Not enemies, but polite strangers, preoccupied with their own private emotions. Weeks pass without an embrace. Beth does not use contraceptives. It is part of her attitude of drifting, of her decision to be indecisive. She regards Theron's sexuality as neither important nor a threat to her. When he wants her, she will screw almost lazily with him and most times she comes but it doesn't mean very much to her. It means a brief forgetfulness of her troubles, but it does not change anything for her. Beth never considers that perhaps her feelings of isolation and panic might be caused by the poverty of their sexual life. She never makes the first approach to Theron. She does not ask herself why a young couple married less than two years should make love so infrequently. She is incapable of asking these questions, for she cannot look about herself with any clarity, she cannot consider the matter; it is only Ash, Ash, and the past . . .

And her husband is haunted.

SEVEN

THREE days before her death, Vellet and Theron argued violently. It began with a minor disagreement about the untidiness of the house. (Beth's tidiness was one of the qualities Theron valued, one he noticed particularly.) Vellet had hesitated for a moment but then turned on Theron, pointing at him, and shouting hysterically,

'I see your blasphemous books and I see your armies destroyed and once I thought I saw you slain by your own son. Remember, Theron, there are times when a slip of the tongue is high treason!'

'For god's sake,' yelled Theron, having heard all this before, 'just forget it, ok ?'

But this response only infuriated Vellet and she shouted more shrilly,

'I carried my doorway under my arm, my heart made snarling noises but no one heard.'

She shoved him out of her way and ran out of the room.

It was on this occasion he became certain that he could not go on living with Vellet. They had friends coming to supper that evening, but all afternoon Vellet stayed in her room and refused to answer Theron when he attempted to persuade her to talk things over. They'd only been married two years at this time, and Vellet's always excitable temperament had in the last few months grown violent, morose and neurotic. Theron sat in his study that sour afternoon, his papers unread. He reflected that despite his academic qualifications as a military historian he could find no strategies to help in this situation. Vellet's sickness, as he had come to think of it, was a great sorrow, the greater since he had known Vellet from her childhood, from the time she and her father came to live in the village. Her father had died soon after the move, and as Theron was a distant (in fact the only) relation, a cousin several times removed, he became the old man's executor and guardian of Vellet. They had married immediately Vellet was legally of age.

The marriage caused talk in the village but Theron chose to disregard it. However, he acknowledged privately now that the gossips had been right, the marriage was a mistake. Vellet was too young, and he had exerted too much pressure on her, to persuade her into it.

He recalls her intent yet puzzled expression when they sat together in the summerhouse and he asked her to marry him. She had been reluctant, had caught her breath suddenly, in surprise or fear he could not tell.

He spoke to her persuasively though always in a straightforward and honest manner. To Vellet he seemed, as usual, withdrawn, grim in manner. And she had other more complex motives for not marrying him. He was an intruder, she felt. She sat beside him, gathering the green material of her dress into pleats, nervously moving in her mind between timidity and anger.

But all she said was that she had to think about her future before she could answer. He watched her walk away across the lawn, green and green. He watched her and began to gloat.

It was an evening some weeks later when she said yes, she would marry him. She accepted almost incoherently, unaware of real consequences. That afternoon she'd had a bad shock but she told Theron nothing about it. He had been over at the university all day and Vellet had gone secretively to meet a young unreliable friend. They had argued, the boy had come at her, grabbed her, word-blind, and she only just escaped from some violence, by ducking away, running out of the cottage, getting lost in the market crowds. When she got back home she locked all the doors and then decided, full of panic and foolishness, that she'd grasp the way out Theron offered her.

It was an evening with a grimy sky. The summer was going. The garden was shifting between white and black. After the words were said, all was set, planned, arranged, his touch and kiss no longer postponed, the shadows lapped around her, a dilapidation, and she was full of resentment.

Just before Christmas, on the day after her birthday, they were married, in the village church. The church was draughty, the parson disapproved of the whole business, the best man, a colleague from the university, had a bad cold and spoke his words hoarsely. That night Vellet told Theron she was nervous and so he went to his own room, touched by her ignorance. Vellet, in her room, the same room she'd occupied since she was a child, moved from bed to mirror to window to bed again almost blindly, fumbling and swearing. Her groin felt cold as ice. She went back to the window, stood there, trapped. How Vellet hated the thought of the life ahead of her, how, to her mind, she would be humbling herself every day.

She tried to avoid him, was very wary. He acknowledged her shyness and inexperience, but his patience did not last out the week. He had wanted Vellet since she was a schoolgirl. He had been patient a long time and he was sure it would work, this marriage, for his own emotions had been reflected upon Vellet for so long that he believed she was as intent upon their union as he himself. He went to her room. It was evening again, tense weather, not cold enough for winter. He paused, stood behind her, watching her in the mirror. She watched his reflection, without expression. Kindly, he asked her how she felt. She shrugged, then turned to him and tried to smile, yet she felt her body grow stiff, like a breakwater on a beach. He held her. For her this was exhausting, a punishment. There was a secret in her, old habits. She was unwilling to let Theron learn of or be responsible for those debts. She searched arduously for an excuse but found none. When she was naked he touched her cautiously. The bed was like half the earth's surface, they were so separated on it, so much distance between them. When he touched the hair between her legs she found the sensation very unpleasant and could not hide her reaction from him. He thought it was her shyness.

The deep sound of pain that she uttered as he fucked her he mistook for a virgin's cry.

It was not.

The months went past until Theron sat in his study and thought of Vellet simply as a bringer of bad luck. That evening she came downstairs and prepared a meal for his guests. She enjoyed cooking. He watched her but she did not speak to him.

'You will speak sensibly to our guests?' he asked.

She looked at him and laughed sneeringly.

He turned away.

Four people, two men, two women sit around the table in a brightly lit room. Vellet has been silent so far. Theron has been talking nonstop to Bob and Lina but he cannot relax, feeling the radiation of Vellet's sullen discontent. His friends are shocked to see how bad things have become between Theron and Vellet and exchange sympathetic embarrassed glances.

Vellet broke her silence by saying that the dolphin is noted for the brilliance of its colours when dying. Theron poured out more wine, ignoring the remark.

'The meal was lovely, Vellet,' said Lina, smiling. Vellet sniffed.

'How are your silver mines in Joachimsthal, Bob?' she demanded, grimacing at him. He looked at Theron for guidance, but he only shrugged helplessly. Vellet laughed angrily. She poured the wine down her throat. She sat in her stiff petticoats, aching. She was sure that Bob and his woman were leering at her. The conversation turned to the presidential election, ignoring Vellet. She fingered the necklace that had been her mother's and wished she was outside in the dark, running through the winter darkness, climbing the hill to lie within the white boundaries of the giant and perhaps he would be waiting for her, the one she had wanted to escape, who had frightened her into this dead marriage, this abnormal event, she thought viciously. He cleared off when he knew the wedding was for real, went back to the city, left me here. If he hadn't threatened me . . . None of these people trust me. *He* did not trust me in the end and I got frightened of him, ran off, got into this mess. There are no more nights on the giant's back for me.

'Vellet?'

It is that woman with her dress decaying on her back. I stare at Lina.

'Are you coming to the concert next week, Vellet?' I lean forward across the table. Lina smells of pale mauve flowers.

'No.'

'Why not ?' she asks.

I can't be bothered to answer. She opens her mouth as if to say something more but changes her mind. I saw her look at Theron, there was lust in her glance. My brain ached as I listened to the calm conversation around me. Then I stood up, I had to, and I danced around the room, I wanted them all to move, to dance, or to break, these solid bodies, I wanted us all to start screwing, wanted the night to keel over and for us all to copulate, I told them what I wanted, I told them, and their faces loomed towards me, simian and pale, cold, so calm, bloody calm. I wanted to dance, yes, and to fuck, to sing and shout, break out of this foreign territory. But all they did was to speak to me in warning voices. I saw how they looked knowingly from one to the other. Theron said something to Lina very quietly, I could not hear it. She took hold of me and tried to lead me out of the room. I was swaying and sobbing, and I felt sick, I shouted at her, your mouth is full of shit, but she was stronger than I was and she dragged me upstairs and I couldn't fight them any more, I lay across the bed as if I was paralyzed, and then when she thought I was asleep she went downstairs. I heard the murmur of voices in the hall as she and Bob left, hushed voices as if in a hospital or mad house. When Theron came and stood by my bedside I pretended to be asleep and after he'd gone I thought, all of this is killing me.

EIGHT

BETH said, 'supper's ready.'

Theron flinched.

'Must you interrupt me when I'm busy,' he asked bitterly, not looking at her.

'Didn't you hear me come in?'

'No,' said Theron, 'I was thinking.'

He was thinking of how Vellet got up from the bed and pulled the curtain back from the window and all they could see was night and she said, I cannot stroke night with my open hand, can you?

Beth stood beside her husband, watching him. Then she shivered, moved, knelt by the fire. For an instant she had seen a shadow leaping over his body.

He was thinking of how Vellet laughed at him and told him there was a lot he didn't know about her, she screeched at him and he slapped her across the face, but she went on laughing, and he thought he did not dare go on living with her any longer because he did not know what humpback secrets she was concealing. He had been afraid of her then. I am still afraid of her, he thought, unaware of Beth's gaze, of her possible compassion. She watches from the fireside. I am still afraid, he thought, Vellet is in the doorways, guardian of the doors. She is on the other side of all doors and she will not let me live in peace. She will transmute me from silver to a base metal. She will not stop haunting me.

'Shall we eat now,' asked Beth.

He scowled at her.

'Don't you know the dangers,' he muttered.

Red and silver fish swam along her veins. She shook her head. He pushed his chair back roughly and went out of the room, out of the house, doors banging. Beth did not know what violations she was guilty of. She remains on her knees by the fire. She wanted to thrust her hands into the flames but she did not dare. The pain she endured was sharp, she wanted to replace it with a physical hurt, but she did not dare. I feel torn to pieces by this man who is always edging away from me. There in the flames I see a woman's face, not mine, nor the face of Ash. A stranger, a very young woman, very unhappy. Who is she? I begin to think that I must approach Theron more boldly, and learn what troubles him. I am frightened of doing this but I think we will both suffer a great deal more if we remain locked in our two solitudes. He is calm for long periods of time, calm, easygoing and then he behaves like this, so driven and inexplicably angry. Why? I must ask him straight out. I must have an answer. And I will tell him about my problem, my unresolved interest in Ash, which I don't know whether to call love or not. The days come and go with such vehemence and our questions must be answered.

Beth hears the wind and rain tearing through the rose-garden. She pictures her husband walking along the dark lanes between the fields, across the land salted with prehistoric bones.

She puts her hands against her cheeks scorched from the fire and says, I won't give another thought to Ash, or to the past.

In the room there is a woman's violent laughter. It is not Beth laughing. She jumps up, switches on the light. She is alone in the room. She looks all round the room, opens the door, goes out into the hall. The house is silent. Only the fire spits and crackles. Beth shrugs, settles to read the newspaper, to wait for Theron's return.

On Giant Hill in the dark, who is the woman dancing the egg dance? Who follows Theron when he walks in the woods where certain leaves throw forked shadows?

It is Vellet. She follows him. And sometimes on these night walks she fawns on him, whimpers, and the white of her drowned body is like the white of a bird's egg. She pleads for him to touch her and he must put out his hand, touch that chill breast, that chiller sex, before she will leave him.

Theron returned to the house, alone, disgusted, exhausted. In their bedroom south of Moscow he lectures his wife irascibly and she listens in silence, as if under an assumed name. She is sitting up in bed, an old crocheted shawl round her shoulders, and she notices how drawn his face is, how tired he looks. Suddenly he shouts, making her jump.

'Nobody must touch your watery shadow! Nobody! Nobody must finger your damp hair!'

Who is he talking to?

He bends over Beth and shouts in her face,

'Do you understand?'

He glares at her and the supperless girl brushes the night aside with her hands.

'I understand you,' she answers. She recalls their picnics on the beach, their walks in the snow, happy scenes, and she obliterates these memories with one inward dove cry. Then she turns out the light.

Theron fucked Beth but he was a receiver of stolen goods and he knew it. When he was asleep, Beth slipped out of bed and sat by the last of the fire. Her orgasm was useless for it was an experience unshared. It must be shared, she thought fiercely, letting her head loll between her hands, too tired to sleep. She was contained completely within the night now, dark and stale. She stared at her fingernails and smelt the stench of dead flowers in the room. She thought of knives, but only from a coward's point of view. If there was a place of safety, a protected place, she would go there and make Theron accompany her, no matter how many gangsters and ordeals stood between them and the sanctuary. But there is no safety, she reflected, only an endless series of cruel and grinding tasks in the day and at night orgasms so meaningless they become menacing. There's no bright world of acrobats and dancers, only the world of the wedding ring and the dark, prayers and semen, the night's events.

NINE

A COLD day in the late spring of 1972 with little weary patches of sun and the hollow roar of an east wind. Beth is walking through the village, greeting acquaintances, smiling, nodding, but she does not pause to converse. She walks on, climbing steadily up, until she is clear of the village and at the crossroads. She does not pause here, but turns and takes a familiar road.

On either side of the road, rough fields spread out. The light brown stony earth is also familiar to Beth. It is high ground here and the wind is colder. The sun deletes shadows far off into distances.

The house stands alone, at the edge of the moorland. It is uninhabited, no one wants to rent a house in such an isolated position, unmodernized and chilly.

Beth had been brought up in this house by her aunt. To keep the child company, her aunt had adopted a boy, Jake, a year younger than Beth. But this arrangement never took, the boy was never at home in the house or with the woman and the little girl. He'd been overseas in the army when Aunt Ann died. He'd joined up when he was sixteen, as a private soldier. Aunt Ann had regarded this as an act of defiance, for he could have waited until he was older, she said, and gone in with a commission. She never forgave him for enlisting, and left her house to Beth.

Beth went on living at the house on her own. There was just enough money left, carefully managed, for Beth to get by on, and she started her studies at the nearby university.

It was at this house, during the summer vacation that her friendship with Ash developed, a summer friendship that turned cold, left them both prey to shivery fits of sadness, the chill shadow of which reaches out to

Beth now, at the gate, as she thinks back over the days before her marriage.

In all the windows of the house she sees reflections of that past summer, catalogues of happy evenings, walks with Ash, gardening, growing tomatoes in the greenhouse; and other reflections, of loss, misery.

Jake turned up at the house unexpectedly. He was out of uniform. It was in the evening, at the end of their summer. Beth and Ash met him on the back lawn, on the way home from their ride on the moor. He was looking up at the bedroom windows. When he turned to speak, Beth hardly recognized him, hadn't seen him for over two years. But her first thought was, he wants Ash.

The empty house stands in a tangle of old overgrown paths and marigold lawns now. The orchard has been swindled out of its picnics long ago. Beth pushes the gate open, walks around the side of the house, her feet scrunching on the gravel. She peers in through a window at sheeted furniture and quiet bare fireplaces. Across the lawn, beyond the greenhouse and the air-raid shelter, a dank pool lets the sky fall into its keycold waters. Beth stares down at the water, deep enough to drown in, and watches the wind ruffle the surface. She turns to look at the house again, at the sky reflected in the windows. Squarish, constructed of local grey stone, overlooked by no neighbours, the house keeps nothing hidden in its history. It is an ordinary house. No murders were committed in this house. No wizard rushed from room to room on the top floor, no planets sizzled from his fingertips. No mad naked lady wild for elopement ever wrestled with her brothers and sisters on the stairs. No robbery, no fire, no plague. Even the air-raid shelter turned out to be unnecessary, despite the wartime airbase only ten miles across the moor. No bombs fell. No tragedies, only the commonplace events, natural death, ordinary arguments, moments of happiness, partings, the ending of friendship. Only the usual days and nights resembling sleep happened here. Marriage and birth, divorce and death, generations following the fossil-footprints downward.

Beth sits on an old bench by the pond and looks up at the far window, the room that was hers, when she lived here. Then her gaze moves across the brickwork and down until she stares at the back door. She is too far away to see the horseshoe nailed on the door, but she knows it is there, pouring out good luck.

She closes her eyes. A few cold drops of rain are in the wind, the tough wild daffodils, small and pale, are entangled in the wind, there is a sudden spurt of moorhens across the water.

Beth opens her eyes. One autumn morning very early, mist sprouting everywhere, the back door was opened by a young woman in a long fur coat who hesitated in the doorway for a moment and then ran across the lawn, her thoughts like blood-birds, her feet protected only by thin slippers that were soon heavy with dew. The girl ran until she came to the pond. She stared down at the water, her hands clenched by her sides. Beth recognizes herself, no-one's daughter. On this autumn morning she is not yet married to Theron. The ceremony is to take place this afternoon. Beth watches the video of her memory. Her thin body is going back, she has almost become that memory, crawling into its skin. Her younger self paces the marshy edge of the pond. Between words and between gestures, thinks Beth, watching, I rediscover myself.

The autumn version of Beth looks back at the house, her face changes from one season to another, and Beth sees in that face the last of her own countrified virginity. The girl is gone back towards a future Beth has not yet understood. How often, she thinks, in that autumn and winter did I find myself standing by my bedroom window, our bedroom window, staring out at a frozen garden. I remember the frost, the snow, the life in a different house, how I felt marriage to be a sort of conscription. I did not care then where I was, or what my life meant, but now I require more than indifference, more than the chill that preserves but does not nourish.

She gets up from the bench. The clouds are blowing across the sky, she catches a glimpse of the blue lawlessness of the sky.

I feel I can swing free from the next winter if I can only recall one suitable word for the ice and ache of winter, if I can find a password to transform winter. I have nearly six months grace. My mouth will not be colder than winter this time. When I turn away from the window I will not go down into darkness. There have been too many of those days, when I have watched winter, frozen to my unreal bones. It must be different next winter.

She closes the garden gate, walks back to the crossroads. Beth wants something better than gardens of cold flowers.

Twilight was beginning when Beth reached the village. The streets were deserted. She could not say exactly what the visit to her old house had taught her, other than the warning against winter, but it seemed to her that the afternoon had given her some important knowledge that she must learn to translate. She walked along slowly, thinking over her experience, when she was suddenly surprised to hear Theron talking to someone. She looked around and saw in the dim light her husband and a young woman, a stranger to her, conversing at the end of a narrow passage leading to Church Street. Beth called out to him but he didn't seem to hear her. She began walking towards them but stopped short when she heard him say angrily,

'I see the shadow of lichen growing on your face . . .'

Struck by his strange words and the passion of his tone Beth paused and then drew aside into a doorway in the alley. She could not recognize the woman Theron addressed for she was in shadow. The woman laughed and said,

'The god of doors is blind, Theron, he cannot see my face.'

The woman's voice, cold and complacent, frightens Beth. She presses back against the damp brickwork, then peers forward, listening. The woman whose identity is hidden from Beth speaks again.

'Pretend Sunday is my birthday, Theron. Will you celebrate with me? Will you laugh at my vaginal jokes?'

The woman's laughter echoes down the alleyway and hits Beth with the force of a reptile believed to be extinct. She shivers. Then she heard Theron say,

'Fires in my skull died down when Beth came to me.'

The woman swore then, viciously, obscenely about Beth, and Beth, shuddering, thought, I am walled up in the rain.

Theron said roughly,

'You offered me dry inedible fruit, how could I exist on that? Did you expect me to be content with that?'

Beth edged closer, trying to catch every word.

'I offered you freshly-killed hearts,' the woman told him tensely, 'I offered you the full moon penned in a glass bottle. I showed you how to march up to the Giant and get whatever you wanted.'

'No, no,' he said, 'you wore a dress of dragon bones and offered me the executioner's domain.'

It is as if the words choke Theron.

The woman said,

'I walk every night and see the moon disappear into the clouds of night. I see trees, ditches, rough grass. I am alone. I walk every night. Last night I came to the church and looked up at the bell-tower. An ugly old woman leaned out and cackled at me. Can you possibly imagine how cold my existence is, Theron?'

He answered,

'Liar, you liar, you always were. You could sleep amid bones and bodies forever. All that you complain of you brought on yourself.' She drew her breath in sharply. Then she muttered,

'I foresee the death of your son. I foresee you lost amid fishes and flowers and firearms. All your wives are crazy. I know these things. I am certain of it all. I try to keep the records straight, Theron, even though I feel like a computer invaded by spiders.'

'Shut up, you bitch, shut up! I've had enough. I'm sick of conversations like crossword puzzles, I'm sick of you. Why don't you leave me alone, you know I won't give you anything.'

The woman moved a little away from Theron and to Beth it seemed that she was considering him sadly, and she spoke quietly,

'If my words are distorted, it is by a virus I can't be cured of. You have isolated me. You know the place I inhabit and you chose it for me, Theron. Can you blame me for clinging to you, Theron. You are my only link with the old ways. I cannot help it if I can only meet you in these dark places. I do not choose the time or the place for my . . . manifestations. I want to speak clearly, to speak and live the truth. But I am silted up for good, with no hope. The first and strongest emotion I experience is anger: it is my major key. I see anger in the snow-geese of winter, in the headlands, the sea, in all the duties of this existence of mine that is no existence. I taste anger in birdseed, I hear it in the songs of birds. All the rooms I inhabit are warped. All my memories are waterlogged. I am unable to make sense of my aloneness. I'm still on the brink of the river, at the brink of my death.'

Then there was a silence like an archaeological investigation of the blood of the man and the two women. It was now quite dark and the rain was falling steadily, promising sleeplessness.

Beth crept closer until she was near enough to reach out and touch Theron's shoulder. She shivered, drenched with the rain. She crept closer until she saw the lichen shadow on the other woman's face, her skin stained with waterweed.

'Who are you?' Beth cried out, in terror.

Theron swung round and stared at Beth.

'There's no one here, no one,' he gabbled, 'come away, there's no one here . . .'

But Beth saw the woman and pushed Theron aside, with the strength of her terror, and he fell against the wall, he groaned. The woman began to back away, very slowly, her pale eyes fixed on Beth, her smile decaying in the rainy shadows, retreating into the street beyond the alley. Beth followed her and asked her quietly,

'Who are you?'

The answer came in a voice of no simplicity.

'Vellet.'

And the echo went down the alley, into the darkness which it charred.

TEN

IT is morning and Beth and Theron are eating bacon sandwiches for breakfast. It is very early, an iron-hard light with no sun. Outside, the wind slews round. Beth gets up from the table, leans on the windowsill and stares out at the rainy day that is coiled like a snake about them both.

Last night he refused to answer any of Beth's questions. He did not get angry. He did not respond in any way. He was armoured against each attack. She wept, she screamed, she coaxed, she threatened. He would not answer one single question.

'Why did she call herself by your first wife's name? Who is she? What is wrong with her face? Do you sleep with her?'

He shook his head.

'Who is she?'

'Don't ask me these questions, Beth, please,' was all he said, over and over again.

Now he drinks his coffee, looks understandingly at Beth, asks her to rest today, says no more, except that he'll be home at the usual time. Then he leaves the house.

Fifteen minutes later Beth is thinking, no, not blood, not bloodstains today, please, no blood when I wipe myself.

But there is blood. The blood flows from Beth's womb. Her back aches, pain presses her breasts in its cramping bodice. She pauses as she is about to switch on the washing machine and thinks, what kind of man have I become wife to?

Last night he had caught Beth and stopped her from running after the other woman and getting any information from her. By the time she had struggled free, the street was empty, the woman (was there a woman?) had gone.

Now Beth is without any plans or ideas about her own future. Can I possibly expect a good end from such bad beginnings? Beth shakes her head.

Later that day she went to sit in the little back sitting room that looked out on her favourite part of the garden, where the roses grew. She sat by the window, an old cardigan thrown over her shoulders. On her lap is a book and she is studying a picture of the Creator carrying the sleeping Adam. She concentrates on this, memorizing every detail, for ten minutes, until a sudden whining gust of wind makes her jump. The window sashes rattle. The book slips to the floor. She makes a movement as if to pick it up but changes her mind, scratches her arm, stands up, stretches, yawns. She buttons the cardigan on and peers out of the window at a dull afternoon, a conversation in another language. Taking a couple of tissues out of her pocket, she wedges them into the window frame, to stop the rattling. She kneels on the windowsill and glares out at the fuzzy sky, the few stealthy birds, as if her angry stare might alter the weather. She remembers the colour of rainwater that collects in the hoofprints the cattle leave on the hillside of the Giant: it is the colour of her thoughts. She thinks of the other house, beyond the village, high up on the moors, and wishes she were I here.

The half-touch of cramp still lingers but the blood has settled to an even flow and only her slight pallor might hint at Beth's menstruation. She breathes on the window and on the misted glass writes with her forefinger, Ash . . .

But she is thinking of Theron, and the mystery woman. What does his silence mean? Is he afraid? Of me? No, more likely of her. How did she manage to vanish so quickly? I heard no car drive away. What is between Theron and this woman who has appropriated his first wife's name?

Beth sets her lips, determined to show her contempt for the threats of this woman. She does not know that Vellet has cursed Theron, put an attacking army in his mind.

She rubs out the name on the window and quickly gets her coat, goes outdoors, uneasy with desires she only half acknowledges, disturbed by the strength of her concern for Theron. She'd married him in a careless way, liking him, admiring him, but also detached from any deep sustaining relation with him, she had wished only to blot out all memories of Ash and of the house on the moors where she and Ash had been happy for a while. It was an offhand beginning, straight out of the pain of losing Ash, and Beth is disturbed now to find how deeply she cares about her marriage and fears for Theron's safety.

Up to now their life has worked, drifting, not going deep, but bringing something into their lives, mutual support and shared interests. Beth moves slowly across the garden, through the snarled passages of rain. Now that Theron is intimidated by a stranger and has become more remote and troubled, Beth feels all her emotions roused. She knows she must learn what is isolating him. She does not know that whenever she walks towards Theron, he sees a ghost over her shoulder.

She heads out of the garden, away from the village where her enemies are too strong for her as yet, and walks up through the woods, through Rowden Foot Coppice, until she comes to Giant Hill. At the foot of the Hill, beside the little spring into which she often throws a coin, but not today, she meets the old tramp the villagers call Funeral Jo. He grins at her. He was sitting on a tree trunk, wearing an old grey plastic rain coat, a torn pair of corduroy trousers and layers of newspaper. 'Hello, Jo,' said Beth, 'when's summer going to begin?' He just shook his head wisely. Smiling, Beth walked on through the abbey ruins and began climbing the hill. As she went up through air cold as interrogations she thought, it is not the sky that this giant supports on his shoulders, but the land and all of us on it, all our blindness and recklessness. The grass is slippery and Beth has to go carefully. Another woman watches Beth struggle up the hill but Beth does not see her. The woman who watches from a never-to-be-discovered hiding place whispers, go to the snout of the dungeon, Beth. Beth does not hear these words. The woman with the skin of a hunter sits in her cold forest.

At the summit of the hill, Beth looks along the white expanse of the Giant, the archaic form. Lost in thought, Beth stands for some minutes without moving a muscle, then breaks away, as if out of a spell, looks down to see the long distance of flowing water, the river that skirts the foot of the hill. But she looks again at the giant and moves to meet him, fearfully, with the indistinct vowel sounds of supplication rising to her lips.

She sits or rather squats down between the eyes of the giant. It is not fitting for her to sit on his breast or on his penis. The white yards of him stretch about and around her. She crouches on the cold grass. Her blood flows. The landscape is grey mostly, like a bad smudgy drawing, and the rain has become fine and constant.

Beth offers the giant her loneliness that is like the biting of some animal.

All my life, she thinks, I have believed in the giant. Perhaps I am the first person for many years to love the giant. I am the first enemy of any darkness that hates him. Local people either ignore this huge figure cut into the chalk thousands of years ago, this marcher, this fertile sign, or, if there is any reaction, it will be an embarrassed snigger, a gesture of obscenity. Though perhaps I am being unfair, too hasty. I believe that there may be some, women, perhaps, or young men, who turn towards the giant, seriously, considering his advice. I have tried to keep faith. When I was in my teens, I would cycle over here in the school holidays or at weekends, and read, or think, or dream. He is a focus for dreams, here the energies of dream come into the everyday life, bringing incisiveness, strength, beauty. Or so it was for me. And there is a peacefulness here that I never found in a church. And always behind the peace is energy, which gives me life, and yet which some people, Ash, yes, and Theron, say they find too much to cope with, too alien a sensation, an electric shock, that causes them to have nothing to do with the giant. In the summer, coaches come and strangers on day-trips clamber up Giant Hill, and I've seen them flinch behind their cameras from the prehistoric man, dancer and warrior.

Seated between his eyes, below the summit of the hill, Beth is sheltered from the wind but the rain drives at her. She touches the chalk of his left eyesocket with her left hand, and speaks to the giant.

I remember an autumn years ago when Ash and I sat here. It was sunny but getting on for evening. Ash still had long hair then and as she told me a strange story she plaited and unplaited the ends of her braids. I remember watching her face, the expressions changing, sadness, sustained courage, shame, anger.

This was her story.

When I was sixteen (said Ash) I left home and got a job as a waitress in a café in the poorer district of the city. I had lived in the city all my life and the ugliness of it had had years to get right behind my eyes: crowds, noise, traffic, the silent howl of the living, the violence at the edge of everything. At night, Beth, at night when I slept I did not dare dream. I went from day to day without looking backward or forward, an automaton. I did not dare enter any church in the city although I needed rest and sanctuary. I did not read any newspapers because disasters frightened me, drew me in to their dark to erase me. Obliteration was everywhere. I felt my own blood pour out on the pavement of the city which sheltered so many terrorists. Bomb-blasts deafened me. I worked in that filthy caff, numb and frightened, for nearly two years. One winter morning, the rain pouring down, a tall well-dressed man with a loud hoarse voice came into the stuffy room and glanced at me without smiling.

(Ash paused, took a deep breath, glanced around her at the fields, at her friend listening intently, and resumed.)

For no apparent reason, I was afraid. Even more afraid than usual! I looked away and deliberately took another customer's order. I saw the tall man talking to the manager and at one point in their conversation, I saw both men look over at me coldly. That evening I packed my belongings in a single cheap suitcase and left my room in the boarding house. Carrying one book in my gloved hand I went to the address the manager had given me.

The tall man, whose name does not matter, opened the door. He took my suitcase and smiled formally. There was something motionless about him, a stillness beneath his skin. Who are you? I asked roughly. He offered me a drink. I shook my head. I am not one who guides people through the dark, he said. I did not understand him and I said so. It does not matter, he answered. The room was very cold, I shivered. He switched on an electric fire. Then he stood by the window and looked at me intently, although the room was dark and my face lit only by the fake logs of the fire. Listen, he said quietly. I nodded. He spoke for sometime without looking at me. When he'd finished, he asked, do you understand? Yes, I said. Don't tell lies, he said sharply.

(Beth started to ask Ash a question, but Ash motioned her to be quiet. She went on speaking very rapidly now, to get the pictures out of her head.)

Very well, I said to the man, I don't understand. He was silent. He tapped on the window with his forefinger. It will be a comfortable life for you, he said, softly. You will not have to work all day and half the night in a miserable fish restaurant. This existence of yours in the city will become . . . extinct, as it were. I live a long way from here. You will find difficulties at first, it will be strange, but you will settle down. Do you follow me now? I said, I think so. I thought, Beth, of fool's gold and of the Chevalier Raoul. My head throbbed, I felt feverish. He came towards me and looked at me. I could tell now that he was still young, in his thirties, but tired. You are poor, he said, and, I suspect, desperate. Do you accept my offer? I said nothing. He frowned, then sighed. The dark room stirred with rape and horror. I knew that came from *outside*, from the city, not from him. I looked out of the window at those streets and alleyways and I shuddered. Yes, I said, yes, I agree, in a voice I hardly recognized as mine. Yes. Yes. Good, he said casually. We'll set off first thing in the morning.

He showed me to a small bedroom and here I passed the night alone, without sleeping. In the morning we left the city by car. It was still raining heavily. I was so happy to be leaving. I glanced at the man. I saw no hump on his back. I thought of my hands, Beth, full of money! We drove all day and in the early evening stopped at a modest hotel. Again we had separate rooms. The idea of his sex scared me, yet fascinated me. I had this persistent idea in my mind, I must have read it somewhere, that the empty silken garments of a lover can be abandoned to bring fair weather. As we ate breakfast, he asked me if I was pleased with the new arrangement. In my life, I supposed. I said I did not know. After breakfast, while I was packing, he came into my room and locked the door. He talked to me for nearly an hour. Then we set off again. The rain had lifted and I looked out of the car window curiously at green hills and fields. I was excited. Think, Beth, the city girl's outing. This journey took place in the second month of the year. Yes, I was excited, but I felt tense, little daggers touched my breast.

We arrived at our destination in the afternoon. It was a big house with well-kept grounds. When I walked into the house, my clothes felt dirty on my skin. A woman, older than the man, came slowly downstairs to meet us. She looked ironically at us. You see, said the man, I have been successful. He gestured lightly towards me. Have you? she said coolly. So my life in that house began.

That night I gathered the threads of the life together. He came to my room but did not touch me. He took off his clothes and put on the clothes of a woman. He looked at himself in the mirror for quite a time and then asked me to dance with him. It was a formal dance, without music. As we danced he said to me, my sister won't do it, and my wife's dead, so you see I need you. I stroked the folds of his dress, as he suggested. I vowed to avoid anger, lust, cowardice, malevolence in this new life.

I was introduced to visitors as his secretary, but I suppose a good many of them guessed I performed another function. At first I managed, the man was kind, demanded, you see, almost nothing. The sister hated me, what else could you expect. I stayed there for nearly a year, a lazy life, really, with plenty of freedom, money, better than working in the caff, away from the city. But then contempt built up in me, for him and for myself, and I found unexpected strength in myself, enabling me to break away from that corrupt association. No angry event precipitated my leaving, all happened in a civilized manner, and we parted friends.

Beth is shivering in the rain. Another of Ash's histories. Another of her anecdotes. Beth knows them by heart.

She makes her way home.

On her table there is an open bible and a glass vase with a bunch of lilies blue as the mountains of Jephthah's daughter.

When Beth came in her feet felt bruised as if she'd been walking barefoot and her head ached. She went straight to the living room and lit the fire she'd laid this morning, kneeling down to witness the sacrifice of summer trees. Little flames soon glide through the twigs and the odour of woodsmoke appeases Beth. An alphabet of unhappiness burns away in the fire, relieving Beth's tension for a while. A fire for the giant, she whispers. There is silence except for the fire and Beth sees pictures in the flames. She sees stars, the ships of the left hand, a woman with honeymoon claws, a child dressed in membraneous clothes, sneakthief faces, the serene smile of the hobgoblin.

Beth jerks her head up. She was almost asleep. She moves back from the heat of the fire, sits in the comfortable old colonial chair she'd brought from her own house. She felt a strange indiscriminate peace now, the calm of the last day of a saturnalia. It is because of my period, thought Beth, and it will not last. The arrears remain. But I will accept it while it lasts, without bribery, threats or promises.

And still Ash is behind all Beth's thoughts, numinous, like a sun or a star.

But did I ever, thinks Beth, really believe any of the accounts of herself Ash gave me? Surely I always knew they were her fantasies? Not lies, no, but elaborations of smaller far less exciting adventures. When I think of it, I know nothing at all about her life before she arrived at the village, out of nowhere.

Ash, you were walking along Half Moon Street and I almost bumped into you as I came out of the grocer's. Where are you going, I wondered, at once drawn to you, inexplicably then, but now I believe it was because at that time you and I were so similar that we made the perfect reflection, one to the other. It was late in the afternoon, and the shadows would have hidden me, but I did not dare follow you. Your face was, without doubt, one I was unable to read, and yet felt compelled to consider. The reflection, you see.

Now, years later, I am possessed by the desire to know whether we are still the same reflection, split into two halves, or whether we have grown to be different. I want to know, I suppose, whether we have grown up. I am listening to the past, as to a wound, and I need to change that habit. Blood's given language could map our hearts, if we met now. The masks of twilight crowd around me, whispering, Ash, Ash.

And drowning out that sound is the engine of Theron's car revving up and then stopping outside the door.

ELEVEN

A FORTNIGHT after the encounter in Church Street, Theron and I walked over the fields to the river. It was late on Sunday afternoon. I could sight-read the trees, I saw the summer coming towards me, its glossy green candles and its white anointments. But when Theron glanced at me, I saw the sky become dank and graceless rain threaten. His voice was cold and calm. He spoke of an article he'd read in the morning's paper. He tells me that in his opinion abortions are illegal operations. I felt no need to reply.

We walked along the towpath in silence until we came to the bench donated by a former mayor of the village where we sat down. A little further upstream two boys were rowing in an old dinghy but no other vessels were on the water.

I looked at Theron. He has been sleeping badly and he holds his body in a rigid way, as if avoiding some disgrace. I am afraid he is becoming ill. I do not think he has seen the woman again but he will not speak of that night at all. We've only made love twice since then. I have stopped asking questions. He ignored everything I said. I have just the words of one language at my disposal and my dialect can only cope with so many riddles at any one time. So I've stopped asking questions.

Beth puts her hand gently on Theron's shoulder. The sunlight glitters on the brown water of the river. The little boys row to the opposite bank and are calling to their friends, who help pull the boat in to shore. Theron's smile is forced, cold as the shadow of a dog. Beth sees how his unhappiness encumbers him. Specks of blood are falling on the page of a book of jokes.

'Lets walk on, shall we? To Giant Hill?' She spoke softly. He nodded and for an instant Beth smelt the body of his first wife rotting in the orchard, but she pushed this image away with the damp groping hands of a timid child. Oh this man is to blame! she thought savagely, irrationally, knowing she was being unfair.

Theron opens the wooden gate at the end of the towpath and they walk along a street of settled houses surrounded by bright flowers and quiet cultivated lawns. Theron's remark startles her, the more so in these domesticated surroundings.

'Beth, your hair whispers like her . . .' She turns sharply on him.

'What? My hair? Like hers? Whose?' She tugged at his sleeve, bringing her face close to his.

'Whose, Theron?'

He shrugged, was suddenly petulant.

'Forget it, it's nothing. Just a dream I had, last night. A fragment, remembered. Just came into my head. I was thinking aloud, that's all.' Beth relaxes and slips her hand into his. This is the first real confidence he's made for weeks, the first real contact.

'Tell me, please.'

Theron walks on rapidly, pulling her with him. The windows of the new houses are stone deaf but not blind; Theron and Beth flash in each window they pass like a newsreel.

'In my dream,' he said, 'it is twilight in a moon city, and the wives of senators are decked out in their pearls. I am one, I think, but I have no wife. I drink but the wine makes me weep. My mother comes into the room and a veil is clinging to her hair and makes me think of spidery crabs crawling there. She twitches the veil off and says to me, blood keeps me clean, son. I shout at her, red flowers, mother, red flowers I accept, but no blood. And that was my dream.'

Beth and Theron turn out of the street and enter a leafy shadowy lane.

'No, wait. There was more. I remember now. In the dream mother says, you act the fool but I know that you are clever enough when you choose to be. Her voice is very soft, Beth, and it is like hair moving in the breeze. She says to me, I will walk another mile and then I will rest. I am collecting Vellet's excrement.'

Theron gasps out the last sentences as if rebelling against them but unable to help himself. Sweat stands out on his face. Beth does not know what to say, hesitates. Theron takes a shuddering breath. They are at the foot of Giant Hill. The sun is moving restlessly among clouds and the air is growing colder. Theron remembers his dream with bitterness.

'You know who Vellet is?' he asks Beth.

'Yes. Your first wife.'

He nods, can't speak, lights a cigarette.

'It is perhaps natural to dream of your first wife,' she suggests, frowning anxiously.

'It was so repellent in the dream, Beth.' He is calmer now, draws on the cigarette. They pause by the stile, do not climb over.

'There must be a meaning in a dream, always, so I've read,' says Theron, 'but what is in this dream?'

'It is hard to read dreams, Theron, hard to lift them out of their dark, and no one meaning will ever be found, only the variables, which must serve.' Beth spoke with profound tenderness, leaning towards Theron. 'Can you recall any more of the dream, my dear?'

He concentrated, fixing his gaze on the ground.

'Yes,' he said slowly, 'yes. I see my mother holding excrement in her gloved hands and smiling at me. She offers it to me. Eventually I take it. It feels cold and dry. My mother goes away. But Vellet comes into the room, brushes her hair in front of the mirror. She says to me, *something swollen, Theron? Heart?* I have no answer. She goes out of the room, looking back over her shoulder, contemptuously. That is the end of the dream. What can it mean, Beth?'

When Theron looked at her with such unfamiliar intensity, such new dependence, fear like a sniper behind his eyes, Beth did not know what to say. She knew that if she found the right answer, the true answer, their lives would be changed and be immeasurably strengthened. But his dream had depressed her and she could think of no positive meaning in the dream, it seemed to her only another sign that Theron was very disturbed and that his dream was a symptom of some illness. She did not even want to think about the role his first wife Vellet still played in his life and this factor inhibits her sympathy. She does not know how to answer him without hurting him. Perhaps I should hurt him, she thought.

'Beth?'

She looked up.

'I think . . . I think it means there is some unresolved and unsuspected grief in you still, Theron, about Vellet. Some guilt? But why feel responsible for her death? Do you? It was accidental, her death.'

He struggled away from her embrace, uttering a long incoherent rambling string of words, a lawless bellow, anger choking him.

'Then consult a doctor,' she shouted after him, but he did not answer, he went on down the lane, leaving her by the stile, frightened and resentful. It was his bloody dream, she thought. She wanted at that moment to pack up her things and return to her house, on the high ground above the village. I can't help him. There are no clues. Unless the dream is a clue. But how complex to unravel. I sense Theron is travelling new and difficult distances within himself. These take him not just away from me, but from all who might help him. That dream frightened me. He has become so changed lately. If I am to help him, he must give me all the facts. All the information, not keeping anything back. If it were a lecture, he would give all the facts to his students. He must do the same in this situation we're in. All the facts. How can I advise him otherwise?

She sat on the stile as the summer twilight came on. A remnant of travellers stumbled down through the trees and as they climbed the stile greeted her. She smiled and watched the two couples disappear around the bend in the path.

The idea of a summer spent alone at her own house fills her with pleasure but she will not go unless their troubles grow worse. I will not be driven out of this marriage until I learn more of Vellet. That is the heart of the trouble. It lies in the past. I'll ask in the village about his first wife. I'll ask Tabitha. She'll know.

Beth sits for a long while in the musky evening, thinking half against her will about Theron's dream, about his mother, the red flowers, the blood, Vellet, and her excrement, her contempt. When she walks home, the branches of the trees are like the strong tendons in the necks of animals. The moon is sewn to the church steeple.

But I am not ready, thinks Beth, to enter whatever labyrinth Theron and Vellet spun around themselves. I am not ready, but how can I avoid it. Something swollen? Heart?

When she got home, he'd made the supper and nothing was said of any dream or argument. He came to her room to say goodnight, last thing. He sat on the edge of her bed and apologized for his outburst.

'I was all on edge.'

Beth smiled.

'Why did that dream upset you so much, Theron. We all get these weird dreams.'

He shrugged, moved away from the bed.

'Overwork, I guess,' he said.

'Tell me about Vellet,' said Beth placidly, pulling her shawl around her shoulders. She was sitting up in bed, she'd been reading when he came in. He deliberately adopted an expression that was both stupid and solemn.

'It was a tragedy,' he said, 'we were very happy and then there was the accident. There's nothing to tell. She was very young. She was headstrong. She insisted on going for a swim though I tried to persuade her against it . . . I did not know she'd slipped out of the house that night, I thought she'd taken my advice. It is when I get overtired, then I dream of her. And dreams, you know, they are only distortions of our daytime thoughts, a sort of re-run, only jumbled and rotten.'

'Are they?' asked Beth.

'I brought you a book to read,' he said, placing it on her bedside table.

'Thank you, dear.'

He stooped and kissed her goodnight. He was aware of the sinews and ovaries of her body warding him off, she knew that.

He closed the door behind him. She picked up his book. A detective story. She throws it on the floor. I want none of his propagandas, she thinks, I want the truth. How neatly his mask fits! But it will suffocate him.

After he'd said goodnight to Beth, he tried to settle to some work, and went into his study. He drew the curtains, sat at his desk. As soon as he sat down, he remembered the night it began.

On that first night he could not sleep, so he got up and wandered out into the garden. It was a hot airless night. He was a widower, recently bereaved. Vellet had been buried barely a month.

He sat in the summerhouse and did not notice how the July air got strangely colder. But when he stood up to go indoors he saw her.

Oh god in the dark I saw her, a woman without shoes on her feet, without any garments.

She said, 'I am the water's woman, you cannot bring me back to life.'

I looked at her face and my darkness lifted.

I saw her sensuous shadow, her lap of luxury.

I did not know then her way of destroying, by inches.

She called me, 'Theron.'

She said, 'you know my name.'

I said, 'you have no name.'

But I was fascinated.

Aproned with storms, she came towards me.

I put myself into her hands.

So she trapped me. So began my haunting. So began the resurrection of Vellet.

Theron left his room. It was almost impossible for him to move but he lifted one foot and set it down again in a new position, carefully shifting his body in the direction of this new position, and so again with the other foot, and so on, until he managed to walk. He got to the kitchen and made himself a cup of chocolate, sat drinking it, still puzzling over the dream.

It never occurs to him that he might enjoy being haunted. It never occurs to him that he could exorcise Vellet, if he were to put his heart into it. To tell Beth about Vellet, that's unthinkable. So the haunting goes on.

TWELVE

IN a medieval cathedral in a European city, Ash looks up at a stained glass window representing the biblical girl Tamar.

Beth trudges across muddy fields near the village of the giant.

Ash steps up into the pulpit and reads silently from the huge open bible: 'Eat your flesh as fire.'

The rain slackens but Beth strides on. The man is cold, she rages, the man is cold.

Ash smiles slightly, flicks through the heavy pages of the bible. '. . . all the curses that are written in this book shall lie upon him . . .'

Ash's gaze returns to the stained glass window. Her Madonna wanders slowly through the snow. Her Christ's kisses darken her heart, as if Ash were exposed to wind and weather. She turns another page. '. . . the captive exile hasteneth to be loosed . . .'

In the black morning Beth hears white bells toll. She grips the field gate with her wet hands and imagines spiders pierced with golden needles. It is Theron who tortures them, she mutters. I want to face those sort of dangers without flinching. I know I am the life my fingertips fear. His unkind words this morning are none of my concern. Fuck him. I have to think of the anticipations of Eve, I have to quench my own thirst.

'. . . I have set her blood on the top of a rock . . .' Ash closes the book. She descends from the pulpit, she does not dip her fingers in the stoop of holy water. She goes out of the cathedral barn back into the city. She was weary. Yes, woman comes to it, approaching the edge, followed by the thieving birds of her shadow. She is intricate as lace-making, struck dumb by the risks she takes.

Meanwhile, Beth travels on to a bleak place, much feared by strangers. Yes, the man is cold, she thinks, but her rage has stilled. She has been crying and hitting out at her thoughts with her fists.

Now there is a sensation of steady driving warmth throughout her body and she takes shelter in an abandoned farm building within sight of Giant Hill.

The image of a red shroud flaps in my mind, as in a wind ripping down from the hill. This morning Theron and I discussed that dream and we argued again. We concentrated on his problems but mine were tucked well out of sight. I ask him about that woman but he refuses to answer. If we argue in the middle of summer, we are bound to argue next winter, when conditions are more generally unfavourable. When I have so little knowledge of my own self, how can I give him back the mystery of his dream, solved and safe for him to contemplate? I said to him, the dream is the message of the instincts, what it foretells will happen of itself, you do not have to do anything but allow the process to continue. When I told him this, which was the best I could do, he answered coarsely, you smooth stupid cunt, how would you know? He was pallid and his lips were puffy, like those of a premenstrual woman. There we stood, this morning, in the kitchen, surrounded by the shadows of pre-Christian men and unbaptized infants. On a threshold. Both of us at the border of a route that leads either to an orchard of lemon trees, paradisal, or to a cage of ooze, the slime and algae of our end.

But she will not leave Theron. She has the strength to cope with events of this morning's nature. There is much strength in Beth and she is beginning to understand this. Beth lives in a place where Vellet cannot go. She cannot slither into Beth's life. Vellet is afraid of this woman who has found calm, who can sit and think at the end of her rage, who has a delicacy of intellect that Vellet never possessed.

Vellet is watching Beth, from the other side of the rain. Then she turns to the Giant, her companion.

'Blindman, who am I?' she cries out. 'Who is this woman? How can she be so strong? Beth? Is this Beth? Giant, who is she?'

No answer for Vellet. Silence in the region of the Giant, that handicaps Vellet. I hate the woman, she thinks, and yet she cannot get close enough to Beth to communicate her hatred. There is a barrier preventing Vellet from contaminating Beth with her blue face and red rump, her bird's beak and her drowned hair.

'You look angry, Giant. You look angry all the time, to me. Is it because Beth's child will die one hundred years from now? Why were you blinded, Giant? Did you see stars that were forbidden, a moon with a woman's face? Why was I drowned? Why am I kept in this limbo, half-flesh, half-ghost? I had made up my mind to haunt Beth but she cannot, will not see me. What force is she exuding, that puts me in so close a paddock, eh, Giant? Are you giving her a helping hand? Help me too. Take these handcuffs of water off my wrists, Giant. Give me back my body, my breath. I won't get into unintelligible regions next time, I promise. Give me a new life. Let me go back and begin again.'

'There is a way to the next stage for you, Vellet,' the giant answered, in a delving voice, 'but you must find the door before you pick the lock. You are not ready for any new life yet. You still retard yourself.'

'Fuck!' said Vellet defiantly. And then, after a moment, sadly, 'who else will rescue me ?'

'You have not asked the right question yet. Ask that question and you will be rescued.'

The two shadows, the two shades, converse between weathers, between fluctuations in the air, spirits of the place, perhaps, or the imagination of the hill searching for an utterance.

'I'm tired of all this talk, I didn't ask to be put here, stuck here with you, why should I stay here? There's no pleasure in it. Do you remember, Giant, years ago, when that boy and I came here at night to make love on the slopes of your hill? That was not Theron, but the other one, who I loved, but who frightened me, so that I ran off to marry Theron, and so lost him. We lay down on your slope and exchanged our greetings. There was a little moon that misled me and I let him do it. Did you feel it, Giant? Do you join in?'

Vellet paused, looked mischievous, but there was no answer from her companion.

'Anyway, it was the first time, for me. It was like walking on tiptoe down a steep valley towards a garden. Then he thrust into me, a man groping for a door in the dark. I knew he was thinking of another girl's face but I was too excited to care, I heard my body's havoc and I felt the world revolve wetly in the orifices of my body. I did not come but afterwards I realized I had been able for the first time to look deeply into the downpour of myself. Then he and I sprawled out on your hill, like victims of a bombardment. I trembled violently. If I had known my future, which death would I have chosen? Death by air? By fire? By water? Or by burial in the earth? But I knew nothing of my future. Is this story ammunition for your magic lantern world, Giant? No. You are hard as the earth you are carved from. I am a lost woman in a desert begging you for charity and you will not help!'

'I cannot help you. You must solve the riddle yourself.' The giant is falling back into the uncomprehending earth.

Vellet laughed unpleasantly. She climbed into the boughs of an elder tree and sat among the white flowers and black fruit.

'I suppose I am too wicked to be helped?'

'No. But it is not my business to help.'

'What is your business, Giant?'

'To remember the thinness of my own self. To understand my blindness.' This is the voice of the earth itself now and turning to dust. Vellet does not understand and dances across a red planet and back again to the edge of the giant. She rattles her anger in her throat. In her mouth, she always tastes the necromancy of a great salt lake.

'But I would eat my children as soon as I caught them,' she said, removing her gloves and taking the coins from her eyelids. She will not look at Beth, climbing the stairs to her bedroom. Vellet bleeds from breasts, hands and knees.

'Did you hear me, Giant? Eat my children!' The Giant laughed.

'You are clever at twisting words, Vellet.' Vellet laughed with him, for he was her puppeteer, her manipulator. He said sharply, 'Don't laugh.'

'I am the princess caught under the spell of an evil sorcerer,' she said. But she did not laugh.

Beth wielded the sharp knife expertly and sliced the raw meat. Theron watched her exact movements eagerly, but in silence, admiring her neat interlocking gestures as she prepared the meal. Suddenly he felt the alienness of himself return, felt a buffoon there in the kitchen, doing nothing.

'I'll go for a walk, the sun's coming out.' Beth nodded, absorbed in her task. Theron felt himself turning unavoidably into many shapes, none of them were what he wanted. He waved goodbye through the window. Beth waved back, her fingers bloody. Theron's own fingertips sighed on the black gate. Recently, he had read about the dwarf who mourned the death of his friend, a blind giant.

She sank beneath the water, he thought. And now paths of hawthorn and spittle mislead me.

The words of a man planning rebellion are always confused.

As Theron came down through the trees of Morning Well Plantation, he saw her by the gate, waiting for him. The sun encourages Theron to smile, but he does not notice the sunlight now. He is tired and his face looks worn.

She has followed me again, he thought dully. I have been walking along Vellet's corridor, that territory passing through a land to which it does not belong.

She put her hand out and touched his chest and said in a whisper,

'I saw you, Theron, naked and berserk, sweating with gaol fever. Why did you throw my photograph, torn to shreds, down the privy?'

He does not answer, begins to walk away. She follows him. 'You see, you have two wives,' she explains, smiling.

He opens the gate, walks rapidly along the path. A little stream glitters and winds beside the path. Vellet jumps and lands on the water, she is walking on the water. Theron watches this trick out of the corner of his eye disdainfully. Vellet careers over the water, stares down to see her own apparition heavy on the stream. In the field, a scarecrow is waiting, drenched in sun, but shivering. The summer fields swept away behind him, dry and bare.

'Don't get your feet wet,' he said sarcastically.

'I am not a thief,' she sighed, 'I will not steal your wife. I am not your cold twin, your glittering leaf bud, am I?'

He did not answer. She looked at him and predicted twilight in several languages.

'You smell of dry rot,' he said spitefully, 'it is your death I smell.'

Then the ghost jumped on him, got hold of him. Her wet hair! He almost screamed, pushed her away, throwing her back into the stream. She came at him again, the sodden ghost, and grabbed him. He pushed at her again but his heart wasn't in it. She threw her whole weight at him and they both fell to the ground and she slid his hand up between her legs. He expected cold dead flesh but she was warm. It was a hard decision for him to make and he hesitated. She said, 'I'll rechristen you, dear.' He was trembling and his lanky prick quivered, a lady killer. He rubbed himself up against her blue skirt and touched his wary sex with his right hand. She was silent, she was reconstructing signals for his flesh. But she felt no pleasure. There was no sensation in her cunt, ever. Dead. To him it felt warm, because she intended him to feel a warmth, but to her it was like clay, her dead sex, cold and unamplified. Theron was gasping and fingering her hairy ghostly cunt. Even though he knew this was a hoax, he glanced around to make sure no one was watching, not a soul, and unfastened his pants. He gestured to Vellet and she laughed. They both rolled on the bank of the stream.

He looked at her face and forgot she was dead, a pool of stagnant water. Almost soberly he embraced her. She shifted her body and thought, yes, he is playing the giant excellently.

It was nearly midsummer and he mounted her unhesitatingly in the warmth of noon. His penis travelled slowly at first through waves of a remote fire. Vellet hitched her legs up higher. She grimaced like a grotesque doll when he entered her, squinting, twisting her mouth. She had no pleasure to gain. He moved faster, bewitched. She felt nothing in her cold place, no rift, no gulping ache, no orgasm, no absolution. He pushed into Vellet hard and holy, approaching the pure colour of a clear sky in his body and his mind. His body was shining around him and before his eyes she was glowing, a moist tumult. He could already taste orgasm, feel it, talk to it, love it, press against the mother-of-pearl strength of it — and then there is just the echo of Vellet's laughter and his penis plucked out of a woman's body that had never been there and he moved his closed hand fast over his penis and heaved once or twice, groaning slowly and it came out stark and whinnying, no longer beautifully pent but slimy, uncanny. He crouched on the bank of the stream feeling the watery air on his body and he heard the echo of her laughter, merry and horrid, smelt the odour of decay she'd left behind. The violent memories of his first marriage stank in his nose. He cursed her, the ghost of veins. He remembered how she drowned, like a wooden doll denying he possessed any part of her. Her husband, the darkest possible bugger, stands in the shadows and does not dive into the river to rescue her. He hears her cries but does not want to rescue her. The other man also turns away from the drowning woman. This is the frequently recurring image in Theron's mind. How he watched but did not move, watched, as if his hand were poised over a table containing sharp surgical instruments.

The little wooden hands splinter and bleed thin sap. A writhing dolly weeps, confesses her infidelities. A woman drowns. Men walk away from the scene of the tragedy.

On this summer day, he grovels beside the stream amid the scum of his seduction.

THIRTEEN

BETH in a sunless room, standing at a window, watching summer fail. Why do I exhaust myself thinking of Ash and of the past? Why am I wrenching my life out of shape? If I could forget Ash, I would be better able to help Theron and leave no dirt in our lives.

Theron walks slowly across the lawn, carrying a basket. He is going to fetch apples from the orchard. Beth watches him. The shadow of Ash grows thinner but still maims me. I fear the thought of her more than the armies of Arabia and Abyssinia.

Bridge-building. That is what Theron and I must learn. We must exchange confidences. That solemnity with which he speaks of the dead Vellet! What does it conceal? Theron and I must be helpmates, not enemies. In this chill summer, our marriage is turning into an icy circus without clowns and where we are the trapezists, strong men, acrobats on horseback, lion-tamers. It cannot continue like this. Theron goes about with such a serious look, as if heavy responsibilities were all he thought of, as if he'd been charged with the task of writing the gospels out in letters of gold.

Beth does not know that for Theron there is always the woman walking in the fields, always the woman slowly advancing towards him, offering him broken bread, broken sex. He turns away, he will not eat the dead woman's food.

Beth grumbled to herself a little longer before she made up her mind. Then she ran outdoors, across the lawn, through the air too cool for June. She found Theron in the orchard, murmuring a short and hurried prayer over a huge collar of fungus growing on an old apple tree.

'Isn't it magnificent,' he said. He looked happy and stroked the fungus.

'But there aren't many apples,' she said.

'No,' he agreed, 'it's too early.'

This conversation relaxes them both and they walk companionably through the little trees. But Beth is still trying to decipher all his silences, his casual remarks. She watches him as if her eyes were mirrors.

'Are you afraid of me ?' he said suddenly, harshly.

'No,' she said evenly, 'no. Afraid for you.'

'Ah,' he said, and laughed. 'Afraid for me, in the fields and meadows of my burning.'

'Why are you burning, Theron?'

At the orchard gate, they face one another, the basket tilted on the grass, the few apples green and sour.

'Let me help you,' she said.

He shook his head.

'Soon I must meet the guardian of the necropolis, that master of mummification. I am strong, Beth, but not strong enough.'

'What are you struggling with . . . ?'

He shook his head again. Between the branches of the nearest tree, Vellet is peering at them. He will not look at the ghost in the tree, but he winces.

'What are you afraid of?' asks Beth urgently. 'You must tell me soon or we shall be separated, driven apart by your fear. And by mine, for make no mistake it is contagious.'

'It might be best . . . for you to go away for a time . . . till I know if I can tell you. Until I am certain of my fear.' He speaks nervously, half smiling at her.

'Look, I don't want you to face your trouble alone,' she said.

'I don't want you to suffer because I'm tainted.'

'Tainted?' Beth is shocked. 'Tainted? By what, Theron?' She kisses him but he only submits to her touch, does not respond.

'I won't leave,' she said quietly, 'our marriage is a habitation I share with you.'

'But it can't be any good for you, nor can I,' he said desperately, 'not yet. If I can work this out for myself, then we'll be happy, then.'

'No,' said Beth, 'that is dangerous. I won't leave you.'

He looked at her and smiled but heard Vellet hiss.

'Don't hoard your unhappiness like a miser,' Beth whispers gently.

'I don't. Do I?' he answers, still smiling, tired.

'Tell me what taints you.'

'I can't,' he said, and shrugged, grinning sheepishly. He picked up the basket of apples. She caught at his arm.

'It is about Vellet, isn't it, all this,' she asked breathlessly, 'you feel guilty about her death, don't you, oh, but you know it was not your fault, you know that. You are relishing your damn guilt. Stop it! Let us live.'

She stops as if her throat is dismantling her. Her sudden anger is caught between an old warm moon and the ice of the new crescent. Summer whirls in the grey garden, freezing Beth and Theron to their fears. Then his obscene answer to her questions starts a long cry of pain in her head.

When she had spat the taste of it out of her mouth, he'd gone. She was in a silent landscape. Haunted? she thought. He is ill. Yet hesitation rises in her, she will not accept that he is sick. It is grief, she thinks, as she stumbles back to the house, the folds of her skirt heavy as timber. Her thoughts loop and twist and entangle her. The riddles? What does he mean? A ghost? Haunted? And that look of fear in him that Beth cannot lull.

As soon as Theron told Beth he was haunted, he had regretted it, and swore at her. Then he saw the girl with the goose in her arms hurrying towards him and Vellet drove him out of the garden, away from Beth.

Vellet leads him to the river and tells him, 'my fingers are locked to your sex.'

'Will I see this ghost?' Beth had asked, out of her shock.

'You saw her once,' he said, over his shoulder. And then he had gone. A harsh jog, a disjointed lope.

Where does the midwife live? On the highlands of the moon? Where does she live? I need her help. How am I to be born?

This is Vellet's question, after Beth has walked by her, unseeing. Vellet stood beside Beth as Theron stammered out his story and she thought, now Beth must see me! But Beth did not. Beth moved through the ghost, noticing nothing, no feather, no sediment of the phantasm.

The midwife's hand renews shadows like me, thinks Vellet. I look earthwards and I'm afraid. How am I to be planted again in warm flesh, how possess a spinal cord, a brain, blood, fibres and bundles of nerves? To feel my lungs heave with breath again, to be alive? I hear the songs of slow constellations, yes, I know the darkness of apples. I move quickly through the fiery cities. I study with the giant, hard lessons. But no one sees me. I am dead. I wander slowly through the snowy woods. No one sees me. I drift into summer. No one sees me but Theron. He sees me sometimes, not often. He closes his mind to me. I am the real nonentity. I want Beth to see me. Look at me, Beth. Turn to me. Drink my ice-water. Beth, can you hear me? Beth. How many times must I ask you? Give him back to me, that man. He must take me to the midwife.

Beth hears Vellet's summons but she outlaws it. She mistakes Vellet's voice for the voice of Ash. The house echoes with Ash's voice. Beth hates Ash sometimes, and would inform against her, the accomplice. Leave me alone, she yells, and out of the corner of her eye a shrivelled little old man stood watching her and grinning.

Beth rushes from room to room, trying to shift the burden of Theron's confidence, but she cannot get away from it. It is an immovable thing now, the knowledge he has passed on to her, like an inheritance, a house or piece of land. She cannot dodge it. It casts its shadow.

Haunted! Is he crazy?

She is suddenly ravenous and stands in the kitchen gobbling thick slices of bread, lumps of cheese.

Ghost! How often does it appear? If there is a ghost, I'll capture it and tame it, that's a promise.

The food in her mouth is like raw flesh. Her thoughts are a network of painful legacies that she cannot untangle.

She comes to rest by the open window of her sitting room. She stares out at the rich fertile yet obscure light that falls on the garden and the hills beyond. My abundant possessions, she thinks angrily. Beth is a woman carried forward on a long swelling wave she cannot control. Yet her vigour remains with her. She will stay with Theron. She will not go to her safer house on the moor, not yet, not until there is nowhere else to go. She is a strict observer of her own rules. The sources of her strength are uncertain, but they serve her well.

The long melancholy of summer afternoons remains though, sunlit and with the voices of children calling from distances . . .

Beth sits by the window. Her book waits, unread. The piano waits, silent. The sun falls on the yellowing keyboard.

How can you subject me to such afternoons, Ash? How can you invent such blank hours for me, Theron?

Outside, the calm casual summer evening at last begins springing from the roots of an imperishable moon.

Even though he's left Beth fatigued and half unable to believe his confession — I'm haunted — he thinks of her as a stronghold. Her fortitude is my only chance, thinks Theron. He can find nothing to complain of in Beth. In his mind it is he alone who is guilty of the felony that is coming between them.

He has been running hard and is ready to drop. His limbs flail through the sites of summer. But he cannot outrun Vellet.

Theron rests at the boundary of a little coppice. Behind him, the young trees. Ahead of him, a rural skyline complete with cattle and ruined buildings. Also he observes, at the centre of this landscape, Vellet, the young dead girl. It could not be otherwise. Just as Vellet has not learnt how to release herself from her death, her husband has not learnt to be free of the crusade he is still organizing against Vellet. He calls her up, they are equal partners. But he will not acknowledge this, does not consider it. He walks towards Vellet. Her face is too harsh for a young girl and often it is invisible among shadows. Her death virginity rasps against her, against him. The wands of evening beat them both. He shivers. Vellet comes towards him. There's a luminous area all around her, like that produced by the application of pressure to an eyeball, by a finger, say.

'Tomorrow's my birthday,' she whispers.

He shrugged.

'How old will you be?'

The ghost shouted with laughter, then frowned like a stranger who has adopted women's clothing unlawfully.

'I miss music,' she said, 'I cannot hear music now. I always liked loud music. No cradle-songs or serenades for me. I liked loud music. I've asked that giant pinned to the hill to sing for me, but he won't. Hairless white giant. I hate him. I'm lonely, Theron.'

Then he looked at her as if he'd never seen the ghost before.

'Lonely,' he said, startled, and then smiling against his will, 'you mean you can feel that, loneliness?'

The ghost blushed.

A light summer rain fell on Theron as he sat by the roadside. The saplings in the plantation became more delicate, each leaf seemed handsewn in the rain. Theron stared at Vellet, puzzled. She stood by the plantation fence, her face turned away.

'So lonely,' she continued, 'I don't have flesh, Theron. I am a blue air of loneliness, my lips and tongue, my earlobes and eyelids, clitoris and nipples are only shadows on the air. I am always cold. I have nothing to look forward to. I am locked in a small room of haunting. I cannot take the next step, I do not know how.' After a moment, he said,

'I don't know how to free you either, Vellet.'

The ghost turned her head to look at him, hurt.

'Why did you let me drown, Theron?' Her voice is subdued. 'I hated you,' he replied immediately.

'Yes,' she said, 'I understand.'

'I could not lift a finger to help you that night,' he told her. 'And it has ruined us both. I followed you out of the house, I saw you meet your boyfriend, watched you, heard you arguing, saw him push you away from him, hard, heard you cry out, then saw you fall, gracefully, into the water. But I could not help you.'

'He did not help me either,' said Vellet, 'perhaps he hated me too.'

'Perhaps,' said Theron, pulling a leaf off the nearest tree.

'But I was so young,' she cried out.

'I loathed you,' he said, 'your presence in my house revolted me, I was going to turn you out, when you drowned I was glad to be rid of you, it was something I was wholeheartedly in favour of.'

'But you are not rid of me, my dear.'

'Not yet.'

'You never will be, believe me.'

When he turned to answer her, she had gone, the rain was heavier, the sunlight slanted through it, broken.

'I will be rid of you,' he said. 'This haunted husband will exorcise you.' He heard his heart beating, simple rhythm. Fear left him, briefly. Laplandish summer, he thought, and walked on smartly to get warm.

That evening Beth climbs Giant Hill, resisting changes in the weather.

I saw her! That night; the ghost in Church Street, accosting Theron. I saw her. I do not want to see her again. I don't want to walk on any wet paths prepared by a ghost.

She is sitting very still on the shoulder of the Giant. The night comes, like a door closing.

Theron is in his garden, moving among the long spikes of flowers.

Darkness bleeds into the moonrise and turns the sheets of all the beds scarlet. Beth is an old moon kept in the deepest recesses of the sky. The giant's forefinger is nine inches long. His eyes of chalk are blind. Who gave birth to him? His mother was a pioneer, mistress of the landscape, labouring among stones.

I could detach the smiles from Vellet's face, thinks Beth grimly. I could throw her smile down the well. Why should I be afraid? Anger floods Beth, almost uncontrollable. Your hooves are silent, Vellet. Where are you?

But tonight Vellet is afraid of Beth and hides on the other side of the giant.

So is there a dead woman? thinks Beth. Or does Theron wallow in some dream? Some nightmare he wants to put on me? Breathe your uncanniness on me, Vellet!

But the ghost does not come to Beth. The ghost's flowers are bleeding.

Theron opens his eyes to a vista of scented alphabets. He is looking for Beth in the garden and cannot find her. His empty skin flaps in the breeze and the night steadily tightening around him appals him. He glances up at the moon that reminds him of Vellet and he is afraid again. He is soaking with sweat. Where can I escape? Go abroad? No. The answer is here. I have no bullets, bombs or torpedoes to destroy Vellet. I can only end the haunting by remaining here, keeping a close watch on her, the ghost, and bearing with this fear. He blunders out of the garden and down the lane, looking for Beth.

Beth's limbs are stiff. She gets to her feet, stands at the hilltop and lets the moon flash its messages upon her and the moon-white giant. Beth thinks of her heart coiled like a shell. She watches the giant and sees his white ribs rise and fall with the breath of the night. She hears the voice of the giant, stressing her name. 'I am listening, Giant.' Her voice is quieter than her shadow. 'Listen, Beth. That woman, so suggestive of waterfalls, the woman who haunts, she needs help.'

'Help?'

'Your help.'

'Why ?'

'Show her how to travel her death and then she will be free to start again. She will no longer haunt your man.'

Beth is rebellious and speaks raucously.

'And how am I supposed to accomplish this?' There is a sigh like ice from the white mouth of the giant.

'I don't know. I only know it is from you the knowledge will come.'

Beth is about to reply angrily again but stops, hears those harsh words drop away into the night like stones into deep water. 'Will Theron be free?'

'If Vellet is freed, yes.'

'Where is Vellet now?'

'She is stroking her body beneath the water. She will not visit tonight. Listen. You do not need to outwit Vellet, it is not that kind of solution. You must understand her, contemplate her.'

Beth's body is clammy, she hears her blood clatter, and fears that her time of albino orgasm is past. This is a problem of different dimensions and brings fear shining brightly through Beth. She moans as if flames surround her and pulls at her hair with her fingers.

'Giant, where's your whip, your other torturing instruments.'

'No, I am not a monster. I am a prisoner of this hill. I wish to get up and walk, to be made of flesh, not chalk. But unlike Vellet there's no way for me to move on. I am to be here always, I know. I am in pain here. A great hammer vibrates in my skull. All darkness is here for me to consume with my white vigilance. I am the guardian of ghosts, Beth, and I am lonely, shunned, and too close to earth and sky. I have no black wings. I cannot escape. I have no doors to close behind me. I must stay on this hill, watching the world with my blindness.

Beth is within the giant's domain and says,

'I will try to help.'

She tries to recall the face she'd glimpsed in Church Street but her memory is too frail: the lines of Vellet's face twist like snakes, shading in abnormalities. Beth sees a skull that dances, a caterwauling mouth.

'But black wings brush at me,' she said to the Giant. There was no answer. 'Fool,' she told herself, 'staying out half the night, getting chilled, talking to yourself.' But she is reluctant to go back home. She stares across the valley at the fields of wheat on which the moonlight glints. The fields are webs rocking in the wind. Beth has been so deeply embedded in her own life these past weeks that she has not noticed the wheat growing, ripening.

Now Beth feels large and heavy. In the pale askew moonlight she has a strange shadow. She lifts her hands from her sides and snuffs up the odours of the hill, damp and vegetative. In her mind's eye she sees her own downcast reflection. She presses her right hand against her left. The boorish behaviour of her husband cannot be explained by a ghost! He is hoodwinking me. Beth's jaw aches with tension, her eyelids feel dead, her thoughts are a whirlpool of little wet lips. Silence comes at her without warning, hurtling towards her and the soft pulpiness of fear sickens her.

The giant inhales the innuendoes of the girl descending his steep slope.

He looks down at the village.

The giant knows there is no such thing as an easy death.

The giant plays no card games.

The giant wears no loin cloth.

The giant sings of his blindness.

He breaks the evil bride's neck.

He has no name, he does not drink blood.

The giant looks at the hourglass.

He plucks his own heart out, gazes at it, replaces it, roaring with laughter.

The unworldly giant stammers. Easter candles blaze with light. He puffs them out.

The giant has no harlot.

The giant awaits the return of the ghost with mud on her skirt and waterweed in her womb.

He settles to sleep: the galactoid gaps in his memory must be repaired.

Hoodman-blind, Theron moves through the empty village. In the back of his mind is an idea unclear and indistinct that frightens him. A few lights glow in bedrooms and sitting rooms. He pauses outside one house. Should he go in and speak to someone? As he hesitates, his hand on the gate, the light goes out. He drags himself on down the street. It is his loneliness that makes him ungainly. He longs for company. The ghost does not trouble him tonight. Her drugged starfish face does not loom towards him. But he is so tired, he hardly values the respite. The moon makes grey staircases in the sky that turn white and move with an appearance of truth. He shambles on. A dog barks somewhere and then a child cries in one of the cottages. The grey hulk of the church does not interest Theron. He wanders by, not looking at the graveyard. The son of god, thinks Theron, feeble creature, with his long pointed shoe what son, what god? But there was no passion in Theron's complaint. He has his mind on other matters.

He hurries along the lane as if to a consummation. The little stream flows quietly at his side. He is walking and looking back over his shoulder, unaware of doing so. He remembers his dream the previous night: I am sitting at a devil's table and my mouth is dry as a diamond. I am very hungry and very thirsty. I ask for food and drink, in a voice that means what it says. The black folk bring me my fare. They set it out on the devil's table; drowned mice, drowned cats, drowned dogs. And I must eat. I eat. I bellow like a child. Two women come running, their hair loose, their voices crooning anciently, the juice of ripe fruit running from the corners of their mouths. And then I woke.

The path brings him to a wooden bridge across the stream. He waits here, hare-lipped by the moonlight. His anus itches. At length he saw a shape moving through the trees on the other side of the water, shape of a woman in a long skirt, hair loose. But he cannot tell which wife it is.

'Beth?' he calls nervously. 'Beth?'

'Yes, it is me.' Her voice is a remedy for him. He smells the amphibian odour of her sex. He sets foot on the bridge. She meets him halfway. They embrace like refugees and fend off the night that carves its initials in their flesh.

They walk home together, slowly, through the moonlit village, and they promise themselves that the days of easy anger are over.

This promise is like a narrow strip of land between two seas, under constant threat.

FOURTEEN

MENAGERIE of unopened letters.

Beth watches the postman trudge down the muddy track. She stoops, gathers up the circulars, bills, two postcards, a letter addressed to her, from Tabitha. Beth rips this open, scans it quickly, frowns, screws the envelope up and tosses it in the rubbish basket. Tabitha is back from her visit to London. Beth puts the rest of the mail on Theron's desk.

Ash writes me no letters! I ache between two extremes, two ghosts, women I cannot catch hold of, cannot meet. His ghost and mine. His and hers.

Summer shadows fall on Beth through the frosted glass of the front door. From the radio left on in the kitchen, a throbbing of lickspittle music.

Ash, my nature's sister, recollection of you is brief and blinding. I fear your shape-shifting, even from so far away, so long ago. I still find myself adopting, practising your gestures, your facial expressions. In the place where love is legally coined, you dog my footsteps, and make me ask myself, what am I doing here, living with a man as haunted, more haunted than I, so that Theron and I are made of one colour, no contrasts: dark molecule of our marriage. What will happen to us?

Ash was running across the field. She was obeying the brackishness of the day. It was the last time I saw her. Ash . . . We won two out of the three games, but the third game we lost. When Jake said, I guess it's time to be on our way, you said yes to him and not to me. The continuous sound of your name, Ash, Ash, Ash . . . I can't get away from it, and now it's becoming like an impurity in the blood.

You went away with him. He'd learnt a lot on his travels and you needed to be taught. He was wealthy, he was sensual: did he remind you a little of your first 'lover', Ash, the one who took you from the city to witness the spectacle of his onanism? Jake gave you more than that, I suppose, but you never write to tell me about your life now.

Beth does not like to think about these events, the meeting of Ash and Jake. She prefers to believe that they left only a slight trace on her life, that she was not wounded deeply. Ash and I had a summer, she thinks, there was no way of making that last, and neither of us wanted it to, not that much. Tougher needs arose in us both. Yet that summer still haunts me, encloses me, obsesses me.

It was in the autumn that Jake arrived, bringing change. He and Ash were married at Christmas. I lived in the house all winter and all spring, alone, as if it was a membraneous bag or pouch in which I curled. One day at the beginning of the next summer I was in the market town, browsing in a little bookshop, when a man, who looked vaguely familiar, introduced himself to me. He was a lecturer at the university, in the history department, and we had met once at a college dance. He asked me if I'd like a coffee in the restaurant next door. I said yes, off we went together, and so Theron and I met. It was a comfort, to talk to someone, be with someone. He seemed calm, easy to get along with, our friendship developed, eventually we married. Ash and Jake did not come to our wedding, though they sent an elaborate gift. Ash has not written since.

One morning I thought I saw Ash hanging from a tree, her virtues spattered with blood, but it was just a shadow.

Beth sits down at the kitchen table to write her grocery list. She has a slight burn on the index finger of her left hand where she caught the hot oven door yesterday.

In the sunny kitchen she is a dark abrupt silhouette, as if left behind by the rain.

Sun skirts through the village gardens.

The giant grows whiter against the summer green of the hill, against the blue of cloudless sky. All the ghosts play slapstick games in the summer. Beth lifts her head. She thought she heard someone speaking in the next room. But all is quiet. She stares at the calendar on the wall, at the girl naked but for boots and parachute.

Last night Beth and Theron met on the bridge and became entangled, bodies driven together. In their watertight bedroom, they blushed, forming a complicated sexual pattern, pressing their wet hot faces together, discovering ultimately a composure of flesh. Beth stares at the wall, considering last night's complicities: husband, giant; giant, husband. Even from herself, she keeps secret the extent of the pleasure she experienced last night, as Theron curved inwards, reaching deep inside her. The compass of her delight seems like a warning now.

She stares at her hands folded on the table. Her hands glow, as if part of a great conflagration. But was Jake right, to accuse me of letting Ash fall asleep in my world? Was she a sort of sleeping beauty, as he said? Was he right? Was I suffocating her? Was my body like the scum of molten metal, harming Ash? When he accused me of that, almost lightly, but with such accurate timing and inflexion, letting his power fall delicately upon Ash, he convinced her.

Yet, a few days before the final break, she ran from me across those fields, as if running from Jake also.

But she went with him, and my life became . . . unfinished . . .

Ash is sitting in an armchair by the window, sewing a button on her yellow blouse. Beth is kneeling by the fire, bending over a book. The man stands at the open door, smoking a cigarette and watching the birds wheel and caw above the evening lawn. The sky darkens, clouds take on priapic shapes. Beth glances up at the man, suspiciously.

God with his long sharp knife carves the moon-meat of the women and they bleed.

Both women are menstruating. Ash is bleeding heavily, she is at the beginning of her period. Beth is on her last day and the towel between her legs is hardly stained.

Beth rises to her feet. She longs for her body and for the body of Ash to turn to gold. She wants this man, with his dangerous outspoken demands, to freeze, to congeal into iron.

Ash looks up from her sewing, glances angrily at Beth. Ash does not look at Jake. The blood of virginity has visited her unexpected; she was not due for another week. It is the tension, the fight between Beth and Jake, with her as the prize, that has brought her period on.

She has shared this summer with Beth, living at her house. It has been a summer of deft mornings and wooded afternoons. Ash had seen the little handwritten advert in the post-office window, room to let, and that same evening rang Beth's number. They met the next morning and took to one another at once. It has been a summer of long walks, of bathing in the river, of gardening. They spent their evenings reading, or playing the piano and singing together. Since that first afternoon, sitting on the lawn, when Beth reached out and touched Ash, plunging headlong into an echo, the sound and shape of one woman has been reflected in the other. They have had a summer of blossom, egg and ache: identical creatures. Until the summer day with a sky coloured like a long snaky fish, an eel, the man interrupted their life. Ash wonders if she is depleted by her experiences with Beth, if she might not now prefer the man's riddle to the woman's. She is very careful to avoid looking at Jake as he stands in the doorway, but the blood thrusting out of her with such great vitality warms her. What Beth offers seems scanty. She thinks of the other man, who brought her out of the city. She remembers his stumpy penis rearing up. She bites off the thread of her sewing cotton.

Beth frowns. Jake watches her calculatingly, like a moneylender. He stubs out his cigarette. He walks across to Ash. She does not look at him.

'Ash,' he says.

Ash looks at Beth. Beth bends over her book. She will not help.

'What is it, Jake?' Her voice is unsure, Ash, a scarlet spider in her throat. Jake smiles, looks out of the window at the evening sky and the clouds grown warty, like a muster of witches.

I have lost, thinks Beth, not moving, not defending her claim, it is Jake's evening, and the embarkation of Ash amid leaves and moons.

Jake touches Ash on the shoulder.

'Come out for a walk, Ash. Come on,' he said.

They all remember the fierce argument this morning, Jake and Beth shouting at the tops of their voices in the white room. The way Beth pranced about the room, hysterical. How Jake had been very calm, very decided. How Ash had watched, and listened: and looked sulky because she was frightened. Jake speaks of our kind of love as knowledgeably as a fisherman who never saw a fish, Beth had sneered. Do you want his wet embrace, Ash? she had cried. But Ash kept silent. The stench of flames bursting between Jake and Beth was too acrid for her, she couldn't breathe, and she barged out of the room with an angry embarrassed grin, leaving Beth and Jake staring at each other, their gestures callous and mediocre, filling them with disgust.

But now, evening: Jake touches Ash on the shoulder, lightly, lovingly. Ash gets up, smiles at him, then leads the way out into the garden. He follows her without glancing at Beth.

Beth has lost. She is lost. She bends over her book. She is a young woman with a wooden heart and she knows what the interior of her rectum looks like. Also she knows that Jake asked Ash to wear her red dress this evening and that Ash had refused, pointing wordlessly to the red flowers in the garden. My uninterrupted possession of happiness is over.

That evening, Ash and Jake walk slowly through the lady-crab shadows of Beth's garden. Ash thinks, the hound was petrified with the vixen, to end their perpetual chase.

'Beth was struck by lightning as an infant,' says Jake. Ash stared at him doubtfully.

'It's true,' he said. 'It was a miracle she survived.'

'So I imagine,' she answered slowly.

'I don't imagine Beth will ever get married,' he said.

'Because of the lightning?'

'Yes.'

Ash smiled.

'The dream sees through you, Jake.'

'What do you mean?' he flared up. He turned to her angrily, they stood by the greenhouse, the half-moon was reflected in the darkening panes of glass.

'What do you mean?' he asked again, more quietly.

'I mean, Jake, that what you say awake is different from what you say asleep.'

'And what do you think I say when I'm asleep.'

'Different things.'

'Will you ever find out what they are? Will you ever listen, as I sleep?'

'You must remember them yourself,' she said tartly. Her hands ache to touch wood. His hand touched her throat, her breasts. The blood hummed between her legs.

'You're full of tricks and artifice,' he said, 'Beth taught you those. I'll teach you other things.'

Ash says nothing and tries to think of suns and starfish, but instead the story of a girl comes into her mind, the girl who walked along the suburban avenue pushing a yellow pram packed full of dynamite. In the shadows she sees old hands of bronze gathering up the night.

Jake leads her into the greenhouse. She stumbles and falls against him. He supports her. There is the odour of warm earth and tomatoes. In the summer Beth and Ash often worked in here. At the far end, there's a pile of old sacks. Ash looks down at them. She hears the native language of the stars, twisty and mournful, but she cannot utter any antidote. She gasps at Jake's oaths, his suggestions, his pledged words. The river is the wet tongue of the giant. Ash's dress is a biblical blue. She is lying on the sacks, dry and rough against her skin and the earth smell is strongest here. The moon sees her. The moons know.

'Ash,' the man said, touching her. He stretches at her side. She whispered to him, 'I'm bleeding . . .' 'I know . . .' he answered, 'it doesn't matter.' He began to stroke her, calmly, easily.

'With your body, you could walk into church naked and marry me like that.'

'No, don't say that,' she tells him, 'I don't want to marry naked.'

But she is nearly naked, with the blood flowing. The blue dress lies alone. Night shines against the fox sleep of Ash's breasts and night freezes in the ice of her pubic hair. His fingers comb through her earthy hair. She touches his penis clumsily.

She says, 'I am clean.'

He laughs, low in the darkness. She smiles in the dark. Her breasts sting. She raises her knees. She watches his jagged shadow snared in the moonlight. He snuffs up her brine and eases himself into her warm red virgin cunt. Her blood makes her first time easier. He is an early settler in new country. She begins to make dark cries. The penis moving in her is like an unexpected obstacle which both wounds and sensitizes her. He lifts himself and shudders, reading her body's alphabet. She spells out his. They'll learn of their imperfections in the future but now every second is valid, blossoming. On the ground, lying in the dirt, she tastes the kiss of the giant preserved in Jake's mouth, and moans when the itch-ache of virginity is suddenly sluiced and she is made open, elastic in orgasm. Frosty fire licks her lips. This is the married bonfire. Her blood and his spunk marry together.

When they return to the house, it saddens them, this couple, the lovers, to see Beth's face grimacing, the hack-work of a dauber.

Yes, they returned to my house, hesitating, their clothes dirty, and both of them, stumbling, half-asleep. Next morning, they packed up and went. For Ash, it was the best thing. They are still together, I suppose. I wish she'd write and tell me how she is. But she does not write. Not in one of seven languages, not one. Beth sits stiffly at the table, an old address book in her hand, her mind clouded by imaginations of that first coupling: Ash and Jake.

Beth is afraid to write another letter to Ash, afraid of the silent rejection, or, worse, a scribbled postcard that says less than nothing.

'I am not strong enough,' Beth muses, turning away from the picture she had made of the lovers.

In a half-shadow doorway, Vellet watches Beth. If I whisper now, she thinks, Beth might hear me. But Vellet is not ready to speak to Beth yet. She watches from the shadows, her freshwater fingers and thin buttocks hunched in warfare. A stingless shadow.

Odours of iodine rise from the garden where rain has just fallen. Beth tastes her own ghost.

Ash! she trembles. I am following you through a sewer. Should I rename you Cloacina ? Or is that my name?

'Can you translate my name into Latin, Beth?' said the voice in the blue doorway.

Beth whirled round, turned sharply, just in time to see the apparition fade, the face made nomadic by death, the watery lace at neck and wrists ...

'You!' she cried.

But then was silent.

Theron is coming downstairs. He is whistling and looks very relaxed. The sound of the guns reverberates against the windows of the house. Men are shooting rooks or rabbits beyond the common.

'Over in Hare Coppice, from the echo, and the distance,' said Theron.

'Think so?'

'Yes. There, or maybe even as far away as Well Field.'

Look! There again. Vellet is smiling at Beth. Beth squints at the sunlight, at the muggy air. But Theron cannot see Vellet. The ghost steers her tissue shadow out of his reach.

'Beth? Beth!'

'Yes. Sorry, I was miles away. What did you say?'

'I said, it is not pleasant to be shut in a cage, but believe me, I am trying to get free.'

'Yes, Theron.' Beth smiles and embraces her husband. 'Yes, Theron, I know. Between words, between gestures, we are rediscovering ourselves.'

'Last night . . .' he kissed her gently.

'Yes,' she agreed happily, 'it was lovely.'

Looking happier than he had for weeks, Theron got his fishing gear together and went out. But the shadow of the saboteur has fallen on Beth. Vellet covets Beth's fields and blue fathoms of ease, her calmness.

'But ghosts are out of fashion!' said Beth aloud. There was no answer. Beth sighed and got on with her housework. Polishing the first wife's furniture! While she was dusting, it seemed to Beth she saw Vellet again, the room was like the room of an annunciation. The ghost looked sideways at Beth, giggled, spat and vanished.

FIFTEEN

WEASEL woman in the shelter of the rain.

Today is an unlucky day for the woman with her aching haunted head. She walks slowly, as if dragging havoc behind her. The rain shuns her. Beth hears the cry of wild geese; a mated pair, necks outstretched, fly above her, towards the sea coast. The sound grates upon her for she is distrustful of everything this morning.

She walks without seeing the landscape, skimping the horizon.

It had seemed to Beth that things had been improving, that she and Theron had drawn closer together in their trouble, sharing it. When he'd told her he was haunted by Vellet and they had talked at length about the ghost, penned the apparition up in simple words, descriptions, rationalizations, Beth had believed that their marriage, contracted carelessly by her, unwisely and obstinately by Theron, might blossom into at least a working allegiance: that there might be a way for them both to move out of jeopardy. But after her initial encouragement, after his original outburst and the strength and power of their lovemaking that night of their meeting on the bridge, there has been a withdrawal again. He has grown secretive and silent. The coldness of a flimsily constructed life has begun again. All week an inaudible conflict has been developing between them. He turned away from me, Beth insists to herself, it was him, not me. But she cannot deny that she has been shut up in her own private world, where Ash reigns. So have I not given him enough of myself? Has he sensed that I have another allegiance, a ghost of my own that I haven't entered in our logbook? Does this give me an unfair advantage over him?

The field hedges smell of the rain. Beth breathes in the green air, stares across at the giant veiled in fine rain. The sight of the giant adds to her irritability.

It is hard for Beth to believe what she saw last night. Are we sharing hallucinations, Theron and I? she thinks. She had awoken suddenly, out of a neighing dream, soaked in sweat. Her thoughts were great blocks of stone crushing her. It was very dark, timeless, no moon. She was alone in the bedroom. She switched on the bedside lamp and glanced around the neat bedroom. The door was open. Her dream, details of which eluded Beth, had frightened her and, despite the return of their estrangement, she wanted Theron's company. I suppose he couldn't sleep again, she thought, and slipping on her dressing gown she went downstairs.

It was when she reached the foot of the stairs that she heard the groaning begin and the sound touched her smooth skin like vomit.

The sound is coming from Theron's study. It is not a groan of a man in pain. Beth has heard this sound before, on other nights, less dark than this. Beth approaches the door of his study, she cannot help herself. A chill voice is repeating words in her ear — I see the lichen-scars, the river-scars on your face . . .

The door is open and in the candlelit room Theron is abandoning his kingdom. He is sprawled, half-dressed, in an armchair, almost like a hostage, and there is a stink of rancid water in the room. Theron groans again and for an instant the Vellet ghost materializes, her incubus mouth clamped over Theron's penis, which is pointing erect towards death. He groans again with pleasure and writhes in the chair while Beth watches, stunned and sad.

Who will help Beth? Her brother the giant lives far away, over many mountains, and she does not like his advice. Beth stands in the doorway, remote and sad as a wave. Vellet is invisible at the moment, but Beth smells the foul gas of her presence in the room. Theron gives a final moan and the spurt flies up in the air, a white arc, and he sags down in the chair, eyes closed, satisfied.

Vellet puts her hand on Beth's shoulder. Beth feels the cold seep through her robe, numbing her. Beth shudders but forces herself to stare into the pretty and unspoilt face of the drowned woman.

'Almost every night,' whispers Vellet, 'when night burns its beautiful fire, I come to him and lead him towards my mouth, or my hand, or my sex.'

Beth looks around the familiar room, recognizing nothing. There is no help, not from books, paintings or flowers. She must remain and listen to the confidences of the ghost.

'I am his wife,' coos Vellet, 'and his sex is mine. I have him, Beth! There's not much left for you, is there?'

Beth blushes. Now she knows she has a rival, one she cannot sue for divorce, one she cannot assassinate. This is why Theron does not want to make love to her. Beth's cunt froths with jealousy, she is toppling backwards down a twisting staircase. She does not know how to answer, how to respond to her husband's mistress. Or is it wife? Or hallucination? Or are we both crazy, Theron and I? Is it a ghost that beckons to us and divides us, or is it our own failure to love that confronts us, dressed up as Vellet?

'You should call Theron Mr Blindman,' laughs Vellet. 'He cannot see past me.'

If I answer her, thought Beth, it will be nothing more than the untruths of brides exchanged defiantly.

Who will help Beth? Can a ghost be inseminated? she wonders, in a sudden fright.

'No,' hisses Vellet, answering Beth's unspoken question, 'no.' And her face looms like countless pryings before Beth, bringing bad luck. Beth hurls silence at the ghost and because of Beth's strength and her living blood Vellet flinches.

'I am still his bride, Beth.'

Then the ghost is gone. Beth did not see her vanish. Perhaps a slight glow pastelled against the wall; perhaps one candle was the beacon through which Vellet disappeared.

Beth stoops over Theron, to comfort him, to seek comfort herself, but he shakes her off angrily.

'Did you hear?' asks Beth.

'Hear what?'

'I was talking to Vellet.'

Theron fastened his pants and laughed bitterly.

'Talking to Vellet! My, you are making progress, Beth.' Beth hesitated, then said nervously, tentatively,

'You feel it, then, do you? Really, when she touches you? Pleasure?'

He didn't answer.

'Doesn't the touch of Vellet feel cold, Theron?' He shook his head.

'No. No, it feels like a woman touching me.' Theron wavered, almost moved towards tenderness, but then his face grew harsh again and he determined not to make any excuses to Beth for his encounter with Vellet. It is not my fault, he thought. I am not to blame. I am the victim of these hauntings, when Vellet repeats the actions of past lovemaking. He scowls at Beth. But she is no longer frightened by his anger, the nature of his responses. It is Vellet she fears.

'How can it feel like a woman,' she persists, 'it is a dead thing. A dead thing,' she muses, speaking more to herself than to him.

'Christ, if I knew why it felt so real . . . I'd be happy,' Theron yelled, 'if I knew why I want it, it would not terrify me, stupid bitch!'

She swerved from the blow he aimed at her, and he made no further attempt to hit her. She took no notice of this violence, merely dodged it, and dismissed it. There are more important matters. She wonders if Vellet's ghosthood were fathomless, or whether there were limits, places where she/it might be made powerless. What laws govern Vellet? What exorcisms could be used?

'Now do you see,' he said desperately, 'what I meant by the haunting, by being tainted? How can we stay together when that thing, that perversion is my companion also?'

'Can't you protect yourself from . . . these . . . assaults?' Theron shook his head. 'Why do you think I wanted to remarry? I thought I would get free of it then.'

'But you are not free,' said Beth, shaken.

'No,' he said. Then he shrugged savagely and left Beth alone. She sobs once and the giant opens his eyes. Beth spits in the direction of the giant.

'You say I should help Vellet, Giant,' she cried, 'but how? Vellet is sucking the marrow of our marriage away, humiliating him, destroying me. How am I to help her?'

Then the silence and the darkness closed in on Beth.

Now on this rainy morning she walks into the village where all the streets are dirty. She passes the shops without stopping and enters the village church, pausing in the porch to tie a white scarf over her wet hair. She walks slowly towards the altar, her footsteps echoing on the stone pavement. The church is full of fear that belongs to Beth. The man approaches her as she sits in a devout attitude. His face is marked as by smallpox. She looked up at him and said, 'I want to walk in an unhaunted house, to have an unhaunted garden, an unhaunted man.' He said, 'Beth, you must try to arrange your thoughts without ambiguity.' She said to him, 'there is bad weather in the bible.' She spoke crossly. He said, 'listen. You can hear it? Time, ticking away? Decide. What do you want? To end the haunting? Or to understand the haunting?'

Beth cannot answer. Her silence is long and emaciated.

The man walks away.

Beth wanders through the back streets, past dustbins waiting for collection. The rain is deducing Beth's character from the shape of her skull. Beth knocks at a cottage door and is welcomed by her friend, Tabitha Irons, a small dark woman who smiles and speaks to Beth in a low rapid voice, leading Beth along a narrow hallway into a small brightly lit untidy sitting room.

'I haven't seen you for ages, Beth,' she exclaims. Beth apologizes, smiles tensely.

'Is everything alright, Beth?'

Beth shrugs, does not answer. Tabitha hurries out of the room, calling back over her shoulder, 'take your wet things off and hang them to dry, Beth.'

Tabitha came back with the tea tray and the two women settle by the fire, drinking hot tea out of big chipped enamel mugs.

In the old days, Tabitha's cottage was traditionally owned by the village jailer and the portrait on the chimney breast, a faded daguerrotype, is that of the last jailer's wife. Upstairs, in the old chocolate box where she keeps her jewellery, mostly fake, Tabitha has a pair of gold earrings that belonged to this lady, given to her so that she would put in a 'good' vote at the election. But Tabitha is no descendant of jailers. She and her late husband bought the cottage from the great-grand-daughter of the last jailer. Tabitha never wears the election earrings, a present from the great-granddaughter, who had taken a fancy to Tabitha, but keeps them, as good luck emblems, belonging to the house, and keeping Tabitha in touch with the earlier occupants.

Tabitha is nearly ten years older than Beth. She is a widow and has lived in or near the village all her life. Irons had been a painter of some note. Upstairs in a locked room, five of his paintings remain, the five that Tabitha will not sell or exhibit. The first canvas is of a drunk woman womb-wounded, all shades of red. The second, a pair of long-necked griffons crouched by the pages of a treatise advocating sexual love. The third, and largest of the canvases, Jesus touching the veil of the Virgin. The fourth, Tabitha's favourite, the saint sipping blood, her face alight, and behind her, shadows like bruised armour. The fifth canvas, a portrayal of Tabitha and Harry as lovers, he rising through her like smoke, and, sheltering them both, the golden appletrees of the psalmist: lovers in an orchard. These are Tabitha's five icons. She cannot bear to let anyone in this room, except for the rarest occasions. Beth has been allowed to see these paintings once.

Tabitha is dark, hair and eyes nearly jet, and ornamented with necklaces, rings, brooches and bracelets which suit her more than they would most women. She wears long skirts, often with untidy hems, and there is a gypsy caravan feeling about her house. Tabitha is now not wife, nor virgin, nor mother: she is herself. She is outgrowing the pain of her widowhood and has little need of rewards. Her smile has many syllables.

Beth has confidence in Tabitha's wisdom. Tabitha sees how troubled Beth is, that a night horizon has torn her open, but she waits patiently for Beth to say what is wrong in her own time.

At first Beth keeps the conversation on a mundane level, sticking to safe topics, village gossip. Tabitha answers in the same language but watches Beth intently, seeing that Beth has worn sleep out. Yes, Beth is trying to wind her ghosts on to new spools. The voices of the women linger in the room, waiting for the storm to break over them. Tabitha is leaning forward, the flat palm of her hand unconsciously extended to offer Beth comfort. What is Beth thinking behind her calm conversation? In her mind she passes a rope set with thorns through her tongue and lets the blood drop on to her skirt. Beth's face is stark and reminds Tabitha of the black days of her own marriage, a man and a woman sharing frugal and bitter meals. She remembers Irons shoving her out of the cottage on a winter night. Wearing only her nightgown, she crouched shivering, beaten by a crowbar of solid silver, icy moonlight. She remembers crawling back into a terrible bed, wearing an iron collar, being fucked from behind, defenceless. Tabitha's wisdom has not come from an easy apprenticeship. She recalls the one-eyed husband who, even now, enters her dreams, commanding Tabitha to kiss unknown animals. So now she leans forward and touches Beth gently on the knee. Beth starts violently and catches her breath, thinking; Vellet!

'Whatever is it, dear?' asks Tabitha, worried.

Beth's lips twist from some sourness and she gets up, walks to the window. With her back to Tabitha she asks,

'Will we be of interest to archaeologists? Our bones, some day?'

'Yes, surely,' says Tabitha briskly, 'our bones will tell their stories.' The moon is running backwards for Beth. She catches words in the folds of her skirt. Dark-odoured, she moves back to her chair, and tells Tabitha her story. The whispering of centaurs, that rain outside, and the thread of Beth's story moving through it.

'There is trouble between Theron and me,' she began.

'I feared as much,' said Tabitha.

'Tabitha,' she blurted out, 'I am jealous of Vellet. It is Vellet who is breaking up our marriage. She comes creeping out of some labyrinth and I am frightened of her power. She is taking Theron from me.'

Beth's voice is harsh, she is trembling with anger and fear. Her face is flaming with emotion. Tabitha lies back in her chair, eyes hooded, unshocked. She lights a cigarette. The little burning mist consoles Beth. Although she is not a smoker she breathes in deeply, with relief.

'Theron cannot put it behind him, then? Her death? He mourns for her still . . . ?'

'No!' Beth jumps up from her chair. 'No, you don't understand.' Her voice breaks. To speak of Vellet and Theron denudes Beth. She is ashamed. She feels that it is she who is perverted, she who is the ghost. Her mouth is dry. Is this the summer, is this the frontier of my home, is this me? I am bungling my chance to get some support and advice from Tabitha.

But Tabitha does not find Beth's behaviour so strange. She sees how disturbed she is. She does not come forward to embrace Beth. She lets a gentle silence grow up between them and then she says, in her low voice,

'Come now, explain to me . . . explain what I do not understand.'

Beth sighs.

'Explanations for this matter can only humiliate us both,' she says.

Now there is another silence between the women, who have both given up spinsterhood. Tabitha waits for Beth to reveal this mysterious indisposition, this anger about Vellet, a dead girl.

Beth wheeled round suddenly and came to kneel beside Tabitha. 'Tell me about Vellet,' she pleaded with the older woman, 'tell me something about her. I know nothing about her. I never bothered with village talk about her. But they did gossip about her, didn't they? Tell me. What sort of girl was she? Theron never talks about her. It is our forbidden territory. But what is she like?'

'Is?' queried Tabitha sharply.

'I'm sorry. I mean, what was she like?'

Tabitha touches Beth's hair, a sisterly gesture. Tabitha is unnerved by this insistence on Vellet. But she will not fail her friend.

She realizes that Beth is approaching the kind of weariness that comes after repeated stress and knows that eventually such exhaustion will reduce Beth to a shadow, existing only among the uninvited guests in her skull. So, although the subject of Vellet is repugnant to her, Tabitha speaks, as Beth asked. Her voice grows deeper, her sentences are curt, she does not look at Beth.

'Valet! Little tramp! That's what she was. She filled in her census form with misleading answers. Her lies were always hard to decipher. She was a skilled negotiator with dark things, the dark side, that one.'

'But you aren't lying to me, are you? Don't tell me lies.'

'It's the truth,' said Tabitha solemnly, 'I'm telling no lies, dear. When Theron married her, I was very worried for him. Unlike most of the villagers, the marriage did not surprise me. I knew he'd loved her for years, since she was a child, he told me so. But when I met him in the village soon after the marriage, I warned him, be on your guard. He laughed, I don't think he understood at all. Of course he was the only one who didn't know. The whole village knew about her tricks. She came to stay with me and Harry once, when she was a child. Spoilt! Expected to be waited on hand and foot. Even at that age, what was she, about twelve, she was trying it on with Harry . . .'

Tabitha got up and walked about the room, her memories of Vellet sucking at her, producing grating noises in her mind like unoiled hinges, and her hand on the door, opening, on to the tumbled room, Vellet's thin cry of fright, Irons' curse. Tabitha shivers.

Beth curled on the floor, says,

'Yes, what a cold summer.'

Tabitha does not answer. The pigments of pain, she thought, the little model with the saucy smile! Little Madam! Little Bitch! Better dead. Like Irons, better dead.

And yet Theron never suspected Vellet, never knew she had other men . . .

Tabitha shrugged and came back to her chair. She looked down at Theron's wife and crammed her own memories back into the dark. Where they belong, she thought. She shook her head slowly.

'Did he? I don't know. It's hard to say, Beth. Maybe towards the end he was beginning to catch on. She was out meeting one of her men friends the night she fell into the river, I'll be bound. Did you go to the inquest, Beth?'

'No. Why should I? I had troubles of my own at that time, and took no interest in village affairs.'

'Then you don't know she took drugs?'

'No. No, I never knew that. Was she high when she drowned?'

'Yes.'

'Poor Theron. How could he have been blind to all that?'

'He is a man who idealizes women. Or used to, he did Vellet. He never considered the possibility of her deviating from his vision of her.'

Beth looked into a future without light, in which she is exposed to peril. The palms of her hands are cold, damp. She knows she will not be able to make Tabitha understand about the ghost.

'Where did Vellet get her drugs from, Tabitha?'

'From her boyfriends. She took anything she could get. Why, I met her one evening, walking along the edge of Giant Hill and she lurched against me and said, "t-h-i-s r-o-a-d l-e-a-d-s t-o M-a-r-s-e-i-l-l-e-s. W-h-y d-o y-o-u w-a-n-t t-o t-r-a-v-e-l i-t? T-h-e i-s-l-a-n-d-s a-r-e c-o-v-e-r-e-d i-n i-c-e a-l-r-e-a-d-y?" Then she staggered on. I followed her, made sure she got home safely. Theron must have been away that night. I watched her reel into a dark house.'

Beth stretches her cramped limbs and shifts into a crosslegged position.

'You never told Theron?'

In her mind's eye, Tabitha sees Vellet, the naked model with the darkish pubic hair, the menace of her.

'No, I didn't. I realize now, maybe I should have done. But she was not one to call up compassion.'

Beth stares down at her clasped hands and thinks, once I could have lost a hand for a trivial offence. She glances up at the severe wife of the jailer, in the faded grey photograph. Beth will try now to explain the haunting to Tabitha.

'Tabitha, the real problem is that Theron blames himself for Vellet's death, it is making him ill and . . . he thinks . . . that is . . . I think . . . Vellet comes . . .'

Tabitha wrinkled her face and shook her head, interrupting Beth.

'No, Beth, no. Look, she was promiscuous, she was on drugs, she was unbalanced, out of control, out of anyone's reach. He's not at fault. He saw in her only what he wished to see, was blind to the rest, and she let him see only what he wanted, needed to see. He's not to blame.'

Beth looks helplessly about the room and her gaze comes to rest on a little work table of the utmost delicacy, its top surface mounted with a plaque of turquoise blue porcelain enriched with gold and painted animals. The beauty of this makes her weep, is the threshold of her weeping. She puts her hands over her face and sobs. Tabitha watches her, does not touch her, lets her alone.

'It's not often I'm like this,' gulps Beth. Her uncritical friend kneels beside her. The voices of the women reverberate.

'He says he is haunted, Tabitha! He says he sees Vellet's ghost. Haunted, he says he is haunted. He regards her as a person, a reality. He has sex with her, with Vellet, with the ghost, not with me!'

There is a code of grief in Beth's voice, an unbroken code, that silences Tabitha's immediate response.

'He cannot come near me most of the time, because Vellet won't allow him to come to me.' Beth weeps again, quietly. Tabitha examines the irregular pieces of her thoughts.

'How long has he had this delusion?' she asks. Beth does not answer, she sobs harder and clenches her fists.

'Look, Beth dear, he must see a doctor, he is sick, very sick.' Beth takes her hands from her face and howls aloud once, the cry of the cheated interpreter.

'God, Tabitha, then I am sick also, for I've seen her. She speaks to me also. She touches me. I find her long dark hairs in Theron's bed, on my bedroom floor, inside my purse, in the bath: and neither Theron nor I are dark, we are both fair. So I am sick, and crazy too, Tabitha! Me too!'

The two women stand at the doorway with subdued smiles, saying goodbye. Beth is very pale. Despite washing her face in cold water, it is obvious she has been crying. She has failed to convince Tabitha that Vellet's ghost is tormenting Theron and herself. She has failed to convey the reality of the ghost. She has had to agree with Tabitha's explanations, that she is overwrought, yes, tired, afraid of shadows, searching out far-fetched excuses to cover up the difficulties in her marriage. Yes, yes, she agreed with Tabitha, to silence her friend's gentle banalities.

Tabitha was out of the reach of ghosts. Common sense is her strong point.

'Look, you must have a long talk with Theron,' she urged Beth, 'get him to see a good psychiatrist, for heaven's sake. He's infecting you with his delusions. He is using the ghost motif to veil his sexual inadequacies, Beth.'

Beth nods obediently. What else can she do? She cannot penetrate Tabitha's defences. The two women kiss goodbye and Beth walks down the street, suddenly aware of being childless. She turns at the corner and waves back to Tabitha who stands watching in her doorway, watching her friend carefully, as if Beth were an invalid who might fall down in the street.

Beth waves again, then turns the corner. She acknowledges to herself that Tabitha is a wise woman but she overestimated Tabitha. Her wisdom does not touch on ghosts. The ghost will not reflect itself in Tabitha's mirrors. Tabitha knows no exorcisms. She is not trained in such matters. So I must solve the matter myself, thinks Beth.

She stands at the thresholds, in the empty street, in the cutaneous rain.

Thresholds? which way for her?

One way leads to the river, another to the Giant.

The river is the place from which unwanted creatures rise in an uprush of blue, foetal, obstinate. The Giant is where these creatures might hide. Beth thinks of a bedstead covered with fresh clean white sheets, woollen blankets and soft pillows, and of a man who will embrace her, after he has washed his hands.

She sets her foot on the uphill path, away from the river, through the twilight towards the Giant.

SIXTEEN

THE giant never tells lies.

Do I lie? Beth wonders. No, it is my dumbness that ruins summer, not my lies. If I knew the word that would disperse Vellet! Understand her, the giant said, understand her. How can I understand her? I want to obliterate her! How can I understand the ghost of a drugged and whorish girl?

Beth struggles on up the muddy lane. The moon is also a girl kept prisoner in a grey tent. Vellet rises now from her flowerless grave and begins to search the marshes for the embryo she lost there.

I couldn't explain it to Tabitha, I couldn't get it across to her! The thoughts drum in Beth's mind. Why couldn't Tabitha see it? She wasn't afraid when I told her about the hauntings, because she hasn't experienced anything like that. And yet, those paintings of Harry's, the way she shuts them up, imprisons them, are they not five ghosts she has lived with for nearly as many years? How out conversation has tired and depressed me, and left me feeling very lonely. The worn-out words we both used, her long gaze when she leant over me, the lack of any useful answer . . . Who can help me, after that travesty of friendship? Not Theron. Not Jake. Not Ash. Ash, in my dream, carrying her breasts in a silver dish, with Satan in sunglasses walking behind her, Ash, with a flower sprouting from her neck-stump, her severed head half-hidden behind the curtain: no, no, I will not think of her.

And Theron does not want his 'life' with Vellet to be disturbed, altered, ended. The rain will not wash his weakness away. And I see the shadow of rain each evening, I feel my own memories sweating blood: how she sucked him, how he panted for the ghost's tongue against him . . .

Beth comes to the abbey ruins. The hill of the Giant rises sharply above her. She walks rapidly through the old graveyard. There are no ghosts here!

There is much to be done, she tells herself, many waiting rooms to be experienced before I defeat Vellet. But I will defeat her. I will make my name, BETH, stick in her throat and lodged there it will choke her out of being.

Beth is climbing over the stile when a shove from nowhere sends her sprawling and she falls headlong into the hoof-printed mud and muck of the field. A voice laughs, taunting Beth.

'Come on, Beth, join the suicide club. It's a grand life.'

Beth scowls, she is on the blind side of the ghost. She picks herself up, wipes her hands on her raincoat, and stares suspiciously about her but the ruins, the fields and the hillside are empty of people and ghouls. Beth looks ruefully at the mud caked on her shoes and stockings but will not turn back. I will go up to the Giant, she says aloud. And begins to climb the hill. Vellet returns to her own flooded lands, pleased to find Beth so open to her haunting. She will try more tricks with Beth another time.

Seated on her giant's rainy shoulder, Beth feels that she is the sea: carrion and coast, waves and sea-wrack. Above her, the evening sky is a grey groin forced open. I am the sea, thinks Beth, a sea that lives on drownings, of mice, voles, insects, horses, sailors and many crazy women. From her slipshod seat in the wet turf, she cries,

'Giant! Show me my enemy! Show me Vellet, as she was, living. Show me!'

It is a half-moon that slithers between rainclouds, cut in half by Magdalen as she wanders through the pastures. Beth thought she saw the limbs of the Giant move once, whitely, snakily, and then, in place of the white chalk limbs, Beth sees a woman, a young woman holding herself stiffly, determined not to weep. It is Vellet.

Beth holds her breath and watches.

Vellet is speaking. She says to a man Beth does not recognize, 'I am the woman you may kill by inches.' The man does not reply. Perhaps he smelt

Vellet's monthly blood. Perhaps he sees her plasma shroud. Vellet flinches from his silence, she moves into the blackness of her own silence in this sordine room. 'Please . . .' she whispers to the man. He turns away and the door closes behind him, leaving Vellet motionless beneath towers of silence on which great birds of mars perched. 'By inches,' she whispers.

'You! Vellet,' mouths Beth.

Out of a night of insects and animals, night of woman, night dividing pain from pain, night thrusting out its raw lips, treeless night in which a man and a woman both stand four miles tall, Vellet wakes to find Theron standing in the doorway, speaking her name, irately. He says to her, 'No, you will always exist, Vellet, you and your kind.' Vellet does not answer. When he'd got what he came for, and left her alone again, she was thirsty. She got up and drank a glass of red wine. The wine tasted of meat. She has an appointment which she fears to keep yet dare not break. She listens at Theron's door and hears him snoring. YES and NO throb in Vellet's head, contradicting her, wounding her. In the addict's garden, Vellet sees a man sitting on the ground, waiting for her. He is the man who will sell her what she wants. What she has to have. YES. NO. YES. NO. YES. NO. Like a drum that man in the garden is beating.

Beth watches the tableau the giant shows her, biting her lip. She remembers that in far places mothers will eat a stillborn child so that the spirit may be reborn through her.

Before Vellet made her decision, to go to the man, to buy what he offered, she saw clowns veiled in red taffeta, she saw rivers flowing too fast, too dark, she saw the locked door, she saw her own key that would unlock that door. The clowns wept and ran away from Vellet.

The man watching the house shifted further back into the shadows. He is the same man who refused to give Vellet the stuff yesterday. Get the money, he insisted.

The side door of the house opens slowly and a woman appears, aphis woman, walking towards the yew tree where he is waiting. Vellet is not weeping, though her hands quiver with the treachery of white seabirds; she needs to score. He spoke to her. 'The money ?' he said, not even bothering to colour his words with contempt. She said nothing, smiled slightly, said not one word, moved through the shadows, as if she really were the calm good daughter of the philosopher. She brushed back her hair with a gesture he did not understand, a raindark smile he hated. He looked into her face. He held out his hand for the envelope of banknotes, checked it, sighed as he handed her the package of drugs. She took the parcel in her left hand, she betrayed none of her eagerness, except that her smile twitched almost imperceptibly. 'Be careful,' he said. 'Do not fear,' she said formally, 'I value every grain, you can trust me.'

He watched her slip in through the side door, heard the key turn in the lock, then he moved away through the trees, silently. Beth is wounded by this vision of Vellet.

'Poor Vellet,' she said, truthfully. Poor Vellet, goes the rain. The scab-skin of night has formed. The wind off the east smells of fish oil. Beth is exhausted by her glimpse of Vellet and is about to trudge downhill, go home with her worries, when she realizes the giant has more to show her. Reluctantly, she settles to watch, pulling the collar of her gaberdine raincoat higher about her neck and hugging her arms around herself for warmth.

In this next vision of Vellet, it is another kind of night, warm, sultry, rainless. Vellet is wandering along the path at the foot of Giant Hill, munching an apple. She seems to be waiting for someone.

Beth waits. In this entangled situation she finds it hard to remember that she is the real girl and Vellet the phantom. She is sure that by the manner in which Vellet is pacing, waiting, that something terrible will happen, branding both of them. Beth dislikes spying on Vellet, especially as the idea of the winged skull of Ash keeps coming to her, with its shadow. But Beth has to see what happens next.

Vellet is still pacing up and down the little path and Beth can smell the jeremiad that moves with her. Vellet throws her apple core away. The soundtrack sighs, the sculpture of a woman on the hillside cries out in loneliness, and there is no exit.

Can it be, Beth wonders, that Theron actually prefers masturbation to me, and that because I am insulted by his preference, I have invented this ghost to deny my responsibility, to camouflage Theron's rejection of me. Is Vellet my poltergeist phenomenon?

Two men are approaching Vellet. They are young men, dressed in leather jackets, jeans, the proper gear. Vellet stands on the path to receive them, greet them. It seems as if she is asking them a question. Then she offers them something from a paper packet. They are eating what she offers, her technicolour host. Vellet and the two young men sit on the grass and talk, laughing, kidding around. Beth cannot hear what they say. She hears only her own blood beating against her eardrums. Vellet, you are the odour of sickrooms, she thinks.

Beth does not want to go on watching. The trio of her vision have such an air of violence about them. They are smoking now, they pass a cigarette from hand to hand.

Beth wants to get up and run away, but she cannot move. The giant says to her: 'I am the wifeless giant, I go back as far as anything can. I will pass my knowledge on, Beth! Stay here. Watch. Learn. You must understand Vellet. Do not be content simply with rejecting her. Think of her as a part of yourself, denied and repressed. Watch Vellet and her two boyfriends, Jo Silverpiece an Vic Coppercoin. Watch her.'

So Beth watches. She watches Vellet, Jo and Vic in their nakedness, their dance between the eyes of the giant. She saw Vellet dancing like a blind ballerina. This is a riddle, thought Beth, and it is not just about a ghost, it is about a woman. It concerns me. Fearfully, she watches. The long pricks of the men joggle as they dance and the mouths of the men are open, their heads thrown back, and their mouths yelling slowly. Vellet dances between the two men, her breasts like two inkblots in the moonlight. She is crouching between the two men now and urinates on the ground. The men are smiling, still dancing, but more slowly. Vellet turns her back on the men, and waggles her arse. First Jo Silverpiece, then Vic Coppercoin kneel down and kiss her arsehole.

Beth's eyes ache and burn. She peers down at the three lovers and tastes the thumbnail of the murdered woman.

Now the men stroke their own erections while Vellet watches, seated on the giant's prick. Her smile is martial, her demeanour vigorous. She watches the men with the red eye of her cunt. She lies on the earth, limbs spread-eagled. The men begin to abuse her.

'No,' said the Giant, correcting Beth, 'no, not abuse. They are only carrying out orders, Vellet's orders.'

Silverpiece has his penis in her mouth. Coppercoin is fucking her. Beth sees Vellet's body quiver and convulse. Coppercoin and Silverpiece change places. Then Coppercoin fucks her in the anus, while Silverpiece winds her hair around his prick.

These sexual acrobatics make Beth's skin burn. She tastes her disgust in her mouth. She feels faint and thinks, God, if this woman's corruption was so strong that she created a ghost for herself, to keep her image abroad in the world after her death, then how can I free Theron of such a wife? Vellet, Vellet, that stink of bowels is you, then!

The antics of the trio continue but Beth closes her eyes and refuses to watch the giant's show any more, so with the palm of his hand he wipes the vision away.

Beth sat on the wet hillside, her flesh stuck full of needles. Now she realizes Vellet's strength. How Vellet's fingers will always reach for the fruit of the tree of voluptuousness. Dirt! thinks Beth. But I have undertaken this work, of ridding Theron of Vellet, even though the work may be beyond my strength. Beth cannot bring herself to stir, even though she is cold and wet.

What happens now, Giant, she thought listlessly.

There is no answer.

The eyelids of Hades close . . .

Beth's sigh is like chalk crumbling in her hand. She still feels sick, cannot get the events she has witnessed out of her mind. How long ago did that orgy take place? How long after that night did Vellet drown? Did Coppercoin or Silverpiece push her in the river, rebelling against her leadership? Beth feels that her own undergarments have been abused. She looks around, almost guiltily. Now Vellet approaches, she cannot smell or sense the ghost's presence, it is the replay of Vellet's adventure that is sickening Beth, and yet at the same time she would like to insert her fingers deep into her own vagina.

I must either help Theron, or leave him.

She shivers violently, cold as if she were standing up to her neck in a stream. Might just as well be, she thinks, and gets up stiffly. Her sweat is beginning to smell rank.

From a long way off, Vellet watches Beth go downhill over the dark grey grass. She sees the broken branches of her own kith and kin. Vellet looks at the man in the moon. Then she whispers, so you showed her, Giant. Why? What are you planning for me? He did not answer her. She sank down in the river again, despairing. Beth's pain is no comfort to her. Beth will be on her guard, now, even stronger an opponent. Vellet cursed, and cats and dogs shuddered in the village. Her open mouth screamed as the Giant chastised her, and the river mud filled her lungs again.

Beth walks briskly to get warm and although she still feels horribly sick, she knows she has been toughened, that the Giant has taught her the use of her eyes, that she knows what she is up against. She has, in fact, been given a shield of defence against Vellet, having seen her at her worst, and she understands that Theron need not feel guilty for her death. Such a woman will inevitably find her death early, violently. It is this guilt of Theron's that Vellet trades on, Beth realizes. If I can remove that guilt, will he be free? Perhaps.

Despite the shocks she's had tonight, and those on top of the frustration of her meeting with Tabitha, Beth feels her sickness ebb away and her spirits rise. After the strain, euphoria. She knows she should not trust it but she does, and she is singing quietly to herself as she comes through the village streets. The odour of beer comforts her as she passes the pub and she is glad to be down among the ordinary houses and the village people. Every lighted window cheers her up and she feels nothing will stop her dealing with Vellet and putting a stop to all this trouble and worry.

Then she crossed the road and saw, in the gutter, a dead black cat, stiff and swollen, a parody cat, a stilted animal waiting for the garbage collector in the morning.

A message from Vellet, thinks Beth, and walks on soberly.

SEVENTEEN

TOWARDS the end of June, Theron asks Beth what she would like for her birthday next week. She frowns, tells him she will go up to town and look around the shops. But she is thinking, secretly, what I want for my birthday is to spend the day at Ash's house, invisible, silent, just overlooking her life. Beth walks quickly away from Theron, so that he will not guess her thought. Her cool response returns Theron to his isolation, to his birdlime ghost.

Beth lifts the lid of the piano and plays a favourite tune, one that always reminds her of rocks and cliffs, of the sea. Her left hand and her right hand move delicately over the keys. She goes on playing, thinking of nothing and no one, her hands imitating shadows.

As I play the music mingles with an odour of slowly decaying fruit in an overripe room. The sullying of fruit amazes me, the malcontent of apples rubs at my groin. Beth jumps up from the piano stool and hurries to the table. She opens the bible with sweaty fingers. She bends over the black blood of the book. She wants to know everything. She would give anything to know . . . But when she tries to read the words the edges of her eyelids feel raw and she is half-blinded with fear.

For the third time in as many hours, Beth unlocks her polished wooden box, bought in the village junk shop, and takes out the six photographs of Ash. Sitting on the edge of her bed, she pores over the snapshots. Beth took them herself with her aunt's old camera that summer five years ago. The smile of Ash is like the roar unidentified in a distance at night, her expressions shift like smoke of that old summer.

Ash, murmurs Beth, poor years since you went with Jake. Nearly five years since I caught the fever of you that still burns me up, even though neither of us are those girls any more, those virgins are no longer us, no more than a soldier's a soldier after he's been demobbed. We're women who never write letters to one another. Yet my life is still jammed up by this ... interest I have in you. And you? Are you still running from me? Do you ever think of our summer? Or doesn't it enter your head?

In the room of sporadic sunlight, Beth locks the photographs of Ash away, safe.

Strange name, strange power.

Beth is taking off her clothes.

I am not able to practise the calligraphy of my love for Ash, not even on the walls of public lavatories, that way is not possible for me. I cannot proclaim my love that way. There are always my doubts ...

But sun and moon maim me, and I keep my right hand prepare for pornographic tasks.

Alpha, Ash, Alpha ...

Beth shouts silently to the women of Jerusalem.

A child's pink hair ribbon lies on the dusty carpet. Ash stares at it. It is the shape of the lower jaw of a horse. It is the fin of a fish. It is a ribbon, her child's hair ribbon.

In the darkening room, Ash shuts her eyes. The life drains out of her, fluid from a wound. The day, boat of hours, has drifted away from her. This morning, first thing, when she saw the morning mist on the ground, the trees scratching the green sky, she felt she could look into the day and not be afraid of it.

But between her and her existence within the day, her wholeness, have come the heavy weight of other people, their words, gestures, demands: husband, children, friends, the gossip that follows tappings on the door, the thriving of trivia. So Ash's day has gone and now it is twilight, a stone of great size beneath which she is pinned, against which she heaves with no result. And the hours that passed, into which she could not see, could not hold close like flowers or pages to contemplate, those hours are mildewed.

She bends down and picks up the hair ribbon, opens her drawer and drops it in, and is about to close it when she pauses, reaches in the drawer and takes out another ribbon, of black velvet, on which she sometimes fastens a silver medallion depicting a crescent moon. She rummages about in the drawer till she finds the medallion, clasps it in her hand until it gets warm. Then she threads it on to the ribbon and ties it around her neck. Comforted, she goes downstairs.

Last night she had dreamt she was slapping a small child, a little girl, and on waking she thought, but there is no danger. During the day she became certain there was danger, for her.

EIGHTEEN

The Giant in Summer

The giant looks up at the sky.
The giant inhales the innuendoes of the afternoon.
The giant laughs at the idea of an easy death.
The giant outwits god at card games.
The giant wears no loin cloth.
The giant sings of his blindness:
   'the herbage of my eyes'.
The giant breaks the bride's back.
The giant drowns his verdicts in the fountain.
He has no name.
He does not drink blood.
The giant looks at the hourglass.
The giant plucks his own heart out, gazes at it,
   replaces it, roaring with strength.
The unworldly giant stammers and candles blaze.
The giant speaks the word 'snowdrop' in French:
   'perce-neige'.
The giant listens to a wireless, message that glitters with evil.
The giant watches the apparition, her shimmer.
The giant understands the sleepwalker's language.
He hears the driftwood's mirth.
The giant pricks his finger sewing baby-linen.
The giant smells the sorrel odour of the rain.
The giant meets with thieves and clubs them with his white
   umbrella.
The giant meditates amid the wooden torrents of the afternoon

on secrets everybody knows.
The giant hires a harlot.
The giant awaits the return of Ash, with mud on her skirt,
    and oak leaves in her womb.
Then he sleeps.
The galactoid gaps in his memory must be repaired.

NINETEEN

B ETH turns off the ignition, sits for a moment in the parked car. What will happen after the flowers? she thought, after this pale summer of abandoned orchards? She heaves the two shopping baskets from the back seat and struggles to the door with the week's provisions. She fumbles for the house key, then gets in, dumping the bags on the kitchen table.

Her head aches with the thud and clang of the supermarket. She always goes once a week but wonders whether the double stamps are worth the ordeal of crowds, ill-tempered women and bawling children. A village of shoplifters, anyway, she thought bitterly.

Beth lit a cigarette and sprawled in the fireside chair, though there is no fire in the grate. It is July, although the weather is dull as secondhand clothes. She draws the smoke deep into her lungs. For the past fortnight she's been sleeping badly and her body feels fussy, disorganized, her strength going, everything changing, her own face like that of a different woman reflected intermittently in mirrors and windows.

I've scratched myself on Theron's barbed wire cock, she thinks.

I held your hand, Theron, last evening as we stood at the foot of the stairs. I held your hand, you clutched my fingers, you said, 'I'm afraid, Beth,' with your head you made the gesture 'no', and I saw her falling towards us down the stairs in a shadow, passing us like a chill breeze, and you clutched my hand, hurting my fingers, you shuddered: and Vellet's ghost left behind her a hard auriferous sensation that parted us yet again and Theron and I began to run away from one another in this house. It is no laughing matter, we ran all night, our words so unkind, so cruel, we ran with our quarrel, our rage burning us like the edge of a moon, and we could not stop, not until I screamed and shrieked and hooted with hysteria, a real attack, no rumour, and you saw that it was me, Beth, me and not Vellet: you saw the danger of your mirage. We calmed down, we were both shivering, sweating. I pushed the hair back from my face, got up from the bed, naked, and staggered under the shower, warm water on my face, tits, ankles. 'I'm not afraid now,' you called out. I nodded, exhausted. 'She won't visit again tonight,' he said confidently, when I came out of the shower. I was so tired, and wounded from the fight. The silence moved between us again. I stuck my tongue out at it. You laughed, Theron, and hope revived in me, that you might free yourself of Vellet, shuck her off.

But can I trust to that? My mind turns more often to my own house, safe escape, high up on the moors. My house, untenanted, unhaunted. Vellet will not follow me there. It is Theron she wants. I am coming closer and closer to the break, I feel it, I know that one day, in the dark time before dawn, I shall creep out of this haunted house where there is not enough room for two wives. Vellet will have won. As I leave I'll laugh without making a sound for my head will be full enough of noises. Poor Theron. I shall leave you and be free of the mewing of Vellet, free of the ghost swimming towards me in the naked night.

Often, Theron appears to enjoy his ghost. Oh he protests to me no, Beth, I do not enjoy it. But she has a hold over me (he says) and somehow, it is as if, when she is here, I don't care what she does or how she does it. I said to him, 'you're welcome, Theron, go ahead, have your fun.'

He said then, 'Beth, I understand your angry words, I know how you feel, squeezed into a tiny lonely jealous room.'

'Do you,' I said.

Last night, the moon turned aside when I looked up at the sky

Last night, when we were hoarse with our dispute, I put out my hand and scratched his cheek with my long nails, drawing blood.

Later, in bed, I was almost asleep when I felt you shift, Theron, move, your touch on my shoulder, and then the weight of your body, coming down on mine. You were excited and you caressed me without satire. Without speech, no explanation, no word, you touched my thigh and then to acknowledge a reconciliation you fingered my cunt. Last night was the first time we'd had sex for weeks.

Beth stubs out her cigarette, begins the tedious chore of unpacking groceries, the eggs, butter, bacon, flour, bread, apples, oranges, coffee, raw meat.

She opens the larder door and smells the cold summer in there too.

All the while her thoughts are creasing and wrinkling and she feels she is moving rapidly away from any solution. There is no cure for me and Theron. Nothing to salvage from what might have been a shared life. Vellet is a gag thrust into my mouth. I have only silence and retching left to me.

He gets strength from Vellet, even though he says he hates and fears her. Perhaps they are operating a two-way vampirism, sustaining one another. Where does that leave me?

Beth is almost weeping but will not give in, pulls herself together. Putting the kettle on to boil, she glances through the kitchen window at a miserable sky with bits of blue the size of midges. I feel I've lived as long as the giant, she thinks.

Theron fingered my cunt as calmly as if he didn't have two wives. I felt the pummel of his cock against my buttocks. He weaved his touch restlessly but delicately. After his encounters with Vellet, I didn't want him to fuck me, but the weeks of chastity had been too long, left my body unwieldy, so I didn't push him away, I couldn't, I gasped, he was trying to catch fish in my nets, I was fresh from the furnace, he was groaning above me and I was panting and swearing, heaving myself up to the many-seeded man, my throat marked with red blotches, and sinuous flames darting up my spine: yes, we sped on our way, hearts banging loud in our ears.

Beth sips her tea.

Now I am disgusted with myself, she thinks, exactly because I am not ashamed of what happened last night, that consummation. I should be, but I am not. I know he's turned on by the ghost of his first wife, and is slaking himself on me. But I wanted it. I should be revolted by that, but

I'm not. I just don't know how long I can go on with this strange tension. I ought to clear out, go back to my own home. My love is being clipped, my branches lopped off. To make me grow straighter? I don't know. If I go, am I running away? If I stay, will I grow straight, or crooked and crazy?

Beth strikes her hand repeatedly against her hip. What am I to do? The phone rang. She jumped up.

'Yes?'

'It's me, Beth.'

'Hello, Theron.'

'You know that bookcase just by my desk?'

'Yes.'

'On the top shelf, you'll find my annotated copy of Bullock's Hitler. I left it behind this morning. Can you bring it in to the university for me, dear? Before three this afternoon? Does that upset your day?'

'No, Theron, no. I'd enjoy the drive anyway.'

'Fine. See you about two thirty ?'

'Sure.'

She put the black receiver back on its cradle gently, then ran upstairs and brushed her hair vigorously. Then she made the beds, cleaned the bathroom, came downstairs again, got the hoover out of the broom cupboard, cleaned the house while her thoughts piled up like dirty dishes in the sink.

And out of all Beth's confusion, what? No decision, no way out discovered, no exit from her embattled area. These are the quicksands of Uranus, she thinks, as she parks her car in the university yard. For me, there's little difference now between singing and screaming. I must get free before it's too late.

She left the book with Theron's secretary, he was busy in a tutorial session. The secretary wanted to talk, glad of an excuse, but Beth did not stay, she was trussed up in the same ghostly inflorescence that had been hers all day. She drove out of the town and along a narrow road between fields. She feels her mind stretched across regions of brilliant metal, with no place to rest.

How can Theron go on with his lectures, his krieg-talk to the students, sit and discuss old battles and strategies, when his own life is so jagged, war-like, his world tightening around him, invading him. But perhaps he does not notice the danger. I come back again to the same question. Should I leave him? Because he is happy with his ghost wife. Let him have his formal masturbator's life. Let him look deeply into the eyes of the ghost. The impeccable mouth of the ghost!

Beth drew into a lay-by and got out of the car. At least I am out of the house, away from those silent rooms with their slavonic clocks. Perhaps one day of some sort, the day after tomorrow, or one day next month, a warmer day, the door will unlock, this door I'm facing, this door I'm hammering against, and it will swing open easily on the prospect of glittering lakes and fountains, and I, one day, without warning, will be invited to that country, and Ash, you'll step forward, and lead me into that place.

Beth crosses the road and walks across a field. On the other side of the century, my life stretches out freely, with flowers and friends, days the colour of wheat, not these pale chill days. The wind drags her thoughts through the grass. She looks up at the giant. He is three miles walk away. She sees him preening his whiteness.

'What are your habits, giant? Do you catch fish by poisoning the waters with your own urine? Do you live on bones, nerves and embryos? What are the names of your daughters?'

'These are the names of my daughters,' said the giant, his breath billowing like dry ice.

'My daughters are called Amulet, Ash, Ararat,
Beauty, Beulah, Breast,
Cunt, Coffin, Crown,
Dog, Dream and Dust,
Eve, East and Egg,

Fish, Flamen and Famine,
Gospel, Grace and Glass,
Hallow, Hag and Husk,
Iron, Itch and Island,
January, Juniper and Jackdaw,
Kerosene, Kaleidoscope and Kale,
Lamp, Luck and Lapwing,
Moth, Map and Mask,
Net, Newt and Night,
Oak, Orgasm and Ouija,
Palfrey, Prairie and Plough,
Question, Quilt and Quartz,
Rubble, Ring and Rain,
Shadow, Shore and Shrapnel,
Tree and Turtle and Twilight,
Udder and Umber and Uterus,
Vagina and Vampire and Veil,
Waltz and Wave and Wimple,
Xanthin and Xenolith and Xylophone,
Yew and Year and Yoni,
Zodiac and Zona-Pellucida and Zephyr.
These are the names of my daughters, Beth.'

Beth goes on looking at the rough bluish sky behind the giant. The giant's erection turns Beth's clothes to tatters. The wind flaps the remains of her skirt around her legs.

'How many wives have you, giant ?' she whispers, her mouth dry.

'None,' he answers softly. 'None.'

Now Beth feels herself plunge headlong into her own womb 'Vellet? Is she not a daughter of yours?'

'No,' he answers. 'She is no daughter of mine. She is no one's daughter.'

His voice is laborious now, his blind eyes pits of chalk. 'How many sons have you, giant?'

'No sons,' he says, 'I have no sons.'

'And tell me,' asks Beth fearfully, 'What is the name of my daughter?'

The giant does not answer Beth's question. There is only silence, and the wind moving across the field, down from the hills. Beth stares at the giant cut into the chalk hill. Then she begins to move cautiously back to her car, her flesh creaking with random guesses. And the lining of her womb is woven so as to change, colour, according to the time of night or day.

Singing or screaming a lunar song?

Beth cannot distinguish between the two modes. She moves stealthily. She stands at the gate of her own house. The moorland is cold and quiet around her. 'Where was the tree?' she sings. 'In a garden,' she croons.

In the porch of the house there are snuffling shadows. The red paint is peeling from the front door. Beth turns the key in the lock. It is stiff, she exerts pressure, hurting her fingers, but the resistance gives, and the door opens.

Beth pauses on the threshold of her house, the names of the Giant's daughters reverberating in her mind. Why do those names remind me of the little pearly birthmark on Ash's left cheekbone, that splash of moon?

On the doorstep, Beth hesitates, afraid of the dusty loneliness inside the house, petrified of the mirrors that once reflected Ash.

The sky shudders with the irritation of a botched summer. The overgrown garden murmurs retarded proverbs. With a surly smile Beth enters her house, re-enters the sheeted rooms of her adolescence. In the house she discovers a leviathan stillness. All is muffled, stifled.

How long has it been? thinks Beth. Over a year since I've been inside this house. Usually I peer in through the windows, just staying in the garden. This house has been empty too long. It's become sad, sadder than when I left. My house is uncared for . . . it should be lived in, made alive. Shall I run out of the house before something catches me? I can if I want to . . . No voice will call me back, no ghost detain me.

Beth pulls the front door to, shutting herself in. The hall is dark. The house smells damp.

Slowly she climbs the stairs and goes into the little lavatory built into the alcove at the turn of the stairs. She pulls down her pants and urinates. Then she tries to shit but finds it is only wind stretching her bowels.

How can Ash be one of the Giant's daughters?

I don't know.

She glances out of the lavatory window, down at the old greenhouse, and beyond that, the yard in which they used to keep chickens.

Beth pulls the chain.

My body aches, thinks Beth, as if I were a sword-swallower, an inexperienced one, a novice. She is at the top of the stairs. Her movements are slow. She opens the doors of the bedrooms, as if unlocking a harem. The bare iron frames of the beds are harsh and ugly in the thin light. Heavy wardrobes loom. Beth opens the windows. The chill air comes in, butting against the dirty curtains. Beth holds her own invisible afterbirth in her hand.

She puts her head out of the window and yells,

'Howdy, Vic Coppercoin! Welcome, Jo Silverpiece! Where are you, Vellet?'

Her voice goes palsied through all the neglected rooms, across the coarse garden, but there is no answer. None of the guests accept Beth's invitation. Beth's challenge goes unanswered.

'There! I knew your real name was Mr Blindmaker, Giant,' Beth grumbles. Leap years and lunar years, white languages and black: all yours, Giant, and you can keep them. What did planchette say to me, years ago, in this room? Ash insisted on calling up planchette, though I told her I was scared. It was a hot evening, we'd been drinking vodka, drinking pretty heavily. Four times Ash received a message and each time all planchette said was, go away, Beth, go away, Beth, go away, Beth, go away, Beth.

Planchette's command or Ash's desire?

I went out of the room that night, I tiptoed out of our room and along this corridor, listening to the sounds of my body. That night the clock rode naked until dawn. But that was a long time ago.

Another night, not in the same room, but downstairs, on a calm unelaborate summer night, with the french windows thrown wide open and a moon with its roots in us and stars like stepping stones: on that ghostless night I sat at the piano and Ash sang. Her song was called *A Secret Understanding* and the words made us both blush. Later that night Ash unplaited my hair with her long fingers. That night I wandered out of my cage and (because the puppet wanted to be human!) went to Ash. Female bears with honey on their paws. It was a long time ago. Another night we washed our feet in clear river water. Even now when I think of Ash, explosions of an unknown but terrifying nature go through me.

How can she be a daughter of the giant?

One night shortly after Jake's arrival, he and I went out for a walk. It was dark and moonless so Jake brought a torch with him. In fact, Ash suggested he take the torch, so that we didn't stumble in the dark.

'How have you been, Beth?' he asked, after we had been walking some time.

'Great!' I answered expressionlessly, 'no wars, no floods destroyed me.'

It was a warm autumn night but iron hooks clipped the stars to the sky. I shivered, smelling Jake's strength, sensing his intentions. We walked in silence by the pond. The trees by the waterside were old and hard and I knew they had voices and they could speak and when they did what they said would be terrible. Jake walked faster and then turned, asking,

'Are you happy, Beth?'

I couldn't answer him.

'Are you?' he repeated, making me look at him, shining the torch full on my face. He was not angry, he spoke quietly, but I knew I had to answer him, I knew it, even if we had to stay there until dawn and its billowing smoke. How well I remembered his gestures from our childhood, the wrench of his mouth, the narrowing of his eyes, his head and hand and heel, the stranger he'd grown up into. I remembered one day in particular when we were children, his clothes spattered with red paint, and how he teased me, dabbing me with the wet paint brush until I cried.

'Are you happy?' he repeated, softly.

'I was,' I told him. 'Yes,' I whispered, 'I was.'

'Before I came?'

'Yes.'

'When you and Ash were alone?'

'Yes.'

When Jake smiled, there was a darkness at all hours of the clock. He pointed the torch towards the pond and flicked a beam of light this way and that carelessly across the water.

'But you know it can't go on . . . don't you?' he said, almost lightly.

I said nothing.

'You realize how crazy it is, you two girls?' He laughed. How did I feel then, knowing he despised me and that he would take Ash away? I felt I was the rain, the dirt, a nun's shadow, no more.

'Do you understand, Beth?' he asked sharply, his grip tightening around my forearm.

'She must decide,' I said weakly.

He relaxed his grip.

'Why, yes, that's fair, surely,' he said, grinning, 'we'll let Ash choose.'

I nodded my head.

'That is fair, isn't it?' he asked a minute later, in a sing-song voice. I nodded again. I did not want to be Beth any more.

We leaned on the fence and stared through the darkness across the moor. Jake lit a cigarette and the escarpment of smoke hurt my eyes. There was a dog barking somewhere far off, and the sheep moved in the darkness. I was the only casualty in the night. All of this was years ago, though.

Beth, the coprophagan, stands again at the edge of the pond. It is the present now, not the past. Her conversation with Jake, years past, echoes and fades. Her body feels luminous. She must not linger in the twilight much longer. The rain begins, whisper of latinisms. Beth will sell her body very cheaply this evening. Where are the customers, the soldiers, the sailors? She ran out of the old playroom because the old black-faced goggle-eyed fantastically-garbed toy lying on the windowsill frightened her. But even so she might have to return to this house to live soon, leaving Theron, carrying coldness in her hands, to keep night-vigils among the hanks of dream.

Ash wails in darkness, callously. She will not offer Beth any of her uneasy lullabies. Beth must creep back into her own shadow regions alone, accepting her own penury.

Theron and I cannot answer the important questions we have both posed, therefore I think our dialogue must dissolve. We must take our questions elsewhere. Beth stares over the pond towards the fog of long grass; beyond that, the moorland. She bites the jagged fingernail of her left forefinger. The back of her thighs ache with tension. She looks up at the sky where the greeny light reminds her of someone rubbing glass with a scrap of silk. Beth's heavy hair is bound in two long plaits, reaching almost to her waist, and its weight is increasing, it seems hardly possible that she'll be able to get her body moving again, she is taking root here by the water. The broken thoughts of exhaustion confuse her, and it seems as if her mother's silhouette is reflected in the grey waters of the pond. Beth gasps, touches her sweating forehead with her thin hand.

'Your fires and lamps are to be extinguished,' said Jake, that night he told me he and Ash were to be married. Ash had gone up to bed but Jake and I still sat talking, the empty bottles of wine littering the table. Then he cut the cards and said, 'do you want to know your fortune?' He smiled covetously. 'Tell me,' I said. He moved his hands rapidly over the pasteboards. 'It is never new enough for you, Beth,' he said, 'the new year, the new moon: beware, Beth. The man you'll marry will live up a one-way street, sensual but too silent.'

That night Jake told me ancient jokes.

'I have had many wives in many languages,' he boasted.

'All obese, I bet,' I answered.

He snorted with laughter. I survived until the next page. But he took Ash and left me with a body that looks like that of a young woman but to me resembles the body of a dismantled ship, unwieldy, unseaworthy.

Crossing the lawn, Beth sees the triangle of dancers standing still, too late to begin dancing, Ash, Beth, Jake.

Beth hurries through the garden.

My brains are in my arsehole, my womb is kept in a polythene bag stored under my bed, she thinks feverishly. All that I had has gone, is different, and I hear the calendar combing her hair.

Vellet does not haunt me here. She has no need. I have my own ghosts here, to whom I am addicted. In my dream last night Jake called up the baby-bat hurricane. Jake lifted the jugs one by one, filling them with September cider. 'Do I make you afraid?' he asked me fiercely. I did not answer. I saw Ash in the background, opening an iron cupboard. She was dressed in a military uniform of some kind.

I've had enough of these reminiscences. I'll go back to Theron, to try a little longer, before the sacred bone of my pelvis wears out with trying. I'll leave my house, this dangerous refuge, with its half-healed wounds, and go back to Theron's world.

His world: the puzzle, the charade of the stallion's shadow, the place where night begins.

Beth and Theron are reading. On the radio, a music perseveres. Outside, the rain is taken for granted. A moon is drizzling down also.

Theron exclaimed suddenly and looked up.

'Beth,' he said excited, 'Beth . . .'

'What?' she said, not looking up, absorbed in her detective novel.

'Do you know what the first vertebra in the human neck is called?'

Beth stared at him.

'What a strange question, Theron. No, what is it called?'

'Atlas!'

Beth looks bewildered and glances around the room, as if the ghost might enlighten her as to the significance of the vertebra called Atlas. But this is the ghost's night off.

'I don't understand, dear,' she said.

'But don't you? I meant how poetic the names of the various regions of the body are, unsuspected, hidden beneath the skin. The first vertebra, Beth, that holds up the neck, called Atlas, because Atlas held up the world. His figure is often put on the title-pages of atlases to this day. And the vertebra supports the world of the head.'

'Ah, I see now. Yes, that is very neat, very exact, Theron.'

'I thought so,' said Theron, pleased, and smiling at Beth. She looks a little tired, he thinks. He goes back to his book, but only a few moments later interrupts their reading again.

'By the way, isn't it strange we never hear from Ash and Jake now? You never hear from Ash nowadays, do you?'

Beth's wrists and ankles ache. But she does not look up from her book.

'No,' she says abstractedly, 'no. I had a few letters soon after she and Jake married, but not now. She's busy. With a young family, you can't expect . . . why do you ask?'

'It seems strange to me . . . your own family never in touch.'

'We were never close, you know that.'

'He and Ash might have died, for all we know.'

Beth shrugged, felt sick.

'So you didn't get on? You and Jake?'

Beth threw down her book. Theron ignored her gesture.

'No, we didn't get on.'

'And Ash?'

Beth hesitates, watching Theron. He is only gossiping.

'I hardly knew Ash,' said Beth quietly.

'I thought she lived with you?'

Beth got up and walked to the window, pulled the curtain aside, peered out at the rainy evening. What is Theron's reason for this conversation, what is he hinting at? Or is he only passing time, tired of his book, of the idea of Atlas?

'She lived with me just a few weeks during the summer of the year she married Jake, she met him while she was staying with me. It was lonely for me, you know, up there in that big house, so isolated, not a neighbour for miles. Ash didn't pay any rent but she helped out with shopping, cleaning, instead. When Jake came home, he and Ash hit it off.'

'So you were a matchmaker,' said Theron, laughing. Beth turns on him sharply, but his laughter is innocent enough.

'As you say, I was. And it is strange that we never hear from them.' Beth sighs, sits down again, takes up her book.

Then Theron says insolently,

'Had quite a fancy for Ash, didn't you?' The silence splits into two equal halves. In one half, Theron waits for an answer. In the other, Beth struggles for breath. No ferries cross the cold river between Beth and Theron. Beth is sure that her skinny body is emitting an offensive odour.

'Bastard!' she whispers, digging her nails into the palms of her hands.

He heard her.

'I'm not the only one with a secret then, am I?' he said angrily. 'Did I say you were?' she replied.

'You didn't tell me about Ash. You implied that you were perfect. You left me to be the shitty one.'

Beth threw herself back in her chair and slashed with the blades of her hands through the air. Her skin is metallic, she does not recognize the abuse she is mouthing.

He got up without a word and beckoned to his wife.

Beth hesitated, then stood up, a culprit, uttering light rapid incoherent sounds. She followed him upstairs and into their bedroom.

Unhurriedly, he smeared a clear cold ointment on her bum, his kind of witch's ointment.

TWENTY

ASH is hunched over her sewing but keeps glancing up out of the window at the shortcoming of the grey sky. She is menstruating and she is gloomy. Her shadow bites the unfinished dress and her hands are penetrated by the sharp points of her thoughts. Her embroideries anger her. Also there are the old spellings she cannot erase from her mind. A slender blind red snake moves in her wet place, nipping her.

I used to visualize my great grandson's life, shining in a cat's cradle mirror, the face of the future. This vision used to sustain me through bad times. Now I do not care about the generations.

Jake is pursuing me. That is the manner of our marriage. I cry superstitiously. He runs after me. My many escapes exhaust me. I am holding my bruised hands out in front of me as I run, to brush aside the leaves that threaten to hit me in the face. I run but hesitate suddenly, cannot decide which path to take. I cannot elude my pursuer, I hear him close behind me. He is chasing me. My son and my daughter are chasing me. The percussion of their voices tortures me.

I am caught.

He will not let me escape.

Bride-harlot, he called me.

Now I ache all over, I clench my muscles tight as one of god's smiles, I throw my sewing down. The afternoon says to me, why aren't you running, Ash, home to the giant.

I gasp and hold my hands over my ears.

Who will write a requiem for me, if I leave Jake? He will follow me.

My other head sprouts, laughs, has its own dreams, eats roots and skins of fruit, plants tomorrow's starvation. As I look at myself in the mirror, I see my hair turn to leaves, my hand is a branch, my cry is mud. I spread my name upon the wounds of Christ.

Last night I stood beside Jake, motionless. He frowned. He took hold of my skirt in both his hands, wrenched and tore the fabric, asked me questions.

'Why do you want to go back there? Is it just sentiment? Why do you want to go back, to the village of the giant?'

I shook my head, tired of all this.

'Why don't you answer me?' he shouted. Then he forced an entry into my trance. His thumbs pressed against my throat. I crawled away from him, a broken woman. I saw in my mind's eye Beth weeping blood as she got out of the train and came towards me. Her hair was blue as the sea. She soaked me in her embrace. I'll teach you star-archery, Ash, she promised. Moons of Europa fell on us.

Now leaf-shadows ache on the afternoon wall. A leaf-ghost trembles against the white door.

Ash unlocks the door of a cupboard and takes out a wicker basket, similar to a picnic hamper. She places it on the table and stands looking at it, her expression taking on a severe radiance.

She lifts the lid of the basket, which gives off a strawy creaking. She takes a deep breath. Inside the basket, a jumble of old pages, old notebooks, coffee-stains on the covers, diaries whose pages she never completed, all the stories of adolescence unfinished, only half told, postcards of cathedral towns, overthrown republics, long dead movie stars. Letters from Jake when he'd been overseas. Ash dabbles her hands through the mementoes. She's never had the courage to burn these memories.

Now she will confront them.

Methodically, she begins to sort the papers. There are forgotten things here for her to rediscover, versions of herself come to light again this afternoon. It is almost unbearable, this thinking back, looking back across wind-beaten years, but her life demands it, and it is harder to turn away from the task now than to complete it.

She reads the poems she wrote long ago in the city, and then the other poems composed in the houses of strangers: the misshapen stanzas remind her that she is a woman now, established, respectable, the mother of children, having a place in the world. It is a long time since she was a girl working in a cheap fish restaurant. But her pride in her position does not last. My unhappiness is not to be washed away like that. Difficult lessons take the longest to be learnt.

She stacks the poems neatly in a pile. How thin my handwriting was then!

She picks up several letters that she wrote to Jake, when he was away in Madrid last summer. She'd never posted them, despite the hours they'd taken her to write, the nights they kept her from sleeping, with the things she wanted to say to him, how they were full of her unhappiness with Jake, yet how she depended on him, loved him. Ruefully she turns the sealed stamped envelopes back and forth in her hands, but cannot bear to open and read her messages. It was very bad then, my depression. I have gone on from that, I see clearer now.

But Ash knows she will never be free of her own silence, her undelivered messages. She feels she is made of mirrors.

Then she smiles light-heartedly. Here are the photographs. Alison, her first child, and James, born a year later; many photographs, from babyhood to first day at playschool. Ash lingers over the photographs with the skin feeling of her babies creeping warmly over her body.

Then suddenly she is very cold. Her tender smile grimaces.

This is not a photograph of children.

This is a photograph of the two girls, untidy, innocent as alphabets. Beth and Ash, arms linked, laughing into the camera help gingerly by Tabitha Irons.

This photograph is like an alarm clock set to awaken Ash from her long sleep, when the moment is ripe.

But why should I suddenly find myself thinking of Beth, drawl back to her? I haven't thought of her for years. Why does the photo of me and Beth shock me, feel like a signal?

Slowly Ash packs the papers, including the last snapshot, into the basket again, locking it away in the cupboard. She is growing angry. The pendulum of her blood swings. Beth and Jake are the same creature: they are both pursuers. Leave me alone, both of you!

She reaches down a book from the shelf, taking one at random, and opening it to read a poem about a woman descending a flight of old steps down to the sea.

Futures were still wailing in her when Jake pushed the door open to see his wife seated at her table, immobile, desolate and dumb. His heart sank.

'What is it?' he asks anxiously, setting down the cup of tea he has brought her. He looks at the book lying on the floor, spine broken from the violence with which it has been thrown down. He stoops, picks it up, sets it on the table, beside the cup.

Ash looks up at Jake and laughs, hard and humourless. 'Happy Anniversary,' she cries, quoting from the inscription written on the flyleaf of the book, and then rushes out of the room, leaving Jake to pick up the book again, which she has flung away from her.

About what did you dream last night, Ash? thought Jake. And why are the sunlit streets of the early afternoon so desolate to you? They always have seemed so, you told me. Why does it seem to you that our children play doomed games? This is all part of the riddle called Ash. I preferred the period she had last month, she was calm, if deformed, sad among her spiders. There was not this fury.

Jake is groping for a door in the dark. He loves Ash. He has loved her since their first meeting in Beth's garden. He frowns at the thought of Beth. Beth, always resisting him, jealous of the adopted boy, always turning down his friendship. But he'd got Ash. His love is bearing down on Ash more and more each day. She feels the black-gloved hand on her shoulder, beneath which she must bow. His army defeats her, an army made of two children. Yet Jake loves her. And she knows it. It is what shames her, what splutters in her mind like a burning sea-coal. It is what keeps her here, it is what prevents her considering what she would rather have, in place of her accustomed life.

Ash walks in the garden, through the wastes of summer. Her thoughts are illegal activities. She knows that Jake is standing at the window of her room, sipping a cup of tea, watching. In pursuit again.

She will not look up at the window, not wave to him.

She walks by the roses that recoil from her and each other in the windy sunlight.

Why does the recollection of Beth rise up in me now, as from some unsuspected dark place in me? Why does the thought of that long past summer nag me now, why do I feel that in leaving Beth I took a wrong turning? These thoughts are new and strange. I do not want them but perhaps I have nothing else. Why now do I feel the pain of separation? Why not earlier? It was the newness, the excitement. To be married, to have my own house, and then the children, like confirmations of myself, assurances of my own existence. Now that spell is wearing off, and what is left? What is to be done now?

Do I have to go back to the village of the giant?

Always I feared the giant, his white outline dominating the hill, the countryside around; giant, priapic moon-man. I don't want to go back to his domain. But Beth is there, and the end of the story that began for us is there. How afraid I am to go back, to climb Giant Hill and hear what he has to tell me, what I always refused to hear. What will spawn in me then?

Isn't Jake right when he tells me I should be content here? That I have all I need. Yes, he is right. But I cannot curb the sense that a vital element has been left out.

I was content with my placid life, suckling children, taking care of the house, walking dogs, playing with the children, reading and sewing in the evening, sometimes visits to cinemas or theatres with Jake, yoga at the technical college. But this past year my content has worn out. Is it because the children are older, and take less of my time, leaving me alone too much? I looked forward to some peace, as the kids got bigger. But it's not working out like that. I am discontented and Jake merely defers a punishment that might shatter me.

Shall I have another child? Would that put me in a stronger position, regarding Jake? No. He wants me to be pregnant, sees me safest in that condition, and the advantage to me would be only temporary. My womb has done its work. It has grown its creatures.

Why do I want to see Beth again, want to talk to her, ask her advice? I want her as my friend, no more. Years ago, I hated Beth. Beth, who made no effort to keep me out of Jake's custody, who put up no fight, but let him overrule us both. Beth, whose betrayal made me think I hated her until now. Beth, who I've hated and forgotten. I turned to Jake and found strength in him that delighted me but now scares me.

Whichever way I turn, I cannot spring back into fresh life, I only remain hurt, as one who is hunted can only be hurt.

If I run to the giant, what then?

Her husband's shadow approached, fell over her.

'You do not know me,' she told him scornfully, not turning to him.

He sat down beside her, beneath the limetree and spoke to her quietly until he had swept her clean of her fiery-redness, until he had dissolved that war-dance. She is no longer sinewy. She is meek, she floats like a kite and he holds the string.

TWENTY-ONE

AFTER weeks of cloud and the grey summer growing taller and thinner, the weather clears. The sun brightens the paths and linden shadows with its pendulous yellow.

Early in the morning, Beth is pinning up washing to dry. She is wearing a light summer dress, the green material patterned with small white flowers. The sun soothes her, enables her to act without thinking. It gives her a natural body. The damp garments hang motionless on the line.

Beth picks up the empty laundry basket. Since the arrival of the sunlight, she has forgotten the cold stories and the torn marriage map. When she woke to see the sunlight streaming through the curtains, she took a deep breath of relief, as if she'd received a royal pardon. She got up quickly and showered, noting that the soreness in her anus had eased. Alone in the sunny rooms she busied herself happily with various tasks and now strolls by the moist cobwebs of the early garden.

But when Theron awoke in his sunny room, he looked out of the window and saw Vellet. She is holding what seems to be a fan and she is looking upwards as if in fear.

Like a sleepwalker on the motorway, Theron moves around his room. Unlike Beth, he is not changed by the new weather, sunlight does not lighten his load. Vellet smiles at him from the front page of yesterday's newspaper. Theron jerks away from her tabloid grimace only to meet another of her reflections in the sunny mirrors: she is swallowing gold coins and pearls, and laughing. Theron raises his fist to punch the mirror-ghost but now there are only reflections of branches in the mirror, an image of the calm garden's sunlit trees. Theron feels a pulpiness behind his eyes. This is Vellet's first visit for three days.

'Why have you come back?' he asks, smelling the damp address of the ghost.

Vellet sits on the edge of his bed. She murmurs: 'captivity . . .'

'What do you mean, captivity? Mine, or yours?' asks the haunted man unhappily.

'I do not want to be a ghost,' says Vellet. 'To be a soft mean vagrant. I do not want to whine for a touch of love that cannot come to me.'

Theron watches his first wife from his position in the sunlight. Vellet sits in shadows, a spider-tamer.

'Every moment is a lucky-dip tub for me, Theron, and when I thrust my hands in among the shavings all I bring out are booby prizes.'

She falls silent amid the rubble of her death.

'I'm sorry,' says Theron gently.

She nods.

'Your picture, as it seemed to be, in the paper, frightened me, Vellet.'

The ghost of a smile touches Vellet's face.

'Yes,' she agrees, 'I know. But you realize, of course, Theron, that I have permission to haunt you.'

'From whom?'

'Why, from you. If you tell me I must go away, then I will. You will give me no choice. I'll go away and I will not return. If you tell me strongly, honestly. Otherwise, it will not work. And being dead I can recognize your lies. It is you who call me, demand to be haunted.'

Theron shifts in his chair.

'Yes, I have feared as much.'

'Am I to go? Will you let me go, Theron? I too want to be free, not to be this sickly waltzer between light and dark. Let me go!' The ghost looks up at him eagerly.

But he is silent, shakes his head. Vellet slumps back into the shadows, disappointed.

'I see that my attractions still call you,' she says bitterly, 'that you cannot resist me, that I am still bound to you. It is a defect in us both.'

Theron begins, 'look, Vellet, I want . . .' But she has gone. Theron moves swiftly to the window and peers down into the sunlit garden. In the early morning he sees Vellet culling dew from the rosebushes to rinse the blood from her sandals. He unlatched the window, leaned out and cried, 'Vellet!'

Beth comes forward, squinting up at him, then smiling. 'What did you say, dear?' she asks pleasantly.

'I only wondered, is breakfast nearly ready?' Beth nods. Out of the corner of his eye, Theron sees Vellet skipping away through the orchard, handcuffed to haunting. He closed the window. As he walked downstairs, he thought of himself as an amputee, still feeling the phantom limb, Vellet. He is anxious to get to the university and to his work, where Vellet rarely disturbs him, because, no doubt, he does not have the leisure to conjure her.

At breakfast, Beth tries to say something important to Theron, but he is abstracted, his attention elsewhere. She wants to say how sorry she is for not telling him about Ash, to tell him he was right to be angry and that she bears him no malice. Beth feels that with the coming of sunlight she has fresh hope that they might both work their troubles out. But when she begins, 'Theron, I am sorry I didn't say about Ash and explain . . .' he interrupts, reproaching her for having brought the subject up. '. . . so let's forget about it, shall we?' he says shortly.

Foliage of the succubus, thought Beth penetratingly, but said nothing. After breakfast, she went to the lavatory and emptied her bowels.

Behind the mirrors, Vellet laughs at the pair of them. She is the shitless ghost. She polishes the giant's halo. She laughs at Beth and Theron. She laughs at herself, a laughter springing from a gross pain.

Theron kisses Beth goodbye, like a miser, and then hurries out to the garage.

Beth stands by the garden gate, waving to him. The car disappears in clouds of dust, turning down the track. Beth's backward grammar did not reach Theron. She wanders from the gate across the lawn to the rustic summerhouse and sits inside, twirling her thumbs.

'Is your back breaking, dear?' asks Vellet. The ghost is sitting beside Beth, shading her watery eyes against the sunlight. The false black birth of the ghost hurts Beth. Her throat, her cunt ache. Ash is tiny and lost in the distance while Vellet brings her ugly song very close.

'Is it you then?' Beth says coldly, 'why don't you go away, Vellet?'

'Tell your husband to send me away,' said Vellet archly, and vanished.

'That would be the answer,' murmured Beth.

Scarlet, the folds of my vagina, she thought. The sun hesitates on the lawn, then grows stronger, and Beth responds again to the opening of the air. The brown birds flit in the garden, from branch to bush. Scents of flowers rise and drift. Amid all the disturbance of her life, Beth does not cling to uglinesses. Theron's angers, lack of sympathy, his slow speech and his dedication to the ghost . . . Beth sets herself free from them. She will release herself from him when she comes to the last of her strength. It will be soon, if Theron does not dismiss Vellet.

It is the garden that concerns Beth now, the green and the gold, the unviolated enclosure of flowers, of flaming light and flushed shadows, this is where Beth is at home. She is keenly aware of the late burgeoning of summer and she loves its voluptuousness. She feels the patina of leaves against her skin.

Last night, shortly before midnight, as Beth was preparing for bed, she'd glanced out of the window, expecting to see the full moon, its achieved shape, and the humility of moon-watching was in her. But she'd received a shock, for instead of the white and perfected circle of the full moon she saw, low in the sky, a planet she could not recognize. She was afraid. What has gone wrong? she thought, and could not at first understand the lopsided crescent slung across the sky.

She called to Theron as he was coming upstairs, soon realizing that she was watching a lunar eclipse. She looked up her astronomy book and found tonight there was a partial eclipse.

Beth and Theron put on coats, took the binoculars and went out in the garden to observe the eclipse.

She lifted the heavy glasses and focused the lenses. The shadow of earth had fallen on the moon. Only a thin crescent of moon was left free, the rest of the full moon was dimmed to grey by the penumbra. A greenish light hung all around the moon and a red tinge also appeared close to the rim. The slant of the eclipse filled Beth with joy. I go through my eclipses also, she thought, the red rim is mine also, and she relished her childlessness. I am the one inhabiting the foam of my womb!

After a few moments, Theron said, 'I'm cold, I'm going in.' Beth stayed out a little longer, gazing at the earth-shadow that was edging further across the moon. Then she shivered. The acreage of stars was too much for her, she felt giddy, a bit drunk. She went upstairs to bed and slept soundly until dawn, when she rose and went about the rooms and the garden, watching with delight as the sunlight washed the greyness from the world.

As she picks flowers, the giant speaks to Beth.

'A woman is a time machine; even when she is turning her head from side to side disagreeing with everything and everyone, a rhythm is diffusing through her, like moonspray rising and falling. Through the moon-time of woman, world-time gushes and stains.'

'Is it so, that I am timed by moons ?' said Beth, aloud.

'You are moon-time,' says the giant, 'so why do you wear that wristwatch ?'

Beth smiles.

'I'll keep my watch for a while,' she said, 'because I feel, giant, that behind the moon is a whip cracking which I must obey.'

'The whip is yours,' confided the giant, 'you must wield it, not jump to it. It is your own possession.'

Beth is silent, looking towards Giant Hill. Though she cannot see the giant for hedges, hills and plantations, she smells his spoors. 'My own possession . . .' she muses.

'Yes!' The Giant laughed. 'You were always faithful to me, Beth. I shall not abandon you. When Vellet committed her adulteries before my eyes, her veils ensnaring a brief moon, when the woman Vellet and her consorts danced on my prick, when she shouted: "earth, moon, sun, stars, you'll never destroy me!" when she danced lewdly, showing me her conspicuous vulva with its shining mucus, then I knew Vellet would need help one day. You must help her, Beth.'

Beth frowns, almost petulantly.

'So you say. Have said for ages! But why?'

'You know why, Beth. To help her complete her death, and to free Theron.'

'Theron! Oh he'll never let Vellet go. That is what I am beginning to think.'

'You must help Vellet. Then your husband will be free. Don't you want to rescue him?'

Beth is silent, sullen. The garden ceases to be a place of refuge.

'All loves will ease and resolve themselves when Vellet is free of her half-death,' says the giant quietly. 'Your loves, too, Beth.'

White clouds appear in the sky, a wind from the Atlantic begins to strut through the leaves. Beth picks up the mood of the wind and strides up and down beside the orchard fence, with long steps.

'You must grip the thorny veils that bind Vellet, grip them and tear them off,' instructs the giant.

'Won't I hurt my hands?' she whispers, fearfully.

'Perhaps,' says the giant. 'Yes, perhaps you will hurt your hands. Perhaps the skin of your lips will peel like old paint from a door and perhaps the night will shudder in its cradle. But the time cannot be postponed very much longer. Remember, Beth, in the giant's mirror, all broken creatures can be healed.'

'Why can't you heal Vellet, then?'

'I am healing her now. It is you who look into my mirror, and reflect. Vellet is blind to my mirror. I send you as my reflection, to that ghost, Vellet.' The giant speaks gently, reprovingly to Beth, and she flinches.

She walks slowly from tree to tree. The sky is cloudier. The branches move and sway in the wind.

'Beth! Hi, Beth! Beth!'

This new voice startles Beth, she shies round nervously, then smiling, hurries towards her visitor.

'Tabitha! Hello . . .'

'I'll just scribble a note for Theron, in case he comes home early.'

The two women go into the house through the conservatory, laughing and talking, relaxed in one another's company. In the kitchen, Tabitha perches on the table while Beth looks for paper and pencil. Beth is excited and thinks, soon it will be the longest day of the year.

She scribbles on the back of an envelope, 'gone for lunch to Tabitha's, back about four, love Beth.' She props the message up against the clock on the dresser, he is bound to glance at the clock; then she combs her hair, and is ready.

As the two women stroll along the lane, commenting on the clear sky, Tabitha remembers what her late husband once said to her. 'If I had as many women as I have valves in my heart, Tabitha, then I'd be happy, Tab, happy . . .' And then she'd felt his hands on her shoulders, heavy, dragging at her. Around her, the ruins of the abbey are still the man's allies. Now the sun is hot on her uncovered head.

Beyond the next turn of the path, the stream is glittery as forceps with the sun on the water. As they approach, Beth suggests that they sit down for a while. She pulls off her sandals and plunges her feet in the cold earthy water. She wriggles her toes in the water.

'It's lovely, Tabitha, lovely and cool.' Tabitha smiles and nods her head, but does not copy Beth.

'How have you been, Beth?' she asks, more seriously.

'Better for this sunny day,' Beth answers sleepily, stretching out full length on the grassy bank of the stream.

Tabitha sits upright and stares at the water. Last night her own screams, almost pure white with terror, had ransacked the house and even the hen-houses out in the backyard. What had she seen? Harry's eyes, like two silver thimbles stolen from the headmistress. Dead cats and dead children in his arms. Smiling, without feeling, as always. Up the big mountain of night, I went climbing with Harry. After I woke screaming, I didn't dare sleep again for fear my fingers would turn to mould. And I thought I was free of all that!

She looks down at her hands, frowning. Perhaps we have to give the dead some undamaged region in our hearts, and if this is not given, then the dead begin their impeachment. I am no longer so confident of my ability to walk backwards into the future and salvage what I need from it.

'What are you thinking about, Tab?' asks Beth drowsily. 'Ghosts, dear.'

Beth turns on her side and looks at Tabitha. Her wrists throb with questions. The questions rise up in her, she clutches at them before they become indecipherable.

'Why ghosts, Tab? That's unlike you.'

Tabitha hesitated, then said rapidly,

'The past two nights I've had bad dreams, nightmares. And this morning, early, with its beautiful gold light that seemed so fortunate, this morning, I opened the back-door and stepped out into the garden. And in the garden I saw hens and pheasants and colts and quails and rabbits and hares and turtles and elks and deer and asses and hounds and wolves and mallards and mares and oxen and goldfinches and tame swine and sheep and lions and herons and kine and foxes and geese and bears and goats and nightingales and horses and doves and kittens and moles and whelps and porpoises and ferrets and rooks and boars and apes and starlings and whales and larks and at the centre of this crazy menagerie, a man, amid the stench and cries.'

Beth moves closer to Tabitha.

'Who was the man?' she whispered.

Tabitha looks away and says, 'It was Harry. I saw his face. It was him. He smiled, raised his hand in greeting, waved, vanished, and all the animals too.'

Beth puts an arm around Tabitha's shoulders but Tabitha disengages herself gently and says, 'So it seems there are other ghosts beside little Vellet. What do you think?'

Beth shook her head slowly and the sunlight streamed off her body, as if repelled by a grease.

'I don't know, Tabitha. Perhaps it is all our own creation. That there are no ghosts, only us: the palpitations of our plagues, our own dark cupboards which aren't full of ghosts but only old clothes.'

'I think all husbands are called Lazarus,' says Tabitha roughly. Beth smiles, then says firmly,

'We must not be trapped, we must read the runes of these apparent ghosts. What are they trying to tell us?'

Raising her eyes from Tabitha's frowning face, Beth saw on the opposite bank of the stream, Vellet, riding on her black hoyden horse with the docked tail, riding between the green branches, like doggerel. Beth's soothing advice dries on her tongue. But she does not point across the stream, does not ask Tabitha if she saw Vellet. Tabitha did not see Vellet, Beth is certain of that.

'I don't care what a ghost has to tell me,' protests Tabitha, 'why should I?'

Beth sighs and lies back on the grass again, looking up at the sky. That was what I said to the giant, she thinks. Why should I listen to the ghost, try to help the ghost. What are you called, Giant? she ponders. Giant Wheatland? Giant Cattle-Dung? Giant of the Ruins? Giant Cockcrow? Giant Blackmailer?

Beth looks up at the cloudless sky and thinks of clouds. Cumulus congestus, cumulus fractus, cumulus humilis and cumulus mediocris. The Giant may have his head in all of those clouds.

In the garden this morning Harry smiled at Tabitha from the richness of his animals and now Tabitha blushes, looks up at the clear sky and sees two martian moons. She smiles secretively, anarchic. Zatertag, a man's voice murmurs in her ear, Harry's voice.

In their separate cages of haunting, on a sunny morning, two bruised women sit by the water, watching butterflies; heartbeats of a marsh fritillary.

'I saw Harry,' says Tabitha in a low voice, 'and all his menagerie, and I took one step towards him and then all had gone, all but for my own chickens left scratching in the dust.'

Beth says, 'our wraiths are washed ashore.'

'Yes,' agrees Tabitha.

'What's happening, Giant?' yells Vellet furiously, 'what's happening?' She stamps her foot on the Giant's breast. 'What's Beth up to? Things are happening that I don't understand? Why isn't she afraid of me?'

The Giant said, 'look, Vellet.' She looks at the giant's open book and watches the pictures as he turns the pages for her.

'There's Theron!' she cried.

Theron is walking about the forbidden room, Vellet's room at the top of the house, the room that is dusty and unused. He is experiencing a nostalgia he cannot explain. He does not understand the emotion. But it could be the beginning for him of a life without Vellet. He glimpses a way out, and smiles.

Vellet gasps. 'Are they over?' she asks, 'are they over, Giant, the stiff miles of haunting? Is that what is happening to Beth, to all of us? Am I changing? Are we coming to a freer place?'

'I do not know,' said the Giant. 'I only reflect what you ghosts and lovers experience. Look at the pages of my mirror, Vellet.'

Now Theron is seated in an old leather armchair by the fireside in the forbidden room. He researches the past and the fogs that usually brood in his head clear. He thinks, perhaps I can make up my mind, decide which wife I want.

'Which wife does he want?' whispers Vellet.

'Hush,' says the Giant.

Theron opens the wardrobe door and takes out a long roll of paper. It is a poster. Carefully he unrolls the tube of paper and places a book at either end of the poster, laid flat on the table, so that it will not curl up again. He pores over the poster. It is a photograph of a drowned girl. It is a large coloured grainy photograph and the girl is very beautiful, cast up on the night shore, her short white dress plastered against breasts and thighs, her arms pinioned behind her. She is a woman undistinguished by fortitude or noble deeds. A woman drowned, unrescued.

'Ah,' groaned Vellet, 'he drowned me just as surely as if he'd pushed me in and held my head beneath the water.'

'Perhaps,' said the Giant calmly.

'Yes, he did,' said Vellet, 'look at the river-scars on my face, giant. He drowned me.'

'I know,' said the Giant.

Beneath Vellet's skin, stars leak.

'It will not be long, now, Vellet,' promised the Giant. 'They will let you go.'

The ghost wept. She wept, and hid beneath the floor of the summer house. She dug her cold fingernails into her heart and wept.

The Giant sends Vellet back to the living women, to study them, to learn from them.

Yes, thought Tabitha, with the sunlight drenching her skin and trickling through her bones. Yes, when Beth brought me her ghost story, I thought she was just compensating for a failed marriage, covering up the mess with a romantic story, the useful smokescreen of Vellet as ghost and revenger. But now my own strength is under attack, and my commonsense can't cope. The tide of my ghost is rising. I thought the dead faded away, with an expression of anger or of gratitude, into the pale green clay and our recollections. I told myself I had understood Harry's death, and adjusted. But I was wrong. In the darkest corner of the barn, he waits for me to let him go. To tell him it is time for him to depart. One word is required. But how can I say that word? What will I have left, if I cut the cord and let my ghost go? My muscles are stiff, my head is full of the sparse thoughts that follow an evening's drinking, and I see him still waiting in the musty shed, by the feed-bins, pouring grain through his hands, from one hand to the other, and back again. He has been there all the time but I have only been able to see him since Beth told me of

Theron's relapsing ghost. Do I hate her for that? The unveiling she brought me? On the thin rim of my life, there is an arctic region where hate might exist, but I will not encourage it. What Beth has helped me to see, must be seen. I made a museum for Harry but he does not need it. I must travel up and down my own spine and unlock Harry from his bondage. I will let him go.

'I'll let him go,' she said aloud.

Beth looks at her sadly.

'It will not be easy,' she answers. 'For he'll require something of you before he is able to go. They see through all lies. It is only the true desire to free them that they can accept. Between their fingers and thumb they hold a key. Into us, they insert their key: and can only turn to freedom when the combination is correctly given. It is a process of learning for both ghost and haunted.' Tabitha closes her eyes. 'I am very tired,' she says.

'Naturally, we are tired out by these guests,' says Beth gravely, 'but we invited them. We must endure them.'

Tabitha smiles.

'Do you think we can?' she asks eagerly.

'Yes,' says Beth firmly, 'I do.' And although Beth heard a sharp abrupt scream of anger, although she saw Vellet standing behind Tabitha, Vellet trembling in her wet and thorny veils, even though the ghost harangued Beth and spat at her, she did not flinch, she did not cry out to Tabitha, 'look out, behind you!', no, she adjusted her idea of the landscape so that she could accept the ghost, and with another howl, Vellet, confused and disappointed, merged into the hot summer air.

Beth and Tabitha go on their way, the ovary shadows of the women soft on the water. Beth crosses the stream, balancing barefoot on the stepping stones.

'Be careful, it's slippery,' she warns Tabitha. When Tabitha has crossed over and stands close to Beth, smiling, Beth touches her shoulder timidly.

'Tabitha?' she says shyly.

'Yes?' The strain has eased from Tabitha's face, she is lighthearted again. 'Yes, dear?' she encourages Beth, 'what is it?'

Beth hangs her head and her hands are not real hands nor is her womb a real womb. But she must ask.

'Tabitha, I know this is asking a lot, and you've had a bad time lately, but please, do you think, can I, can I see Harry's paintings, please, please, it would be such a help to me, now . . .'

The words come out in a rush. Beth watches Tabitha anxiously. Sunlight drops slowly through Tabitha's head. She saw a shadow space-walking. A shadow. A shadow sucking the flowers. Tabitha recalls her aborted child wrapped in the robes of his blood. I must give, she cried inwardly, I must give Beth what she needs, must answer her hard request. This is a way of beginning to release Harry, the pain I experience is my own business, none of her concern. Yes, I will try to help Beth, so that she may cure the paraplegia that threatens her marriage. I will take my friend to my house and lead her upstairs, I will unlock that room for her, the room of deceptive calm. She agrees to Beth's request, agreeing to her own dethronement.

Beth sits at the old piano in Tabitha's parlour, playing and singing a Russian song. Tabitha stands by the window, thinking, over and over again, perhaps it was a shadow. Perhaps it was not Harry I saw but a shadow. It was a shadow. When Beth's song is finished, Tabitha turns and says, as if cursing Beth,

'Shall we go up, then?'

Tabitha unlocks the room where the paintings are hung, her mouth twisting, her wrists aching.

The two women enter a room as sad as the nursery built for Queen Catherine Parr's child.

A hot dry wind moves the stiff curtains. Tabitha stands by the door while Beth looks at each picture in turn. Tabitha watches her. Hundreds of miles away, Ash is writing a letter to a blind lady. Beth looks at the first painting: the intoxicated woman clutching her useless womb.

Tabitha watches intently, a woman who says 'no' in the language of the Saxons. Now she moves to the window, a polished stone, picked up from the shelf, in her left hand. She is smiling to herself, roughly playful with her own thoughts. On the brink of prison. Her back is turned to Beth now, straight, tense.

Beth is staring into the face of the drunken woman. Is this the one who will tell me what to do? I feel so strongly that in one of these paintings of Harry's, I'll find a message, an answer, the clue I need. The face of the drunken woman is only a waxwork, this is no answer. It is Tabitha as a younger woman. Horrible. The vomit on her lips, the womb where she burnt her fingers. Behind the drunk woman, a man walks to the block with the ambitious Lord Seymour. Beth peers into the shadows of the painting. Vellet, by her side, holds her breath. Beth glances at Vellet and smiles. Vellet, unsmiling, whispers to Beth, 'not this one, no, not this one.' Beth shrugs. 'I know. But which one then?' Vellet vanishes. Beth turns, away from the twilight of the drunken woman.

Tabitha has descended to the second degree of her soul. She is the waxwork widow. She hears Beth's footsteps on the wood floor as she moves to the next painting.

The griffons with necks like snakes squat on the book of love.

Tabitha thought, he abused my undergarments. Then I heard a death cry from the garden. I heard the shot. I found him with his head blown in. There was blood on the shells of the snails that crawled over the rose trees.

Beth craned her neck, trying to read the words on the page of the book of love, and gets a shock. '. . . *he whipped her with his sodomite's whip.*'

Beth half turns and says, 'Tabitha?'

But Tabitha does not turn from the window, does not answer, and Beth dare not ask her a question. The griffons glare but Vellet says, 'not these creatures, Beth.'

He wrote a scholarly monograph on medieval pigments, thought Tabitha with the old amazement, but he shot himself through the head just the same.

Beth moves on and looks at the female saint sipping menstrual blood in a shadowed place. A homespun woman with a monthly thirst. Beth smiles at the saint. This saint, she thinks, could open the door to the waterfall and proceed through the wondrous waters. Is this the answer? Is this the way to find an honest answer for Vellet? To help Theron? To enable me to understand Ash?

Beth would like this to be the painting. In the shadows are alpine flowers and huge boulders. Tabitha lights a cigarette, inhales, rattles the box of matches in her hand. The polished green stone gleams on the windowsill. She puts the matches down, picks up the stone again, still warm from her hand.

Beth smiles at the saint. To her eyes, the saint's face is that of Ash on the verge of orgasm, the deadline of delight. *And there I saw four and twenty damsels*, thinks Beth joyfully, *embroidering satin at a window.*

I slipped my hand into the hollow tree trunk, recalls Tabitha to herself, I unfolded the scrap of paper on which he'd scrawled, meet me in Black Hill Barn tonight. I tore the message up but kept the appointment. I kissed the bark of the hollow tree. I arrived on schedule. Not even the evidence of shadows made me unhappy in those days. In my mind's eye, I still see my hand, blue-white as a blown egg, hovering over the latch of the barn door. I entered the barn and instead of him, it was Harry waiting for me, his one-eyed vigilance that broke my bones.

Beth and the saint still commune. There is a fountain in this shadowy garden of the saint. The waters spring, noble blood. Beth imagines herself kneeling naked beside the bloody fountain, and that a bull of gold and a unicorn of ice appear beside her. Dark toads with lamenting cries approach. The saint strokes my shoulders, irresolute but able.

'No, Beth, no. It is not here, what you are looking for.'

Vellet warns Beth to move on, showing her white teeth. Vellet is a wanderer from the prison-places, Vellet of the Seven Scars. She must be listened to . . .

Tabitha stubbed out her cigarette. She stared out of the window but did not see the giant. She did not see the daughters of the giant, alphabetical in their robes. She did not see the sun shining on the fields. She does not consider gathering bluebells in the moonlit valleys. She imagines strangers laughing at the crude jokes they have made about her. The room has thrown its noose around her throat and it is tightening. Harry said to her, I'll plant babies in the cabbage patch for you, Tab!

Beth glances casually at the study of lovers, Harry and Tabitha. On my way here, she thought, I knew this was not the painting. The orchard is too perfect, the lovers too accomplished. Lovers at dawn, seeking the wild ox's alchemy, do not help Beth. But she enjoys the painting even though it is not her solution. As she turns away, the lovers' laughterless shadows tell her, you are one of the descendants of the children of Hamelin.

Very likely, thought Beth, amused.

'Move on, move on,' urged Vellet.

Tabitha is afraid of this room. Her whole body itches an sweats. Harry said to her, there are fifty empty milk bottles under the sink but I cannot move them, because that would mean I am manipulating reality, and I cannot do that.

'Move on, Beth.'

Beth confronts the final painting. It is the largest canvas. It is of Jesus and the Virgin.

Tabitha lays one hand on each breast. There is a pain like infanticide in her body. Frost blackens her summer garden. I am hammering my omens into shape. Behind my back, Beth is learning what she came to find out. The tribes of the sea flow through me and I am lonely as a bow and arrow. Water laps against my closed doors.

In the painting the Virgin holds a fish in her hand. The Virgin is veiled. Beth stands very still. She does not panic. But she is crawling towards knowledge, not walking upright.

The torches of Tabitha's mind are flickering, a black basket of candles. Autumn will not help her. Blindfolded wives wave at her in the halfblood storm. My dark takes many shapes. Rectum or vagina he said I don't care I said he wound a cloth tightly round my mouth so I could not shout blasphemous words Harry gave me two coins he shaved my cunt with his razor he refused to believe in anything supernatural he painted his face with rouge a chill settled on the wife for her lifetime beheaded cold jointure the ghost gave off sparks when struck I waited for him he was late he had been working he said I withdrew my complaint . . .

'I see,' cried Beth suddenly, excitedly, 'I see!'

'Yes,' said Vellet softly, 'you see, now you see.'

Beth runs across to Tabitha and pulls her towards the painting of Jesus and the Virgin. Tabitha allows herself to be dragged in front of the canvas.

'Look,' said Beth, 'it's incredible, it is what we were saying this morning, how the ghosts grow together. Look, do you see, haven't you ever noticed?'

Beth points at the Virgin, she is trembling with her discovery. 'What is it?' asks Tabitha, exhausted, afraid.

'Haven't you ever noticed? Look at the Virgin's face. Beneath the veil. Don't you recognize her?'

Tabitha goes up close to the painting and studies it closely. 'I still don't see what you mean, Beth.'

Beth fidgets about the room, amazed at Tabitha's blindness. Vellet watches the two women wistfully.

'Look,' urged Beth, 'look!'

Tabitha looked. She saw.

She groaned. 'Oh god!' she groaned. In that early spring Harry had knocked at her skull and then gone out to his studio to paint this . . . Tabitha hears again the crude laughter she hated years ago and the polished green stone turns cold again in her hand.

Vellet watches her compassionately, watching as Tabitha pulls the painting off the wall and throws herself to the floor with it, tearing at the canvas with her fingernails. Vellet watches as Beth struggles to pull Tabitha to her feet, to save the painting from her destructive hysteria, watches Beth slap Tabitha and try to hold her down. She listens to Tabitha's screamed obscenities and observes Tabitha fight Beth off. Beth, unable to stop Tabitha from weeping and yelling, runs in a panic downstairs and out of the cottage, the door catching to behind her. Tabitha stretches full length on the floor, writhing and banging her head repeatedly, then staggering to her feet and tearing her clothes off, stripping to her skin and rolling on the floor again. Vellet watches her own face, disguised as the Virgin. Tabitha spits on that face over and over again. Vellet, the Virgin. Vellet, the artist's model and mistress. She watches the canvas curl up in the shadows where Tabitha has hurled it. She watches Tabitha limp out of the room and into her bedroom, where she takes two pills and crawls into bed.

Beth meanwhile is running home thinking: connected with death connected with death we must be connected with death Tabitha must understand that she cannot ignore it she must let the nocturnal visitors in I tell her she must love the dead her hair dark as a parsee her mouth wide and shrieking her face dark and thin I was so frightened her splotchy skirt her hands grown cold from weaving ropes for the hanged I could do nothing to help her connected with death we must be connected with death her hysteria is below the threshold of my heart her hatred invaded my moon she must let the dead in and accept them I was right to show her that Vellet was the Virgin she must have known all the time but never let herself look at it but only let the whisper perch by her heart she will understand when she recovers she must not let herself be defeated how she screamed but it is not a battle all this trouble it is a learning my children will need my children need it to become alive and bright with flower and flute . . . if I can live with my dead and study their shadows in clean rooms if I can give the eyelids their chance to live in pentagrams of blood . . .

So Beth thinks, as she runs home through the sunlit woods Vellet loping by her side, keeping pace.

TWENTY-TWO

VELLET the Virgin.

Vellet, the Virgin!

Beth tramps through the sunlit trees, rejoicing, amazed, a bezonian woman watching great changes in herself, in all around her. I have found the key! I have discovered the clue.

'Perhaps,' murmurs Vellet demurely.

'It is the harvest of Orion!' cries Beth, and her shadow falls lightly on the genitals of the spider.

'Perhaps,' Vellet coos.

I saw the Virgin's face beneath the veil of grey-blue paint and her features were those of Vellet. Vellet, the ghost with her epidemic of love-bites, Vellet, the faithless wife with her drugs and her albino bowels, Vellet always tracing out the skidmarks of her marriage. How I have hated her, hated her soothsayer's feet dancing over our bodies, hated her keys of belladonna opening our eyes when we should have slept, Theron and I. Always, her tantalus presence in our garden. I have hated her. I have been the dorsal bride to her ventral, I have trembled with rage in Theron's arms, dancing with him only a pessimist's waltz. From the moment she emerged in the dark rainy lane, I have hated Vellet.

Theron hates her. He hates her shadowy riots. He puts his head out of the window, say, and she is always there on the lawn, grinning up at him. Vellet Frithborn, her hectic skeleton gleaming in the wolf-pack's dark. She has shown him her brochure of tall stories, made him follow her calendar. And he hates her.

Beth slows down and dawdles across a field of dandelions.

We have hated Vellet, she thinks, but have we the right?

'I was not allowed to choose my death,' says Vellet. But Beth does not hear her. She is deafened by the shock she received in Tabitha's house, amid the paintings, and now the aftermath of Tabitha's hysteria is making her feel queer and lightheaded. What I have discovered may still be an undeliverable letter. I have yet to explain to Theron the significance of Vellet as Virgin: to convince him of the sadness of the ghost: to teach him we must love Vellet before she can be free and we free of her. We are both too used to hating Vellet to find that love will come easily. We have our implacable side, each of us. We may be at a standstill between love and hate for some time yet; yet I have seen her true face now, her other' face. And I know that soon I will be able to love her. A Virgil , a little goddess, a transformed one.

Beth stands rapt by the field gate. The hot sun bathes her. The trees are without wild ancestors. The blue sky is all tender execution.

Vellet stands sadly beside Beth. Beth cannot see her yet. The translucent ghost is becoming shabby. She watches Beth and is apprehensive. Vellet is grasping the fact of her disfigurement, is beginning to long for and yet also to fear the next stage of her death, that substance of emotions with which Beth and Theron will disinfect her and send her on her journey. Vellet is frightened, thinking, they will tear me limb from ghost-limb, there is no other possibility, my dislodgement will hurt more than my death.

Beth climbs over the gate and continues home across the flaming landscape. I can teach Theron to love her! she thinks excitedly, to love her!

Vellet trails disconsolately behind Beth. Words in her mouth are something she has forgotten.

And still, amid the fieriness of the afternoon, there remains icy material in Beth's head that will not thaw. All at once a sickness heaves into her stomach, turning her hopes and ambitions into a grainy semaphore. Poor Tabitha! she thinks, and approaches the stream gloomily, sitting at the water's edge. Poor Tabitha. I have taken too much from her. I have taken her carefully constructed survival from her, left her desolate among the unclean animals of the bible. I have shown her Harry's last insult, his fifteen-year-old mistress painted in the guise of the Virgin. I have let uninvited guests into Tabitha's head, let the ghost get to her. How many years has she been fending off that ghost? Must she now return to that twilight where Harry waits for her, laughing. Should I have spared her that, let her go on with her unblemished life, fearing nothing. I don't know. It seemed there was no choice. When I realized that the Virgin was Vellet, the shock and joy of my discovery went through me like a leap in which I turned head over heels and alighted firmly on my feet, I thought that Tabitha too would benefit from this knowledge, find it a doorway into a region of steady light and clearer understanding. For her it came too late? Perhaps.

'Vellet, how could you pose for Harry as the Virgin?' asks Beth, half-amused, half-reproving the ghost who is tapdancing on the waters that are like a sheet of glass in the sunlight.

'I can draw a full-size goose egg through any lady's wedding ring,' remarks Vellet, and slips invisible into a notch of sunlight.

Beth sits alone by the waters, quietly thinking of Ash. Of Ash at the green throat of this same stream. Of the slight pause between the two sentences Ash used to say goodbye. Felling Beth with her unknown language.

TWENTY-THREE

H E gazes into the folds of fire. The dry garden refuse makes a good bonfire safely contained in the square mesh box of the incinerator. He watches, relaxed, enjoying the odour of garden-smoke, with its atmosphere of mild untruths.

It is cool now in the evening. Theron is glad of the cooler air that hovers behind the heat of the bonfire. The morning and afternoon had blazed like that bonfire and he and Beth sheltered indoors all day, out of the strong heat. It was at the tips of their fingers like explosions. But indoors they were calm and resourceful. Beth prepared a cold lunch, a salad. She has a natural aptitude for this. The wine was white and very cold. Beth's serenity transmitted itself to him and in her shelter of cool calmness he felt safe. He smiles, and stares at his hands caked with earth. He looks about his garden with pleasure, the smooth lawns, the well-kept flowerbeds, the roses, the staunch hedges clipped and shaped into animal-forms. He is at peace with himself and his world.

The fire crackles and grumbles, a chattering of incognitos. Within the flames is the possibility of munitions, he thought suddenly, and he saw flame-throwers directed on the bodies of soldiers. The folds of fire contain all the colours of last month. The grey smoke has a sheen like a valuable fur and as Theron stares he sees that Vellet is the grey creature of smoke rising slowly from the flames.

'No,' he says. 'No, not today, Vellet, don't spoil it.' He backs away from her.

She goes on rising from the flames. He turns, runs to get the hose, douses the fire, but she is still in the garden, over there, by the fuchsias.

'What of my unborn son, Theron?' she appeals to him.

'I don't know,' he stammers, the smoke arid in his throat. Vellet delves into her long smouldering hair and laughs.

'Death is but the midpoint of a long life,' she quotes.

'Don't come near me,' he said menacingly. But he knew it would make no difference. She would come towards him, with her hottentot shadow, her gravest smoke. She will write 'hallucinosis' on his tongue. 'Sleepy sickness', she whispers in his ear. Between the dying fire and the coming shadows, he can hardly breathe. 'I hate you,' he told the ghost. 'I know,' she said, 'that is the trouble,' and her eyelids were immobile, her tongue divided snakily at its end.

Indoors, Beth is closing the windows against the chill of twilight. Then she turns on the table lamp and begins her small imperfect stitches.

Theron's hands are dirty but Vellet's are clean, her fingers white, scrubbed. 'Get away from me,' he moaned. Vellet takes his hand. She leads him into the summer house. He is afraid and his mind is full of the echoes of pain, of the frozen, of the burnt. Vellet smells of imprisonment and when she comes close to him he does not see her face but the hideous mask of an old woman. She presses up against him and he closes his eyes. His little finger aches with cold but his cock throbs with heat. He began to recite the names of stars aloud, to keep him from capitulating, 'Mesarthim, Algenib, Tarased, Adhara, Mirsam, Jabbah, Mintaka,' but as he stammers the list, he hears Vellet laughing, and her body is pressed against him, her damp shawl oozing over him, and he pulls up her grey-green dress to rub himself against her misty thighs. Carefully he buries himself in the reeds of her cunt and begins to fuck the ghost.

Beth hears Vellet wailing from beneath the waters. She runs out into the garden. Where is Theron? She pauses by the blackened cinders of the bonfire and listens. She hears sounds from the summerhouse and is already weeping herself. The beard growing beneath her legs bristles. She goes helplessly and angrily to the threshold.

Her husband is wanking inside the summerhouse. Beth watches him. Theron takes no notice of her. Some people seem to be whispering behind Beth's back. She watches, as if seeing all this in a mirror. As she watches

Vellet gradually seeps into view. Beth sees how Vellet has fitted her ghost vagina over Theron's prick.

'Theron, you are being tricked,' said Beth sadly. Vellet looks at Beth scornfully, her black wings held stiff and high, and then becomes invisible again so Beth can only see Theron jerking himself off. He licks his lips and groans, 'Valet, Vellet,' and comes, his spunk flicks out across the summerhouse wall. He sighs, wipes his fingers on his pants.

'This won't do,' said Beth, deeply concerned for him.

'Shit on you!' said her husband, turning away, zipping his fly. 'Look,' she said, 'can't we talk? Vellet isn't real and . . .'

He pushed her to one side and left her alone in the little stuffy shed.

Vellet watches the metal bird moving in the night wind, first north, then east, south, west. She watches Beth weep. She wants to say something to Beth but she is afraid of her and creeps out into the fields. She rests in the giant's hand, her eyes wide open.

Beth stops weeping and says to herself, he thinks he can do anything, does he, just because he has married me with wine and water, cunt and prick, but I am not staying with him much longer! Let him complete his own jigsaw puzzle! Her anger makes her a bit tipsy, she digs her fingernails into her forearms, her thin skirt feels icy against her legs. I may have to abandon this whole business as too difficult, she thinks, smiling tensely at her earlier optimism. She is in shock though. She cannot forget the white sperm pumping out thick and warm. She feels that her mouth is enormous, that she has swallowed some peculiar large object, perhaps something alive. Her repressed excitement at the memory of Theron's orgasm grows like a pale light in the darkness. All this goes beyond the demands of a dowry, she thinks. When she passes Theron's window, she can see him standing naked, looking out at her. Her skeleton moving like dew, she comes indoors, upstairs, towards him, and, her mind stopping and starting, she pulls him against her hip, begins panting, half-weeping. They make love standing up, without words. Her orgasm is chill and foggy. Afterwards, Beth is afraid of the dark thoughts of the giant.

She looks at Theron, sprawled asleep on the bed, then turns away, goes to the bathroom to sponge her cunt with warm water.

TWENTY-FOUR

I N the church there is a cruel gold eagle who carries a book shouldered upon its wings. There is a green satin cloth of embroideries bursting into flower and star. Stained-glass men and women are looking at a woman sitting in a pew, she is like a piece of broken colourless glass, alone in the church.

The sunset presses her into folds of stone. She has come here to learn which part of her life to choose: the past or the future. But there is no answer here, just as there was no answer in the familiar room where a dim light burnt, no answer in the summer darkness, nor the close-calls of sleep.

Late this afternoon, she sat in a wicker garden chair beneath a tree whose long slender pliant branches dipped into the water of the pond, and watched the wild waterfowl pluck the surface, drawing folds of shadowy water in their wake, unconcerned, at ease. The sky grew cloudy and rain threatened, she heard the wind in the branches, like the faint singing of old men.

The chair creaks, it is old, discoloured by sunlight and rain.

The wind moves slowly and gradually across the pond, the reeds, the branches of the willow and the bones of the seated woman. She reproaches herself for her inaccurate thin garments and rising from her chair, she walks back to the house, with no answer.

The book she was reading lies forgotten on her chair. The wind flicks the pages over, the words are broken up. Now night will read this book.

Ash went out into the rainy sunset and sat in the church.

When she left, the rain had stopped. She walked aimlessly and came eventually to a tawdry new block of flats. In the courtyard that opened out on to the highway stood a group of nude cupid-like children who looked at her silently.

She walked on, aware of a decision at the edge of her mind. She remembered the story Jake once told her, after they'd quarrelled, and after she'd listened, the bitterness of moons became apparent to her.

She paused, glanced back to see the group of children, but the road was empty, no figure, trees or animals.

She came to a decision then, walked on rapidly for several moments, stopped, heaved open the door of the phone box fumbled in her pocket for a coin and for Beth's number, an dialled.

Darkness gathers up hot pence, the stars.

Ash sits by the open window and waits. She is no longer afraid of the consequences of flight. She waited until Jake had gone to work and then she had driven the children to the house of a friend, Ruth, whose children were roughly of an age with Ash's. She told Ruth, I have to go away, it's an emergency, can you . . . ? Ruth nodded then leaned forward and kissed her.

She drove away, knowing Jake would pick the kids up that evening or the next day. But without hesitating, she drove to the station, and now waits in Beth's old house, for a message, for an arrival. She feels tipsy, her nightdress sticks to her sweaty body.

If she does not come, thinks Ash, or if she rejects me, then must go back to Jake. But I had to take the chance. I felt the time had come to return here. I need to know what drew us together five summers ago, whether it is still vital to us, or whether it is only our memories we need to refresh, not our lives. We both have to be free, surely, to get this business clear.

I come here as a messenger, and I may be bringing snow into her summer.

When I got out of the taxi and looked up at the house, I was depressed by the neglected garden, the grimy windows. But then, I accepted my responsibility for the dilapidation of our landscape. I should have visited sooner. I should have written, answered Beth's letters.

But I could not. I had turned away. The journey of the gamete bubbled its heat through me and would not let me write letters, or think of myself in any other role but that of mother, wife.

Now the melting flesh of my month browses deep in me, as I wait. My belly aches. I recall Beth and myself, our smiles impaled upon old photographs.

In this house, my white downy thoughts go about their duties, just as I went about the house, removing the dust sheets, opening the windows, letting the fresh air and the sun in, cleaning the grimy mirrors, restocking the larder. The electricity was off, but the warm air is drying the house out, and I've lit the kitchen range so that the night does not chill and spoil my work.

I'd gone straight to the old outhouse when I arrived, and there, as always, the spare key hung on its hook in the darkest corner. I let myself into the house and touched surfaces, mantlepiece, stopped clock, poker, cupboard door. I left my fingerprints everywhere.

Veiled faces of myself watched me from the past as I cleaned and scrubbed the years away. In the thicket of a bedroom I saw myself with a bunch of thin flowers from the moorland clutched in my hand. My younger selves dappled the mirror's vault. Never once have I seen Beth's new image in the house I am reclaiming for us. She must bring that reflection with her. It is that I am waiting for. I am at a crossroads. Only contact with this house, with Beth, will show me which of the offered roads I am to take.

A wingless rain is falling now, the heat of storm recedes. The rain is very slight, inexperienced. It reminds me of my children's tadpoles, earlier this year. The tadpoles jerked, carnivorous, in their moonstruck waters. I remember them, their pensive heads and witty tails. I have been moving myself about slowly, piece by piece in these rooms. It is as if I have been eaten into by moths and my skin frays in my hands. The house is clean and alive once again and yet I can smell decay in myself, the canals and cavities of my body. Their mucous nature puzzles me.

I do not know which way to turn now, not to the rain, nor to the reflections. The rain smells of minnows and leaves. I want to belong to myself. Will Beth show me how?

The desperately unhappy events of last weekend, the fighting with Jake, turned my life into an area of land sown with mines. I could not remain among those mishaps until I came back to the place where I was most myself.

On the phone Beth was guarded. She would hardly say anything. I do not know what welcome she will give me.

I estimate the smallest possible amount of sadness I can expect to experience from my return, and I find it is too large for me. I could leave tomorrow.

But will not.

I will sleep. Perhaps I will dream of a world without flying creatures, no eagles, doves, sparrows or humming birds. There the men and women are clear-sighted, unenchanted by the furling of feathers, never saddened like me by the aerodynamics of birds soaring above ruins into the blue, the open sky.

Next morning, long before Ash wakes in the old house, Beth drives slowly through the empty village streets, past the church, past the pubs, past Tabitha's shuttered cottage. The car moves almost stealthily through the dawn.

That dead girl in the summerhouse. She is sharper than a sword and thinner than a hair, thinks Beth. I am much afraid of summer and Vellet. It is a combination that has proved too strong for me. I've thought and worried about Vellet so often and I thought I was just about to solve the problem she set us, but I was wrong about all that.

When I said to Theron, 'but I saw the painting, and Vellet was the Virgin, don't you see? There are other aspects of Vellet we've not even begun to consider yet, we've limited her by our own narrow perceptions, and we've driven her to act out a baneful ghost's drama because that is our drama, not hers. If we can allow ourselves to love Vellet, we'll all be free . . .' he turned away, shaking his head. 'I don't see what this has got to do with me,' he said, 'It is your illumination, Beth. It works for you, fine, ok. But I am still in the dark.'

Theron turned his back on me, on my attempt to explain the ghost to him. He went away to look for his own solution. Perhaps I was wrong. Perhaps Vellet posed as the Virgin with a cynical jokey attitude, and she has fooled me. But I cannot believe that. The purity and grace of her expression could not be a fraud. It was true, and shone out.

Beth drives like an automaton, her destination known and terrifying.

The phone had rung and it was Ash and I thought that death is like this. 'I want to see you, Beth.'

I could hardly stammer out an answer, just said she must go on up to the old house.

My heart, newly exposed to the air, turned brown. There is no certainty that a white raven won't be found tomorrow, though past experience would make such an occurrence unlikely.

Ash.

Her voice pierced me. I am afraid now.

The first crest of sunlight appears on the hills, at this time of acute danger. The yellow tint creeps forward, making narrow inlets on the grey. Gates, fences, tractors in fields, horses grazing, distant farmhouses on hilltops are sharpening in outline. Their shapes fill out, a jigsaw puzzle rising out of the grey dawn.

Suddenly she pulled the car off the road and parked on the hard shoulder close to a patch of common land. She opened the car door and stepped out into the odours of dawn. There is still mist in Yellcombe Mead and the thin trees of Morning Well Plantation are only just emerging. Daylight is a loud noise in Beth's head. Dawn had hidden her but now she is out in the open, exposed.

She begins to climb uphill over the rough grass.

Lifelong maps are written on her hands.

When she reaches the top of the ridge, she hears a woman crying for help. She looks all around the empty fields, up at the pale inbred sky, up at the moon. Who called out, 'Help me'? Who?

As Beth stands on the hilltop in the early dank sunlight, she hears the murmurings, mutterings, hummings and whisperings of many women all around her. The sound rises to a crescendo, a burliness that mocks Beth, and then suddenly cuts out, leaving only silence with no escape. Silence, like a hole scooped in the ground.

Beth is alone. Those women are elsewhere. And she could not make out the words they were uttering. Something about standing between the victim and the knife? Beth shrugs, angered. She stands on the edge of the hill and rolls her imaginary children down, like cheeses.

Which way now, Beth? She is gasping for breath. Which way?

Blue sky and mauve hills, brown fields, landscape like a manuscript containing a later writing written over an effaced earlier script. Which way?

Beth is sobbing and throws herself full-length on the damp grass. I am finished with impersonations. I can no longer be a wife mediating between ghost and husband. I must go back to my own perception of myself.

She scatters the words of her wedding on the ground and then she runs, fast as she can, across fields, ditches, over streams, running, for she must catch up with the shadow at the edge of the giant, or he'll tie her veins together.

She falls to the ground, tripping, she is within the boundary of the giant, out of breath she crawls forward and kisses his chalky penis.

'Help me, Giant, before I grow any weaker. The naked baby blocks my path, lisping, Beth, carry me, carry me. I do not want to. Help me, Giant. Look, I can pay, I have money. Look in my purse. I have denarii and sovereigns, guilders and half-marks, sesterces and one louis-d'or. I have dollars and kopecks, nickels and sequins, centaros and farthings. Look.'

'Put your money away, Beth, and look in my mirror, instead. Look.'

Beth looks where the giant points. When the reflections settle, she sees herself running along a dim gallery in an old house. No, it is not her. It is Vellet. Vellet turns and smiles. The mirror clouds, then clears to show a man gutting a fish. It is Theron. He does not speak and does not hear Beth call.

'I don't understand,' said Beth.

'Watch,' said the giant. 'One of my pictures will answer you. Wait. When it comes you will know it.'

In the mirror Beth sees the face of her grandchild.

She sees herself going on a pilgrimage, a steel collar around her neck.

Theron steps forward from the mirror and mouths inaudibly her.

A lazy girl plays the guitar fretfully.

A morning of serpents, a room of women.

The reflections gather and break up, reform.

A small white room where Jesus and his mother wait.

Beth's mother, cracking open the sun.

Night: armies of the moon turning to cold water.

Beth flinging herself down on the bed and the man beside her speaking of ghosts.

In the giant's mirror two rooms are reflected: one room is untidy, daubed with clothes, books, records, unanswered letters. The second room is clean and neat. A girl stands in each room, each girl is nursing a newborn baby. Beth passes from one room to the other, singing a peace treaty. The girl in the untidy room is bitter. But the girl in the white clean room smiles and says, are you clothed in skin and flesh, now, Beth?

'I have not seen my solution yet,' said Beth to the giant.

'Then go on watching,' he said.

Beth's eyes are sore but she goes on watching.

She saw herself and Theron standing side by side in a ploughed field, a concourse of seabirds circling above their heads. It had been a time of happiness then, even though she knew he would break his promises.

Other pictures: angels dredging the sky, Tabitha wearing an old-fashioned dress the colour of oysters. A man setting fire to himself. Beth diving into the left ventricle of the apostle's heart. Rooms flashing past. Moons hoeing the sky. Fountains, where girls wait averting their faces, murmuring windswept words. A figure of a man made of compressed snow that stands all day on the lawn. A child's toy that rattles when shaken. And to each picture Beth says firmly, not this, not this, not this.

A group of six women are standing beneath the rose-window in the church.

'What is this?' says Beth.

The women are Eve, Sarah, Tamar, Rhahab, Ruth, Bathsheba. Eve asks Sarah for a handkerchief.

Sarah plaits Tamar's hair.

Tamar laughs at Rhahab's joke.

Ruth looks serious.

Bathsheba dips her fingers in the font.

Bathsheba points to the man of letters, silent in his wooden cage, and cries,

What is his answer?

He has no answer. This makes the women restless. They want to leave the church. But the doors are locked.

Who locked the doors?

When Ruth dared to open the sealed order they read, lock the doors. Who locked the doors?

It is cold and damp in the church. Outside, autumn is calming down the trees.

Whose blood stains the altar cloth?

Bathsheba says, not mine.

Tamar says, not mine, not mine.

Ruth laughs and says, not mine, not mine, mimicking exasperation.

Sarah shouts, not mine.

Rhahab swigs from a can of beer, then says, not mine.

Eve is silent and her five companions watch her.

It is mine, she says, the blood is mine.

The six women swing round rapidly and stare out of the mirror towards Beth. They all wear the same face now. Beth recognizes the face. It is the face of Ash, repeated six times, weaving back into the mirror, until the mirror has gone, sunk back into the green turf, and Beth is alone with the Giant.

Without a word to him, she stumbles downhill. The giant looks about him in an abstracted listless manner, with the eyes of an old horse. Vellet, approaching from the direction of the river, does not dare speak to him, creeps back to the water.

TWENTY-FIVE

THE giant has unlocked his mirror.

Beth will meet her reflection. She will cross to the other side of the mirror. She will enter the abyss of the mirror.

On other occasions rain and sperm have made Beth's fingers wet but now it is sweat that makes her hands slippery.

She gets out of the car, trembling. Why does the house look different? Why are the windows open? Why is the door open? Beth knows the answer to her questions.

Who waits for me in my house?

She knows. Ash waits.

On the threshold, Beth prepares herself for the meeting. She is very frightened. What if it has all been an illusion, my recollection of a perfect season, of Ash's beauty? Suppose the girl I remember is changed and lost? What if the girl Ash remembers has gone away, in some dark nebula?

The sun has risen, it is long past dawn. This is terrible, thinks Beth, I don't want to meet her, it will hurt far too much, I am going to turn and run.

But she stumbles into the hallway. After the brightness of day, Beth is blind in the dark passageway. Through the darkness of the house, down the stairs, someone is coming.

'Who are you?' asks Beth sharply.

'Don't you recognize me?' said the other woman quietly, coming closer.

This woman is wearing gentle yet chaotic colours. In her hand she carries a half-eaten apple. Beth looks at her and as her eyes grow accustomed to the shadows, she sees in the stranger, no stranger. Beth looks at Ash for the first time and for the thousandth time. She shares the ceremony of courage Ash is inaugurating, by coming to this house. She sees Ash and all Ash implies. Yet she dare not move towards Ash, to elicit the first greeting.

Beth turns away, she has seen that Ash is flawless.

It is too much for Beth. She feels like an outcast. Twice she to speak to the woman who is watching her silently, compassionately. But twice she fails, twice savage waves of sweat debauch her and chill her to silence. She hears her silence like the clatter of an iron key on the stone floor of the kitchen. The stupidity of her silence echoes around them.

She opens a door and walks into a room without looking back at Ash. This room has always been called the library, although there are not nearly enough books here to warrant the title. Beth feels she will be safer in here, hidden from this strange summer. The room smells of polish, and fresh flowers. The dust has been swept away, the windows are cleaned. Beth peers at the books on the shelves, long-out-of-fashion novels, obscure biographies, foreign dictionaries, all taken asylum here.

Ash is standing in the doorway.

Beth takes a deep breath. She likes this room's quiet, she had forgotten this was her favourite room. She takes a book from the shelf, reads at random.

'What is that book?' asks Ash in a low voice.

'Descriptions of old gardens,' says Beth, tense again. She feels Ash's hand on her shoulder and turns to see in Ash's grey eyes the promise of an unskimped friendship. Beth trembles and she moves out of the shadow as she hears Ash say again,

'Don't you recognize me, Beth?'

Beth nods.

'Yes,' she whispers. 'I know you. But I am afraid now. You are too much of a phantom. I've thought about you so much that it doesn't seem possible to me that you too look back at our time together longingly. I am at a loss. Your phone call shocked me with its reality. You have been a dream to me. Perhaps you should go away before we are both hurt.' But Beth says this last half-heartedly.

Ash smiles.

'Go away? Of course not.'

'But I'm afraid, Ash.'

'I'm afraid too,' said Ash, 'what of it?' When Ash touches her, Beth feels that her own body has taken on the shape of a giantess.

Her thoughts are cold, a garden of needles. She hears the voices of defiled heroes telling myths and legends. Ash's fingers stroke Beth's hair, recalling Jake's eyes speckled with silver as if he had never seen Ash before, as if her sex were still to be named and learned. Ash sighs and urinates shadow. Beth is relaxing, leaning against Ash, her limbs no longer grotesque.

Hugging tightly, the women stumble upstairs. In the bedroom at the top of the stairs, Ash takes Beth's hand and kisses her forefinger. Beth and Ash stand naked in the shadow of the mirror. Their bodies move together in a cumulus. Embracing rediscovered flesh, they bite breasts, they kiss cunts. 'I am piecing you together,' gasps Ash. Beth catches her breath. The two women tremble on the edge of carnival then fall slowly into a silent bed, a grey raft in the room.

Afterwards, in the sunlit room, Ash sleeps soundly but Beth falls into a torpor and does not know what thoughts she is thinking or why.

When they wake, it is late morning and rain is streaming down the windowpanes.

Rain streams across the mirror of the giant. The predictions of fine weather have not come true. But the women are immune to weather today. They are still piecing one another together, gathering up the lost fragments.

Splashing and singing, they bath together. The steam on the bathroom mirror hides nothing from them.

'I knew you'd come! I knew you'd come to me!' crows Ash happily.

Beth smiles and squeezes the sponge between her legs. She has no regrets. Her long hair is wet through, it is plastered against the nape of her neck and her shoulder blades. She leans forward and looks into the far-reaching regions of Ash's eyes. Ash does not look away. She stares at Beth, concentrating in turn on her friend's features.

Outside, the summer trees carry the rain easily in their thick foliage. The white five-pointed flowers are whiter in the rain.

Beth says, 'the day after you and Jake left, years ago, I went into the village and the first person I met was an elderly lady who was selling small paper flags, to be worn as a sign of having given to charity. I bought one of those flags. I still have it, it is in my purse. I took the pin out and kept the flag.'

'All that time,' Ash murmurs, 'I was busy with other things . . . '

Beth trickled the warm soapy water through her fingers.

'Yes,' she said softly, 'yes. After you'd gone with Jake my emotions, my body, my spirit were overtaken by the sensation of an incombustible arson: intolerable conflict. At length I married the first man I got involved with.'

'And it hasn't worked out?' asks Ash, stepping carefully out of the bath, pulling a towel off the rail.

Beth still pours the bath water from one hand to the other. She shrugs.

'I don't know. This break may be final, or this may be a respite. Here, staying with you. An interval, and then perhaps, a fresh start with Theron.'

'Yes,' Ash agrees, 'it is the same with me.' Beth stretches out in the bath, her unshaven armpits are soapy.

Will Jake come here after you ?' she asks casually.

'No, no, he won't try that. He'll find enough to keep him happy. He'll manage.'

'And your children ?'

Ash slips on a dark blue towelling robe with a purple border.

'They'll be OK,' she says carelessly, 'we have an au-pair cum nanny, she's very reliable, we left her in charge of them earlier this year for several weeks, while Jake and I were in the States. She'll manage until the autumn.'

'The autumn,' queried Beth, sitting up suddenly, with a sharp emphasis on the first syllable of the word autumn.

'Yes,' says Ash, not looking at Beth. 'Yes. By the autumn have decided what to do. Hey, you'd better get out of the bath now, Beth. The water's getting cold.'

'OK.'

Beth stands up and pulls the plug out of the bath. Ash wrap warm towel around her.

'You get finished up here and I'll go down and make us a quick lunch.'

Alone in the bathroom Beth wipes the steam from the mirror and says goodbye to her reflection.

After they've eaten and done the dishes, Ash opens the back door. Beth stands beside her on the threshold and the rainy air drenches them both. They feel they are standing by a waterfall and are invigorated. The slight tension that had remained between them, scraping their skins roughly, recedes, and their gestures again become gentle.

'I love the rain,' says Ash, 'it makes all my flesh as sensitive as the quicks beneath my fingernails.'

Their first real journey through the house begins in the kitchen and as they go through each room in the house, remembering the events that happened at various times in the rooms, they relive their first summer by a series of almost formal questions.

'Do you remember the first night I came to your room ?' asks Beth, shyly, as they enter the little back bedroom. Ash's only answer is a smile.

In the bedroom with the yellowy faded wallpaper where Jake had slept, the women are silent, overdosed with memories.

In the junk room they try on costumes, giggling.

By the airing cupboard they embrace, quickset women.

On the landing, Ash says in a shaky voice, 'will you release me from my captivity, Beth?'

Beth stares at her.

'Will you release me from mine, Ash?'

In the straggly light of a rainy afternoon, Ash turns and looks at Beth wordlessly.

'I will try to release you, my love,' says Beth hoarsely, 'I will . . .'

Before I came here to meet Ash, Beth thought, my throat was sore because I had been considering only one side of the problem of our relationship. Now when I wake Ash is next to me and her roots are delving deeply into me. That problem of mine: what is happening between me and Ash? makes more sense when I am with her. In isolation it frightened me. Now we are together it is the naturalness of us that strikes me most powerfully. With Ash I am no longer pretending. And I do not have to think of Vellet. The ghost cannot bring her quicksands here.

The girls have dragged the old mower out of the greenhouse this afternoon and are taking it in turns to mow the lawn. They laugh and pant, struggling with the heavy old machine, and the familiar and somehow multilingual odour of the cut grass roams in the air.

Later, in the twilight, Ash lights candles in the kitchen. Beth stands by the window and looks at the livid bank of night cloud moving rapidly across the sky.

The warren of the moon is part of the night, and Ash is pressing her hands down on Beth's shoulders surreptitiously.

Like the inhabitants of a small island, the women grow nervous at nightfall.

Daylight is their domain.

But at night the flowers droop in intolerant vases. Ash walks in the garden. Beth sits by the window in the candlelight, unable to smile. We will grow more used to the night, she thinks, I am sure of that. But her tongue aches.

In the second week in August, Ash and Beth are walking between the tall trees and their voices, low, sibilant, are like part of the mist rising from the valley.

It is early in the morning.

They are speaking of their respective husbands, recalling intimacies and hard times, comparing their experiences.

'Jake was always bad-tempered at weekends,' said Ash.

Sombre thoughts about men are present in the minds of the women today, and they speak of the riddles each woman discovered at the heart of her marriage.

'And they will swallow us up greedily,' exclaimed Ash angrily, turning to Beth, 'until their houses become uninhabitable to us.'

Beth slides her hand into the oven glove and lifts the lid of the casserole dish, sniffing the meaty aroma. She gives it a good stir and then, satisfied, she re-sets the oven's timer and goes swiftly from the kitchen down the three whitewashed steps to the scullery. She inhales deeply here, breathing in greedily the damp smell from the hempen sacks of potatoes, the odour of earth clinging to the potatoes and to the gardening tools that she and Ash have been using for the reclamation of the flowerbeds.

The big white ghostly freezer clicks gently, going through its rhythm of electrical coldness, but Beth forgets about the frozen vegetables and opens the top half of the old-fashioned backdoor to lean on the edge of the lower door and peer out across the still-warm evening garden. Beyond is the green hill of the giant, the slope which discoverers climb when it is necessary for them to change, to transform themselves.

These reflections please Beth. She smiles, is rapt before the scene, turns her head from the hill and looks across the moorland, at the tiny far-off sheep in their heavy fleeces. Her gaze continues until she comes to the roofs and smoke from the chimneys in the village at the foot of the hill.

Between the world of the giant and the world she has found with Ash, Beth hesitates. Ash does not want to climb the hill of the giant. Beth has suggested they walk up that way several times but each time Ash got that secluded look on her face.

'I went up there once on my own, before you arrived,' Ash protested, 'I don't like the atmosphere of the giant, anyway . . . I get nervous there . . .'

So Beth did not urge a visit. She smiles, is relaxed for the first time in months. The holiday feelings delight her. Her life with Theron has dropped away from her, the burden gone. This August experiment, the refreshment of her body, the daily contact with Ash would have seemed, a few weeks ago, an unattainable fantasy. Now Beth revels in their adventure in the old house. She exists without past or future. It is the same for Ash. We are adding the finishing touches to ourselves, thinks Beth, we are almost complete. The network of our bodies, from retina to follicle, bone to eyelash, cannot be queried.

Ash's blue nightdress hurtles from north to south, arms billowing as the warm wind buffets the clothes of the women pinned up to dry. Ash stands at the bedroom window, watching her blue nightgown speculatively. I am happy, she whispers.

Ash and Beth sit on the bench by the garden gate, laughing at old jokes, reminiscing. Over the past three days, they have overcome their fears of giving their love to one another again and seeing it disregarded or mocked. Beth, especially, has decided to live in the moment as it grows, as the embryo in the womb must do. She clasps her arms around her shoulders and looks hard at Ash.

'Why, you've cut your hair,' she said in surprise, 'I hadn't really noticed it until now.'

'Yes,' said Ash, 'I had it cut short ages ago. Have an apple.' She hands Beth an apple and Beth bites into the flesh of the apple. 'It was a windfall apple,' says Ash.

'It's nice,' mumbled Beth, her mouth full.

Next morning, Ash took Beth's car and drove down to the village to do the shopping.

'I think it's better if I go alone,' she pointed out to Beth, 'no one will recognize me down there.'

'Theron might . . .' began Beth nervously.

'Then I'll worry about that when it happens, OK. Bye!'

Beth waved as the car disappeared down the lane.

Theron, she thought uneasily, I know where you are. You are at the other end of all the telephones. The phone box at the end of the road is where you live. When the strong summer wind gusts, the phone box door blows open and stays open. I have a strong urge to slip inside the red kiosk, to close myself in the small red building, lift the phone and speak to you. I know where you are. But I turn away from the temptation. I will not call you. You know where I am. Come and find me, if you want. Christ, I know your trick. Letting her cool off, you'll call it, that's what you'll say to yourself, when you sit in the summerhouse, a cigarette in your mouth, waiting for Vellet. While I am living with Ash, our life of sunlit reflections, you are living with the dark mirror of Vellet, dark, underwater, dead.

Beth pours herself a cup of coffee and settles herself in the windowseat to read through a batch of magazines, five years old. But it is her own story she reads, not the print on the garish pages. This is the story of the summer when the giant's mirror held out life to me. And I picked out what I wanted, from the reflections I was offered. As if plucking silky flags from a conjurer's shiny top hat. Here is the reflection I chose then: Ash. The lasting reflection.

Beth lets the magazine slip to the floor.

What about the other reflections I chose: what have I done with them? From the mirror I picked out moon, clock, menhir, leaf, arrow, star, sun, bee, candle and Ash. Ash, from whom I draw strength, who draws strength from me. When our bodies touch and embrace, we are learning all that our skins have to tell us, these soft rinds that cover flesh, bone and blood. We contemplate one another and discover we are new women. We compare notes, and reshape ourselves accordingly. I have plunged down into the depths of Ash these past few days, this is what I have longed for, and what I have always needed. The sympathy which existed between us, in miniature, as it were, has flowered and blessed us now.

Does it matter now that I have lost or sold the other reflections, given them away, squandered them?

In that mirror long ago I saw the fountain of my life. As I stared I wanted to sleep but I was not allowed to sleep. The fountain swayed and began to flow over me, silver water and red blood, moonlight and seeds, and in the water I saw the face of Ash. I saw the face of Ash and I did not speak. The menhir taught me silence. I saw the face of Ash and I bled: the moon bandaged me. I saw the face of Ash and leaves burst from my body. I saw her, the fountain of my life. My companion.

Flaxen shadows flickering, curving.

Afternoon, and the bare flank of Ash's body, the freckled arms of Beth. The women are stretched out on a rug on the lawn, sunbathing. In an hour's time the first gnats of the evening will appear and drive the women indoors, squealing and slapping their flesh, but at the moment there is no flaw in their relaxation.

Their bodies are brown from the reflections of the sun. It is over a month since the morning of Beth's arrival and after the rain of that first day the days have been clear and hot, enabling the women to spend most of their time in the garden, happy tenants regardless of the length, long or short, of their stay.

But the weather breaks.

With a flick of a finger against thumb, Beth comes indoors, out of the rainy garden.

'Your hair! Your clothes! You're soaking wet!' cries Ash. 'Summer rain,' said Beth, 'It'll do no harm.'

Ash put out a hand and touched Beth tentatively, she touched her where her nipple showed against the wet cloth of her blouse. Ash looks shy and blushes.

'You look beautiful, Beth, all wet,' she whispers.

Outside, the rain runs off the sword-shaped leaves. Ash presses herself against Beth, against Beth's wet clothes. She is flushed, her tongue flicks against Beth's lips, her throat, her hands knead the damp cloth of the skirt she is pulling tight across Beth's buttocks.

'I'll call you Cloacina today,' gasps Ash.

On the stairs, she strips Beth of her wet clothes, leaves them lying in a heap on the landing.

Beth is straining tight against Ash, she is alert for all Ash's instructions.

Ash is shivering in the warm room and web-like blotches appear on her skin, especially noticeable on her breasts.

She pushes Beth on to the unmade bed and stands at the foot of the bed, watching her, then watching herself in the mirror as she struggles with the husks of her clothes, pulling her bra and pants off. Still looking in the mirror, she parts her pubic hair and strokes herself. She looks over her shoulder at Beth, who is sitting up on the bed, and smiles coolly at her. Beth can see that Ash's clitoris is swollen and rigid. A pang goes through her own body. She scrambles forward off the bed and kneels before Ash. Bending her head she tastes Ash, her tongue roves against the taut projection of flesh and laps against the warm open cunt. Ash moans and shifts her weight to stand with her legs more widely astride, leaning her arms against the mirror. Beth uses her tongue to make Ash writhe and she can feel Ash's clitoris swell even more, like a delicate bulb. Beth's tongue is rotating faster and the pathway of Ash's vagina is alight, swirling with furnace sensations. The whole of her body presses against Beth's tongue until with an ache that pinches and floods her Ash comes and relaxes against the wall. Beth helps her to the bed and they lie down.

After a few moments, Ash slides her hand up Beth's leg.

'No,' says Beth, shyly.

But Ash can feel her quivering and she slides her finger cautiously up Beth's cleft. Beth is wet inside and she moves her finger slowly up and up until Beth groans and spreads her legs to give Ash more room to manoeuvre. Ash rubs Beth very slowly until her cunt was like strawberries crushed and mixed with cream and she was sweating and laughing and humping her behind until Ash brought her off just as Beth turned her head to stare at Ash fixedly and fiercely. She came, superhuman, with a wrenching orgasm, and collapsed into sleep like a star.

*

'This morning when I was in the village doing our shopping,' said Ash, 'a young man with longish blonde hair and old but clean clothes stopped me in the street and said, clearly and simply, "Will you give me a shilling to get something to eat?" '

Beth looks up from her book, startled.

Ash nods. 'Yes, strange, isn't it ?' Beth looks at Ash and is afraid for her safety. She sees threats, pain, injury.

'He didn't menace you?'

'No, oh no. He was quite gentle.'

'What did you do ?' asks Beth.

'I looked into his unstarving eyes and at his healthy body. I asked him, "how long since you've eaten?" He smiled sweetly and told me, "a long time." '

Ash is silent, lost in thought.

'And?' asked Beth impatiently.

'And what?'

'Did you give him any money?'

'Yes. Yes, I did.'

'I think you were foolish,' Beth told her quietly.

'Perhaps,' said Ash lightly.

'He didn't follow you home? We don't want him here, that sort.'

'Don't fuss, Beth. I'll never see him again, he was on the road, bumming around.'

'You liked him,' said Beth angrily.

'Maybe I did.'

Ash got up and began to brush her hair.

'Maybe I did like him,' she repeats, 'I am ashamed that I hesitated before giving him the money. I should have given it to him without shame. Perhaps he was laughing at me, perhaps it was a dare. But perhaps he was simply hungry.'

Beth snorts. 'You're a fool, Ash. You're too easily taken in.'

Ash puts down the brush and leans across the table towards Beth, speaking distinctly.

'But Beth, perhaps he had left all his friends and gone off alone by himself, and discovered that hunger was the worst part of loneliness?'

'Perhaps,' says Beth doubtfully.

'I think he was brave to beg, I was the one ill-at-ease, graceless, embarrassed. Why was I shocked, Beth?'

'I would have been shocked also,' said Beth, 'and perhaps refused to help at all.'

'Why are we so conditioned, so incapable of spontaneity, lacking any trust? Why do we hesitate to open our purses? The fuller our purses are, the tighter we close them, keep them closed.'

Beth remembers one time when she sat on the hilltop, spilling the dirty coins in her lap.

'Yes,' she whispers, 'those of us with purses full of money, we have most to learn.'

Beth stares at the flowers in the vase on the windowsill, blood-red flowers. She gets up from the table carefully, and goes upstairs to the lavatory.

Ash sits in the kitchen alone, letting her cup of coffee get cold, thinking of the beggar, the boy, his gaze.

'Wait!' said Ash, in that moonblue twilight.

'What is it ?'

'Ssh! Over there!' warns Ash. 'I thought I saw someone in the shadows, over there.'

'I see no one,' says Beth. 'No one. No beggar, no ghost.'

Nervously, hand in hand, the women approach the patch of shadow at the side of the greenhouse.

'You see,' said Beth, 'there is no one, only the shadows.'

After a night of heavy rain, the deep and glowing colours of the garden amaze them. They stand at their bedroom window, exclaiming at the beauty of the day.

After breakfast, Ash peels the potatoes. It is her turn today. Beth watches her in silence for a while then she says,

'Sometimes, Ash, in the past, I longed either to be you, or to wipe you from the face of the earth, obliterating all memories of you.'

'Did you?' said Ash calmly, smiling.

'Yes. Your image on the few snapshots I had and cherished gave me pain. But now, these last weeks, all that lockjaw has gone. In the past I looked into the mirror and spat at my reflection. Now I can bear to look at it, and beyond, and can bear whatever comes to us, the long separations that no doubt we'll have to accept, the verdicts of our husbands and friends, the reunions in the future, you and I back here together again, the salvaged times. Angry shouts from the wilderness of men will try to wear out the strength of our womanhood, Ash, your children will summon you back with their cries, their demands, but we will survive it all.'

'Yes,' Ash replied, still peeling potatoes, 'we will survive, Beth.'

Afternoon, like a handheld mirror, flashing, sparkling light. The two women are out walking on the moor, rambling with no destination in mind.

Vellet looks at the giant and calls him by his first name. The giant cracks his knuckles and laughs. Often in the sickness of her limbo Vellet has planned to hunt the giant down. Vellet looks at the baby through a magnifying glass. She sees the yellowness of Jupiter and night comes ashore and her embroidered wings shiver.

'Do you see the two women, Vellet?' asked the Giant mockingly.

'I see them,' said Vellet shortly. 'Yes, I see them.'

The giant's eyes are open all night. His mirror is approaching the full.

'So, you have seen the two women, have you?' he says to Vellet, teasing her.

'Yes!' she exclaims, 'but I can't get near them, you know that. There's no place there for me. But what I want more than anything is rest. I want to sleep . . .'

Vellet, the sleepless ghost.

'I want to sleep,' she cries again, 'and to get away from the barbarism of my existence. What is holding me back? Why can't I break out of this orbit? Why can't I look into your mirror, Giant? I know the answer is there.'

'One day, after toiling hard,' answered the giant, 'you will have finished your tasks, Vellet.'

'When?' she asks eagerly, 'when?'

Long past midnight but hardly dawn yet. A hot summer night, a night that is not dark, where a perpetual twilight has taken the place of the dark. The moon is full, the moonlight reels about the lawn, the moorland; the moon is reflected in the glass of the greenhouse.

The two women sit on the lawn on the rug, wrapped in shawls. They have been drinking white wine since early evening and are conversing drowsily now, tipsy but not drunk.

Ash touches Beth and lets her hair loose into the moonlight. 'Jake's smile was becoming the smile of a collector of birds' eggs. I had to get away, Beth.'

Beth lies on her stomach, her cheek resting on her folded arms. 'And you, Ash, what were you becoming?'

'I? I was becoming the wife. A background, no more. A healthy young mare, unregarded as anything else.'

Beth turns over and stares up at the sky, the filmy boneless clouds. She has not said anything to Ash about Vellet. That has no place here. Beth will not bring the matter into this garden.

'I always liked Theron though,' drawled Ash, 'A bit dull perhaps, but decent. I expect it is different, being married to him.' 'Yes,' said Beth absently, 'It is, yes.'

Ash glances at Beth and decides to allow the events of the night to take their natural course. She is happy. Beth is happy. They need use few words. They are suckling each other back to strength. Love is shining softly between them. This is the Lammas month we were not wise enough to experience those years ago, thinks Ash, now we are able to accept our feelings for one another without shame, without peril.

'We are sharing the night, Beth.'

Beth nods slowly.

TWENTY-SIX

NOT hand in hand, Beth and Ash are walking across the field of knee-high grass and buttercups. From the direction of the village comes a chime of bells. It is Sunday. The clang of bells reminds Beth of bones, teeth, keys. She glances at Ash, who is intent on picking her way, bare-legged, through the rough thistly ground. Beth is thinking about the past month of unhaunted days and nights with Ash. Beth and Ash pay one another homage, yet are careless as adolescents, giggling at their own shadows. Now in the pre-storm hush, under the dull sky that is tight with thunder, buzzing with electricity, the two women walk slowly, suddenly tired out. Beth feels that her lips are swollen, that her expression has grown ugly. She notices that Ash is frowning at her, and then speaks to Beth with a new vigilance.

'We love each other, Beth. Beneath the foundations of our separate lives that love is our strength, the source of our energy. But we cannot isolate ourselves forever. From now on our meetings, our holidays' (she smiled here) 'will be frequent, we shall meet here in this house where we first recognized our affinity. I shall come alone, or sometimes, if you permit it, with the children. The house will be our sanctuary. But we have responsibilities elsewhere and cannot abandon those. I've refreshed myself here, at a time in my life when I thought there was no possibility of refreshment; I found the part of myself that was lost, the other side of me that you represent and reflect back to me. But if we stay together, you and I, we will stifle what we have. Do you agree? We have come to the end of our discoveries, for this visit. We must go back to the others in our lives, take our good news back. Do you agree?' she asks again, touching Beth's shoulder lightly.

Beth nods.

'Yes, Ash, I agree. After this month nothing will be the same again. We shall never lose sight of one another again. We are stronger now, stronger than we believed possible. And we must take our strength back into the world, and resume our places. We can reanimate our old lives.'

'That is what we must do.'

Now Beth and Ash run for cover, they shelter in the hedgerow. The storm is breaking. There is no lightning. Only the ache of thunder, and then the syllables of summer rain.

On the first day of September, Beth and Ash stand by the garden gate. It is a dark deaf morning. The women are quenched by yesterday's storms. Clouds exhaust the sky. When Beth mentions the giant, Ash is at first angry, then silent.

The women are on edge, the time of leave-taking is here.

The lawn the two women are crossing slowly seems, to Beth, to be pitted with craters. The colour of Ash's mood is red, the heart of a harp. Beth's colour is black, black as the flea's shadow.

Indoors, they cover the furniture with dust-sheets, the bed is stripped, the garbage packed in a black polythene bag and set by the gatepost for the dustmen to collect tomorrow morning. The house is returned to its solitude.

Ash's suitcase stands in the hall.

There is a hesitation in the women's speech. Now the time has come, they want to be far away from here, very quickly.

'We'll write, of course,' says Beth, 'and phone.'

'Yes,' murmurs Ash, and fidgets with her shoulder-bag. She is acting hardbitten. It is the only way she can survive. She stares at Beth arrogantly.

'We are right to do things like this,' she says loudly.

'Of course,' says Beth, opening her eyes wide.

The taxi blares its horn and Ash pulls the front door open violently, she lunges down the path with her case, Beth following behind.

The taxi driver puts the case in the boot of the car.

'Goodbye, Ash,' says Beth with composure.

Ash looks round the garden, up at the house, at Beth . . . She looks scared.

'Don't worry,' says Beth compassionately, 'don't worry.'

Ash smiles, relaxes, leans forward and kisses Beth, then gets into the car.

Beth bites her tongue. She is alone in the garden. The sky is without energy, is grey and stony.

Ash, Ash . . . She cannot imagine how she will be able to leave the house, with its many impressions of Ash, the hundred reflections, the cup Ash drank from, the knife she peeled apples with, her traces everywhere.

Depression, heavy and sour, is settling on Beth as she enters the house but her concentration is broken by a woman's cry.

Beth wheels round about to say, Ash! But instead she sees, very faint in the dull light, Vellet standing a few yards behind her. Vellet has a joyful expression on her face.

She looks like the Virgin, thinks Beth, and does not dare to move.

Vellet stares at Beth, yet does not approach.

'Yes, I see what love is, Beth, I see it now. You and Ash, coming together, parting, planning to meet, involving others in your love, taking no selfish course, binding no one. Yes, I see. I can look into his mirror, now, look deeply into the mirror. Yes, and in the mirror of the giant, I see what I could never perceive before: love moving between all of us like fine weather, like a good moonrise, renewing us; like warm blood in our veins. I see far beyond the struggle for small rewards, possessions and territories, beyond the struggle that has kept me in one place for so long. Ah Beth, I am dissolving in this witnessed reflected love . . .'

Beth sees that Vellet's fingertips, breasts, eyelids are beginning to turn misty, an ectoplasm, the last of the ghost.

'The pangs of my ghosthood are erased,' whispers Vellet, 'and I open out into a hemisphere of water and light, blood and warmth and oh how easy it is, how easy, how simple at last, the freedom, I am lifted from my prison, I am on a new pathway, I see, I see . . .'

As the figure of Vellet fades wafting into this misty exhalation, Beth darts forward and cries,

'Vellet, wait, tell me . . .'

'Yes,' answers Vellet faintly.

'Vellet, will you follow Theron any more, will you haunt him again?'

A light and calm laughter.

'No, Beth, I will not haunt him any more. You can tell him, Beth, I forgive him for murdering me, it is of no importance now . . . I am on this new pathway that I have seen in the mirror of the giant, that moon-mirror held up for me to look into, and I go down into a necessary dark, Beth, a dark redolent of the half-remembered smells of womb and atom. I am set free and I see my new reflection, my new beginning. I am . . .'

The mists of the ghost disperse. There is only the grey and solid morning. Beth walks cautiously towards the spot where Vellet vanished. The air tingles but there is no other indication of anything out of the ordinary.

Now I must help Theron bear the loss of his haunting, thinks Beth. And all the time the knowledge of Vellet's transformation thrills through her. Such knowledge cannot be left behind, forgotten. It will always nourish my life, thinks Beth, for now I know Ash and I belong together, like twins, reflections, for our love freed Vellet. She enters the house gladly now, able to relish the touch and smell and aura of Ash that inhabits the house.

TWENTY-SEVEN

H E is lonely.
Sometimes he sees all objects turning red.

I am afraid of blushing, he thinks.

It is a chilly evening and he would like to shun the garden. But by half-past six he can wait no longer and walks briskly across the lawn and into the summer-house.

There are autumn leaves on the summer-house floor.

Worth less than my good name, he thinks, scuffling the leaves with his feet.

He sits down to wait for his visitor.

He is ashamed of himself but cannot break the habit of coming to this place most nights.

My excrements frighten me, he thinks.

He can smell autumn forming in small drops in the air. He misses Beth badly. He would like her to come back. She is up at her old house, I know. But I'm not going after her. Let her come back here.

He wishes she would.

It is as if his loneliness is draining him of blood. His visitor is late tonight. Theron's body feels dull, slow-witted. Perhaps I have called the night by the wrong name, he thinks. A tiny animal of the arachnid class scuttled along the seat. He watches it, grimaces.

The dampness of autumn has entered the summerhouse. He can smell the fungus growing in the corner.

Where is Vellet? Although Vellet is unhappy, he feels no pity for her. He knows he is using her, but that is her tragedy.

He gets up and stands at the door. He looks up at the burr of the moon, at the thick shrubs of the garden. The mass of the house is grey and quiet.

Theron would like the night to smell of acrobats and clowns but it is scented only with tomorrow's rain.

He saw Vellet coming towards him across the lawn, and he starts forward to greet her.

But Vellet wears on her head a hollow silver horn, rearing itself upward obliquely from her forehead.

She whispers, 'Theron, I am in deep water now, but I shall not drown . . .'

'Vellet,' he calls, but she's gone, leaving him steeped in silence. The night is thinking deeply about Theron.

His laughter brays out across the garden. He is gaunt, there are loops of wire twisted around his heart and he hears Janus calling loudly. Will a man's nativity emerge from the flames of Theron? There is a fishhook caught in each of his ten fingers. He continues to resist the shadow of his sex. He is nailed to the threshold of the summerhouse, as if it were a leprosarium. It is as if I have half-forgotten some secret, some vital information, and my life depends on the recovery of this secret. He walks up and down the lawn.

'Am I haunted?' he asks out loud, 'or has the ghost abandoned me?'

'Vellet has gone,' Beth answers softly, 'Vellet has begun her next journey.'

Beth is walking towards him, from the shadow of the house. 'Why has she gone,' asks Theron resentfully, 'and where?'

Beth does not answer. She stands beside Theron, who does not touch her, moves a little away, stiffly.

'It was you and Ash!' he shouts suddenly, 'You two have driven Vellet away!'

Again Beth does not answer. She shook her head and walked towards the summerhouse, leaving Theron to gather his thoughts. He is as deep in thought as if calculating the moon's age.

Smiling to herself, Beth sits in the dark summerhouse. Theron stood in the doorway and asked,

'Will I see Vellet again?'

'No, never,' said Beth quietly, not moving, not looking at him.

Then the questioner approaches her and she looks up at him, smiling and gentle. She takes his hands and shows him how to celebrate the riddance of the ghost. She shows him the pinnacles of her body, with its new confidence gained from loving Ash, she takes him further than Vellet into the burning cascades, further into the woman, she loves him until he begins to sing with the vision of it, descending into the hollows of her body, gaining his freedom, his independence.

The lovers have gone beyond emergencies. A new partnership has begun. Now the roots and branches of Beth and Theron twine together and whatever storms attack them will not easily despoil their growing landscape.

TWENTY-EIGHT

As they walk by the river in the late afternoon, Beth says to he husband,

'All over the world, men and women are longing for peace.' Theron nods. 'It is true,' he said.

'We are free of the ghost,' said Beth wonderingly. The autumn evening is a gauzy cupboard within which thin flowers blow.

Theron is growing accustomed to the place Ash has in Beth's life now. He is no longer jealous. He finds the matter strange

Strange, exciting. Last weekend, on the phone, Jake had said to him, 'can't you stop Beth interfering with Ash and me?' Theron had laughed and said, 'does Ash want Beth to stop interfering?' After Theron's long affair with Vellet, he finds in himself a sympathy with unorthodox love.

When Vellet left him, when the pressure of guilt and ghost lifted from Theron, he'd felt even lonelier at first. He realized his dependence on Vellet, was both ashamed and proud of it. She was like an elixir, he thinks, and I move less agilely without her. When I make love to Beth, I think of Vellet sometimes. But less often.

My memory of Vellet gets thinner each day and night. I am full of hope for the future and I love Beth. I accept the exodus of Vellet. Ash is part of Beth's life and therefore part of mine. When I come to the end of my loneliness, the time when I never think of Vellet, then I too will be able to grasp the extent of my good fortune.

Beth is thinking of Ash's letter. 'I was so happy . . . all that month . . . I think Jake will see the sense in it eventually, accept if as Theron does, that you and I experience the love, and more, of sisters . . .'

On his hill, the giant is silent. His white silhouette is frail as autumn frost.

Theron sighs, a long audible breath. There is no mirror for him yet. Beth glances at him, determined to resolve any existing difficulties in their life. For we are still composed of dangerous elements.

'What are you thinking?' she asks quietly.

'Of Vellet,' he answered at last. 'Sometimes, in the evening, I think of Vellet. She is a component of my twilight depression. Alone in the house sometimes, too, I think of her.'

'It is natural,' said Beth, 'there will be some trace left for a while. But we have whole years before us without the ghost.'

Theron turns to her gratefully and touches her body, breast and stomach. There is my mirror, he thinks suddenly. Our unborn infant is in his warm water laboratory, growing fast, unstoppable.

Theron kisses Beth. He does not want to solve anything. He is perfectly happy with the gleam of his thoughts, the ease of his heartbeat. It is as if a blindness caused from many hours of adoring flowers has dropped from him and he sees Beth welcoming him. He kisses Beth again.

Penelope Shuttle has lived in Cornwall since 1970. She is the widow of the poet Peter Redgrove, (1932-2003). She has a grown-up daughter, Zoe Redgrove.

Penelope's most recent publication is her Iota/Shots pamphlet, *IN THE SNOWY AIR, Templar, June 2014.*

UNSENT: NEW AND SELECTED POEMS 1980 – 2012, appeared from *Bloodaxe Books* in October 2012.

HEATH, a book-length sequence of poems on the theme of Hounslow Heath, written in collaboration with John Greening, will be published by *Nine Arches Press* in Summer 2016.

WILL YOU WALK A LITTLE FASTER, is to appear in May 2017, on the poet's seventieth birthday, from *Bloodaxe Books.*

Her work is widely anthologized. She has given readings at many festivals, including Ledbury, StAnza and Aldeburgh, as well as in the United States. She is also a tutor and mentor,and for ten years (until 2014) was Chair of the Falmouth Poetry Group. She is a member of the Cornwall Contemporary Poetry Festival Committee, which is currently planning the 2016 Festival.